I can only find Torvan; the rest are dead or blind or deaf. He says, 'Why did you have to leave?' and I feel it, the weight of those words, and he grabs my hand and drags me to The Terafin's Council chambers.

"She's dead. There are three knives in her body and she lies across the Council table. Gabriel looks up when I enter the room; there is fighting, of course, the war for succession. He is aloof from it, but bleeding anyway. And he says, 'You *left* her to die.'

"The Terafin sits up. Her eyes are dead eyes. Her wounds don't bleed. And her voice—it's not her voice. Her head rolls awkwardly on her shoulders as she turns in my direction. She says, 'Another lesson. The hardest lesson. There will be blood on your hands no matter what you choose.

"There will always be blood on your hands. Glory in it, or weep at it, as you choose—*but when you choose who* must *die, choose wisely.'*

"And before I can answer, before I can ask a question, she gestures and the—and the—city rises."

"The Shining City." Avandar's voice.

"Yes. And the screaming starts. . . ."

The Finest in Fantasy from
MICHELLE WEST

THE UNCROWNED KING

The Sun Sword: Book Two

Michelle West

DAW BOOKS, INC.
DONALD A. WOLLHEIM, FOUNDER
375 Hudson Street, New York, NY 10014

ELIZABETH R. WOLLHEIM
SHEILA E. GILBERT
PUBLISHERS

DAW Book Collectors No. 1097.

DAW Books are distributed by Penguin Putnam Inc.

First Printing, September, 1998
1 2 3 4 5 6 7 8 9

DAW TRADEMARK REGISTERED
U.S. PAT. OFF. AND FOREIGN COUNTRIES
—MARCA REGISTRADA
HECHO EN U.S.A.

PRINTED IN THE U.S.A.

*This is for my mother and my father,
because I don't say thank you often enough.*

ACKNOWLEDGMENTS

Sheila Gilbert has been patient above and beyond the call of duty for this book. It was late and although I plead unusual circumstances, it certainly wasn't *her* fault.

The usual suspects were also extremely helpful—and I'd particularly like to thank Kate Elliott and Tanya Huff because it's always nice (my penchant for understatement is showing here) to have someone to call when I've hit the middle-of-the-book-and-I-hate-every-word stretch of the novel.

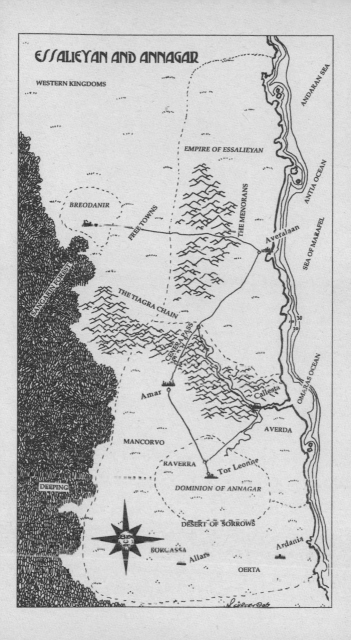

Annagarian Ranks

Tyr'agar	Ruler of the Dominion
Tyr'agnate	Ruler of one of the five Terreans of the Dominion
Tyr	The *Tyr'agar* or one of the four *Tyr'agnate*
Tyran	Personal bodyguard (oathguard) of a *Tyr*
Tor'agar	A noble in service to a *Tyr*
Tor'agnate	A noble in service to a *Tor'agar;* least of noble ranks
Tor	A *Tor'agar* or *Tor'agnate*
Toran	Personal bodyguard (oathguard) of a *Tor*
Ser	A clansman
Serra	The primary wife and legitimate daughters of a clansman
kai	The holder or first in line to the clan title
par	The brother of the first in line; the direct son of the title holder

Dramatis Personae

ESSALIEYAN

AVANTARI (The Palace)
The Royals
  King Reymalyn: the Justice-born King
  King Cormalyn: the Wisdom-born King
  Queen Marieyan (an'Cormalyn)
  Queen Siodonay The Fair (an'Reymalyn)
  Prince Reymar: son of the Queen Siodonay & Reymaris
  Prince Cormar: son of the Queen Mareiyan & Cormaris
  Princess Mirialyn ACormaris: daughter of Queen Marieyan &
    King Cormalyn

The Non-Royals
  Duvari: the Lord of the Compact; leader of the Astari
  Devon ATerafin: member of the Astari and of House Terafin
  Commander Sivari: former King's Champion (at the Summer
    Games)

The Hostages
  Ser Valedan kai di'Leonne (Raverra): the heir to the Sword of
    The Dominion
  Serra Marlena en'Leonne: Valedan's mother; born a slave;
    granted honorific "Serra" because her son has been
    recognized and claimed as legitimate

  Ser Fillipo par di'Callesta (Averda): brother to the Tyr'agnate
    of Averda
  Serra Tara di'Callesta: his Serra
  Michaele di'Callesta: oldest son
  Frederick di'Callesta: youngest son
  Andrea en'Callesta: his concubine

Ser Kyro di'Lorenza (Sorgassa): the oldest of the hostages
Serra Helena di'Lorenza: the only wife he has; he has taken
   no others
Ser Gregori di'Lorenza: his son

Ser Mauro di'Garradi (Oerta)

Serra Alina di'Lamberto (Mancorvo)

Imperial Army
The Eagle: **Commander Bruce Allen.** Commands the First
   Army
The Hawk: **Commander Berriliya.** Commands the Second
   Army
The Kestrel: **Commander Kalakar.** Commands the Third
   Army & the Ospreys

THE TEN:

Kalakar
Ellora: The Kalakar.
Verrus Korama: her closest friend and counselor
Verrus Vernon Loris: friend and counselor
The Ospreys:
Primus Duarte: leader
Alexis (Sentrus or Decarus)
Auralis (Sentrus or Decarus)
Fiara (Sentrus)
Cook (Sentrus)
Sanderson (Decarus)

Berriliya
Devran: The Berriliya

Terafin
Amarais: The Terafin
Morretz: her Domicis
Jewel ATerafin: part of her House Council; also seer-born
Avandar: Jewel's Domicis

THE ORDER OF KNOWLEDGE
Meralonne APhaniel: Member of the Council of the Magi; first circle mage

Sigurne Mellifas: Member of the Council of the Magi; first circle mage

SENNIEL COLLEGE
Solran Marten: Bardmaster of Senniel College
Kallandras: Master Bard of Senniel

ANNAGAR

The Tor Leonne
General Allesso par di'Marente - par to Corano; General to the former Tyr

General Baredan kai di'Navarre: General to the former Tyr; loyal to Leonne

Widan Cortano di'Alexes: the Sword's Edge

Lord Isladar of the kin: the link between the Shining Court and the Dominion

THE CLANS

Callesta
Ramiro kai di'Callesta: the Tyr
Karro di Callesta: Tyran; half-brother (concubine's son); the oldest of the Tyran
Mikko di Callesta: Tyran; half-brother (concubine's son)

Garrardi
Eduardo kai di'Garrardi: the Tyr'agnate of the Terrean of Oerta

Lamberto
Mareo kai di'Lamberto: the Tyr'agnate of Mancorvo
Serra Donna en'Lamberto: his Serra
Galen kai di'Lamberto: the kai (former par)

Leonne
Markaso kai di'Leonne: the Tyr'agar
Serra Amanita en'Leonne: the Tyr'agar's Serra
Illara kai di'Leonne: the heir
Serra Diora en'Leonne: also *Serra Diora di'Marano*

Ser Illara's concubines:
> *Faida en'Leonne:* Oathwife to Diora
> *Ruatha en'Leonne:* Oathwife to Diora
> *Dierdre en'Leonne:* Oathwife to Diora

Lorenza
Jarrani kai di'Lorenza: the Tyr'agnate of Sorgassa
Hectore kai di'Lorenza: the kai

Marano
Adano kai di'Marano: Tor'agar to *Mareo kai di'Lamberto*
Sendari par di'Marano: his brother; Widan
Serra Fiona en'Marano: Sendari's wife
Ser Artano: Sendari's oldest son
Serra Diora di'Marano: Sendari's only child by his first wife
Sendari's concubines:
> *Alana en'Marano:* the oldest of Sendari's wives
> *Illana en'Marano*
> *Illia en'Marano*
> *Lissa en'Marano:* given to the healer-born
Serra Teresa di'Marano: sister to Adano and Sendari

Caveras
Ser Laonis di'Caveras: healer-born; his wife is *Lissa en'Caveras.*

THE RADANN
Radann Fredero kai el'Sol: the ruler of the Radann
Jevri el'Sol: his loyal servitor
Radann Samiel par el'Sol: youngest of the Hand of God
Radann Peder par el'Sol
Marakas par el'Sol: contemporary of Fredero
Samadar par el'Sol: the oldest of the par el'Sol

THE VOYANI

Arkosa
Evallen of the Arkosa Voyani: the woman who ruled the Voyani clan
Margret of the Arkosa Voyani: her chosen "heir"

Havalla
Yollana of the Havalla Voyani: ruler of the clan

AIDAN: I

8th of Lattan, 427 AA
Averalaan, Hundred Holdings

Men were fighting in the distance.

It made the people who trudged their way to and from the Common, laden with baskets and awkward panniers, stop a moment beneath the cover of the trees for which the holdings were famous. Those trees towered at a height great enough to give little relief from sun's light this early in the day, and they were as thick around the base as a small knot of men, which meant they were easy enough to hide behind. That no one did said more about the demands of the festival season than anyone's bravery.

Swordplay was something to stay clear of, no question.

An older woman shouted into the thick of the crowd. Aidan recognized her, although he didn't know her name; he bought the odd curiosity from her in the Common when he had money. These days, though, that was never.

A tall man made his way through the crowd at the sound of her hawkish voice, and this man, Aidan *did* know; he was Primus Telarus of the magisterial guards, a regular man with slightly broader shoulders and a squarer jaw than most, but with gray hair that grew in a fringe around what was otherwise almost black. Like his dad, except for the hair.

"Over there," the woman said. "Can't you hear it? There's swords being used!"

Primus Telarus bent down, said something to the woman. Made her angrier, from the look of it, but a lot less frightened.

"Damned foreigners, who do they think they are? There are *rules* in this city!"

Whoever they were, they kept on fighting.

Magisterial guards, in the streets in somewhat larger numbers than usual because of the approaching Festival season, didn't even blink an eye. Whatever the swordplay was, they knew about it, and they didn't much care. The Common's regular merchants were made skittish by the influx of cartwheeling hawkers and peddlers, keen to stake claim to good ground as the travelers—and they were legion—made their way to Averalaan for the Kings' Challenge. The magisterians were here to prevent the skittishness from developing into something uglier and more permanent. People were decent when it was easy to be decent, and when it was hard—well, that's what guards were for.

That they didn't blink twice at the sound of swordplay probably meant that someone had gotten a permit for it. You had to have a lot of money for that, but at this time of year, there was money in plenty to be found—in everyone's pockets but Aidan's. It was the Challenge season. Merchants from as far away as the Dominion's deserts on one side, the winter principalities on the other, came in droves, almost like the cattle that was sold and traded for in the Common.

You could see people tossing sharp daggers in a circle that started and ended with their hands; you could see them sword-dancing; you could see them throwing torches, lit with orange fire; hells, you could see them *eating* fire, here. Off the thoroughfare, which was as wide as any in the hundred holdings, there were tents and wagons— old wagons, fine as the best carpenters and wainwrights together could make—and in them, the future waited, if you had the coin. 'Course, if you didn't, men with bigger muscles than brains waited instead, and usually in a bad temper; Aidan strayed close enough to admire the wagons, but not close enough to be noticed—and in this crowd, that was actually fairly easy.

The Challenge festival was in the air, in the smell of food and ale and sweat. But the air carried other things as well: voices as perfect as those of the bards of Senniel College, and often Morniel College as well—the Morniel bards were known to be fond of ale over fine wine, good company over the gatherings of the pretentious patriciate.

You could hear almost anything if you listened hard enough. Even swords. Especially swords.

Aidan knew it was high summer, and he knew that the champions would soon be here, to try their luck, and then their skill, in a test the Kings set. He glanced at the shadows on the ground, then slapped himself on the forehead; there weren't any that he could easily see. No one could, there were too many feet in the way. Still, sun was low across the eastern sky. Morning, mid-morning at the latest. Tomorrow was when they'd start. The tents were up in the Common—he could see the poles and the flags, but he wasn't allowed anywhere near the tents themselves. No one was.

Kings' guards were all over the place, securing this and that and barking out orders as if they were selling them. The magisterians didn't much like it, and Aidan couldn't say he blamed them; having a bunch of people whose only real claim to power seemed to be an extra sword up either side of a magisterial crest suddenly become top dog in your holding—well, he couldn't see liking it all that much either.

But he wasn't a magisterian; he was just Aidan, and this was the best time of the year, even with the heat. Because—there, there in the distance—there was fighting. Clearer than bard's song.

Of course, he couldn't actually *see* the fight, not yet; he approached it, breath held, feet light against stone and packed dirt. He didn't need vision to know it was something tremendous—a clash of long steel swords, slide of metal against metal that daggers were too short for, a silence that was free from the sounds of anger, of ugliness. You couldn't drink and fight like that. You couldn't just swing a large fist, pick up a ladle or a tureen, lash out with a heavy foot. Swords like *that* meant you had to be special. He knew it. He'd seen it before.

Seen it when he was younger, before his father's foot had gotten trapped by a turning wheel in one of the wainwright's wagons and gotten all twisted up. Had twisted him all up.

It hadn't been so long that he couldn't remember when his father had been a whole man, when his strength had gone into moving things, lifting things, learning to make them.

But it had been long enough that the memory of the one man, strong and certain and silent, made the reality seem so much worse. If you started out at the bottom, the bottom was all you knew. But if you fell, it was different. Hurt more, for one. And things had been good. They had.

I won't be like that. Something bad happens to me, and I won't be like that. I'll just die. I'll die first. Aidan couldn't understand why people were so afraid of dying. You went to Mandaros, is all. Everyone who ever listened to one of the Mother's priestesses knew it. His mother had known it, too. She hadn't been afraid of death.

Probably why she'd died.

He shook his head to clear it; the sun was hot, and there wasn't enough wind to carry away the smell of sweat and food and horse manure—someone was going to get it for that—and fire. He held his breath past the worst of it; breathed through his mouth until he'd gotten past the thick of the crowd. The tents, with their limp red-and-blue flags, were at his back. But the swords were closer, he was closer to them; he only wanted to catch a glimpse of them, of them and the men who wielded them.

They never shouted. They never swore. They never spoke when they held their swords. And they didn't swing wild when they swung. They seemed to know where to strike, and where the other would strike. Magic, he thought. He'd never seen magic.

And he wanted to.

This year, he wanted to.

He hadn't eaten today. Wasn't worth it, to try to come up with something to eat. His father had woken earlier than usual because of the heat, and he was in a foul mood. Heat made some people slower. Not his dad.

Try to understand him, Aidan, his aunt had said. *He lost his livelihood and he lost your mother in the same year.*

What about me? Aidan had shouted back. *I lost them both.*

She'd nothing to say to that; that's what she did when he'd said something true enough that she couldn't speak over it or past it. In the silence, she'd run her hands through his hair—his white, white hair, that had nothing of either his mother or father in it. And that's the way he wanted it. Here, in the street, drawing closer and closer to the sound of swordplay, of a magic that neither his mother nor his father had had time to dream of.

The King's Challenge was a little over a week away.

In six years, his aunt told him; in six years, he might be big enough to try; he'd be old enough. To find a sword, and maybe learn how to use it. To impress the men who chose among the hundreds of supplicants, and to *be* one of the challengers.

Six years ago, he'd believed her. Six years, one at a time, had taken that belief away in bits and pieces, until the only time he had any of it left at all was now, during the challenge season itself. And he kept it tucked away, behind a still face, the words to express it lost with his mother's and father's lives.

He knew that these men had trainers, teachers, weapons that cost more than his father made—when he'd done real work—in three years. Knew that six years from now the only way he was going to even have a sword was if he was lucky, there was a war, and the army was stupid enough to have him.

That's what he wanted. At twelve, it wasn't going to do him any good. But at eighteen—at eighteen, it could change his whole life. So he waited, and he prayed.

And during the challenge season, he loitered around the fighters, when he could find them.

It would have been easy enough to catch a glimpse of them in the streets, but Kalliaris had never made anything in Aidan's life easy. He was used to having to work around her. Barely noticed it, in fact. Now if something went *right,* he knew it was time to worry; you paid for the good things with bad, and it was always much worse.

He was stupid, though—he prayed to Kalliaris, same as anyone. He was probably the only boy in the city trying to find men *using* swords. But he knew this part of the hundred holdings fairly well—there weren't many places they could be and still be that loud. He stopped, as if he were testing the sea wind, listening to the blades.

They stopped, and he froze a moment in bitter disappointment. Even started to trudge back the way he'd come, hands clenched in loose fists, face set into the scowl his aunt hated. But he didn't get far before he heard them again.

There.

They didn't fight in the streets, but close enough to them; the courtyard of the building that housed so many foreigners was open to the traffic of the large manse. Merchants came with the produce that the kitchens required as well as the fabrics that were to be used in the rooms themselves, as curtains and throws and bedspreads wore with age and use; carpenters came, masons, women from the poorer holdings who were certain to find work during the Challenge season.

All those people. And between them, if one were careful, a boy too small for his age might sneak, head bowed like a servant or an obedient extra son. It was best, in Aidan's experience, to come in with the wagons that carried the food and drink. They were often crowded with people, and the people were the right kind. The cloth merchants were more refined, and no matter how well he washed, his clothing was stretched to the point of breaking and he sounded like—like his father's son, not his mother's.

But he wasn't expected to speak, and if a flustered merchant cuffed him in the head for getting underfoot—and they did—the blow was a light tap compared to many he'd received and it served to push him closer to the courtyard, to the men with swords. How could he mind it? He cursed, but his heart wasn't in it, and the merchant, still flustered, was already beyond him.

The steel was ringing in the early morning air. The courtyard itself was dark with shadow, but the men were forced into the sun when they fought; they squinted against the light. So did Aidan. It was cast by polished steel, and the steel was brighter than sunlight, sharper, quicker. You could look away from the sun, but if you looked away from the swords, you missed the fight.

He counted twelve men in all, although he saw a couple sitting in the shadows cast by awnings that were unfaded by sun, unstained by years of rainy season. New, Aidan thought, for the Festival. As if it mattered.

What mattered were the twelve men. Two pairs of six, they seemed to fill the courtyard—and the courtyard here was large enough to house the wedding of two children of large, moneyed families. But those people would be vacant spectators, and these men were things in motion, slick with sweat, shiny with effort and the grace of effort. Some wore armor, some did not; he couldn't tell if there was rhyme or reason to it. He was certain there was, and that he wouldn't understand it, and besides, if he asked anyone, they'd notice he was here and kick him out.

The swords were loud here, louder than they had been on the city streets. And no wonder. Twelve men. His head darted side to side, like a bee near a cluster of flowers, and like that bee, his gaze eventually came to rest upon two of the twelve.

He lost the courtyard, the open sky, the sunlight; what remained was shadow, sharp reflection, and the way the swords spoke where no words could.

"They're foreigners, you know," someone said.

He ducked his chin into the hollow between his collarbones. He'd learned not to be angry, or at least not to show it; he didn't have the size to get away with it. But he *was* angry. He wanted to be left alone. Just that: to be left alone to watch. The Challenge would start soon enough, and then the fighters would vanish across the bridge to the isle itself, where no one without money or cause was allowed to go.

Certainly not Aidan, the wheelwright's son.

Not no one, the treacherous little voice said. *Remember, the witnesses. They each choose one witness, from the streets, on the first day.*

Right. A handful out of the whole city. He hated to dream. More than that, he hated that he couldn't stop it, because he never got what he wanted, he *knew* he wasn't going to get what he wanted, and it still hurt when even the chance slowly slipped away, champion by champion.

This, this sitting, was as close as he was going to get to the real fight. It was closer than he had gotten in far, far too long. He *had* this, and he didn't want to lose it.

But his tormentor wouldn't take the hint.

"Why do you come to watch them? If they win, they'll bring honor to the Dominion, not to the Empire."

Aidan shrugged, staring at the swords. At the men. At this man's shadow.

The shadow shrugged in reply, the movement more elegant than Aidan's, perhaps because it held no anger. When he spoke, he spoke loudly, the words meant to carry across the courtyard's width. And the language he spoke was only familiar to Aidan because he heard it in the holdings, spoken by the dark-haired, dark-skinned Southerners who somehow escaped the Dominion's net.

The two men he was watching so intently froze at once.

It took him a moment to understand the connection between foreign words and foreign swordsmen; the utter conviction the cessation of all movement held. The two stopped in mid-swing, frozen in place more completely than the statues along the courtyard's wide, rectangular walk.

He scrambled to his feet, then, trying to take back his sullen silence, his terrible lack of words. Because the two men looked past him to—to the man who had asked the question. The man he had ignored.

In a rush, the words came, and he felt his cheeks darken. It almost stopped him from speaking at all. But not quite. Not quite.

"It doesn't matter who wins and loses," he told the man, who appeared to be ignoring him as completely as Aidan had done in his turn. "I won't see it anyway. It doesn't matter if they say the South won. Or the North. Or the Northern wolves, and they win most of 'em."

Without looking down, the man—and he was old, Aidan saw, older than his Da, older than his aunt, and yet somehow whole and stronger than either of them—said, "Yes, the far North carries the wreath most often. The Queen, Siodonay the Fair, is from the North." He spoke with an accent. Aidan had heard stronger in the crowded stalls of the Common. But there was something about the words themselves that was different. Better.

"The South almost never wins," he said, and then cursed himself. *Good. Insult him. Get yourself thrown out, idiot. Kalliaris' curse.* "I—I just like to see them," Aidan said. "The ones that come—the ones that are chosen—they don't fight because they're angry. They don't get bloody. They just—they just use the swords as if that's all they know."

"Yes." There seemed to be a question in the dark eyes, and Aidan knew he was being tested. He hated that; he almost always failed tests. But he'd already offended the man once, and he knew that if he didn't pass this one, he was back out in the streets again. This man, *this* man, was the trainer. The teacher. He would've known if he'd looked up. If he'd just bloody looked.

"And sometimes—sometimes they get that look in their eyes, on their faces, and you just *know*—you know who the best ones are. You know the ones that won't break. They *mean* it."

"Mean what? I'm sorry; my understanding of your language is perhaps imperfect."

"I—" He looked away. "I don't know. They just look like they have it."

"You see the fire," the older man said softly. "We call it Lord's light. Some men will burn with it, and will be extinguished by the flame they carry. Some will burn, but instead of guttering, they will be tempered. You cannot tell when you first see that flame whether you deal with wood or steel, but it becomes clear, with time."

"You—you're teaching them."

"I try," the man said, a smile turning up just the corner of his lips, and only for a second.

"Do you—do you teach a lot?"

"I? In the Dominion, I am not called a teacher," he said. "I am called a master. I do not teach, as you put it, but rather, I find." His smile broadened; their eyes met for a moment, and Aidan felt his shoulders straighten out, as if a burden had fallen from them.

He spoke again, in the foreign tongue, and one of the two men looked, quite deliberately, at Aidan.

Who cursed every minute he'd listened to Torra and ignored it as foreign babble. "What—what did you say?"

"I told them," was the serene reply, "that you have good sight. Vision. You understand what you see. It is . . . rare. They will spar for a while longer," the old man said. "You may watch as you like." He turned, and then turned again. "But I must ask a single question. There are almost twelve men gathered here—why are you watching these two? Not any of the others?"

"Because," Aidan said, settling back down into bent knees and the known safety of a wall at his back. "They're the ones who get that look the most. They just—you know that they're both the best, if you watch 'em."

The old man smiled. "Yes," he said. "I do." He turned away. "They are unused to the humidity of this city. I would prefer that they fight unobserved; the younger man—not much younger in age, but younger in carriage and bearing—is too aware of his audience if it is large."

Aidan said nothing at all.

"And I explain myself to you, a boy of Averalaan's many streets." The words were not said unkindly. "We will be here for three days; after that, I'm afraid there will be no further opportunity for you to bear witness."

Aidan nodded, pressing his lips together as tightly as possible in case something stupid came out. He wasn't good at speaking.

"I make warriors," the man continued, "the way some men craft sculptures. And perhaps I, like that young man, still desire an audience that appreciates that work. Even be they," he added with a slight smile, "as young and untutored as you appear to be. You see well.

"Come, if you will, and watch."

Aidan nodded. And he stayed, shifting position only to catch the shade the walls made. The old man did not speak to him again that day.

"Where in the Hells have you been, boy?"

His father's voice.

His father's rooms. He stood, a shadow in the door, a boy looking in on a life that he both wanted and loathed. "The Common," he said at last. Took too long to say it, too; he could see his father shift in his chair. "I brought food." It was true. He'd helped Widow Harris with her cart and her mule—and that mule was as difficult as his father—got himself a bruise that was already turning both purple and black, and had been offered food as recompense. She knew.

"Tell him he's hiding behind his leg, same as some men hide behind their wives' skirts," she said, salty as the sea. "You tell him I said that—tell him it's a shame to make his boy beg when he's still got strength and a brain. Well, maybe half a brain, but it's better than nothing."

He thanked her profusely for the bread and the cheese, and her frown got considerably sharper. "Never you mind," she said. "I'll just tell him myself."

And she probably would, too. That was Widow Harris. But she was busy, and would be until the threeday after the Challenge had been won and lost. She was also pretty noisy, so he'd probably have time to get out of his father's way and stay out after her visit.

"Well, don't just stand there. Bring it in." He stood, bracing himself against the table, a broadly built man with a back so bent that he looked a foot shorter than his height. He didn't like the crutch he'd been given by his friends and his dead wife's family, and it had cost—Aidan knew it, even if his father couldn't acknowledge the truth—so he hobbled around the house, leaving handprints on the walls, loping like a one-footed giant. Like, Aidan thought, although he never said it, a monster that's been injured by a hero who can't be bothered to finish him off.

In the old house, his mother would have chased him around with a broom, swatting him, which would have been easy. She'd make him laugh, which wouldn't. Then she'd've made him use the crutch. At least she'd've made him clean up the handprints and the dirt on the wall.

But he didn't want to think about it now; he thought about it every other day of the year.

Aidan scurried into the room, set the food down on the table. He got a knife that looked like a knife unless you examined its edge and cut the loaf in half. Cut the cheese as well; it was a hard cheese, so it took a bit of work.

His father sat down, dragging the chair across the floor. They'd had complaints about that in the old place—but it had been a long time since they'd been able to afford a real home. Here, it didn't matter much. He went from wall to chair, settling down with a thud, and he sat there for a moment, staring at the bread, the knife, and his son.

What his father said next nearly killed Aidan.

"Got some work."

Tricky situation, that.

He almost believed his father. He *did* believe his father. But he didn't trust his own beliefs anymore. He wanted to walk a little closer to his dad to see if he'd been drinking. Probably had, but it wasn't so bad if he had to walk by to check on it, and Aidan was grateful for the little things life offered. Especially today, when it had offered so much.

"Doing what?" he asked, before the silence got uncomfortable. His dad liked to take silence and build accusations out of it. Especially when he'd been drinking.

His father shrugged, deflated. "Wainwright needs some help. Merchants are coming in from all over the continent—and they've wagons that need repair, wheels that need either righting or outright replacement."

Which wainwright?

"What's the matter? You don't think your old man can be useful around *wheels?*" Large hands slapped flat out against the kitchen table; it teetered. The floor was sloped beneath one of its legs, and no one was going to fix it; a wobbly table was just another fact of life. Like weather. Or anger.

"No, Da, I didn't say that."

"You didn't say anything." His father picked up the bread as if it were a weapon. On the other hand, it *was* a pretty hard loaf.

"I was waiting for you. To finish," Aidan added. "To finish telling me about it."

"Not much to tell. There's work, and I've got experience." He grimaced. "Not much but experience. It'll do for now."

"What—what happens after?"

His father shrugged. It was the single gesture that Aidan least liked.

"Maybe if you do a really good job—maybe if—"

"Aidan, shut up and eat."

Kalliaris, Aidan thought, in the darkness of a night punctuated by snoring and moonlight. *Give my Da his life back, and I'll give you anything you ask for. Give him back his life. He was the best. He wasn't what he is now.*

Gods were a tricky business. That's what his mother used to say. Tricky. They were like a combination of powerful men and crazy dogs; they held all the cards and you never knew when they would turn on you—but when they did, that was it.

So you weren't supposed to ask for anything, because *if* they felt like giving it to you, they asked for something big in return, and no guarantees that what they asked for wouldn't make it worse either.

Aidan's god of choice was Kalliaris because you *saw* both her faces, and you knew what she was. Knew she'd frown if she felt like it—and she did, gods knew—knew that you could coax a smile from her when things looked darkest. Smile. Frown. Fact of life.

Give him back his life. I'll give you anything you ask for.

He rolled over on the patchy mattress. It was far too hot for blankets, although the worst of sunlight's bite had been driven back for a moment by the night's grip. He felt as if he'd forgotten something, even something important.

Oh. Right. And thanks a lot for letting me find the fighters. For making that old man let me watch. Thanks. I owe you.

He returned to the hotel's grand courtyard the next day, slipping in once again with harried merchants, and sliding out from their moving mass with the same practiced ease. Better, because this time he didn't earn a stray swat across the back of the head as he left. He was worried because he didn't hear the sound of swordplay.

No. He said he'd be here three days. He said I could watch.

He didn't speak out loud; there wasn't much point. But he stopped a moment, just a moment, to wonder if this wasn't an answer to his prayer. Weighed it: Da's job, and his life, and this day or two of swords and magic.

Wasn't an easy choice, and he didn't much like that it was made for him. But gods were gods as his mother had said. He turned around to go back the way he'd come, and because he was looking at his feet—his toes clipping the ground because they'd grown over the worn lips of his sandals—he walked into the old man.

Old man. Not fair, not really. His hair was still dark, although the whites had gotten to it, and his chin didn't have that sag that some old people's chins did. His arms were dark, and his face; and both looked hard, like finished, polished wood. And he wore a sword.

"You're . . . early," the old man said when he spoke.

Aidan flushed. "I thought—I thought—"

"That they don't have to eat? That they don't have to perform other tasks, other exercises? This is the Challenge, boy, not a sword fight." The words were harsher than his expression. "They run, in the streets of the high city; they will run for the better part of two hours yet. Tomorrow, we will ride." He smiled then, softly. "But, yes, boy. In the South, in the Dominion, it is the test of

the Sword that defines a man. Even here, in the North, where so
much else about power is political and effete, the crowning test
of the Challenge is always the test of the Sword. They'll be back,
and they'll spar." He smiled. "I am, myself, just newly wakened.
Would you join me in breaking my fast?" He waited, and then, after a moment, added, "I am not familiar with all of your language. I am going to eat, and I would like your company."

Aidan nodded. He didn't trust himself to speak.

The hotel's rooms were grander than any rooms that Aidan had
ever lived in, and this was not the very finest of the hotels that
the holdings boasted—although he'd heard, and who hadn't, that
there were hotels on the isle that were finer by far than any in the
holdings could ever hope to be.

He couldn't imagine it. The cloth merchants had found their
customers in everything here: the chairs were covered in embroi-
dered fabric, in plush, heavy silks, all of which were vibrantly,
brilliantly colored; the curtains that hung about windows taller
and wider than even the jeweler's in the Common; the knotted throws
and hangings that adorned the walls. The walls themselves were
pale, but that was fine with Aidan; he found the colors so dis-
tracting he almost forgot about the food.

Wasn't actually that hard to do. There was hardly any bread,
and what there was of the food was cold and covered in something that looked sort of like sour milk. Tasted all right—he had
to eat it, he knew that much about manners —but he wouldn't have
paid for the privilege.

The actual dishes were nice, though, and he thought about pock-
eting the silver. Thought long and hard about what would happen
if he got caught, and reminded himself that to be here at all was
so lucky, he was due for a good dose of Kalliaris' ill-favor. He
left the spoons where they were.

"You don't eat enough,"' the old man said.

"I ate as much as you did," Aidan shot back before he could
stop himself. He froze, but the man laughed genially.

"Yes, you did. But you are a young almost-man, and I am an
old one; I have built the body I live with, you have not. Come;
I've paid in good coin for the meal, and I would hate to see it
wasted."

Aidan picked up a spoon.

"Do you watch your own fighters as carefully as you watch

ours?" The old man asked the question before the spoon had left Aidan's mouth.

"If I could," he replied, around a mouthful of something that had probably once been egg. Bread would be nice. And some cheese. Some meat that looked meatlike. He wondered how much money the meal cost. Worried, for a minute, that he might be asked to pay for part of it.

"Ah. But I believe that there are Imperial soldiers who are practicing within the holdings."

"Probably. Probably all over. But you've got to get a permit, and you don't get one for a place like this without—"

"Money."

"Ummm, well. Yes." Aidan shrugged, self-conscious. You didn't talk about money, for two reasons. If you had it and someone who didn't heard you, you might not have it for long—especially with so many strangers from so many places just waiting around—and if you didn't have it, and someone who did heard you, they were like as not to look down their nose and treat you like dirt.

The old man laughed again. "You are Northern, boy, and I forget myself. I did not—I did not always occupy my present position, and I have had to learn much to live up to it." He laughed again. Lifted his hand, picked up a stick on the table, and struck something that Aidan had assumed—until that very moment—was a bowl.

It resonated in the air with the sweet, clear note of a bell, of a perfectly crafted bell.

A man appeared out of nowhere; that he was standing at all was the only thing that made him appear not to be groveling.

"Bring us something Northern. Bread, meat. Your food."

"At once, sir." He disappeared.

"How many times have the Northern Imperials taken the Challenge Crown?"

"The wreath, you mean?"

"It is formally called the Challenge Crown," the old man said soberly, "but, yes, that is what I meant."

Aidan thought about it for a minute. That was all it took. "Just over three hundred. Three hundred and two times."

"Can you name all of the men who were so victorious?"

"Not the middle ones. The early ones, yes. There was Eadward Wegnson; he was the first. He was the first of the Challenge Champions, and he won the wreath and gave it—gave it to the King Cormalyn's wife."

"Yes. It caused unrest in the court, I believe. He was known for his admiration of her—but young men with swords and brawn often admire women of beauty. It was said she was also known for the fact that she returned that admiration." He was silent for a long while as he stared across the table at Aidan. At last he said, "In the Dominion, that would have been her death."

"What? Because he gave her the wreath?"

"Because she accepted it with cause," the old man said gravely. "A wife has only one husband, and if the husband rules the land, she *must* be seen to be both pure and untouched."

Aidan shrugged. "Doesn't seem fair. A husband doesn't have to have only one wife in the South. Not like here."

The old man was quieter for a much longer time. "No," he said at last. "In the South it is common for a rich man to have many wives."

"If you have a lot of wives," Aidan said, and he said it without thinking, "maybe it doesn't hurt as much when one of them dies."

Silence.

He looked up, the old man's face was like stone, like his father's face the day that Widow Harris had come in, come running from the Common, to tell him that something bad had happened to his wife. He'd had to hobble, he'd had to cling to walls, just to get around, and he wouldn't do it in front of "that Harris woman." So he'd stood there, while she urged him to follow, while she offered help; stood there, being a man. Like that. Stone. Aidan had run, at Widow Harris' side. Because his mother needed someone. But he'd left his father behind.

What little hunger was left in him died the minute he saw the old man's face. He dropped the spoon, but it fell into his lap, making no noise.

Twice. Twice he'd opened his mouth, said something stupid. But this time—he knew that expression. "I—it's my father—he—my mother—"

The old man said nothing at all. Aidan knew he wouldn't. But Aidan wasn't made of stone yet.

"She died last year. Over a year ago. An accident in the Common. We couldn't get her to the Mother's Daughter in time. It didn't hurt her —that's what she said, the Mother's Daughter—she died quickly, without pain."

"Then she was fortunate," the old man said coldly. "To die without pain."

The silence was awkward. Only when the man, forgotten until

this moment, came bearing bread and meat and cheese—and fruit!—did the old man speak again.

"You know a lot about the Challenge for a boy who has never witnessed it. You might as well eat it, boy. It is not food that is overly much to my liking." But even as he said it, he picked up one of the loaves and broke it, messily, in half.

"I went once," Aidan said. "When I was younger. With my Da—with my father."

"A good father, then, to expose you to things that are as important as the Challenge." He picked up the meat with his hands, ignoring the slender fork that rested on the silver tray for just that purpose. Aidan relaxed then, and did the same.

"I think so."

"How many men from the free towns have taken the wreath?"

"Harder to say." Hard to speak, too, around a mouthful the size that Aidan had taken. He chewed as quickly as he could and swallowed. "The free towns are made up mostly of people from other places. Mercs that settle down. People that are too poor here to want to stay. Things like that."

"Spoken," the old man replied, "like a boy who has grown up in Averalaan. Still, how many men who have claimed the free towns as their homes have taken the wreath?"

"Eighteen," Aidan said promptly. "But my Da says—"

"And from the Western Kingdoms, as you call them?"

"Twenty-three, although if you break that down, then most of them have come from just one of the five Kingdoms."

"Let us not break them down that far. How many men have come to the crown from the central Empire?"

"Seventy-four." He said that without pause.

"I would not be mistaken, I think, if I assumed you could name them all."

"There was—"

"And I do not believe I have time to hear about seventy-four such illustrious men." He smiled. "What of the South?"

"One."

"One?"

"Well, yeah. But he won twice. He was called Anton Guivera."

"In the South, I believe it would be styled Anton *di'*Guivera."

"Oh." He chewed on that, and on the meat, thinking he should probably tell his father that, and then thinking better of it. "Well, he came from the South, and he won the wreath. Shocked everybody. No one was expecting it. I say, good for him. The North gets too complacent."

"Your father's words?"

"Well, yeah, but I agree with him. Anyway, when Guivera took the wreath, he didn't give it to anyone there—he said it was for Marianna en'Guivera. I think that was his wife. But she wasn't with him, you know," he added. "She died in a bandit raid a couple of years before. He hated bandits forever after that. They say, on the way here, he cleared a path between Raverra and Averda all by himself."

"I believe," the old man said wryly, "that anyone from the South knows full well the story of Anton di'Guivera. He achieved some fame there for his effort."

"Here too." They ate together in a companionable, if delicate silence. "Do you think you've got another Guivera here? Di'Guivera, I mean?"

"Here? A master does not discuss his students and their capabilities with any but them." The old man's eyes narrowed ever so slightly. "You, however, are no such master. Tell me what you think."

Aidan hated to be tested, and he was being tested. But the old man had paid for the meal, and besides, Aidan had a sense that he'd *know* a lie, even a polite one. "No."

"No?"

"No."

"How can you judge if you haven't seen the rest of the field?"

Aidan shrugged. "I don't know. I think that two of 'em are really good, but I don't think it's a sure thing. If a man can win the Challenge two years in a row, it's a *sure* thing. I mean—that is—I think."

"Good enough. I don't know who you are, boy. You don't know who I am. But we have an interest in common, and I am in a foreign land, far from the comforts and familiarity of my home and my family.

"The testing begins this afternoon, after the midday meal. We will, of course, eat early and late around that test."

Aidan was silent; he hoped that his lips weren't moving in time to the fierce, desperate prayer he was repeating over and over.

"You, no doubt, know that this set of tests, incomplete though it is, will result in the choosing of the hundred men deemed most suitable as candidates and allowed to pass over to the isle as competitors."

Aidan nodded.

"There are probably a thousand, possibly two; most will be passed over instantly."

He nodded again; his hands had found their way to his lap where he was now wringing them.

"I would be most amused if you would care to travel with my party when we attempt to gain entrance to the Challenge itself."

AIDAN: II

9th of Lattan, 427 AA
Averalaan, Merchant Holdings

There were some things you didn't need language for.

Aidan couldn't understand a word the old man's students spoke—but he knew from the widening and the narrowing of their eyes that they weren't much pleased that he was to come along with them. There was even an argument or two among some of the men—but that died the minute the old man came into ear-shot. At least that's what Aidan would have thought—but judging from what followed, all of it in words that were completely foreign to him, the old man's earshot was a damned sight better than any of theirs.

They were humbled.

They shut up.

They ignored Aidan entirely. And he'd learned, with time, that to be ignored by the bigger and the stronger was at worst a mixed blessing. At worst. Today it was just a blessing.

The only uncomfortable moment came when they left the grand building—because instead of walking into the streets themselves, they headed toward the stables.

"What—what are you doing?"

The old man looked down his shoulder at Aidan. "We are retrieving our horses."

"Why?"

The corners of the man's mouth lifted a moment. "Because we are riding to combat, be it limited, unsatisfying, or unchallenging; we treat it with the respect combat is due, and therefore go as men."

"But there are—there are more than ten of you!"

"There are, I believe, thirteen at the moment."

"You—the streets are really crowded—you—"

The old man's smile deepened. "Have you never been on the back of a horse?"

Aidan went mute. He wasn't going to look like a complete fool in front of everyone.

But the man's voice softened slightly. "Boy, you are young. There is no crime, there is *never* a crime, in being what you are, in being true to what you were born to. Some struggle and strive to surpass that, and there is no crime or shame in ambition—but to be what you *are* is the test of any man, be he seraf or clansman, warrior or no.

"You come from the North. Your traditions are not our traditions. Your bravery is not our bravery—but I have seen the Northern warriors, and I have seen them exercise their control and their prowess defending those things that *are* considered a matter of men in the Empire. I am not a fool; I respect the respectworthy, and I know it when I see it.

"Wish *I* did," Aidan muttered.

"You have good instinct," was the old man's reply. "Trust it."

The horses were brought. They were huge. Far larger than the carriage horses that the rich used, or the wagon horses and mules that the merchants did. One of them, big and black and sharp-hooved, snapped at Aidan, his teeth closing on the air an inch in front of Aidan's face.

Aidan leaped behind the old man.

The old man's students burst into unpleasant laughter.

He spoke sharply, the old man, and one of the men sauntered forward to grab at the horse's reins. Aidan dearly hoped the huge beast would snap at the closest hand, but no such luck; the demon beast snorted and allowed himself to be led away.

And it wasn't just the one horse that was dangerous; it was about half of 'em. They even snapped at each other, moving restively against dirt and cobbled stone. There was going to be damage to the grounds, that much was clear, and the stable hands all looked queasy.

It was the old man who spoke again, and Aidan found the cadence of the foreign tongue almost comforting, although he was grateful that he wasn't on the receiving end of the incomprehensible words themselves. The horses were forced apart by sullen men, mounted, and ridden out the gates that led from the stable yards to the street.

"Do they know where they're going?" Aidan asked.

"No. But I thought you might wish to mount without the benefit of an audience. We will join them when you are ready."

"Mount?"

"Yes. You do not have a horse, but the one I have—I call her Abani—will serve us both very well." He smiled. "I am an old man, and I have proved myself time and again. The choice of a mare over a stallion does not seem to cause me any loss of status."

"They were *all* stallions?"

"Not all, no. There are some men for whom the patina of success, and not necessarily success itself, is important; half here ride stallions that would beggar small families. The other half ride mares. You do not know my two best students. They are studies in opposites. The desire for obvious glory does not, sadly, preclude success—and perhaps it does not even hinder it. But come; we are guests here, and supplicants of a kind; we do not wish to be late for our granted appointment."

Aidan closed his eyes, opened them, closed them. The old man's hands were as sure as, as strong as, his father's had ever been when Aidan had been younger and easier to lift. When his mother had been alive.

The horse was *wide*. He thought his feet would dangle over either side of the saddle; he was not large for his age.

"I will sit behind you; you will have to trust that I will not let you fall off."

Aidan nodded.

The old man's mount was graceful and easy; he hardly disturbed the saddle whose bridge Aidan almost straddled. They settled into their place upon the horse, and the old man reached round Aidan to either side and grasped the reins. As if it were actually safe to ride, the creature began to move forward at a stately, almost smooth, walk.

"You trust," the old man said, "far more easily than many a Southern boy."

Aidan shrugged. "You told me to trust my instincts."

He was rewarded by a low, brief laugh. "We are often caught by our own words. Very well, boy. The Challenge."

It was a long, winding journey from the hotel to the testing grounds, and until they were mired in the height and the ancient facades of the many buildings that comprised the Merchant holdings, Aidan wasn't certain where they were going. He rarely ventured this far into the Merchant holdings; the merchants tended to hire their own guards, and if the guards broke the laws the Magisterium set out, they would eventually be in trouble—but you had to survive them, and if they broke something like an arm, leg, or a jaw—yours, of course—you usually just had to pray that it turned out all right in the end.

Healing cost money, after all. Everything did.

There are things that money can't buy, Aidan, his mother had said, and he could hear the lost sweetness that had been her voice; it was one of her favorite things to tell him. But he'd learned the hard way that if there *were* things money couldn't buy, they weren't really things he wanted anyway.

His mother would have loved the Merchant holdings. Stonemasons had done their work here, and although the trees in the Common were her favorite, she also loved the great cut stone buildings that signaled wealth, as if money could build a fortress in the streets of the city. She loved the gargoyles and the way that both gargoyle faces and building walls seemed to stand unchanged with the passing of years; no staining and wear with time, no timbers to be bowed by moisture or worse.

But she did not often walk among those buildings.

Certainly she had never come to them riding on the back of a beast several times her weight and with a vastly poorer temper.

People stopped to stare, and although the roads here were almost as wide as the roads in the Common itself, they became crowded with curiosity seekers. Crowded, and hard to pass through. There were children underfoot—it astonished Aidan, to see children here, in the stronghold of the merchants, and he wished irritably that they would go back to their fathers or mothers or nursemaids.

But even wishing it, he knew, guiltily, that had he been lucky enough to be in the streets when so many armed men were riding by, he would have stared, too. From a safer distance. Maybe.

It was hot. Heat was one of the tests a man faced when upholding the Lord's honor. So the old man had said. The heat had never troubled Aidan.

"That is because you've never spent a day in armor, let alone when your life depended on the wearing of it." He lifted a hand before Aidan could speak, although how he knew Aidan was going to speak, Aidan didn't know. He certainly couldn't see it from the back of his head. "In the Dominion, there are two kinds of armor that men wear. The most obvious is the armor you see on Andaro there; leather, metal, a thing upon which life depends. It can be bought if you've the coin for it, fashioned if you've the skill. It is second to only your horse or sword in importance. But armor wears; it breaks and it can be stolen. A fool with money can purchase the best. It takes no skill to wear it and little enough to learn how to put it on.

"There are men who define themselves by the things they own, the things they buy. Owning these things, they put much of their wealth into hiring others to protect them." His tone of voice was deceptively soft. Aidan heard the steel in it, the winter chill. "But hiring others guarantees nothing. This is a lesson that the Tyr'agar himself—the king, if you will, of the Dominion—learned, to his regret. We all learn it, Aidan: there are times when the plans of other men will prevail." His voice became soft, and Aidan heard in that softness a hint of his mother's thoughtful distance.

What are you thinking? he would ask her when he saw that look. As a young child, he'd asked not because he wanted the answer, but because answering would bring her back to him, and he hated when she was far away. But as she got older, she would smile, sometimes sadly, and tell him, *I am thinking of far away.*

Very far?

Not so far that I can't reach it by making a quiet space for myself and taking time to think in it. And not so far that I can't be called back by you.

That was how she told him she loved him.

And now she was too far. He couldn't bring her back with anything as simple as a question because she couldn't hear him ask it.

As if he could hear the sudden ghost of old pain, the old man continued, returning from the place that he'd been, just as Aidan's mother had. "There is armor that we wear in the service of, for the glory of, the Lord. And there is armor we wear as protection *against* him, for he tests us, always; he destroys the things that weaken us, and if we prove weak, he destroys *us*. He will not be served by the inferior.

"This second armor I speak of, nothing pierces, nothing destroys. It cannot be bought, have you more money than a Tyr, and it cannot be made by any hand other than your own. Forge well, boy, and the world will never know that it can hurt you, and it will find some weaker man to torment in your stead."

"Do you have it, this armor?"

"Yes." The old man chuckled. "It does not stop pain, boy. Only death does that. But it prevents you from revealing the things that cause you pain. If they do not know the difference between the things that hurt you and things that do not, your enemies can make many mistakes."

Aidan was quiet for a long time. At last he said, "So can your friends, though."

The old man's arms tightened a moment; Aidan should have worried about being tossed off the horse. But he didn't. "You are young," the old man said at length. "You don't yet realize that in truth, we have no friends. There is the will of the Lord. The will of powerful men."

"There has to be more than that," Aidan said.

"Does there?"

"Yeah. Why else would you come to the Challenge?"

"What makes you think that I do not travel at the will of other, more powerful men?" Bitter, bitter words.

"Because," Aidan said, "you're the master."

Silence, punctuated by the clipped weight of shod hooves on exposed stone. "You are very observant, boy. If you stay where you are in the life that you have, it will be a crime in the Lord's eyes."

"The Lord doesn't rule these lands."

"No, perhaps he does not."

"Can I ask a question?"

"You have asked more questions in this last hour than anyone of my acquaintance has dared to ask in the last ten years," he replied.

Aidan took that as a yes. "Why do you serve the Lord? You don't even sound like you like him."

"You do not particularly care for *Kalliaris,* but if I had to guess, I would say that you pray to her far more often than you pray to any of your other gods."

Aidan shrugged. "She is what she is. But I like the Mother, and the Kings' fathers."

"They are none of them powerful enough to stand alone," the old man replied, with the faintest hint of scorn.

"Maybe they don't feel they have to. They don't have a lot to prove."

Dry chuckle. "Your point, Aidan. Perhaps if I lived in the North, I would believe as you believe, worship as you worship. But the Lord *is* the Dominion, and he shapes us all. I do not follow him any more than you follow *Kalliaris.* He *is.* I am. But before the winds take me, I will stand up to his heat; I will stand. And if he destroys the things I value, I will have vengeance.

"Because creatures of power only understand power; everything else is in a tone too delicate, a nuance to subtle, to catch their attention, to force their acknowledgment."

"Nobody lives alone," Aidan said. "My—my mother used to say that."

"She was a woman of the North."

"She was smart."

"Wise, I think, would be the better word. What else did your mother say?"

"All the old stuff. Stand up for what you believe in. Do the right thing, even when it's easier to do the wrong one. Give when you can. Take only what you need." He shrugged, uncomfortably close to himself, to the fact that he was slipping away from his mother's words because he couldn't figure out how to live with his father. She'd've hated that. "Stuff like that. Girl stuff."

The old man said, softly, "Once, there was a woman in my life who said very much what your mother said. I, too, thought her very foolish. Very, very foolish."

And Aidan, who found his eyes stinging a moment as memory blending into the present became sharp and twisted, understood that this man had lost someone, and that he, too, would take no comfort at all in the telling of it.

One hundred men.

One hundred men would be chosen out of this gathered, hopeful crowd. Aidan was not very good with numbers, but he was certain that the long, thick line of waiting men, on this first day of the trials, far outnumbered that. Some, he knew, would be turned away immediately; they were perhaps a year or two older than he was, and worse, looked it. The Challenge had rules just like the army's; you had to be Old Enough. Aidan wasn't that mythical age. He wondered if he would ever reach it.

"What do you see?" the old man asked.

"That we're not the only people here on horseback."

"That is unusual. It is seldom that we see Northern riders, and for the Northerners, the horses are large and fine. Who are they?" There was an awkward pause before the old man said, "Forgive me, boy. You know so much of the Challenge's history and ritual that I had almost forgotten that some of these things—horses, mounted riders—are foreign to your way of living. I . . . see the horses. I do not see the riders."

The old man didn't sound at all pleased about it either, which is to say that he suddenly ceased to speak Weston at all. Had a lot to say in the Southern tongue, though. Aidan promised himself that he would learn to speak that language. He tried to listen to the sounds the old man's words were made of, clinging to them as if he could hold them in memory for long enough to eventually unlock their meaning. But the only words he could sift out of that fluid stream of oddly musical sounds were "tor" and "leonne"; they were said sometimes together and sometimes apart.

The tone of the old man's voice as he spoke was all alley shadow. Aidan wouldn't have dared to interrupt him had his life depended on it. He was certain that if it had, he would be dead.

They joined the line; the horses brought a combination of the magisterial guards and the Crown guards. Before either of these groups of officials could speak, the old man handed them a set of curled papers. The magisterians read them over so carefully you could almost hear their eyes scraping paper. But the royal guards hardly glanced at them at all; it was as if they'd expected to see over a dozen huge horses in the trial lineups.

"Commander Sivari," one of the King's men said. Aidan froze. He recognized the name. Sivari. It wasn't all that common.

The old man said, quietly, "It is time for me to dismount, boy." He offered Aidan a hand down; Commander Sivari met him halfway. The Northern officer looked at Aidan's white hair and soon to be blistering pale skin, and raised a dark brow. He did not speak, however.

"Commander Sivari," the old man said. He bowed, the gesture so unexpected to Aidan that the boy froze in surprise. "I expected to be met, but not by a man who has worn the Challenge Crown. I am honored."

Aidan's jaw dropped. This man—this man was Effarin Sivari. Kings' Champion. It had been a long time since he had earned the right to that title, but as he was one of the few champions who had been born and bred in the Empire's heart, and not its Northern remove, Aidan knew his name, and even some of his history.

He was speechless. A god could have tapped him on the shoulder and it wouldn't have surprised him more. He was beyond surprise.

Or so he thought.

But Commander Sivari returned the bow; if possible, it was lower, more formal. "Who else would they send," he said as he rose, an expression that Aidan didn't understand on his face. "Who else would properly honor the only man living who has worn that crown twice?"

Why didn't he tell me? Aidan was still speechless. He was also mortified. He had spent the last two days with a man who practically defined the word champion. He had even—oh, the humiliation was boundless—told him the stories about *himself,* stories he probably sounded completely stupid, at best, repeating.

No Southerner knew so much about the Northern Challenge; they almost never sent their best North. The fact that he'd shown the interest, and knew so many of the answers—that should have been a dead giveaway. Dammit, he should have *known* who that old man was.

He wondered if the old man had enjoyed laughing at him.

"You are . . . quiet, boy."

Aidan said nothing.

The old man returned his silence with a silence that was shorter and less awkward. "I would have told you," he said at last, "but by the time it became relevant, it would have been awkward. You have a vision and a simplicity that no one involved in the Challenge with me will have. Not this Challenge. I found it refreshing. I am not a political man." He laughed. "And yet, life *is* politics; the politics of the sword, the politics of power, or position. I wished a reprieve, and you were that reprieve.

"Forgive my duplicity." He bowed.

Aidan was stunned. "But aren't you—but didn't you think I was stupid for not *recognizing* you? I should have," he added, speaking because the old man had spoken. "They all practically worship you. They'd stop breathing and turn blue if you told them to hold their breaths. Hells, they'd probably parade around the Commons without any clothing."

"But not without their swords surely," was the old man's sober reply. "You mistake them."

"No, I don't." Aidan shrugged. Balled his hands into fists and crossed them behind his slightly bent back. "'Because I'd do the same damn thing, if you told me to. If you'd accept *me* as a student, I'd do it, too."

"I think," the old man said quietly, "that I would not take a student who had so little sense of self. They listen to me because I speak of the sword and the Challenge when I speak to them at all, and they know that my knowledge in this regard is superior to theirs. Were I to speak, instead, of women, I think they would

humor me because of that knowledge—but they would take no
orders of mine. Two of them are better riders now than I have
ever been, and if they had beneath them the mount that I was
given for the Challenge, they would be unstoppable here. But we
two, that horse and I, we were chosen for our strengths; riding
him, *I* won the race. That man," he said, pointing to one of his
students, "will win the rider's wreath." There was no doubt whatever in his voice. "But I digress. They listen, but they do not worship me, boy. I am not the Lord."

Aidan would have argued, but he realized that at least two of
those students suddenly looked less friendly than they had only
moments before—which said a lot, as they'd never looked particularly friendly. It hadn't occurred to him that any of the other
Southerners could speak Weston until that moment, and it made
him feel at a disadvantage.

One of the men, the one, in fact, that the old man had pointed
out, opened his mouth. Spoke two words. The old man—no, he
had to stop thinking about him that way—*Ser Anton di'Guivera*
lifted a hand and swatted them away as if they were flies. Well,
more exactly, he crushed them.

Aidan was distinctly glad that no part of his life depended upon
the goodwill of that student. It was too bad, though; he was one
of the two really good ones.

Talent, his mother used to say, *tells you nothing at all about
the man. Don't judge anything by it.* It was true, but it was always
disappointing when someone who was living his dream didn't
live up to the dream itself.

He glanced to the side and found that the old man's eyes were
upon him. "He doesn't understand most of what you say," he said
with a wry smile. "He merely dislikes you on principle. He wishes
to be surrounded by his peers, and has enough wit to be suspicious of the unusual—you, in this case—without any instinct whatsoever to fall back upon for discretion's sake.

"He is also," Ser Anton added, "preparing in his own way for
the trials. He likes too many things, too much: food, wine, the
company of young women. But he has a sense of respect for his
art, and although there is no question at all that he will be accepted as one of the hundred, he will give these trials the same
respect as the Challenge itself. That alone sets him apart from the
many rather unremarkable young men he resembles. It's not just
about talent, although talent does count. Focus. Concentration.
Ambition. Without these, no man amounts to anything."

"In the eyes of the Lord," Aidan said quietly, thinking uncomfortably of his father.

The old man raised a solid brow. "Indeed," he said softly. "In the eyes of the Lord."

The trial administrators were a bored group of men. They resembled, more than anything, merchants, as they sat in high-backed chairs behind their solid, heavy desks. They even had paper and slate, ink and chalk, before them. Names were taken, and numbers given, numbers written down.

The old man—Ser Anton—smiled a little grimly. "This," he said, "is where most of our day will surely be spent."

"Do they do this where you live?"

"They do 'this' as you call it," Ser Anton said, "in every land I have ever visited. Not for the same things, not precisely. But yes. In the Dominion, it is more gracefully hidden. A family must enter—with small fee—the name of their chosen contender or contenders. The Radann perform the office that these magistrates perform here, and they do it within the confines of their temples. They also," he added, "have the good grace to do so where the rest of us are not forced to bear witness.

"You must excuse me. Few of my students speak Weston well enough to answer these questions—and almost all of them, without exception, take poorly to being asked them."

Aidan was left alone.

No one chose to question his right to be here; he obviously carried no sword, so he wasn't trying to sneak in as a contender. He stared at his feet, feeling his size and lack of weight, and almost despising both.

And because his vision was so turned inward, and unpleasantly at that, there was very little to distract him from one of his favorite sounds. Metal. Metal. The clash of weapons. He lifted his head. For the most part—or so he had been told—the men who had come to trial came to prove they had swords, but they were tested in this first round, with wooden swords. Practice blades. They were required to wear their armor, to show their bows, but steel and steel for such a test as this was rare.

He'd wondered about it, because the old man's students certainly used real swords. And perhaps what his Da said wasn't true. Wouldn't be the first time, although it would be the first time he'd been wrong about the Challenge.

He thought the sounds of fighting would stop, but they didn't,

and he couldn't help himself. He was carried by them as if by
music; to Aidan, they were. They had their own timing, their own
distinct feel, and as he approached them, as the sounds grew louder,
as the bodies in front of him became sparser and sparser still, he
felt the hair on his neck stand on end.

The coliseum itself was huge, and it was mostly empty—those
were the rules—but attendants, such as he, were allowed to sit and
bear witness to the fairness of the trial's many judges. He was aware
of the seats, but he did not take one; he walked across the ringed
floor to the railing that separated him from the two men who now
fought in the circle's center.

A flag was flying under the open sky, and beneath it, a banner
had been driven into dirt. He did not recognize it immediately
because he was not familiar with banners that didn't have something common, like bread, a keg, or a lute sewn across them, but
when he saw the gold glinting off the full height sun, when he
saw the golden curve of the sword beneath it, he knew that this
man was a foreigner.

He crept closer, then froze.

There were two men. He recognized one of them.

Commander Sivari.

The other, he had never seen before in his life—but he would
remember the grim set of his face, the dark, straight flat of hair
pulled back and bound very, very tight. He wore no helm. His Da
would have said that was the last act of a young idiot, the lack
of helm.

But Aidan knew, watching him, that it was more than that. He
moved. He did not falter, not once. The sun caught his blade, his
hair, the curve of his armor; he and the Commander seemed to
be, in this dance, in another place entirely. A place where heat and
the sea-heavy air could only watch, as Aidan did: without touching.

He did not hear the footsteps at his back, although they were
heavy, and there were many of them. He did not see the old man
appear at his side. But he heard the old man's voice because the
old man was watching these two through the same window that
Aidan was.

"Why do you watch him, boy?"

Aidan felt a curious resentment—a muted echo of the same resentment that he had felt when the old man had asked a similar
question the day before. He wanted to *see* this. He knew that he
would never, never have this chance again. To watch even the

others—even the two best of the old man's students—wasn't quite the same.

But because it was Ser Anton di'Guivera and not just any old man who asked, he answered. "Because, Ser Anton, I don't think I'll ever see anyone as—as perfect as he is again."

"He is far from perfect," the old man said, his eye the more critical, the more intelligent, his experience the more telling.

"Look at his eyes," Aidan replied. "Look at his face. The sword—it's so much a part of him, I don't even think he knows that the sword is there."

Ser Anton said nothing; they watched together, in a silence born of awe on Aidan's part, and of something else on the old man's. Another voice spoke—in the Southern tongue—and in it, Aidan heard a hint of what he himself felt.

The old man's reply was sharp. No one spoke again.

They watched; they waited.

In the end, the judges intervened; they called the halt. Commander Sivari heard them immediately, but Aidan wasn't so certain that the young man did. He stopped only when Sivari stepped across the thin stone circle that had contained them both within the fighting ground.

The old man's words were Southern, foreign, and soft.

At once, as if that were a signal, the men at his back began to speak, their words clashing and colliding in a cacophony of tones.

"Do you know who he is?" Aidan asked. "That banner—it's Southern."

The old man's laugh was a brief, angry bark. "I know well whose it is," he said curtly. He started to say something else and then became completely still. He was angry; that much was clear to Aidan; perhaps this young man and his own students were somehow rivals.

"He is—not what I thought he would be." The old man reached out with both hands, dwarfing the railing in them. It was only then that Aidan realized that the old man was actually very large. "I came to the Empire to make his acquaintance. He is Valedan kai di'Leonne, the last living member of the clan that once ruled the Dominion of Annagar." He spoke again, something soft, and raised his face to the sun.

"What are you saying?" Aidan asked quietly.

"I? I am telling the Lord," the old man replied, "that a worthy enemy is not always a warrior's blessing. Now come; we have seen what we were intended to see, and we are required to ready ourselves for the judges."

He turned, the old man, in a quiet that wasn't quiet, and spoke in a tongue that Aidan was grateful, just this once, that he couldn't understand. Ser Anton di'Guivera and his students began to walk away, but Aidan turned to watch the man that the old man had called *Valedan kai di'Leonne*. The distance between them was larger than the length of the crowded coliseum; it was vast as the distance between the harbor and the merchant ships at the farthest edge of the horizon on the days when he watched for the sea winds.

And as he watched, this man, this Valedan kai di'Leonne, turned to look into the empty seats that surrounded the fighting ground.

Their eyes met; Aidan felt a shock of something that he couldn't even name. They stood staring in silence until two men came to break their regard: Ser Anton di'Guivera and Commander Sivari.

Aidan watched the old man's—*Ser Anton, you idiot*—students as they performed for the trial judges. They were uniformly better than he had ever seen them, and he thought he knew why; they had seen a rival, and they knew that they had to live up to his performance. Not for the sake of the judges—even Aidan wouldn't have been that stupid—but for the sake of the man who taught them. But there was a self-consciousness about them all that day, and he knew that he could watch the entire trial, and he wouldn't see Valedan kai di'Leonne again.

And he wanted to.

Not much, he thought, as he felt the familiar refrain that was the prayer to Kalliaris start up in the back of his mind. *I wouldn't have to see much—just a little. A bit. Let him ride past me on the way to the isle. Just that much.*

He promised himself that he would find a spot by the road that the challengers would travel; he knew the whole route. Anyone who paid any attention at all did. He was going to hold that spot, sit in it, and keep it for himself, as he hadn't done since he'd been eight and his father had let himself be wheedled into it.

He was going to watch the procession.

And maybe—*Kalliaris, please*—if he was very, very lucky, he might, once in this lifetime, be chosen as Challenger's Witness. There were a hundred challengers, after all. One hundred chances.

Out of tens of thousands. Get real, Aidan.

Still, he made his plans. And after he made them, he went to talk to Widow Harris about both food and errand running during the Challenge itself.

CHAPTER ONE

Evening of 4th of Lattan, 427 AA
Averalaan, Terafin Manse

He knew, by the quality of the younger men's silence, that he would arrive too late; that death had come and gone and taken with it the patient that they sought his care for. This late in the eve, there were those among the six who stood in the hall, weapons drawn, who could use his time and attention—but the House member for whom they had come at a run, to judge by the rise and fall of their mail-plated chests—was beyond him.

But Alayra, semiretired captain of the best House Guards in the Empire, waited just beyond the rank of six bone-weary, blood-ied men, and her face was an expressionless, steel mask, save for the slight whitening around the edges of old scars. She had never had a pretty face; had gone out of her way to make sure that she never would. A glimpse of her younger self shone through a moment in eyes that saw less well with each passing day; a glimpse of his younger self responded.

They had fought in a war together, the healer-born Alowan who, although he had served Amarais Handernesse ATerafin, had never chosen to take the name she offered him for his service, and Alayra ATerafin, trusted above all among the Chosen hand-picked by The Terafin at the time of her ascension.

Sleep left him completely; he straightened his back, reach for the cane that supported his weight, and said only, "A moment." Turning, he shouted a single name. One of his young assistants, the one first roused by the banging of the mailed fists, came peer-ing out from around the healerie's fine plants. "Terrisa," he said softly, "wake the others; have them bring the stretchers and meet me—"

"Alea ATerafin's rooms," Captain Alayra said quietly. She turned away then, the steel of her face cracking as if under great or sudden pressure. He lost sight of it a moment as his eyes closed.

Terrisa's eyes were still round and unblinking when his own opened. "Terrisa," he said, his voice thick and foreign to his own ears, "now is not the time. Be quick."

The cane was necessary to take him from the narrower halls the healerie occupied to the grand halls that separated the manse into its wings; he asked no questions. She offered no information. On all sides, the heavy, even steps of men who were used to walking—and working—in unison set the tone of their journey: grim, certain.

He, who had seen his share of deaths, was never prepared for it. The healer's blood cried out against it, an accusation of a type, but to whom, and of what, no healer was ever fully certain. They defied death where *any* hint of life remained at all—if they dared. The cost was high.

Healer Alowan had dared, and dared, and dared.

And his bones—or something akin to them, something buried within the flesh and the blood, buried within the moving body— ached with the memory of all of those lost half-selves; the healed, the people that he had had to love to bring back to light at all.

Four of the Chosen stood guard outside of the closed double doors; he recognized two of them at once: Arrendas, still dark-haired, still unruffled by the passage of a decade and a half, and Torvan, grayer, paler, but unfettered and unbowed. They stopped him; it was perfunctory. Alayra gave them a nod sharp as a knife's edge—a knife that she'd own—and they stepped aside at once.

He paused, hand on door, hand on door handle. It was cold to the touch, but a soothing cold, a comforting cold; nothing about brass and iron was meant to move, to breathe, to speak with the rhythms of movement and breath. His head found the fine, heavy density of wood that was older than anyone present; he pressed his forehead there a moment.

He thought, *I am too old.*

The captain of the Chosen took her place beside him, as if to offer comfort, or receive it; hard to say. They had seen a war together, and it had scarred them irrevocably, but they'd fought it so they would never have to fight it again.

Thus the hope and the fire of the young.

Alayra said, her lips barely moving, her hand against the closed door, "I'm too damned old for this."

Their eyes met.

Alowan straightened out a white-crested head, unbending at the shoulder. He pushed the door in, steeling himself. Taking the blow; absorbing the shock of sight, of vision.

Five bodies lay in the room.

Three fully armored, but all armed. He didn't recognize the three armored men, but they wore the crest of the House Guard. *Imposters,* he thought, but no part of him believed it; they would take these three dead, and when they were presented to The Terafin and the captains of the House Guards, they would be identified as part of the Terafin Guard, no more, no less.

One of the Chosen lay dead as well; he was not so well armored as the three men in regular guard uniform, but better armed. He paused as he stepped over the body, his glance enough to tell him what he already knew.

It was not for their own that the Chosen had made the summons.

Alowan the healer knelt by the side of the bloody bed where the remains of Alea Rose ATerafin had been laid to rest. He reached out—he could not help himself, although the answer was writ clear in the way that the neck was half severed.

Ice, beneath skin; the coldness of a question asked that will never, never be answered.

He did not look up, seeing in the trademark attempt to separate head from shoulders—failed though it was—more than an echo of an earlier war. It was the harbinger.

"Alowan?" Alayra's voice. Over his shoulder and a step back.

"She—she has to be called," he said softly.

"I know."

Bleak, these two. The Chosen who bore open wounds, sweaty weapons, dented armor—they were silent; the battle had exhausted them and tempered their surprise.

It was Arrendas who was sent to wake The Terafin.

The Terafin wore the black and the gold.

Over the years, she had been forced to it many times, and they were colors that she had come to loathe because of it: the colors of respectful mourning.

The dress was perfect; it always was.

He saw to that, when the details were too petty or too small to occupy her time. It was the life he had chosen when he had reached the age of his majority, although it had not been the life that he had foreseen for himself in his youth: service, servitude, silence.

Of the latter, it was silence that he had achieved at the highest price, and silence that he set aside when service demanded it.

She stood in front of her mirror, and he, behind her, saw only her back; her reflection was taken by the dark folds of cloth and the perfect positioning of her back. Not, he knew, an accident.

"Terafin," Morretz said. He was one of the very few men who could come, unannounced, into her presence, and perhaps the only man she allowed to approach her vulnerable back. Especially now. He was aware of it as both an honor and an inevitability: he was domicis, she was master. Nothing but trust could exist between them if they were to hold this relationship.

She turned.

The silence between them was taut with his disapproval. Strange, that in her youth at the helm of this great House she had seen so much of his disapproval, and in her prime, so little. She had become used to its lack.

Or perhaps she was tired. For she *was* tired. She let it show.

The lines of his frown softened slightly; they would have smoothed away completely had he not been required to hold the sword for her. To gird her perfect dress with its ungainly weight. She knew him that well.

And he, in his fashion, knew her. He knew, of course, that she allowed him some hint of her vulnerability to forestall the argument to follow. But he also knew that such a tactic was almost beneath her dignity, and used so rarely that it could not be disregarded. Not entirely.

The sword was heavy in his hands. The Terafin sword. It was seen only during time of war, and her choice to bring it now—to the funeral of a member of her House, no more and no less—was a statement which he thought it wise, at the very least, to avoid.

Justice, the archaic Weston that ran the length of the blade said, *shall not sleep.* Terafin The Founder had proved the truth of that saying during a history in which the spillage of blood counted for less than the spillage of cheap wine. Death. War. Triumph.

"Amarais," he said, his knuckles whitened as he gripped the sword's dress scabbard. "Why now? Why this?"

She turned away again, because there was only so much vulnerability she could expose, to him or anyone. It was her nature; one of the things that he both admired and disliked. What weakness there was in her was buried, and buried deeply; he was certain it existed only because he had been so well trained in the guild of the domicis that he knew all power had its complementary weakness.

"Who killed her?"

Silence.

"Morretz?"

"We have not been able to ascertain that yet." Pause. "And if we had, you would be the first to know." The last was almost chiding.

"I know," she said softly. "But Courtne is dead as well."

As was Corniel ATerafin, but it was to Courtne and Alea that The Terafin had looked for quiet support and counsel; their opinions that she had trusted, always, to be in the best interest of the House itself, and not of personal political gain.

She lifted her arms, to better expose her hips to the width of the sword's belt.

Courtne's death had been a bitter blow. He was there when the news arrived; there to see it stiffen her spine and pale the already classical complexion of her face; there to see her hands tighten a moment into slender fists as she placed them behind her back, hiding them, hiding the truth that needed expression in some gesture, be it a small one.

Captain Alayra of the Chosen had delivered the news; she was still bleeding from the battle that had brought about Courtne's untimely death, and had bypassed a gruffly intemperate—a grieving—healer to do so. Old wolf, old wintered battle-axe of a woman, she understood what the word would mean to Amarais Handernesse ATerafin. To The Terafin. And she'd delivered it in person to spare her the company of strangers.

He remembered that they had stood as they so often did in informal matters of House business: The Terafin by the long, empty library table at which she took informal meetings, Alayra, reflection a sheen of blurred light against fine, fine wood grain across from her, and Morretz one step to the side.

Silence, in that room, after Alayra's terse announcement, broken at last by The Terafin's single word.

"Who?"

There had never been a satisfactory answer. Had there been, had there been, there would have been at least two deaths that night.

But Alayra was not one to shrug and turn; she offered names instead, the names that he himself would have offered in privacy. Haerrad. Rymark. Elonne. Marrick. Corniel.

Because, of course, they were the surviving contenders in the eyes of House Terafin: the men and woman who strove to succeed to the House title and take the House throne.

"Not good enough," The Terafin had replied.

"Then kill them all and have done," the old captain had said wearily. She had seen House War once, and the blood of five of its most prized members troubled her very little compared to the blood that *they* would spill.

It had surprised neither Morretz nor Alayra when The Terafin tendered no reply. But it surprised them both when she dismissed them.

That night, she watched dawn from the roof of the great manse, in the solitary comfort of the oldest piece of clothing she owned. And the day after, she prepared—as she did today—for a funeral. A leave-taking. Had she cried?

He was certain of it. She shared her tears with *no one,* not Morretz and not the men and women in whose hands she placed her life. But she shed them; he was certain she must shed them, and she was given room in which to choose pride over public display. Dark times, those few days.

They were nothing compared to Alea; she was, had been in her fashion, the closest thing to a child The Terafin had allowed herself to have. Amarais had given her life to the House, and the House had become entirely hers for the sacrifice; for companionship she had her Chosen, her domicis, and her Council.

Only one other death, Morretz knew, would be—could be—as painful as this one.

Jewel ATerafin's.

But Jewel was not considered by the Council to *be* a contender. Her past as a street urchin—a thief, if the truth were baldly stated—and the speed with which she reluctantly learned to treat the patriciate as equals on their own ground—slow—precluded her. If this bothered her at all, she showed it as often as The Terafin showed tears.

She was reliable in her fashion, but prone to a certain impatience, a certain wildness, that never harmed the House—but always hovered on the edge of doing so. Amarais trusted her in spite of, or perhaps because of, her past. There was affection between them that was on one level completely different from the affection she had offered Alea, and on the other, absolutely the same.

As if she could hear every word he was thinking, she looked

up, her eyes hitting the surface of perfectly silvered glass to meet his. "The sword," she said softly.

Jewel was in a fury.

They all knew it. They could hear her clattering about the kitchen in isolation; she'd purged it entirely—in one sweeping curse—of both her den-mates and the one or two servants she grudgingly allowed to clean and tend it. Carver hadn't moved fast enough, which is how they'd learned that fury was the right word: she'd sent a tureen—an empty one, but nothing in Terafin was cheap and light—flying into the wall four inches to the right of his head just to catch his attention.

Caught it, too. He left. They all left. No one stayed to ask questions.

Luckily—in a manner of speaking—she'd thrown Avandar out as well. First, of course. He wasn't the den favorite—he had never become part of the den in any significant way—but they'd developed a sneaking admiration for his ability to deal with her graceless temper; he wasn't a man who looked like he was used to hearing a single angry word, let alone what Jewel usually said in the heat of the moment.

"What happened?" Angel said, straightening out a spire of hair and looking at the closed door beyond which a small army's worth of noise could be heard.

Avandar Gallais looked back over his shoulder before he shrugged. He was older than any of 'em, dressed better, spoke better, and knew how to read every language they'd ever encountered even better than Jewel did. They suspected that he could actually *use* magic; he sure as hells recognized it when he saw it coming. They didn't know, though; no one had ever asked him directly. He wasn't a man who usually answered direct questions—even Jay's, which really pissed her off.

Avandar was, as he most often was, silent and thin-lipped. This meant he was both angry and resigned. Angel had already turned away, and almost missed the answer; it was curt and to the point.

"Alea ATerafin."

"Oh."

They knew what it was, then. Alea ATerafin had been about the only member of the upper echelons of Terafin that Jewel Markess ATerafin had actually *liked*. Quiet woman, in her own way, and in Finch's opinion a little on the watery side, but she was probably better than any of the rest of 'em.

And Jewel, seer-born, had never learned to accept that the only life her gift would ever let her save for certain was her own. They all had, and they all did. But not her.

Carver shook his head. "Glad I'm not you," he said, as he pulled away from the kitchen door. "Funeral's in two hours, and you're going to have to dig her out of there and get her ready."

The phrase "if looks could kill" took on significant meaning only if one knew Avandar Gallais well enough to understand the subtle sourness of his expression.

It wasn't a rainy day; it wasn't a dark one. It was the type of day that was so mild and so beautiful it made toil of any sort seem almost an insult to the benevolence of the weather gods—whichever gods those were at the moment. Changed a bit, with time.

Jewel hated it.

There should have been rain, storm, something that showed the displeasure of the heavens at the unjust, the unfair, the unacceptable passing of a decent woman. There should have been mourning, and if not that, than at least weather drizzly and gray enough to keep people from good cheer and ease. Petty thought, that. But Alea was dead, and the death should mean *something*.

She hated black. She hated gold. She wore them both for Alea because Alea would have insisted on it. For the good of the House, of course. For the sake of solidarity.

What she'd chosen not to wear spoke volumes, and indeed volumes had been spoken by Avandar all the way from her rooms to the edge of the grounds.

"You cannot leave your House Ring; it *is* the mark of your status as part of the House Council."

"The House bloody Council," she'd replied, "can choose to go straight to *Allasakar* for all I care."

That silenced him for a moment. The name of the Lord of the Hells was rarely, if ever, spoken. In matters of protocol, however, he was rarely silenced for long.

So she tried a different tack. "Look," she said, "you're not an idiot. I'm not an idiot. We're standing on contested turf right now, and Alea's death was just like Courtne's—part of a turf war. There are two dens forming up. Maybe more."

He was quiet another minute—which allowed her to get from her room to the great hall—before he spoke again. "Four."

"Four. Or five. I don't know. But I do know this. I don't have the funds or the soldiers to throw away in a turf war over a House that's not even up for grabs. The Terafin's not *dead,* Avandar."

"But the—"

"And the House Council *is* the collection of den leaders who are sharpening their knives. Who've already blooded them. Alea is *dead* because they've started their skirmishing. Who's left that's worth respecting? Courtne's dead, and he was considered the un-impeachable heir to the title. Gabriel? Rymark's his *blood son.* And I've already said enough about Rymark.

"Look, I've seen it before. I thought—because I was an idiot— that I'd never see it again. You think I want to be part of them right now? Think again. You want the ring?"

"You don't insult *them,*" he'd said, "You insult *her.*" Avandar spoke of The Terafin, not the dead, and Jewel knew it. "You are her choice, as you well know, and your inclusion on Council was a matter of harsh words and politics."

That almost worked.

Almost.

But she ached when she thought of Alea, and she could think of nothing else to offer her. She wanted to make a gesture. So it was childish. So it was a waste of time. It didn't matter. She wanted to, and this was the only one she could think of.

"If she's insulted," she told the domicis gruffly, "I'll grovel in private later. But I have to say something, and if I can't say it this way, I'll actually *say* it."

He didn't surrender gracefully. Never did. But he shut up, which was the best she could ask for.

They made it to the grounds in the relative chill of his anger and the relative heat of hers; her den were smarter than he was and walked about five yards behind her temper, letting her cool off the only way she knew how.

She was glad of them. Glad that they understood what she just didn't want to put in words. Not now, not ever. Loss—it was the worst thing. The thing she hated most. Even speaking about it was somehow letting it in.

But she discovered that the strength of her loss was selfish, centered around her own fear and her own rage; discovered, to her surprise and her dismay, that she was not the only member of Terafin that somehow felt a gesture *must* be made.

That she was by no means the most powerful member either.

It should have comforted her, to see it, to see the act of defiance and anger and to know that even The Terafin could be pushed too hard, too far.

But when she saw the sword, her heart froze. She'd thought there wasn't anything left in her heart *to* freeze; she was Jay, and she was stupid sometimes, and she constantly underestimated her ability to be surprised. Being a seer did that.

But this sword she'd only seen girded once before, and that time was one time too many. It still came back to her in nightmare: darkness and death, the madness of the mage-born, the godborn and the Allasakari. The deaths of too many of the Chosen.

Justice shall not sleep.

She knew Morretz just well enough to know that he disapproved of the sword, but it barely registered; her eyes were caught, everywhere, by the faces of the men and women who lined the walk in preparation for her coming: the Chosen. The men and women handpicked and trusted absolutely by The Terafin. The men and women who had each seen that sword at least once in their tenure: It was the sword upon which their oaths were taken, and to which a ceremonial amount of their blood was given. A sword of war, yes, but much, much more.

It chilled her.

"You see?" Avandar said softly, quietly. "A gesture has been made. How does it comfort the dead?"

Later, she'd remember to keep her face completely rigid in Avandar's company; she usually managed it, but the sonofabitch could see so damned clearly it only took a twitch.

The phrase "cold comfort" took on a whole new meaning. *I'm not sixteen anymore,* Jewel thought. And she looked across the grounds to see that The Terafin's gaze had stopped a moment to meet hers. Saw herself in those eyes.

Jewel lifted a ringless hand in salute.

10th of Lattan, 427 AA
Kalakar, Averalaan Aramurelus

The Black Ospreys were the lone company that had not been given leave— indeed, given specific orders to the contrary—to expand their number. Duarte had expected no less, and was resigned to the lack before recruitment started. Secretly, it did not displease him; the Ospreys were a handful at the best of times, and an increase in their numbers usually called for a pruning that he found, over time, he had lost stomach for. Dangerous that.

Michelle West

An Osprey was, after all, a bird of prey—you could fly it, hunt it, give it freedom in which to take its kill, and even force it to feed from your hand, but the relationship was a delicate balance of will and mastery, a subtle acknowledgment that, at the right time, the bird's flight *was* the bird's flight, and all the more breathtaking for the uncertainty it inspired.

But the Black Ospreys were more than just captive killers; they had their pride.

Duarte was no fool. When Fiara burst into the room, her eyes narrow and cool enough to freeze water where it stood in the pitcher on his desk, he knew exactly what was coming, and wondered briefly if holding both halves of the conversation—if such an encounter could be graced with that word—would make his point. He doubted it.

"Sentrus." A warning, of sorts.

She snorted. "Duarte," she began.

"Sentrus."

It stopped her, but not cold. "*Primus* Duarte."

"Better."

"Duarte—"

He sighed. "What?"

"Every company in Kalakar is recruiting in the streets of this city. Every company in Kalakar is going to be recruiting in the West—and in the North—after the King's Challenge." Fiara, dark-haired and dark-eyed, was an anomaly; she came from the Northern kingdoms where a sword served as well as most speeches, and the people were as pale as the ice and snow that surrounded them for so much of the gods-cursed year. Duarte had done his time in the North, and had no desire to return to it; the ice had crept into his hair there, and the wind had frozen lines into his skin.

I am not a young man, he thought, accepting it as truth although it troubled more than his vanity. War was coming.

"I *am* aware of that, Fiara. It may surprise you, but as Primus and therefore commanding officer of this company, I actually do manage to hear a few words before the rest of you do."

She had the grace to flush, but that was about as much grace as he could hope for; she was an Osprey, after all. They all were. Misfits, killers, mercenaries more than soldiers—their only real law was the loyalty they held to each other. And, by extension, to the Kalakar House Guards. He had gathered them; they were his.

But it had been well over a decade since he had pulled their hoods from their faces to let them see the light of the open sky. To let them catch sight of their quarry.

And that, he thought, was taking the analogy about as far as it could go without losing it entirely.

"Sentrus," he said quietly, in a tone that brooked no interruption—even from an Osprey, "the time for peace is almost past. If you wish to be offended by The Kalakar's order, be offended *in silence*. What I accept from you in peace, and what I accept from you in time of war are, of necessity, two different things. It's been long indeed if you've forgotten it."

"Primus," she said, tapping her chest with the curled tips of her fingers.

He closed his eyes a moment. House Guards were expected to drill *and* present. Even the Ospreys. Given their reputation, probably especially the Ospreys.

Still, no war had been declared, and the Callestan Tyr, or so rumor had it, was certain that *if* war was to be declared, it would be declared by the height of the Festival of the Sun. The eighth day of Lattan had come and gone; it would be two days yet before word could be expected to arrive in Averalaan, carried most likely by members of the bardic college. The Kingdom had time to mobilize.

No doubt that was what the Dominion intended to do as well.

"Primus Duarte," Fiara said, her voice rather chilly, "permission to speak?"

"Granted."

"We've never been allowed up to our full tally. We took the brunt of the slaughter in the valley—"

"We were one of three companies, Fiara."

"We were the only company that counted, as far as the Annies were concerned."

"Ah, Alexis. I was wondering when you would decide to join us." His smile never started. "The term *Annies* is not to be used under this particular tour of duty." His tone and his expression indicated clearly that they'd both agreed to this at least a dozen times.

Nor did she argue now. "News," she said grimly.

"What news?"

"You aren't going to like it."

"Alexis."

"Do you want to finish with Fiara?"

Fiara's dark gaze had started to drill a small hole in the side of

Alexis' face—or it would have, if eyes had that particular strength. Alexis, apparently, did not notice. Which fooled neither the woman standing beside her nor the man sitting in front; she was sharp as a Maker's blade; she missed nothing.

"Yes," he said at last, hoping that he'd remember to tell her that, as Sentrus, she was being unconscionably rude—hells, as Decarus, before she'd been busted down a rank, it would still have been poor behavior among Ospreys. Of course, correcting Alexis in public had its own special consequences. It made Duarte uneasy a moment. This woman was his companion, as much of a soul mate as he had ever allowed himself to find. But that bond had been built *after* the war's end—formed in the fires and grime of the Annagarian dead. Formed, he thought, by a need to escape the war's cost, the war's loss.

They had never faced combat together as a couple; he'd half-thought they never would. And he wasn't at all certain that the shift from peacetime friction to wartime rule wouldn't destroy what they'd built. He wondered, idly, if she ever thought about it.

"Duarte?"

"My pardon. Sentrus," he said, turning to Fiara AKalakar with a grimace, "You might recall that not one of these soldiers came to me without passing through the ranks of either the House Guards or The Berriliya's regiment first. You might, if you care, further recall that more than a handful of those that *did* come to me were given, without pause, to the Kings' Justice.

"I built the Ospreys. I know how to build the Ospreys. But they're built out of war, *in* war. They cannot be tempered in any fire weaker than that. The Ospreys are mine, Fiara. It appears that you've forgotten that."

She stared impassively at his face for a moment; he thought she was actually going to argue the point. And then her face cracked into a sudden grin. Her salute was far less feeble—if far from perfect.

"It seems that *Sentrus* Alexis also has her concerns, and I would like to take them in private."

"Primus."

How the hell was he going to beat them back into army standard? And had they ever really been up to army standard, or was his memory being exceptionally—and uncharacteristically—kind? He leaned back in his chair and gazed up into Alexis' neutral expression. It was the one he least liked. Temper, if unpleasant in every other way, lent a color and a richness to her face. Also a certain deadliness, but as Duarte had founded the Ospreys, he was not a man to shy from danger.

"Well?"

"It involves our . . . current tour of duty."

She was right. He didn't like it at all. The current tour of duty was one that most of the Ospreys were not completely confident in to begin with: instead of killing, covertly or otherwise, they had been assigned to preserve and protect. And the boy—which, as he was fully of age, was an unfair word, but used regardless— whom they'd been assigned the protection of had already tangled with one of the Ospreys, been wounded, and kept his mouth shut, placing, by that action, one foot across the circle that separated the Ospreys from outsiders.

Unfortunately, it was a tour of duty that couldn't be failed. There had only been one assassination attempted since they'd taken over their role as personal guards. It had cost them one life; it wasn't an amateur attempt.

It had its value, though. If it wasn't war, the single death of one of their own cemented their dedication—such as it was. It made the shadow enemy a real one. He waited for Alexis to continue. Waited a bit longer.

He hated these games, small though they were. "Alexis . . ."

"I'm not certain if you're aware that the Kings' Challenge is just around the corner. You've been kept so busy," she added sweetly.

"Alexis." She knew damned well he was aware of the Kings' Challenge—there wasn't a House raising troops for the Kings that wasn't. All of the hopeful young men with any brawn and little enough brain made their trek across the continent in search of a challenge, a way to make their names, and a golden reward. Those men, disappointed in their attempt to reap a greater glory, were often easy pickings for army recruiters.

As a mage-trained scholar, Duarte had avoided recruitment; as a man indentured to Kalakar by the cost of the Order of Knowl-edge's training, he had not.

"You've too much on your mind, Duarte. Let me spell it out for you.

"First: Take the Kings' Challenge. Big contest, full of young men with more brawn than brain. Contestants arrive from as far away as the Western Kingdoms and the Southern Terreans of Oer-ta and Sargasso—even this year, when war is so close, and the Kings should damned well know better than to risk the influx of spies or assassins. But I digress—and that's your trick. So, take the Kings' Challenge, in which everyone without a real brain feels he should try to prove himself to every other person without a real brain.

"Next: Take one young, very fast, very competent man, who's been sword-trained and dagger-trained, born to the saddle and gods alone know what else. Make him a man who, of all these entrants, *does* have something to prove." She smiled as Duarte went suddenly pale.

"Alexis, if this is a joke—"

"Not even I have a sense of humor this grim." She waited, and then, when Duarte did not deign to interrupt her silence, added, "Valedan kai di'Leonne has undergone the trial, before judges, and has been chosen as one of the hundred men who will undergo the King's Challenge."

"This is *insane*. The boy's sun-mad!" Ramiro kai di'Callesta felt the chill of the night winds stretching across a continent. Here, in these so-called Annagarian halls, there was water and wind and the touch of the open sky. And men who did not wish to risk the scouring of the wind stayed inside, in safety. An old adage.

This day, this single day, he would have given much for the company of his wife, the Serra Amara, known across the width and breadth of the Dominion of Annagar for her gentle qualities. But although they stood beneath the warmth of the same sun, toiled beneath the blue of the same sky, the boundary that separated them, one from the other, was more than mere distance: She resided within Callesta, the city of his ancestors, in the heart of the verdant and much-prized Averda—and he, he stood as honored guest within the palace of the Imperial Kings, Reymalyn and Cormalyn. A nation stood between them, and the ghost of each old war that had moved the boundary of Annagar or Essalieyan by mere tens of miles every few decades or so. He wished her momentary advice and her silliness—for she, alone of many, could evoke laughter from his dourest mood.

But she was there. He was here. He made do. "The boy doesn't realize what he risks."

His brother, Fillipo par di'Callesta, nodded grimly. "Perhaps he will listen to the Wolf of Callesta, where he would not listen to a mere par." He leaned back into the shadows cast over the fountain by the light of morning sun; his hair, removed from the glinting light, was as dark as his brother's, his eyes as narrow. There was, between these two, a very strong family resemblance; it had often been said that the clan Callesta was doubly blessed: first, for being graced with two men of such high caliber and second, for the real affection and loyalty between them. Both were true.

Ser Kyro di'Lorenza snorted. He ran a hand through age-paled hair before returning it to its customary repose atop sword hilt. He was Annagarian bred and born, a man with little taste for politics and much for war. "I fail to see the insanity in it, Tyr'agnate," he said, his tone neutral with respect. He was both beholden to this man—they all were, for his coming had sealed their survival—and suspicious of him. Ramiro di'Callesta was known across the Dominion as the Imperial Tyr.

And he knew it. His smile was brittle indeed as he acknowledged Ser Kyro's comment. "Baredan?"

"I am not in a position to comment," the General Baredan di'Navarre replied. "But if the boy succeeds—"

"There is no chance that he will succeed, brother," Fillipo said quietly.

"If he fails, he will lose more than he gains if he succeeds. Why take the risk?"

It was Ser Kyro who answered, and at that, only after the shadows of the day had grown visibly shorter. "There are clansmen here who will take that same test. They need only know that he can best them, and they will be impressed."

"It is not as simple a thing as that, Ser Kyro."

"It is *exactly* as simple a thing as that, Ser Ramiro. You play a Tyrian game, and you play it exceptionally well. I do not. And although it might pain you to admit it, most of the men—the Lord's men—do not. We see clearly because we desire simple things: A good horse. A good wife. Strong sons, a strong sword, a battle worthy of killing and dying in. But more than this, a leader worthy of following."

Even Baredan had the grace to wince slightly at Ser Kyro's words. Ramiro grimaced. "Thank you, Ser Kyro."

Ser Kyro frowned. He started to speak, stopped, started again. "General. Tyr'agnate. You must, of course, feel free to speak with the boy. But I tell you now that he will not listen. He has made this decision.

"I will also say that the—that his guards, his *Imperial* guards, find the situation at least as distasteful and questionable as you do."

Cold comfort indeed, to be in agreement with the Black Ospreys of the Kalakar House Guards. For a moment, an old anger caught him by surprise; he felt pain, heard the cries of the dying across a bridge of years made of memories too strong for a single lifetime to shake. He did not speak; the cloud passed.

"Baredan," he said at length, "what does the boy do?"

"He trains," the General replied evasively.

The evasion was not lost upon the Tyr'agnate. His eyes narrowed. *Is this the way it is to be?* he thought, as his eyes glanced off the General's. But again, he did not speak. Baredan was the Tyr'agar's General, and Ramiro di'Callesta, in time of peace, the Tyr'agar's subtle rival. They had their duties and their roles.

"I do not believe that speaking with the boy will change his mind," Baredan said quietly. He paused. "No word has come from the Tor Leonne."

It was a question. Ramiro shook his head. "No word."

No war, then. Not yet.

But it was coming, as inevitably as the rise of the sun and the fall of the night, the Lord's time and the Lady's. They were, each of these four men, seasoned by war, anointed by it, elevated by it—and wounded by it. But they were warriors born; the wounds, they buried deeply beneath the facade of proud scars.

10th of Lattan, 427 AA
Terafin, Averalaan Aramarelas

He had served as Chosen for almost twenty years. Taken up in what, at this remove, felt like his distant youth, he had stood his ground in the face of demon and darkness; he had proved his worth time and again.

But he had not fought in the Terafin war. The grizzled veterans— and that, they were—of that early battle had about them a mystique and a confident wariness that the younger among the Chosen envied. He was not so young now. Not so foolish.

Or perhaps it was because they were dead, those veterans, with a few exceptions, that their early years of glory and loyalty were no longer such a siren's call. Captain Alayra, one of the last of The Terafin's first Chosen to continue to serve, retained her title in a form of retirement that honored her early service.

He had never seen her look old before.

"News, Torvan?"

He saluted her. "Nothing out of the ordinary."

She nodded, her eyes on a spot someplace beyond the windowless walls. Seeing, he thought, the war. Old battles. He had been blooded in the South, and he knew now that such a blooding, in a foreign land, at the hands of distinct and clear enemies, was the easier introduction to death.

She rose from her solid, simple chair. She walked with a cane during the humidity of the summer months; it was beneath her slightly gnarled knuckles as she made her way to him. "Arrendas?"

"Ready."

"And you?"

He nodded grimly.

"Good. The Terafin's waiting."

He saluted. Lowered his hand. Alayra was still bent, still old. *We've fought demons,* he thought, *and mad gods. We've fought the South, twice, and won. We've fought Darias, we've fought Morriset. We've never done it without you.*

She met his eyes. "I've lived through one succession war. It was . . . enough. I did things in that war that I've been able to face because of the peace and the justice that followed it."

"Alayra—in war we all do things we wouldn't otherwise do."

"A war for succession happens *after* the death of the reigning Terafin," she continued as if he hadn't spoken. "Why now, Torvan?"

From anyone else, the question might have been evidence of the torment and the shadow of a war they both saw coming, inevitable as a sea storm. But, from Alayra, it was what it was; it demanded a real answer.

He thought about it a long time in the confines of the simplicity of her rooms. At last, he said, "I don't know. At this point, it's not clear who gains if Terafin is severely weakened."

"No. It's not." She turned. "You're escort, Torvan." Pause. "I've assigned Chosen to Alowan. He won't have them. It's your job to force him to accept them."

"Gracefully?"

Her turn to wince. "At all. I don't care about grace."

By House rules, any member of the Council proper was allowed two attendants and two guards when the Council sat in session. It was a formality; a governing rule written into the House constitution—or whatever it was they called the rules; Jewel couldn't remember and didn't particularly care—during years that The Terafin preferred to pass over when she spoke about House history.

Funny thing.

Every member of the House Council save three—Gabriel, Cormark and Jewel herself—had, surprise, surprise, two attendants and two guards. The great chamber, which was called "the bowl" by anyone who had to work in it or clean it, had room enough that the addition of three or four bodies per member didn't make the room seem that packed.

But the lamps had been lit along the light rails, and they cast a brilliant, cut spectrum of hard edges against a tabletop that was completely free of fingerprints or grime. No food here, no water, just the sheen of polished wood. It was a very fine room in the way that the largest part of the cathedrals on the isle were fine: Grand, high ceilings that were meant to make the occupants feel even smaller than they were. The tapestries added to that effect, as did the curtains and the towering windows; this was not the hall for a war council.

Jewel had the single attendant she was forced to accept by House and guild law: Avandar Gallais. To leave him behind was, unfortunately, to absent herself from the meeting as well; both The Terafin and Avandar had made it clear enough in their early years together that it had become a fact of life.

Fact as well that Avandar was possessed of unspecified magical abilities that made him both servant—although the exact definition of the word *serve* had yet to be offered—and guard. Apparently good service and full disclosure had nothing to do with each other; Jewel could see when he used magic, but she couldn't see what was available to him.

His job was to see that she neither embarrassed herself—he called it the impossible task, which might have been true if his standards for so-called embarrassment weren't so damned high— nor died, although, as she tartly pointed out, she *was* a seer.

He was in a vigilant mood today. She'd learned, over the years, to figure out what was vigilant from what was sour; it wasn't all that easy, given that most of the statues in the Terafin grounds were more expressive than he was.

"Well," she murmured for his ears alone as she took in the guards, the attendants, and the weapons that adorned the ATerafin Council like so much gaudy jewelry, "looks like Angel wins."

Avandar frowned. "At eighteen, it was, if not permissible then at least understandable, that he turn everything into a wager. But at his current age . . ."

She laughed. "You tell him. Me, I'd be happy if he'd lose more often."

Her laughter, unguarded for a moment, caught attention. Just what she wanted.

The doors to the great hall were left slightly ajar; they would be left that way until The Terafin's arrival announced, by presence alone, that the Council meeting was in session. At that point, the Chosen who accompanied her would close the doors at her back as she took her chair at the head of the long table.

Nice to see that at least that custom had not changed, although Torvan ATerafin noticed the slight space between two open doors not because he was overly watchful—although today, he was— but rather because the low, deep laughter of a familiar voice wafted through them like an autumn breeze after a scorching summer.

The Terafin raised a peppered brow, her lips turning up in the only half-smile that had reached her face since news of Alea's death had become known.

Torvan said nothing; he was well-trained to present the perfect dress face when the occasion demanded it. Today, if ever, was such an occasion. But he wondered, inwardly, what Jewel was laughing at, and hoped that it wasn't—as it so often was—another one of the Council members. She could take laughter, herself; she always said she hadn't much dignity to lose. But the men and women who marked the Council with their powerful presence were not in the habit of joining a social inferior in a joke at their own expense. She had offended Elonne and Haerrad more than once in the past year; she had offended Rymark and Corniel a dozen times each. Cormark and Alea had indulged her; Alea's indulgence was over. It left Cormark as her sole staunch ally on a Council that had suddenly become more dangerous than any Southern Empire. Marrick had a wicked sense of humor, and dealt well with her gibes. Unfortunately, the only thing to recommend him over the others *was* his sense of humor, and Jewel ATerafin was no idiot, for all that she had come to the Council a young girl. Charm alone didn't buy her allegiance.

What did?

Torvan smiled, and the smile was also genuine. Of all the ATerafin High Council—as opposed to the Merchant Council, for instance, although the High Council itself was a subset of what was usually considered the "working" body of Terafin—Jewel ATerafin held a special place in his memory.

She had, after all, saved his life when both he and the lord he both served and admired had determined that the only wise course was to end it. Why?

Because she was moved by a simple act of kindness. And he was impulsive enough to have offered it to a street urchin and her den of petty thieves, all desperate, one dying.

He had become the Chosen of choice when she required a special guard—and because of her talent, which was so very, very hard to keep hidden, it was required often. She was irreverent to the point of offense, but he found it hard to take any; there was about her the same dogged determination and the same sense of duty and responsibility—albeit to entirely different things—that he had long admired in The Terafin. If she had only taken to the finesse of political life as well as she had taken to the duties of merchanting routes—but she was Jewel ATerafin. Might as well ask for pigs with wings.

The Terafin paused, took a deep breath, and lifted her chin ever-so-slightly. It surprised Torvan; it was almost a gesture of . . . vulnerability. He gazed at Morretz, but all Morretz presented was a finely but simply dressed back.

It came to him for no reason, and it came with force. *Jewel,* he thought, almost missing a step between the threshold of hall and hallway, *stay clean. Keep out of the politics.*

They were gathered there like vultures, and she saw them clearly as exactly that for the first time in years. It was not a comparison much to her liking. Courtne had been cunning; his had been the formidable intellect. But Alea had had the heart of the House, its pulse her pulse, its people her people.

Beheaded, heart stilled, the Terafin responsibility fell across the shoulders of the woman who had once been merely Amarais Handernesse like a blow and a mantle. It had aged her, the taking of power, but not so much as the keeping of power had. She was tired.

But she was not yet dead.

The anger surprised her, although she had lived with anger for much of her life and had learned to make a weapon of it that was single-edged, aimed outward. She drew herself in now and looked at them all.

Cormark was old. Over the course of a day and a night, the age that she denied had seeped into his face, his hair, the line of his shoulders. She trusted him, but she thought, seeing him this day, that she could not lean heavily on him for support.

She was *The* Terafin; support was not required.

Elonne was, in carriage and poise, her match. She did not raise her voice, did not resort to tactics of raw power. Her size was diminutive; the only person in the room smaller than she was Jewel ATerafin, and Jewel ATerafin had never been considered a threat. Her hair was as dark as Amarais' hair had been fifteen years ago; her back was unbowed by the daily requirements of labor. She was responsible for the merchant routes in the far South and the far West, and she had gained much in prestige and power by her handling of House fortunes in those areas.

She sat now with one hand, palm down, upon the surface of the table. Her House Ring caught the light of the chandelier above; a quiet statement. She met The Terafin's eyes without flinching; without offering any reaction at all save a very, very slight inclination of head.

Was she capable of murder? Certainly.

As was Marrick, easily the most charming of the House Council, and almost as physically perfect as Devon ATerafin; he wore his age like the glowing patina on her most perfect silver. Nothing stooped or bowed him. He dressed well, but not flamboyantly, and spoke in a soft enough voice that he could seem, for long stretches at a time, to be almost self-deprecating; certainly self-aware. She liked Marrick; she had always liked Marrick. But she labored under no illusions. His heart was as remote as Elonne's, and his ability to take a life with the same charm and good grace that he hosted a dinner had never been in question.

Still, it would hurt to know that Marrick was Alea's killer. A pain she would never share with him.

Much better, for her, if Haerrad were the killer. Much better for them all. He was the throwback to the earlier years; there was not much in the way of civility about his temper, and his temper was prone to peak at unfortunate times. He was a brilliant strategist, Elonne's equal where, sadly, Marrick was not—but he played too close to the line, and there had been an unexplained caravan slaughter or two that had forced her to political extremes in order to protect her House from censure. It had also forced her to remove Haerrad from all but the Southern routes. In the South, the deaths were often not reported, and it was just as likely that the caravan lost would be Terafin; the Voyani and the poorer clansmen were bandits by less pretty names. There, battle driving him to prove himself in the way he loved best, Haerrad shone.

His nose had been broken at least twice, his jaw once; his face bore scars of early encounters on the trade routes. He had a rough charisma about him—but it was the charisma that came with power, not the charisma that led to it. She had taken him onto the Council because her only other choice had been to kill him—and she had considered it very, very carefully. His death, on balance, would have hurt the House, but it was a near call.

She regretted that decision. Unfairly, but the silence behind the perfectly composed mask that she now wore was a safe place in which to be unfair.

That left only Rymark; Rymark ATerafin.

Of the four Council members with strength in numbers, support, and financial means, Rymark ATerafin was the most careful to keep to the shadows. She herself did the same; to hide behind a careful, studied neutrality was a trait that in most cases evoked respect, if warily given.

He was his father's son in looks; taller than any other Council member, gaunter in build. His hair was streaked gray—and it had always been gray, even in a youth that she did not clearly remember. But he was his father's son in looks alone, and the family resemblance was superficial enough that she only saw the father in the son when she turned to look at her oldest adviser, her oldest supporter, her most trusted ally.

The father had never sought power. The son sought little else. He had taken his first step on the road under the tutelage of the magi. That had been a relief to her, for it was the only strain that lay between her and Gabriel in their long years together: he had wanted his blood son to be ATerafin, and she, as always, was cautious about the giving of her House name. Of *her* name.

But the magi had given him a skill, and that skill was a thing of value; in the end, and perhaps foolishly, she had granted Gabriel his one selfish desire. And it was a single desire; he had never asked her for anything else so purely personal in the long years of silent service he had offered. Gabriel. Right-kin. And compromised.

Do you suspect your son, Gabriel? Parents could be so blind where their own children were concerned, but she could not—not quite—believe him so willfully blind. She wondered, idly, if Rymark was his mother's son.

And her gaze passed on. Three Council chairs stood empty. Courtne's. Alea's. Corniel's. The last she had shed few tears for—the same tears, in fact, that she might shed if any of the four who remained were to perish: Elonne, Marrick, Haerrad, or Rymark.

But beyond those empty chairs, set apart—as always—by the most convenient method given to her, sat Jewel Markess ATerafin. No longer the young girl, she seemed, still, an embodiment of things youthful. A sign, The Terafin thought, of age, that a woman over thirty can feel so much the defiant youngster.

Jewel's dark hair was not so unruly today as it usually was, and her clothing was, indeed, of a fine material and an acceptable cut. She alone had chosen to bring no guards or attendants, but Avandar towered over her like a shadow, like a death for any whose approach was careless or inimical.

Of the four—Elonne, Marrick, Haerrad, and Rymark—The Terafin thought that it was Marrick who stood the best chance of protecting the House and gaining for the House what the House needed in the future from the both the Council of The Ten and the Crowns.

But it was to Jewel ATerafin that her gaze returned, time and again, before she at last began her address.

Council meetings were often bearable because they represented a rare opportunity to catch up on sleep—if she were subtle enough about it not to catch Avandar's attention which was, admittedly, not often.

But today there were no odious reiterations of a previous meeting's minutes, no descriptions of what was to be discussed (although this often proved more interesting than the discussion itself), no maneuvering behind the scenes (which in this case often meant causing one) for presentation position, or worse, for "support." There was *The* Terafin, and there were the ATerafin, separated by the chairs they occupied across the gulf of the suddenly huge table.

She sat; they sat. She rose, and when they moved to rise, she gestured them down with a cutting motion of hand through air.

"This will be a brief meeting," she said softly, and for a minute Jewel could almost believe it would end in an execution. She cast a glance at the right-kin, but his complexion was going through a serious color change—enough of one that she knew he was as surprised by The Terafin's tone as any of the other members of her Council.

For just a minute, The Terafin seemed to shake her age, gaining inches and power in the process.

"Courtne is dead. Alea is dead. Corniel is dead. For the last, I offer no great grief, as you are all intelligent enough to suspect. I will do you the favor, behind these very closed doors, in the privacy of a Council chamber that it is in your best interest to leave private, of not insulting your intelligence. Or taxing it overmuch."

Stiffening, there, especially across Rymark ATerafin's features. Jewel was certain that once Haerrad figured it out, he'd be purple. Elonne's face did not change at all, and Marrick, damn him, actually smiled.

"I do not understand why you choose to play these games now—and they *are* games, make no mistake. A war of succession is generally held after the death of the ruler one wishes to succeed.

"I will remind you all that the decision of heir is made in Council *by the council's recommendations* in accordance with my decision. I will further remind you that the last time a House ruler was assassinated, the House in question lost prestige in the Imperial Court, and for that reason, lost a great deal of both power and influence.

"The question of succession has been—and in future will be—left to the House; it was agreed upon when The Ten came to the Kings at the beginning of their reign over four hundred years ago. But in turn, it was agreed that the Houses would abide by the greater martial laws imposed by the Kings we had chosen to support."

Restive movement from all of the House members but Elonne. Jewel didn't much like Elonne, but the woman was made of steel, and steel was necessary in the rule of a House.

"Ah. I see you understand the rudimentary costs of a House War. I will, in that case, refrain from belaboring known history." She put both hands, palm down, upon the table and leaned toward them, captive audience by force of her will alone. "Courtne was a reasonable choice as heir. He is obviously out of the succession. You will now, no doubt, argue among yourselves for the honor of a clear recommendation and a clear choice. I have no . . . difficulty with this.

"I have difficulty imagining that when the heir is finally chosen, there will be more than two of you left standing, and again, I have little difficulty with this. But Elonne, Marrick, Haerrad, Rymark," she said, her voice soft, her gaze harder than Elonne's, "I *will not* see this House torn apart by your ambitions. Whether you die or not is of little consequence to me; it will be a loss to the House. Do not kill those who follow *me* because they have chosen to throw their future in with *you,* or worse, because they will not.

"Do I make myself clear?"

Silence.

Haerrad said quietly, "And if they die, Terafin?"

Jewel held her breath. It was not a question that needed asking, but having been asked, it was not a question that could be ignored. The Terafin did not utter threats; she did not rule by such extremes. What steel there was in her was sheathed until the last possible moment, and if she was capable of death—and she was—it was the death that more than simple expedience demanded.

She thought that The Terafin would make no answer; the silence stretched. Stretched for long enough that Jewel realized she'd forgotten to breathe while she waited.

And as she drew breath, The Terafin replied with a single word. "Justice."

She turned then and left the room.

CHAPTER TWO

Evening of 10th of Lattan, 427 AA
Averalaan, Terafin Manse

Jewel had not had dreams like this for almost fifteen years, although she woke often from nightmare, and some of those nightmares twisted truth. No dreams like this since she had started to learn the limits of the talent she was born to. Not since she had accepted that the instincts by which her life was ruled could, occasionally and with great cost, be *pointed*. Not since she had run from the streets and the warrens of the twenty-fifth holding, the remnants of the gang of children—her den—that had survived their first contact with an old and terrible magic under the thin stretch of her shadow.

Seer-born.

The days with the den returned to her. Years in the most powerful House in the Empire would never remove them entirely; she had come to know, and accept, this truth. It made her something of a mystery to most of the powerful men and women who partook in the rulership of House Terafin; truthfully, it made her something of an object of disdain. But the disdain that there was was whispered and hidden—as if she was too stupid to be aware of it—because if she was from the streets, she was also of value to the House.

Seer-born.

She was Jewel, born Markess, raised to ATerafin, and she still felt the rawness of a scream against the walls of her throat as she sat bolt upright and waited in the darkened bedroom for the wing to come to life around her.

It happened slowly; the swing of doors in the distance, doors well-oiled enough that they did not creak, but not stiff enough that they did not slam—either into their frames or into the walls as they were pushed open or slammed shut. Then the shouting:

There, Teller's voice, just outside of Finch's door; Jester's voice outside of Angel's. Carver was—ah, there. Swinging lamplight bobbing beneath the crack of her door. Light.

Her own lamp was guttered.

And, of course, no matter how familiar these friends, no matter how welcome, they would not be the first to arrive. There were three doors that led to this room. The first was the door from the sitting room beyond which lay the hall and the rest of her den. The second was a door that opened into an office—a room she still rarely used, preferring the comfort and the familiarity of the late night kitchen seen through oil-lamp light and sleep's lack. The third door opened into the chambers which her domicis occupied.

And always, always, always it was that third door that opened first.

No exception tonight; in the shadows, Avandar crossed the threshold, neither lingering in the doorway nor appearing to hurry. She could see in the dark about as well as anyone else, but if Avandar was a shadow, he was a shadow who had substance and color and personality, all rooted firmly in memories, most of which still irritated her.

As domicis, he was, technically, her servant. As Avandar, he was like a keeper, but of what, she had yet to determine—and they had been together, as uneasy allies, since her sixteenth year. There probably wasn't another domicis in the guild's long and honorable history who could abide by technicalities so well without conveying *any* of the spirit of the law.

He's handsome, Finch had said, *and powerful; you can feel it.*

Yeah. So's a demon, and I wouldn't want one serving me—you never know when the damned thing'll get loose and rip out your throat. Or worse.

If the Terafin thought he'd be the best domicis for you, it probably means she thinks you'll see a lot of trouble, Jay.

The years hadn't made him any uglier.

Or any less arrogant, for that matter.

"Jewel," he said. He knew better than to touch her.

Before she could answer, the door to the outer hall flew open; Angel and Carver stood abreast in the wide frame. Lamplight was at their back, held aloft by a slender, strong arm: Finch's, she thought. She smiled as she saw the light glinting off steel too short to be sword. It was her first smile.

"Jay?" Teller's voice. He sidled around Carver, shoving his forelocks out of his eyes and squinting into the shadows. In the darkness, she was sixteen again; so were they. There were instincts, she thought, that they'd never lose because more than half their life had gone into the making.

"It's—safe," she said, swinging shaking legs free of blankets and planting her feet almost delicately against the nubbly cotton rug.

"You were dreaming." Not a question.

"Yeah."

"Bad."

"Yeah."

"Kitchen?"

She laughed. It was a wobbly sound. "Yeah."

The lamp helped. It sat on the table in its customary place at her left elbow, flickering with warmth and orange light. Her elbows, propped against the smooth, hard surface of sturdy, unornamented wood, were like a silent commandment; only when she lowered her hands from her chin and shook herself would anyone speak. And she wouldn't do either of these things until her gaze was focused on them, and the present.

She could barely see them at all. She wanted to, but the *reality* of them deflected the edge of the dreaming as if both were blades. She felt Avandar settle into his customary position to the left of her, back to the wall. Almost told him to sit. She hated the feel of his shadowy presence where she couldn't—quite—see it.

But she opened her lips and said instead, "Terafin is burning. The fire is black, but the heat—the heat is white." She swallowed. "There's sand on my clothing, in my hands, my mouth; I'm dry and hot and I can barely move. Someone calls my name. I turn toward the voice.

"Behind me, there's a woman. She's my age—" She stopped, absorbing the words, realizing how untrue they were. It had been a long time since she'd returned to that age in the dreamscape. The age, for Jewel Markess, of demons, of fire, of magic. "She's the most beautiful woman I've ever seen. She's sixteen, seventeen— and her eyes are filled with fire; she kneels, as if she's supplicant, but she's wearing a thin crown, and a bloodied sword is staining the silks she wears.

"She tells me—that I cannot turn back." Hard, to speak those words here. Jewel swallowed. Continued. The vision's hooks were things of fear, of terror—but although the emotions would sustain themselves, the vision itself would pass into memory, and memory was imperfect.

"The Chosen are scattered. I can only find Torvan; the rest are dead or blind or deaf. He says, 'Why did you have to leave?' and I feel it, the weight of those words, and he grabs my hand and drags me to The Terafin's Council chambers.

"She's dead. There are three knives in her body and she lies across the Council table. Gabriel looks up when I enter the room; there is fighting, of course, the war for succession. He is aloof from it, but bleeding anyway. And he says, 'You. You *left* her to die.' " She pushed unruly brown curls from the edge of her forehead so that she might better see the light, feel its distant heat across her cold, cold skin.

"Where," said the only person in the room who refused to learn better than to interrupt her, "is Morretz in this vision?"

Morretz, The Terafin's domicis. Jewel frowned, bit her lip to stop the sharper words from leaving her mouth, and then shook her head. "I don't—I didn't—see him."

"Strange. Go on."

It was so hard, with Avandar, not to snap. "Why, thank you," she said, grinding her teeth. Losing her clarity. It took her a moment to find it again.

"The Terafin sits up. Her eyes are dead eyes. Her wounds don't bleed. And her voice—it's not her voice. Her head rolls awkwardly on her shoulders as she turns in my direction. She says, 'Another lesson. The hardest lesson. There will be blood on your hands no matter what you choose.'

"The color returns to her face; the knives fall out; she shakes her hair down and stands. She's not dead, and she's not undead; she's alive. She keeps speaking, with the same voice, as if life or death doesn't matter to what she has to say. 'There will always be blood on your hands. Glory in it, or weep at it, as you choose— *but when you choose who* must *die, choose wisely.*'

"And before I can answer, before I can ask a question, she gestures and the—and the—city rises."

"The Shining City." Avandar's voice. Avandar's unwelcome, solid voice. No shadow in it; no shadow would dare.

"Yes. And the screaming starts." She shuddered, then, and her arms relaxed, hands falling almost nervelessly across the tabletop. "I remember the baby—"

"Jay." Teller rose at once. The shadow of Henden in the year 410 fell across their faces like the blow of a drunk parent across a captive child's; they flinched, and hid from it, as they could. But it was there. Always there. Finch glanced furtively at Carver, but

Carver was staring at the tabletop, at the diffusion of light across the wood grain.

"Did you recognize the voice?" Avandar asked, speaking almost gently. For Avandar. Which meant slowly, and without that slight clenching of jaw that accompanied many of his questions.

"The voice?"

"The voice she spoke with. Jewel, you said The Terafin spoke with a voice not her own."

"No," Jewel said. And of all her den—yes, dammit, *her den*— gathered at this large table, the only person who knew she was lying was, as always, Teller. He raised a brow, his expression shifting, and then shifting again, so quickly that she was certain only she had caught it at all.

Finch stopped writing. "Anything else?"

"No. Yes."

"Which is it?"

"Yes. Can you arrange a meeting with The Terafin?"

Jester frowned. "Jay, you might've forgotten that you're to spend half of tomorrow with the Flight."

"With," Avandar said quietly, "the three Commanders."

"Yeah. Eagle, Hawk, and Kestrel." Jester smiled, his teeth a flash in the lamplight.

"Jewel—"

"Jester."

"Fine." He held out his hands and surrendered with about as much grace as she expected. Sadly that was about three times less grace than Avandar considered acceptable. "But that's what everyone else calls 'em."

"If *you* call them that, I'll pick it up. If *I* call them that, I'll kill you."

Angel laughed. It was nervous laughter. He scraped his chair along the kitchen floor as he rose. "Jay?"

"What?"

"Are we going South or staying?"

She loved these men and women. Everything was obvious, and nothing had to be spoken in more words than were needed to get the point across.

That fact that she rose, turned, and left the room without an answer was lost on no one. Especially not on Jewel herself.

She went to the shrine, of course.

Not immediately; at first she returned to the dubious comfort of her bed and pulled the comforter up to just under her chin, burying every part of her body beneath its folds. She even closed her eyes, willing her hands to relax the firm grip they had on the thick, dry linen. She'd become an optimist over the last decade.

Or an idiot.

With something that was decidedly less quiet than a sigh but more heartfelt, she pushed the comforter to one side and then groped around on the floor for her shoes. She thought of changing from bedclothing to real clothing, and decided, practically, that no one was going to see her anyway; she took a large cloak as a compromise, intending to drape it across her shoulders until she'd cleared the wing and the halls of the manse itself.

Somehow it never quite came off her arms, which was unfortunate, because it made her look not unlike a servant woken for some household emergency at a late hour.

And at a late hour, at such an obvious disadvantage, was not how she would have chosen to meet Rymark ATerafin.

Of the Terafin Council, he was the man she least trusted—possibly because he was, in Finch's estimation, the prettiest, and Jewel had never been one to trust a pretty face. She almost managed to avoid him, but the cloak was heavy and more cumbersome than anything else she normally carried from one end of Terafin to the other, and it didn't fit into the convenient alcove beneath the torch rings that separated the wing that had been her home for fifteen years from the main hall. That hall, wider from side to side than the small tenement in which she and her den had once lived, was well lit, with silvered glass and towering windows at even intervals from end to end.

If you didn't want to be seen, the great hall was not the place to be. Unfortunately, it was also the fastest way to get out to The Terafin's private grounds, and the four shrines that it harbored.

She knew that he'd seen her when she saw him approaching her. And she knew who he was because he had a distinctively graceful way of walking; he was almost as catlike as Devon ATerafin could be. And a helluvalot less pleasant.

"Why, Jewel—what a pleasant surprise. I'd hoped to be able to speak with you before the next Council meeting." He crossed his chest with his hand in a civil greeting that lacked nothing. He even bent his head, granting her a measure of respect that she could only dream he'd show her in an actual Council meeting. Lamplight made the sheen of his greying auburn hair look like warm, contained flame.

Fire. She shuddered in spite of herself and rather too obviously; his face took a chill expression for a moment. But only a moment. He stepped closer, smoothing his thin-lipped silence into
a friendly one. "Have I . . . interrupted an assignation of some
nature?"

"Yes."

The curt, short word stopped him cold; it was not the way people with rank or station often responded to innuendo. If she were
honest with herself, it wasn't the way Jewel usually responded
either. But she wasn't a sixteen-year-old girl in the first blush of
youth anymore; she was over thirty, and she wasn't to be thrown
off-balance by anyone, let alone this particular ATerafin.

But she took a step back, into the wall, as she thought it. Rymark was one of three ATerafin that she knew wore not only the
House symbol but also the symbol of the Order of Knowledge:
the three phases of the moon, with the full moon quartered by elemental symbols. That platinum medallion reflected the burning
flame as he bent to speak to her; he was a tall man, and made the
most of the difference between their heights. "I see. I assure you
that this will only take a moment of your time. I have no desire to
interfere with affairs that are not of my concern."

Mages always made her nervous. The only mage that she halfway liked was Sigurne Mellifas, and that because there was something about her that reminded Jewel of a grandmother who was
almost—but not quite—made gentle and perfect by memory.

It was not Sigurne she faced, but Rymark.

She sighed and resisted the urge to massage her forehead, a
gesture that she often used when either bored or irritated. Instead,
she shoved her curls out of her eyes. "What, exactly, did you want
to speak to me about, and can't it wait until tomorrow?"

He shrugged.

"This is not a discussion you want to make an appointment
for."

"Perceptive, Jewel. But then again, I would expect that of you."

She had always been given a choice of two behaviors in response to her talent: awe or nervous humor. Rymark added a variant that she didn't particularly like: Possessive humor. "What do
you want?" The words came out shorter than she would have
liked, too clipped by far, given how close he was.

His eyes narrowed, changing the contours of his face ever so
slightly. "I want," he said coolly, "what at least four members of

the Council—or members of the House who are not yet privileged with a position upon the Council—will want before this is
over."

"Which is?"

He smiled, leaning over again, leaning into the edge of the
boundaries that she defined as personal space. She really didn't
want to take another step back, but by presence alone he almost
forced it; the wall hit her hard, made her look even more awkward than she already did in her soft cotton nightdress and soft-
soled night shoes.

If he touches me, she thought, *I'll cut his fingers off.*

Except that her dagger was in her room, with the rest of her
clothing.

"Jewel, play no game. If you will not choose a side intelligently, *do not choose sides.*"

She knew, then, exactly what he wanted. She'd always known
it, but she'd ignored it until now.

"The Terafin," he said softly, "has . . . begun to speak openly
of choosing her heir."

Not the interpretation she'd have put on it, but she wasn't the
politician. "She's not likely to die tomorrow," Jewel snapped, unable to think—although she had given it much thought over the
years—of anyone else at the helm of the most powerful House in
the Empire. When she'd been younger, she'd thought it might be
her. Youth was stupid. Seeing the way it aged The Terafin, understanding what it meant, had taken time. Had offered her a truth she
didn't particularly want to see about a responsibility she no longer
dreamed about shouldering, although nightmare once or twice had
brought her close.

He smiled, his lips turning up in what seemed an infinitely
lazy gesture, a self-indulgence of an expression. "Your loyalty is
to be commended. You've never been made one of her Chosen,
but you're infected by the same spirit. I admire it, Jewel. I would
like very much to be able to count on it in the future." He lifted a
hand, palm up, his fingers slightly curled.

"You can count on my loyalty to The Terafin," she replied curtly,
lifting her chin slightly to avoid the tips of his fingers.

"Jewel, my dear," he said, and the coolness was suddenly
matched in his words by a kind of awful heat, "you cannot always
be the girl who says 'No.' You are no longer the child, although
perhaps in your current attire that would not be so obvious."

"I told you," she replied, quelling any heat with the ice of her words, "that I'm already otherwise occupied for the evening."

"Ah. And if it's not something as simple as an evening that I desire?"

"Then you can make an appointment, same as anyone else." She lifted her hands, placed them as quick as she could in the center of his chest and *pushed*. There were a hundred other things she might've done—but they'd all cause damage. She didn't like Rymark—but for that matter, she thought him better for the House, although it was hard to imagine at this particular point, than at least one of the other four members of the Council to which they were both jointly appointed: Haerrad.

And that meant that she would do her best not to get involved in the type of fight that she knew well at close quarters. Or the type of fight that she now knew at any quarter.

He didn't make it easy, though, the bastard. He grabbed both her hands by the wrists and pulled her suddenly close, yanking her hard enough that she lost the flat of her feet, and the protection of the wall at her back.

If he tries to kiss me, she thought, although her breathing quickened, *I'm going to bite his tongue so badly even Alowan won't be able to save it.* "Rymark, treating me like you treat the household servants is not likely to endear you to me." Icy, keep it icy.

He only laughed. "The girl who says no to the end. In the North, my dear, they would respect this provincialism. You are not in the North now. Do you think, when the Terafin dies, that you will have no need of support? Or would you see Haerrad raise his little army and slaughter half the House to bring it to heel?"

"Not even Haerrad would be that stupid."

"You don't speak with conviction, Jewel."

No, because she didn't have it. Haerrad, gods curse him to the Hells with no further lifetimes of atonement, was, she suspected, much like the ancestral ATerafin it was forbidden to name in his open desire for power and his ruthlessness in his quest to obtain it. That The Terafin had not chosen to have him killed was something that she did not—not quite—understand, legality aside. Instead, to neutralize him, she'd made him part of the Council, and answerable to it. "What do you want?"

"You know it, little seer. I want your support in the Council. When the discussion of the heir is raised—and it will be, for The Terafin believes it is time—I want your vote of confidence. Or I want you to abstain from a vote at all." His grip on her wrists tightened as he smiled again. 'But perhaps I am not only interested in the business of politics; there are many more things in this life."

He bent, again, and she'd had enough. Brought her knee up, suddenly, and found that it was hampered by folds of a too heavy cloak. He laughed, caught the back of her head in one hand, twisting his fingers into her hair. "Lady," he said, his lips a hair's breadth from her own.

And then he cried out in pain; his hands were scoured by a brilliant, brief light, a light that burned blue and then orange before his grip was broken. He turned at once, all pretext of charm—and it seemed to Jewel that there was little enough of it—gone. "You!"

Jewel made haste to stumble around him out of the alcove that had proved such a poor choice of hiding place. She had to scrape skin against stone to do it, but she didn't wait for Rymark to move; he wasn't likely to just to be convenient. She won free quickly, as if the opportunity was going to be a very, very short one.

And there, arms hanging deceptively free at his sides, was the man she least wanted to see: Avandar. It couldn't have been anyone else, of course. It had to be him. He did her the grace of not speaking his mind, although she could see it in the momentary narrowing of his eyes; he never criticized her in any company save that of her den, where he, like only one other outsider in the last fifteen years, had made a half-place for himself by his dogged persistence.

And the last man, Ellerson, she often wondered about; the hurt of losing him had dimmed with time. Dimmed the same way the loss of her father had, even though her father had not chosen his death the way Ellerson had chosen his departure.

"Avandar," Rymark said coldly. "This does not concern you."

Avandar was a domicis. It was not his right to reply. But he folded his arms and said softly, "It seems you are not only imperceptive but graceless. I am not a man with your reputation for prowling—"

"Avandar, you had a choice." It was as close as Rymark ever came to open anger. "You made it. You *serve,* and you serve her. If she does not cry for help, do not seek to interfere in what you do not understand."

Morretz, The Terafin's domicis, would have been deaf to Rymark ATerafin; in fact, he usually was, which Jewel found quietly amusing and Rymark found irritating.

Avandar showed her again—as he usually did—why he was not Morretz. "The function of a domicis is not mere service, ATerafin—and I rather thought you knew that when you applied for the services of one."

Jewel was shocked. *Oh, gods,* she thought, *he's done it now.*

Rymark paled and then purpled. "That is strictly under the confidence of the guild order," he said, and Jewel thought a whole lake would freeze at the chill in his voice if one were available. "And you, *domicis,* have broken that confidence by your words tonight. I will speak with the guild," he added.

Avandar now offered a stony silence in return for the truth that Rymark had spoken; he managed to maintain that silence until Rymark turned on his heel and strode out of sight.

"Avandar," she said, the concern in her words genuine.

"It is not—quite—a disruption of guild confidence," he said, his lips nearly white. "Rymark's original application came through Terafin, and as it happens, those documents are accessible to us if they still exist. I will argue that the breach and the knowledge occurred at *this* end."

"But I've never—"

"You will." He shrugged.

She thought about it for a minute. Thought hard. "I think I can find them. Gabriel's got to have them filed neatly somewhere. An application of that nature is recorded; refusal would be recorded as well, for future reference in dealings with the guild.

"Of course there's a very small chance that Gabriel didn't keep track of the application. Remember, Rymark's his blood son."

"And that," Avandar said quietly, "is an insult to both the right-kin, Gabriel, and all those who have become, through dint of effort, ATerafin."

It stung when he was right, and he was right more often than she cared to admit. Of course, given his disposition and his unbearable arrogance, once was more than she cared to admit, so she supposed it wasn't that hard. He'd not yet faulted her for her appearance, and she didn't want to deal with yet another criticism, so she said, hoping to distract him, "How in the Hells did you know that he'd made that application? He doesn't have a domicis."

"Now *that* would be breaking guild confidence."

"How convenient. I suppose this means you're not going to tell me."

"You suppose correctly."

"It was *you*, wasn't it? You were offered his service."

Avandar said, voice low with warning, "Jewel."

She could not imagine how two men—Morretz, who served The Terafin, and Avandar, who served her—could be so different. He was dark and mercurial in temperament; Morretz was patience and stability defined. She knew by Avandar's tone that she was right, and that he would not elucidate further. Ever. Fifteen years had taught her when to fight and when to give up. She gave up. "Were you following me?"

"Yes."

"Well. I guess this time it wasn't such a bad idea."

"How graceful of you to acknowledge it."

Her cheeks reddened. Jewel hated when they did that.

"You go to the shrine." It wasn't a question.

She nodded, self-conscious.

"I will escort you as far as the path will allow." His offer was grudging; he loathed the exclusion. But The Terafin and the A'Terafin who sought the shrine sought it in isolation.

If the offer was grudging, the acceptance was not less so. Jewel turned and began to walk, her cheeks burning with the embarrassment of the required rescue, her anger directed at Rymark for proving to her, yet again, how necessary Avandar had become to her life in Terafin.

He had not always been so.

Vision.

Torchlight in the darkness. Blue, blue night, scattered across with stars twisting the raiment of moonlight into light, the haze of the heavens. Against that backdrop, leaves and fronds, black— the silhouettes of the puppet theater in the Southern holdings, moving at the hand of the wind, whispering their muted night whisper.

Sight.

Terafin burning. Sands where the gates might be, shadows lapping at the grasses and the flat stones that lead to the shrines. She walked in their center, taking careful steps. Afraid to look left, to look right; afraid that her talent would take her eyes again, show her things she did not wish to see.

Gods, but the visions hadn't invaded her dreams this strongly since—

Since the last time they'd been searching for the Shining City. Unbidden, the ghostly vision of a young woman with dark hair and darker eyes smiled at her from across the way—but the smile was dangerous, half-threatening. Duster. Death.

She had walked this path so many times she could follow it without looking, but she looked anyway, for comfort's sake. There, the Mother's shrine, a flat-roofed presence, surrounded artfully by flowers and plants whose colors could be seen in the torch-light of the rings on each of the four pillars. She bowed at the sight of its murky marble, but did not stop to make an offering; she might have once, but this was not a matter for the Mother.

Nor was it a matter for Reymaris, and that grieved her, because Jewel Markess—the girl she had been before Terafin had both saved and swallowed her life—had believed in that justice, without reservation; the reservations were ones she had learned as ATerafin, and having once learned them, she discovered them to be like spiderwebs, and she the fly; she could not turn back.

Still, she held what she could of her old beliefs. Bowed a moment at the plaque that graced his presence on the grounds of Terafin, wondering how angered he might be at the end of the succession. Wondering if, indeed, there would be a succession war.

War. Although she did not speak the word aloud, it echoed, lingering in air and on the tip of her tongue as if she'd shouted it. Her arms stiffened a moment; she forced them to relax and then remembered that the bundle she was pressing more and more tightly to her chest was a cloak, and proof against this unseasonally cool evening. Hands shaking, she donned it, and then drew it tight, treating it as if it were more blanket than apparel.

To Cormaris' shrine she went; if one followed the path set out by a long-dead architect, there was no choice—it took you to this shrine, this lit and guiding place, and made you stop there, for the path surrounded the shrine in a circular ring.

Cormaris, the god of wisdom, was worshiped, if privately, by more of the older Terafins than she could count, and not all of them the men who made of their lives political tools and weapons. His presence secured more in the way of offerings than the Mother and Reymaris combined, although it was the Mother's name that was most often spoken across the Empire's breadth.

Just behind the gleam of the eagle swooping there was an offering bowl, hidden by the height of the plaque so as not to be too garish, too obvious—but obvious nonetheless to any who knew to come here. Jewel bowed, and as she shifted into a momentary obeisance, light caught her eyes; the torches were flickering across shining brass. The rod, and the ring, each caught beneath the eagle's claws, in bright relief. The ruler and the servant. The ruled and the master.

For most of House Terafin, the path ended here.

But Jewel ATerafin had not come this way to seek the wisdom of Cormaris, blessed though that might be. She took a breath as she rose, expelled it and drew a deeper one, and then brushed her straggling curls out of her eyes.

The path went one shrine farther; there were four shrines in the gardens of Terafin.

It was to the shrine of Terafin, that round-domed, marble structure beneath which lay the altar upon which so many dreams and oaths were offered, that Jewel ATerafin repaired in a darkness that she had not once thought to alleviate by lamplight or torchlight of her own.

She came, bearing the fading reality of a dream that only a seer could know, and climbed the concentric marble circles that made stairs and a plateau upon which the simple, smooth stone of the Terafin altar sat.

There, in the light of lamps that were never allowed to dim completely, she knelt before the stone itself and began to pray. And if she leaned her forehead into the stone itself, more for support and comfort than to offer respect, no one was there who would comment on it.

And yet, someone did.

"Terafin has no strength to give you. If you have strength, offer it and it will be accepted. But the ways have begun to open; there is nothing to take from the altar once you have placed your life there."

She withdrew at once, as if the cool stone's touch had marked her, burned her. As if she could withdraw what she had, in honesty and truth, offered years ago. Taking a deep breath, she rose, unfolding one knee and then the other, feeling her weight upon both. Standing seemed hard.

"Not so hard as it will, Jewel Markess."

She recognized the voice, and she did not; she kept her back to the light, away from the night and the night's solitary visitor. "It's been a long time since I've been called that."

"Yes."

She heard no sound of motion, nothing at all, but she *knew* that the spirit of Terafin, the spirit of The Founder, had drifted closer and closer to her exposed back. She waited without turning.

"Why are you using that name?"

"Because, Jewel, it *is* who you are. The years have given you wisdom, of a type, but they have not changed your nature. You are ATerafin in times of peace."

She turned then, bleakly, her dark eyes the color of night, but wider. And what she saw stilled her completely. For the last time she had spoken alone with the spirit of the Founder, he had worn the face and flesh of one of the Terafin's Chosen, Torvan ATerafin.

Tonight, he wore the guise of someone so different she drew breath: a woman whose face defined Terafin, hair paled by time's touch, but body still slender. Bent, she thought, and oddly fragile, although not until he came to her thus had she recognized any sign of the weakness of age; The Terafin was the signal example of age's strength.

Almost grim, she smiled. "You realize," she said lightly, "that she'd probably kill you if she saw you."

His smile was not The Terafin's smile, although it was The Terafin's lips that framed it. "There are worse fates. I speak from experience." The smile dimmed. "And, although she will not thank me for it, I will tell you now that not only has she seen me in this guise, but she understands what it presages, for her House, that I appear thus to her. Do you?"

"Not her death," Jewel said softly. "Torvan didn't die when you wore his face."

"No. But Torvan was not The Terafin."

Silence. Then, "Are you telling me—are you telling me that she'll die?"

"She is a ruler without an heir. What have you learned of our history, of the Weston history upon which it is founded?"

Jewel bridled slightly. "Enough."

"As much, I imagine, as most of the House Terafin." It was clear that he did not mean it to be a compliment. "And if you could recite our history, end to end, from the first day to the last—and, if it will ease you, I cannot—it would still mean nothing. It is not the event, but the experience that comes out of the event, that defines a man; it is not the experience, but the wisdom that comes out of a full range of experiences, the ability to draw a conclusion from experience, that defines the ruler."

"All right. You're saying that I'm not a historian, and that because of it, I can't draw conclusions." She shrugged. "I won't argue with you. Do you know that I don't even know your name? You were always The Terafin. The Founder."

"What is The Terafin's name?"

"Amarais, born Handernesse."

Her expression—his expression—darkened. "No, Jewel, born Markess, that is *not* her name. She *is* The Terafin."

"And I'm Markess."

"Yes."

"Why did you come here tonight?"

"Should it not be I who asks that question of you?"

Jewel shrugged. Turned away from the knowledge that she saw in eyes that were dead, and yet somehow alive with it. "The dream," she said at last.

He said nothing. He, wearing the form of the woman she respected more than anyone in the Empire. Respected and feared, if only a little. Shadows wavered as the lamps flickered in a cool sea breeze; the winds were stirring. Storm? She lifted her head a moment.

"Oh, yes," he said. "The storm is coming."

"You told me to go South."

"I told you, child, go South if South calls, and do what must be done."

She didn't much like being called a child, and he knew it, but she was old enough now not to bridle at a slight that was not offered with intent. She looked back again, and then, although it wasn't, strictly speaking, correct behavior, placed her palms on the altar's cool surface, and rested her weight against them. "And you've changed your mind?"

"I?" It was the eyes, she thought, as she met them. The eyes were not The Terafin's eyes, just as they had not been Torvan's, or the man named Jonnas, whose appearance he called upon when he offered counsel to the ruler of the House. "No, Jewel." His voice was grave. "Have you?"

The weight on her hands increased. "How much do you know?"

He did not reply. Not directly. But at the last, he said, "I had hoped to spare you this because you are young. But in this generation, no one will be spared. That is the way of it; that we treasure the young and the young at heart, and to preserve them, we sacrifice our own youth. There are deaths, Jewel, that must be faced. Love is not proof against that fact—in fact, love, in times such as this, is the root of all weakness *and* all strength; it is not the battle, but if you surrender to its impulse, it *is* the end of the war, and not in your favor."

"I've sacrificed those that I loved before," she replied bitterly.

"Yes." He drew closer, the lines of his face blurring in the torch-light, becoming as indistinct in her vision as the edges of her dream. "But never knowingly. Imagine this, if you will, an in-dulgence that I beg of you."

She nodded, wordless because she did not trust her words not to give too much away.

"You are standing on the edge of the field of battle. The time is our distant past, during the baronial wars. Two sides are readying for a battle that has been long coming, and upon this battle, the fate of the Empire rests."

"Our Empire?"

"Our very Empire," he said softly. "For out of the last of the baronial wars the Kings rose like birds of fire, and they spread their word, and their law, with the strength of the blade, and the bless-ing of the Mother. Ah, but you lead me astray, Jewel, and I do not have that luxury of time.

"You stand upon the edge of the field in that battle; you have seen skirmish, you have seen war; you have both ridden and marched as a soldier."

She nodded.

"But you are not a soldier now; you have a rank, and a responsi-bility. Into your keeping the standard has fallen."

Privately, Jewel ATerafin had always thought that standards on the field of battle were an artificial mess. A flag, a thing that peo-ple made into something that it wasn't, a way of prettifying some-thing that should *never* be made pretty.

"You know," the spirit of The Founder continued, blurring even more in form, taking on a shape that had never belonged to Ama-rais Handernesse, "that if the standard falls, the hope of the regi-ments fall with it. That you are, while keeping this piece of pretty cloth, and its bearer, safe, succoring those men who cannot see you, those thousands who will never even know your name.

"With you, in this war, is your young adjutant. Teller ATerafin. He sees well; he always has; he watches the periphery of the boundaries set out as your responsibility."

She did not like where this was going at all. Lifted her hands from his altar again, almost—but not quite—leaping away from the name.

"A small group of men, with a mage and the use of two de-mons, is about to spring its trap upon your standard. You have the vision, Jewel, and because of this you see clearly.

"You also see, clearly, that you have two choices: You can go, now, to warn the mage—in which case, the flag will *not* fall to this attack—or you can ride, in haste, to that stop thirty yards away, in which your adjutant is pacing out his nervous attention so as not to disturb you; he has always been considerate.

"You cannot do both."

The spirit of Terafin stood before her, not as The Terafin, not even as Torvan, but rather as a shade, a passing fancy whose voice was still as sharp and cold as a blade's edge.

"Jewel Markess would ride to the aid of young Teller.

"Jewel *ATerafin* would summon the mage.

"You do not have the luxury, now, of being both, and for this, I apologize. Amarais would know her way to the only choice available, and she would accept it. But it is not her war, Jewel; it is yours.

"She will call Council in three weeks. And the matter of an heir will be raised, for she has chosen none."

"I know."

He laughed. "You are lying, but I accept it. I always accept a lie when it's an honest one."

"What the Hells is that supposed to mean?" she said, her voice far too sharp and high, to the empty air.

Air answered. "A lie is honest when you tell it to yourself so strongly that you believe it to be the truth."

He was gone. And she, who had come seeking strength and solace, was no more comforted than she had been when nightmare's grip had been the strongest and Terafin itself was burning into desert heat.

CHAPTER THREE

11th of Lattan, 427 AA
Averalaan Aramarelas, Avantari

The sun traced a slow arc above two men. Rays glinted off armor
joints and helm, becoming such a consistent source of light an
onlooker might be forgiven for ignoring it entirely. What caught
the eye with its lightplay was the sword-work; it made of the two
men proud gods with forks of lightning in play.

Flash, strike, the ringing of metallic thunder.

Clearly, as one drew closer, one could see that of these men one
was larger, muscled in a way that extreme youth did not allow
for. He was also, this older man, more experienced; his attacks
were not wild—not yet—and not poorly planned. Yet if he gained
ground, it was a slow process.

His opponent was younger, slender in the way that youth is that
still knows strength. He was, of the two, the taller, and his blade
the heavier and the one with longer reach—but where the older
man's blade was straight and double-edged, the younger man's
was curved—and the older man used the interchangeability of edge
to his advantage, as he used all else.

Not terrain, though; the terrain was even, flat, and quite lifeless. And Kiriel was used to that lack of life: it was the footpaths,
here, that were still almost paralyzing in their scent, their profu-
sion of color and motion.

It was not as hard for her to watch as she imagined it would be.
This was not a fight—not in a way that she understood it—but
she had been trained to observe, in a fashion, by a creature she
had promised herself she would never again grant the dignity of a
name. That creature had trained her in the arts of war, and Ashaf—

Ashaf.

Breathe. What harm was there, in invoking an old woman's

name? It wasn't a *name,* after all; it was a human conceit, a thing with no power. The sun was cold a moment as she smiled bitterly at the lie she was only beginning to accept for what it was: a lie. The speaking of Ashaf's Southern name caused her more pain than anything in her life save her unnamed teacher. And why?

Flash. Clang. Curse. Lightning against the wall and the ground; the older man used his strength as leverage to half-throw the younger almost out of the field of play. He stumbled. Righted himself as the older man seized the opportunity to unbalance him with a series of quick, short swings, side to side.

Wild tactic; too wild for the young man.

These people, they would have liked Ashaf. In her turn, she might have grown to like them as well, although she never trusted men much. Kiriel rose, restive, and touched the hilt of her sword—but it was no defense against Ashaf's memory.

She almost thought that Ashaf had trained her in the arts of peace—but what peace was there now? She, as the two men below, could *feel* the war that gathered, like storm, like the breath of the Lord of Darkness himself, on the horizon to the South. But only she willed it, waited for it, yearned for it.

She saw, in the older man's heaving motions, his coming exhaustion. They had been working thus, young man and older, in the sun, a long time.

With a neutral eye, she watched them both and knew that the young man was better, far better, than even the Ospreys understood. He fought as if driven—no, better, he fought as if what drove him were a force that could be taken, whole, and *used,* as if it were power. In that, she thought that Valedan kai di'Leonne and Kiriel di'Ashaf were similar. That, and coloring; for they were pale of feature but dark of hair and eye.

In all else, Valedan was gray and light, a thing of distant beauty. Kiriel di'Ashaf grimaced, seeing in him what only demons could see: the choice of his soul. But she was no demon, no *Ktalll;* what she saw, she could not twist or take. It would have been simpler if she could.

Commander Sivari's spirit was paler than Valedan's, almost luminescent. He was at the waning of his life, not the waxing, when the soul itself was often fatigued by the life a human led—although how a soul grew weary, when the life it cloaked itself in was so short, Kiriel did not understand—but he was a man at peace with himself, and secretly, Kiriel hated him for it. And it was hard to hate the Commander.

She heard footsteps; familiar fall of feet against stone—a step too light for a woman, although it was, indeed, a woman who claimed it, who owned it.

"How long have they been at it?"

She turned to face the curiosity in the eyes of the Princess Mirialyn ACormaris. Those eyes were such an odd shade; not golden, not like Kiriel's—or, for that matter, her father's, the King—but not quite brown either. Her hair was the color of new brass, a thing that was at once rich and pale; it reminded Kiriel of Auralis' skin.

"They've been 'at it' for almost an hour."

"They're insane."

"Yes."

The two women exchanged a rare smile. It was hard for Kiriel not to smile at the Princess, for Mirialyn was in all ways a thing of beauty, a thing of grace. More than once, Kiriel had found herself reaching out to touch the older woman, the Princess Royal. But she was used to control, to the necessity of control; she could freeze in an instant, but subtly enough that the sudden lack of motion was not noted.

Kiriel, listen well. I know the dangers of the gray that is almost white; I, too, have seen it. But I do not care for the light, and I do not love it.

Cleave to the darkness, love it, serve it. For the light is ephemeral and fleeting; you might touch it, but you will never *hold it; when the body is gone, so, too, is the soul. The darkness, the darkness you need never mourn the loss of; it can be Taken and claimed for you, and you will have it always.*

She bit her tongue; it bled freely. The taste of blood distracted her. She could control all motion, should she so choose; she could control the rate of her breath, the rise and fall of her chest, the nuance of gesture. But her thoughts were not so well-leashed, and his voice returned to her here, as it often did.

Had he not been one of only two true teachers?

"Kiriel?"

She nodded.

"I think you'd better have them stop. If this doesn't kill Valedan, it most certainly isn't doing anything for Sivari, and we're going to need them both."

Kiriel frowned slightly.

"What concerns you?"

"I have been watching. Not just Valedan, but the men who have come from the South."

"On orders?"

"Primus Duarte's."

"Good. And?"

"They train and they . . . spar . . . I think."

"Spar is the right word, yes. And?"

"Valedan must defeat these men?"

The daughter of the wisdom-born King said nothing for a moment; the moment stretched. At last, she said, "Yes. But it is more than just that."

"You think he needs to win."

"I think, having entered the Challenge, he needs to win. It has not yet begun."

"Will he win?"

"What do you think?"

"He is not what I am . . . accustomed to. In my own lands, none of you would last the fight."

Mirialyn raised a brow and then shrugged. "He can outride any of the Northerners, and probably half of the South; in swordplay he can hold his own against all but the top ten. The javelin, I think, will be the weakest of his skills. But he has the advantage over his distant kin; he can swim, and well. Between us, Kiriel, the one thing that Valedan has is the tenacity of endurance, the ability—and this is so rare in youth—to *wait*. To persevere. He will swim at the top of his form, and he will run well." She paused. "I do not know if he will run quickly, but in the marathon, there is no question that he will take the stand. But in what position, only the gods can say.

"Pole-vaulting favors his build and his coordination. But archery is the sport at which he excels, and it is not considered a man's sport in Annagar; it will avail him little there, although it will move him to the crown.

"He does not have to win every event to win the crown," she added, as if uncertain as to how much Kiriel understood of this odd festival, "but he must win three of eight to have any chance at all."

"Have you seen the others?"

"Not all of them. Some choose to train upon the fields that we provide, and some refuse the opportunity, holding their strengths to themselves until the actual moment."

"And?"

The Princess shook her head softly. "The Challenge has not yet begun. If he can be turned from his course, I think it wisest."

She was the granddaughter of the Lord of Wisdom, the daughter of the Lord of Wise Counsel. Kiriel understood the weight of her words from the way she ended them.

11th of Lattan, 427 AA
Averalaan Aramarelas, Terafin Manse

She thought, when she heard the knock at the door, that she might as well not have bothered to sleep at all, for all the good it had done her. There were accounts, after all, to be kept, and reports to be taken; she had been given, in her tenure with Terafin, the running of two of the smaller merchant routes. They were safe routes, to be sure; they sold pearls from the bay and jewels from the Menorans both to the West of the mountain chains and to the South. Trade in the South had diminished at her command, but the men who actually traveled the route were anxious to be off, and she often put faith in the men who did the real work while she sat behind a too-large desk playing with inkwells.

Inkwells.

The knock was louder.

"I'm coming!" she shouted, and sank a bit farther back into the bed. The last of the dream had left her, but the visit with the spirit of Terafin now carried a greater, a more terrible, weight.

The door opened. It was Finch. "Yeah. Right." She marched into the room, as officious in her own way as Avandar, and threw off the light covers. Jewel didn't like to sleep without covers, even at the height of summer. A remnant of a childhood belief that if, in bed, she was covered from toe to chin, the monsters that only materialized in the dark of a bedroom—and obviously, only preyed on young children—couldn't get her. "Get up!"

"Finch—"

"Or have you forgotten that you told me to make an appointment with The Terafin when you woke us all up in the middle of the night?"

She *had* forgotten.

"And you know you've still got to talk with the Commanders, right?"

"When?"

"*If* you get dressed, you can breakfast with The Terafin; the Commanders are coming here, after all. I think The Terafin wants to feed them, so you'll have some time between her and them to sleep if you need it." Her expression made clear that whatever Jewel thought, Finch thought she needed it. "I brought clothes."

"Avandar's supposed to do that."

Finch shrugged. "I guess he trusts me."

"Hardly."

Avandar stood in the doorway. He held out his arms, and Finch placed the carefully made bundle of day's clothing into them. There was no point arguing with—or making fun of—Avandar. "She's your responsibility," the younger woman said, brushing pale brown strands of hair from her face. "Get her there on time."

"Why, thank you," Avandar replied, "for reminding me of duties that are obviously so often forgotten." His sarcasm, even at this time in the morning, was unpleasant.

No, change that. *Especially* at this time in the morning. "Does it meet with your approval?"

He offered her a very rare smile. "All of the clothing that young Finch has easy access to does. I chose it, remember?"

Whenever he tried to be too friendly, he expected it to be a bad day. She nodded, swung her legs off the bed's side, and shed her nightclothing in one easy pull of flannel over head and shoulders. He offered her her underclothing and she slid into it, hating it in the summer's heat. It was, she thought, going to be a hot day.

"Tell me," she said, as he handed her the pale blue dress that made her feel so insipid—it had a silly neckline and a sightly pinched waist—"what we're going to do about Rymark."

"Any suggestion I have," he replied, his voice light, his smile thin, "would cost rather more money than we could divert without suspicion."

"Oh, ho ho ho. Look, I'm being serious. Here, hook me in."

"I was being half serious. If we were discussing Haerrad, there would be no half about it." He stepped behind her, to the back of the ridiculous dress, and deftly made it tight. Jewel could safely and easily say that this particular year's fashions were meant for young pretty women whose job it was to look, well, young and pretty. She was falling off the edge of young real fast, and she'd never, in her own mind, been up to pretty.

She held out her hand and he plunked a necklace into it—pearls, a show of solidarity with the merchants who mined, in a fashion, the sea's gems. "Good. Let's—"

"Hair."

The part she least liked. "Avandar, it's only The Terafin. It's not like she hasn't seen me—"

"Straight from The Terafin into the meeting with the Commanders. Your hair."

"Look, if I'm late again, I'm going to be cleaning the balconies the pigeons live above. And you're going to be right there beside me." She knew, by his expression, that it didn't much matter. "All right, but *hurry*."

There were fairly strict unspoken edicts about who could run down the wide halls of the Terafin manse, and who could not. Jewel Markess ATerafin was definitely and without question in the class of those who could not. She reasoned, however, as she walked perhaps a little too quickly that there was a difference between, say, a canter and a gallop. Which of course applied to horses, not Terafins, but it was a thought.

The skirts of this season's wear were wide—praise the Mother—enough so that she could take the steps three at a time. She did, but even over the sound of her too heavy footfalls and her slightly labored breathing, the Terafin manse being a large area to cover in the very short time remaining her, she swore she could hear Avandar's teeth grinding.

Jewel did not have to clean the balconies.

But while she did not care for the grand or dignified entrance that seemed so important to so many ATerafin—and to Avandar, if she were honest—he did. It wasn't that it didn't impress The Terafin; Avandar often showed a remarkable nonchalance when it came to the perfect good opinion of The Terafin herself. No, it was rather that it showed some sort of imagined flaw or weakness to The Terafin's domicis, Morretz.

One day, she thought, as she watched them both, and saw the peculiar tensing of either man's jaw, *I'm going to find out just what in the Hells it was that made you hate each other so much.* She'd had no luck so far, and it had been well over a decade.

One day—and then, she *felt* it, and she knew that what she had just said to herself was the truth. And instead of feeling comforted by it, she felt chilled. Cold, although the heat of the day was already notable.

"Jewel?"

She shook her head and smiled weakly at the woman who had given her her name, her life, and the time to develop the talent she'd been born to. "It's been a long night."

"So I gathered. I received an urgent request from young Finch."

She took a seat at a small table in the room just off the library, following with some speed The Terafin's unspoken command. Food filled a room too small for it with its aroma; Jewel realized, with a pang, just how hungry she was. She hoped it wasn't obvious—not so much because Amarais would dislike it, but because Avandar would kill her. Well, no, not kill her, but make himself unpleasant enough that she'd wish he'd just put her out of her misery.

"You're unusually expressive this morning," The Terafin said softly as she took the seat Morretz had, without remark, pulled out for her use. Before Jewel could respond, The Terafin carried the morning's conversation in the direction she meant it to take.

"Finch took it upon herself to send me this." She held out one ringless hand, and Morretz very carefully handed her two pieces—no, three—of curling paper. She set it down upon the table where Jewel might see it more clearly.

Finch's writing.

Jewel's dream.

Silence surrounded them, permeated with the smell of a morning meal; a summer meal, fruits, cool water, cold breads, early wine.

Neither woman touched what had been set out before them. Morretz gestured, almost unnoticed; but what was not unnoticed, not by Jewel—and she bet not by Avandar either—was the spark of light, of orange heat, that fled his fingers in a fine, delicate web, fading almost at once into the colors of the dawn.

"Jewel," The Terafin said quietly.

Hunger dissolved into ash. Into the memory of ash and sand. "Last night," Jewel answered.

The Terafin looked out, out into the bay that the windows faced. Boats flecked the seascape in the distance, and beyond it, the curve of the old city, the hundred holdings, cathedrals to the gods who were not part of the triumvirate reaching up and pulling the eye with them. At last, she said, "I've been to the shrine."

"Me, too."

"He offered me a warning," The Terafin said, delicately. She reached out for a glass, thin-stemmed and empty; Morretz moved at once to fill it. The wine was almost clear, it was so pale.

"What—what warning?"

Silence again. And then The Terafin said softly, "I must choose—and announce—my heir."

"Word travels."

"Indeed. Angel mentioned, in passing, to Torvan, that Rymark ATerafin thought to gain your support at a rather unusual hour."

Jewel raised both eyebrows and turned on her domicis, who had not seemed to hear The Terafin's words. "I see," she said dryly, utterly unfazed. Not much went on in this House that The Terafin didn't know about. You could fool yourself into thinking that you had privacy, that you operated on your own, that you owned the little territory she granted you.

But you were an idiot if you forgot that it *was* hers. Everything was hers.

"You find this amusing?"

Jewel laughed out loud. It was a good feeling, the laughter; it traveled the length of her body. "I find it funny, yes. I'll strip Angel's ears, but I do find it funny."

The Terafin's smile was a relaxed echo of the younger woman's laughter. "What are we going to do, Jewel?"

"I don't know. I asked, but the spirit, as it were, wasn't willing."

Stillness. Then: "You spoke to him?"

"He spoke to me."

"And was there anything unusual about him?"

"You mean besides the fact that he's dead?" But the laughter died because The Terafin's words brought back the night, and the night was strong. She looked up, met the older woman's dark eyes, and wondered how the spirit could look so fragile when the woman looked so strong. She turned her face away, to the light upon the water.

"If I name my heir," The Terafin said softly, "that person's rule will be contested, either before my death or after it."

Jewel wasn't an idiot. She understood what The Terafin meant: the heir was unlikely to survive the naming.

"So name Haerrad. I'd be willing to see him buried in the infighting."

"If I could bring myself to do it, I would. But there's always the chance, however small, that he would survive—and of the self-proclaimed candidates, he is the least acceptable."

"And what is it exactly that Terafin's Founder will do if the candidate who reigns is unacceptable?"

Silence again. "You know what Terafin is asking of you."

And then Jewel spoke, so quietly that she was surprised the words carried at all. "Yes. And . . . I don't know."

The Terafin was silent again, a punctuation to her still vigil, the watchful clarity of her clear eyes. When she spoke, those eyes were leveled upon the younger woman's face, searching for something buried there. "When I came to Terafin, I came with dreams of power. There was no other reason to join a great House.

"When you came to this House, you did not seek power."

"No." The younger woman stared out at the ocean because it was safer. "I came because Rath told me to come. And I stayed because I thought—I really thought—that here, my den would be safe."

"You came to Terafin seeking safety." Her lips touched her glass as if it, and they, were ice.

"There's no such thing, is there?"

"Yes, Jewel, and no. Most things that are worth seeking exist only a moment at a time. Safety. Strength. Love. A moment at a time, you might build a life; it would certainly be architecture that would stand the test of time."

"But you never—" Jewel had the presence of mind to leave the sentence dangling; she wished she'd had the presence of mind not to start it in the first place.

But The Terafin, this awkward morning, was expansive. "If each of those things is worth pursuit, and each exists a moment at a time, it is also true that each takes time, dedication of its own. I chose to rule; I chose this House. This is as close to the Crown as any man or woman will ever come."

"The Kings marry."

"The Kings, my dear Jewel, have never married for love. You are past thirty; no young girl. You must be aware of this."

Jewel ATerafin rarely saw the Kings; she did not speak with them. And because she was no longer a young woman, she did not bridle at the veiled accusation of ignorance, although it was a near thing.

"The fact that they marry as they do doesn't mean that no love can grow. Nor does it mean that there is no affection, no respect. But they marry for children, and they marry women who understand that the Kingdom will—and *must*—always come first." She paused a moment, the stem of her glass between fingers made translucent by sun's lack. "It seems such an easy thing, to the young, that they think they can accept this; they dream of love with little understanding. But the ability to accept that one will, and must always, come second in time of need is rather more rare than that.

"I sometimes think you've never been young, Jewel. But today, this morning, I look at you and I also realize you've never been old enough."

At that, Jewel Markess ATerafin did stand. "I've always been true to the responsibilities *I've* accepted. I'm not you. I don't want what you want. I never did.

"I want my den. I want to choose my den. I want to build it a bit, I want to surround myself with people *I* trust. But I won't do that if I can't protect them. Because that's what I promised them."

"No," The Terafin said softly, making no move or gesture that might indicate displeasure at the outburst, "that's what you've promised yourself. I believe this interview is at an end. Remember that we are to meet with the three Commanders in the afternoon, and be prepared. Commander Allen, in particular, will view you as a skilled talent which, like any of his soldiers, can be trained and pointed. Watch what you say to him."

"We've met," Jewel replied.

"Ah, yes. I'd almost forgotten."

Jewel didn't snort, but only because she was with The Terafin. "And?"

"He's the Eagle."

The older woman frowned as the younger woman smiled.

"Jewel, you would do well to remember that that's what his soldiers call him. It is not an acknowledged title."

"I've got more in common with his soldiers than I do with him."

"Is that really true?"

You guard the Standard. Jewel turned pale in the white-gold of the sunlight's rays. "It—used to be."

"Jewel—"

"I *don't know,* Amarais."

Silence, long, profound. Jewel did not use The Terafin's given name. Only those who were her equals, or her confidants, did. But she had to do something to stop that question. Oh, she was afraid. She felt it again, and again; The Terafin spirit's words were working their way to her core. She wasn't sure what would happen when they reached it. Half her life had been spent in Terafin; a quarter with her dimly remembered parents, a quarter on the streets of the twenty-fifth holding.

Yet it was true that the quarter on the streets still defined her. Her friends, she kept; her responsibilities, she entrenched. Oh, she could read Old Weston now, and Torra, the tongue of the Dominion; she knew the history of the realm as if it were more than her grandmother's superstitious, dangerous, and terrible stories.

But when she thought about herself, she still *felt* like the sixteen year old who had crossed the Terafin threshold seeking—

demanding, in her awkward, naive way—shelter. She didn't feel like a woman of power, although Avandar assured her she had become one.

It suddenly occurred to Jewel, as she sat in the sun's growing heat, the woman she most respected watching her quietly, expectantly, that she never would feel like a woman of power. Like, say it, an adult. Even if she was one; even if she had to become one. She would always feel like she was groping for the right thing, the right answer, the right action.

For the first time in her life, Jewel Markess ATerafin looked at the woman who ruled and saw past her to her age. And that age, like a web, lay beneath the surface of translucent skin, where all else lay trapped by it.

"You were . . . gentle," Morretz said quietly, long after the thud of doors closing had faded into the silence of birdsong and wind. He glanced at his master's face, but only briefly; there was something in the wide eyes that he felt might sear him if he met it too directly.

"I understand her," The Terafin replied. "I understand her desire to protect those that she can. I am not immune to it myself. She is . . . she is to me what Alea was."

"She is not Alea." Morretz began to remove the fine-stemmed glasses from the table. It was rare that he desired something to do, but when he did, he found it.

"No. She's younger."

"She's stronger," he said.

She did not speak to him of her visits to the shrine of Terafin, but what lay between them was such a visit; she had come, ashen, from it, and had gone directly to the roof, forbidding him access to a moment of weakness that still echoed in the little nuances that defined her. He had tried most of his life to understand her. He tried now.

"Amaris," he said softly, using the personal.

For his trouble, he received her attention, but not as he desired it; she did not meet his eyes, and her shoulders stiffened and rose, as did her chin.

He thought she would remain silent, but he waited, as he had always waited. There was reward, this time, of a sort.

"I wanted," she said, speaking so softly a strong sea breeze would have taken her words, "nothing but the House. I left my blood kin for it, and that was bitter. I had only the approval of my grandfather—but he said to me, the last time we spoke, that I wanted it because I did not understand what it was that I wanted.

" 'Like children,' he added. 'Like first children.' " She raised her head further; her skin caught light, and the light was unflattering in its harshness; it traced the contours of time-worn crevice, bleached the color—what there was of it—from cheek and brow. "What was my first act as Terafin?" Soft question. Hard edge.

He was silent a moment.

"Let me ask a different question, then." She turned to face him, fully, and he almost regretted his desire for her full attention. "Why did you choose to serve me?" She had never asked him before.

Silence again. Stiffness. He did not know how to answer her. To observe, yes. To serve, yes. To comfort in a very oblique fashion—which was as much as she had ever allowed him. But this was to invite her across a wall that had always divided them.

It was the first time he had thought that the wall might be of his own making, and not hers at all.

Her smile was rare; sharp as the sword that defined her rule. "I ask," she said dryly, "because it provides me insight, indirectly, into Jewel born Markess."

"Insight?"

"I might better understand why Avandar would agree to serve her."

"I . . . see."

"Do you understand it?"

"Yes."

"Morretz, what I want, we both want: She is the woman who will best understand the *cost* of power. But such a price cannot be paid unwilling, at knifepoint; it cannot be paid because of the wounded cries—" and here she grimaced, "of those who wish to pass the burden on." It was as much of an indictment of herself as she ever offered, and it was laced with bitter humor.

She rose. "But you have had years to observe young Jewel; as many as I have. Avandar, if I am not mistaken, is frustrated at almost every turn; she is not the master he expected."

"No."

"I will answer the question, and you will answer the question I have not asked. The first thing I did when I took the Terafin sword was to execute the traitor. Not to order it done; not to pass the blood on, but to execute him myself."

He was silent; she had silenced him. There was no doubt in his mind whatever that Jewel Markess would give her last breath in defense of what he, and The Terafin, valued about Terafin itself. But more than that?

"Not all rulers are killers," he heard himself say, but the words were very distant to his own ears.

"No?" She turned. Walked away.

Serra Alina di'Lamberto waited in the cool shade of the halls. Gone were the Northern beds, the accoutrements that Valedan di'Leonne had known all his life; there were maps here, Southern pillows, fans, low, squat tables that gleamed under the new light. There were no scrafs, of course; this was the Empire, and the Empire did not approve of slavery, as they styled it. Nor would she have accepted serafs from the Imperial capital, even had they presented themselves.

Valedan was a threat only so long as he lived.

He lived; she intended that he continue to.

And so the Serra Alina di'Lamberto, no slave herself, and no woman of a lowborn clan, chose to provide what serafs could not: food and graceful care. Watchful care.

She waited, knelt, the tops of her feet pressed to the mats. It had been, in truth, far too long since she had kneeled thus, waiting on the kai of a clan—far too long and not long enough. She had waited willingly, then, because that *was* her life; she waited willingly now because this was her life. But between these two lives, the experience of Alina the younger and Alina the elder, was something that loomed large indeed, a gift from the North: Choice.

She had never intended to leave the Empire.

Listening, she heard the fall of steps against the stone. She frowned, only recognizing them at the last moment, and that, because she did not expect them here. But it was too late to rise with grace, and she was in all things—must be, until she could choose a suitable wife—graceful.

The Princess Mirialyn ACormaris pushed the hanging curtains aside without ceremony and entered the room. She stopped, nonplussed. The silence, between the standing woman and the kneeling one, was awkward.

At last, Mirialyn spoke. "*Serra* Alina."

"ACormaris." Alina rose as gracefully as she could. She felt, in the gaze of this distant Princess, embarrassed, uncertain. Standing gave her the strength that kneeling, in such a correct Southern posture, had taken away. "Have you come to speak with the kai Leonne?"

"I have come," the blood daughter of King Cormalyn said quietly, "to speak with you."

"Then speak. But be aware that these quarters are the quarters which the kai Leonne occupies; what passes here, he will learn of." It was a warning; the warning of a friend to a friend.

And Mirialyn's eyes, brown now under the curved, smooth ceiling, narrowed. Silence took them both a moment.

"So," the Princess said softly, "you make your choice."

Alina was stung by the words; she drew herself up, throwing her shoulders back, lifting her chin. "Why have you come?"

"To speak with the Serra Alina. To ask her, because she has influence, to speak with the kai Leonne."

"About?"

"The Kings' Challenge."

"You do not wish him to run the marathon."

Silence. And then the Princess smiled. Alina knew the cool expression well; it was sharp, as sharp as a blade. "And you do."

"Yes."

"Alina, *why?*" She asked the question as if it had been thrown from her lips, leaping with all of the anger and surprise she might otherwise have chosen to conceal. She had in her veins the blood of the Lord of Wisdom—such a loss of control was no small feat.

Alina took a bitter joy in this smallest of victories.

"Do you know how much he endangers himself? To run the marathon—to run the gauntlet—he will expose himself across the miles of this city, and its surroundings. We cannot stop every archer in the Empire should they choose that moment to attack.

"And it isn't just the gauntlet. He must swim from *Averalaan* to *Averalaan Aramarelas* and back. There are dangers, Alina."

"He knows them," was her cool reply.

"He is a *boy.* You are not."

She realized her hands were balled into tight fists when the nails of her fingers pierced her flesh. This woman, this highborn, respected Princess, was not unlike herself: a woman with no place. Here, in this Empire, the golden-eyed ruled, and the Princess had been born like a mortal, to a mortal. The blood of gods ran in her veins, but it was not purified by the shadowy covenant made between the Queens and the fathers of their husbands.

Years, Alina had lived in the Northern clime, and the one thing that she had never understood—and never would, she was certain—

was the way whole powerful Houses could disavow their kin in favor of some artificial ideal.

Yes, Mirialyn had no place in the North.

But had she been born in the South, there would have been no place for her either.

We are not so unalike, Alina thought, not for the first time. Not for the last.

"He must take the Challenge," she said. "Miri."

The light gleamed off her hair, brass frosted with a patina of pale white. "Why?"

"Because you think he is a boy."

"Taking the Challenge won't change what he is."

"Winning the Challenge will."

"You think he'll win?"

"I think he has a good chance of doing so."

Again, the Princess was silent as she accepted Alina's words, the truth of them. "It's not worth the risk."

"It wouldn't be worth the risk if he had been raised in the Dominion," Alina replied, the edge creeping back into her voice. "He wasn't. There isn't a clansman south of the border who won't think him just another pawn in the game between empires if he doesn't make his name known. Even you must see this."

"I see it. I see the risk as being greater."

"Because you think that word will travel. Because you think that the clansmen will cleave to the blood of Leonne."

"The General Baredan di'Navarre chose to do so."

"It is the only way he might save his life; he was marked for death, and rightly, by the General Alesso di'Marente."

"Ser Kyro—"

"You still do not understand us. Leonne was slaughtered in a *night*. There was no fight, no struggle, no *question*. We are not the North—what softness we have is devoured by sun and wind. Do you think the men will much care about the deaths of women and children? The only thing that matters—that matters at all—is that Leonne put up no fight, made no resistance; he sat in idle splendor and was slaughtered just as if he had been one of his wives. The clansmen will not follow a weak leader—and Alesso di'Marente has proved himself strong.

"No word of Valedan will travel in the Terreans except Alesso's word." She paused. "Unless Valedan makes his mark here. This is the only place he will have a chance to do it, Miri. He will stand in the sight of clansmen—and when they make their trek back to the Dominion, they *will* carry word of his deeds and his exploits.

"If we had another choice, I would counsel him against the Challenge."

"And if he loses?"

"He loses. He will do well enough that they will understand that he is not a mere boy, and not a mere pawn."

Miri's smile was cool. "You don't believe that any more than I."

She drew a breath and held it a moment, understanding that the years of living in the North hadn't softened her so much as she had once feared they might. It was hard to show fear; hard to be vulnerable. She had never faced that difficulty with Mirialyn ACormaris before, because the past and the present had always been foreign countries; she realized with a pang that they would never be so again. "No, I don't. If he loses, it will cost—but not so much as invisibility will cost. These are clansmen, Miri," she added bitterly, "and I understand the clans."

"And you will return to them." Not a question.

"For his sake. For the sake of the Dominion. Do you think I desire the Dominion? Do you think that I desire that life, with no true name of my own, no true title, no power to which I can turn, and upon which I can rely? Only counsel me," Alina said, lifting a hand to touch her friend's shoulder. "Counsel me otherwise, and I will heed you. We will continue to teach each other our language, our history, our philosophy.

"But look well at what he faces. Remember the carnage that you saw with your eyes, and that I saw only through Valedan's. Tell me that there is another whom he can trust, another wise enough to dance the dance the clansmen will force upon him. Only tell me any of these things, and I will stay, because if you say them, I will have no choice but to believe."

"Now you speak like an Essalieyanese."

"Yes. So I know, in the end, that you *have* tainted me these past ten years. But I notice, ACormaris, that you do not speak against the decision you know I've already made."

"How can I?" was the other woman's bleak reply. "I'm ACormaris."

"Will you ride with the armies?"

"I? No. I belong to Avantari, and it is in Avantari that I will remain. The Commanders will go to war." She reached up, caught the hand on her shoulder, and pressed it into the line of her collarbone. "Will you?"

"Yes. I will ride with the armies. And you will hear the outraged cries of Baredan di'Navarre and Ramiro di'Callesta no matter where you choose to hide in Avantari when they are informed of this fact."

"You are too strong a woman to waste your life on the South."

"No," Alina replied, freeing her hand. "My problem was that I was never strong enough. But I am not the willful girl that I was; I am a woman, with a woman's sensibilities. When I return, I will be Annagarian in all the ways that I could not be in my indulged youth."

The Princess bowed, her lips pressed into a thin line. She turned to the door, and then stopped. "One more question, Serra."

"Of course. If it is in my power, I will answer it."

"What if we fail to protect him, and the Challenge costs him his life?"

"Then he is dead," the Serra said softly. "But whether or not he faces the challenge, he will face the risk. There is a death here, ACormaris; many thousands of deaths. We cannot prevent a war, we can only seek to win it."

"Was I good enough?"

Sivari smiled. It was a question that Valedan had asked daily—almost hourly—since the Challenge trials. He sparred; he focused on the fight he was offered. But when it was over, it was to the Southern audience that had gathered on the trial day that his thoughts returned, over and over. "You were better than I've ever seen you. I don't know which gods you pray to—ours, or the Lord and the Lady—but they answered."

"You had best hope," the courtyard's other occupant said quietly, "that the wrong god didn't hear you; you know that gods are an expensive proposition."

He sat between them, his first teacher and his second; stone beneath his thighs and calves, the sound of water at his back. This was his haven, this courtyard, one of the few places in which there was no audience beyond the people whose company he chose and the fountain behind him.

Princess Mirialyn ACormaris had never taken the Kings' Challenge. She was a practical woman; in some things, she accepted that she would be inferior, and she was not willing to take the test and run the course if there was no chance whatever that she might complete—and win—it. Valedan knew this not because the Princess herself had ever deigned to speak of it; she did not.

He knew it because of Serra Alina; the Serra and the Princess were as much friends as anyone, Northern or Southern, might be when so much divided them. It had been the Serra Alina's suggestion that he train with the Princess Mirialyn one year after he had arrived in the capital. At the time, he had thought it strange— after all, the Princess was a *woman*—but because it was Alina of the sharp tongue and the easily invoked displeasure, he had agreed. He had also, as had Alina, neglected to tell his mother. Or the clansmen. But Alina knew. Mirialyn knew.

She did not fight like anyone he had ever met. Did not teach like anyone he had ever met either. She spoke, always, of finding his center; of finding his focus; of finding *the place,* and holding to it. It seemed to him, as he got older, that she cared less and less about technique, more and more about this mythical place, this magical *something.*

And because her regard was important to him at that age—it still was, now—and because Alina's regard was inextricably linked with the woman he had grown to call Miri, he struggled. Worked.

"He's not the best swordsman in the Empire," Commander Sivari said to the Princess. "But I believe he is one of the best that has been accepted for the Challenge."

"And the others?"

"There are four Northerners that I would bet on, if I were a betting man and not an Imperial tutor. But there are also two Southerners who had that look to them; they'll be his fiercest rivals there. They have a lot to prove."

"They don't have as much to prove as Valedan does," Miri answered, all humor—and there was little enough of it—gone.

Sivari did not openly reprove her, but his eyes narrowed and flickered off Valedan's still face.

Valedan shrugged. "She's right." He shifted on the flat stone, trying to find a way to be at ease. His sword was safely—and uncomfortably—sheathed. It was Southern custom to cart one's sword around off the side of one's hip no matter what the occasion. Valedan had always preferred to follow the Northern custom. No more. The days where he was allowed the relative freedom of the Northern court had ended the day he had declared himself in the Great Hall.

"I have not seen the Serra Alina in the halls today," Miri said quietly, changing the subject.

He heard the question in her voice. Heard it, and didn't know how to answer it. "She—she is preparing," he said at last, lamely, and knowing that it was. "Ramiro and Baredan have just heard the results. They are—unimpressed."

"Furious, I'd imagine. At least I'd imagine the Tyr'agnate would be. The General I'm not as certain of." Sivari was thoughtful. When he was thoughtful, he often missed the subtlety of expression in Mirialyn's words; he had missed them in the question she put to Valedan, and there was no way to correct him.

Indeed, it was probably best that no one did. What passed between his first Northern teacher and his Southern adviser, not even Valedan truly understood.

And besides, although he felt it, and felt it keenly, much of his life had been honed and sharpened into just a single question.

"Do you think they'll notice me? Do you think it will make them less certain of themselves?"

Sivari laughed.

"We seldom see you display such uncertainty these days," Princess Mirialyn ACormaris said softly.

He was instantly still.

Her smile faded as well. "What are you thinking?"

"That there was a boy," he said, "who watched me fighting. I did not see him until after we were done."

"You didn't see anything," Sivari said.

Valedan ignored him. "And that boy watched me, as I might have watched my father, or Ser Anton di Guivera himself. I've never seen that expression from the outside before."

They were silent, these two, waiting upon the question that would inevitably follow.

"Why is Ser Anton here, Miri?"

"I don't know," she said, but the pause before the words was long. Significant.

As significant as the fact that he did not ask her why she thought he was here.

The first time Jewel had set eyes on Commander Bruce Allen she knew why they called him the Eagle; knew why, of the Flight, he was considered the leader. It wasn't his uniform, for they wore the same uniform, the Kestrel, the Hawk, and the Eagle; bore the same rank, the full circle above the Kings' crest, the crossed rod and sword. It wasn't his size, or his build; almost any of the Tera-fin Chosen—never mind that, the Terafin House Guards—were of greater stature. But he had a sharpness of presence that drew the eye and the attention for no reason whatever that she could immediately think of; he was not a particularly flamboyant or imposing man.

And anyone that drew the eye of a half-trained seer for "no reason" deserved, even demanded, the attention she could give him.

He was not unaware of the attention; she was certain of it, but he accepted it as either his due or her poor manners. Later, she would understand that he accepted it because it was as natural a consequence of his presence as breath was to most people.

Seeing him for the third time, the effect was still strong; she had a desire to give the reins of power that she held so poorly to *this* man, because she felt certain that he knew what to do with them.

And that, of course, drew her up, made her suspicious and cautious. The reins she held were Terafin reins, and this Commander was affiliated with no House. He owed his loyalty to the Kings, and she was certain that the Kings received it. Certain that Terafin meant no more, and no less, than any of the soldiers he deployed in that duty.

She thought, suddenly, *How many men died? How many men did you order to their deaths in the war twelve years ago?* But she did not ask it; it was a young girl's question, and it would not be as easily forgiven coming as it did from the lips of a woman past thirty.

"Commander Allen," The Terafin said, bowing slightly. "Commander Berriliya. Commander Kalakar."

"Terafin," The Kalakar said, her lips rounding slightly in a familiar smile, the lines around the corners of blue eyes crinkling. "This is a change of venue."

"And a change of topic, as I suspect our merchant lines are not an issue in this discussion." The Terafin's smile matched The Kalakar's; that they were peers in all things was made clear by the ease of their discourse.

"They weren't entirely at issue in the last discussion," The Kalakar said, but shortly.

The Berriliya's frown was both slight and unmistakable. Jewel had seldom seen a man look so continually sour. Well, if you didn't count Avandar, and she didn't. She looked over her shoulder and saw, without surprise, the center of his chest; he stood closer to her than usual. Her colorful shadow. Protector, of sorts. Domicis, whatever that meant.

How had she gotten so used to him?

Commander Allen left the three—Berriliya, Kalakar, and Terafin—speaking; he moved to the table upon which lay a large, marked map. Maps like these were probably scattered across *Averalaan Aramarelas*. Merchant caravans and their inroads into the Dominion were the best source of the lay of the land—with the possible exception of the bardic colleges—and each House had merchants who used slightly different routes, or visited different Tors or Tyrs depending on the goods that they traveled with. Members of the Order of Knowledge—and members of the Imperial army—were at work combining the knowledge that was, in most Houses, more carefully guarded than all but the persons of the ruling members of the Houses themselves; it had been, and remained, a very tricky subject, and Jewel suspected that at least one or two of the merchants had deliberately been less than truthful. Knew it for fact, although she hadn't bent her mind to finding out which ones.

Because, of course, the Houses were to see the finished map in its entirety; they'd insisted on it, as The Berriliya and The Kalakar would be so privileged in the course of their duties.

It was hard, to have two Commanders who were also the heads of their Houses. In the history of the Empire—the brief history, Jewel thought, and knew that her understanding of its history had indeed changed her—it had only happened once before, and that at the Empire's bloody founding. The Ten had ridden to war.

The Kalakar ruled her House; there was no question that it belonged to her. No question that it would be there, loyal and unswerving, upon her return. The Berriliya's hold on his house was no less secure, but Jewel was not as certain that the House itself would not require some careful cleaning when the war was over.

If, she added bleakly to herself, they won.

"We *must* win this war," she surprised herself by saying. And, as usual, the words immediately silenced the conversations that had dappled the room with their little noises. There were days when she hated the gift she'd been born to.

The Kalakar smiled. "Then we will."

The Berriliya frowned but said nothing; Jewel wasn't certain she wanted to see the day when they both smiled in unison. But she knew, suddenly, that she would.

Commander Allen turned from the map to the younger ATerafin as if the map had never been of much interest to him. His eyes, she thought, were bright with something other than color; it was as if he saw clearly a thing which no one else in the room could.

Unfortunately, that thing was Jewel.

She felt, rather than saw, Avandar take a step to her left, coming out of her shadow, as it were; becoming more solid. He did not speak; it was not his place, and in that he was almost always painfully correct. But the warning in his presence was clear; perhaps too clear.

Jewel could not recall Morretz ever being so threatening in his silence. In fact, until this moment, she had—as she habitually did—forgotten that he was in the room. Their eyes met, and The Terafin's domicis actually smiled, as if Avandar's presence had drawn from them both the same thought.

Commander Allen chose not to notice Avandar; it was the wisest course of action, and she thought that he, like The Terafin, was a man who favored the Lord of Wisdom, if he clearly otherwise followed the god Cartanis, Lord of Just War.

"ATerafin," he said, offering her a nod.

"Commander."

"Your tone of voice suggests some further knowledge."

Not a question. She shrugged, and caught, for her trouble, the minute frown on The Terafin's face. "We've done this one before, Commander."

"We have." He waited; it was clear that she could speak as formally or informally as she liked and his reaction would be, as it was to most things, opaque. She had the sense that he could wait like that forever, as if he were Morel's statue.

And she would be damned if she was going to stand in his shadow for another minute. "My tone of voice is always going to suggest further knowledge that I don't have. If we're going to work together, get used to it."

"Jewel," The Terafin said, her voice, and Avandar's expression, blending into a stern warning that could—almost—not be ignored.

"I resent," Jewel continued, "the implication that I'm withholding information, if I can't immediately explain to *your* satisfaction something I've said. You aren't a stupid man—at least by all reports—so I'll grant you what little knowledge there is of the powers I've been born to. You requested them, after all. But we might as well begin here. I don't like to be treated like a lowly House spy.

"I'll work with you anyway; I don't have a choice." Not entirely true, though true enough on ethical grounds. "But I'm not your soldier, I'm not your adjutant, I'm not part of your Flight."

"*Jewel.*"

"I'm not beholden to you, and I'm not going to be questioned

by you as if I were a common criminal; you don't hold my oath.
Is that clear?"

"Perfectly," he replied, his voice dry as Northern winter.

"Good."

The Berriliya's expression was also as cold as Northern winter, which was fine. The Terafin's was even chillier, which was not. Oh, she was going to suffer for this later. She didn't even bother to glance at Avandar.

But she was surprised to see that The Kalakar's expression, if anything, was—faintly—approving. Approval was worse, in some ways, than disapproval, because it meant you had something to lose.

And loss was something that Jewel had never dealt well with.

"I don't think," Jewel said, as cautiously as she could, "that this war is the only war."

"Meaning?"

"It's a big battle."

"And you say this because?"

"Commander Allen, I say it on *instinct*. It's the instinct that I was born with. If you asked me to bet my life on it, I would."

"And how many other lives would you bet on it, Jewel ATerafin?"

"As many as you have," she replied. "If we don't win this battle, somehow, we've lost the whole thing."

" 'Whole thing'?"

"The Empire," she said. "The Western Kingdoms. The Dominion. Everything." It settled upon her, around her, within her: It was truth. Having spoken it, she could not turn back, and she knew, as her glance skirted The Terafin's stiff features, that the spirit of Terafin had known it when he had given her permission, even indirect orders, to go South.

"You will," the Commander said quietly, "allow us to speak privately for a few moments before we continue this interview." The Berriliya and The Kalakar had already drawn closer to his back, but he didn't turn that back upon her; he waited. Showing, no doubt, that his manners were vastly better than hers.

Still, it wasn't a request. She nodded, afraid. Because she knew—not as a seer, but as an intelligent young woman—that the war that was coming was in his hands as much as anyone's, and if they were to win it, it must remain that way. The Eagle was the only thing that could effectively bind and lead the other two. The Hawk. The Kestrel.

CHAPTER FOUR

"Well?" Commander Allen turned to the man known as the Hawk.

"She's known for her capabilities. It is rumored that when she is certain, she's infallible." Dry now. The Berrilya had the best information-gathering network in the capital; he valued it with a cool sort of pride.

"Infallible. Ellora?"

The Kestrel's eyes were still upon the door that had just closed. "I wouldn't," she said, half to herself, "want to be the unfortunate fool sent to kill her. That domicis of hers is only barely a servant, if I'm any judge of character. I wouldn't have had him if he hadn't come from the guild."

"You wouldn't have him if he did," Commander Allen said; her scruples were well known.

"We are not speaking about the domicis," The Berrilya said, a bit too sharply.

"They come as a pair, Devran."

The Hawk subsided. The Kestrel continued. "But the young woman?"

"She's at least thirty, Ellora."

"She's young for thirty, in some respects."

Commander Allen did not argue the point. Instead, he waited. Ellora AKalakar—no, *The* Kalakar—had instincts that had been tested in battle; honed by death, by the dying. The Berrilya relied on structure, on order, on a clean rationality; The Kalakar took her chances upon the sword's edge. Both had survived, which was the test, perhaps the only true one.

"I'd trust her."

The line of his shoulders fell ever so slightly; he lifted a hand to his eyes a moment, as if to clear them of dust. "With your life?"

"My life, certainly."

"The lives of your men?"

Her answer took longer, but he knew her well enough to know what it would be; he wasn't disappointed. "Yes. Even if she swore no oath to me."

"But?"

"But I'm not certain that I would trust that girl with the deaths of my men. Or yours. Or his."

To someone who had never been a Commander in time of war, the words might have held no meaning. But to Commander Allen they were cutting.

"Devran?"

"Concur. The girl can barely follow The Terafin's command; I doubt that she will follow ours if it does not suit her purpose."

"That's not what I said." The Kestrel dropped her hand flat against the tabletop, slapping Devran's reflection. They were powerful, these two, but they were not above heat and ire. To Commander Allen's abiding regret.

"It is not at the heart of what you think you said," was The Berriliya's cool reply, "but it is at the heart of the matter. She will do what she perceives to be 'right,' rather than what *we* perceive to be necessary."

"And do you counsel that we leave her behind?"

The Berriliya said nothing.

"Bruce?"

"No."

"Why?" Devran turned his back upon Ellora.

"Instinct," the Eagle said, his smile sharp. "Hers and ours. She means to come, and I think that means we need her."

"How will we control her?"

"Crowns' mandate."

"The Crowns' mandate," The Berriliya said balefully, glaring at The Kalakar, "doesn't even keep our own in line."

Ellora's smile was cool. "It doesn't keep us under *your* control, Devran. I believe you've forgotten what the Crowns' mandate *is*." Before he could answer—and there was no doubt whatever in Commander Allen's mind that a reply was forthcoming—she turned to the man whose lead they both followed. "We've given you our opinions, and as usual, they're . . . diverse. I note that you've withheld your own."

"Perhaps because I haven't formed one."

"I don't believe you."

At that, Commander Allen smiled. It was something that Ellora, direct and to the point, would say; Devran would think it, but keep his own counsel. Neither of them would be fool enough to believe that he had drawn no conclusion. "Time hasn't dulled you at all, Ellora. You're right."

"You like her." No question.

"Yes."

"You think she'll make a terrible soldier."

"Yes."

"You never had any intention of leaving her behind."

"True."

"Then why this discussion?"

"Because I've been wrong on occasion, and my understanding of people like this Jewel ATerafin is often . . . limited." He raised a hand and placed it almost absently upon the hilt of his sheathed sword. "She is no soldier."

"And that," Devran said unexpectedly, "is a pity, because I believe by the end of her tenure in Terafin she will either learn to be one, or she will not survive."

Commander Allen turned sharply. "What do you mean?"

"The girl is not a killer. You are, Bruce. Ellora is, I am. The Terafin is."

"Why, thank you," Ellora said wryly.

"This is House business, not Crown business," the man called the Hawk added, his eyes sharp and clear as his namesake's. "But the rumors are stronger than they have been in fifteen years."

"What rumors?"

Ellora and Devran exchanged glances, and Commander Allen reminded himself that they, these two and he, were not yet upon the field of battle; they were *The* Kalakar and *The* Berriliya, and his concerns and theirs, in this so-called civilian life, did not meet or touch often.

It was Ellora who replied. "Even Kalakar has heard the rumors—and fielded requests."

"Requests?"

"For support."

"Ellora, Devran—time *has* passed if you've forgotten how little patience I have."

Devran answered. "The Terafin is being pressured to choose an heir. There are, that we know of, four candidates, and of those four—Rymark, Haerrad, Elonne, and Marrick—two have emerged as the true contenders: Rymark and Haerrad. Regardless, all four have quietly petitioned The Ten for aid and support should they be the chosen heir of Terafin."

"I see. And?"

The silence was uncomfortable.

At last, Ellora said, "You serve the Kings, Bruce. As do we when we wear these uniforms. But the requests came not to the uniforms, nor to the Crowns; they came to *us*. It is House business."

Which meant, Bruce Allen thought bleakly, House succession war. The Kings did not interfere, not directly, in a House War, unless it grew out of proportion. And proportion, to the Wisdomborn King, was a hundred deaths, not ten. It was within The Ten that those who sought power tested themselves, and weeded themselves out. The Twin Kings were proof against the succession wars that had devastated human empires for centuries, even millennia, before the birth of Veralaan. "Were there only four?" he asked.

Ellora and Devran glanced to and away from each other so quickly their expressions hardly had time to shift. It was Ellora—always Ellora—who finally said, "There was a fifth. Possibly a sixth."

But more than that, she would not say. And his intelligence, within the Houses, was not up to the task of finding what she did not offer. He could ask Duvari, the Lord of the Compact, but that would draw attention of a type that neither the Hawk nor the Kestrel ever gracefully accepted.

He would say nothing.

But he wanted, in his own way, the simplicity of a war that could be fought in the open.

"We'd best speak with the girl, then," he said at last. Thinking of Duvari, he added, "we won't have her services until the last serving member of the Kings' Court has been officially cleared by the Lord of the Compact—and I believe he intends, with The Terafin's permission, to use the girl's peculiar vision."

12th of Lattan, 427 AA
Avantari

Five days.

Valedan kai di'Leonne rested a moment beside the fountain that had never once ceased its quiet cry. Blindfolded, the carved statue that had been an affront to so many of his compatriots stood in the center of the water that came from his cupped hands. *Justice*, its maker had called it. *Tyrian Justice*. They translated *Tyrian* to be *Annagarian*, and perhaps it was; either way, it was clear to those who had come from the Dominion what its intent was. An insult. A slap in the face.

Usually the intent of such a slight was lost if you were not from the North, with the rain's water and the frozen winter for blood—after all, slavery was a fact of life, the Lord's will; the Lady's stricture. This statue had been carved by the branded hands of an escaped slave—one of the few who had probably stolen enough that he could bribe the Voyani to bring him across the borders.

No. Be honest. He knew, because Mirialyn ACormaris had chosen to tell him, that although the man's hands had been those of a slave, he had been revered in his fashion, for he could make, out of stone, an almost living, breathing boy, an accusation that could not be ignored.

Not even by the clansmen of the South.

North, Valedan thought bleakly, or South. Where did justice fit in at all?

He was exhausted. His joints, even with no movement on his part, ached; he carried bruises that had only just turned yellow-gray. Purple, the more common color, decorated his shins, his forearms, but Commander Sivari was no longer able to touch his chest, his ribs, the side of his head. That much, he'd won for himself. He had hoped to hide his skill; had hoped to take them by surprise. A boy's hope. A fool's.

Five days. He could run the footpaths until he was exhausted, and then continue his run, the heat of the sun bearing down upon his clothed flesh, his dark head. This was Avantari, the palace of Kings, and in it, he was as safe as he could be. But the gauntlet was not to be run within Avantari; it was to be run within the hundred holdings—and beyond.

Five days.

Ah. He rose and turned, twisting his back slightly as he plunged his hands into the waters of the fountain, cupping them beneath the surface and drawing water toward his face. He felt guilty because he hid here, instead of returning to his rooms—but he could not bear the teary sight of his suffering mother for an instant longer than was completely correct.

It was hard enough to have made the choice, to have petitioned the Kings, and to have been accepted into the ranks of the many who would attempt to qualify themselves as worthy contenders for the wreath the Kings offered their Champion. Hard enough to know what the cost would be if he failed, worse to know that every step of the way he was exposing the entire fate of his clan—and he could say it now, with a perverse pride, a quiet and dogged determination, *his* clan—by the turn of his back beneath the open sky.

But worse was to have to justify it, again and again, to a woman whose worst fault was that she did not want anything to happen to her beloved, to her only, child.

Let Serra Alina take care of his mother.

Or Ser Kyro, if he was not fast enough to move out of her way.

The stones beneath him were cool; the shade, however, was moving as the sun rose in deliberate reminder of the time, of the lack of time. He swallowed a deep breath of air that was too warm to be refreshing, and then he picked up the unstrung bow that lay on the stones by his side, well away from the spray of water, from the glare of sun's heat. Fighting, and running, and swimming he had already forced himself to face in the course of the early day; it was time for the targets.

Peace, there. A moment's peace.

He thought he would like to see the Princess Mirialyn ACormaris, for it was her hand that had guided his to the bow that had become his strength, to the sword whose use so surprised his compatriots, the clansmen who were too busy to notice the activities of the son of a concubine. But he was no longer Valedan the boy hostage, to be permitted to run from room to room like an indulged child seeking the most indulgent of his gentle keepers.

He was kai Leonne.

But Mirialyn ACormaris would have recognized that boy in the way that this young man momentarily bit his lip before gaining his feet and throwing his shoulders back. Before leaving the courtyard that was, and had been, his sanctuary.

". . . and it's supposed to be the single best way to prove that you're better than anyone else without actually going off and killing someone."

"Why?"

"Why *what?*"

"Why do all of that just to avoid killing someone?"

Duarte saw Auralis lift both hands to his face in a gesture that was only partly theatrical. The leader of the Ospreys was still not quite comfortable with the newest of his recruits, and watched her often, sometimes openly, sometimes surreptitiously, and sometimes by chance and serendipity. This was, he hoped, an example of the latter.

Auralis had been put slightly off his stride by his encounter with the young man who would be Tyr; the fact that, dagger to dagger, an apparently inexperienced boy could not only hold his own, but best him, had done more than cosmetic damage, although that aspect of the damage, fading fast, was hardly in evidence.

No; that wasn't accurate. He wasn't *slightly* off his stride. He was restless, a little too wild; Alexis was certain—or at least she was convincing when she spoke with Duarte—that he'd taken to drinking in the hundred holdings without the benefit of his companions. Probably true.

And everyone knew that meant he was looking for a fight, preferably a deadly one.

"Auralis," Kiriel continued, her dark eyes completely unblinking as she stared at the cracks between the older man's sun-browned fingers, "these men—they will all be soldiers, yes?"

"Not all."

"But almost all."

It was when she was like this that Duarte found her most compelling, least difficult. She had about her a childlike insistence, a terrible, strange need to know, that made the desire for knowledge seem a thing of dark wonder. He froze; often, if there were too many witnesses, she ceased to ask questions at all. As if the mere asking of questions were a weakness.

It was, Duarte thought, if he were honest at all.

"Yes, Kiriel," Auralis said, pushing his hands up from his face and through hair that was only slightly darker than his skin at high summer. "Almost all of the men here will become soldiers."

"Then, they'll kill."

"Yes. Then."

"Why not just have the war, and judge by that?"

"You don't have a war just to choose a single man as Champion."

Careful, Auralis, Duarte thought, seeing suddenly where she was leading.

"But that's exactly what you do do," she replied intently, no hint of the victory her words were about to gain her in her voice, or the lines of her peculiarly delicate face.

"It is not—"

"Yes, it is. We are going to war to choose a Tyr."

Duarte saw the whites of Auralis' eyes as he rolled them. "Kiriel, we *don't* ride to war every year. And if we had a choice—"

"You'd ride to war every year," she told him softly. Her voice changed, then, as it often did, turning suddenly cold and dangerous, as she revealed her edge, that dark perception that came from the mouth of a child.

They were used to it, in part—but it was hard to stay used to it, the turn from clawing kitten to overland cat was so sudden. He thought Auralis might react badly, and he prepared to intervene.

But Auralis' face shuttered as if it were a window. "Yes," he said. She seemed nonplussed by the surrender.

"Every day. There are men I'd kill in a minute. Less. And not slowly either. There are women I'd take. There are enemies I'd give eternity to have in my power—in my complete power, for hours. Minutes. Is that what you need to hear, Kiriel? What you want to hear? I won't deny it." His voice was ice, as cold as the Northern winter.

For just a moment, the winds changed; Duarte felt that the intervention needed might after all be on Kiriel's behalf, and not Decarus Auralis'. "I joined the Ospreys because I *know* who I am.

"Can you say the same?"

Her hand came up, but it came up empty; she clutched the strands of silver that held a pendant she was never parted from—a heavy, crystal thing that was, as far as Duarte could tell, a gaudy, near valueless bauble. That and the single, unadorned band she wore on the third finger of her left hand were, as far as any Osprey had been able to ascertain, the entirety of her nonessential worldly goods. She had sword and armor, but they seemed so much a part of her, no one thought of them as possessions.

"Who are you, Kiriel?"

"I don't know," she said softly. "Choice waiting for consequence to occur." She shrugged; the chain slipped back into the folds of her loose, pale shirt. "But you're more like I am than anyone here, Auralis. Doesn't matter what you hide, if you hide it at all. I can *see* it."

He shrugged. "What of it? Do you think I care what you think?"

"No."

"Good. I don't." He met her gaze, unblinking. "And it wasn't me we were talking about. It was the Challenge."

"Yes." As if his lack of pain had taken the wind out of her sails, she shrugged and returned to the matter at hand. "Why can't we cheat?"

Interesting.

"Ask Duarte."

Said Primus exercised his imagination as he mentally cursed the man who was unofficially his third in command.

Auralis turned, with a sly smile, and Kiriel followed his lead. Duarte was half-certain that the girl had been aware of his presence all along; she rarely missed anything as obvious as a mage shielding himself from easy detection.

"The Primus will say no."

"The Primus," Duarte said, with what dignity an eavesdropper could muster, "would indeed say no. And not for the reasons you think."

Auralis bared teeth in a smile; the sun fell upon them all in the midafternoon heat as if it were the gaze of the Justice-born King in anger. "We'd get caught."

"We'd get caught. Kiriel, every possible trick in the world has been tried at least once. The magi themselves sit in attendance over the Challenge to ensure that no magic of any variety is used. They handle the weapons that the combatants will take into their combats; they manufacture the javelins for the throw, the poles for the vaulting, the reins and saddles for the riding. Do you understand? There is no way to cheat the Kings' Challenge magically.

"And to cheat it in other ways is likewise difficult; the mages watch everything."

"If we knew how to do it," Auralis said, "We would. We could make a *killing*."

She frowned. "Why," she began, and Auralis held out a hand, palm out, in frustrated, if theatric, surrender.

"I meant, of course, that we could make a lot of money."

"Why is money so important?"

She meant it. Someone who could pierce the carefully cultured surface of Auralis to see the darkness beneath his mask, who could pinpoint him as the most dangerous, the least honorable— and there wasn't much honor, all told, in the Ospreys—of them all paradoxically could not understand the concept of *money*.

Duarte and Auralis exchanged a knowing glance. "I think," Duarte said softly, "that would be far too complicated a lesson for what's left of today. Valedan is about to join the Commander for the afternoon session. Your watch, Kiriel di'Ashaf."

She nodded then, all business, completely at her ease.

As if, Duarte thought, as she turned and walked away into the sharp, short shadows of the afternoon, this watchfulness were the only part of their life that she understood so well it was, of all things, natural.

* * *

Four days.

The Serra Alina di'Lamberto, fingers sweet with the fragrance of some delicate blossom that Valedan could not, sweat-stained and sullied as he was, identify clearly, massaged his shoulders, his exposed back.

"You did well," she told him quietly. "Mirialyn was watching your bout with the Commander; she was impressed." Highly impressed.

" 'Well' won't be enough," Valedan said, into the cushion of his forearms. " 'Impressive' won't be enough. Sometimes I think that nothing will."

Her hands stopped their forward motion; she stilled. "Do you wish to turn back?"

"How can I?"

"Withdraw."

"They'll know."

"They might." She did not lie to him, nor he to her; she was not certain, could never be certain, that he understood what she gave him, because she knew that he did not value enough what he gave to her: his confidence, his trust. *If I had had a child,* she thought, as she started to knead the muscles just beneath his shoulder blades, *would he have been half of what you hope to become?*

No. Because her child, had she had one, would have been born and bred to the South, claimed by the ways of the clans.

This boy, this man, this pretender to the Tor Leonne, although dark-haired and dark-eyed, was not. All Southern in birth, the North had ceded him much that the South could not. She glanced to the wall and back; his bow cast a fine shadow, a long one. It rested, unstrung, against the stone of the Arannan Halls.

"Miri says that you will have one challenge on the range, if that."

She saw his cheeks lift as he smiled; the smile was tired and half-hearted, but it was genuine. Happiness was like that, in the South: too brief, and often not sharp enough to touch and take root. Grief, on the other hand . . .

"She says," Alina continued, "that in swimming, you will best your Southern kin—save, perhaps, one man, who hails from Callesta. That man has spent time in the coastal villages this spring, and half last summer; he is shorter than you are, but he is older; he has reached his full growth."

"Wonderful. I'll better the men from the Northern cities as well—but not the ones from here."

"She says you are one of ten men who can run the gauntlet to its full length without pause."

He was silent a long time, waiting.

"In swords, you will face your stiffest competition; you do not have the advantage of size, yet. In a year or two, but not yet."

"Swords define the Southern combatants."

"Yes."

"Alina—"

"Yes?"

"How long has she been watching?"

Alina smiled, well-pleased. "I don't know. I do not believe she is alone in her concern; she and a few of her advisers or servitors have been watching the practice sessions that have been allowed within the coliseum."

"Most of the Annagarians haven't set foot within the coliseum."

"I was wondering if you would catch that. Very good, Valedan. No, none of the Annagarians have chosen to accept the time offered them. But there are ways in which their worth might be measured that do not require their entrance upon lands owned solely by the Crowns."

The Tyr'agnate Ramiro di'Callesta was not a welcome presence within the great hall situated at the heart of the fifteenth holding in the old city of Averalaan. He might have been less unwelcome, but one or two of the men who had traveled to the Empire's greatest city recognized the crest upon both his cape's clasp, which was not significant, and upon the black length of his sheath.

Which was.

Set in red, simple in design, the crossed strokes of the Callesta clan near glowed in the magelights that provided brilliant day to a building closed to the sun's light. The sight, Ramiro thought, of the Lord.

It would never have occurred to a Tyr to leave his sword behind, not even this most practical of Tyrs; he acknowledged the truth with a wryness that did not reach his face. For leaving the sword behind would have made his work easier by declaring far less, and less openly. *Bloodhame* was a name better known in the Empire than his own—and it should be; the sword had existed for centuries, through the rise and fall of the Callesta fortunes.

Two of the men here were Averdan, and if they were young, they were not fools. They were trained—well-trained he thought, by the look of them—and immediately ill at ease in his unexpected presence. Such a lack of ease transmitted itself more quickly than disease through the ranks of these men who, like himself, were foreigners upon this soil.

They did not speak, but they offered him no violence and no disrespect. It wouldn't have been wise. He came, as befit his rank, with the Tyran of his choosing; there were, in total, eight. And if these men who trained before him were among the best the Dominion had to offer, they had come for what was, after all, display; the Tyran had experience, and more, the will to use it, and they had come with their sole purpose in mind: his safety.

"Well?"

Ramiro di'Callesta shrugged. The men here were from diverse Terreans, and they were uneasy, but they were clansmen enough to desire not to display that lack of comfort where anyone could see it for the weakness it was. He had hoped they would all be young, and they were.

If the men who trained them were not taken into account.

"I recognize two."

"I recognize more than that." Baredan's face was hooded, neutral. His hand never touched the hilt of his sword—that might have been too much of a provocation. But in everything else, he stood on edge, ready for combat.

Just as, Ramiro thought with amusement, he had always done when he faced the Tyrs who ruled under the Tyr'agar. It must irk him, to know that the threat, in the end, had not lain with the ambitions of the Tyr'agnati, but rather with one of the three men who had been appointed to guard the Tyr'agar Markaso kai di'Leonne against their predations.

"The trainers?"

A nod.

"I believe that man is Anton di'Guivera."

Another nod, a grimmer one. They were both silent as they watched the one man in the building who seemed to take no notice of their presence. He was working with two men, both wielding naked blades, and both much at ease with their weight and heft. Unlike many men who worked at such a discipline, he felt no need to raise his voice, no need to emphasize, with heat or volume, the points that he made. He would raise a hand, and nine times out of ten they were so attuned to his measure they would stop, in mid-swing, to better hear his quiet correction. He was not a man in the habit of repeating himself.

Baredan knew him well; as a young man, it had been his privilege to see Anton in his prime. He was past that now; they both were. But he remembered.

Anton di'Guivera was the *only* man in the history of the Dominion who had come to the Northern empire and taken from the hands of the demon kings the wreaths which symbolized victory. The pride of the Dominion. The proof of its strength.

As if Ramiro could hear the youthful yearning in the momentary thought, he said, "I was there the year that he was declared the Lord's Champion. It elevated clan Guivera."

"Were you there the following year?"

"When he became only the second man in the history of the test to repeat his victory?"

They both smiled, each smile edged in its own way by a past that was both precious and bitter.

What neither man said was that this man, Anton di'Guivera, and not kai or par, for all that he was the only man of Guivera to distinguish himself at all, had been responsible for the training of the previous kai Leonne before his death.

"How long has he been here?"

"He arrived with the men from the Terrean of Raverra. The two he trains with now are two of twelve; they left before the end of the Festival, with the Lord's blessing, and arrived in haste. Alesso—and it must have been Alesso—has sent a greater number than has been sent to the Empire for many years."

"To prove a point?"

"Or to make one."

"And these?"

"I would have said that they were not of the highest caliber; no clan would waste the chance to perform well in the Lord's Test, but they might send those sons who were competent to do what they could here."

"You no longer believe it."

"Would you?"

Ramiro was silent for a long while. At last he said, "No. Not while Anton di'Guivera travels with them." He shrugged his cape back and crossed the length of the hall, dragging his Tyran with him as if they were shadows cast by the lights above. With them came the General, as reluctant as Ramiro had ever seen him.

They came to stand behind Anton di'Guivera. He had aged,

certainly, from his twin moments of glory both in the Dominion and in the Empire; the sun had scorched an enduring darkness into the cast of his skin, and the wind had etched lines there, year by year, that nothing would erase. Yet this particular di'Guivera was like the mountains; he endured all changes as if they did not and could not touch his essential nature.

And part of that nature was this: his ability to concentrate. To insult a member of the Tyr'agnati was no small risk, but Anton di'Guivera undertook it as a matter of course. The only man to whom he paid the obeisance that was his due was—or rather, had been—the Tyr'agar Markaso kai di'Leonne.

But Ramiro sometimes suspected that this was more due to the fact that the Tyr'agar had enough respect for his own dignity that he did not attempt to interrupt his premier trainer when he was at work. Because, of course, a refusal to acknowledge a man of his rank in the Tor Leonne would be met with—*must* be met with—death, but no one threw away a man of Anton's caliber without cost.

They were not in the Tor at the moment.

With cold respect, Ramiro di'Callesta folded his arms across his chest and waited.

As if that were a signal, the men slowly resumed their bouts, reluctant to stare at a Tyr'agnate, but equally reluctant to expose the weakness of their training mistakes—if indeed they made many this close to the competition itself. They did not, Ramiro noted, seek to take the title; they sought, rather, to take the single rod upon which the man-to-man combat depended. Or so it seemed; no man lifted a weapon that was not a sword within the confines of the hall.

But the two men with whom Anton worked continued without pause that was not caused by their master, until in the end they were slick with the sheen of summer heat in a building that hid them from both the sight of the Lord and the cooling touch of the sea-laden wind. Even then he pressed them, watching their feet, their feet's placement; correcting their shoulders and the arc they made when they swung. At last, when it was clear that they could do no more, he stepped in, drawing his blade in perfect silence.

The younger of the two unknown men grimaced; the older readied himself.

Anton di'Guivera was an older man. Against two who were new to the fight, he was no longer guaranteed an easy or a complete victory. But against these two, tired with training and the rigors to which they were subjected, he was a joy to behold, a thing of almost perfect grace.

And he taught them in this way; by being what he told them to be. Ramiro could see that the line of his arm and the extension of the blade were perfect; that the only time the edge of the blade wavered was when it turned, edge to flat; that Anton di'Guivera, twice chosen by the Lord, was still blessed by him. No doubt they would bear scars, these students, but Ramiro could believe, watching the flat of this man's blade play against the light, that those scars would be deliberate gifts or medals, not the chance slip of the blade, not the misstep of underconfident youth.

He disarmed them both.

And then, as if that were his introduction, he pivoted. Bowed, not to the Tyr'agnate, but to the absolutely silent man who stood by his side. "Baredan."

"Anton."

"Have you come to compete?"

The General's smile was as narrow as the edge of the master's blade. "Yes," he said softly.

"And I, I think." He lifted his sword; held it a moment parallel to the straight line of his body. "I did not think you would survive, but I am not . . . unhappy to see you."

Ramiro glanced to the side in time to see the color of the General's face seep away into that peculiar paleness that was often called white, although it wasn't.

"You were a part of the assassination?"

"I?" The older man's smile was as thin as the General's. "Baredan, had you been a decade younger, you would have been among my students, I think. And I would have served you better than your previous master by beating out of you the sense of loyalty that drives your life.

"You are not *Tyran*. That was not the life you chose. Nor," Anton di'Guivera said, sheathing his sword almost—but not quite— as silently as he'd first drawn it, "was it mine."

"You trained the kai Leonne."

"What of it? You supported Alesso di'Marente."

Stung, Baredan snapped, "Not in this, Anton. Never in this."

"Oh? And why?" Anton di'Guivera had never been a small man, but he rarely chose the arrogance of making those about him feel his height. He chose it now, crossing arms that no amount of time would soften across the breadth of his chest.

"Because the clan Leonne—"

"The clan Leonne was a weak clan," Anton said coldly. "Not a single member of that clan survived the culling of a simple night's work."

Silence. And then Baredan smiled, brightly as a sword in sun's light, fencing with his expression. "You know."

Fencing, sadly, with a master. "I know that the son of a concubine remains alive in this Imperial City."

"Not even you could deny him the legitimacy the waters—and the Tyr'agar—granted."

"Does it matter, Baredan?"

"Of course not," the General replied. "I've traveled to this city only to watch your half-trained men lose the foreign challenge."

"General, " Ramiro di'Callesta said, breaking the cadence of their conversation before Baredan could embarrass himself, "I believe that we have as much answer as we came to receive." He bowed. "Ser Anton di'Guivera."

"Tyr'agnate." Anton di'Guivera bowed. And then, as he rose, his eyes widened ever so slightly. Ramiro noticed that they remained at the level of the brilliant crest that broke the simplicity of black and gold. *"Bloodhame,"* the older man said faintly.

"Bloodhame," Ramiro replied.

"You are not like Baredan di'Navarre," Anton di'Guivera said, rising. "His folly is not your folly. Yet you stand by his side, with that sword; it is clear that you have made your choice."

"We all make choices. Some of them are irrevocable." And as he spoke, he placed his hand upon the hilt of the Sword of Callesta—the surest symbol of his commitment, and the only one, in truth, whose declaration meant much.

"Yes." Anton replied, distant and distinct. He bowed, again, and turned; where he might fence with the General, he did not seek to cross words with the Tyr'agnate. Anton di'Guivera had never been a fool.

But as he turned, he spoke. "I hear a rumor, in the holdings, that we are not the only men of the Dominion who seek mastery of this Challenge."

"Rumors are always a dangerous thing to put faith in."

"Indeed."

"We will see your best upon the field."

"And I, General, Tyr'agnate, will be most interested to see yours."

"Anton—" Baredan began, but Ramiro cut him off with a slight gesture. The gesture that he gave his waiting Tyran was less subtle; it snapped the attention that they had been giving the legendary Anton di'Guivera as if it were thread that led directly from them to the swordmaster. As a man, they took their positions.

"Ser Anton," the Callestan Tyr'agnate said softly. "Do not always trust what you have been told."

The man's head snapped around in the most gratifying of fashions. As did Baredan's. The swordmaster took a single step forward, as if drawn. "And will you tell me," he said, his eyes a sudden dark fire, "that Alesso lied to me?"

"You are what the Lord made you; you are what you have chosen. You have always made weapons. It is, and has always been your calling—to be the best; to make the best. Judge for yourself."

"I want," Anton di'Guivera said, his face hardening into a neutrality that did not quite sink roots deep enough to take his voice as well, "what the wind wants."

"Then stand against us, Anton, and you most certainly will receive it."

Declaration. Movement. Commitment.

Baredan di'Navarre and Ramiro di'Callesta left the great hall. But only Baredan looked back.

Later, in the questionable comfort of the Arannan Halls, the two men sat alone. It was odd, to sit thus; Baredan di'Navarre had yet to become accustomed to the lack of serafs in the rooms in which they sat. A man of his station had few, but he had them, and they were a constant presence, like weather, or breathing—a thing only noticed if it caused difficulties, but never otherwise questioned.

There was food here, and it was obviously made by the hands of a Southerner—but again, there was something in its flavor, some herb or spice, some barely discernible difference, that made him realize that the most the North could offer a man from the Dominion was the facade of familiarity, not the depth.

He wanted to go home.

But he said none of this; instead he noted, with some residual bitterness, that Ramiro di'Callesta was affected by none of these things. He was at home here, as at home as he had been in Callesta, with a foreign tongue spilling from his lips just as frequently as the Tyrian court tongue, and just as smoothly. Not all that was said about the Tyr'agnate of Averda was merely the rumor of the envious.

"It is not so lovely a view here," Ramiro said, as he sat back on a chair—a chair, of all things, in this hall, a hard piece of dark wood and fine cloth that could not, in Baredan's opinion, ever be as comfortable as good, solid mats and cushions.

"It's a better view than I ever had."

"Ah. Well." The silence was uncomfortable; there was, between them, a single question that Baredan di'Navarre had spent the better part of two hours wondering how best to ask. Two hours. He shrugged. He was, after all, expected to be a General, not a ruler.

"What," Baredan said, as he lifted foreign wine in a thin goblet to his lips, "did Alesso tell Anton di'Guivera?"

He thought that Ramiro might smile, but in this he was mistaken; the Tyr'agnate's lips pressed into a line thinner than the rim of Baredan's glass. "What did Alesso tell him, or how do I know?" He lifted wine, but did not drink it; Baredan noted that although he accepted hospitality wherever it was offered, the acceptance, like much about the man, was a facade. "Baredan, you are a General; you will serve Valedan kai di'Leonne in this war. And if he somehow succeeds in his intent to claim the Tor Leonne, you will serve him as Tyr'agar.

"The interests of the Tyr and the interests of Averda seldom coincide completely. We will not be such good friends then, such willing allies."

This was the Tyr'agnate that Baredan knew so well. He smiled. "True."

"But there must be some trust between us, a gesture if nothing else; we will fight this war with everything we have, and many things that we do not know we have.

"Therefore, while I will answer your first question, I do not choose to tell you how I know what I know. Although I'm surprised that you don't know. Perhaps you know it already, but have not thought to make the connection." He set the goblet down, untouched.

"This is only a story, Baredan. A rumor, you understand, a thing that cannot be verified at this remove."

"Anton is no fool. A rumor that was only rumor would not have—"

"Would not have this effect? Baredan, he is *the* swordmaster, if the Dominion has one—but he is not the lofty nobility of Leonne's once great height. He is a man, just as I am—and just as you should be."

And why are you here, Ramiro? But he did not speak. Instead, he sat back, feeling the uncomfortable hardness of the curved chair's top along the line of his shoulders. Sun came in through windows open to the light of the courtyard; the leaves of plants too numerous to name—and Baredan was not a court clansman, to name all variety of plants such as these—caught that light and made of it a colored vista, a landscape in miniature of a world that was too varied to be quite real.

"Do with this story what you will; if Alesso has spoken it openly, it is open."

"Tell me," Baredan said, as patient as he could be.

"The story goes thus: That when Anton di'Guivera was a young man, his skill with the sword came so easily that he came to the attention of the kai Guivera. Guivera is not a well-known clan, and for good reason; Anton di'Guivera, at that time, had already chosen the one wife his own labor could support, and had by her one child."

Baredan picked up the goblet again. "Ramiro, I *am* familiar with the basics of Anton's early life. He lost that wife, and that child, to bandits; it is for that reason that he chose to become the warrior that he did."

"Humor me," Ramiro said, adding with a smile's edge, "if you're aware of this basic conversational courtesy." It was not a comment that he could make in a room that contained serafs, or women, or Tyran or cerdan; only here, with one witness, and that the man being so prodded, did he have that luxury.

"He was foolish about the wife, as many men often become, and she had not grown so wind-worn that she did not find his prowess flattering. She was, indeed, proud that he had been called by the kai Guivera. Prouder still to find that he had been noted by the man who, at that time, trained the Leonne heir.

"But it was not just the trainer who noticed the skill of the young Anton di'Guivera; it was the Tyr'agar himself."

"That would have been Maredan kai di'Leonne."

"Yes. Valedan's grandfather. He wished to see the young man trained to the full extent of his ability, and so he relieved him of his duties as cerdan to the clan Guivera, paying both the man and the clan that had nurtured him handsomely. The young wife, and their son, he brought to the capital.

"And there, the work began."

Baredan waited.

Ramiro turned away, to look at the finery and splendor of growth that the Kings chose to call the footpaths. His voice changed subtly, although later Baredan could not quite have said how. "But the trainer watched the young man and although he was impressed, he was also, it is said, concerned. He saw, in Anton di'Guivera a weapon—but a weapon without an edge. He approached the Tyr'agar—remember, Baredan, that this is story and rumor—and he told the Tyr, "this man will be the Lord's Chosen twice over if he but devotes his time and his attention to the discipline."

"And the Tyr'agar said, 'He devotes all of his time now to just that; the mornings to riding and the afternoons to the sword." It must be said that he was not, coming as he did from a clan one step from serafdom, well-versed in riding.

" 'He devotes his time, Tyr'agar, but only his time. When he leaves my circle, he leaves it; he goes to his home.' "

Baredan paled.

" 'What will this young man be, if he gives you what he gives you now?' the Tyr'agar is said to have asked.

" 'A champion, perhaps; there are no certainties.'

" 'And if I grant you the student that you desire?'

" 'He will be two things: A swordsman beyond compare.'

" 'And?'

" 'And the only man to go North and return with the cursed wreath of Kings.'

"The Tyr'agar heard these words, and reflected on them a long time. At last, he said, 'I will give you the warrior that you desire. Deliver, for this, the champion that you have promised, and the Lord will consider our work here well done, and judge it accordingly.'

"Six months later, Anton di'Guivera and his young family returned for a visit to the clan Guivera. There, in the small township that Guivera administered, his young wife and his child were killed by raiding bandits, along with half of the villagers."

Baredan leaned forward in the chair, leaned forward so that he might momentarily cover his eyes, his face, with the comforting shadow his palms might provide. For the Lord *had* judged, and he did not wish to betray his own judgment of that judgment to the light that streamed in through the windows; the eyes of god.

But Ramiro had not yet finished. "Anton di'Guivera lost everything he valued in life but his skill, and it was to his skill that he turned the whole of his attention. He has never turned away. The winds have scoured him almost clean. There is no new wife; there are no new children. He exists outside of life, almost outside of time.

"His only regret, the only failing in his long life, was that he never found the bandits responsible for the death of the family that had been his life. He led many raids against many bandits—I believe he still does from time to time—but he never found their killers."

Baredan rose because he had to. Some men, when they receive ill news, are frozen with shock; some become stricken, dumb and cold as stone. And some are moved to act, to do *something,* long before they know what it is they must do.

"Alesso told him this."

"Yes."

Neither man questioned its truth. Truth had its own ring, even spoken as it was by a man famed for his ability to bend truth to suit whim.

"What does a man do," Ramiro said softly, "when the last of his demons have been confronted?"

"Have they?"

"They were, with the death of the Tyr'agar."

"The clan is not dead. The boy remains."

"Perhaps."

Sunlight grew warmer in the still air; Baredan longed for the wind of the plains. Home. "I've known Anton di'Guivera for most of my adult life," the General said quietly. "Certainly since the Tyr'agar accepted my service, and gave me my rank after the Imperial war. He is a swordsman, but he is not a butcher. He's not a young man anymore, Ramiro; the passions of youth cannot drive him so long or so hard."

"Neither are we."

"True enough. Very well. What would you do if your demons were dead?"

"I think that if the death of his wife's killer had been the sole focus, the sole force, in his life, he would have seen the Tyr'agar dead, and then he would have laid down his weapons, disavowed their use; it was for his talent, after all, that his family was slaughtered.

"But he cannot quite deprive himself of that talent; it *is* what he is. I spoke no lie. Therefore, he must do one of two things: He must make peace with what he has become, and accept the history of his forging, or he must continue the war that he has already begun."

"You believe that he will try to kill the kai Leonne."

"I believe," Ramiro said bleakly, "that is what he came North to do."

CHAPTER FIVE

Four days.

Four days; long days. Sun too hot, wind not dry enough to take away the sweat of a day's labor. A life's labor.

Jewel ATerafin sat in a room made dark by heavy curtains. Light illuminated the folds of fabric that skirted the ground by an inch or two, as if the window were waiting for her attention.

It was a struggle, for Jewel, not to succumb to its call—even given the weight of what was at stake. She rose, unfolding her knees, tilting her chin to the ceiling and lifting her arms as far as they could uncomfortably go. If she sat for another minute, she'd grow roots and branches.

And not a thing had come to the dark corners of the room. Not a thing to the corners of her vision, the seer's gift.

At her feet there was water; Teller had brought it before Avandar let the curtains fall. She lifted the goblet and drank; the liquid was the same temperature as her mouth; it spilled down her throat as if it were almost nothing.

"Nothing?"

Avandar's voice. Even deprived of the stern expression his face habitually fell into, she couldn't quite pretend his presence was welcome. He always made her feel slightly on edge, slightly uncomfortable, although she trusted him daily with her safety, with more than her safety. She shrugged. Seventeen years of history could do that, although she'd never have guessed it at the start.

"Nothing. Allen's not going to be happy."

She felt, rather than heard, Avandar's more crisp version of a shrug. "Then he'll be unhappy. If he seeks to use you as a reliable source of information, it's best that he learn your limits here, where the risks are few."

Few. Her neck cracked as she turned her head in a slow, deliberate circle. "They don't want to lose the boy."

"Then they should put their foot down and refuse him his place in the Challenge."

"Avandar—"

"At the least, he should be given no leave to run the gauntlet."

"It's been suggested. You've even been there. Let's give up for an hour or two; we'll eat something, try again."

"As you wish." The line of light beneath the hang of curtains was broken as Avandar stepped in front of them; it wavered further as he began to draw them apart, to let the day in. Here, up in Eagle's Remove—although why this room in particular was given that name, she didn't know—the windows were long and wide, with seats for the room's occupants to sit in, so that they might look down, and down again, and see clearly all they were missing by being stuck here.

There were no shelves, no desk; but there was a grate for the burning of wood, a mantle around it, two comfortable chairs, and enough leaded glass to bankrupt a lesser House.

She had grown to hate the room.

Avandar preceded her to the door, placed his hand upon the old, iron handle, and froze in place. She had seen this only once before. He was not a man given to expressive gestures; all of his movements were economical, spare. It shouldn't have been so obvious when he stopped moving at all—but it was.

Her dagger was out in an instant, her knees slightly bent. What he felt, she now felt; the edge of darkness, a shadow that held ice and death within its folds. He was the only man in existence who would have felt it before she did. And she didn't know, couldn't say, why. Later. "What is it?"

He did not answer her; not with words. Didn't need to. She saw the ripple that surrounded his hands, taking shape and form as it crackled into bands of color: blue and gray.

Blue and gray—

"Avandar, no!"

The light froze, just as he had, held in abeyance not by her words, but by the quality behind them, the force of something that was, and was not quite, Jewel. She sheathed her dagger at once and walked to the door, shunting him urgently to one side.

And then, taking a deep breath, she opened it, half-prayer already dying on her lips. There were guards outside these doors; Chosen by Terafin, Chosen for trust and trust's sake. *Please,* she thought, *don't let them be dead.*

They weren't.

She took the time to notice that they hadn't even drawn their swords; it was a cursory observation, a short one.

"Kiriel," she said, as her eyes met the darkness that waited outside of Eagle's Remove. "Come in."

Kiriel di'Ashaf crossed the threshold as if it were the edge of a blade, and she barefoot. Her teeth showed briefly between dark lips, a flash of white not unlike a hound's. But she did not draw the sword she wore openly, and she did not—did not do whatever it was that Jewel felt certain she could do, even if the details weren't clear.

The darkness that shrouded her golden eyes would never quite leave them; of that, Jewel was suddenly completely certain, and for a moment she felt a profound sense of loss, of compassion, and even of pity. They came in a rush, these things, unexpected and unlooked for. Jewel had learned to school her face well over the years.

But not from this: vision, a thing not felt that *would be* felt—in an unnamed, distant future —about the almost sullen young woman who stood uneasily before her. Dark eyes narrowed to slits; Kiriel backed away.

"Kiriel," she said again, holding out a hand, realizing the gesture meant nothing. She let it drop, and then spoke again. When she spoke, she abandoned Weston entirely in favor of Torra, the Tyrian tongue. "I'm sorry—I mean you no ill will, and no mockery. I'm—I have to admit that I didn't expect to see you here."

The younger woman's eyes widened in such a way that it almost hurt to see them. Tyrian. *di'Ashaf* was a Tyrian form. And what line, Jewel thought, was Ashaf? No clan name that she recalled, but that wasn't saying much; her knowledge of the clan hierarchies was abysmal.

"I didn't expect to come," Kiriel said, in such a way that it was clear she begrudged every word. She drew breath.

"Then why," Avandar said, uninvited and as unexpected in his interruption as Kiriel had been in her arrival, "did you?"

She looked at him as if seeing him for the first time—which, Jewel thought, she might well be doing; it was hard to remember when Avandar did trail her and when he did not, so much of a shadow had he become. "Does he speak for you?" she said at length, coolly.

"No." Jewel's reply was less friendly than Kiriel's question.

Avandar did not seem to react at all to the less than subtle hint. She stopped hinting. "Avandar, leave."

"I don't think it wise."

"I don't care what you think. Leave."

"Jewel, I'm not certain if you understand what it is, exactly, you face—but it is not what it appears to be. You—"

"Avandar."

"I-will-wait-outside-the-door."

"Good."

He opens his mouth again, Jewel thought, *and I'll kill him.* She folded her arms, her lips pressed into a tight line.

He walked out the door, slamming it shut behind his back.

Kiriel looked from one to the other—the door that seemed to reverberate with the force of its closing, and Jewel, as if what had just occurred was the only thing, so far, that made any sense. As if the desire for sense and stability was so strong she could suck the scene out of the air and hoard it.

Her hair was dark, her eyes dark; when she lifted an ungauntleted hand to brush the one from the other, Jewel expected the hand to be dark as well, wreathed in cloud and black shadow. It wasn't. Of all things, it was the only part of her body that seemed human, free from shadow and shadow's claim, from the darkness that had devoured the Allasakari, in their time, one by one.

Shining there, faintly luminescent, a star in the depth of night sky and not the radiant, warm sun, sat a simple, unadorned ring. Jewel felt the ground beneath her feet shift; she took a step back.

Kiriel immediately began to lower her hand, aborting the gesture. "I mean you no harm," she said, moving slowly and steadily, bringing the hand, palm up, to the level of her waist, where Jewel might better see it.

"I—know. It's—I'm sorry. I wasn't expecting you."

There were two chairs in the room; Jewel hesitated before one, but did not choose to take it; she knew that Kiriel would stand, and did not want to lose the advantage of equal height.

"Where did you learn to speak?"

"Torra?"

"Is that what you call it?"

"That's what it's called in the Empire, yes." Jewel turned away from her visitor, although every instinct in her screamed as she exposed her back. Deliberately ignoring instinct was difficult for the seer-born; she steadied herself by letting the visual panorama provided by the open window distract her. A little. "I learned it from my mother."

"You were born there?"

"No. Here. There are Southerners—and those, like me, descended from them—across the hundred holdings. But mostly," she grimaced, "in the poorer ones."

"Was she a seraf?"

"No!" And then, realizing not what she'd said, but how, Jewel added, "No. There are escaped slaves in the city; enough of them. But my mother was an insignificant member of one of the Voyani lines. She was free."

"Free." Kiriel came slowly to join her; they stood side by side, appreciating the view, as if they were two visitors to the House with nothing better to do. The sea breeze was laden with salt, heavy with moisture. The open windows let it in, where it curled the ends of Jewel's hair. Kiriel's hair seemed heavy enough to be impervious to weather.

"Where did you learn the Tyrian tongue?"

"In the Court," Kiriel replied. "And Weston as well, but later."

"Kiriel—why did you come?"

"Because if I speak to anyone else, I—" She stopped, bent her chin almost into the length of her neck. "Because of what you said," she replied, quietly.

"What I said?"

"That I'm a killer, but—"

"Yes?"

"It's not all I am." She toyed with a slender chain that encircled her neck as she spoke; the gesture was a nervous one. "I've never had to hide what I am; only what I'm capable of. Knowledge is power."

" 'Knowledge is power.' You sound like Meralonne." Jewel touched the younger woman's shoulder. "I told you, Kiriel: Tell me that I *can* trust you, and I will trust you."

"Does it matter? Does it matter, if I've already decided to go with you, to fight this war?"

"You tell me."

Kiriel turned to face Jewel, her eyes golden, like light, like sunlight. "Yes. It matters," she said simply. She lifted the chain, and from its end fell a large crystal; it was surrounded by a lattice of light that moved so quickly Jewel couldn't quite see the color of it, the colors that made it solid. "I'll fight this war, but I have to fight it my way. My father—"

Silence.

"I don't love him," Kiriel said, as if forced.

"I don't care if you love him," Jewel replied, as if she were un-aware of how singular a statement Kiriel had made. "I don't care if you hate him. I'm not Mandaros, Kiriel; what he decides, he decides. I don't judge you."

"Neither did she."

This time, Jewel did not ask. She wanted nothing to interrupt the words, the shaky trickle of them, that Kiriel so haltingly, clumsily offered.

"I spoke to Valedan," Kiriel said. "About you. He says, if you want to travel with us, you can."

"Thank you."

"Do you?"

"Yes."

Silence again, Kiriel's, not Jewel's. The moment was broken for Jewel when she realized that no birds had come by this win-dow at all since Kiriel had approached it.

"I don't want to go to Duarte yet, because he'll have to tell The Kalakar."

"Tell her what?"

Hesitation, fine and edged. For a moment she poised at the win-dow as if she was bunching and gathering her muscles for sudden flight. And then it left her, that tension, in a little sigh of breath, of uncertain commitment. She reminded Jewel of the dead, the much loved, the much remembered dead. "There are kin in the streets of the city."

"Kin? You mean—" She stopped, knowing exactly what Kiriel meant. "You've seen them?"

"No."

"Then how do you—" Jewel stopped at once, as elusive under-standing finally stood still long enough to be caught. "You won't say how."

Kiriel shook her head. "Can't," she whispered, as if it were true. "But *you* don't have to. They've come to kill Valedan." Absolute conviction in those words. "You tell them where the kin are, and they'll believe you without question because that's your gift." She turned her eyes groundward through the wide, stone sill to greenery and life. "I'll go with you, when you hunt them. If you do. I'll be your whatever it is—adjutant, assistant, Verrus. I'll take you to where they are. No one has to know who leads who."

"Kiriel, no one understands the abilities of the kin well enough.

Tell them that you can magically sense each other and they'll believe you."

But Kiriel looked at her and said a single word. A name. "Sigurne."

Jewel couldn't argue with that. "All right. I'll do what I can." She paused. "We've got four days to hunt them down."

"If you wait until the Challenge, they'll be easy to find."

"If we wait until the Challenge, we probably won't be able to reach them without carving our way through spectators, most of whom will be utterly helpless in the face of kin magic. I'll do what you ask, Kiriel; I won't ask questions. If you need me to lie, like this, for you—I'll do it. It seems harmless enough." A lie, all right. "But I won't risk those deaths. Not the innocents. Not the children. I've seen enough of 'em. I won't risk more, ever."

Kiriel met her eyes and stared at her for a long time, and then, of all things, she smiled. A real smile, almost devoid of her natural intensity.

"You can," she said softly.

"Can?"

"Trust me."

You couldn't lie to a seer.

Teller told himself that, as his hand dipped quill slightly shakily into inkstand.

It wasn't one of the many truths about seers that was widely spread, like children's stories and overblown fables, across the wealth of bardic songs or ancient texts, but it was true.

Or sort of true. You couldn't lie about much that was important to the seer herself. Little things—what you thought of her clothing, for instance, or what you thought of the meal she'd prepared with her own painstaking labor on one of those days when she and Avandar had had enough of a disagreement that he'd been banished from most of the wing—those you could get away with. But not big things. Not truth.

Kiriel spoke the truth. Jay'd heard and accepted it.

Hearing, and accepting, she invited Kiriel to leave Eagle's Remove, and together, they adjourned to the kitchen.

She'd told them all as much when she'd asked them to gather there; that this young woman had asked for help and offered her own in return; that she was to be considered, in any way they could, as a member of her den. A new member.

Hadn't been a new member for almost twenty years.

Twenty years? He didn't feel twenty years older. Didn't feel twenty years smarter. He was thirty—near as anyone could figure—and it only showed on the outside.

Kiriel, he could tell, was uncomfortable with the idea of the gathering but Jay insisted: These were her den; she trusted them all with her life, just as they trusted her, as they *could* trust her—and they'd accept Kiriel if she did because she was—

She was Jay Markess, their leader.

Oh, her hair was longer and maybe even a little bit straighter most of the time—not during the humid season, mind—and her back was a bit more bent; she had a couple of new lines and a woman's body, not a girl's—but something burned at the center of her eyes when she spoke—a window into a past that you could only share if you'd been part of it.

They were hers. She was theirs. It worked.

Teller ATerafin watched them almost silently as they spoke. He found that he did not much like Kiriel di'Ashaf, although he couldn't say why; there was something about her that made him feel more naked than he'd felt since—since his life had been a lot harder and a lot more desperate.

Not a feeling he wanted to relive.

Angel and Carver had the same half-neutral expression on their faces; they sat back from the table, chairs on a tilt, soles of worn boots facing inward from the edge of the tabletop. Teller knew them both well enough to know they'd crossed arms over their chests to prevent their hands from straying weaponside and staying there. Arann couldn't be summoned on short notice, and Finch and Jester were out in the Common, doing gods only knew what. It was a tough time to go out to the holding's markets and back; the streets were lined with merchants big and small who'd come to the capital for the Challenge itself, following the trail cut by hopeful, too young men who wanted a life outside of farming a small stead in the middle of nowhere. Movement in Averalaan was at a premium; horses were forbidden during the Challenge season unless one could prove Royal Exception, and there were few enough of those to go round. Certainly none for either Finch or Jester, who hated riding anyway.

But Finch was going to be angry.

He looked up from the notes that he was taking to study the side of Kiriel's face—as if the only time he could examine her face at all was when it was turned away from him. Her eyes were so dark a brown they were black—to his vision, anyway—and she had about her the wary air of a trapped predator. Hungry predator, at that.

I'd better not be food.

As if she could hear the thought, she snapped 'round, meeting his eyes even as he sought to attach his gaze to anything else in the room. He swallowed air, steadied his hand, and thought, clearly, that he hadn't felt this uncomfortable since the day that Old Rath had smashed through the boards over the windows of their old haunt, and gazed down at them as they fled through the city's streets at Jay's unfathomable command.

Jester, Finch, and he had run; Arann had dogged their steps like an overgrown shadow, until he'd heard the scream.

He could still hear the screaming; could feel himself freeze at the sound of it, the terror it contained, the certain death. He could hear Arann's breath, see his shadow suddenly recede from theirs as he twisted the club in his hands and started to head back. To Duster.

Duster.

We don't say good-bye to the dead, he thought, as he stopped trying to evade Kiriel's gaze. Dark-haired young woman, blemishless face, hair that fell heavily enough across her shoulders it looked entirely out of place given her weapon, her armor, the ease with which she wore both.

He knew who this woman was supposed to be, even as she turned away from him, back to the conversation that she could only barely share with the rest of Jay's den.

Oh, Jay, he thought. It had been easier, when he'd been younger. He could look at Duster, bruised and bloody, shaking with anger— or the need to outfight whatever it was that put fear into her— and accept that this killer was *their* killer, that she would do for the den what some of the den couldn't do for itself. Be the heavy. Be someone who could face down—permanently, if necessary— other people's enforcers.

The idea of right or wrong hadn't come into it.

Just survival. Survival was everything.

Jay, we're not the same den. We're not boys and girls, anymore— we're adults now; we don't live in the shadow of fear.

Even as he thought it, he set aside the thought. They didn't live in that shadow, but who they were had been tempered by it. And if they were all fifteen years older—more—they all remembered, more clearly than the vows they'd made to Terafin—the vows they'd made to Jay.

Angel hadn't chosen to take the Terafin name, although it had been offered to him. He, of all of them, was truest to the youth that Jay had rescued them from. He knew that he served *her,* and if she served the House, that was her business, not his.

Watching the young girl, Teller wondered.

She wore the crest of Kalakar across one shoulder—and that crest, the House Guards' crest, one didn't just get for free. It wasn't service, but life, that you swore by.

He didn't see that commitment to Kalakar in the young woman. He didn't see much of any commitment about her—except in the line of her shoulder, the tilt of her head, the oh so slight change in the timbre of her voice when she spoke to Jay. Had Duster been like that, truly?

Jay, he thought, as he turned his attention, at last, to his leader, and not the girl she'd brought in from the heights of Terafin's contemplation room, Eagle's Remove. *One day, some day, the dead have to be dead. You can't just see 'em in the living—not when the living are so bloody dangerous.*

He chose to say nothing, as usual.

Because he knew it wouldn't do any good. And he knew that this girl, this Kiriel, had given Jay her word that she could trust her, and that Jay'd accepted it.

You couldn't lie to the seer-born.

Please, Kalliaris, you couldn't lie.

Later that afternoon, army business and den business aside, Jewel isolated herself in her kitchen to think about what she least wanted to dwell on: House politics. Had to be done sometime.

Rymark, Haerrad, Elonne, and Marrick.

She spoke the names to herself as if they were a mantra, something to meditate on, a collection of syllables that made no sense, and promised to make less sense with repetition.

"Jay?"

"What?"

"Someone here to see you."

Jewel pulled her elbows off the kitchen table—where else?—and rose. Finch was a bit too quiet. "Who?"

"Haerrad ATerafin." It was not Finch's slightly delicate voice that answered her question—but given the lack of surprise she felt, she was certain on some level she'd expected it. She motioned with her head, a slight toss of loose, dark curls, and Finch stepped quickly out of the path of the oncoming visitor. Much as if he were an oncoming wagon pulled by maddened horses.

There was more than one door that led to and from the kitchen—something Jewel insisted on. Fires started in kitchens, after all. Finch passed Jewel's back and headed for the nearest door.

"I'm afraid," Haerrad ATerafin said, in a tone of voice that belied his words, "that I believe it best if your young . . . aide . . . remains here. The interview will be brief."

"My aide," Jewel said, as carefully neutral as she could be, confronted by another's orders in the heart of her territory, "is not your prisoner, Haerrad. If you've come to negotiate, this is a poor first stance to take."

"Your value to me is not, at this moment, high," was the older man's response. He cast a short shadow in the daylight; it was the color of his hair, his eyes. "Girl," he added, as Finch moved again toward the door, "don't take that risk."

She took a breath; Jewel saw it clearly in the slight tightening of her shoulder blades. And then she pushed the door open. It swung, loosely, on well-oiled hinges.

Between the open frame and the hall stood a man with drawn sword; Terafin by crest, a guard. Not Chosen. He did not utter a threat; the sword did it for him, catching the sun's light and breaking it. Jewel did not think she recognized him, but she was certain she would in the future. Very certain.

"Finch."

"He wouldn't dare."

"Finch."

Finch nodded reluctantly and stepped back, wary in her movement, angry.

"I do not wish any unfortunate interruptions," Haerrad said genially. "Especially not those tendered by your domicis, whom I note is thankfully absent.

"Let me come to the point. The Terafin has agreed that she will announce her heir shortly. I intend to be The Terafin. You may join me, or you may follow your current master when she dies."

"Neutrality?"

"There is no such thing in House politics, Jewel, not among the powerful. You serve me, or you serve no one. You are far too dangerous as an opponent, and even if you chose not to serve me, you would still remain far too dangerous in an opponent's hand."

"The Terafin still lives," Jewel said, keeping her tone even.

"The decision, for one or the other, has not yet been made. I do not feel a great pressure to make one."

"You should. You have her ear, where so few of us do. You will begin before her death as you mean to continue, and I will note it."

"And you?" she said softly. "Will you begin, before her death, as you mean to continue?"

His smile was soft. "I already have." There was nothing to like in the smile; there was no veneer of civility, no veneer of legality. She could not remain in Terafin should Haerrad somehow rule.

"I do not advise you to leave the House either," he said, just as softly as he smiled. "But I believe that our interview is at an end. I have come to offer warning."

"I've been offered a good deal more than warning and threat," Jewel said, the words sharper than she'd intended.

"No doubt. Rymark has offered you his bed—and possibly money to enter it. Elonne has made no offer yet. Marrick has made none. And I? I offer you your current circumstance and your life."

"How generous. I'll keep both in mind."

"I'd advise—"

The door blew off its hinges, carried by the weight of an armed and armored man. Both slammed into the air two inches away from the western edge of the table, and then clattered to the ground with a grunt and a thud.

Haerrad's brows went up in a dark line as Avandar stepped into the room, dusting his hands lightly against the sides of his robe. "I'm afraid," he said, with a minimal bow to his master, "that a man posing as a Terafin guard attempted—unlawfully—to refuse me entry. Shall I have him removed?"

"With prejudice," Jewel said.

"Not necessary," Haerrad said. "Avandar. Pleased to renew an acquaintance."

"And I," Avandar said, bowing with as much sincerity as Haerrad spoke.

"I don't believe that it will be necessary to bring up this unfortunate misunderstanding in the Council," the older ATerafin said. "We understand each other almost perfectly. Or we will."

"What do you mean by that?"

"Only that you are a perceptive young woman, with a clearer understanding of action—and consequence—than many. I bid you farewell, Jewel ATerafin, and I look forward to your support in the Council."

He turned then, pausing to wait for the guard to gather himself enough to take to his feet. He did not offer his assistance, and the guard, quite intelligently, did not ask for it. Standing, in armor, this man was three inches shorter than Haerrad; he was formidable in bearing if not overly handsome in look.

If she could have killed a man, it would have been Haerrad, at this moment. Jewel waited, Finch and Avandar at her back, in a grim silence that was only broken once the shadows Haerrad cast left the room.

And it was broken by Avandar in the worst possible way; his voice was unaccountably gentle until the words cut. "Jewel," he said softly, "Teller was injured on the way to Avantari. A rider, unidentified, apparently lost control of his horse in the High City streets."

"Injured? How bad?"

"Jewel—"

"How badly?"

I sent him, she thought, as she ran. *I sent him to Avantari.* She hated it, and hated running. Haerrad's gods-cursed spies would no doubt see her—would know *just how much* this meant, how frightened she was, how much he'd hurt her. She had to stop running. And she did try. Failed each time, the healerie seemed so far away and time so much of the essence.

She cursed her gift, hating it. Hating that she'd had *no warning,* gods curse all, no damned warning of any danger. Finch was at her side; Avandar was wherever Avandar went when she couldn't quite bear to have him witness her weakness. She caught herself, slowed down to a walk.

Deep breath. Deep, deep breath. If they knew how much this meant to her, they'd just keep at it, all of them. Keep at it, until—

"Jay." Finch's hand, on her shoulder. Not many people touched her at all; she froze a moment as instinct gave way to instinct, each as old as the friendship that bound them. "You'd know, if he were dead. We've got time. He's with Alowan."

"Alowan," Jewel snapped, "is older than the empire. Every time he uses his talent, it brings him that much closer to the death he's managed to dodge these past ten years. What if—"

Finch lapsed into silence.

Jewel gave herself a swift kick. Hers wasn't the only fear, and it wasn't the only loss. "Finch—"

"I know. Come on. We're almost there. Smile, Jay. Don't let 'em see it."

Taking her weapons out of their sheaths and leaving them in the box by the door was second nature to Jewel when visiting the healerie; first nature was to cling to the edge when one had enemies that could send one to a healer, or worse, send one's den there. She struggled a moment, as she'd never struggled, and then bit her lip as Finch easily deposited both of hers into the healerie's keeping. *The only death that comes through these doors isn't carried by human hands.*

"Finch—"

"C'mon, Jay. We're here. We can find Alowan."

They opened the door together because their hands found the handle at the same time, overlapping in both purpose and urgency. It made them both smile, if briefly, as the door opened outward and they stepped across the threshold into the arborium. There, surrounded by the greenery and silence of momentarily stilled birds, they followed the simple path that led from the door. Winding beneath and around the leaves and the vines and, yes, the birds who began their fluted chirping the moment the doors were closed, the path led to the fountain, the simple, quiet fountain, that stood at the heart of the arborium. Jewel remembered when the fountain had been completely visible from the door. But that, Alowan had told her, was the nature of life—change, growth, an unpredictability that comes only with absence and time.

The fountain was still there, still the same; stone, and not life. The chalice, held by stone hand and stone arm from the water's surface, overflowed gently, brimming as if it were Moorelas' and could raise the dead with a trickle of its liquid light.

A young woman, seated at the fountain's edge, looked up and smiled; she seemed far too young to be stationed here, where the injured and the sick were routinely brought.

"Hello," she said. "Are you Jewel?"

"Yes, I am. This is Finch; she's with me."

"Alowan told me to expect you. He's in the healerie at the moment, but he says it's safe for you to visit him there. If you'd follow me?"

She didn't wait to be asked twice.

Teller was in a bed, and that bed was stained in two places with the russet trails of dried blood: his. He was awake.

Jewel felt her legs lose all ability to carry her as she reached

his side, as if, having reached the destination, all strength gave
way to the face of fear's fact. She locked her knees.

"Jay?" His left eye was dark with bruising, swollen enough
that it distorted the look of his face, his slender face.

"Daydreaming again?"

"If you call *this* dreaming." He looked up at her face as she
touched his with a shaking hand. To see how it felt; to see if it
was cold or warm, hot with fever or damp with sweat.

"What happened?" Her voice almost broke; it was a near thing.
But she didn't want him to see how worried she'd been, so she
kept her voice lean, the words spare.

And it would have worked on anyone but Teller. He met her
eyes for a long time, and then said, "I was ridden down, I think.
I thought—I thought it was an accident."

She cursed inwardly, knowing Teller *always* caught her lies,
even if they were lies of omission.

"I was hit and thrown."

"He fell well," Alowan said, his voice neutral. "And no, before
you ask, the fall wasn't fatal, or near fatal. He broke ribs, and his
left arm and leg; I think that if he weren't one of yours, his head
would be softer and easier to damage." It was said in a tone that
was gentle, teasing even; if Jewel had said the words, they'd've
had humor in them, but they'd be harsher.

"Did you—"

"No. The left leg is barely fractured, and will heal in a matter
of a week or two. The arm, we can keep immobile without risk,"
the healer said quietly. "I'm not a young man, Jewel. He is. He
can get though this well enough on his own, unless you need him."

"I can't think of a place he'd be safer."

"Jay."

She turned back to Teller, her hand now warmed by his cheek.
"Don't ask, Teller. You always know when I lie."

"All right. Finch?"

"Haerrad," Finch said, without blinking.

"*Finch*. This-is-not-a-matter-for-the-healerie."

But Finch shrugged a still-slender shoulder. "He'll find out
anyway."

"I believe," Alowan said, clearing his throat, "that it is not Teller's delicate sensibilities that she wishes not to offend, but my
own."

"Yours? But—" Finch shut up then, and about time.

"If I might speak with you?" the healer continued.

Jewel sighed. Nodded. "You'll take care of him, right?"

"Of him, yes." Alowan's face adopted stricter, darker lines than she'd ever seen it take. "Come. No—not to the fountain. The plants have ears, or the birds do. Follow."

Jewel had never been invited to the quarters that Alowan called home; few of the ATerafin actually had, although it was rumored that Alowan did entertain visitors from time to time—healers on the odd occasion, children of the Mother, bards.

It hadn't occurred to her to wonder what his life outside of the healerie might be like. The moment one stepped across the threshold that separated the rest of Terafin from the healerie, one stepped into another world: Alowan's world, a place of peace and tranquillity, of rest.

She thought his rooms might be like that, somehow; that they might be similar to the mixture of finery and simplicity that Amarais so preferred. She waited patiently for the keys in hands that shook ever so slightly to reach the door to see if she was right.

She wasn't.

Alowan's pale brow furrowed as he watched her expression change—slightly, as she'd managed to absorb something resembling manners over the years.

"It's not what you expected?" he asked, as he took hold of a slender, simple cane that stood propped by the door.

"No."

"It never is." He opened the door wide and Jewel took a careful step into the room itself. It had to be careful, there was so much on the floor. There were crates piled high in the corner, obscuring what she assumed was still a serviceable chair, clothing dropped in a pale pile that had expanded into the room's center, a plate, or two plates, both meticulously clean, on a small, almost perfect table beneath the low, wide window.

There was, she thought, a lute in the corner of the room; it had a chair to itself, and frankly, from the scratches that were evident at this distance, it had seen unfriendly use—or cats, as was more likely, given the room's slightly musky air.

"Don't you—"

"No. No one cleans these rooms but I or my assistants."

You need new assistants, she thought, keeping the words, with some struggle, to herself.

"Please," he said, as he lifted the lute, "take a chair."

"There's only one."

"I prefer the window seat, myself."

"How can you find it?"

He raised a white brow.

She had the grace to blush. "This isn't—"

"What a man who commands as much money as a healer should have?" He laughed. "It's funny, that *you* should say that to me. I've heard from too many of your den over the years; they say that the fanciest desk you actually use is the kitchen table. Not the dining room table, which has the advantage of making sense— but the kitchen table. The young girl there, Finch, has even said that you'll work while she's cooking."

"I can at least *see* the top of my table."

Alowan shrugged, the smile still at play in the network of lines around his lips. She suddenly wanted it to stay there; some instinct told her that it would be one of the last of its type that she would see upon his face.

But her anxiety must have been obvious, because he sat, heavily, upon the stone sill, crossing his legs and letting the cane carry the brunt of his forward weight. "Haerrad," he said, looking oddly like a mage, and not the healer that he had always been.

She tried not to meet his eyes; it wasn't easy. "I don't want to lie to you, Alowan."

"You don't have to. Jewel, what have you seen for The Terafin?"

She was silent, as she often was; at length she said, "I don't ask you to tell me what ails your patients, great or small, unless that information is information that is necessary."

"Or unless the injury dealt has been dealt to one of your own."

She nodded.

"Jewel. Let me tell you what I've heard, even kept away from the thick of the political infighting as I am.

"There is going to be a succession war. It will be started by one of four people: Elonne, Rymark, Marrick, or Haerrad. You might be familiar with these people; you sit on the same Council." He drew breath, and before she could speak—although there wasn't much chance of it, really—he started again. "The skirmishes have already started. There were three more. Alea, Corniel, and Courtne."

"Yes."

"The Terafin has not recovered from the loss of Alea. I should not say this, but I will. I do not think she *will* recover from that loss. Nor will Cormark, of the Council. Gabriel supports The Terafin, but he does not look too closely at the alliances being formed because one of the four is his blood son; he is abjuring his duty as right-kin, whether he knows it or not—and Gabriel ATerafin is not a stupid man.

"Who will we have as Terafin? Who will be heir to the most powerful House in the Empire? Will we bow before Elonne ATerafin, Rymark ATerafin, Haerrad ATerafin, or Marrick ATerafin?"

"You know . . . a lot for a man who stays out of politics."

Very bitterly, Alowan leaned back into the window, pulling his staff from the ground as if it were rooted. Perhaps it was; Jewel thought she could detect the vaguest aura of magic traveling round its girth in a shimmering ring—but the daylight was bright enough at the old man's back that it could have been a trick of the sun, no more.

"Because, my dear, a healer doesn't stay out of politics during a House War. The only way to leave it is to die." His expression grew grimmer, paler. "Not just this healer, my dear. If we are not careful, or not well-protected enough, the unscrupulous will involve us all. But I digress, and if I choose to follow that road, there will be no conversation—only silence in the face of the wrongs we do each other for the sake of power, whatever that means." He closed his eyes; she watched him count, could almost hear the numbers that did not pass his lips before he spoke again.

"Corniel and Courtne. I was called across this threshold far too late to save either. But not too late that it wasn't completely clear to a man who's seen one succession war already what their deaths presaged. They died the death that will undoubtedly and undoubtably take all but one of the Council who desire the title. A death they deserved.

"But Alea . . . desired no such power. She was a lesson, I think."

She was almost shocked, to hear him say the words so bluntly. "Alowan," she whispered. "A healer—"

"Reveres all life. Yes." He bowed his head into his hands, and then raised it. "Forgive me, Jewel. I am tired, and I am—worse—weary. When I was younger—and I was never a young man in the service of the Terafin—I could join the fray; I did. I refused the services of these hands—" He lifted them; they trembled as if the memory of his denial could not be expunged. "I refused the services of one born to offer them to any of the factions involved in the war save one."

She took the seat that he'd cleared for her then, because her knees were weak. "You—"

"Yes. For The Terafin."

"Why are you telling me this?"

Even before he spoke she'd half lifted her hands to cover her ears; a child's gesture—a way of denying a truth that one doesn't want to hear—visceral, instinctive. "Because," he said quietly, "I will not survive this war."

She wanted to shout at him, to tell him that it wasn't true.

But she wasn't a good liar. Had never been one. She *felt* the words sink into her as if they were her own, and she'd swallowed them, and they were never going to be released again. "Alowan—"

He was serene, as if, having said this, the turmoil had been given over to one who could better deal with it.

"I am an old man, Jewel. If not for my gift, I would have died twenty years ago, maybe a bit less. I am weary of this; I should have died before Alea's body crossed my threshold. Alea was one of three people that Amarais trusted on the Council. Gabriel was another, but he is . . . compromised. Rymark is his blood son. I never considered the appointment of that one to be wise, for just that reason."

"This is a *House,* Alowan. Blood counts for nothing."

"You say that as if you believe it, and I believe, given your background, you probably do. But there's a reason that we swear blood oaths, that we become blood brothers, or brothers under the blood. And there is a reason that, from the dawn of time to now, parents have let kingdoms fall to preserve the lives of their children. A reason, young Jewel, that the Kings are born to the gods, and not to men.

"Enough. I have not asked you in to debate this with you. The Terafin trusted Alea, and Alea, trusting and foolish, is dead. She trusted Gabriel, but he is involved, and distant because of it. There is only one person that The Terafin can trust."

"Why are you telling me this?"

"Because I don't think that you want to think about it yourself. Do." He turned to look out the window. "I am not the only person who will not survive this war."

She sat too still.

"I will not heal for Haerrad or his faction," Alowan said softly. "I will put the word out. I will not heal for Haerrad, or for anyone who contests the heir The Terafin chooses."

"You know," she said, "who The Terafin will choose?"

"No. But I know that under no circumstance will she choose Haerrad."

He rose. "I am tired, Jewel Markess ATerafin. I would sleep. Think on what I have said."

CHAPTER SIX

They watched the boy spar, and not only because so much of their future—and, worse, the future of their bloodlines—depended on it.

Not, of course, that they watched for the same reasons, if compelled by things other than survival; these two men, Ramiro di'Callesta and Baredan di'Navarre, had lived under the same sun, but within the force of different gales, different winds; they were alike to those who did not know the Dominion, and as unlike as two men could be who still professed to understand the value of honor.

Baredan watched Valedan with a surprise that dispassionate assessment could not—quite—subdue. He had watched the boy spar from time to time, but never like this: Flash of blade, of forged, heavy steel, twist of torso, shift of leg, of knee, dip of shoulder, all of these a part of the dance, as if, indeed, this session *were* a blade-dance, and he, one half of the partnering of trust and skill that such a dance required.

He was simply not there when his opponent struck, and he parried by diverting the weight and the thrust of his opponent's lunge, as if some subtle sense, some voice of the capricious wind, told him where it would fall.

"How long?" he asked, his voice much softer than he would have liked it to be when speaking with a woman, even this one.

"An hour," she answered, in a tone as respectful as his; as awed, even. He thought that he liked this foreign Princess, this noblewoman who was the only one to be born *of* the blood of Kings. This is how the golden-eyed—or their descendants, set their traps; not by force or display of power, but by the seductive expedient of being honorable, and of honor worthy. "An hour," she said again. "I think he's found his stride."

Baredan nodded. "Have you?"

"Twice," she said, her hand touching the hilt of the sword she almost always wore. "Only twice in all the years I've been a competent swordsman. You?"

He laughed. "Once," he said. "But I do not think that this is that moment of transcendence for Valedan."

"No, nor I."

He hesitated a moment, his eyes still upon the boy and his opponent. At last he whispered a benediction, to the open sky, to the Lord of the Sun.

Ramiro di'Callesta, beside him, frowned.

The sea breeze had a saltiness to it that he, as Tyr'agnate of Averda, was familiar with, if not accustomed to, but he found it unpleasant in the languid heat of an afternoon sun that, if not at its height, still shortened his shadow, made of it something squat and unattractive. Certainly unpowerful.

He watched the contest, but he watched it, his eyes on the man who had once been Kings' Champion. Commander Sivari. Impressed by the man, impressed that he was so certain of himself he allowed two Southerners to stand here, in this private place, to watch the work of the Northern man-at-arms.

For without question Valedan di'Leonne was a student of the master; in no other way could such a young man have become so proficient. Ramiro di'Callesta made it his business to know and understand the workings of the Empire; they were his enemies, and even in time of peace, they gathered their strength and waited until some fool of a Tyr gave them the excuse they needed to cross the border.

Or so it often appeared. He confessed, in the privacy a man has with his thoughts, that he did not understand these men and women half as well as he would have liked. They were not uniform in their behavior, although they accepted one law—and that law, with the minor, minor exceptions the Houses managed to obtain—applied equally to both the lowest of common thieves and the Princes of the realm; they had power, but they had no serafs; indeed, the closest they came to serafs were men who *sold* their time and their allegiance, by contract, to masters of their own choosing: domicis.

He did not have Baredan's difficulty with armed women, women of danger; he was not so naive not to understand just how powerful the powerless could be.

Just how powerless the powerful could be.

Because he stood, beneath the open sky, under the Lord's gaze, watching a man who could be his enemy train a boy who would be—*will be*— his only master.

Baredan, he thought, as his hand strayed, almost with the exact motion the woman's had, to his sword hilt. *What are we witnessing?*

The moment was profound. Uncomfortable.

He could see, in the boy, the wind, the sun, the grace that legend lent to the Leonne clan. For a moment, he could see the Kings' Challenge as a springboard for the young man. But only for a moment, and that moment became insubstantial, inconsequential. Because he could see the Northern hand in the forging of the Southern weapon, and he did not know what the weapon's temper was.

Northerner.

Yes, the Northern Imperials could wage war against the South, and yes, they could win it; he had always acknowledged self-evident truths. But could a Northerner *rule* what he had taken?

And if he could not, would it be of benefit to Callesta in the long run? To Averda?

The sun was hot and merciless, as always; the wind was too humid. Ramiro di'Callesta watched the boy who looked like a blade-dancer in his grace and his focus. In a moment of doubt, Ramiro had traveled to the Callestan Swordhaven, seeking an answer to Baredan di'Navarre's fate in the only constant—besides blood— of his clan. In a moment of folly, he had made his decision; he accepted both that folly and the decision that came of it.

Decades of politics and pragmatism, dashed in a single gesture. It would haunt him. And cost. The Tyr'agnate of the Terrean of Averda took a deep breath, an even breath, a long one.

We have left him to you for far too long, he thought, drawing the Sword of Callesta.

Light caught the blade; noise carried the slight sound of steel against steel, the scrape of blade's flat against scabbard's mouth.

Baredan di'Navarre turned, mouth slightly open, to face the unsheathed sword, *Bloodhame.* "What," he said, his voice as steady as he could make it, "are you doing?"

"I am testing the temper of a sword," Ramiro replied, distantly.

"Not that sword."

"This sword?" The Tyr'agnate's voice was soft and momentarily chill. "No. I know this sword better than I know my kin."

He raised the weapon, pointing it as if it were an extension of his hand, his arm. "That one."

The boy. Valedan. Baredan was no fool.

"Ramiro, let it be. What the Commander cannot teach him, we cannot; there are three scant days before the gauntlet is run."

"What do you see when you see him?"

"A man. A Leonne. My Tyr."

"I see what you see, but more. I am an old man; it should not be so much of a challenge."

Because the Princess was with them, Baredan did not snort. "You are one of the finest swordsmen in all of Averda."

The Tyr'agnate's smile was sharper than *Bloodhame*. "The sword," Ramiro said, stepping forward, "is drawn."

"Tyr'agnate," Mirialyn ACormaris said, her voice smooth as steel, and just as soft.

"ACormaris."

"If I am not mistaken, that sword is the Callestan clan sword."

"You are not mistaken."

"And if my memory serves, once drawn, it is not returned to its scabbard unblooded."

"Your memory," Ramiro kai di'Callesta said, "is the memory of Cormaris, lady."

The argument caught their attention. It was loud, and inasmuch as they could be, they stood downwind of the play of words among three voices: two men and a woman.

They broke at once, drawing out of the invisible circle that bound all their movements, all of their attacks and defenses, their thrusts and swings, counters, parries. Shadows which fell short against the ground became two things, not one; they turned, almost as a man, to the spectators that they had been, at best, peripherally aware of.

Valedan would have recognized the woman's voice anywhere. He lifted the lip of his helm, squinting through bright light to shadow, the shade of bowers above the open courtyard.

"Valedan," Sivari said, letting the name carry the full force of his voice.

Valedan nodded. They both looked to the naked blade of the Tyr'agnate of Averda. "Treachery?"

Sivari's laugh was brief; it held both amusement and a trace of bitterness. "Always. He is of Annagar. But if you're asking me if

I think he means to kill you, then no; it is his vanity and not his sense of safety, that has been somehow pricked. Stand ready."

Valedan shrugged; metal joints clanked slightly as his shoulder rose and fell. Without another word, he crossed the stones, holding his sword, unsheathed, by his side.

"Tyr'agnate," he said, nodding.

"Tyr'agar." The Callestan Tyr brought his sword up, as if it were weightless. "You are better with your weapon than I thought you would be."

Valedan fought to keep the smile from his lips; to keep his pleasure from showing. *To show pride is necessary. To show pleasure in praise is not—not when your allies are men such as the Tyr'agnate. It will make him question your youth; it will make of you, in his eyes, a boy. Men accept praise as their due when it is their due. You will be his Tyr.*

Do not forget this.

"I am not a young man, Tyr'agar. I would be honored if you would allow me to take the Commander's place for the remainder of this session. I seldom have cause to practice, and I would be in your debt."

"It is not a—"

Valedan raised a hand, asking for silence from the Princess Royal. Receiving it.

"As you can see, I am armored; there will be no delay. We had cause to venture into territory that might have proved . . . inhospitable before we returned to *Avantari*."

"If the Commander wishes to cede his place," Valedan said softly, "I would be honored."

Both men—the younger gleaming with the effects of the session's exertion—turned to look at Sivari. He lifted his helm.

"I will cede my place," he said. "But with your permission, I will watch." His tone of voice made of the request a command; his eyes were blue as sky, unblinking, as he stared past Valedan at his challenger. As if he were suddenly dangerous. Or as if Sivari were finally willing to acknowledge that he *was* a danger.

"Granted," Valedan said, before Ramiro could reply. "Tyr'agnate?"

"I am ready."

They circled each other like wary animals, two of a kind. Swords glinted in sunlight as one or the other shifted his stance minutely.

"What is he doing, Baredan?"

The General shrugged. "What the Tyr'agar has accepted." It was clear that he was not pleased by either challenge or acceptance; clear, also, that he was fascinated by it, by the movement of two men, one still slender with youth and the other—the other fettered by power and power's rein.

Soon, he thought, as he watched the Callestan Tyr. *The boy has stamina. He bides his time.*

In matters of war they were not so different as all that, the General and the Tyr; they noticed the same things, fought many of the same fights. Ramiro di'Callesta struck before Baredan's words fell into memory, stepping in with his left leg and swinging with his right arm. Neither man had chosen to carry a shield; their skill served in its stead.

And the shield was a Northern style for a combat such as this.

He watched; the sun was lower now, but it cleared the trees and the heights of all buildings save those the cursed god-born ruled. The shadows it cast lengthened, blending as boy and man clashed, as curved swords glanced and slid and separated.

The boy was tired. The man was not—quite—up to his edge. Even so, they should not have been evenly matched. Death changed a man, and killing more so; Ramiro di'Callesta was blooded in both ways. Valedan, in neither.

He drew breath, but did not release it.

Circle. Strike, parry, strike strike strike—pressing the advantage Valedan's exhaustion gave him, pressing it as hard as he could. The boy gave way, but he gave ground slowly, holding his own.

Witness, Lord, Baredan thought, his hand a fist atop the pommel of his sheathed sword. *Witness. Grant us a sign.*

And it came.

Valedan broke, at last, coming out of the circle, foot upon the interlocked brickwork that led into the footpath's menage of life. Ramiro pressed him, hard. Pursuing, Baredan thought, a little quickly. A Northern combat would be over, but by unspoken consent the two who sparred did not follow the Northern convention of the circle's boundaries. Still, if Valedan left the training ground, he would be expected to end his combat, declaring it a victory for the Tyr'agnate.

A victory without the proof of blood *Bloodhame* required.

The Callestan Tyr came on and Valedan stopped, suddenly freezing in place, his sword up and across his chest, his hand on the back of the blade. He pushed, and then drew the blade across air as if it were weightless, as if it were the steel, and not the man, that guided the movement.

Sunlight flashing.

Blood.

Ramiro di'Callesta stood beneath the eye of the Lord in the courtyard of the foreign Kings, the fight over. He raised a gloved hand to his cheek, touching the cut that the tip of Valedan's blade had left there.

He spoke, but the winds carried his words away from Baredan's ears; Valedan bowed his head slightly and walked back to the circle's far edge, where he lifted a cloth. There, he wiped the blood—and there was little enough of it—from the blade's sharp edge. His hands were trembling; not a good sign, but still, one that could be overlooked for this day.

Lord, Baredan thought. *Your servants bear witness.*

The Tyr'agnate joined the boy by the bench; he spoke again, but again the words were too faint, too personal, to carry.

And then Baredan's mouth opened to shout a warning as *Bloodhame* came up in a glitter of sunlight, a hidden whistle of wind.

The warning died.

Because Valedan kai di'Leonne's blade rose to greet it.

Baredan knew a moment of perfect peace then, although he heard Sivari's curse, felt rather than saw the depth of Mirialyn's frown. The boy had been bred in the North. Had been born to a wife not Serra, and at that a terribly weepy, overly dramatic, unattractive woman. He had been sent here to live and die as a means to end a poorly fought war.

But the South was there, at the core of his heart; a Northern boy would have taken the cut that Ramiro desired to offer—because a Northern boy would have trusted the guise of both ally and the formality of "rules."

Still, enough. For they were in the North, and it was the Northern armies that would be their best weapon. He had no intent of letting the Tyr'agnate further antagonize either the Princess or the Commander.

"Ramiro," he said, drawing close, the tone of the single word genial, the hand upon his sheathed sword not. "A good fight. I trust that you have what you came for?"

The Tyr'agnate spared the General a glance, and then he smiled thinly. "Not entirely what I came for, Baredan. But I am . . . satisfied."

"Sheathe the sword then, and be done."

"As you say." Ramiro di'Callesta lifted *Bloodhame,* and ran her edge lightly across his cupped palm. She bit, but not deeply, not in his hands.

"You are not," the Tyr'agnate said, turning from Baredan to the master he served, "what I feared you would be. You . . . fight well, and you are wary enough. Be so, and you may survive what follows."

Valedan did not smile in return. Instead, he sheathed his own, unnamed, sword. "One does not have to be treacherous to understand treachery, Tyr'agnate."

"Not in the North," Ramiro said softly.

"Nor in the South," Baredan added. "There is a difference between cunning and treachery, Tyr'agnate, at least to most clansmen."

"Not the clans who rule, General."

"Not all of the clans, no."

They bristled a moment, the General and the Tyr'agnate.

It was Valedan kai di'Leonne who took the edge from their words. "You did not come here," he said, his voice betraying some weariness, "to argue among yourselves." It was a question, and a statement.

Baredan had the grace to bow. "No, Tyr'agar, we did not."

"Good. You have news?"

"We have."

"Join me in the baths, then, and let me hear what you have to say."

"Alina," Valedan said quietly, as he fitted himself with the soft, silk robes that were meant for evening's use, "What does it mean?"

"What," his closest adviser replied, "does what mean?" She motioned to the mats on the floor, and after loosely tying the sash around his waist, he knelt there.

"Anton. Anton di'Guivera."

He felt her sigh wuffling through the back of his hair, a soft breeze rather than a sound. He was tired, but if his legs and arms would cease their near-endless ache, he thought he might be momentarily content. Today he had accepted the sparring challenge of Ramiro di'Callesta—and he'd bested him, although it had been a near thing. Commander Sivari was, after all, a better swordsman than the man whose life had been forged in the fires of the Lord, and to come from the first to the second had given him an edge he wasn't certain he'd have otherwise.

She said nothing, but he felt the smooth strength of her palms against either side of his neck; she lifted one hand and pushed his head forward, murmuring a graceful request that he relax.

"Alina?"

She sighed. "You *must* relax. Tomorrow, you will run and you will ride; you will swim, and you will fight. And the next day. And the day after that."

He did not reply, not directly. But as she massaged his neck and his shoulders, he shifted, lowering the full length of his body into the coolness of the mats. He buried his face into the arms he crossed beneath his chin.

"He trained my half-brother."

"Valedan."

"Do you know what they told me?"

"That he is here? Yes. I'd heard."

"And you didn't mention it?" Valedan knew better than to rise; he let his words carry his surprise.

"The Princess told me," she said quietly. "But I knew that Ramiro and Baredan would have that information—and more—brought to you. It is better, with men like Baredan, that they feel they are being useful."

"Do you know what—what our enemies—told Anton di'Guivera?"

"No," she said gravely. Her hands stilled. "Do you wish me to know?"

It surprised him. "Alina, what's wrong?"

"Nothing."

He sat up and turned; she knelt against the mats, her hands uncharacteristically folded in her lap. "You've been almost too quiet all evening."

"And I am usually too loud?" Her smile was, for a moment, *her* smile, not the smile of an attendant. It left her face quickly.

"Have I done something to offend you?"

"No."

"Then what?"

"I spoke with Miri before I came," she said, her eyes upon the lamps, and not his face.

"And?"

"Your combat with Ramiro kai di'Callesta—you did not choose to tell me how it ended."

"I did not— Oh. That."

"Valedan—I would not have guessed that you would escape

the scratch he intended to give you; not I, not Baredan, not Sivari. Only Mirialyn was not surprised."

"So?"

"You are not the boy that we think you are; you are already more of the man that you must be. Not one of us clearly understands you—but until this afternoon, each of us, born and bred beneath the Dominion's sun—thought we did."

"The sun is the same anywhere," Valedan said, almost absently. "Sigurne from the Order of Knowledge teaches that—"

She laughed fondly. It eased the stiffness that he did not care for out of her features for a moment. "Even I would have guessed that you would have been cut, measure for measure, as Ramiro was. Why weren't you?"

As if it were a real question, and not one posed almost entirely to herself, he answered. "He was angry," Valedan said softly. "Gracious about it, but angry. He didn't sheathe his sword; I assumed he was waiting until I was . . . less prepared."

"He couldn't sheathe the sword. *Bloodhame* requires blood before it's returned to its scabbard—at least, that is the Callestan legend."

"Oh."

"You didn't know this?"

Valedan said nothing for a long moment, weighing the truth, weighing a lie, glancing, as he balanced the cost of each, at the neutrality of the Serra Alina's face. She was the only person who both understood the Dominion and whom he trusted, and he did not want to lose either her affection or the sharpness of her mind; it was a weapon at least as graceful as the Callestan sword, and perhaps more deadly.

Lie? Truth?

"No," he said at last, reluctantly, "I didn't know that."

Her dark eyes widened in surprise, and then she laughed, and he saw the shadows leave her eyes. "The Lady protects you, even when the sun is at its height. You must never tell either the General or the Tyr'agnate what you have just told me.

"But come. Tell me," she said, "about Anton di'Guivera."

He did, hesitantly at first.

Because he knew that he had lied to the Serra. And that she believed it, because he had never lied to her before. But he knew, then, that the lie would ease her where the truth would not—and he was young enough to need that ease, and that confident affection, old enough to know how to best get it.

One day, he promised himself, almost guiltily, one day, he would tell her the truth.

The moon was high above the manse, the air almost cool, although at the height of any other season, no one would have called it so. Everything was relative.

Jewel ATerafin stood on the path not ten yards away from the shrine of Terafin, moonlight shining like half-lit silver along the bent leaves of flowers that night had brushed color from. She had not traveled this distance alone, and it galled her, but not so much as the idea that one of the remaining two ATerafin—Elonne or Marrick—might come upon her unprepared and unaware. As Rymark had done.

As someone had done, to Teller.

Teller.

She drew breath and balled her hands into fists, feeling the bite of fingernails against the flesh of palm. She did not want to think of it. Could barely think of anything else. It brought old memories back; removed the patina of experience from the years she had spent here.

Like silver, she thought; take away the tarnish and the stuff underneath hasn't changed all that much—but it certainly looks different in either state, cared for or careworn.

Avandar was the shadow over the face of the moon's light. He did not accompany her to the shrine, but there he was, like an awkward third arm, or leg, a thing to be gotten around. And he knew it, too. She wondered, for a moment, how a man like Avandar could make it his life to *serve* when command seemed the natural inclination to him; she had never really wondered that of Morretz. Or of Ellerson.

There. In the shadows beside the shrine, sitting on the lowest of the steps.

"Stay here," she told her domicis.

The domicis raised a brow—she could see it, although she didn't actually look at his face; his face, his plethora of expressions, was etched in memory, a conscience of sorts to pull out when she needed one and he happened to be elsewhere. Or to be avoided, when he happened to be present.

But he followed her gaze, and when he saw the man on the step, he gestured. "Very well," he said. "But I will wait here, Jewel."

"I'm not a target," she snapped, irritated.

"If that were completely true, you would not have agreed to my escort."

Worst thing about Avandar was that he wasn't stupid enough. She muttered something less than graceful under her breath and started out across the path, shaking her hands slightly to take the edge off the tension balled fists always produced.

Devon ATerafin looked up as she approached. He smiled, but the smile was half-hidden by the poor light, and Jewel did not carry the lamp. "You summoned me."

"Yes."

"But you did not wish me to meet you in your quarters?"

"No."

"Very well." He stood. "Why?"

"I'm being observed, and my routine is known. No one blinks twice when I make my way out to the Terafin shrine. Anyone interested might do more if I make my way out to Avantari on business that hasn't passed through Council or Gabriel first."

"You have your own concerns," he said mildly.

"Yes. But they aren't, apparently, *solely* my concerns." She passed him, taking the steps two at a time until she stood by the altar, beneath the domed roof, where light might make the lines of his face—and the expression they fell into—more clear. He followed with his usual grace; the years had taken nothing away from the quality of his movement, and very little away from the speed.

Nothing away from the quiet force of his personality.

"Something happened," he said quietly.

She started a bit, and then laughed. Ugly sound, that—too weak by half. "Two things. I need your help with one—and you'll want to give it, so I consider that I'm doing your office a favor."

"I see. And the other?"

She looked away. "Since I'm doing you a favor, I want a favor in return."

"It's House business." Not a question.

"Yes."

"It is not . . . always safe to involve me in House business, Jewel."

She looked up at him, met his eyes. "I know," she said at last, acknowledging what was not often acknowledged within Terafin proper: That Devon ATerafin was one of the very, very few men of any power who owed his allegiance, in truth, to two lords. Acknowledging what had *never* been acknowledged by The Terafin, because of course it could not be: That the allegiance to the Crowns was stamped so thoroughly across every nook and cranny of his beliefs and endeavors that there might as well have been only one lord.

The Terafin had always liked Devon, in her fashion; Jewel believed that she found it convenient to have a man who served so close to the heart of the Kings' security. It was clear that the Kings understood that Devon was ATerafin; equally clear that The Terafin understood he was a member of the Compact, Astari. Devon himself was a gesture of The Terafin's political confidence in the Crowns, a sure statement that the woman who ruled the most powerful noble House in the Empire was certain that between the just and wise rule of Kings and the ambitions of the House, there would never be conflict. Practically, however, he was also a source of contact with the Crowns in an emergency that went to the heart of the matter through channels that were unpredictable and therefore nigh impossible to block.

But not even she would have given her House name to a man—or allowed him to keep it—had he once publicly avowed the greater loyalty to the Twin Kings. She had never asked, although they had walked that line time and again, finding anew how sharp it could be, and how close to cutting.

Jewel had never asked. Had never needed to.

"I know it's not often done. But this isn't just House business, and it's not—yet—officially Council business, so I can talk about it if I damned well please."

"Jewel—"

"Haerrad had Teller ridden down. Not killed. Just injured and left in the road."

"Jewel—I tell you again, there are things that we do not discuss—"

"I *don't care* what you don't discuss with The Terafin." She pushed her hair out of her eyes. Thinking, as she bit her tongue and got control of the level of her voice, that it never seemed to matter how often the damned thing was cut—it still skirted the edge of her lashes or worse. "I need your help."

"Do not ask me," he told her, his voice as formal as it had been in over a decade, "to choose sides in this. For the good of the House that you love, do not even force me to speak of the sides that exist. Jewel—House Wars are prohibited by the Crowns."

Bitterly, she said, "And the Crowns are hypocritical enough to look the other way as long as the death toll doesn't get too high.

Four, five, six—they won't blink. And six is all it'd take to wipe out what's left of my den."

He was stiff for a moment; she saw his lips thin at the open criticism of the men whose lives he was sworn to protect. "It's not hypocrisy," he said at last, coldly, "but wisdom. We are what we are, Jewel, and the Kings are what *they* are. The Houses are what is left of the old order, and if they've changed over time, what hasn't is this: Men seek power that they can rise to. The Ten provide the magnet to their steel."

"And the grindstone," she snapped. "And the blood." She lifted a hand to her eyes for a moment, and then said, from beneath the safety of that hand—and in a much smaller voice, "Sorry. It's not your fault."

"They want you to choose a side."

"The two that have managed to find me, yes."

He reached out almost gently and pushed the hand away. "Why is she doing this, Jewel?"

"Mandaros knows," she snapped. "I don't—"

And then she was struck by the lie in the words that she had spoken. Four words. Simple words. She wanted to tell Devon, then, but she couldn't quite bring herself to speak of it openly. Death. Loss.

"Without her," she managed to say, "this won't be home."

"No. But it will be a House." He was quiet. "Jewel—"

"I can't." She reached for her hair again, pushing it back, nervous habit. "What about you, Devon? Surely they've come to you?"

"Not one of them, however many there are," he replied, and she *knew,* suddenly, that he knew exactly how many there were, exactly how many there had been, and exactly who was left. "They are all wise enough to know what you won't know—that this is House business, and that the less a man who also serves the Crowns knows, the better. I'm sorry, Jewel." He paused. "If it helps, you are valuable to the Crowns, and valued by them."

She smiled grimly. "Tell that," she said, "to Haerrad."

He offered no response. "If you wished my aid for this —"

"No. I should've known what you'd say."

"Yes. But you're young for a full Council member, and I won't mention this transgression to The Terafin."

"Why thank you."

The sarcasm was lost on him. It wasn't always. "You said there were two concerns?"

She placed her palms on the altar and leaned slightly into them, letting the stone support her weight. She drew a breath, looking intently at his neutral expression. At last, she said, "You aren't going to like the second one."

"I never do. What is it?"

"There are kin in the hundred holdings."

She had a childish desire to see some sort of shock or surprise across his features, and she set it aside immediately as his face became rigid and cool as the stone beneath the flat of her palms.

"Where?"

It was not impossible to keep anger from his face; it was just difficult, and Devon ATerafin was used to this. There was a fine difference between acting in anger and acting after the fact, when the anger itself had quieted into the depths of a cool, implacable determination; it had been long since he had given himself over to the former. But not that long since it had been tempting; that was the nature of anger.

He listened as Jewel spoke, naming the seven holdings among the hundred that were the more densely populated and therefore harder —much, much harder—to easily investigate without drawing attention.

Also more dangerous to fight in, to kill in.

Oddly, the presence of the kin was not what angered him.

The kin were not creatures that he understood, he could not judge them. They were not human, had been birthed, so far as he knew, in the fires of the Hells, under the grip of, the dominion of, the Lord of the Hells himself. It was a source of argument among several of the priests of almost any religion save the Mother's whether or not these creatures had freedom of will; it was agreed that they were malice personified; malice made grand and infinitely dangerous when it managed to escape the Hells.

He did not hold the kin responsible for their actions any more than he might hold a rabid dog responsible for its; what was true in either case was that the creature must be killed in as efficient a way as possible. The kin were intelligent in a way that rabid dogs were not, and therefore more dangerous. But they were what they were.

No—his anger, when it found him at all—was always engendered by and for people. And Haerrad had—he was certain of it, now, although the spies within the House beholden to the Astari had been less than clear—threatened Jewel. He did not speak of it because he could not; he did not lie to her when he made clear the lack of wisdom she showed. But it angered him nonetheless.

The more so, oddly enough, because it was not the threat to her life that frightened her or moved her; rather, it was the threat to Teller, a man who had never quite achieved full growth, who seemed in some ways ageless adult and in some ageless child. Of all the den, all her unusual and loyal den, it was Teller to whom she was most attached.

And he hated the fact that loyalty and love were rewarded, always, by this terrible weakness: the threat of loss, the fear of it.

Accident, illness—these took lives, where the healer-born or the Mother-born chose not to—or could not—interfere. Age did the same, regardless of choice or decision. But willful death, murder . . .

"Devon?"

He was almost embarrassed, but it didn't show; very little did unless he chose to reveal it. "I'm sorry," he said. "I was— remembering." He felt a twinge of guilt when he saw her expression shift.

Between them, the mutual memories of kin and their ravages were strong, profound. To use those memories, to invoke them, to hide a more natural emotion, was probably wrong.

To use them, with Jewel ATerafin, was also foolish, but it was easy to forget, with Jewel, that the future existed: She was a woman who seemed to live in the present, with earth-deep roots, a practical, unsentimental mind.

He saw her eyes narrow, and he shrugged in response, remembering that there were some lies that never got past her.

Some did. She rarely called him on either.

"What do you need from me?" he asked her quietly.

"Your support," she replied, softly, so softly, he almost lost the words. Would have, if a sudden breeze hadn't picked them up and carried them to his ears.

"Jewel—"

"I know. You can't. Or the Kings will get involved."

He heard the bitterness in the words.

"I'm not one of your den," he told her softly. "And you're not— quite—one of mine. But I promise you this: Not a single one of the heirs presumptive, as they style themselves, will be foolish enough to touch you."

"They couldn't anyway," she answered starkly. "*My* death, I'd always see in advance. They're ambitious, Devon. They're not stupid."

He lifted a hand to touch her arm, and she stepped away. "You think I care, don't you? You think I care about all of this?"

"About Terafin?"

"Yes."

"Yes," he replied, carefully, neutrally, "I do. Will you try to tell me that you don't?"

"No. But what Terafin means to *me* and what Terafin means to the rest of you—it's not the same. Do you think I care if the Kings intervene, do you think I care if they stop this stupid war before it takes the lives of our own? It's only our own that'll die in it."

"Terafin is not a collection of children, to cry into the pleats of their parents' robes," Devon told her stiffly.

"No. It's a collection of murderous thugs with fancy accents, fancy clothes, and a better class of hidden dagger."

"Terafin is Teller," he told her. "Angel. Carver. Finch. Jester. Even Arann. It is me, Torvan, Alayra, and even Alowan, although he, like Angel, has never chosen to take the name that has been offered to him. More than that, it is you, Jewel."

"And if it were me, would you still give me the same damned answer?"

He didn't answer the question for a moment, because he almost didn't understand it.

And when understanding dawned, his mouth went dry; his face lost—for just a few seconds—the neutrality that the Astari so highly prized.

"Is that the game?" he said softly, bitterly. "Is that the game you desire to play?" He was disappointed. Worse, but the rest of it would come later. The silence was awkward between them, foreign. "The years have changed you."

"Maybe," she said, offering him the shrug that passed for nonchalance among her den. Their eyes met, and she looked away. "I want you to get me a writ of execution."

"For the kin?"

"No, for the rodents in the holdings," she said, sarcasm shaky, but definitely hers. "Yes, the kin."

"Done."

"I need a writ of execution for those who attempt to aid and protect the kin."

"You know we can't grant that. We can evaluate the crime itself behind closed doors in the Hall of Wisdom, but for that, you know we need to call in one Mandaros-born to judge."

She shrugged. She'd known. "I also need a writ of exemption."

"That is less quickly done. The Mysterium grants the writs of exemption in conjunction with the Magisterium and it—"

"That's not my problem," she said curtly, even angrily. "We're not going kin-hunting without the ability to use the magic we've got."

"And you've got a mage traveling with your den now?"

"In a manner of speaking."

"Who?"

"None of your business."

"Jewel—"

"No. I mean it. You're no part of my den," she told him angrily, throwing his words back at him as if she'd aimed each one. "You want the kin out of the holdings before the Kings' Challenge— more particularly, before the gauntlet is run. We can do it, but we can't do it with ceremonial daggers—we need to be free to use what we've got at our disposal."

"We?"

Her lips pressed themselves into the line he least liked, thin and white-edged. "No," she said, at the same time as he said, "I'd like to join you."

"Jewel—" he said, starting over.

"You don't trust me, if you can think that I want what Haerrad wants."

To the point, and cutting. There was nothing of the delicate sadist in Jewel ATerafin. Nothing of the diplomat either. "I trust you with the hunting of the kin," he said. "We've done that before."

"We were on the same side before, Devon." She turned then, to face the altar that had been supporting her weight. Showing him, with stubborn finality, the flat of her back.

"We're not on opposite sides now," he said, the heat of anger permeating each word, no matter how measured he made them.

She bent, placing her hands against the flat of the altar; he could not see the expression upon her face, although perhaps that was better.

Anger. And then: Wonder.

The altar began to glow, softly at first, but more and more brightly; the sky lost the patina of silvered moon, of night color. He knew that this was not a magic of Jewel's creation; she did not have that ability.

Before he could speak, she cried out, wordless, and stepped back, and back again; her back hit his chest with a soft thud. She froze, there, the circle of his arms not yet closed. Not closing. You couldn't close her in, couldn't trap her, couldn't offer her safety that she didn't ask for.

That had always been the rule.

"I don't want this," she said softly, and he was certain that she didn't speak to him, although—if one ignored the distant presence of Avandar—he was the only other person present.

"What does it mean?"

"I *won't* do it."

"Jewel—Jay . . ."

But she did not even look at him. Instead she turned, ran down the steps of the altar, trailing past a startled Avandar in her flight. He knew, then, that she was as afraid as she had ever been.

What would you give, to protect the Kings?

The silent night held no answer but the echo of her last words. His own accusation.

CHAPTER SEVEN

13th of Lattan, 427AA
The Shining City

Serra Diora di'Marano.

Close his eyes, and he could see the perfect stillness of her face. He could even think it lovely, in the way a perfect sword was lovely when it was held by an enemy's hands and turned, in silence, against him. And she, barely a woman, had lifted sword against *him,* against them all. The Sun Sword.

If the power existed in a Widan's hands to destroy that Sword, it would have been destroyed long ago; if the power to steal it existed, it would have been stolen, hidden, copied. But it rested, luminous and defiant, in the Swordhaven that the first Leonne had built for it in ages past, after the end of the Shadow Wars.

As if there could ever be an end to such war. As if, he thought grimly, fingering the long, fine strands of his pale, peppered beard, that bloody, murderous battle had been anything but a skirmish, a pale shadow of the war to come.

The mountain winds came in through the open arches, lifting his cloak and his hair in the strength of its grip. Such arches as these had never existed in the whole of the Southern Dominion while he lived, and only the whispered echoes of a history before the gods themselves gave hint that such structures as this—this stone work, this scion of mountain and magic and shadow, this Shining Palace, was not unique in the history of the world. It boasted no gold, no wood, no Northern masons. Only the hand of a God could have accomplished this: the stone was of a piece. End to end, depth to height, it was seamless; embellishments added for the human court had been added with the Lord's permission, as afterthought that did not, ever, diminish or add to the grace and strength of his achievement.

The mage stood, planted there by spell and Southern defiance, as the winds at the height grew stronger, and stronger still; the Northern Lords repaired at once into the great chamber, drawing their furs and their magics and their cloaks tight about their bodies, forgetting, in a moment's discomfort, that the kin watched and waited, circling weakness in the way that vultures circled above the dying in fields made fallow by battle's end.

Cortano di'Alexes neither forgot the watchers nor fled the cold; he had lived with the wind all his days, and in a Dominion where the wind and the sand scoured the soul in perfect harmony, the Northern wind was not so much to be feared; it was a fact, the wind, and it comforted him to feel its threat so far from home. The comfort was, as the wind, cold.

Serra Diora *en'Leonne.*

Oh, she was more than her father's daughter, that pale-faced, black-eyed child. And he, surrounded by men who defined manhood by three things, war, riding, and women, had been outmastered by her maneuvering; outmanipulated by her helpless facade; almost undone in the sweep of a few well-placed words, at a ceremony that he had been the original architect of: The crowning of a new Tyr.

Not even the death of the Radann kai el'Sol was a death he could take pleasure in; for it had been used against them all, a reminder that the only way to truly disarm a warrior born was to kill him, and brook no delay.

Very few of the women in the Dominion were born warriors. Still, he should have seen it. They *all* should have seen it.

The wind drew tears from his eyes, and those tears struggled down the folds of his skin, freezing slowly in the cold air. Soon, he would have to leave this perch; a show of strength was one thing, but it could be . . . overdone. Almost disdainfully, he stepped forward to the stone rails, and stood there a moment, between the folded wings of a stone dragon in flight. His gaze rolled down the length of its neck and beyond: for in the distance made of height and wind, he could see, clearly, the gate. Demons guarded it, standing at each of its five points, invoking its magic—mind, heart, spirit, body, and place—with theirs as sustenance. Hours from now, they would be replaced, and hours from then, when the sun was well and truly hidden, the Lord himself would take to the pit and begin to call forth the kin.

He had their names.

Each and every one.

Turning, his hands edged in white, he made his way back to the great hall in which fires would be burning.

Burning.

For a moment, just a moment, the Widan Cortano, Sword's Edge, the most powerful mage in the Dominion of Annagar, paused. He was beside himself with rage, and that rage, concealed behind a necessary mask, was like the fire itself, and the wood; it consumed. She was a *girl* and he a *Widan,* and she had taken, in silence and meekness, the weapons that she required to injure them all.

No, it was not that she had taken them; it was that she had used them, to advantage. She had won. Had he been a political fool— or a man to take those chances—the girl would be horribly, terribly dead, a sure warning to any who thought to follow her example. Cortano di'Alexes was not a man who lost at anything. Ah, he was angry; he was angry, still, and he dared not show it, not here.

For he stood within the great stone halls—the cold stone halls— of the Shining Court, and here, such an expression was almost an open admission of weakness. He was not a fool; a foolish man could never have both wielded, and been, the Edge of the Sword of Knowledge. He knew that the *Kialli* watched, always; that no human lord of this Court was ever safe; the *Kialli's* memories were long and near-perfect.

And why should they not be? The *Kialli* were truly immortal. Kill them here, and the Hells opened in the distance to draw their essences home to the winds of the Abyss. Their bodies, made by some pact between the sleeping earth and its ancient children's names, burned to ash, and less, like discarded clothing.

At least, he reflected, this was how a Summoning worked. But the gate that the Lord of the Shining Court built, with the aid of Cortano, Isladar, Krysanthos—a man Cortano respected and disliked in equal measure—and the Lord Ishavriel and his strange, wind-scoured child-woman Anya, was not a summoning of that nature; it was a bridge. It made, slowly, a single place of these two worlds: The Hells, and the lands of man. And if these two places were one, then what?

Cortano let curiosity eat away at the edges of anger, for he was known for his curiosity; it was a weakness that he was, conversely, proud to own.

The sun was in position. The meeting was about to start. He played no games of waiting here; his power was understood, and it was valued.

* * *

"Lord Assarak, Lord Etridian; your objections in this matter are trivial and must be overlooked. I need not remind you that you were invited—and accepted that invitation—to show your vaunted prowess by seeing to the destruction of a boy. Not even a man, but a magicless, powerless boy.

"Your failure there—and our enemies' ability to use our weakness to advantage—has placed us in a more delicate position. The plan that I've outlined is the only plan we will consider."

The saying of the words afforded Cortano di'Alexes a certain amount of pleasure. He turned toward the shadow that waited patiently by the door, and that pleasure diminished greatly.

The shadow bowed. "Sword's Edge," he said softly.

"It is . . . not common . . . to bring a guest to these meetings." Lord Isladar rose.

The shadow sauntered into the light that was brought as a subtle accusation of weakness into the council hall; the *Kialli*, after all, did not require it. "I am hardly a guest, Lord Isladar." He bowed, but not to the *Kialli* with whom he spoke; instead he turned to Lord Ishavriel of the Fist of God.

Cortano was not pleased, but the presence of this particular man—and by extension, of the men with whom he served—had never given the Sword of Knowledge pleasure. In the Empire, the Order of Knowledge—a weaker and less focused body—did one thing that Cortano desired to emulate: They destroyed mages who were not under their auspices and their quaint law. Somehow, that destruction of the so-called rogues had not brought the Order to its knees, and it had started no long and bloody war between rival factions. Power in the North was a strange creature.

Not so, not here.

The shadow rose, shedding magical disguise, and adding it. Bold, here. "I am . . . the humble merchant, Pedro di'Jardanno." Humble. Older. Rounder. The beard that suddenly graced his face was streaked with white; the rings that adorned his fingers were tight around overly soft flesh. "I have been granted permission, by the Tyr'agar's new edicts, to travel North for the Festival season; I am late to arrive, sadly."

"Is this meant to impress us?" Etridian said, with studied contempt.

"No," Pedro replied genially. "But the Brotherhood of the Lord will test its mettle against the coterie that protects one simple human boy. Perhaps," he added, equally genially, his smile a studied fold of flesh, "it will impress the Lord, where his Fist has failed to do so."

Etridian rose like the fall of lightning.

Pedro crossed his arms; there was a clash of something that sounded almost like steel, and lightning, indeed, did come. "We are not *Allasakari*," he said, with some contempt. "We do not seek to be the Lord's vessels. I have no doubt that should you decide upon it, you will kill me—but your own survival might then be at question; it will be a costly kill, Lord Etridian."

The Brotherhood of the Lord.

Cortano understood much then. It was not a title that had been claimed in centuries—not a title, in fact, that Ser Pedro had dared to claim when they first began their negotiations. Something had changed, was changing, and Cortano liked it little.

What, he thought, *have you been promised?* He did not ask; he would, later, but indirectly as was his wont. The brotherhoods—Lord's or Lady's—did not take kindly to direct questioning.

Etridian's hand left claw marks in the surface of stone and wood; it drew the Widan's attention and ended the unfortunate silence.

Of the five Generals—the fist of God—he preferred Lord Ishavriel, who had the advantage of being subtle. He had no other advantage, however; he was, as were all of the *Kialli*—with the notable exception of Lord Isladar—condescending and arrogant when dealing with the merely mortal, so the preference was slight, and had he the upper hand over that General, he would not hesitate to apply it. Cautiously.

"You will not take my kin," Etridian said. "When we were instructed to do away with a so-called magicless, powerless 'boy,' you neglected to inform us that we would be facing the darkness-born." He turned his neutral expression upon the Lord Isladar, who had until this point kept his own counsel. "You gave your word," he said softly, "that she would not be a threat to us."

"I gave my word," Isladar replied, softer still, "that she would not defy our Lord's command."

"It is his plan that we follow."

"And he has not chosen to speak against her." The single Lord in Allasakar's service who had asked for no demesne offered the glimmer of a rare smile. "Kiriel has long lived by the law of the Hells, Etridian. You have offered her no alliance, made no pact, granted her none of the respect due her position."

"Position," Assarak said, "is a function of power."

"Indeed. And had she none, she would have died long ago."

"She has yours, Isladar."

"Not now."

"No. Now, she holds—"

Silence descended at once, cold and sudden; all eyes glanced a moment off Cortano's still curiosity, off Ser Pedro's implacable good humor.

"*Enough,*" Lord Isladar said. "Enough, Lord Etridian. This bickering is pointless. The kin will be taken from both the ranks of yourself and Lord Assarak—and the Lord has graciously agreed to summon one who can take the physical form of another creature, and not the mere appearance.

"The boy must die. His existence is an affront to our ability, and our strength."

"And your . . . student?"

Isladar was silent a moment; Cortano watched with interest—always interest—as the will of Ishavriel and the will of Isladar clashed openly, and in complete silence. It was the only way he had seen them test power against each other. Of all, Ishavriel was Isladar's greatest threat, and it was hard to gauge the depth of that threat; Cortano had seen each of the Generals display more power, and at that openly, than Isladar had ever displayed.

Which is why it should have come as no surprise to him that Isladar spoke first. But it did. "If Kiriel is hunting the kin, and I suspect there is a chance that she will do so out of spite, we must be prepared."

"How much can she sense, Isladar?"

Again, Cortano caught a flicker of glances, all touching him briefly.

"I do not know," Isladar said at last. "But I believe we can circumvent it—or better, use it against her."

"How?"

"She is young; she is not experienced; she has not dwelled long among the humans. I believe, with the expedient use of magics, we may be able to convince her that there are kin where indeed none exist.

"In the event that we have that success, I believe she will likely kill—and with some obvious force—an innocent human, perhaps several, and in Averalaan, that will mark her. Let her run from our enemies, and draw their attention to her unique capabilities in the process."

"And what," Etridian said coldly, "makes you think that our

enemies will be her enemies? It was in the hall of their Kings that she chose to attack me."

"True enough. However I believe that until that moment the allies that she had did not realize her true colors; it may be that they will never do so without our . . . aid. They will look, and closely, when that same girl is busy slaughtering the citizens of their city with talents that only the darkness-born might possess."

"They believe there is no such thing as one darkness-born."

Isladar's frown was a momentary crease of smooth skin. "Indeed," he said softly. "Perhaps," he added lightly, "they will assume her to be Allasakari."

Etridian spit. "They will not. They will know—or the triumvirate will—that she is god-born. Just as you, or I, would know the kin, whether they chose the talents of the *kialli* or the use of man-made sword to spread their law."

"Then let us pretend that our enemies are not fools. They will know her for what she is, sooner rather than late, with the aid of our misdirections."

"And her death?" Ishavriel said quietly.

"If they can kill her," Isladar replied, "then they will kill her. She has been raised in the Shining Court; she understands the price of that particular weakness."

Lord Etridian nodded, well pleased; there existed no fondness for Kiriel in any of the *kialli,* save Isladar—and what his interest was, what his plan, none comprehended.

Not even Cortano di'Alexes. But he was, in this case, in the company of his peers; he found the ignorance on his part equally galling.

He turned and caught the profile of the chubby merchant's still face; all smile was dimmed, and in the recess of a flesh formed partly of magic and partly of reality, the Sword's Edge saw a glimmer of the knife's edge, and was disquieted.

Who are you, Pedro di'Jardanno? What do you want from the Lord? More questions. He felt he would have their answer, and even that made him uneasy.

CHAPTER EIGHT

"Uh, Jay?"

She was up from the kitchen table in an instant, nervous at the sound of uncertainty in Finch's voice. It was hot enough that the papers she'd been writing on clung to her hands as she lifted them. "Is it Teller?"

"No—he's fine. Honest, sit down, he's fine. Torvan's set up a guard around the healerie; subtle, but definitely there."

"Torvan wouldn't know subtle if it tried to run him through." Pause. "How did you know that?"

"Arann told me." She was silent for a moment, and then she shrugged. "You've been really busy," she added, in a tone that meant she was about to offer an explanation.

Jewel hated it when Finch felt she had to explain something—because in Finch's book, an explanation was in line with an apology or an excuse. "And?"

"Well, we thought—with Kiriel and all—you'd need some help."

"What kind of help?"

"Well, Carver's ATerafin, and Angel's not. So Angel's gone out hunting in the thirty-second and the thirty-fifth."

"Alone?"

"Not quite."

"What the Hells does not quite mean?"

"He took Jester with him."

"Finch—"

"We figured if there are kin, there are likely to be disappearances, deaths—something suspicious. We know those holdings better than almost anyone." She took a breath. "Those and the twenty-sixth. Right next to our old holding."

"Finch, I told you—we can find them."

"Doesn't hurt to find out how they got there. Look, Angel fits in there."

And I don't? Jewel wanted to say it, but she didn't like the way Finch's gaze skittered off her face. Better not to ask when she didn't have time to be pissed off about the answer. "Okay. Arann and Carver?"

"They're in charge of the watch around the healerie."

"Well, at least you know how to mix good with bad. They've got a clue. Torvan doesn't."

Finch smiled. "We can take care of our own, Jay. You take care of—"

Silence. Jewel hated it. Because she knew what they were all thinking. They were like Chosen to her because she'd chosen them. They weren't, and could never be, counselors; they didn't have—excepting only Teller—the skill it took with numbers, the understanding of the broader political concerns, external or otherwise, that seemed to dictate the House course. But she didn't need another counselor beyond Avandar, and she could barely stand him.

"Oh, and Jay?"

"What?"

"One more thing before you go back to your papers."

"What?"

"There's a long-haired mage waiting in the sitting room to see you."

"Long-haired— Finch! Why didn't you tell me right away?"

She smiled. "I hate the way he thinks his concerns are more important than anyone else's. But I suppose his temper's worse, too. I'll send him in now."

"You'll do no such thing! I'll meet him in the—"

But the door was swinging in the wake of the slightest, and most cunning, of her den. Oh, no. None of Jay's den would ever make a good politician; pool their skills, and you'd come up with one mediocre politico among them.

Excepting only their leader. Their leader, damn her, had shown some skill at word-dances and postures.

Meralonne APhaniel came into the kitchen.

It was not the custom of Jewel Markess to meet him there; indeed, anyone she did not consider part of her circle of intimates was confined to the library or the small meeting hall, where she could wait upon them in all manner of correctness.

She had servants assigned by The Terafin to her wing; that they were, each and every one, ATerafin, had escaped no one's notice, least of all Jewel's. None of these servants came, however, to the kitchen without her express permission, and very few—except to cajole her with food—interrupted her by so much as knocking. Their pay was from the allowance The Terafin granted, and Jewel was generous enough with it, seeing in them as much ready service as she did in the Council members themselves.

Jewel rose as the unmistakable sheen of long, white hair caught the light that came in through the windows. "Member APhaniel," she said, covering her momentary discomfiture with a low bow.

He favored her with a perfunctory one in return, fixing her face, as she rose, with the cool gray of steel eyes. "ATerafin," he said.

She was comfortable around Meralonne APhaniel in the same way she was comfortable around Duvari; she knew that she could trust him absolutely to do all in his power to protect the things he had vowed to protect. If that meant throwing *her* life away, she could count on that as well—but she knew where she stood, and that was something.

Meralonne was tall; old, although age seemed to be a thing he could slough off at will, and his presence was such that she always wanted to take two steps back when she drew his particular attention.

In fact, the only time she was ever truly comfortable with him was when he'd forgotten himself enough to curse like the rest of her den did; it made him seem human, when so little else did. "W-what may I do for you?"

"I believe that you are about to embark upon a dangerous task— one which it is in our best interests that you not fail."

Jewel pushed the hair out of her eyes and exhaled. "I'm not sure what you're talking about."

"You should be, Jewel ATerafin; you are not, as most of your compatriots delight in being, dense and unobservant."

True enough, although she could do without the gratuitous insults to her den. On the other hand, Finch *had* kept him waiting. Observant. She looked at Meralonne APhaniel and didn't at all like what she saw there, because she knew, of a sudden, that he was girded for battle. His robes were not the usual robes, and he wore, of all things, a shield. No scabbard.

"You have," he continued, when she didn't take advantage of his silence quickly enough, "two full days until the running of the gauntlet. Three days, including this one. The hour is still quite early, but I see you've not chosen to depart."

"Depart?"

"Jewel—ATerafin. Duvari, the Lord of the Compact, chose this morning to deliver—in person—a writ of some urgency. It seems he wished to demand a writ of exemption from the Mysterium and the Magisterium."

Jewel ran her hand over her eyes. It was a gesture that was becoming far too familiar. "Let me guess," she said. "The Council of the Magi was only willing to bypass the necessary investigations and magisterial seals—even though the demand came from as close to the Kings as possible—on condition that one of the Magi selected, of course, by the Council, accompany the person or persons the writ's intended for."

"Very good."

"Not acceptable."

A silvered brow rose. "I see you pay the same respect to authority you always did."

She shrugged. "I joined it."

And was rewarded by a smile. "Yes. Jewel Markess ATerafin, this is not the first time we will have worked together, looking for signs of the kin in the streets of the city. Indeed, one might say that we have the leisure of knowing that this time, only a few lives, and not the whole of the Empire, are at stake."

She wasn't fooled by his manner.

"I don't need your help, Meralonne."

"You don't have a choice. You want the writ, and I accompany it."

Before she could speak, there was a gentle knock at the door; an expected knock. She bit her lip—bad habit, that—and looked at the mage. His legs were planted slightly apart, his arms crossed. She didn't much care for pipe smoke except on odd occasions, when the day was lazy and the hint of a father long dead was carried by it. As she was never that peaceful around him, he chose not to smoke. He'd ignored it, when she was younger. She couldn't remember, suddenly, when he'd started to pay attention.

Jewel. Markess. ATerafin.

"Meralonne—"

The door swung open.

Framed by it, frozen in place the moment her eyes lit upon Meralonne APhaniel, was the newest, and the youngest, member of Jewel's den.

Kiriel di'Ashaf.

"I see," Meralonne said softly, but completely without surprise. He gave Kiriel a bow that showed Jewel just how little respect a member of House Terafin garnered by comparison; it was a deep bow, a thing of back and head, an elegant, graceful movement that somehow seemed too fine for Imperial courtesy.

Her dark eyes moved from his bent form to Jewel's face at once.

Jewel didn't like what she saw there, but she wasn't surprised by it either. Suspicion and certainty. "I didn't send for him," she told Kiriel.

Meralonne, damn him, said nothing at all.

But then again, she didn't need his corroboration. She took a breath, feeling her age for the first time in years. Thinking that at sixteen this would have been easy, because at sixteen it wouldn't have occurred to her that someone she'd taken as one of her own could ever *doubt* her intentions. She had to find the sixteen-year-old in the thirty-three-year-old, and for the first time, realized that they weren't the same. Oh, she knew it, she'd always known it—but the intellect and the heart didn't learn at the same pace.

"Why is he here?"

"I told you about the Magisterium, right?"

"Yes."

"The Mysterium?"

"Yes."

"The Council of the Magi?"

Suspicion gave ground to irritation. "Yes. Why is he here?"

"Use of magic in the city—where it can be proved, or where it's reported—is illegal without the writs. Certain places get writs the way we get fresh bread, and you expect to suffer through magic if you go to them."

"And?"

"We need a writ of exemption."

"Then get one."

"We also need a writ of execution. In combination, if we're to—" She exhaled heavily. "Meralonne," she said. "Leave."

"No."

"Leave, or I'll summon the Chosen and have you escorted out the hard way."

His smile was thin, his gaze thinner. "I don't believe that that would be the wisest course."

"And I should care what you believe?"

Kiriel drew her sword.

It should have been silent, dammit, it *was* silent—but the sword drew the attention and held it. It was not in motion, but it was; there was about the blade an eternity of a darkness that Jewel had seen only once. Her hands were in motion as her gaze was held captive; she knew that she was drawing dagger by the cold feel of its hilt in her palm. Stopped, then, because no matter what, Kiriel was one of hers. You could hit 'em, shake 'em, shove them if you had to to get their attention—gods knew it wasn't always easy—but you didn't pull a weapon on them.

Especially when the weapon they'd pulled was theoretically pulled in your defense.

"Kiriel—"

Meralonne APhaniel did the unthinkable.

He pulled *his* sword. Or rather, he called it. And she remembered his sword. His shield was dim and ordinary, as if it could no longer be touched or tainted by magic, but his sword was a match for Kiriel's, day to its night, blue light to its black darkness.

"She asked you to leave," Kiriel said softly.

Meralonne did not reply.

"APhaniel," Jewel said, "this is a poor way to start."

"Is it?" He did not look at her; did not look away from Kiriel or the weapon she bore.

"Yes," Kiriel said softly. "There is truce between us. We fight the same enemy here."

"Then you must have no complaint about my inclusion. We are, after all, allies. Do you know who she is, Jewel?"

"Does she know," Kiriel countered, stung, "who *you* are?"

Silence.

Jewel broke it. *Jay* broke it. "Yes. I know who she is."

"Oh?"

"She's Kiriel di'Ashaf, and she's taken the only oath I ask for. She's part of my den."

His momentary surprise was palpable. It did not last. "Have you seen fit to mention this . . . shift in allegiance to The Kalakar, or her Ospreys?"

"Arann ATerafin is one of my den," Jewel replied, defiant, and irritated to be so. "He serves the House with no less binding an oath."

"You do not know the oath Kalakar requires."

"I don't much care. We're not talking about Kalakar here."

"Kiriel will be Kiriel di'Ashaf AKalakar if she serves well, and if that is her desire."

"So?"

"Jewel—"

"Meralonne, leave it be."

"No."

"I know what I—"

"You are perceptive, as befits the talent you were born to. But might I remind you that you did not see the near-death of young Teller?"

Stung, she opened—and closed—her mouth. Years under the service of The Terafin gave her at least that. "How do you know about Teller?"

His smile was disarming, not so much because it was sudden and unexpected—although it was both—but because it was almost rueful. "We are all on edge, and the edge dulls our caution and our wit," he said softly, turning to face her. "Devon."

"The man who can't choose sides," she said bitterly.

He raised a pale brow.

"But he runs to you."

"He appreciates my experience; you obviously do not. I apologize for my . . . intrusion. If you desire the writ, you will have my company—and my aid."

He sheathed his sword.

She did not, could not know, what he granted her in the face of the threat of Kiriel's sword unsheathed.

"He doesn't trust me," Kiriel said.

"No one does."

"You aren't as stupid as you look."

"Except me."

Kiriel's laugh was brief and bitter. "You mean it. That's what I don't understand. You mean it all. You even think—you even think you understand what I am, and you still mean it."

"I see it," Jewel told her, "I see what Meralonne sees in you. What he sees when you draw sword. What he sees when you smile at someone else's discomfort. Do you think I'm blind, Kiriel? I'm *seer-born*. I can't help but see it." And then, before she knew why, she added, "But I'm not the only one who both knew it and trusted you."

And the moment she said it, she *knew* it was true.

She thought Kiriel would leave the room; her hand whitened against the hilt of her sword until it seemed all of a single color, and that, ivory. But she stayed her ground; the moment passed, by common consent, before she spoke of the matter at hand. "If we refuse to hunt them, they'll kill."

"Yes."

"Then go to his Council of Magi, and tell them that. You won't take them where they need to go, so unless we go on our own, the deaths are on their heads."

"Why, Kiriel? Meralonne doesn't trust you; it's clear to me the lack of trust goes both ways. I trust you, and oddly enough, I trust him. You can work together in this. He'll come to understand it—"

"They have to understand—*he* has to understand—that we're not in their power. If we do as they say, on their orders, with no volition, if we bow to them, if we *obey*—"

"Kiriel."

The young woman met the eyes of the older one; neither looked away, although Jewel wanted to. There was something, in the lines of Kiriel's mouth, in the intensity, sudden and heated, of her words, that was feral, wild.

That was, Jewel thought, very like the kin themselves.

"If we play those games," she said slowly, as much to gather her breath as to be understood, "helpless people die. Innocent people."

"They'll die anyway," Kiriel replied, her words sharpened by certainty.

Jewel shrugged. Turned away. "I'm going to go hunting with or without you. I know the holdings—I owe you for the information, no matter what you decide—and if I don't know the exact location they've chosen to hole up in, I *know* a demon when I see it. I'll do what I can to protect you from censure; you're one of mine, and I won't desert you. But I can't make you do anything. I won't."

"You decide for yourself."

"But the magi will *win*."

"And if they do, then what? Meralonne already seems to know more about you than I do, and if he hasn't used the knowledge by now, he's keeping it to himself the same way he hoards every scrap of information that crosses his desk. What exactly happens if they, as you put it, win?"

"We'll lose."

"Yeah. We'll lose." Jewel Markess ATerafin walked across the length of a kitchen that was suddenly too small for two people.

"I'm going to talk to the mage. Join us if you want to. Stay here if you don't."

The second surprise—and annoyance—of the morning came one hour later, in the guise of a messenger, delivering the writ of execution. That writs of this nature were rarely granted was attested to by the seals that framed them, one in each corner of a rough-edged, rectangular page, joined by the finely drawn blades of swords: King Cormalyn, Queen Marieyan, King Reymalyn and Queen Siodonay the Fair.

Jewel expected the writ; indeed, she had been surprised to find that the Mysterium had responded before the Magisterium had.

What she did not expect, given the conversation of the previous eve, was Devon ATerafin. Unexpected use of her gift had taught her a few things in her time, and the one that came in most useful when her eyes lit upon the actual face of the messenger was this: To keep any surprise hidden. Devon did not stand as ATerafin in the sparsely populated—but still populated—hall that served as the entranceway to her home; there was something about his posture that was not quite right. It was an affect he was good at assuming; Devon ATerafin did not so much hide when he worked as blend in with people who were occupied with daily tedium.

She could not, however, mistake his face for anyone else's once she'd seen it; nor was she intended to. Had she been, they would have sent someone else.

"ATerafin," she said.

He stiffened. It was, in effect, an insult—and in intent. Among members of the same House, it was more than permissible to use given names—it was acknowledgement of family, of a mutual bond. His eyes narrowed, obscuring color; he bowed as stiffly as she spoke. "ATerafin," he replied.

"How may I help you?"

"I'm afraid," he said, knowing her better than Meralonne the mage ever had, "that it is I whom am put in the uncomfortable position of being forced to aid you."

Jewel had heard of the mountains in the far South that occasionally gave vent to heat and air—and she thought she know how one felt at just this moment. "You might as well stand in line and join the crowd."

"Crowd?"

"Let me guess. You've got the writ we need, and you come with it."

He shrugged, little surprised at her surmise; it was, after all, what *he* would have expected.

Or at least that's what she thought she read in the momentary shrug of his shoulders, in the unremarkable expression on his face.

Just at that moment, she loathed confident men.

Of course, that was pretty much all of the ones she had to deal with day to day. Gods, she was in a foul mood. She was also in no mood to argue with Devon; certainly in no mood to lose another argument, and sadly, certain that she *would* lose it.

But at least she had the comfort of knowing that Devon's orders were from the Kings, and not a handful of smarter-than-god-in-their-own-opinion-mages. Cold comfort was better than none.

"You might as well go into the kitchen," she told him curtly.

"Oh?"

"You can keep the mage and Kiriel from killing each other."

"Kiriel?"

She had the satisfaction of seeing a momentary astonishment ripple his brow. And the guilt that followed the indulgence of such a petty thought. "Kiriel. Devon, until the House is settled— one way or the other—we're not going to be on speaking terms. We'll be on civil terms, and certainly, we'll be allies in the bigger fight.

"Don't expect more, and don't ask for it." She wanted to close her eyes a moment; turned her back on him instead. "And as long as I don't lose any of mine in the war," she said, each word dragged out of her throat by the pull of lips into near silence, "we'll be friends again. As much friends as you're allowed to be in the role you've chosen."

"Friendship," Devon said, closer to her back than she would have thought, given that she'd heard almost no movement, "is an indulgence that you'll have less time for than I, Jewel."

"I—"

"And I suppose it is worse to have less time and a better understanding of what the word means."

She was surprised at the bitterness of his tone; not surprised enough to relent, but surprised enough to face him. He'd gone.

Damn, she thought, for no particular reason. *Damn, damn, damn.*

Teller's eyes were closed as Finch spoke, and he didn't trouble himself to open them. His hands held no slate, his fingers no quill, and thighs angled toward the ceiling were as close to the kitchen table as he was going to come for some time, if Alowan had much to say about it.

"What can she do?" he asked Finch.

Finch shrugged uneasily. "Don't know. But Jay took her in for a reason."

He nodded. "Don't worry too much about me," he said, and meant it. "They've done what they intended. Made their threat. I'm not useful now, and they wouldn't kill me in the healerie anyway." He took a deep breath, wrapped his words in it, and spoke again. "She knows what she's doing, Finch. You've seen Meralonne fight the kin before."

"Yeah. But that time we had all of the Chosen and the House Guards as backup."

But Teller knew enough of Jay to know that in this battle, she thought Kiriel di'Ashaf was a worthy replacement for almost a hundred men. He knew she was on their side; Jay had said so, and Jay's word couldn't be doubted.

But he was troubled for other reasons, because he also knew what Kiriel was: god-born. No girl, no single girl, even if she was that, should have so much power.

It was time to think about killers.

Angel came, with Jester, into the kitchen, swinging the doors smack into the wall. She hated it. Avandar's frown bit the back of her neck because she knew he hated it more. It was disrespectful, and Mandaros knew the only person who was allowed to treat her with disrespect in his eyes was Avandar himself.

But the doors' wide swing was a type of alert; they didn't have bells here, or horns, and they rarely raised their voices in shouts or screams— if you didn't count Jewel's nightmares, and she didn't.

"Jay," Angel said, without preamble.

"Sit?"

He shook his head. Stopped for just a moment to look at the white-haired mage, the grim and silent Astari, and the youngest member of Jewel's den. Jewel nodded, perceptibly and irritably, and he shrugged.

"You're not going to like it much."

"What?"

"We didn't find much in the thirty-second, or the twenty-sixth. We didn't even bother with the Common; stopped just long enough to pick up some rumors, gossip. Food," he added quickly.

"And?"

"This is the bad thing. The list of holdings you gave us—no disappearances, no strange deaths, nothing."

"None that've been leaked anyway."

"They'd be leaked—you can't hide the really bad deaths, Jay."

She shrugged. "Why's that bad?"

"Because there *have* been bodies. Disappearances and then discoveries. In the fifteenth," he told her grimly.

"What the Hells is in the—isn't the fifteenth one of the foreign quarters?"

"It's where a chunk of them hole up, yeah."

"Well, that would make sense, I guess." She turned and whispered two words to Avandar; he left the room and returned, wordless, with a rolled map.

"The fifteenth," Devon ATerafin said, as Jewel unrolled the map, "is particularly significant this year."

"Why?"

"Spoken like a Terafin," he answered. "You might remember that this *is* the time of the year for the Kings' Challenge?" At her glower, he continued. "There's a large contingent of Annagarian contestants for the Challenge this year. They train under the auspices of the only man from the South who has ever won the title."

Angel whistled. "He won it twice," he said quietly.

"How do you know that?"

"I pay attention, Jay."

"Great. So what you're saying is that one of the contestants is a demon?" She snorted. "It's not impossible, Devon. With what's happened the last two months, no demon would survive half an eye-blink if he tried to enter Avantari. There's no way they'd try it."

Kiriel, silent until then, stepped forward. "They haven't. Or if they have, he lives elsewhere."

"In one of these holdings?" Jewel said, indicating the map's penciled positions.

She nodded grimly.

"Your call," Jewel said to Devon.

"We've a watch on the Southern contestants already," he replied.

"And?"

"No."

"No what?"

"No, they don't leave the fifteenth holding—and when they do, they travel in groups of no less than six." He fell silent a moment, and then added, "a group of six men is hard to miss."

"Maybe," Angel said, "They're the killers. From what I've heard—"

Jewel lifted her hand; he subsided at once. "Where?"

"In the Common."

"That means—"

"Yeah," Jester said, speaking for the first time. "Everyone in the city knows it. Or thinks it, at any rate."

"Doesn't make any sense," Angel added. "If I were going to kidnap and kill, I'd make damned sure the bodies were dumped in another holding."

"Maybe someone did," Meralonne said softly. His eyes met Devon's across the bent heads of Jewel's den.

"Everyone in The Ten Houses has heard tell of the demon that killed the priests in the Great Hall," Finch offered helpfully. "It was trying to kill the rightful king of Annagar."

"The Tyr'agar," Kiriel said softly.

"Whatever. The point is that the demons are already known to be working for, or with, the Dominion."

Devon and Meralonne frowned, and Jewel was struck by their similarity of expression; something at once focused, intent, and cold.

"What?" she demanded, speaking to Meralonne.

"I think that whoever it is who is killing in so obvious a fash ion either knows the city well—or has been commanded by someone who does. We cannot have the Southerners killed in this city by an angry mob—"

"Seems like it would solve a lot of problems," Angel said, shrugging.

No surprise that Meralonne continued as if uninterrupted. "—and it may be that our efforts to protect Valedan—and our own—will be severely tried in the next several days; we'll be forced to split our forces to defend the very people sent to be a threat to him." He reached for his pipe, avoiding the sudden narrowing of Jewel's eyes. Stuffed it with leaf, too—but didn't quite go so far as to light it. "To put us in the position of protecting his probable would-be killers takes a . . . certain frame of mind. I would say that the girl is right: the demon will not be found among the Annagarians."

"They can take care of themselves," Angel said.

"They can be left to take care of themselves," Devon agreed, rather affably. "But if they die, they become another symbol; they are here under a peaceful flag. Valedan's cause will be hurt

by their deaths, if we ever make it as far as the Southern borders—
because they'll be Southern deaths at Northern hands during a
trial of prowess; a statement that the only way Valedan can win
the trials the Kings set is by killing the only 'true' challengers.

"You're right, Magi," he said. "Someone understands the city
well. And if it's a demon . . ."

Kiriel di'Ashaf looked up across the table, at Jewel, as if she
were a tossed ship and the den leader a momentary anchor. Her
face, Jewel thought, was perfectly white, her eyes obsidian; the
shadows surrounding her grew until Jewel could not breathe for
fear of what they presaged.

And Kiriel said, "He is."

They left two hours later.

Devon armed them, although both Meralonne and Kiriel fastidi-
ously refused the weapons he offered. There was about the group
a silence of purpose; it descended and it would not be lifted, Jewel
thought, no matter what words were spoken within its hush.

She was torn between leaving Finch and taking her, and in the
end, she chose to leave her, praying to Kalliaris for a smile, just
a smile. Haerrad was here, after all, and in some ways worse than
a demon. He was on the inside.

Angel and Jester came; Arann stayed, but Carver joined them
before they'd left the gated grounds. They walked three abreast,
ahead of her, as they'd often done, and she felt more at home,
watching their backs, than she had in months. Years, possibly.

Kiriel walked beside her to the right, Avandar to the left; Devon ATerafin and Meralonne APhaniel behind. They walked with
a light step, an easy confidence, that suggested they might be going to the Common, and no more. But Meralonne at least was
known in the high city, and what passersby there were stepped
well out of the way of any group that he accompanied.

So it began.

It should have taken time. There should have been investigations, conversations, bribery (because, alas, there were always
magisterial guards who could be wheedled into parting with information that didn't threaten the guards themselves) and threats.
There should have been a retreat then, a planning session, something official, intellectual, something that showed they had control.

But it happened quickly; quickly enough that Jewel felt as if
all steps taken, from the moment of her nightmare to the crossing

of the bridge between *Averalaan Aramarelas* and Averalaan proper, had traveled a single, fine edge. It cut her now.

Kiriel's head rose, her eyes widened. She lifted a hand, staring into a clear day's sky as if the clarity itself were a disguise, something that her god-born eyes could pierce, with work. She worked.

Jewel began to ask her a question, and Kiriel di'Ashaf lifted a hand in command; it was all Jay could do not to take a step backward. She did not stifle the small cry that escaped her lips as the darkness suddenly imposed itself upon her vision.

Nothing escaped the Astari's notice; Devon was no exception. She felt, rather than saw, his presence at her elbow. She knew it couldn't be Avandar; there was something about Avandar that was unmistakable, some unseen, but much felt familiarity that the years had built between them in place of affection and respect.

Kiriel lowered her arm.

Meralonne said, *"Kialli."* It was not a question.

The younger woman nodded, shadowed, and Jewel knew then, *knew* then, that she was more of a danger than any demon could ever be.

"We will follow, Kiriel. I only ask that you take care to remember who runs behind."

Her smile was grim, but genuine, dark, but warm. "I'm half what they are, APhaniel."

And if that means you've got more in common with us than with him, Jewel thought, and let the thought wander off; she wasn't certain where it had been going. What she was certain of was this: Kiriel di'Ashaf took to the streets of the city at a measured run; Meralonne paced her. Behind these two, Jewel's den ran, and the bustling crowd of midmorning merchants and workers alike were carried to either side in their wake.

The past grew a shadow that was longer and darker than Kiriel's receding shroud. Jewel knew how to navigate the city streets. And she knew more than most people in the city of Averalaan should ever have to know about the kin. It was the combination of these, kin and running, that drew her back across years.

Almost involuntarily she looked to the side, and saw that Devon had dropped into Kiriel's place beside her. He drew a pained smile from her by offering one in return. Fear was a taint that pulled their lips down, but it gave them the strength that running requires, and they made use of it.

After all, it wasn't as if fear was something that she wasn't going to have to get used to, one way or another. The House War.

The Southern War. And now this: Demons in the hundred holdings. It was as if time was twisting backward, and a doorway into a past that she never wanted to return to had opened to swallow all her pretensions of wisdom and experience, to strip them clean away and leave her as lean and hungry as she had ever been.

She *knew* that if they ran very quickly, they might just be in time. But she didn't know in time for what.

The fear bit her, and she bit it back with a fierce, brief grin. Bravado, but what the hell; you took what you could get at times like these.

This was the first time she'd ever run *toward* a demon.

She didn't know where they were running to until they came across the crowd. It did not, at first glimpse, seem so very different from the crowds that they had slipped through as they traveled—but it became clear, and quickly, that the difference was significant: This crowd was angry, anticipatory—and it was knotted and dense as thick undergrowth. It did not part for their passage.

"What's going on?" she called to Angel, who was taller than either she or Carver.

It was Avandar who answered. "I believe we've found a mob."

She started to say something sarcastic—at least sarcasm was the gloss that she would have put over the words—but a crackle of blue light and black fire caught her attention.

It caught everyone's. The crowd's intent shifted around the edges that contained Jewel Markess. Problem was, although she had no idea where the fireworks had come from, she had a bad feeling—and if she was right, the writ wasn't going to be a lot of use.

The humans standing in a bunch, like tightly penned cattle bound for slaughter—which Kiriel had watched with fascination as a child, beginning to end—did not move. Did not, in fact seem interested in moving. It angered her, and she reined the anger in, but she did not want to hold it. Because she knew that these people formed a ring, a protective wall of curiosity and savagery and flesh, in the center of which hid one of the kin.

The kin itself was not her concern, not exactly; she struck the master she was certain it served. No more, no less. But she had to strike *quickly*. It was too much, to be surrounded by these, with their taste for violence, their hurt and their anger, their smugness, their superiority—their savagery ready to be unleashed, barely contained at all—and not feel it herself; the desire to see violence done. To see suffering.

But she was no human to want to hide behind the guise of *justice done*. There was a blackness in them, gray and dark all, a fear and a desire, that she knew well. And she felt at home in it a moment.

She hated that.

She cried out—snarled—a guttural warning, but only three or four of those who crowded there heeded it, and she would not, could not wait; her blood bucked against her, and she rode the impulse, but only barely. She had to unleash it soon or it would devour her, and there was only one safe way to unleash it. She had to reach the kin.

She drew sword.

And Meralonne APhaniel grabbed her left shoulder.

The light flared and traveled; the darkness answered. The storm had started.

The snarl became a roar; she felt it, rather than heard it, a complexity of muscles in the length of her throat, the depth of her chest. *How dare he?* She turned.

And heard the voice.

"KIRIEL! No!"

It stopped her; opened her eyes. She saw white light and gray, felt the welcome horror of disgust and fear, and felt her own disgust and fear reply.

She was what she was.

And she was more.

Ashaf!

She had to be more, or the death meant nothing. She would not allow the death of Ashaf to mean nothing.

Swallowing her rage, choking on it, Kiriel di'Ashaf lowered her blade.

And as the rage released her vision, she realized that Meralonne APhaniel had never drawn his. His face was the color of stone; it had that hardness beneath it that goes from surface to depth without change. But his silver eyes flickered as they met hers, golden now, and glanced off, as much of a strike as either would make.

He turned as Devon reached him, and pulled out two things: the first, a medallion that she recognized: The triple moon, the whole moon quartered by the symbols of the elements, and the

second, one that she did not recognize: Crossed swords. Light
glinted off them, obscuring them as he raised them into sun's light.
As the brilliance passed, she saw that she had been wrong; the
medallion's cross was formed by sword and staff or rod. It was
bounded by crowns.

"I am Meralonne APhaniel of the Magisterium *and* of the Order of the Magi."

His words did what her sword had not been allowed to; they
parted the crowd.

People drew back as if they were curtains, and there, upon the
stage, men were fighting for their lives. Blood ran in the cracks
between hard dirt and planted stone; there were dead here already, although in what number Jewel could not immediately
say. She drew sword, although the sword was not her weapon.

Angel and Carver did likewise; Jester drew long dagger and
disappeared. Devon now carried the colors of the Magisterium,
and besides that, carried a sword with an ease that spoke of practice, experience, and the casual will to use both. His glance at Jewel
burned; his glance at Meralonne she couldn't quite catch. Just
as well.

Kiriel and Meralonne vanished into the fight; Devon began to
secure the crowd, to disperse it. It was to Devon, in the end, that
Angel was sent; Jewel took out the colors of her own House—
for she carried them, and made much of the signet ring up on her
hand, the ring that denoted her membership upon the House Terafin Council itself. Governing body. It was the first time she had
deigned to wear it since Alea's death.

She'd never thought to return to the streets as an authority.
And she blessed the privilege, although it took her away from the
fight, from Angel and Carver, from Meralonne, and especially
from Kiriel.

She'd seen that Kiriel was a killer, but she hadn't seen, until
the black and the blue, the light and the storm, how big the game
had gotten, how complete. Against her, Duster was nothing, and
nothing to control.

Later she'd remember that it was one of the few times that she'd
forgotten to worry about whether or not the rest of her den would
survive.

She had two goals, only two: the first was to save the lives of
the onlookers by scaring them the Hells off the streets. The sec-

ond was to stop Kiriel from cutting down everyone who held a sword in the circle the crowd had made.

Devon recognized the livery of the Annagarians the moment the crowd had parted at Meralonne's threatening command. This in spite of the rents therein, the blood that disfigured them. They had arrived, however, in time; they were not all dead, although of the six, he was certain that two would never walk again.

He didn't recognize the attackers; they wore nothing that identified them as anything more than citizens of Averalaan. He was certain they were citizens.

He casually slapped a man, hard, his mailed glove giving the blow an authority which sent the man flying. He disliked a mob of spectators in the same way that soldiers disliked vultures, but vultures at least had the intelligence to remain circling until the dislike had been dissolved by death.

Devon commanded as if he had been born to it; he had certainly been trained to take control of almost any situation should the need arise, and he was old enough now that there was no question about identifying the need, and none whatsoever about resolving it. But even he found himself distracted a moment when he heard the roaring that filled the streets and set the shingles that hung from the buildings closest to the crowd to swinging.

The roar, on the other hand, stopped only him; the crowd, it set to flight, accomplishing his chosen task in the space of perhaps ten seconds.

Ten seconds was more than enough time to kill a man; he knew it for a fact, although experience removed none of the urgency of death's hovering.

To the south, perhaps ten yards away, perhaps less, Angel, Carver, and Jester; Jewel and her domicis were carrying the last of the fallen Southerners to join them. It was not only the Southerners who had fallen; the Essalieyanese had perished, and in far greater numbers from the looks of the scattered bodies, than the two Annagarians.

Three of the Annagarians appeared to be tending, with caution, their fallen companion; Jewel joined them, speaking quickly and with the animation that urgency provoked in her. They responded in kind, in their fluid, foreign tongue, seeking reassurance from this child of expatriate traitors or Voyani settlers. They couldn't know which, and it was clear that they didn't care; they turned, after her reply, to watch Anton di'Guivera.

Devon followed their gaze—after all, it was only the responsibility of the moment that had taken him away from the source of the roar—to see four people. Kiriel, Meralonne, Anton di'Guivera, a man he'd much admired in his youth, and something that could not, could never, have been mistaken for a human.

Devon ATerafin had been in the Great Hall when the creature that Kiriel had called Etridian had collapsed the ceiling and destroyed by living fire the priests the Court held in highest esteem.

Kiriel knew that to lose control here was to lose what she had built, what little of it there was, in this complicated city, with its weave of lies and rich deceptions, and the truths that shone so brightly in spite of—or perhaps because of—them. Jewel watched her, and she hated the fact, but she accepted its truth: She did not want the den leader who trusted her to understand the truth, the whole truth.

And besides, this demon, this one's name spoke to her across the arc and the curve of their crossed swords. His was the subtle art, but she could sense the ties that bound him. Blood ties. It shocked her, muted some of her anger a moment—a demon of this one's power was *never* bloodbound; destruction was preferred. To bind the blood was to bind the whole. Only one creature controlled the *Kialli* against their stated whims, and he, the Lord of the Hells.

Her father.

He recognized her, this creature, and she him: Abarak. Named, his own, a lesser lord.

Whose blood? Who could force such a thing?

As if he could hear her question, he spun, and the whole of his focus was devoured by her: even Meralonne APhaniel, even he, fell beneath the range of his notice.

"You," Abarak said. He laughed. "When I send your head back to your master, he will be ill-pleased."

She saw his shadow as he saw hers, and he drew back, falling behind the sword and the sword's defense, as he began in earnest. With his shield, he shunted Meralonne aside; a mistake, but not costly enough.

He came bearing down upon her; she felt the shadow's edge devour her waiting, her desire for anonymity—and then he answered her question; he cried out in a terrible fury, a trembling of lips over perfectly formed teeth.

"He wants you . . . alive."

She did not name his master, but said, through this creature that had been made his, "Come then, and get me." And swung.

It was Jewel who saw it coming; the loss of the Kiriel that she knew to the Kiriel-that-was. She cried out to Kiriel, and knew that Kiriel was beyond her voice's reach, beyond caring for the words the voice held.

But Kiriel was a girl; she was Jewel Markess', and she had chosen. Jewel didn't give up so easily. She turned, her voice clipped and perfect, to Avandar, to Avandar who hovered above her like a shield, so unlike her den, and yet so much a part of her life.

"Hide her!" she cried.

He started and then he understood; he understood what she could not put into words in the face of the watching Southerners. *Hide her.*

She saw the distaste take his features and transform them; she was certain that asking him to slowly torture a small infant to death would have been preferable to what she had asked. But he drew on his magic, and she had seen enough of it over her life to know the color of illusion. Violet light shrouded his body with the crackle of its aura.

She trusted him, but it was a trust that had come with time; it was not what she felt, odd though it might be, for Teller or for any of the rest of her den.

The Southerners, unless they were mages themselves—and none of them bore the marks—or seer-born, saw nothing but Avandar's unnatural stiffness, and he was of such a condescending disposition that they probably wouldn't notice. Hells, most of her den wouldn't.

She had to give him one thing: He was fast.

The shadow bloomed for her eyes, for hers, and Avandar's and Meralonne's; she knew that Meralonne's eyes would pierce any illusion that Avandar could create. But she thought that Devon, that the lone Annagarian who fought, on his feet, by Meralonne and Kiriel, that Carver and Angel and Jester, would see the snarling fury of a crazed, a lunatic, killer, nothing more.

Glancing over her shoulder, she wondered if they'd even see that; they were transfixed all right, but not by Kiriel; it wasn't the familiar that tempted or held the vision.

For just a moment, as Jewel turned back to the whirling of a dark cruelty that was blade and more, she could see what they saw: the terror of the kin, and the beauty, the perfect, unutterable power that he held over life and death. He held her gaze that moment, and held the others for the duration of his shadow's bloom.

But she could see what they could not: what Kiriel was, at that moment. For the first time in years, Jewel ATerafin began to weep, quietly, in awe and fear.

She cried out his name, pinning him with it, as he cried out hers; she had no intention of leaving the site of this chosen battle until she scattered his ashes right to the doors of the Abyss itself. She saw the gray one, saw the other, darker, torn in his little human way by the life he had chosen; she threw up her hands in a final motion: this was her battle. *Hers.*

Meralonne APhaniel was not so young that he did not understand what the crying of the names meant; nor so young that he did not recognize a naming when he heard it. He was old enough to know himself a Power, and wise enough to know that power's limitations, or at least wise enough not to test it unless the cost of doing otherwise was great.

And he was wise enough to know that the lone Annagarian who stood, stunned a moment, by the twin cries, sword catching no sunlight, as if no sunlight could touch these streets again, was not a man he could sacrifice to the battle of two such as these. He was tempted; he knew what Anton di'Guivera signified, by his presence, at *this* Festival. He knew the harbinger of war.

And he knew, oddly, the duties that he had come to accept. Shielding himself from her coming wrath, he leaped above the battle to the kin's flank, and there, rolled into Anton di'Guivera, taking care to protect himself from the certain edge of the swordmaster's reflex. The swordmaster's steel.

He carried them both to safety—such as it was—before the cobbled stones erupted in a spray that shattered glass and pocked wood and masonry down the length and breadth of the street.

They were smart enough to leave her alone when she cried. Angel. Carver. Jester. Even Avandar. They knew.

She watched, her vision blurred by sheen of water, as these two fought, seeing no swords now, no physical blows; seeing in their movements the movements of oceans, of mountains. It was over; she knew it must be over; she held her breath a moment as the hum of names—for there were two, twining round the fight in a circle made somehow of sound, some twisted, bardic working—broke and faded until one remained.

She had never doubted which name that would be.

Kiriel.

Kiriel roared, and the streets shook.

Now, Jewel thought, weeping, and wiping her eyes with the folds of a shirt she'd thought too heavy for the summer's humidity. Now. She straightened out at the knees, rising, as the name began to grow in volume.

Now.

Still, she hesitated.

And so it was that the half-god in glory met the gaze of the slender, fragile woman who moments ago had been her only concern. She stood, the outline of her sword coalescing slowly as the sun reached its height, stood wavering, as if the sunlight at its height was still a thing to be denied.

It was good to be here and to be victorious, and to let that victory be known. It was good because there were others, and she meant them to understand her intent.

She turned, she was ready to leave, and saw the face of the woman, and she noticed that the face was smooth, but the lines around the eyes were somehow deeper, that the eyes themselves, dark enough to be mistaken for black by anyone but Kiriel, were rounded and reddened.

Reddened, she thought, with weeping.

Weakened, she knew, by fear.

Because she did not want to remember it, it took her moments to acknowledge that she had seen this before. Or perhaps it wasn't denial, perhaps it was due to the differences between the face of that woman, that older, that dead, woman and this one.

"Kiriel," this woman said, her voice nothing like the other woman's voice. It pained her, to hear the difference, when the expression was so exactly the same.

She wanted to be cruel; she could feel the ability to wound with words, and words alone, that would be far more painful than the dissolution she had inflicted upon the kin whose name the silence had taken. The shadow filled her eyes, touched her lips, moved her hair as if it were the charnel wind.

She spoke.

"Jewel."

"You've finished," Jewel said. "You don't have to do this anymore."

It wasn't what she'd thought to hear. She didn't know what she'd thought to hear. What had Ashaf said?

"I didn't come all this way to learn how to love—"

Ashaf was frightened, but she struggled to hide her fear behind the mask of anger, as if Kiriel couldn't sense fear better than she could sense life.

"I won't have you do this, Kiriel. I can't stay to see this." Her body was bent by the weight of the words; by the weight of the sight of the daughter, Kiriel knew, of the Lord of Night. Evil Incarnate, if Ashaf understood what evil meant at all.

Kiriel stood by the window. She turned her back to Ashaf; turned it to the waning moon's slight face, scant light. "What," she said to this momentary stranger, "would you have of me?" She lifted her hand and shadows filled it, and she knew that if she learned a bit more, just a bit more, she could unlock them all, all the shadows that were her birthright, and she never need fear the Court, human or kin, again.

It was the night after her investiture. The ceremony of Allasakar. The rites of passage. And Kiriel had survived them, and more. She was not the girl that she had been. Time, then, and time perhaps finally, for Ashaf to recognize this and have done.

"I don't—I'd have you give it up," Ashaf said then, and the tears started. "You have what you had. You have Falloran—"

"Falloran is the Hells' version of an ignorant beast. Kept in check by compulsion, *bloodbound* to serve me, probably stupefied into thinking that that's what he wants."

"But you—"

"Ashaf, I'm not human. If you came here thinking you could make me human, you're a fool, and you always were one."

Oh, she remembered the saying of those words, and they cut her and cut her and cut her because she remembered the dark joy the pain they caused brought. Because she hadn't meant to say them, and then, having said them, she was stopped from taking them back because of the heightened sensation, the *awareness* of the fact that they did hurt, they could hurt.

Regret and pleasure.

Pleasure and anger.

The shadows fled at once, done, drained by her need to scour herself clean of the taint that brought those memories back.

But she was fooling herself; she was as much a fool as Ashaf had ever been, and ever would be, had she survived her stupidity. She was never free, never clean; they were with her, her father's gifts.

I came, Ashaf had said, with dignity, although the pain made her wrap her arms around herself and take a step back, *because I knew how to love you.*

And then she was gone. The triumph of the night was gone with her, gone with the warmth that she alone carried. Had Kiriel forgotten that warmth? Yes. For just long enough. For long enough.

She looked up, diminished, at the woman that she had led here. She spoke again, and again, she chose to express herself with a single word.

"Jay."

Jewel Markess stretched out an open hand, and after a moment, hesitant and suddenly far too tired, Kiriel di'Ashaf took it.

The sun was high, the shadows as short as they would be all day.

A continent away, surrounded by the blight of rock and lifeless waste, the towers rose, and he rose with them, taken by wind's whim to the heights.

He had witnessed the fight; the fight itself stirred some ember of something akin to pride; pride, after all, was no stranger to the *Kialli* race that had once walked these lands. It was no stranger to them when they ruled in the Hells, and human pride, he thought, was infinitely lessened without the *Kialli* to set a fitting example.

It was an idle thought; Lord Isladar of no demesne did not cherish idle thought. He had watched Kiriel fight; that pleased him.

What had not, did not, please him was what occurred after the circle of names had been broken: The human woman.

He had already suffered a setback—the only setback—because of the designs of a single, ignorant woman, and he ill-liked the notion that he might suffer as much again; for Ashaf kep'Valente had been confined to the rules and the laws of the Hells, her influence broken by the lessons and the strictures that survival placed upon their mutual charge.

The wet tuft of cloud distracted him; the coldness of the high air.

The demon that not even demons understood spun in wind, came, slowly but surely, to face the south and east, a single name upon his lips, two words.

Jewel. Jay.

CHAPTER NINE

16th of Lattan, 427 AA
Averalaan, Fifteenth Holding

Ser Anton di'Guivera was wounded; he felt his age keenly as those wounds were washed and dressed by the hands of the physicians he had brought with him. It had been many, many years since he had taken a mark in a fight.

Many years, indeed, since he had fought in earnest. A man could forget, over the years, that a fight was something less— and more— than art; it was, in the end, about living and dying. Winning or losing were only pale echoes of the twisted braid of survival, after all.

But it truly galled him to be here, beneath the Lord's gaze, solely because Northern Swords had chosen that moment to interfere. There was no question whatever in the mind of Anton di'Guivera—or those that had survived the attack of the mob of angry peasants—that they had lost the fight; what remained to them was only the chance to make their enemy's victory as costly as possible.

"Enough, Mikal. Enough. Go away and leave me alone."

The doctor sputtered like an angry cat, but he had argued enough for one day; he pinned the bandages perhaps a bit less carefully than he might otherwise have done, and left. Anton di'Guivera was not known in the Dominion for his forgiving temper, and for good reason, although it was true that his demands were far less exacting than those of the members of the court proper. Mikal sputtered and argued with Anton; he would not have dared that with other men. The Tyr'agar. The Tyr'agnati. The Tors. He, Anton, had never had those pretensions, and because he did not, he felt free to see through the pretensions of others. They were men of power, after all, and men of power made poor allies to the unwary.

He rose and retrieved his sword.

Girded himself stiffly, feeling the ache in his side that would not leave him from this day until he returned to the drier air of the South. Wounds did that in this unnatural clime.

He could taste the salt in the air; it parched him, and he hated it. He hated much.

Including the duty—the only duty, other than the art that he lived for, the shaping of warriors—that he had chosen for himself on this, the last day before the start of the Challenge itself. It was with great distaste that he called for pen, for paper, for ink. His penmanship was not good; he was considered of the court, but the prettier skills of the men therein had eluded both his interest and his time. He knew how to speak well, and speech was the medium of communication in the Dominion. But here he had no serafs to send with a message—and there, in the rooms of a palace not meant to house the Lord's men, Ramiro di'Callesta had no serafs to receive it. They were both bound by the stupidities of this kingdom.

Instead, he sent a man out into the streets to find one of the Northerners. It took half an hour—the Northerners were angry indeed at the deaths that were occurring in this quarter, and they chose to blame it upon his students. Himself.

Had he expected justice from them? Had he believed that North was any more fair a place to live than South? It was myth, as all else about the city was. The Lord was not worshiped here, but he saw all.

The Lord.

Anton di'Guivera had made a life in the Lord's service. A name. A legend, of a type. The Lord's service.

The anger was still too new to him to be easily shunted aside once he had stepped upon its path; he shied, turned, fell back into what was left him: his role. He was master here, and he knew, better than any, what the cost and the benefit of a life wed to the sword was.

Duty. The writing of a message.

The message was eventually taken up, eventually delivered; he was certain it would be. If not by an urchin of ill-repute, then something better: his enemy's spies. They were, after all, watching his every move.

"What does this mean?" Fillipo par di'Callesta passed the letter back to his brother. "Are you certain it's genuine?"

"Yes."

"Why? I don't recall that either of us have ever seen Anton di'Guivera's writing, and it seems with good reason."

Ramiro nodded absently; the writing itself, blocky and ink-heavy, was graceless at best. "I am certain it is genuine," he said, as his brother started to ask the question again, "because it was delivered by members of the Crowns' personal guards from the hands of Anton himself."

"What?"

"No one in the quarter was willing to carry the message for any price they were willing to pay; it was eventually taken by one of the boys who've been set to watch the building."

"Was it sealed?"

"Yes, although not well."

"Broken?"

"No. Which means we can expect a visit, although from which of the Kings' servants, I'm not certain."

Fillipo was silent as he studied the curt sentences; there were two. One was what might pass for a civil greeting in a Terrean court, and the other, a stiff request, made of Ramiro di'Callesta. He desired, he said, a meeting. "Will you attend him?"

"Yes. If he wishes to speak with me in person, I will go."

"Why did he not summon the General?"

"An interesting question. I don't know the answer." Ramiro disliked, on principle, any profession of ignorance. But he was a practical man, when among kin whom he trusted—and he trusted none as well as this pair.

"Ah," Fillipo said, looking over Ramiro di'Callesta's shoulder. "Your answer."

The Tyr'agnate turned as the sound of booted feet against flat stone grew louder. He was curious.

From the far end of the courtyard, shadowed by the wall in this early morning sun, came Commander Sivari, accompanied by Princess Mirialyn ACormaris.

"I would say," he said quietly to his brother as they approached, "that they already know the reason for the summons, and that we are about to hear the first of it now."

Commander Sivari bowed stiffly, the Princess who was also ACormaris, fluidly. They wore armor and bore arms as casually as did any Tyran, and they carried themselves as men of import might. Even the Princess, especially the Princess. She was not self-conscious, and Ramiro was certain that she had never been, in her life, victim of that foible of uncertain youth. She was so close to her grandfather in temperament that he wondered that any blood separated them at all.

But it did; she was the blood child of one of the two men who now ruled this Empire, and she would never live to take his place. Instead, they would turn over the thrones upon which they sat to the children of the wives they had chosen—the children of their fathers.

Ramiro was not a suspicious man; he could not afford to be so ignorant and yet deal with the North. He knew what they professed the golden-eyed to be, and as he had a man whom he trusted in steady contact with the periphery of that profession, he had come to understand that in some wise, the gods of the Empire *were* gods.

And it was not that the kings were golden-eyed that disturbed the Tyr'agnate. It was that they could, with equanimity, surrender their *wives*—not their concubines, or mistresses as they were called here, but the women through whom the legitimacy of rule *must* pass—to their *fathers*. The thought made him grimace with distaste.

The women they chose would raise their half brothers to prominence. And to this, this very rare, this legitimate child, what would fall?

Nothing.

Nor in the South had she been born there, if he was honest; there was something so clean, so sharp and straight about her, that he could forget that she was in fact a woman, and not just in seeming. But in the South, she would be bartered for marriage, and the line would pass to an uncle, or perhaps an illegitimate son. Was that truly so very much more difficult than this, the bloodline passed over?

They rose, and he left his musing; he did not grant the Princess any show of his momentary discomfort. For she was, if not to rule, then to guide, and her father listened to her above almost any other adviser when she chose to give her advice—or so it was said.

But it was said by the Serra Alina, and that meant something.

"A long bow, ACormaris," he said softly. "The news you bring, or perhaps the inquiry, is prefaced by little good, I fear."

Her smile was brief and genuine, a flash of white in the open sun. "By no good whatsoever, depending on how you feel about the man who penned that message."

"Do you know its contents?"

"No."

He believed her, although he knew it would be possible to ascertain the gist of the message without breaking the seal; there were mages here, and in number, that served when the Kings commanded. In all, he thought, a larger organization than the Sword of Knowledge—but somewhat less cumbersome; they had been brought to bear, and they obeyed. No one controlled the Sword's Edge.

"It is short," he said, "and to the point, not unlike the man himself. He wishes my attendance at the hall during the Lord's hour."

"No sane Southerner travels during the Lord's hour."

"He knows," the Tyr'agnate said with a smile, "that the ruler of Averda is a man from the Northern clime." The smile that he returned was briefer than hers but not less felt. When it vanished, however, it was gone. Smiles rarely found a lasting purchase in the lines of his face. "Why does he wish to see me?"

Sivari looked toward her, but she was steel; she did not meet his quick glance. "Yesterday afternoon there was an incident in the fifteenth holding."

"That would be the holding where Anton currently resides."

"Where most of the Southerners reside," Sivari added.

"Indeed. What incident?"

Before she could respond—and indeed, she made no attempt to reply—another man entered the courtyard. And it was to his surprise that Ramiro found himself mistaking the untried Valedan kai di'Leonne for a man. His stride, perhaps, his bearing? He was not certain, for when he recognized the face, his impression was once again that of youth that has taken no scars and made no history.

And that youth was his future. He knelt at once to the ground; his brother knelt also, to the right and behind, as befit the captain of his Tyran. Fillipo had not filled that role for years, but there were habits that were etched in a man so deeply they were not lost.

Ramiro was pleased.

"Rise," Valedan said and they obeyed with ease; Ramiro was not used to the rigors of the inferior position, and his knees were not so young as they had once been.

'Tyr'agar," Mirialyn said, and she bowed, offering him the

respect that she granted her father, but not more. "Thank you for granting my request." Turning, she said, "we can begin now."

"I see."

"In the fifteenth holding, for the last week, bodies have been discovered. They are always bodies of citizens who are not Southern in either descent or birth, and they are always hideously disfigured, horribly killed."

"A body can be disfigured after death."

"Yes. And these were not."

"I see." And he did. His expression was grim. "These murders are being blamed, no doubt, upon the Annagarians in that quarter."

"I wish I could say they were not. It is an internal matter, Tyr'agnate, and I would not have brought it to your attention for that reason. The officials have taken the situation into hand."

"I see. What has this to do with the Tyr'agar and myself?"

"Yesterday, a mob attacked six men."

"Six—" He raised a hand to his forehead. "Continue, please."

"One was killed, one crippled unless his family can afford the price a healer will charge. And yes, they were men who had come to the North for the Crowns' Challenge. Anton di'Guivera was one of the six."

"I see."

"It is . . . slightly more complicated than that."

"That is not in and of itself complicated," Ramiro said quietly. "Had Anton di'Guivera died, it might have served our purpose, or the purpose of the Tyr'agar, whether or not he would desire such a death." The last he added for Valedan's sake; Valedan had about him the Northern taint, and perhaps for that reason, that combined with his youth, he was not a practical, nor a political, boy.

She nodded. "That was the preface."

"Is there more?"

"Yes, and it is . . . unfortunate."

"ACormaris, you are oblique. It is both refreshing and unlike you."

"Very well. The mob was led by a demon. It was his intent to destroy the Annagarians, or so it seems."

"So it seems?"

"The creature was destroyed before it could complete its attack. We believe—although we have not yet confirmed—that it was neither here alone, nor working on its own."

He took the words in quickly, digested them. Spoke. "You believe the creature was responsible for the deaths that are being blamed upon my distant compatriots."

"Yes."

"Why is it here?"

"If you mean by that, do we know who summoned it, then the answer is simple: No. The streets are being combed by our own forces, and the citizens in the holdings are becoming both fearful and angry; the story spreads, and as is common, grows out of proportion."

And it was not, Ramiro thought, within a reasonable proportion to begin with, as far as much incidents went. He said nothing.

"We are therefore put in the position of being forced to defend the contenders."

He shrugged.

"It is difficult, within the holdings there are too many elements that are outside of our control. We therefore desire you to offer Anton di'Guivera the protection of *Avantari*."

"No."

"Tyr'agnate—"

"No."

"We can watch them well from here."

"You cannot watch Anton; he is too dangerous."

It was Valedan who spoke. "They are splitting the forces they will need to protect *our* interests in their attempts to protect these men."

"They will split those forces anyway," Ramiro replied, wishing for a moment that Baredan were beside him. "We are not the only Southerners in the quarter."

"*They* are not," Valedan said. "But the deaths are occurring— or the bodies are being discovered—around that hall." He was quiet a moment. "I ask it, Tyr'agnate."

"You wish to see Anton di'Guivera here? He means your death, Tyr'agar."

"Indeed. But if anyone is to be my death, it will not be Anton." He paused. "I have seen him fight, three times, when my brother was training. I was young. He was—the best."

"Tyr'agar—"

"Tyr'agnate." He took a breath. Held it a moment, and then released it around carefully chosen words. "The kin are not here to cause trouble for Anton di'Guivera. They are here, we believe, to kill me—and they will choose some point, or points, along the marathon's course to launch their attack.

"If our forces are spread across the the fifteenth holding until the final moment, they will be in conflict with citizens, they will be injured, or forced to injure, their own. How well will they protect me?"

"They will not be split when Anton and his men join the Challenge."

"Anton is not running the marathon; neither are most of his men. They will no doubt be training for the test of the sword—and they will train in the fifteenth. The Imperials will not follow the marathon; once they have seen some portion of it passing—or perhaps before or after—they will take things into their own hands. Perhaps with encouragement."

"Are any of his men running the marathon?"

"Two. There would have been three."

"I see. I understand your concern, Tyr'agar, but must say that I continue to think it ill-advised. If they cannot protect themselves, let them perish. They mean you harm."

"They are the message I will send to the General Alesso di' Marente. They *must* survive to carry it."

At that, for the first time, Ramiro smiled. "You have an edge, Tyr'agar, that you hide too well. Very well. If you insist, I will offer. But Anton di'Guivera is a man with his own mind, and if he refuses, the refusal cannot be ignored or overridden by any but the Tyr'agar." He stopped a moment as he realized that he had made a very rare mistake. Because, of course, there was only one Tyr'agar—the boy he had offered *Bloodhame* to.

"By the Tyr'agar," Valedan said smoothly, "of his choice. Understood. But you will do your best, and the best effort of the Callestans very seldom ends in failure."

Ramiro bowed; there was nothing left to say.

In the valleys, there were wolves, and in the depths, sharks; in the high lands there were the great cats, and in the jungles as well. But the desert? What hunter did the desert breed?

Only men; the Lord saved his ferocity in the face of the sands and the wind for desert men. They were, or so it was said in the South, his finest. Anton di'Guivera had spent half his youth in the desert; the insignificant part of it. Leaving the desert for the milder climate that lapped at its edges, he found the woman who was to be his life: His first life, with child, when the weight of responsibility had descended upon him, when he had realized that that boy, that woman, were his not only to defend against any outsiders who meant them ill, but also to feed, to clothe, to shelter, and be as gentle with as he could.

It had been an odd thought for a man raised to the sword—born to it, as his uncle had often said—perhaps even an unmanning one. He had struggled against the deep humiliation of it, and in the end, in the end he had chosen to hide it as he could from men who might otherwise perceive it as a weakness. For seeing weakness, they felt obliged to exploit it—and who could blame them? It was the Lord's law, after all; the Lord's will. The strong ruled, and the weaker obeyed.

Yet she had, hidden, been his strength.

As she was now.

Mari. Her name. *Antoni.* His son's. Not a good name for a child; too hard to make into the diminutives that made of a boy a thing a woman could love. But they'd managed, and besides, it was, as his wife obstinately insisted, a fine name for a man. Her husband's name. His own.

Their child would have been better served by a boy's name; he had not survived to take on the man's.

Aie, it did him no good, to fret and wait. His men knew he was distracted, and he knew they thought it was due to the encounter with the foreign creature, the unnamed thing that had darkened the streets with Southern blood. Perhaps some part of it was. They did not know what he knew, and if they had, they would not have credited it with his discomfort—for Mari was a woman, and only a woman, and Anton di'Guivera was the finest swordmaster in all of the Dominion.

His sword was sheathed; he folded arms across his chest to watch the interplay of swords unfold before him: two men. He lost their names because their names did not matter. He knew how they gripped a sword, how they swung it, what their faces looked like before a feint, a parry, a strike—it was one of the first things he tried to lessen. He also knew that this was not a true test, this sparring; these men knew each other well enough by now to dance the sword-dance if they so chose.

Of course, if they did, he'd have to kill one of them. They could not be wasted on such frivolity, such useless purity of purpose. They were here for one reason: to serve the interests of the Dominion. And of Anton di'Guivera—a gift, of sorts, from the General Alesso di'Marente. A gift and an order.

What did it mean?

The presence of the demon he could attribute to the Northerners and their desire to protect their puppet—the last of a broken line. But the presence of their high clans? No. He'd seen the girl, and he knew the crest that marked her finger in gold and gold relief, for he knew the crests of the Ten Families. They had flown in their time in the Tor Leonne, until the ill-advised slaughter.

Terafin. The House that fancied itself first among equals. He knew what the raised ring meant, be it wielded by woman's hand or no: She was of import, and she would be obeyed.

Yet why send a demon to kill, only to intervene?

Politics?

Did they truly think that he was naive enough to trust in such coincidental salvation?

And yet. And yet. There were rumors. And the Northerners had proved—with one exception in their history that he was aware of, the *Black Ospreys*—that they had no stomach to sacrifice their own for the greater good of victory.

What would you do, Ser Anton? What would you do to finally avenge the deaths of your wife and your son?

Anything.

He bowed his head; the flash of steel caught it. Almost grateful, he fell into the fight and the lines of the fight; it was more natural to him than anything but breathing.

Anything.

Ramiro kai di'Callesta traveled with four of his Tyran, but it was noted immediately by the men who barred his entrance into the hall itself that one of these four was the captain of the Callestan Tyran: Fillipo par di'Callesta, the favored brother.

An escort of Imperial Swords stood in loose formation around the building itself; they had seen to the safe travel of the Annagarian clansmen, for they did not trust their commoners to behave. Fillipo could understand that reluctance; in the streets of this holding, and the one previous to it that they had passed through, the mood was grim. Four Tyran, armed with swords, were likely proof against it—provided no supernatural occurrence came to the aid of men who lifted not swords but common implements, as weapons.

"The Tyr'agnate Ramiro kai di'Callesta is here at the request of Ser Anton di'Guivera," Fillipo said smoothly. "As the summons requested speed, we have come quickly; it would do neither of us good to keep the Tyr'agnate waiting."

The cerdan exchanged a glance; the older man nodded slightly. "Wait here," he said, but it was formality.

They waited less than five minutes before they were granted entrance.

"Ser Anton wishes," the cerdan who had stood guard said, "to speak to you in private."

"I bring only my Tyran," Ramiro said softly.

"He wishes me to say that he will have no cerdan in attendance."

"Nonetheless," Ramiro replied, "Ser Anton knows that in any but one's own territory, it is considered impolite—and even impolitic—to ask a man to strip himself of his guards. These are *Tyran*, and they are not Leonne. They serve my interests."

It was meant as an insult not so much to the clan Leonne but to the men who ruled in its stead through the treachery of Tyran. Such treachery was one of the few that was—almost—unthinkable, even in the Dominion. The man stiffened slightly. But he nodded and said merely, "Follow."

As a concession, Ramiro chose to bring only the captain of his oathguards into the meeting with the man who had once trained Tyrs. The Tyr'agnate was known for his practicality, and the room that Anton had chosen—a small thing with one window, and it unglassed—would not comfortably accommodate a single man; five were out of the question. He did not stoop to wonder if it had been planned; Ser Anton had chosen the only space in the open hall that was enclosed.

The swordmaster bowed.

The Tyr'agnate bowed.

They were both perfectly correct, which was surprising, if one knew the swordmaster.

"Please," Anton said. "Sit." He gestured to the cushions that lent the room its only color. "Water?"

"Thank you, but no."

Ser Anton nodded gruffly; he poured for himself, clumsily; water dripped down the goblet's side to the planks of the rough, low table.

"It's only at times like this that I truly appreciate a good seraf. Lord's lesson. All clansmen should be forced to come North at least once in their life." He sat.

They were not comfortable in their silence, although both men had been raised to it. "You summoned me," Ramiro said at last, at the same moment as Anton said, "You wonder why I summoned you."

It was awkward; the Tyr'agnate was not used to awkwardness. He was also unused to the company of the swordmaster. They all were; the man avoided the court assiduously; he was to be found in the sun, beneath the Lord's full gaze, working always with the sword and its students. They watched him, they listened to him, but they did not converse with him, in part because he was like a sword, and they did not wish to be the cause of his death. He had never quite mastered the art of politic intercourse. Nor, Ramiro thought, watching him drink, would he.

But there were none here who would remark upon any offense he gave, intentionally or unintentionally, for Fillipo would not.

"I wondered, yes," Ramiro said neutrally. "We have chosen our sides, Ser Anton."

"Yes. But this . . . war . . . is not a sword, and I am most comfortable with them. There are more than the two sides, many more, and each has its complexities and offers its death to the unwary.

"You said, Tyr'agnate, that I should not believe all I have been told."

"Yes, I did. I note that you did not summon the General."

"No. He is what he has always been, and well chosen; he has cunning, but in truth, he has the heart of a Tyran." At this, his lips folded up slightly in a smile. "I mean by that no offense, Ser Fillipo."

"And had you, I would still take none."

"He follows his master, and I believe that he has chosen poorly; it will be his death."

"It has not been his death yet," Ramiro said softly, "and greater odds were against him for that first attempt than you will be able to muster again."

"True enough. I did not say he was a fool, not precisely. He has cunning and wit and determination—but it is coin offered to another and not spent on his own behalf. Enough. I did not summon you to speak to you of Baredan di'Navarre; he will not listen, and you will have your own use for him."

"Very well. What is of urgency?"

"You will, no doubt, have received some intelligence of the . . . difficulty."

"Yesterday's?"

"The very one."

"Yes."

"I was inclined to think it an attempt at either assassination, manipulation, or both."

Ramiro was silent as he accepted and digested the words, as he built the interior, the political vision, of another man's mind, testing it against his prior knowledge.

"But I understand the foreign tongue," Anton continued. "I have forgotten much of it over time—but I learned it when I came to the Challenge, the first one. Language is part of an enemy's arsenal."

"I have often said the same, but I am treated with contempt."

"It was only the language I adopted," Anton replied.

Fillipo bristled slightly; Ramiro did not even darken. It was an old accusation, so oft-considered that it bothered him only slightly more than a discourse about the color of his hair might have in its inanity.

"You heard something yesterday."

"Yes. It appears that the people who chose to attack us were accusing us—and the Dominion—of allying itself with a god the Northerners fear and have fought. Allasakar. They called us *Allasakari;* they claimed to be avenging their dead."

"This is unlike you, Anton. The Northern gods are not our concern."

"They are. Or you do not understand the language so well as you think."

"The language is not concerned with the worship of foreign gods."

"Only commerce, eh?"

Again, Fillipo tensed. "Rational commerce, yes."

"What a man worships or fears *defines* him. I am surprised that you do not remember this."

That was an insult. "I remember it well enough, Anton." He spoke his words on the edge.

"Very well. *Allasakar* is the name they give the Lord of Night."

Silence. Fillipo met his kai's glance and looked away, toward the light streaming in through midday windows. The air was still, although no Northern glass blocked its entrance into the room where the three men stood.

"You know what I speak of."

"No."

"You know what *they* spoke of, then. You understand their accusation."

Again the brothers exchanged a glance. "Yes," Ramiro said at last. "You know of the deaths in the quarter?"

"Peripherally, until yesterday; I am fully apprised of them now. It was not, I think, of those deaths that they spoke."

"I believe that it was. But the men for whom you toil miscalculated as well."

"That is surprising."

"Perhaps. During times of crisis, the Kings of this land meet with their counselors, their advisers, their—*citizens.*" He used the foreign word because it was the only word he could use; Torra did not contain the concept well. "Among those are priests." He shrugged. "A demon was sent into their midst during one such meeting, and it slaughtered many before it made its escape." He rose. "If that will be all?"

Anton nodded quietly. "But one question, Tyr'agnate."

"Indeed?"

"Why had the Kings gathered?"

Ramiro said nothing. Fillipo said, "Tell him, Ramiro."

"No."

"Tell him."

"Why? Will it reveal anything that will aid our cause?"

"Tell him, or I will. We owe the boy that much."

"I advise against it, Fillipo."

"Command against it, brother."

Ramiro was silent.

"You were present, no doubt, for the slaughter of the hostages in the Tor Leonne." Fillipo's voice could not—quite—cleanse itself of an angry contempt. "That certainly was the act of true warriors—a paeon to the Lord and his law."

But if he hoped to discomfit Anton—and it was clear that he did—he made no mark; the swordmaster was already parrying, and in silence.

After an angry moment, Fillipo continued. "We were meant to be slaughtered for the slaughter, a convenient instrument of vengeance. We were gathered in an open courtyard like so much cattle, and left to wait upon death.

"But Valedan kai di'Leonne chose to assume the title that his father's death, and his kai's death, dropped upon him, and he sent both a summons and a challenge to the Kings' Court."

At that, Anton raised a brow. "And you will tell me that this was not your doing?"

"No. I will not insult your intelligence, although it is tempting. It was, indeed, my intent."

"Then—"

"He took the title, and he took our oaths beneath the open sky."

"And you had weapons with which to offer it?"

"Of a kind." Fillipo shrugged. "He was granted his audience, and that audience was not before the Kings alone, but before their counselors; the mighty of the realm. He spoke for us, and against their action, and in the end, the Kings granted him his life, and his line's life."

"I see. Obviously, yours as well."

"No. Our deaths were mandated."

"The condemned are not given free run of the city," Anton said dryly.

"They are not. The kai Leonne refused to stand apart."

"What?"

"He refused to stand apart. Granted his life, he chose to stand with the men whose oaths he had taken."

"Ah. I see. Another fool."

Fillipo fell silent. His face was reddened, but the words that might have accompanied the anger did not follow in the presence of his brother. "Yes. A fool. He held *Bloodhame* when the Tyr'agnate came into the hall as witness, as proof that not all of the Tyrs supported the slaughter. He held *Bloodhame* when the servant of the Lord of Night came up through the marble floor as if it were a thin layer of water or oil; he stood his ground when that creature attempted his destruction.

"Do you remember your history, Ser Anton? *Bloodhame* was created for another war, by a greater swordsman than even you. And *Bloodhame* knows the truth of it; that the kin of demons was sent against Leonne, and it failed, as it did when Leonne first rose against the darkness at the Lord's behest. Had we not chosen to follow the kai Leonne before, what choice have we now? The Lord of Night works against him, and we will not turn Averda over to the Lord of Night again. Not while a single Callestan still bleeds.

"You are the fool," he said at last, but coolly now. "For you serve the Lord of Night, whether or not you wish to acknowledge it. Go down in darkness, Anton, and let it devour your body; it has already devoured the rest of you."

He turned then, and made his way to the small door that stood in place of hangings.

"Ser Fillipo?"

"Yes?" he answered, although he did not turn.

"You speak with a great deal of passion, and yet if I were to guess, I would say that it was not you, but your brother alone, who was in that hall."

"You would guess poorly," Fillipo said. "I was not in that room, not present—but the Tyran were, and they are as much a part of me as my sword is. What they saw, they spoke of, and what they spoke of was truth." He did not turn. "Lord's light," he said softly.

Ramiro heard the rest of the curse. *Scorch you.* He did not call his brother back; it was a dramatic, even a reasonable exit—for one who did not have the duties of Tyran to uphold. But he would not humiliate his brother in public if his own actions had not already achieved that. Judging by the expression on the swordmaster's face, they had not, by some miracle.

Ser Anton di'Guivera was silent a long time.

At last he rose, stiffly and heavily. "I thank you," he said, "for your attendance."

"I have one other duty, Ser Anton."

"And that?"

"I have been asked to convey an offer of hospitality to you and the men whom you train."

"And that?"

"You are to be given a hall upon the grounds of *Avantari,* the home of the demon kings. There are training grounds there, and ample protection against—distraction."

Anton's smile was thin. "And a chance, no doubt, to observe us before the fact."

"No doubt. Although if you think you have been unobserved here, you are almost as naive as you would have Baredan be." Ramiro di'Callesta rose. "I hope that you will consider what the captain of my oathguards has said. And I hope that you will consider the offer made to you."

Anton said, "I have. And I believe, Tyr'agnate, that I will do you the discomfort of accepting it."

Serra Alina was quiet.

It was not, as it would be with many of the younger ladies of the Imperial Courts, a bad sign in and of itself, but the Serra had taught Valedan, by both instruction and the far more valuable example, that every silence had about it a quality of its own, a hidden portent if one knew the person well enough to know how to look, and how to listen, to the things that were not said.

The things that were not said, today, were wrapped about her like the finest of silks.

"Alina," he said at last, when it was clear that her silence was not for the gathering of words, but for the keeping of them, "what's wrong?"

She did not like to lie to him, or so he believed; she said nothing.

"Serra Alina?"

But she could not choose to say nothing forever—not without offending the rank she was trying, by example, to teach him to honor. "It is Ser Anton," she said quietly.

"You do not want him in *Avantari*."

"I would be happy," she replied, "if he had perished in the fighting. Happier still if he had perished before he brought his chosen students to the North." She rose then, lifting a crystal decanter, a thing she said was different from the niceties of life in the home he would return to.

"Why?"

"It is clear to me that he has been sent, as he was before, to prove a point. But it is not to prove that point to the Empire; here, he has nothing to gain. He has been sent with men of quality to take the Crown of the Challenge. To prove that it was Leonne weakness, and not Annagarian training, or its lack, that has always been at the heart of our poor performance here."

"Alina," Valedan replied softly, "that much is obvious to me."

"Then think, Valedan," she said, with a hint of her old sharpness, her scratched pride, "what it means. He has these men, the best, and they did not perform in the Lord's Test. Think: He has been training them in the tasks of the *North*. For how long?"

He started to speak, but having begun, he saw that she meant to continue.

She turned away from him to the open window, to the sunlight of the late afternoon, the lengthening shadows. "He is there among them, even now," she said softly. "He speaks to Mauro and to Kyro, he courts them; he talks with Ramiro's Tyran, with Fillipo—with everyone but you."

Valedan shrugged. "He serves a different man, Alina. We did not expect that he would come to us to pay his respects."

"No. But he *is* respected, Valedan. He has that in the Dominion, and he will always have it. He is no Court politician; he is more dangerous than that. It is not to the head that he speaks—

not the rulers, not the Tyrs or the Tors. It is to the heart. He is an
enemy, Valedan."

"Alina, I know this."

She turned to face him again, white as the Northern Queen. "It
was his hand," she said softly. She waited for the understanding,
but it did not come; her pupil, and her lord, waited patiently for
the words the silence did contain.

"It was his hand," she repeated at last, "that killed the Tyr'
agar, Markaso kai di'Leonne."

He rose, then. Bowed stiffly. "Serra," he said gravely.

He left.

The sun in the North was hotter than he remembered it, and he
was no stranger to sun; the heat alone didn't even darken his
skin. No, it was the sea that bothered him. Days, he had been in
this foreign city, and the salt touched everything, turning even
the innocuous gesture of licking dry lips into something unpleasant and distasteful.

He was old, to be here.

He had thought never to subject himself to this place again.
But twice, twice he had done; had come with swords strapped to
his back, and himself strapped in turn—loosely—to the back of
the finest horse it had been his privilege to ride, before or since.
He had practiced with the three men sent for just that purpose,
each of them bitter at their exclusion from the *true* test, at the
height of the Lord's Festival, and he had quietly entered himself
into the Northern ledgers, making a mark that was only graceful
in comparison to the crude symbols drawn by many another, all
barbarian.

He had been tested, briefly; had been chosen. It had never
been in question.

And he had won that year; he had been the first, the only, man
to take the wreath from the North and bear it to the South. *Kings'*
Champion. For her. For Mari.

The next year he returned, riding the same horse, bearing the
same swords, and facing the same Challenge. And that, too, he had
won. For Antoni.

He had thought, the day that he rose from his bow to face the
crowded amphitheater a second time, that he had paid his wife
and son the highest tribute that he could; he had given, to the
South, the gift of his skill in their names.

That they might be at peace.

He had failed them in life. In death, he meant their names to be *remembered*. And gaining the twin wreaths was, he thought, the only way he might achieve such remembrance. Because they were of the Dominion, he, his wife, and his son, and in the Dominion, only the names of men counted. His son was so far from being a man that had his father been a greater clansman, he would never have been seen outside of the harem. His wife—Mari—

The wreaths, he had offered to the Tyr'agar, and the Tyr'agar had accepted them as the prize that they were. Ser Anton di'Guivera became in all things a rich man; gold was his, and his choice of horses, his choice of swords; he was given lands within the Tor Leonne's city, and leave to train those he saw fit. The sons of the clansmen of wealth and power—if the two could be easily separated—were sent to him; his name lent credibility to skills that were often meager. He took their money.

Once or twice, a boy showed promise, and on those rare occasions, he accepted no barter, or trade; the chance to temper and hone the weapon was enough. It *was* his life, all the life he had left him, and he was too afraid of cheapening the memory of the dead to choose another life, although many were offered him.

The wreaths were displayed in the palace itself, that the clansmen might witness this proof of the superiority of the Lord over the Northern demons.

And while those wreaths were displayed, Anton di'Guivera had become a legend, to young boys and old men, and the range of power that falls between either extreme. For his wife and his son had been killed in bandit raids—along with half of his village, and all but a handful of his clan—and it had become his lifelong obsession to see banditry ended. Each season, he was given young men in their prime, and they traveled across the width and breadth of the Dominion, seeking, always, the men who had been responsible for the death of Mari and Antoni. Of so much of Guivera.

The wreaths hung, for the nobility to see; Anton fought for the serafs to see; from the heights to the depths of the Lord's and the Lady's service, his was a name and a presence that was known.

Even here. Even in this Northern Empire, with its demon Kings, its lack of tradition and respect, its law against the owning of serafs, those born to serve, and raised to make it a fine art. He was known, in this place. For it was here that he had twice earned the title Kings' Champion.

With the death of the Tyr'agar Markaso kai di'Leonne, the wreaths had returned, dented and slightly bloodied, to him.

And he had taken them, one and the other, and he had repaired to the lands that were his, in the city that he had come to hate, the Tor Leonne. In the privacy of a night sky, the moon itself so slender a crescent of light he'd carried four lit lamps into the darkness to see by, he'd returned them to their rightful owners: His wife. His son.

The dead were the worst taskmasters. No matter how you struggled, no matter what you sacrificed, what you lost, what you paid, they gave you no nod, however minimal, to show their approval. No benediction. No absolution.

Carlo was flagging.

He frowned, as the lackluster sparring caught his attention. His frown spoke volumes; it was the expression that no one of his students had ever been able to ignore, be they deaf to the words that followed. Carlo was no exception.

"It's the heat," the young man said, wiping sweat from his forehead before it reached his eyes. "And the air. It's so thick you can hardly breathe it."

Andaro's subtle shift in expression was as good as a cringe in a lesser man.

"That," Ser Anton replied, "is why we fight *here*. The Lord will not destroy the ocean overnight so that you can have the fight you're accustomed to. A warrior fights the fight he's confronted with; he doesn't whine for a different one. We are not Serras longing for different shades of green silk so that we may best present ourselves; we are *men. Learn.*"

Andaro, thankfully, was silent; his face had fallen into that perfectly neutral mask that he used when he wished to convey nothing whatever to a possible enemy. That Ser Anton was that enemy in the young man's eyes did not give the older man cause to worry; they were students, these two, and of them, his finest. He expected them to be wary.

Unfortunately, the fact that Andaro was wary enough for two did nothing whatever to instill such a wariness in his closest rival and friend; Carlo spoke too much, complained too frequently, drank too much, ate too much—and admired foreign women too much.

He had never been a man like Carlo, although he had served beside many; it was Andaro, silent and measured, who best reflected his youth, and perhaps because of Andaro, he had been too indulgent with the friend.

When Anton folded his arms across his chest, it spoke in a fashion that words alone could not; the two fell silent and returned to their sparring with a passion that spoke of anger, annoyance, and perhaps a touch of shame. Together, they could best him. On a very, very lucky day. No doubt they considered it from time to time, like any sullen children. They were wise enough not to try; there were tricks that one did not teach champions. And Anton's early skill had been honed in a place where the sword decided not honor and glory but life and death; the imperative of survival could make a man cunning, and low. If the Lord judged, he did not judge harshly.

He did not need to.

The sun was high, hot; it bore witness to this, the beginning. *Bear witness,* he thought, *to an end. Let there be an end.*

Old. He was old, now, to think such thoughts at the height of the Lord's power. He turned his anger out; Andaro and Carlo were not the only two men who served his purpose here, they were merely the best.

The woman watched.

Her hair, brass and silver, her eyes brown with hints of the gold that spoke of her demon heritage, she stood straight-backed, her head tilted to one side as if listening to the cadence of metal and metal's strike. He had been guaranteed privacy when he had accepted the offer—her offer, he was certain of it now—to accept the protection of the Kings' Swords within the palace itself. That guarantee could easily be invoked.

Ser Anton knew it because he had done it, not once, not twice, but ten times, forcing spectators to withdraw. He was not afraid that they would carry tales of his students and their exertions; very little that could be said about either Carlo, Andaro, or the rest of his men, could damage them.

But this woman—he could not deny her her observation. Because she had, upon her face, that intent concentration that spoke not of war, not of spying, not of prurient curiosity, but rather of mastery, of comprehension.

Such a vanity, in a man his age, with so much at stake. But these eyes reminded him of a young boy's eyes. What was his name? It was gone; he could see, clearly, the white, white hair that in the Dominion would have been both so rare and so highly prized, and he could see, more clearly than that, the intensity of his desire to *be* what Anton created. She did not have that desire.

He very much wished to see her wield the sword that hung at her side. But he did not ask her to spar, and she did not offer.

Who are you, demon daughter?

Princess Mirialyn ACormaris. Too valued by her father to be married off to any who might come asking. When she came to stand above them, in the rounded stone of balcony that was one of many in these halls of cold, tall stone, he could not bring himself to demand her removal. It was his weakness, still. Women. Children. It had always been his weakness.

He could not afford to be weak here. And yet . . .

Andaro disapproved of the decision—although not obviously, and not loudly enough to endanger himself or to truly anger Ser Anton di'Guivera. He was prudent, in all things prudent.

"She is only a woman," Anton said genially.

"She is a woman in the North," Andaro replied levelly. "And you yourself have said that the women in the North are as dangerous as the men, in their fashion."

"If you think this does not apply to a Serra, you are young, Andaro." Ser Anton shrugged, losing the facade of geniality slowly. "What she observes here will have no bearing on the Challenge."

"It has bearing on Carlo already."

"True enough, but if Carlo cannot concentrate in the face of the admiration of one young woman—"

"She is the daughter of demons, as far as Carlo is concerned."

"—he will be utterly destroyed by the audience gathered in the so-called high city. It is best to face obstacles now, Andaro."

"We face enough; we must fight in the sun and the humidity, in public, like common cerdan."

It was Andaro's pride that Anton least liked; he did not remember his own youth as so prideful a thing. And yet they had so much in common, his younger self of memory and this young man, that he was not now so certain of his own worthiness. Age took it away, that certainty. Replaced it with truth, much of it bitter.

"You will face it for three days. If you cannot fight without collapsing—or turning into sluggards, like Viello—you will fail here."

Carlo and Andaro exchanged a single glance. Words passed in silence between them, some struggle. At length, Carlo began to speak, and Anton braced himself for at best mild stupidity. He counted himself lucky that he had not yet been exposed to it, and he could see, by the dour expression upon Andaro's face, that had the wiser man held sway, the words would be stuck permanently *behind* Carlo's lips.

"Why did the General—"

"The *Tyr'agar,* Carlo."

Carlo ducked his head as if he expected to be struck. Had they been elsewhere, it would have been a safe bet. "The Tyr'agar. My apologies, Ser Anton. Why did the Tyr'agar choose to send *us* to the city? Why could he not just bespeak the servants of the Lady?"

Andaro stepped on Carlo's foot, hard. The glance that passed between them was more heated than the exchange of sword blows toward the day's end, when their tempers had frayed completely.

Anton covered his eyes with his hands; both of them, for good measure. At times it hurt him to look upon such a sincerely stupid face. But he did not correct the boy; Andaro had done as much of that as was safe. "If such servants existed at all," he said at last, "they would not be summoned by the Tyr'agar. The Tyr'agar serves the *Lord,* Carlo. Not the Lady. You are here in service to the *Lord,* not the Lady."

Carlo flushed. "We are here in service to the Tyr'agar," he replied, letting the familiar anger show. "And not as warriors, but as clumsy *assassins.*" He spit the word out as if he could not hold it in his mouth without swallowing its taint. "Warriors? Yes. *That* is what we are. We—Andaro and I—should have been at this year's Festival as Champions, as the Lord's chosen. Instead, we were picked by you and brought *here.*" He kicked at packed dirt with his foot. Grimaced; it was harder than it looked. "Here, to a land where women are treated like men, and men who are barely fit to be serafs rule by *money.*" He spit.

Sincerely stupid. "Carlo, it is wealth that defines power, even in the Dominion. You show your ignorance, as usual, and as usual I find it uninteresting."

"But even you—"

"Uninteresting enough to forbid it. Had you desired to remain in the South, you might have remained."

"You would no longer teach me."

"If you continue this, lack of a teacher will be the last of your concerns. Quite literally. Do I make myself clear?"

Carlo bowed at once.

Ser Anton di'Guivera disliked being forced to make so open a threat, and only among the sincerely stupid was he ever called upon to do so. And yet that stupidity was also the source of much of Carlo's attraction; it was his unrepentant youth, his vitality.

"You are a servant of the Lord," Anton continued serenely. "The Tyr'agar will make us strong, and we are here to gain his favor by doing his bidding. I chose you personally because I trust you both, and if I am foolish in that regard, so be it.

"We are here to kill a concubine's son, no more; a boy whom we cannot even be certain carries the Leonne blood in his veins."

Carlo bowed.

Andaro did not.

"Something troubles you, Andaro?"

"An inaccuracy, Ser Anton."

"And that?"

"We can be certain that he indeed carries that blood."

"How?"

"Have you not received word?"

Lord scorch him. "Word?" Anton was a terrible liar; that he could lie at all was the product of years of exposure to the delicate political balance of the Tyr'agar's court. Andaro had grown up in the fluidity of that elegant way of life; he knew, of course, that Anton had been the first to receive any such word.

But he continued, smoothly. "The kai el'Sol drew the Sun Sword at the Festival's height."

"And?"

"It destroyed him utterly. Had there been no acknowledged Leonne, no Leonne of the blood, there would still be a Fredero kai el'Sol."

A kai el'Sol, Anton thought, *that the Tyr could slowly kill for his disobedience and interference. Ah, Fredero; you chose well. You did not strike to wound, and you had only a single strike.*

"Very well, Andaro, you have bested me with your knowledge. And I am in a generous mood, so I will forgive the insolence and presumption. Get what passes for a bath in these parts, eat what passes for food, and take what rest the heat will give you."

They did not wait to be told twice.

They left him alone.

Fredero. Ser Anton bowed his head a moment in genuine respect. Could one ever respect one's allies as well as the worthy foe? No. That was the warrior's way.

He watched his two best students leave him, and he knew that Andaro understood the truth, and that Carlo would not.

That Ser Anton di'Guivera had not been *sent* to kill Valedan kai di'Leonne—and in the privacy of his thoughts, he granted the unknown boy his just and full title—he had *demanded* it as his right, and as his price for any involvement in the affairs of the General Alesso di'Marente.

The boy had to die.

The boy's blood had to be on his sword, on his hands.

In Mari's name. In Antoni's name.

And then, then he would have peace.

It was not that Anton di'Guivera was a friend; he was not a friend, had never been. But he was *legend,* he was a thread in the fabric of the stories that Valedan had been weaned on. There was not a boy in the Tor that did not know of the poor man's tragic loss, to bandits, of wife and son—his only son, and only wife—not a boy who did not remember the tales of his valor as he roamed the countryside destroying the bandits who preyed upon the villages, north and south, east and west, that lay around Raverra in an ever widening circle.

Those stories were still told. They knew, the four year olds, as Valedan did, how Ser Anton received the scars across his face and arms; they knew how it was that he had first been granted the sword which he'd made famous; they knew that he had been chosen and favored above all men by the will of the Lord of the Sun. But better than that, they knew that Ser Anton di'Guivera had, not once but twice, come to the kingdom of the Northern demon-ruled Imperials, and bested their best.

He could see it, if he but closed his eyes. He could hear Serra Antonia, telling him from the grave—from the vortex of the winds, a gentle breeze—all these things.

But more than that, he could hear her gentle admonition to be, as Anton had been, in all things an honorable man.

How long, he wondered, as he sat beside the fountain that had been his comfort since he'd first set foot in these wide, open halls. *How long have you known?* For he was certain that the Serra Alina *had* known the truth of it.

The boy's graven face—most of it hidden—did not move to give him reply; he stared as the water fell from young, stone hands, like weak Northern blood. The sky's tint was crimson and pale. The Lord—if he existed at all, and according to the Princess he did not, except in the hearts of the men who chose to fashion a god in their likeness—was closing his eyes.

Shadows fell.

And they were wrong, even for the closing of the day. Valedan kai di'Leonne rose at once, hand on the hilt of a sword that he did not remove when he walked any halls but the rooms that had been granted him in recognition of his title and his claim.

There stood only one man, hand likewise on the hilt of a sword which was sheathed. Sheathed or no, it had the power to cut, to wound.

"Ser Anton," Valedan said gravely. He did not bow; he could not; his back was stiff.

The swordmaster did not reply.

He longed to be political, did Valedan; he longed to be wise. But he was alone, and the Lord's light was fading. He could see the lines of the old man's face, and he realized for perhaps the first time that Anton di'Guivera was old, was older than his father had been at his death; was older than Alina or Ramiro or Baredan.

"I wondered if you would dare," he said, "to pay your respects to the clan."

The silence he heard was the silence of contempt. Certain that words would follow, he weathered it. His anger—unlooked for, unexpected—prevented it from stinging, from wounding. "If you take this chance meeting to be a gesture of respect," was the cool reply, "then, yes, I dare."

"I have heard," Valedan continued, because he wanted to speak and there were none but himself to advise against it, "that it was your hand that killed my father."

"You have good ears."

"Was it easier, to kill a student whose skill you put together, year by year, than to kill a man who never trusted you?"

Anton di'Guivera froze.

Valedan kai di'Leonne turned his back upon him, giving him no chance to counterstrike or to parry—no chance but the obvious, blade to blade. He walked toward the fountain. "This," he said, to the silent danger behind him, "was built by an Annagarian seraf who made his way North to build a life in this land. I come here, often; if you wish to avoid me, it is best that you understand this to be *my* territory." He was silent; Anton was silent.

"Justice," Anton di'Guivera said.

Valedan turned, surprised, aware that the surprise was a weakness that he must master, that he must bleed from expression if not gesture. "Yes," he said, although the older man's eyes were upon him. "The statue, the boy, is called Justice. The Lord's justice. The Dominion's justice."

"I have heard much of you," Anton said, his voice completely neutral.

"I have heard much of you," was Valedan's bitter reply. "I may only hope that what you have heard is not so lacking in truth."

This time, this time Anton di'Guivera expected the blow; he was not moved by the words of an angry young man. "Perhaps; I will see for myself what the truth of those words is."

"Why?" Valedan replied coolly.

"Because it is always best, as you would have known had you been raised in the Dominion, to know one's enemy's strengths— and weaknesses. The North breeds for weakness."

Valedan shrugged. "The North won," was his calm reply.

"A point, indeed, in their favor, inexplicable though it is." He met Valedan's eyes, across a distance that was not great enough. They were brown eyes, brown eyes, and anger enough between them, old and young, to start wars.

Valedan did not look away.

"I have come here," Anton said, "to finish what was started, and to have peace."

"You've come to kill me."

"Yes."

"My sword and my skill were not fashioned by your hand; I will not be so easy to kill as my father. But at least my death will not be a betrayal."

At that, at that Anton di'Guivera did look away a moment. "What do you know of betrayal?" he replied at last, his voice low. "Nothing."

"No. Perhaps not. I look forward to the fight, Ser Anton. You were once the most honorable of the Lord's warriors; the best of his line." He bowed, although he had not intended to show this man that respect.

Ser Anton did not return the gesture.

CHAPTER TEN

16th of Lattan, 427 AA
Hundred Holdings

They were sweating with the heat, damp with it; their clothing was darkened to shades that were unfashionable, and in Jewel's case, unbecoming, not that she much cared. She'd worn worse, far worse, in her time—at least these fit. Last time she'd stood this long in the twenty-sixth, she'd worn a shirt that had rubbed through at the elbows.

And she'd been smart enough then not to mill around in the city during the Festival Challenge. She could see Angel's spire of hair—a holdover from his younger days; follow it, and she could see Carver standing beside him. But the others were out of sight, hidden by a moving wall of people that only occasionally let a window open up where it was useful. In her next life, Mandaros willing, she was going to be *tall*.

The streets were packed. Petty hawkers, farmers, bakers, and their families moved and stopped in large clusters, carrying their arguments and their glee with them as they went. Five days of work—this particular five days—would see them through the off-months if they were frugal; and if they had the best position, the right stall, the loudest voice. It was the height of the season; the Challenge festival. Comers had camped in the streets against all magisterial dictate; the competition for space was fierce in those areas where the people who had the right to levy fees didn't think it worth the bother.

Jewel had never understood how such money could be too much of a bother until she'd joined Terafin. There, she'd discovered how much it could cost to collect money owed for such ephemeral enterprises as these; hiring guards, getting the correct permissions sealed and signed so you could actually use said guards, locating the people who owed the money in the first place as more than half of them wouldn't be standing around with money-bags outheld, hiring more guards when you found out that the guards that you'd hired at such a bargain turned out to have the worst tempers this side of the Dominion and were now cooling their heels in the magisterial jails while the Magisterium paid a personal call to Terafin—and even then, it was a pain that she'd've endured had she been the hapless subservient put in charge of collection.

Terafin holdings didn't demand that of her, and she thanked Kalliaris for the oversight every time she was reminded of it.

Gods, there were so many *people*.

So many people, and no more demons.

"One day," she said grimly.

"Longer," her companion replied. "The marathon itself isn't run until the third day."

"I know when the marathon is run, thank you," she snapped. It was churlish; she knew it almost before she said it, but she'd so hoped that Avandar would stay home. Teller was there, and Finch, and Avandar was capable although she hated to say it—of defending them. Better than Jewel herself, gods curse him. She'd tried to order him there, but he wouldn't stay, and she knew that his service wasn't that of a guard or a servant; he was there to protect her.

It would help me, she'd told him, *if I weren't so damned afraid of someone killing* them.

Then let it go, he'd replied. *They serve you, Jewel. Do them the grace of accepting their choice for what it is: clear-eyed. Adult. Do you think they would run away if they knew what they faced? They've faced worse than a House War.* He'd smiled then, which was rare. *I shouldn't say this, but Finch has already spoken to me about the possibility of my remaining with them.*

Oh?

Yes. She said that she'd kill me if I abandoned you.

And that had been that.

Devon ATerafin rounded a wide bend in the road, inasmuch as a man could come round a corner into a crowd packed cheek by jowl. He was tall enough that he was easily seen.

Avandar was tall enough that he was easily seen.

Jewel, sadly, was not. As Devon drew closer, she lost him to the heads and shoulders of men and women trying desperately to

stake their little claims. He'd get through by and by; if it had
been an emergency—and she wanted one, because at least it
would come on time, before the marathon—he'd have made his
way through the crowd more efficiently than a pain-maddened
horse.

Tucked away in less obvious places than the old holdings were
the other, less earthy, merchants. Moneyed people traveled this
time of year to take part in the Festival that surrounded the Challenge itself, and if they were here, they often chose to conduct
business in the Festival environs. Jewel wouldn't have, but she
understood the attraction, even if it was—at this moment—the
last in the world she would have felt.

First, even merchants enjoyed the spectacle and the gathering
that was the prelude and aftermath to the Challenge; there were
bards from every college to witness the events, and to call them—
not journeymen, but master bards, men and women whose voices,
once heard, were woven into a life story as one of the few perfect
memories; there were criers, lesser bards, acrobats, there were
actors and plays. In all, a gaudy, perfect display of humanity.

Second, it was harder to police the city. Those divisions of
the army that were disciplined enough—Berriliya's, for the most
part—earned double their wages by swallowing their pride and
donning the uniforms of the Magisterium—but they didn't know
what to look for, crime-wise, and they weren't used to the give
and take that the magisterial guards ran their holdings by. Despised it, in fact, which meant that cooperation was largely a
theory during the Festival season if the holders didn't know your
face. There were a lot of faces out there that Jewel and her den
wouldn't have recognized.

She stained her sleeve with one swipe of forehead and glow-
ered at a young boy with nimble fingers who had the cheek to
grin before he vanished between two stalls. Merchants weren't
the only people who made a few months' living wages in the open
streets of the festival—as she well knew. She'd done it herself.

More, much more, to lose by not doing it, back then. But gods,
she hadn't remembered there ever being so many people. If a demon started a slaughter here, in broad daylight, he'd kill a dozen
before they'd even manage to reach him. More.

*No. No, that's why we've got Meralonne. That's why Avandar's
here.* But she'd seen the deaths that demons brought; the memory,
like the voice of bards, was a memory that was undimmed and

untarnished by time; it had cut her so deeply she only had to think, just to nudge her thoughts in that direction, and it came back at once: The darkness, the sickly sourness that had grown, and grown, and grown until she had been so overpowered by it she couldn't smell at all; flickering lamplight caught on the backs of insects in the darkness. On the back of insects who had made homes of— the dead.

Too many damned people here. Children.

"Jay?"

She nodded, tried to shake the memory away. It clung. Was it worse to find bodies, or to hear them being made, to see the dead and know that they'd all been far too late, or to hear deaths-in-the-making that she couldn't prevent?

Angel thumped her on the back, hard. She bit her tongue, and swallowing the blood—her own—and the curse that followed as she spun round to give as good, or better, eased the shadow.

Shadow is what her grandmother, long dead, had called memory. What kind of life was it that could make a person think of all memory as shadow? *Babua,* she thought, as she tried to recall that old woman's face as clearly as she could a demon's victims. The face remained blurred and indistinct, but the voice—that she could hear, with all its aged texture, its low, throatiness, its heaviness, and its odd joy.

She seldom came this close to home.

"Jewel?"

She shook herself again. Happened too often, these days, and it had to stop. Devon waited, more patient with the woman than he had been with the child. "Sorry."

"Don't be. Meralonne?"

"Nothing. Not back yet."

"Kiriel?" He wiped his brow with a cloth and looked, if possible, less comfortable in the heat than Jewel felt. The day had started before dawn, for all of them; it would end, if they were lucky, before dawn.

She shrugged. "Gone up ahead. She won't start a fight if we don't—"

She heard it, then. Not a scream, not precisely. It was a cry of surprise, edged with a pain that wasn't quite real, but was close. Shock. Confusion. Child's voice. She had no doubt what would follow, gods, no doubt at all. She'd heard it before.

"Jewel."

He touched her. Avandar never did, but Devon was not often as circumspect in an emergency. They'd been through enough together that he had that right, even now. Surprised her, to think that, but that was all she had time for.

Her hand was on her dagger, and then her dagger was in her hand, and the crowds that were as hot and sweat-stained, as tired—but not as frightened, not as tense—as she, parted before her. No, not quite. She found the rhythm for walking through it, found the spaces between bodies that moved and bodies that didn't, found the openings that were left between one step and another. You had to be able to do that, as a thief.

She was glad that there were things that had roots so deep soft living couldn't destroy them.

It tired him, to travel so quickly between one human place and another. He was not used to expending so much of his power, for he did not believe in gaudy display, in intemperate show of strength. It was not for the regard of the *Kialli* that he lived or struggled or planned; their regard was of little import, one way or the other.

Immortals rarely worried about the passage of time.

But time had become a matter of grave urgency.

In years, the Lord would be ready to ascend with his army; to leave the frozen, rocky crags of the Northern Wastes and take the first step in the long plan that would eventually decide the fate of both man and gods. Years. Not decades, not centuries, not millennia—but a space of human, of mortal, years.

Every person here, every person who did not suit his current plan and purpose, might live to see the coming of the Lord. And today, in the streets of Averalaan, upon land that formed the barrier and the burial ground of a much more worthy city, there were many of these people indeed.

It did not suit his purpose to kill indiscriminately, to draw attention to himself or his nature. It rarely had, although when it became necessary, he made no objection. Of the *Kialli,* it could truly be said that only one was that least glorious of things: practical.

And that one, Lord Isladar of the Shining Court.

He had watched—and it was difficult, for Kiriel's power was strong, if untrained and unsubtle—where he could, and he had seen, clearly, this one thing: Jewel. To get information about her had been difficult, but again, he had seen, clearly, the crest that she bore upon her finger, gold-heavy as humans were wont to fashion things of import. Terafin. ATerafin.

It was a crest with which he was familiar, and it had led to the information he desired. Jewel. ATerafin.

She was unlike Ashaf kep'Valente in all things save this: she had somehow made herself a figure that Kiriel could—and worse, did—trust.

He was angered by it, for he was *Kialli,* and he had that temper. He had made certain that there were none left—save perhaps the great, stupid beast that had served as her dog—that Kiriel trusted. Not Ashaf. Not Isladar.

His plan was not to be undone by a mortal whose life, no matter what she might desire or how she might struggle, was nothing more than the sum of a handful of years.

He knew that she was close; had planned it, just so. Had there not been so many people, he would have arrived early, done his work, and left. As it was, he had had to arrive farther away from Jewel ATerafin than he would have liked. He was properly attired for a human, but he did not sweat with the heat; it was a flaw that he did not have time to correct.

There. He found the child. Not a young one, which was a pity, but without the use of power to bind and to hide behind, the youngest of children were still too close to their parents to be easily taken. He could kill the parents quietly enough, but that would draw attention unless—again—he used the power that he would need to leave Averalaan quickly. Then, of course, he could kill them unseen; they would die on their feet, quickly and horribly, and there would be no sign of their killer. In streets as penned in with life as these, as hemmed by it, as contained, that would bring other deaths, a cascade of injuries and fear too complete for words—from one small action.

He had seen avalanches in the North; had caused them infrequently; they were not dissimilar.

But not today. Not *this* day. The time would come, and Isladar knew how to be patient. But he did not desire to travel twice, so great a distance, without his Lord's aid as he had done this day.

The child was drawn to him; this much he could accomplish with so little power it was natural; there was something in the forbidden that was attractive to children who had been raised without fear. In time, there would be none of those—but he took advantage of it now because it was required.

He led the child away from its parents. He could not waste the death on people of no consequence, and he knew that if they heard the voice, they must begin their search in earnest, might even

reach him before his intended victim did. It must be Jewel ATerafin who responded.

It was not so difficult a task as that. She was, after all, looking
for the kin, and he had them here, at his command. Kiriel was on
the trail of one who had been ordered to make himself obvious to
her; she would not return in time—and she was the only true danger, if not the only threat.

He found an alley, long and narrow, and set about it a delicate
seeming; gave it an aura of shadow, of subtle menace that would
repel without causing alarm. Any who crossed these barriers he
would kill outright, swiftly.

He sealed the alley with his back.

The child turned, sensing his glamour, his darkness. He saw
her eyes widen, saw her smile uncertainly. The smile he offered
gave her no comfort at all.

Come, he thought, as he began his binding spells, *come and
find me, Jewel.*

With one slow cut, he began to summon his intended victim.

He wasn't prepared for her when she came.

She saw it, of course; saw the dark glimmering that went up
about the alley's mouth. It was a blackness tinged and ringed
with violet. The color of illusion; Meralonne had taught her that.
But he had not taught her to see the shadows that billowed in violet confines because the shadows weren't his to control.

Shadow. Oh, she remembered the deaths. The earth had been
the barrier between them, between the dying and the men and wom-
en who desperately needed to help, to fulfill their responsibility—
and it had been unbreachable. She could taste it, suddenly, the
awful dryness in mouth and throat, the slightly salty tang of blood.

She'd bitten her lip.

There were people in the street, and they were safe, she *knew*
they were safe. They let her pass, they let her pass each and every
one, and as she approached the mouth of the alley itself, the crowd
thinned. She blessed Kalliaris.

Forgot about Cormaris.

Forgot about Cormaris until she'd crossed the line that led into
the alley itself. He hadn't expected her, the bastard, hadn't expected that she would come so soon. She knew it because his back
was to the alley's mouth and when she drove the dagger into the
middle of his spine, he didn't—not quite—have enough time to

leap out of the way, over the head of his victim, a girl not much older than ten if Jewel was any judge.

She'd cut, struck; not home, but it was enough.

Or it should have been.

She heard his cry; it was a roar that was suddenly cut away, as if by a sculptor separating stone from stone, essential nature from essential nature, to reveal something far worse: silence, deliberate control.

She knew the dagger she wielded.

She had seen it destroy demons before.

Involuntarily, her gaze went to its blade.

"Oh, yes," this creature said. "It is . . . well crafted, little human. You were . . . closer than I expected."

Jewel caught the girl by the shoulders; she was bleeding, but the cut wasn't deep; it was a long one that had pierced cloth and skin in a single stroke. She'd recover. If she got out of here, Jewel intended that.

She put the girl behind her. "Run," she said.

"She cannot," the creature replied, struggling to speak clearly. "The way is barred, Jewel. The only key is your death."

They were angry. They were all angry until they reached the alley itself. Avandar was unarmored; he was faster than Devon, and significantly more proprietary. He reached the alley before the last of Jewel ATerafin was swallowed by it. And it *was* as if she were physically swallowed; she moved through the alley's shadows and they solidified at her back, blocking all light, all sight of her but the vision that memory provided.

What had been the entrance into a narrow throughway was now a wall, black as Northern coal.

Because he was Avandar, he survived.

Devon could stop on a pin's head. As blue light crackled and flared, he instinctively threw up both of his arms, crossing them in a clatter of metal against metal.

Singed flesh and cursing brought them down.

Avandar was bleeding, and it occurred to Devon, as the domicis staggered and dropped to one knee before bringing his hand to his chest and the ragged edge of cloth that defined its center, that he had never seen the domicis injured before.

At his back, Angel and Carver skidded to a halt; Jester was caught up by the crowd, somewhere at Kiriel's heels.

"Avandar?" Carver bent to speak.

"Get Meralonne," the domicis snarled.

Carver turned and ran.

She had never been this close to dying.

She knew it, and *knew* it, the instinctive for once in perfect harmony with the intellectual. But she did not see the blackness or the death itself, and she took what comfort she could from that. She adjusted her grip on the dagger that was her only effective weapon—her only weapon, really—and bent into her knees, readying her weight for a leap or a dodge.

But he did not approach her.

Stall, she thought. *Stall him for a time.*

As if he were just another power-mad human. As if he were Haerrad, or Marrick, or Rymark, or Elonne. A person of power. A politician who was willing to do whatever it was that was necessary to get what he desired. As if.

"Don't you have anything better to do?"

It wasn't the question she'd been about to ask. She'd thought to utter a threat of some sort, feeble or laughable though it was. But there; she'd asked.

His eyes widened, slightly rounding at dark corners.

"If you wield that dagger," he replied, "you know what I am. Know that, and you have the answer to your question."

"No, I don't."

"No?"

"You aren't frothing at the mouth like a sharp-toothed madman."

His brows, which were dark and thin, rose, and then he smiled. It was a dark smile, but it was edged with genuine amusement. "You have no idea, Jewel ATerafin, how much I wish I could call my brethren to witness this. But I am . . . diminished. You are an interesting human, a foolish one to be so fearless; you are not a power."

"I'm not a mage, no. But—"

He *moved* then.

She was moving before the sentence was complete, rolling on the dirt and minimal garbage, cushioning the force of the fall.

At her back, she heard the scream of the young girl. The alley took it and made it a resonating accusation. She had forgotten. The reason she'd come had been left behind by reflex, by her own desire to survive.

She froze a moment as that realization hit her; moved again as the creature did, slicing cleanly through clothing and a thin layer of flesh. It *hurt*.

But not as much as the whimpering did, because it wasn't hers. She wheeled, fighting instinctive movement because instinct told her to leap away. The girl was alive, but she was clutching the side of her face; her arm was slick with new blood.

He was there, and his face was devoid of the triumph she expected to see; she let instinct take her body—if she survived, she'd pay—and bled again for the momentary hesitation. But worse than that: the dagger skittered out of her slashed wrist.

It only works once. Devon had said it. After that, it had to be cleansed, be reconsecrated. Something.

She leaped.

Carver started down the street, started out at a run. His mouth was dry. Jay was all right. She *had* to be all right. She'd never walked into a trap before.

He wanted to believe it, but he'd seen Avandar's face. Heard his voice. Carver wasn't a grand patrician; he was a part of Terafin, but he hadn't been born and bred to it. He knew fear, he'd felt it so often; he knew gut-deep visceral fear when he heard it.

Avandar's voice held about as much fear as a man's voice could. And he'd never heard Avandar afraid.

Get Meralonne.

No. Carver stopped dead. Jay wasn't the only one who operated on instinct.

Stay alive, he thought, as he suddenly twisted round, knocking two soon-to-be-angry women over. Their curses were a comfort.

Who did you turn to, after all? Who did you turn to when one of your own had been caught by the magisterians, or worse, angry merchants and their guards? You didn't run to authorities; they'd be piss useless.

You gathered your own.

"Jester!" And then, louder, as if his life depended on it, "KIRIEL!"

Why doesn't he just finish it?

She was bleeding from a dozen small cuts; the girl was bleeding from fewer. But while the girl was frozen with fear, as easy a victim as one could ask for, Jewel was in motion, constantly in motion. And it cost her. She couldn't draw breath unless it were noisy, and it hurt now.

"Why," she said, bracing herself against the wall, "don't you just finish it?"

"My apologies," was his soft reply. "I had no intention of prolonging either your misery or my stay."

She would have snorted, but she heard truth in the words.

"The injury you inflicted is the cause of your less convenient death. You have cost me much here, Jewel ATerafin; more, in fact, than any of my brethren, who have both power and time to plan, have done in millennia. To kill you quickly, it seems, requires a magic that I can no longer afford to expend.

"Let me compliment you on your reflexes," he continued, as he moved slowly to close the distance she'd put between them. "I had thought to kill you quickly regardless." A smile turned his lips up. "If you wish an end, perhaps you would oblige me?"

"I'd love to, but you know how it is."

"Sadly, yes." He reached back then, casually; the child screamed.

Jewel had no weapon, or she would have attacked then. Probably would have died, but she couldn't do it; she couldn't ignore him. He had two weapons: the child and the fact that he did not tire.

And gods, she was tiring.

Devon ATerafin watched Avandar's progress. He was not mageborn, not mage-trained, and his sensitivity to magic was more instinctive than real, a thing of imagination that was strong enough, on rare occasion, to cross the boundary of reality.

This was not one of those occasions. He could see, clearly, that Avandar was struggling with something that was almost physical in nature—but with what, and how, he kept to himself, as he kept most things. His fear was strong, but focused, and this, as his magic, he kept to himself.

In at least that much, they were alike.

He waited as patiently as he could. He could feel the sun against damp skin, but at a distance; he was chilled with the need for action. Something caught the periphery of his vision, and he glanced up.

Haloed by sun's brightness, he could see a slender figure whose hair traced an upward spike: Angel had reached the building's narrow height. He lifted an arm, hand palm out, fingers splayed wide. The shout behind Devon's pursed lips died into the hiss and shout of a crowd of people all desperate to make good during the Challenge season.

Angel, not ATerafin, bunched up, shoulders blades deforming his back the way a cat's might have had he been feline, and chose that moment to disappear.

He was through.

The building was not so tall, and the ground not so far, that he paused for more than a moment to think about what he was doing, or how. He looked down from the heights, he saw Jay, and he saw someone who was stalking her; that was enough. He pulled his dagger, positioned himself as silently as possible, and jumped.

It was that simple.

What was not simple: To throw himself clear of the hand that flashed out to meet him, mid-fall; to hold back the single cry of surprise as something that looked like fingers came *this* close to bisecting his chest, and to roll away—all without losing that dagger.

Jay wasn't a killer; he'd known that. And he knew—and learned again, in case he'd forgotten it—that she wasn't an easy target. But she could see a death coming when it was meant for her; he couldn't.

The wound, he knew, was deep; it was not fatal. He thought it wasn't fatal. He didn't have time to think all that much more.

"ANGEL, *left!*"

He rolled with the voice. That much was instinct. Came up on his feet two inches away from the wall that had almost killed Avandar. The dagger, he held in slick hands, his own, where he'd brushed his chest.

There was another person in the alley; he'd been aware of her, but only a bit; it was Jay who'd mattered. She was young, though, by the sound of her voice; she was whimpering.

Take it easy, kid, he thought. *Jay'll think of something.*

The alley was awfully dark, and getting darker as he watched. Magic? Pain.

Damn.

She did not come through the crowds, although it was through the crowds that he was frantically, clumsily, calling. She came, instead, above them, walking two feet over upturned, suddenly silent, faces. He froze a moment when he saw her. Thought, stupidly, *Jay's going to kill us.* If Meralonne didn't beat her to it.

"Carver." She came at once to where he'd stopped the minute he caught sight of her, sprinting as if she already knew what he'd called her for. There she stopped. Her sword, he saw, was sheathed, and he was grateful for it; if she drew it, he thought—was sure— that there'd be sudden panic and people'd be hurt in the crush.

She didn't bother to descend to his level, and that meant that everyone within easy sight—too many damned people for his liking—was suddenly staring at *him*.

"It's Jay," he told her. He thought he'd have time to explain it, but he didn't have to.

"Where?"

"Over by the old mill building—"

She cursed. "That means nothing to me. Give me your hand. Hurry."

He did as she ordered before he'd time to think about it; put his hand into hers. She didn't wear mail gloves, or any gloves at all; he was wearing half-leathers for grip's sake—but he was the one who felt completely naked as his hand met hers. He would've pulled back, but her hand closed like a trap, and she hauled him to his feet, beside her.

Thank Kalliaris, he thought, *we're not wearing skirts.*

It was a giddy thought. He took a hesitant step; followed it by another, firmer one. She gave him that much play and no more, and she didn't let go of his hand; he had a feeling that when she did his next step would be a long one, straight down.

For some reason that he couldn't quite explain, he thought of Duster, and his face broke into a grim smile. "This way."

This was not the way she had run, the first time.

She had no one with her, and no one to carry warning to her before it was too late. What she had, that close to the Lord who had birthed her, was a heightened instinct, an awareness of things that brought pain.

She had not called upon power there. In the stone halls of her father, seamless from depths to height, she had not even run; she had heard the screaming with a curiosity and the intense pleasure that was her birthright. Indeed, she heard it heartbeats before the *Kialli* in attendance raised their faces, sniffing at the winds as if they were charnel, as if, indeed, they were in the confinement of their home of millennia.

Why, why had she not run then?

Pride.

Survival. Haste—the obvious need for haste—was a sign of weakness, and she had been trained too well to show it to those who might consider that weakness a sign of their advantage.

In the Hells, after all, all advantage was pressed and tested. And she had grown up in the shadow of her human heritage, the weakness of a form that demanded sleep and food and breath. She had envied the *Kialli* then. She envied them now.

But in this city, in *Averalaan Aramarelas,* it didn't matter who thought her weak. She left off her chosen pursuit when the sound of Carver's voice shattered a concentration that not even the breath of her great beast, Falloran, could, fiery and dangerous though it was.

She was surprised that she recognized him; his voice was not like anything she had ever heard; his fear rode it, but it was a rare fear; there was something vaguely unsatisfying about it.

"What?" Jester had said. "Kiriel, what is it?" He was tense, his dagger—a weapon that she never wished to see employed— wavering dangerously in his hand.

"I think—I think it's Carver."

"I don't hear anything."

"He's called you. And—and me."

"He's—" Jester's brow puckered, the soft folds of his skin forming deep, lines.

"What is it?"

"What does he sound like?"

"Afraid."

"Is he running from something?"

She'd paused. "No." No.

"*Kalliaris'* frown. It's Jay. Or Angel. It's one of us." He'd turned then, and she felt a surge of fear in him, as unlike the fear he'd carried as he'd hunted by her side as day is to night. *There must,* she thought, *be another word for an emotion that is so different in texture from fear for one's safety, and yet just as visceral, just as paralyzing.*

And she knew that the fear he felt was the fear that Carver felt. Knew it because it suddenly invaded her, as if it had a life of its own, as if it were a human disease, and she only mortal, and already laid low. *Jay.*

She listened; heard Carver's shout grow slowly. Jester had already started to move. The crowd was a maze, and it closed round his back; she couldn't follow where he led because the path disappeared when the arms and shoulders of strange humans touched.

She tried to follow; she almost drew her sword—but hacking her way through the crowd, as she suddenly desperately desired to do—would not get her to Carver as fast as she felt, suddenly, she needed. So she did what she did not do, in this strange place, with its laws and its ordinances and its meekly accepted penalties: She called her magic, draped herself in its shadow, and took to the air, made of it a solid plateau, made it serve the weight of her feet.

She passed Jester with a grim smile. Even in this, in a mutual goal, she felt pleasure at being first, at being—yes—more powerful. And then she forgot it; she saw Carver, saw his face.

She ran, *because* she had not run this way in the Shining Palace and she remembered too clearly what it had cost her to walk.

It cost her something, to take the boy's hand; to take it, feel the small leap of suspicion and fear as he hesitated, and hold on because she needed his help. But she did. She did not know where they were going, how they were to arrive. She only knew what he knew—that they *must* arrive, and soon.

She tried not to snarl at his speed, or what little there was of it. She held onto his hand although she hated the feel of it. She even let him lead without speaking, because she knew that he was struggling with his own reactions. She could taste it, he was so close. The discomfort, the fear. She had gotten used to the peculiar shade of his soul, the odd darkness, the odd light, both so strong, and both so separate. Uneasy alliances there, easily broken.

But they had not been broken yet; she reminded herself of that. Humans were not what they had been in her youth in the Shining City.

"It's there!" he shouted, although shouting wasn't necessary. His breath interrupted his words; he strove for air, and air's weight in his lungs, between his lips.

She let go of his hand, although she hadn't meant to until the moment she turned to follow his shaking finger with her gaze. He fell at once; there was space beneath them, and she heard his surprise grunt as he struck stone and dirt.

She didn't care.

How had he done this? *How?*

She opened her lips and the words wouldn't come; there were too many of them, they were too painful. But pain didn't last for Kiriel di'Ashaf; not here, not in the face of his power. Like lead in the hands of the fabled alchemists, it became something infinitely more valuable, more precious to her: Anger. Fury.

"Isladar!"

They all heard it.

Jewel, who was clutching her side now, clutching the first deep wound. Angel, who was on the edge of a sleep that held no waking. The child who was insensate, driven by fear beyond fear's reach.

And the demon himself.

Jewel saw his expression shift as he froze, as the sound of the single word seemed to destroy his momentum.

Isladar.

"I see," he said quietly.

She was aware of his movement before he made it, of course. Of every movement toward her, before he made it. Because every single blow he struck was meant to be her death, and her body didn't want to die. But she was tired now, bone tired, dead tired. What her body knew, and what it could do, were two different things. He cut again, and cut deeply; she was out of his way only enough to stop the blow from being fatal.

As if he knew that she was flagging, that he no longer needed to distract her or tire her, he left the child and Angel behind; there was only Jewel. Only Isladar.

Death. Death here.

And she was tired enough not to fear it.

Avandar had enough warning to leap out of her way, but in truth, that was little warning, and his body covered a stretch of rock and dirt so quickly he left parts of his skin on his shirt. She was a shadow that appeared, streaked in blackness, reddened and whitened by the cast rage lends fair features. Her sword—the sword that both he and Meralonne APhaniel shunned—was in her hand as if it were just a natural extension of her body. She drove it forward into the wall that separated Avandar from his keep.

No wall in the world would have withstood the weight and the force of that sword. Buildings, he thought, would shatter in the wake of the magic that traced the dark arc of its traveling. There was no doubt in his mind, no room for it, that she would fail to do what *he* had failed to do: breach the barrier. Reach Jewel Markess ATerafin.

Certainty was such an odd thing.

He saw her stagger back; saw the air give way, refuse her its support. It took a moment for him to comprehend what he could not comprehend: her failure.

He heard her. From where he lay—lay?—upon the alley's floor, he heard the sound she made as her sword struck the barrier. He wouldn't have recognized her voice at all, except he'd never much liked her voice, and wouldn't have trusted her if it hadn't been for Jay.

And Jay was the word she shouted. Roared.

He opened his eyes to the barrier's darkness; thought he saw it shivering, as if it were alive. As if it were living shadow.

He thought he was beyond pain, but he was wrong; it *hurt* to move. He could see Jay, and in the darkness that he could not move to confront, he could see what attacked her. No way to reach her. No way.

But he thought—he thought that he might do some other thing. Wondered why he hadn't thought of it before.

Living shadow. Living.

He lifted the dagger that Devon had given him. Lifted it in a feeble hand, a shaking one. Propped himself up on an elbow, rolled. Fell over. Didn't matter. He was close enough. He'd heard the stories.

With no strength at all, Angel sliced the barrier's darkness with a thing of light: consecrated by the triad, blessed by the god-born. Too ornate by half to be useful in any other way.

He had not known her for what she was; had had no reason to know it, although his informant must have. Something to remember. But Lord Isladar of the Shining Court knew it now: She was seer-born, and her gift was as strong as the gifts that blessed those who had ruled in the cities of man, before the cataclysm. Before the desert.

More time, more time and he would have had her. More power, and he could have killed her at his leisure—and the desire to do so, this long thwarted, was great.

But time had run out.

He thought he had killed the man. A mistake, obviously, and a costly one. He could not reconstitute the wall that he'd erected. He was lucky that Kiriel in anger was still much like a child; she did not think to do what that man, pale-haired and pale as he hovered on death's gray edge, had done—to climb the building, to go *over* what *Kialli* Lord had made.

The wall was her enemy, and she did not look for anything to defeat it but a display of brute force. Had he taught her that? Perhaps. When one sharpened a weapon as dangerous as Kiriel one tried to make its edge as predictable and straight as possible.

It served her poorly. It served him well.

He turned as the barrier shattered, feeling the shards of his shadow dissolve, absorbed by both his body and hers.

Like shadow, she stood in the alley's mouth.

"I'm afraid," he said softly, with a very slight bow of his head to the seer-born human, "that you will live. For the moment."

And he turned to face his charge.

The wind took her hair, and it was a wind of her own making; the streets were heavy with humidity and the stillness of sea air. Strands far too long for practical battle fell back from her face as if pulled, and not by the gentlest of hands; she was in the grip of an anger that was deeper than anything she had ever felt, save perhaps—save perhaps that at Ashaf's death.

Ashaf's loss.

She had dreamed of this moment, in darkness, at night when the Ospreys slept, or better, when Valedan did, and she was not required to feign sleep, but rather, watchfulness, which was for her the more natural of the two things. She'd dreamed that she would see him again. That he would fall before her—that he would grovel or beg.

And she knew, the moment she saw him, that it was only that: a dream. Lord Isladar—Isladar of no demesne—did not know how to grovel or beg. And he had taught her well enough that she knew she would do neither were their positions reversed.

He bowed. She had not expected that.

"Kiriel," he said softly. "It has been . . . too long. You have begun to play a game that is greater than you realize. Come home; leave it be. The Lord does not yet fully comprehend the depth of your transgression, and you are his kin, his only kin. Come; if you stand against us for too long, I will not be able to protect you from his knowledge."

The words that she wanted to say would not come; they were not so simple as she had thought they would be. She wanted to

cleave him in two and have done, and she brought her sword up
for the blow. But she wanted more, too, hungered for it the way
that she hungered for pain.

"Why?"

She did not mention Ashaf by name; there was only this one
thing that stood between them.

"Can you ask me that?" he said softly. "You were far too attached to her, Kiriel. You accepted the investiture. You chose, and
yet, having chosen, you sought to retain what you were required
to leave behind: humanity." He paused. "Do you not see, now, how
she has weakened you? Were they to follow you here, any one of
your enemies, even the least of the Lord's Fist, would destroy you
with ease."

"You could have let her go!"

"You do not see it," he said softly. "Kiriel, I have called you
weak. You do not refute it. Have you forgotten everything I labored so long to teach you?"

"I would have let her go."

"That is what you would have done, yes. And she would have
returned to you, in pieces—but not so many that she would not in
some fashion remain alive as a weapon against you. I did not
fashion her to be your downfall, nor did I fashion her to be the
tool of any other Lord."

"Only you?"

He shrugged. "She was not what you are, Kiriel, and in the end,
she would have left you—or worse. Can you doubt that, who could
see her soul? She was beginning to know what you were, just as
you were beginning to know it, and accept it. Was her death really
so difficult?"

"It wasn't her death," Kiriel said at last.

"And what was it, then?"

"I'll kill you," she said.

She was lying. Jewel was certain that, had she been anyone
else, she wouldn't have known it—but she felt the truth that
Kiriel hid behind the words she was willing to speak, and she
knew, suddenly, that she did not want to hear the rest. Knew that
Kiriel—this Kiriel, this angry, hesitant girl—would say the rest,
and regret it.

Lord Isladar. Shining Court. Allasakar-born child. It made sense
only because, as she watched them, girl and man—for he looked

the part of a man, sounded it—she saw the ties that bound them; they were ugly, but they were there. Pain. Fascination. Need.

Not to him. I'll keep you, Kiriel; you gave me your oath. And if I let you go—and she had let members of her den graduate—*it won't be to that bastard.*

Jewel was bleeding now, from eighteen wounds, only the last three of which were life-threatening by her own guess, but she wasn't dead. That she was on her feet at all was incentive to stay that way.

While Kiriel stared at this creature, Jewel quietly bent to the alley floor and retrieved a dagger. It was only that, now. The killing stroke had already been given, and denied.

But Hells, a dagger was better than nothing.

She was wobbly; thought that she would be worse than wobbly in less than a few minutes. As carefully as possible, she took aim, and spared enough of the breath she held to speak a single word, and that a supplication. *Kalliaris.*

She threw the knife.

It struck him. She was good enough to hit a motionless target in the back, especially if it was large enough to be mistaken for a good-size section of barn. The damned dagger—well, the blessed dagger, really—made it as difficult as possible; it was everything that a dagger shouldn't be. Pretty. Ornate. Unbalanced.

But it did its work.

It broke the moment.

"Kiriel!"

They both turned, then—Kiriel and the demon. The darkness of the alley would hide nothing at all from the eyes of the newest member of Jewel's small den. She knew it.

Isladar had time to frown, time to lift a hand in either denial or supplication, before Kiriel's sword bisected him.

Or it would have, gods curse him, had he still been standing there.

"Damn," Jewel said, to no one in particular. And then, as Kiriel reached her side, she added, "Angel. Get Angel." Pause. "And the girl. Don't know whose she is."

After that, there were no more words.

No light, no pain.

But as she slid into oblivion—fighting it all the way because she was Jewel and fighting was what she did best—she saw a familiar face step out of the sun's light toward her. Smiled, or tried to, as Avandar Gallais tried to take her from Kiriel's arms. Those arms tightened, and Jewel realized that she was being carried.

She wondered, before she lost the light entirely, who would win.

CHAPTER ELEVEN

Alowan could not speak with Jewel; she had faded into something too heavy to be sleep, and she could not be awakened. The young woman, Kiriel, had delivered her into the keeping of her den-mate, Finch—but only after Finch had assured her that there were healer-born here who could grant life any miracle as long as some life remained.

Kiriel did not desire to see the healer. Reacted as if it were a shock, to hear of him. Maybe it was. But she accepted Finch's word as if the mention of the healer-born was indeed enough proof of a miracle, and she left swiftly. Left before Devon ATerafin came in, bearing Angel.

Finch froze.

Seeing Jay had been bad enough. Angel—Angel was worse, somehow. It wasn't the blood; they were both covered with it, sticky with it. No, it was his hair; his hair—which she'd never really liked—was flat, its spiral broken. The rest of him seemed intact, but his hair—he never gave it up; it was the last of his life on the street. Not really suitable for Terafin, but it was tolerated.

Angel.

Jay.

Here were *two* people that she loved—she wasn't afraid of that word anymore, they were her *den*—and she knew that a healer could barely survive calling one back.

Alowan came at once, and he looked a long time at them, Jay and Angel, unwakeable, barely breathing—but breathing still. They were in side-by-side beds, out of sight of Teller—which she privately thought was stupid—and he stood between them a long time.

"Well," he said softly. "It comes to this. Was this the House War?"

"No," she said immediately. Knowing she wasn't supposed to

talk about it. Knowing that she would, to Alowan. "It was Kings' business, all of it."

Some of the tension left his expression; none of the weariness. "I cannot save them both," he told her softly.

He was wavering in her vision; she turned her back and rubbed her hands angrily over her eyes, as if she could squeeze them dry. "Will you—would you be willing to—to save one of them?"

A long pause. A *long* pause. And then. "Yes."

Anyone else, anyone else and she would've known who he'd pick. But Alowan didn't judge the way anyone else did.

"Who?"

He smiled at that, smiled wearily. Because she asked. Because she knew that to him, to the part of him that healed, life was life. There were precious few in the House—with its political tensions, its fractured struggle for power—who understood that at the moment.

They both heard the doors to the healerie open. No question who it would be. None at all. Devon had gone at once to fetch her: The Terafin. They entered the room, the armored man and the woman who was so sure of her power it seemed she didn't need armor. Morretz followed in her wake, as silent as always; his eyes flickered over Avandar, who stood apart, who stood alone watching Jay from a distance. Watching her, knowing that that watching did nothing, or so it seemed to Finch.

The healer tensed; she saw his shoulders slump and then rise, saw the line of his jaw stiffen. He turned and bowed. "Terafin," he said.

She wasn't a stupid woman. She must've heard it in his voice, because she said, "You have not begun."

"No. There are . . . two . . . who cannot be brought back by anything but the call."

She was silent a moment. Then, "There is only one who is important to the future of the House. Do what must be done."

"I will." He bowed his head again. "But it will not be to your liking, Terafin."

"What?" Devon's voice, harsh, loud where The Terafin's was soft, for all that you could hear it anywhere.

"We do not argue here, not in this place. It is the healerie, and it is *my* domain. If you wish it, Terafin, I will leave your grounds having achieved no healing at all. But for reasons of my own— good reasons—I believe it is the boy that I must save."

"Boy? He's not been a boy for twenty years!"

"And you, sir, for longer."

"If she dies, we lose her sight, we lose her vision—we lose—"

"What do we lose, ATerafin? You will speak of House matters when The Terafin does not?" He turned away then.

Finch was silent, although she paced back and forth in front of the fronds whose tips touched floor from a height that was greater than Avandar's, pretending not to hear the raised and lowered voices, the imprecations, the near-pleas, the curses.

Avandar moved to stand beside Jewel's bed. He made of silence a weapon, one turned in both directions: outward and inward. Finch had never seen him so grim, so pale, so—downtrodden. The Terafin, she thought, had aged, putting on the weight of years the minute she crossed the threshold between her manse and Alowan's healerie. And it was, indeed, Alowan's healerie, no matter that it was located in the heart of Terafin's finest dwelling. They had forgotten it, at times, because they *could* forget it; not even during the last pitched battle, the aftermath of it, had he contravened any order, ignored any request, The Terafin had chosen to give him.

Finch had nothing against standing up for oneself against power—after all, it was not as if Alowan had ever chosen to take the Terafin name—but she wasn't certain she would have chosen now to do it, if she had been someone else. If she had been him.

But if she'd been him, she wouldn't have been able to act at all. There were some choices that should never have to be made, and this was one: Alowan, hovering between the barely breathing bodies of Jay and Angel. Finch was afraid. Maybe, at his age, there was no way he could bring even one of them back. But if that were the case, surely he'd say it? She bit her lip to stop from thinking; didn't help. Never did.

Jester and Carver had gone, with Meralonne, to find the demon-trapped young girl's parents, to deliver her to them. To hear Devon speak, she wouldn't have found her way home, otherwise; she was in a state of grace that people who've forgotten what pain and terror *really* feels like call shock. Devon was speaking now, and it was clear that what he had to say didn't do much but annoy the healer.

She tried not to listen.

Because The Terafin and Devon were *both* doing it. They were talking about Jay and Angel as if they were just two weapons; Jay was the House sword, and Angel was a well-made, but common, dagger.

She thought—she thought that Avandar would join them. That he would demand, because everything with Avandar had the weight and feel of demand, no matter how he worded it, that the healer heal Jewel. But he seemed content to let The Terafin speak for him. To let Devon speak for him.

"Neither of you understand. I expect that lack from you," Alowan said, frowning at Devon ATerafin, "but from you, Amarais, I expect better."

"Better?"

"You should know who this young woman is."

"She is thirty-two or thirty-three by her own reckoning, Alowan. She is not a child."

"No. But she is not a power, not yet. She is useful. She is necessary—but she is *not* a weapon that can be reduced to the value of its obvious function. You do not know the steel that goes into her; you do not understand, either of you, that *this* is the time when the sword is being tempered." He lowered a voice that was seldom raised. "But you should, Amarais. You should. Ten years from now, I would tender a different answer. But I know what you intend, as she refuses to know it, and I tell you now that if I choose differently, the sword will be poorly tempered; the edge will be brittle."

"If she dies, Healer, and she does approach death, she will not survive the temper." Devon's voice.

"Yes."

"Alowan—"

The old man looked across at the woman that he had served, without name, for half of his adult life. "Call me a coward," he said softly, "if you must. But I have done what you ask of me once—twice—in my life, Amarais. It is how I came to be trapped here, when I abhor things political.

"I offer no lie. What I have seen in healing *you,* I have seen in her. If you could force this choice upon me, it would break her for the House purpose. Understand it. There are sacrifices that one *must* come to on one's own. You did."

"If the House does not have that time?"

"Then, either way, the House will fail. Accept it, Amarais; what is precious in her cannot be forced."

She fell silent then; she did not flinch or blush or pale. She was, in Finch's eyes, The Terafin.

"The boy," Alowan said softly. "The boy I will save. But if you do not leave us, they will both die."

Devon stepped forward and reached out; Finch held breath as she realized that he was going to *grab* the older man. But his hand stopped, froze suddenly, as if the hand and the man were struggling. The man won.

"You have money," Alowan said, as he bent down to place his hands upon Angel's broken chest. "And time, if you wish to save Jewel ATerafin. The boy's injuries are worse."

Time, but not much of it.

Avandar stirred. "You've decided, then."

Not a question, not really. "It's not what Angel would've wanted," Finch heard herself say. She bit her lip; she'd meant to stay out of it entirely.

"No," Alowan replied, without looking back, his voice as gentle with Finch as he himself always was. "And I can guarantee that when I've finished, it will be the last thing he will be willing to face again. Remember, Finch; he is not the first member of your den that I've called back from death's lands."

And she did remember. Arann.

She walked over to the bed. Sat down on the other side of it—or tried to; she had to scramble to find a chair. "I'll wait."

He didn't answer.

But as she watched the lines of his face deepen, she realized that sometime in the last decade he had crossed the line between old and elderly; that his power, the power to heal and comfort, was as tenuous as his life. Angel.

Damn, she wished she could *see*.

"Your pardon," Avandar said softly. "Before you begin?"

"I have little time," Alowan replied, but the heat had given way to a tired coolness.

"I understand why you choose as you do. We both understand her that well, healer, and I will not argue against your judgment; it is, I believe, the least costly of the two choices. But you know that there are very, very few of your kind—and of those, fewer still who will—who are willing—to call a man back from death."

"Yes," he said. "And I know that there are three people in this room who will move heaven and earth—and Hells, if need be—to find one. For her." Softer, so softly that Finch could barely catch the words, he added, "Ten years from now; a decade, and she will be wise enough to understand what it is she must endure. But try to train a man too harshly before his time, and more often than not you break the spirit you wish to nurture."

And Avandar said, again, "I know."

And Alowan replied, "It wasn't to you that I was speaking. Go. She has time, but not much."

Carver came to take up watch. Jester. Before the end of his shift—and they all knew when his shifts ended—Arann walked in, no armor, no sword, nothing to mark him as a House Guard.

Arann'd never been much of a talker. But he'd seen more fighting than any of them—most of it scuffling, some of it fatal—and he knew when he set eyes on Jewel that she wasn't going to make it without help.

"Torvan sent word," he said. "Gave me leave." Always Torvan, among the den. No title. No rank. "What happened?"

They told him. Halting, interrupting each other and falling silent in awkward hesitation; they were nervous. They'd never had an emergency meeting without Jay before.

"Kalliaris," Finch whispered.

"Hells with that," Carver snarled. "Devon. Avandar. The Terafin." They clenched their hands into fists, and waited, watching the old man as he sat like a trembling statue over one of their kin, while the other bled slowly away.

The Queens' Court boasted a healer of skill and renown; the Kings' Court, three. But the healers of the Kings' Court were bound to the Kings' lives, and the lives of their heirs; not even the Queens were given leave to visit, and be visited, by these men.

It was, Devon thought, a good thing that healers were notoriously difficult to assassinate; the three had been targets before, and would no doubt be targets again. Still, they were chosen by the Astari, after intensive scrutiny, and with great care, and they served as law dictated. He knew them, of course; they were not invisible in the court—but the closest they got to healing was in the training of the young men and women who saw to the lesser injuries in the Kings' and Queens' Halls. By law, they could heal no one but the Kings.

He wondered, idly, what would happen if that law were contravened. Realized that he didn't particularly care. They were not useful to him. There was only one man in *Avantari* who might be.

Dantallon, the Queens' healer.

The halls were full; it was always this way the day before the biggest event of the year. Not even the Day of Return boasted such a pride of activity, such a fever of last-minute panic. He could hear the heavy soles of the Kings' Swords as they ran from one end of the palace to the other; this particular year had been difficult, and would be more so before a Champion was crowned.

But for all that they were busy—and irritable—they did not slow the passage of Devon ATerafin, a man they recognized as the most senior of Patris Larkasir's advisers in matters of trade and Royal concessions. A man in his position was a man who was privy to both the secrets of power and wealth—if any of the Kings' Swords could easily understand how these two were separated—and they did not so much as question him.

Dantallon, on the other hand, was never quite as circumspect. He was busy. In the humidity of the summer, he was often faced with certain diseases that, when not contained, could kill far too many of the city's vulnerable inhabitants: The old, the very young. At the moment, he stood, arms folded across a chest that had always, and would always, be slender, his forehead creased, his eyes narrowed as he stared down at the tabletop before him as if it would provide answers, and now.

There was a map on that table, and it was marked in several places with slender pins, each of which bore a red flag. The two men to either side of him wore uniforms; one was definitively the red of a magistrate, and the other, the deep blue of a member of the Kings' forces, a circle quartered and lined up across a diagonal. Across from Dantallon was a man whose back was bent; he dressed well, but simply. Devon waited a moment; the man stood. Dark-haired, then, but grayed. Tall, broad-shouldered.

Devon ATerafin could walk into a room and remain unnoticed as long as no one was looking for him; he chose that moment to make the normal noise of entry into another's abode. His feet fell more heavily and his breath came regularly; he cleared his throat.

The magistrate did not hear him; the Sword and the healer did.

"ATerafin," Dantallon said curtly. "I hope this is not an emergency."

"You are already embroiled in one?"

"In two, if I understand the Sword and Healer Levec correctly."

The man in no uniform turned then, and Devon smiled. "Healer Levec." His bow was low, graceful.

"The Swords are attempting to ensure that a foolish young man survives a foot race. Or survives any injury he takes during that race." It was clear what Dantallon thought of that.

"I see."

"The healer and the magistrate are here to coordinate, with the Swords, an attempt to contain the crippling disease. It is late in the season for it, and it is more virulent than it has been in fifteen years."

"But they—"

"They would not normally be at the palace, no, but they require the cooperation of the Swords at this particular time; the affected areas cross into the areas whose security has come under the Kings' jurisdicton.

"I trust that you have nothing to add to this difficulty?"

Devon was silent a moment. "I do," he said softly at last. "But it is not Kings' business. I bear a message from The Terafin, and it is to be delivered either to you or to the Queen Marieyan."

"Deliver it, then."

Devon crossed the room; placed the burden of his Lord's words into the hand of another man. Bowed. Rose. Watched that man's face. He knew how to watch a face; how to read the thoughts that would become words—and the thoughts that never would—in the shifting lines of expression. He did not know, not completely, what Amarais had written, but he knew before Dantallon had finished what the answer would be.

It had been a faint hope, not a real one.

And this season, with so much at stake, they would not risk the strength of the only healer that was theirs to command as they chose.

Dantallon's hands very carefully rolled up the scroll. "You will express my regrets," he said, "to The Terafin. But unless you can convince the boy not to run that race, I will receive no permission to use my skills in the service to her House." From his expression, and from his own knowledge both, Devon knew that there was no way to dissuade the boy; everything short of incarceration had already been threatened. Dantallon was polite in his refusal; gentle. Pressed, he would show his steel.

Devon ATerafin turned to the man whose healing House was known throughout the Empire. "Healer," he said. "Dantallon?"

Dantallon's frown was momentary, but it was there; so was the hesitation, the heartbeat between the understanding of Devon's request and the follow through. He handed the message to Healer Levec, who read it—scanned it. The seal, he would no doubt recognize.

The healer frowned. "I am here to save lives, not to politic," he said, as he set the scroll aside like so much refuse.

"I have come to save a life," Devon replied. "And the fact that that life has value to Terafin does not make it less of a life."

A peppered brow rose and fell. Healer Levec rarely smiled; he did not smile now. But he said, "Granted. I have my students spread thin throughout the city, and everyone with an injury worse than a hangnail has been sniveling at their hems."

"Violence?"

"Twice. Contained by the magisterial guards." He shrugged. "The students are new, for the most part; they're too soft. They'll learn to grow calluses." He shrugged. "Luckily, they don't have to do it much. I say no for them. What do you want?"

"One of them."

"Any particular one?"

"One who isn't afraid to walk into death."

"No."

"We have a young woman who has been serving the Kings' interests. Today, saving the life of a child, she was almost killed by a—by a rogue mage."

"That is not my affair. That is the affair of the Order of Knowledge. *My* affair is the crippling disease. If you don't mind?"

"I do mind."

"ATerafin—" Dantallon began.

"We would not have won the last war fought in this city without the aid of the young woman who lies dying now," Devon said, through clenched teeth. "You might remember it, Healer. It was the Henden of—"

"The year 410." Levec was silent again. "I . . . remember it. No one who lived in this city then could do otherwise." He shook himself. "But she did her service. She made the choice. I will not sacrifice one of my students to her."

"Don't sacrifice them, then. Give them a choice."

Levec snorted. "And you don't think that one or two of them aren't fools? No one who's done it—who's walked that close to death, and been that entwined with a stranger—ever survives unscathed. Do you let an infant swim out to sea? No. But they *want* to. They even think they understand what that want means. These students—they weren't given into the care of *my* house to be turned into tools. They've their own lives, and I intend to make damned sure they live them."

"Levec—"

"ATerafin." Dantallon now. Using a tone of voice that he rarely used.

Devon fell silent, letting the heat drain from him, from the words that would have followed the name. "If not for her," he said softly, "you would not be here now. Nor, I think, would your precious students. She is not a political entity, Dantallon. She is not an evil powermonger—not even by your definition."

"Will you tell me, with a straight face, that she is not involved in the war of succession that Terafin now fights among its own?"

Devon was white, then. Silent.

"They all have money," Levec said coldly. "And they come to me when they bleed. To my House. Tell me that she's not one of your Council. That she's not one of your contenders. That she's not *political.*"

"She's not what you think of when you think of that. If she were, you would already know it, I think. You insult her because you've never met her, or because your dislike for the patriciate colors your perception. But I tell you now that you need not protect your students from her; they will not be blackened or darkened by the experience. To know her, if that's what it takes—would be the privilege of a student's life, not the ruin."

The healer looked across at the ATerafin; they were of an age, or so it had first seemed to Devon. But there were lines in the healer's face that were more than the product of sun and sea wind. "What do you mean, ATerafin?" he said at last. "Are you . . . fond . . . of this girl?"

"If you mean am I personally involved with her, the answer is no." He did not add, although he wished to, that it was also none of the healer's business. Because he was aware that Levec was known for his temperament, and little things offended him easily. Aware that if there was any chance at all that Levec could, or would, perform this thing, or see it done, he could not afford to offend. "But she has been a part of Terafin, ATerafin, since she was, to the best of our knowledge, sixteen."

At that, Levec did raise a brow. And then, to Dantallon's amazement—and it was amazement; even a man who was completely unobservant could not have failed to note the way his jaw went slack as it fell open—Levec said, brusquely, "I will meet this girl. We do not have the time for it, but I will meet her."

Devon *moved.* It was only when the streets of the high city opened up before them that he realized how odd it was; Jewel ATerafin was in no condition to meet with, speak with, anyone, and the healer must have known this.

Hope, bitter and sharp as a keen blade, made him hold his tongue.

Alowan met them in the healerie, or rather, they met him; he sat on the edge of his fountain, in the quiet of the arborium that he had designed for just this use: the recovery and the care of the patient.

Levec had not spoken a single word from the moment they left *Avantari,* in haste, until he set eyes upon Alowan; then, and only then, did he speak: A word. A name.

The old man looked up at the younger one.

Had Devon the luxury of time, he would have let the moment pass in silence; would have granted them privacy. The vulnerability in the older healer's expression was almost painful to look upon.

Is this at the heart of Angel? he thought, because he could not help but think it. And then, *What would you see, Alowan, if you were to come to death, seeking me? What would you take from the experience? Would you be glad that we were parted?*

Alowan rose. Devon was privately pleased that it was Levec who offered the old man the brace, the strength, of his arm.

"I did not expect to see you," Alowan said quietly. Weakly.

Levec shrugged with his free shoulder; his arm was rock solid. "I'm surprised you waited here."

"I cannot help but wait," Alowan said softly. "Because she is dying, and she was the center of Angel's life."

"Angel?" And then he stopped. "Of course. There *would* be a reason that you would not choose to heal the girl. There were two?"

Alowan nodded.

"But you chose this—this Angel?"

"Yes."

"Why?" The word was soft; the suspicion in it was not.

"Because the boy is worth nothing to the House," Alowan replied, matter-of-factly. "The girl, everything."

It was not the answer that Levec expected; this much was clear. "You serve the House," Levec said. "Surely the House would have say?" He turned to Devon, then. "I assume that The Terafin would have chosen to save this girl's life over the other's."

"You assume correctly."

"I will warn you," Alowan said, "that Meralonne and Avandar have been working here the past hour; the member of the Order has left, but Avandar remains. They are attempting to slow the passage of time in the space that surrounds her."

"And?"

He shrugged. "I heal; I am not a mage. I know only that she is not dead. Not yet."

The younger healer stopped. "Alowan," he began, his voice gentle. "You—"

"I know. But it will be over soon enough."

"I never understood why," he said. "You were, of all the masters I've ever had, the master of my choice—and yet you did what you warned us against; have done it, in *her* service, again and again."

"And you seek to question me?" The old man's laugh was hollow. "Then question me when I have an answer to give you." They walked together into the infirmary in which Jewel ATerafin now lay. Angel was gone; Avandar remained.

"Her den," Alowan said, before Devon could ask, "are with Angel. He needs them; he understands what I knew; that Jewel ATerafin is dying, and that his life was bought at the cost—he feels—of hers. He is remarkable, Devon. I have rarely met a man who can be *this* close and come from it to the world so little changed." He looked down at his feet, his expression shifting in a way that was oddly reminiscent of Angel. Devon had not thought to see it there, so obvious. "I do not think he will survive her death, if she does die; perhaps the choice I made was the poorer one."

"Why is she so special?" Levec said suddenly. "To him. Why? Why, if she's so special, did you heal the boy instead of the girl?"

"Why? Because I understand the girl well, Levec. Had he died, now, she would not become what she *must* become. She was not born to the patriciate and its games; she was not even born to your beloved free towns. She was born to a Southern mother, a Northern father, in the twenty-fifth holding; they died when she was a girl, and she was forced to the streets. There, instead of becoming a part of the street, she made the street conform to her, even then—even at that age; she found her den, formed it."

"She belonged to a street den."

"Yes. They did what they had to to survive, but not more; she's particularly proud of that."

"You've said you understand her."

"Yes."

"Will you allow me to examine her?"

"I do not think it necessary. I can tell you what—"

"Let me."

"If her domicis will permit it."

He touched her face.

Avandar's breath was a slightly pungent wind that crossed his cheek, but Levec was not offended; the domicis seemed to be the only man in the room who dared to draw breath. Certainly Alowan did not.

It pained him, to see Alowan so weary who had once been so full of fire, so full of both himself and the ideals which had been held so dear. Who, of all of his teachers, would he have chosen to emulate in his youth? Alowan, of course. Always Alowan. Was this how heroes ended?

I'm getting old, he thought. And he was. Too old for the school. Too old for the hopeful young faces that gradually acquired the dimness and scars of experience. He loved the hope, and hated it, because he hated to watch it die.

Who had told him, a decade ago, to look on that hope as a flower and a blossom; to see it as spring's natural renewal, to see its death *not* as death, but as wisdom, experience, the profound effect of life? Alowan, of course.

Levec bowed his head, closed his eyes.

"You were the strongest healer I've ever taught," Alowan said, unexpectedly interrupting the reverie. "And I think, although I have no spies in your house, no students who are there to tell me of your behavior or misbehavior as I once did, that you have only grown stronger." His voice hardened. "Take what you need, Levec—but do not take more."

Levec looked up. Nodded. He saw Devon ATerafin's face darken, but that was his problem; he wasn't very fond of the patriciate, and Devon ATerafin typified it.

But a girl who grew up in the twenty-fifth, and somehow made her way here to help save a city, a girl who inspired the loyalty of both Angel, the unknown man, and Alowan, the healer, did not. Or so he suspected. He felt hope; it stung. Perhaps she was the one, this girl, perhaps she would be the key.

If a healer's power was strong enough, he could touch more than just the body when he touched at all; he could come close to a person without the weakening of barriers that death brought. Could read, not just their thoughts—for often, they were beyond thought—but the things that lay at their heart, hidden, as it must be, from others.

Levec was a powerful healer.

He let himself walk the ways that were Jewel ATerafin. Jewel Markess. Jay. He knew who Angel was to her, the space he occupied, the feel of his companionship; he knew what lay beyond sight, and beyond specific event, specific experience. Heart. He knew, then, why Alowan had made the choice he had. Wondered if the older healer had touched Jewel as he touched her now, drawing, from her, feeling stripped of word, of specificity, but not of personality, not of self.

It was Alowan who brought him back, catching both of his hands and pulling them away from the sides of her face, gently but in a way that brooked no resistance.

"Will you heal her?" he said.

Levec ran his hand over his eyes; they were wet. "Do you know what you have here?" he asked softly.

"I know," Alowan said. "Without what you've seen, I still know it." He paused. "Will you help us, Levec? We have no other choices. I cannot go where she has gone; I have neither the strength nor the courage."

"Do you know," Levec said, as if he hadn't heard the question, "how vicious this war is going to be?"

Alowan was silent a moment. "You mean the House War," he said at last.

"Yes."

"I . . . have some idea."

"And you think she can somehow survive it?"

"Given what she is, yes, I do." He was quiet. "I value this House. I know that you don't understand that. But it stands for—it has stood for—things that I admire. Not all power is evil, Levec."

Levec was silent. At last he rose. "I do not do this without misgivings," he said gruffly. "But I believe we may help each other, you and I."

Alowan nodded, almost serene. "I thought as much."

The younger healer's eyes narrowed. "You know."

"I . . . have friends in the healing house."

Levec bowed. "I will send for the boy."

"He is hardly a boy, Levec."

"You think of her as a girl, and she is hardly that. We all have our foibles when we think of those who've wormed their way into our affections."

He returned with a young man. It took the better part of two hours, and Devon and Avandar stood in the room as if pacing was beneath their dignity but the desire for it was fierce. Finch came and went; Carver came and went; Jester came and went. Arann, oddly enough, did not; he stayed, unmoving, apparently unmoved.

Alowan knew well why; Arann, of all of them, could understand Angel's loss, the pain that came with being only physically whole. The old healer was glad that Kiriel had returned to her unit; he did not like the girl, although he did not know why, and it shamed him.

His young aide came into the room in a rush and a bow. "Healer Levec," she said.

"Alone?"

"No. There is a young man with him."

"Good. Send them in."

He watched, waited. A young man entered the room. He was taller than either Levec or Alowan; he was as fair in coloring as Dantallon, the Queens' healer, but he was grimmer in look, colder in bearing; his presence was not unlike that of the domicis, Avandar.

Not a healer by avocation, merely by birth.

Except, of course, that was impossible. Alowan bowed.

"I am Alowan," he said.

"I am Daine," the younger man replied, bowing stiffly. "Healer Levec holds you in regard."

"And I him. Come in."

Levec followed, silent. He made his way between the twin sentries of Devon and Avandar, demanding by presence alone that they give the bed in which Jewel lay a wider berth. They did. "This," Levec said to the stiff young man, "is the girl."

"You want me to heal her."

"Yes."

The young man stared at her a long time. He sat, stiffly, in the chair by the bed. "And if I do not want to do this thing?"

"She will die." Levec shrugged. "I will not force you, Daine. You have suffered that once."

Alowan closed his eyes; turned away. The rumor was true.

"Then I will not do it."

"But," Levec continued, "I believe that you will find a way back from death that will free you from the last journey, if you choose this one." He took the younger man's hand; Daine stiffened but did not pull back. "I *ask* it, Daine, but I cannot command it."

"And if I don't do it, what will you do? Revoke the protection of your House? Leave me vulnerable to the demands of the patriciate?"

"No. I will leave. You will leave with me. I ask it, Daine, but I will in no way compel it." He was quiet. "You were born in Averalaan, if I recall correctly."

Daine snorted. "You know damned well I was born here. It's the free towners you fawn over." Only when those words left his lips did he look his age; younger than Jewel ATerafin or her den, with the exception of its newest member.

"Then you were alive during the Henden of 410."

Daine nodded grimly. "We all were. And we all thought we wouldn't see First Day."

"If not for her, we wouldn't have."

He looked at her, then, as if seeing her for the first time. The ice stiffened in his eyes a moment, and then his resolve faltered. "If you're lying to me," he said softly, "I'll know it. I'll know it when I heal her." He frowned. "Why is she dying? Is it the House War?"

Levec didn't answer.

Avandar did. "She was hunting the kin in the streets of the city. She found one, but he was more powerful than any of us expected; more powerful than we were prepared for. You've heard of the bodies discovered in the fifteenth holding, no doubt."

Daine nodded his slender, pale face. Youth there, now, for a just a moment.

"They weren't killed there. She and the mages have hunted them once; they were doing it again, upon the orders of the Kings."

"We've heard none of this."

"There are too many people alive now who were alive in that Henden; it will cause panic, and the panic will serve not our interests, but the interests of the demons."

"Enough, Avandar," Devon said. "You tread too fine a line. Remember that your service requires secrecy."

"He needs to know it," Avandar replied.

"That is for the Kings to say. Not a domicis."

"We are not in *Avantari*, ATerafin, but in Terafin; it is for The Terafin to decide."

"It is now moot," Alowan said, more curtly than he intended. "Daine, she is worthy of your gift. I have seen her in this House the past sixteen years and more, and she is worthy of mine."

"You didn't heal her," he said pointedly.

"No."

"Why?"

"Two reasons. Briefly: Her companion was also dying; she feels responsible for him, and had she lived at his expense, it would have broken her. Second, because I am far too old. I cannot guarantee that I could walk a death for Jewel ATerafin and separate myself from her afterward. Not for Jewel.

"Angel is different enough from the things I admire and the things I desire to protect; I know where I begin, I know where he ends, and I—I have just enough of myself not to want to remain where I don't belong."

He had not yet been as bluntly honest as this; honest enough that Levec would understand it, but not so honest that either Devon or Avandar would. It was hardest, always, to separate oneself from a person one could trust, could—under normal circumstances, love. "I have enough of her companion in me now that I am not above begging you, if that is what you require."

But Daine had already pushed Levec aside; had taken his place beside her. "She—she wears a Council ring," he said. Alowan thought he detected a tremor in the words, a fear.

"Yes. Therefore you must judge the truth of all of our words for yourself. The ring, she earned by her actions. Not her birth, Daine. Not her ruthlessness; she has precious little of that. Not, we fear, enough—but it is not ruthlessness alone that rules the world. Think of the Kings."

"The Kings are god-born."

"Yes. But we all come from a beginning that knew gods, or else there would be no healers. No bards. No young women like Jewel."

Hands, shaking now, touched her face, much as Levec's had done. "I will—I will try this thing. For you, Alowan. For Levec." His smile was ghostly, thin. "For myself, I think. I remember that Henden. I remember that First Day—it was, the *first* First Day, for me. It marks them all. The screaming and then the silence, the dawn. A miracle." He closed his eyes. "I remember the darkness, Levec. I'm so tired of darkness." All arrogance was gone, all ice, although he struggled to speak the words as if against himself, his better judgment.

And Levec said softly, "I know." He looked away, and there were, Alowan thought, tears in the folds of his eyes. He was stubborn, proud; they wouldn't fall.

The healing began.

"Will he be able to let her go?" Alowan asked quietly.

"I—I don't know."

"Who was it? Who forced him to this act?" There was no worse thing one could do, to a healer—but only a healer understood the truth of that; those without the power, those who did not and could never pay the healer's price, could not conceive of the violation.

"A member," Levec said bitterly, "of *this* House."

"Who?"

"It is not of concern," he replied.

"Does he live?"

Levec tendered no reply. It was reply enough. They watched for a while. "Daine is—he was—a soft-headed, soft-hearted idiot."

"You're fond of him."

"I'm always fond of the stupid ones. It's my worst failing." Levec's jaw locked. "They caught him using a child as bait. Makes me wish children had never been invented. They threatened to kill her if he did not heal the man they wished healed; they . . . injured her. The noble was dying. The girl was screaming. Daine—what other choice did he have? He's stupid."

"He did it."

"Yes. They would have killed him afterward, but the man forbade it." Levec closed his eyes. "And it scarred my boy. He has seen murder, and far, far worse, and has had to live with and through it to call the man who has committed all of these atrocities back from the *Hells*."

"Will he hold her too tightly?"

"I think—I think he is stronger than that," Levec said.

He was lying. Alowan heard it in his voice, but said nothing. What was there to say? There were few enough who would risk the walk to begin with; she did not, in his opinion, have the time to wait until they found another, Avandar's magic and Meralonne's containment notwithstanding.

But he knew, then, that the man whose servants had forced the healing must have been Corniel ATerafin. The only man who had died far enough away from the Terafin manse that his body had not been brought to the healerie. Alowan had not regretted his death then; he did not regret it now.

But he bowed his head a moment, in prayer to the Mother that he might not feel such a vicious, such a terrible, sense of triumph at another man's murder.

He was tired, so very, very tired. Angel burned him; he could not separate his fear for Jewel from the younger man's. *I misjudged you,* he thought, not for the first time.

They watched the boy.

Avandar interrupted Alowan's reverie three times, and each, to ask—by gesture alone—if he might somehow interfere. He understood the risks of a healing, to both the healed and the healer. Each of the three times, Alowan shook his head: No.

Alowan understood, then, why Levec cultivated such a dour, grim appearance; no one noticed, who did not know him reasonably well, when it was genuine and when it was not. Today, it was genuine. He kept putting his hands behind his back, pulling them away, wringing them, pulling them apart. It was odd; he was a big man, a man who projected a certain strength, a force of immovable will. The gestures themselves, unconscious, suited him ill.

He heard Finch, as if she were her namesake, fluttering and whispering in a high voice. Thought he should tell her that lower voices carried less of a distance.

And then he heard it. Over the mutter, the questions, the whispering between members of Jewel's den, over Levec's heavy step, Devon's light one, and the merciful stillness of the man whose calling it was to watch and to harbor, the domicis.

"Jay."

They started, all of them. The voice was so labored it was hard to tell who of the two had spoken: Jewel ATerafin, or Daine of Levec's House.

Interesting, Alowan thought, slightly surprised. *Jay.* Not Jewel.

"Jay," the name came again. Stronger this time. Definitely Daine's voice. She did not respond.

They drew breath then, collectively; they had become, in the intensity of their observation, one person, with one hope.

"*Jay.*"

Too late, Alowan thought, almost numb with the certainty of it. Aware that it was his risk, that he had taken it, as a gambler might. He bowed his head; there was enough of Angel in him, would always be enough of Angel in him, that he knew either way—Jewel or Angel—there had been no way to separate the choice made, the cost of failure.

"Jay—I'd let you stay where you're safe," Daine said, his voice low, intense. "I'd stay there with you myself, and gods be cursed, healers be damned.

"But you know what you have to do. And *I* know it. You *know* what was done to me. Death doesn't change it."

Alowan began to cry. It was not loud; indeed, it was completely still, and the tears were lost in the folds of his skin, lost to light, lost to discovery.

"I won't leave you," he continued, his voice hoarse. "But I can't leave you *there. Kalliaris* curse you, Jay—I've been there. I've been there with *Corniel ATerafin.* I've been living with him for two months. I've been mad with it. I *am* mad with it. You want to die? Tough. Tough shit.

"Come home."

He had never heard a calling so violent. Never heard a calling so angry. And he had never heard a calling so fraught with respect and intent and purpose. But he thought, as he listened to the tenor of the young man's voice, that he might have heard the last of these three things if he had listened to his own voice on a cool, sea-heavy day, over thirty years ago.

Her eyes opened slowly, separating lash by lash into the harsh glare of light, any light. She saw the man who had called her, and she did not shrink from the anger in his voice; instead, she reached up, she reached up to where his hands were gripping her face so tightly her skin was white beneath his fingers.

He thought she would cry.

She did not.

He thought she would be too overwhelmed to speak.

But perhaps, Alowan thought, he had never understood the particular demands of being seer-born. Perhaps this finding, and this losing, was not so new to Jewel ATerafin as it had been to a young Alowan, a young Amarais ATerafin, in a House as much—more—under siege than this House.

"All right," Jewel said. "I'm back."

But she gripped his hands with hers; held them tight.

* * *

Youth and renewal, Alowan thought, caught between bitterness and a brief relief. *The wars return and recede, like the tide. And we have to fight them; it's how and what we fight that defines us. Hones us.*

And of course what was he thinking about? War. Weapons. Death. He was older now, but still remembered what being too young had truly been like; he could see the edges of youth, the pain and the passion of it, carved in the damaged lines of Daine's face.

As if she could hear him, Jewel ATerafin sat up in bed, her hands still gripping the man who had healed her. As if he would leave her. As if, Alowan thought, he could. He marveled then at the things that the seers could see, and the things that were hidden from them; the truths, old and odd, of the heart.

She held him thus a long time, and then Finch—it was often Finch—approached her, tentative as she always was with the injured, the sick.

"Jay?"

They both turned, Daine and the girl whose name she spoke, as if they were one. Finch stopped, awkward now, knowing what she was interrupting. Uncertain, Alowan thought, about how much the healer knew.

"Don't stand," that healer told Jewel, as he ignored his own advice. Levec was there before Alowan could be, and before him—before him, Avandar, his hands under the arms of the collapsing, pale man who had saved his vocation, his chosen master.

Their eyes met; Avandar looked away first.

"Give me my charge," Levec said, when that moment was broken—but not, Alowan noted, before.

Avandar nodded, passing the young man to the older one as if he were both precious and a burden. Levec took hold, and only when his hands were firmly attached to Daine's forearms did the tension leave the line of his shoulder, the set of his large jaw.

"Come, boy," he said, the gruffness surrounding the two words without the slightest ability to penetrate them. "You've done good work here. It's time—it's time to be home."

"It's time," Alowan said suddenly, "for *all* of you to leave."

Finch started to object. The eldest man in the room chose to wield his age as authority, rather than weakness. As wisdom. As command. "No, Finch. No argument. You will all leave this room. Devon. Avandar. Carver. Jester. Follow Healer Levec out."

"But we can't—"

"*You can.*"

They looked to Jewel, but she did not meet their eyes; indeed, she met no one's; her eyes fell flat upon the pale sheets that rested against new skin, old skin, dried blood.

"Jay?"

Alowan felt a moment's anger—surely the result of weariness. But the anger was just that: momentary. Finch, of all the den save Teller, he had a weakness for, a soft spot. Stunted in youth, she would never reach full height, and she seemed to him very like the ideal youth, for all her thirty or more years.

He caught her by the arm. "Finch," he said softly. "We must give her privacy. It is not an act of desertion, but an act of kindness. She will not thank you for staying."

"We're her den," Finch said.

"Yes. But there are things that Jewel has never really shared well with anyone. Come."

She could not be driven away by his words. She could be brought away by his hand, by the pull of his arm.

I am sorry, he thought, but he did not look back.

She was alone.

She had always known it, and she had *never* known it, not until now. Even so, she waited, counting each footstep's echo as if it were a curse. Holding breath. Clenching fists and forcing them, forcing them to relax. She did not dare to look up. She did not want to see him leave. Because if she saw him—saw him *leave* her, she might say something unforgivably stupid. Weak.

You promised you'd stay.

Oh, she'd done with that. She'd done with that when she was ten. And twelve. When she realized that her parents were never coming home. They'd gone to wherever it was that her grandmother had gone, some dark shadowy halls that didn't open for young children like her.

She remembered how much she'd hated Mandaros then.

How much she hated Kalliaris.

How much she hated the Lady.

And it was nothing to this. Or it felt, at years of remove, as nothing to this. Not a child now, no. She wasn't a child. But she felt this pain that was a child's pain, couldn't be anything but a child's pain, this entirety of emptiness, this horrible sense of absolute desertion.

Is this what I did to you, Arann? You must have hated me, then.

I never promised you that I'd spare you the pain. But I will. I'll never let you get that close to freedom again and force you home to nothing.

She was weeping.

She was weeping because she could, now that they'd gone and left her. It had been so long since she'd wept, she'd thought she'd left it all behind.

Daine.

She saw him as clearly as if he were standing before her. She could feel his hands in hers, and she knew where they were callused from writing and weaving—the tasks he'd set for himself as a way of recalling his youth in a noble's house. As a way of separating himself from the longing he felt for Corniel ATerafin. Longing for him, loathing himself for the longing.

She could see, through the lens of Daine, the distorted image of that man, and she thought—she thought that had he lived, she would have had him killed. She, who had never assassinated anyone, had never really conceived of doing so.

She felt that she could protect Daine; she felt that he could protect her; there was a circularity and a completion in the desire.

And it was a lie, and she knew it because she was Jewel and she didn't flinch from knowing the truth; real pain, after all, had the benefit of at least *being* real. What else did she know?

She was alone.

She hated to be alone.

She needed to be alone.

He did not reach the front gate.

Oh, he tried. He put one foot in front of the other. Allowed himself to be led by Levec, as he had always been led by Levec. There was a comfort there, a familiarity, that allowed him to be carried above circumstance. Almost. But the halls were long. Had he been brought to a small dwelling, had the healerie been closer to an exit, an entrance, he would have made it out, into sunlight—if sunlight indeed remained, given the flickering glow of torches and lamps—or the moon.

He had been brought to Terafin.

"Levec," he said.

He felt the older man shudder to a stop, as if the name took time to reach his ears. "What?"

"I can't leave."

"You can't stay," Levec said. "You can't stay with her. Not yet. You know the danger."

"Yes. I—I won't go to her. Not, not yet."

"Then come home. Come back to the house. Gather your thoughts—and if you're still decided, gather your things then. Take time, Daine." Levec's dark hair, dark beard, were the shadows across his face that made the paling of his skin seem extreme and sudden in comparison. "You've gone through this once, boy."

"I knew you would say that," Daine replied, stung, but struggling with his anger. He had not struggled so in two months; the anger had rein. "But it's not the same."

"It's never the same."

"She's not what he was."

Levec nodded. "But she's still a member of the patriciate. She's still a member of the Council of *this* House. What do you think to do?"

"Serve," he said, simply.

"You can't."

"Why?"

"Daine—you've done it twice now. You've walked where even I won't walk. Serve her—serve this House, and you'll be called upon to do it again and again. Look at what it's done to Alowan; look at what it's cost him. We are not so very different in age, he and I."

"After Corniel," Daine said quietly, "I thought I would never, never heal again."

"But you—"

"No, you don't understand. Never *heal*. Not walk to the dying, not go into the darkness—but deny the rest as well."

"I . . . I know. I know," Healer Levec said, as he said all things. Gruffly. Shortly. "But you recovered."

"And now I see her," Daine continued, paying his master's words no mind, "and I see that I can't not heal. She's *here*," he added, thumping his chest. "I know what she has to do. Because I saw what she was running away from. And I know her well enough to know that she can't run, not forever. She *needs* me. And I—I need her. I need to do this, Levec. I need to do more than heal the results of a war caused by men like . . . like Corniel. He's part of me, still. He calls to me, still. There are days I wake up, and I'm already burning in the Hells.

"How do I deny him? How do I deny a man who walked right

through my soul and left marks in places I didn't even know existed? *You* can heal. You know who you are. You know who you were. You might even know who you want to be. Let people come to you, take their money. You *know* you're doing the right thing.

"But I don't. If I serve her, now, I lay him to rest. Do you understand? If I serve her, I deny, *by action*, what he wanted, and what he was. I'll be doing something to prove to myself that I can do something."

"You don't just serve until you feel better," Levec said. "Not a House like this. You don't think Alowan felt the same way?" He was shouting now. On the other hand, it was a minor miracle that he'd prevented himself from shouting for this long. "Look what it's done to him! He's isolated here, he has no peers. He has a little garden in the middle of a pit of vipers. Is that what you want?"

"I think," Alowan's voice said, from some distance away, "that that is not a fair question, Levec."

Levec didn't have the grace to be flustered. "Tell him! Tell him the truth!"

"He's right," Alowan said serenely to the young man. "As are you. And he has not said, although it bears saying, that in the early years, there were several attempts upon my life. None, as you can see, were successful."

"They didn't have to be," Levec said bitterly. "They had you anyway."

"Did you heal her?" Daine asked.

"I was arrogant as a youth. You were not. It was my choice to embark upon the healing; choice was taken from you. But, yes, Daine. I healed The Terafin, and I think I know what you see in Jewel because I think it is stronger in her than it was in Amarais at that age.

"Levec is right. This is not a salve, not a way of easing yourself or comforting yourself. It is a life, and it will be the only life you lead. And there is no guarantee—not now, not from where we stand—that you will succeed in what you intend. Or that she will."

"She saved us, you know," Daine said, although it was forbidden to speak of the healed and the knowledge gleaned by the intimacy of that act.

"I know."

The young man closed his eyes tightly, shutting them both out.

Losing, for a moment, the halls of the manse, the torches, the lamps, the crystal chandeliers that both caught and cast light. Then he turned, just as suddenly, and looked into the tall silvered glass that showed such a stark reflection. His own.

"I can't leave," he said, meeting only his own eyes.

"I know," Alowan said. "I am sorry. Come. Let me show you where you will live." He paused, waited as Daine continued to stare at his image in the mirror as if he couldn't easily discern which of the two of him were the real one. At last Alowan turned, to meet Levec's eyes. To meet Levec's anger.

"I am sorry," he said, in as deep a voice, as sincere a tone. "But the boy was lost anyway, and we both knew it."

"I did not know that you knew."

The old man bowed, and when he rose, his lips were turned up in a bitter, old smile. "I have lived my years in a House built upon traditions of the patriciate, old friend. And I . . . have performed a healing for a young man who has literally lived to serve and protect Jewel ATerafin for all of his adult life. Forgive me this."

"If he survives it. And if you do," was Levec's bleak reply.

When he returned to the healerie's fountain, exhausted and satisfied—if satisfaction could have such a bitter tinge—he found Avandar waiting for him. He had never been fond of Avandar Gallais, not in the way that he was of the woman he protected, of the men and women *she* harbored, but there was respect between them.

Avandar bowed. "The boy has chosen?"

It irked him, to be so transparent. "Yes."

"Will he be your match?"

It was not the question that the healer had anticipated. After a moment, he offered the slightest of smiles. "I am arrogant enough to think that no one can watch as I watch, or offer what I have offered."

"That is not arrogance," Avandar replied. "Or rather, it is a pleasing arrogance, for it is based in fact, and not fancy."

"He does not need to be my match. Young Jewel has gifts of birth that The Terafin does not possess, and they will protect her well."

"It is not Jewel directly whom I fear for."

"No." The healer bowed. "She will be gentle with him in a way that Amarais could never allow herself to be with me. She will ask him to save no lives that she does not value personally. Not yet.

"And the first time that she does, she will break a trust between them, and she will break it because of the cost she sees in doing otherwise. But he will be older then, wiser, and I think he will see it as she does. I hope.

"I am tired, Avandar. Perhaps it is true that I overplay my age to spare myself hardship, but my age *is* a fact. I did not dream— I did not hope. But it appears that a god watches over me, and has seen fit to grant me a successor."

He did not say, and Avandar did not, that he feared the god was Cartanis. God of Just War. Of war.

"I am in your debt."

"No. You are in her service. You have not been tested, Avandar. But I believe that this *is* what you've chosen to devote your service to, and you will have your chance."

Avandar was completely still. And then he offered the healer a smile, one that was, if cold, quite genuine. "We are all more obvious than we would like to be. I *have* chosen to serve power. But we are all changed by the service we take and the service we perform. It is never what it seems at a distance, no matter how great our knowledge, how certain our power.

"She is not like The Terafin. Not like any ruler of any House that I have seen, not among The Ten. She was not raised among the patriciate. She knows enough of their manners to get by when she can be bothered to exercise them, but even that has been an uphill struggle." He offered a rare smile. "We value what we fight for, Healer."

"Perhaps, if she must fight for Terafin, she will learn to value it as highly as your master did." His smile deepened before it vanished. "And perhaps not. I am in your debt, as I have said. I— am grateful that the healer was found."

Jewel Markess ATerafin had finally given in to sleep. In the dark, a honeycombed room away from where Angel struggled noisily in the grip of a nightmare that did not—quite—force him to wake, she was utterly still; only her hands, clenched fistlike around gathers of blanket, gave any hint to the two who watched that she was not peaceful.

But neither were they.

They were both powers within the realm they had chosen, and they had come this distance to speak with a woman who was two steps away from being in the prime of her power. Had come, if they were honest, to take advantage of the weakness that Jewel herself would not own up to, to press her to take the last of those steps.

But they could not bring themselves to wake her, because the sleep robbed her face of all armor; it was a child's sleep, and she was, at least to one of the witnesses, much like a child.

"Do you travel," The Terafin asked her unexpected companion, "as you always do?"

"Yes," the woman in midnight blue robes said softly. "Always."

"Then you did not have the burden of slipping past the healerie staff." Her smile, in the poorly lit darkness, was genuine.

"No." She turned, this Evayne, and The Terafin, who had met her now a handful of times, saw that they were almost of an age; Evayne was perhaps a handful of years younger. It was hard to tell; her cape's hood had folds long enough to cast shadows that softened harsh lines. "Terafin, a question."

"Ask."

"I can see only so far in the life of this young woman." She reached into her robes and drew out the heart of her power, the glowing orb that rested between her hands like living light. "I have seen her here. I have seen that she has gathered to her, at last, the third—the last—of her pillars. If she can grant them the strength they're due, she'll stand."

"Not a question," The Terafin said softly, "but it answers mine, and I am comforted by it."

"Don't be."

"Why?"

She turned, then, the ball gripped in her palm. Started to speak, and then stopped, searching The Terafin's face. The silence stretched out between them, punctuated by Jewel ATerafin's breathing. And then, of all things, Evayne laughed. "I should have known," she said quietly. "He is at work here, even now."

"The Terafin spirit?" It was barely a question.

"Yes. He is not the harshest of taskmasters, but he spares you nothing once he knows you can carry the burden that must be carried."

"The same can be said of all good masters," The Terafin replied. But she felt it now: the edge of her death. "You cannot see beyond my death, can you?"

Evayne's gaze rose. "I can see," she said at last, "beyond it. I can see this young woman at the path that *must* be walked, one of the supplicants who must walk it if we are to find the first paths and face the coming war." Her violet eyes were wide, unblinking; The Terafin could believe, watching her, that she did indeed see it unfolding as she spoke. Like Jewel, and unlike.

"But I cannot see what she does; the choice offered her, I cannot witness. I cannot witness any of the decisions made. The first path can only be walked once."

"What is your question, Evayne?"

"She is like your blade—your House blade, the sword by which you proclaim your office when war or ceremony demands such proclamation. But she is being tempered now, and she has never been sharpened. Will she hold her edge?"

The Terafin's laugh was short, brief. Then she turned to the seer. "I do not understand you, but I understand that the burden you carry has become your life. What will you be when you set it down?

"I," she added softly, "have the comfort of knowing that I'll be dead. Absent. I came to ask Jewel ATerafin to take up the burden that ends with my life. But your presence here marks a larger war; it always has. The demons that run in the city streets and the ATerafin that sleeps in that bed are not separate; they are part of the same war.

"Will it end?" she asked quietly. "If that war takes her, and the best that she has found in this House, if I accept the risk to House and kin and do nothing to stand in your way, will the fight at least *end* the war?"

"I came," Evayne said softly, answering a different question, "to ask Jewel ATerafin to walk the path when it opens for her, regardless of what the House requires." She bowed her hooded head. "Not an answer, I fear." Turned, but before she took a step, turned back. "But I believe, Terafin—*believe,* and do not know— that when the war ends, for good or ill, it will end."

"That," The Terafin said quietly, "is all I require. My own battles, it appears, are destined to be fought again and again."

"The gods value finality, of a sort."

She was gone in a step; Amarais was alone.

In the darkness, robbed of a splinter of a seer's soul for light, she stared at the bed's sole occupant, and then bowed deeply and walked away.

And in the bed, Jewel Markess ATerafin slowly unbunched her fists.

CHAPTER TWELVE

16th of Lattan, 427 AA
Avantari

Two of the kin still walked the streets.

She could scent them on a wind that carried nothing but shadow, but they were far enough away that she could not name them, could not summon them and challenge them.

Jewel was alive.

She did not know how to react.

She had known Isladar for all of her life, had watched him, had learned from him, and had—and she could say this only to herself, and only now, in the dead of night, when the darkness made her as sure of her power as she could ever be—fled from him.

But she had never known Isladar to fail, and he had intended to kill Jewel ATerafin. She should have felt triumphant, because for the first time in her life she had bested him, and this was not the first time in her life that she had tried.

But those had been schooling games, and in the end, they had always been under his control. The world had, until now.

She was free.

She was free, and an emptiness so entwined with anger that she could not separate one from the other drove even the facade of sleep from her reach. There were no languages in which she could curse him, or damn him; he was *Kialli,* and willfully, voluntarily damned—if damnation was the burning wind, the vast expanse, the song of those who have finally made their irrevocable choice. She would not think about that here.

Could not; it was an ache. Like anger, like the thing that fed anger, it turned in upon her. Demanded action.

Her sword, in the Shining Court, spoke for her. This was not that Court, not that Palace; in *this* palace, the only prey was human; the only fight, a fight that was layered with human weight, human desire, human strength and weakness. If there had been anyone that had marked her as enemy, she might have chosen this night to carry the fight to its inevitable conclusion. But to make real enemies, to make enemies whose end was satisfying enough to ease the building shadow, took time, took the intimacy of jealousy or hatred.

She was restless.

But she wasn't the only one.

She heard him before she saw him, and she knew who he was because the particular fall of the step, the timing of it, had become familiar enough to be distinctive, even over the clinking chime of chain mail. That, and the smell of him, the mixture of sweat and scent and—in her heightened state of awareness—steel, old leather.

She did not turn when he came upon her back because she knew that he knew she was aware of his presence; not a single one of the Ospreys had yet managed to come upon her unaware, and most of them had stopped trying—not that many of them had bothered to begin with. They were an odd group; they'd probably die defending her right to be one of them, but they were aware that she *wasn't* one of them. Couldn't be.

"Kiriel."

"Auralis."

Silence. Awkward, unleavened by ale or wine as it often was with Auralis. With the Ospreys. He waited for her to say more; she didn't.

At last, he broke. Unusual. Usually he walked.

"You had no luck today."

That stung. The shrug she offered was her only answer.

"You're going out hunting tonight."

Have I become that obvious?

"Look. I know that officially it's the Terafin girl who's responsible for finding and tracking the demons. I know that the white-haired mage is supposed to augment her ability. You want me to play that game? Fine. I'll even pretend I believe it.

"But when you go out tonight, I want to come with you."

At that, she did turn. "You?"

In the darkness, his face was shadowed, the line of his chin lost to the long line of neck. There was light enough, though, to see his eyes; fire was reflected there, caught, as it was offered, by torchlight, but made brighter. He bore two swords, one strapped across his back, one in the grip of a hand bound by the half-gloves that the Ospreys favored for fighting in what they called this season. She knew he carried at least two daggers, water; that he could—but seldom did—don helm when the mood to fight struck him.

He had often dressed just like this and gone out into the city streets, refusing the company of his chosen companions since his defeat—public and costly—by the younger Valedan kai di'Leonne. Kiriel was aware that the loss of youth was a fear that most mortals labored under once they reached an age. She was also aware, as no other member of the Ospreys could be, that it was not the defeat itself which had humiliated Auralis; not the fact of the defeat which drove him to seek his solace in fighting, in the streets of the city's hundred holdings. No; it was the comparison; it was looking at Valedan as if he were the mirror held up to Auralis.

But she did not understand precisely what it *was* that he'd seen in the mirror that had that effect. Only that it had less to do with Valedan and age than it had to do with his own fear and the past that all humans—that all creatures—hid behind the supple lines of the facades a life helped them build.

She could see the pain, of course. She could even appreciate it. But she couldn't see what caused it. No more than he could see hers, this night. The past. Loss. Isladar.

"What does the Primus say?"

He said something that was meant to be rude, and she understood it as such, but it did not move her.

"I'm not on his time."

"The Kalakar said—"

"I'm not on her time either."

"It is not safe. Even at—not even the mages hunted the kin."

He shrugged. "You take the mages with you during the day. Doesn't matter. I'm no mage."

"Auralis—" She stopped speaking a moment. When she started again, her voice was cooler. "Why?"

He shrugged. "Because you'll find 'em. I've been looking for a *good* fight for almost two weeks."

She shrugged. "Join the Challenge."

At that, his teeth showed white. "Too late for it, or I'd've tried. You know, Kiriel, that's the first time I've ever heard you try to be funny. Maybe a couple of years from now you'll succeed."

Her turn to shrug; she never recalled shrugging so much in the Shining City. Habits. She'd forgotten how easy it was to absorb them, from humans.

"I don't want to take you."

"I know."

"If you die, Duarte will blame me."

"I'll be dead. I won't care." He smiled. She saw his desperation then, hidden in the folds of his smile the way the knife's edge was when the blade was turned away from the light and only the flat was visible. It was hard not to turn that desperation in on itself; hard not to twist what she could see so clearly into a shape that was more gratifying to her.

She would never have tried to deny herself that pleasure had it not been for Ashaf.

Ashaf.

Isladar.

Jewel.

"Yes," she heard herself saying. "You can come with me. But I warn you—I'm accustomed to fighting alone."

He shrugged. "We all are, Kiriel," he said, staring into the moonlit night, the quiet of the courtyard. "Do you think it's any different, just because we're Ospreys? In the end, we all fight alone, because in the end, that's the way we die."

He was good at what he did.

Some men were killers without competence, killers of convenience; some were killers because they could think of no other way of affirming their power. Some killed out of desperation, to protect the things that they valued, some because they had built a life around following the orders of a more powerful authority, and some killed out of boredom.

She could not tell, watching Auralis—for her eyes, in the darkness, were drawn to him again and again, as if he were one of the dangers of the city, and not in fact a willing ally—which of these things Auralis was. Did not know why she was curious.

Did not understand why he was here. Why she let him be here. And she did not want to think about it, so she turned her thoughts, her senses, her instinct, toward two kin in the streets of the city.

How human.

They were not together.

One was stationary, and one was on the move, and it was the one on the move that caught her attention; it was that demon's power that was the greatest. She had been taught, time and again, that to confront the strongest of the kin was two things, simultaneously: It was the best way to proclaim her own power, and it was the easiest way to expose herself to combined attack. She was what she was; the kin constantly underestimated her ability to survive them. Such estimation served her well in an actual fight; it served poorly because it was the reputation of power that protected one from having to fight at all.

That, to Isladar, was of import.

To Kiriel it was not.

Yet she stopped a moment, beneath the moon's strong light.

"What?"

"There are two."

"Where?"

"Different places."

"And?"

"There's a powerful one and a not so powerful one."

"Where are you going?"

"To the powerful one."

She could see his smile in the night shadows as clearly—perhaps more clearly—than she could in the open day.

"I think I understand," she said softly, "why Alexis worries about you so much." And for a moment, she surprised herself, because she did.

Even at night it was hot.

The kin did not mind the heat, as they did not mind the cold; they rose above either, unconcerned. Kiriel, trapped halfway between their power and the frailty of mortality, preferred the cold. She'd gotten used to the heat, but she could not get used to the heaviness of the air itself, the wetness of it.

When she was four years old, she'd tried to stop breathing because Isladar did not need to breathe. She had, in time, grown immune to the cold, as Isladar was, and immune to the heat, and fire in particular seemed to melt to either side of her skin as if it were a prettified variant of water. But air—she needed it just as she needed to sleep. Oh, not so much as the rest of the human court did, but the need was there, a weakness that waited to be exploited.

Everything about her life was weakness.

As if to deny that, she hunted.

She'd learned that. To hunt. To kill. To strip the kin of their physical facade and send them screaming back to the Hells, where their names were so weakened by the journey they could not be defined by them, held by them. She had thought that if she could do that enough—hunt and kill—they would finally fear her. That she would become like Isladar.

Like him.

She needed the anger, tonight.

She needed it, so she let the hurt come; they couldn't be separated, not with her. What had he taught her? Not to trust kin.

What had he hoped to teach her?

Not to trust? No. Too easy.

Jay.

"What?"

"Nothing. I thought I heard a name."

She did not understand this unknown demon's game. She could sense that he moved, and that he moved in a straight enough line that he was either magicked and hidden from sight, or human in seeming. Human, she thought. Human in seeming would make the most sense. If he were here to kill Valedan kai di'Leonne, what better guise to take? There were more humans in this city than there had ever been *Kialli*—she was certain of that—and it would be easy enough to lose one in the crowd.

If one wasn't Kiriel.

But it was hard to force the world to render human image, human form; hard to force the world to render a body that was not unlike the forms the *Kialli* once had when they walked the world of their birth. This world, Isladar said. This world was home, and foreign to them.

Do not underestimate the desire for home, Kiriel, he would tell her. *It is strong in humans as they age, and they never reach the age of the* Kialli. *Home is where we were young, and even though we do not remember our youth as clearly as you remember yours, we desire it.*

When you are Queen, you must remember this. It is a weakness, and one of perhaps two.

The other, she thought, was arrogance.

Auralis ran a hand over his eyes. "Can you find him, in there?"

"Yes."

The light from the tavern's many lamps smeared and cast shadows. It was night, but the moon was high, and on the morrow the Festival would begin in earnest. There were bets being placed, coins being exchanged. Money. She'd learned about money. "Are they comfortable, like that?"

Auralis cast a sideways glance at her, one heavy with suspicion. He was more afraid of humor than venom; of laughter than pain. She could see it there, behind his eyes. She had been so careful not to watch anyone in this city too closely; not to stop and stare, not to study them. They were so different in texture and feel than the men and women of the Court, she might be trapped watching them for hours. But she watched him now because it was easier than asking him questions.

"No," he said, when he was satisfied that her question was exactly what it seemed, "they aren't."

"Then why do they do it?"

"Company. Money. Connections." Pause. "Is he hiding there?"

"I don't know."

"Is he going to kill them?"

"I—I don't think so."

"What do you mean?"

"I—I'm not close enough." She wasn't. She wasn't close enough to see his name, to hear it announced by the presence of his power. But he *was* a power, or she would not have felt his summons from so great a distance. Would she?

"What do you mean, not close enough? You followed him all the way here."

"Yes."

"Can you even get closer?"

"I don't know."

"Can you take him?"

"Not without killing half a dozen humans. Not in there."

Auralis was silent for the space of three heartbeats. Then he smiled. "We can clear room."

What had she learned in *Averalaan Aramarelas?* What had she learned in the Shining City? How did they intersect, the Kiriel before and the Kiriel after? The smell of smoke and sweat and ale was overpowering in the heavy stillness of the air, but it did her the mercy of driving away the smell of the sea and the harbor that otherwise always lingered.

She fingered the hilt of her sword, for comfort more than utility.

"Don't speak," Auralis said. "Let me do the talking."

The command was offhand; he expected her to follow it. Did not conceive of her doing otherwise. She tensed; her grip whitened her knuckles. But she nodded. *This is not my territory.* She said it three times, and then let herself believe that it was not a weakness, to say it. To acknowledge it.

She knew that he was at the heart of the tavern, not too close to the bar, and not near the exit.

"He's where the betting is," Auralis said. "I can't believe he's smart enough to be where the betting is." He cast a sidelong glance at her—as if she wouldn't notice the flickering stray of his eyes. "I guess he's spent more time around people than you have."

"I don't know. I don't know who he is."

Auralis shrugged, and then his eyes narrowed, his expression sharpening because of it. "You don't expect to know every soldier in a war, do you?"

"No. But I expect to know the—the officers."

Auralis said, "You've got a lot to learn."

She bristled. He shrugged, an elegant, graceful gesture. His apology; she could tell it by the way his colors shifted, muted. "Did you kill a lot of people back home?"

"People?"

"Humans. Us."

"There weren't many of you 'back home.' "

"Did you kill the ones there were?"

"I? Sometimes. Not often."

"When?"

"Does it matter?"

"Yes."

She raised a dark brow. Wondered why she let him question her. Why she'd let him follow her. Why she was going to answer him. Because she was. "When they tried," she said at last, "to kill me. Or when our Lord ordered it."

"Did you ever kill for fun?"

"Not—no."

She thought he would press her. Ashaf had pressed her, Ashaf had hated every one of those deaths, although the excuse of self-defense muted her anxiety. But he was satisfied with her answers.

"All right. Do you think he knows you're here?"

"Yes."

"*Right* here?"

"Possibly. Probably."

"Is he hiding from you?"

"I—no." She frowned. "Yes. He must be hiding somehow. But . . ."

"Does he have reason to think that you'll care whether or not these people die?"

"No."

"Do they hire people?"

"Yes . . ."

"I don't think that's the game. What's the game, Kiriel?"

"I don't know."

Blue light billowed like the breath of an ancient beast, hoary with smoke and the thick staleness of too little air, none of it clean. It came up from the floor of the bar, pierced and surrounded its heart.

"Oh, my god!" She froze as she recognized the power that permeated the words, that carried them across the breadth of the room, breaking into every conversation, every noisy argument, every private gathering, with equal facility.

She saw him then. He was tall; taller than Auralis, but not of such a height that he towered obviously over the rest of the men in this crowded, filthy place. But he was fair, where they were darkened by sun and summer's height, and his eyes were of a color, a rich darkness that the word black was too thin to describe. He lifted a hand, pointed. At her. At Auralis.

"Demon!"

"Shit. Duarte's going to kill us."

Clever bastard.

There was a pause; the collective drawing of breath, a prelude to action.

In *this* city, those words meant something.

Oh, in the towns they meant something as well—to small children and their exhausted or angry parents—but if you were living in this city in the year 410, if you'd lived through *that* Henden, and had managed to hold onto your sanity until the break of First Dawn, the word had a resonance, held a terror, demanded an action, whether it be flight or fight.

There weren't a lot of places to flee *to.*

Swords left scabbards, when their owners possessed swords; more often than not they didn't. They all had daggers. In two places, drinks hit the tavern planks in a thud and a spill as tables were overturned precisely enough to make shields of them. Luckily, the floors here were thick enough and old enough that the mess was right at home.

He thought blood would be, as well.

Because it didn't occur to him to doubt that the words of their accuser would be disbelieved.

"I think it's time to leave," he said, backing doorward, hand on sword hilt. The room was frozen a moment, in shock, in the space before deep breath is drawn and battle is entered in earnest. They had just that much time to flee. He'd seen enough action to know when he'd been outmaneuvered.

That was the problem with raw recruits. Raw, *powerful,* recruits. They could be so gods-cursed stupid. It had never occurred to Auralis to consider the best, the dirtiest, the fastest fighter in the unit stupid, until now. He hoped fervently that he survived the misestimation.

"Kiriel, no!"

In a single motion, she drew her sword and leaped across the length between the tavern's door and its heart. If there were men in the way, it didn't matter; the old building's ceilings were high enough to accommodate both her height and theirs, and she moved faster than he'd ever seen her move. He cursed. Because the moment she drew that damned sword, it sucked the light out of the air, it made the accusation not only fitting but exact.

He should've been grateful; the minute she drew that sword, no one really had a lot of attention to spare for him. He certainly didn't.

You'd better hope, he thought to himself, as he quietly drew his own sword, *that someone here kills you, because if they don't, Alexis will.* He could face anyone in the Ospreys, would in fact face all of them combined, before he'd face her.

The silence broke like a wave against the sea wall.

They didn't matter to her.

Isladar had told her, time and again, just how dangerous they could be, these humans, these fully mortal, unclaimed humans, and she'd listened to him, as she'd always listened. In the Shining Court she'd discovered the truth of his words; the humans were as dangerous in their fashion as the *Kialli.* They had their power, their magic, their subtlety, and she had felt the sting of each as she grew.

She forgot that now. She was her father's daughter.

She gestured; it was that simple. Shadows rose, splintering floorboards in a jagged edge, making of them a poor wall, a thing that humans would have to struggle between, or over. She thought they would run. If she thought that much.

The room became one thing, one creature. His shadows touched everything, trapped and blanketed them; it was the force behind his voice, unseen by all but her, unfelt by none. She would have ended the game—*do not let another creature set the terms of the games you play,* his voice said, here, where she least wanted to hear it, where she could not help but hear it, for hadn't he taught her how to survive? Hadn't he saved her life, time and again, from the *Kialli,* from the human Court?—but she could not end it; she could only see her enemy's power. She could not see his name.

No name, and no challenge—not directly. And if he were powerful enough, his name alone could not demand what she desired; Etridian, Isladar, Assarak, these at least stood against her. There were others. But they would not stand against her will forever. They bowed to her father. In time, they would bow to her.

She had been chosen. If the Lord was the Lord of the Hells, he had claimed her as daughter and *heir.* She would be their Lady. She would be their Queen.

And what would not bow before her, she would destroy.

As she would destroy this one.

Auralis was on the outside of the splintered floorboards that rose at the drift of her hand across air. They did not obscure vision, but they marked the boundaries of a circle that she had drawn, there. In the North, they fought in circles; the meaning of the enclosure was lost on no one.

He was surprised that she chose to use it. Didn't understand what it meant.

Someone cried, "Get the magisterians! Tell them—tell them to call the magi!" And Auralis recognized the strangled voice, thinned and weakened as it was by fear. The tavern's owner. Fire he'd seen, and fight; he had two dour, grim men with swords—albeit not of the best quality—who habitually took up residence, arms crossed against armored chests, for just that purpose. But there'd been no magic in the tavern since its opening three generations past—at least, none detectable, none visible, which is probably all a normal man could ever really be certain of—and he'd no method on hand of dealing with that.

No way of dealing with a demon and a sword that looked as if it drank souls. There were stories of those, in the years between suckling and manhood; Auralis had probably heard half of them, and the tavern's owner, the other half.

Someone ran out into the night air, as if the command were a gift from the gods. Young man, thin; the owner's son or nephew. He'd been here often enough that he thought he should know.

The two men with swords looked at each other. Their arms, hanging slack with the shock of the accusation, came up, hesitated, and then dropped. To sword hilts.

Auralis was certain, as they drew these weapons, that it was probably the first time they'd been drawn all year.

The sight of swords seemed to galvanize the inn itself. Most of the men and women here hadn't drunk enough—as if—to want to stay; they bolted for the doors.

The doors slammed shut.

Lord Isladar was seldom wrong. He had not been wrong this time. The creature that served him smiled softly in the haze of the tavern's smoke, its man-scent, its peculiar and poor light.

He was a creature of cunning, not a creature of brute force, although he was capable of either. He was one of the few who had been strong enough to hold the memories of his life during the long passage between this world and the Lord's—*Kialli*. His name was more to him than compulsion, it was identity. He guarded it, as the *Kialli* guarded nothing else but the damned.

He was not far from Kiriel when she landed, but he was completely beyond her vision; her sword, drinking the light, drew all eyes to it, even his, who knew what it was.

Even the man he had chosen as her victim.

The man was a fool, as most mortals were, and as mortals went, not a particularly interesting one; he was young, and tall; overly trusting—not a soul who would choose a place in the Hells for several lifetimes yet, if ever. In youth, humans often showed a surprising, sharp burst of malice that time and experience leeched from them. Perhaps this boy was one of those—the men who flirted with the Choice, but never with any intention of following it to its end. He'd accepted, with wonder and gratefulness, the small purse that he had been offered; it was tied to the wide belt he wore, along with the flotsam and jetsam of his hopeful life.

Within the flotsam and jetsam, the power resided. The patina of power. The heart of the truth that was *Kialli:* Illusion. Lie. Death.

He would hold it there for just long enough, and when the sword struck home, seeking life, he would withdraw. She had already summoned the shadows to her; his power, to draw and detail the dark lights of her eyes, was becoming less and less necessary. No man here would forget what he had seen.

That he had seen her slaughter an innocent. That she was a demon, in their eyes, a thing of nightmare. They would summon the mages, and Kiriel, half-blood and hated for it, would know what it was to be hunted by her half-kin.

The man's mouth was still open in the gape of human reaction. He grabbed his dagger—he was too poor to own a sword, as he'd said several times—and drew it. She allowed that. Waited for it.

How . . . odd.

He felt the fear in the air grow, thicken, and deepen—and it felt *good*. Who could have thought, so very long ago, that one could miss the Abyss, the red plains, the charnel winds? Who might have predicted that the voices of Those who have Chosen would become sweeter than *Kialli* song?

Not he, never he.

And do we sing? he thought, as he resisted the pull of a desire more physical than any that he remembered from his youth. *And do we sing now, that we might compare what we once had with what we chose to condemn ourselves to?*

No, of course not. They could not sing who could barely stand clothed in flesh and form. The ages held them in a grip that was stronger than mortality.

The fear here was thick and sweet, if pale.

Oh, it started.

Auralis saw it first.

He saw her land within the broken circle her hand had conjured into existence; saw the sword cut the air and leave a visible trail through smoke and sight. And he saw her clear a path for herself in a wide, wide arc that, by some miracle of Kalliaris, didn't end in a death.

Men who had stood at those tables had chosen to gamble, and more often than not the tables turned ugly as the evening wore on. But not like this. They were swept away by the lash of her power; thrown, like rag dolls, against the walls that were closest to them.

Kialli power, of course.

Not hers.

He intended, before she'd finished, to take a few lives for his own amusement; to bury the crime in *her* crime. The Lord would not know; Isladar would not know. And he was long away from the home he had chosen and had grown, if not to love, then to need. Need was always the stronger binding.

Daggers flashed in the light; the sword drank their reflection, devouring it. They were thrown, and they glanced off her armor as if they were made of starched cloth. One. One she caught and sent back to its wielder; he stopped short at the force of the blow; screamed as he staggered into the bar. Broken arm

No one noticed Auralis. They came upon him, backs exposed, daggers toward her as if they knew, each and every one, that the daggers were useless. They might have chosen to leave the tavern entirely, but the doors were barred more effectively than they had ever been, lit on each of four edges and two hinges with a bright, bright light.

The light was a warning, to anyone with a brain. Two brains had obviously been devoured by the viscerality of fear; two men tried the door. They had the time to scream, and to scream; burning weed did not hide the stench of burning flesh; the black grime of it.

He heard prayers in the smoky winds.

The two men with swords stood in front of the tavern's owner, implacable. If she attacked, and they defended, they weren't being paid enough, in Auralis' opinion. Not that it counted for much.

"Come," Kiriel said, as she lowered her sword, point first, at the only man who stood too gape-jawed and stupid to back away. "I have claimed this city, and these lands; they are *mine,* and I choose to protect that claim. Your serve my enemy. *Give me your name.*"

And the man, knock-kneed now, struggling with a dagger that shook so much it made the poor light shiver, said, "Richard. Richard Welton."

She laughed, laughed at the sound of his name, the terror in the three words he'd spoken, the vulnerability.

The prayers in the room increased. Another dagger was thrown; a tankard—but it was as if they thought—all of them—that if they let her have her kill, if she destroyed this one man, she would be satisfied; they would be spared. They held themselves still, like mice who smell cat and know death's around the corner. Waiting. Hoping.

Hoping that if they were *very,* very good, the gods would let them live. As if the gods decided fate. As if the gods ever listened when it counted.

He hated it.

He hated it enough that he drew his sword before he could think. The smell of terror—theirs, his own—was thick enough to suffocate.

Auralis knew what she was, of course. He'd always known it; they all had. But she was an Osprey. And he had sworn, in the streets of this city, that he would never run from demons again.

He just hadn't known, then, what the Hells it meant, that swearing, that oath.

She was an Osprey. He was an Osprey. The Kalakar forgave them both their pasts. She did not question them. But Duarte— Duarte was slightly more selective. Auralis was no fool; he knew that several of the accidents, training and otherwise, that occurred in the early days and weeks of the Ospreys' formation were Duarte's, start to finish, the pruning of the hard cases that could not be brought into line.

He'd survived.

He suspected that Kiriel would have.

But he knew, without question, that she *could not* survive this. What he didn't understand was why she stopped in front of a man who looked as if he were about to give consciousness over to terror. *This* man was no demon.

But she enjoyed his fear . . .

What do we know about her? Precious little. That she was capable of this. And yet she was an Osprey. And he was certain that she was hunting the mythical worthy opponent, because he recognized that spark of kinship between them.

She was young. She was powerful. She thought she knew everything. They always did. He had, and learning otherwise had almost killed him more times than he could count.

It was obvious to Auralis that this man was no demon. It was obvious to Kiriel that he was. One of them had to be wrong—but it seemed too much of a setup, somehow. Kill him, looking like *that,* and she was dead. The mages, the Kings, The Ten, the entire damned city—they'd all be hunting her, and power or no, she wouldn't survive it.

Why?

And then, unbidden, *Maybe the demons don't think we know who you are.*

He moved past the bar's patrons; past their fear, and their pathetic last minute preparations; past the two who were foolish enough to try the door and now lay on the floor, blackened husks of what they used to be as young men. Letting the reflex take the panic, letting the sword arm slacken as he readied it for use.

I wanted a fight.

She raised her blade.

The creature before her smiled.

"Do you think I am so inconsequential, little half-blood, that you can have my name for the asking? You are not your father's daughter. You are an abomination; a child of weakness and human artifice."

"And you," she said evenly, "are less than even that. You gave up what you were born to; you have nothing but what the Lord grants."

He snarled.

"And I will own it. *Give me your name.*"

Had he not been standing to one side of her focus, had he been at the center of it, he would have answered. As it was, he almost did; his lips formed the syllables, but his will prevented the movement of air and magic that would have given them sound and meaning.

What is this? Isladar—you promised us that she had no training, no ability; that the investiture was in all things a deception, a failure of power.

But no; he could see it in her.

He could see it in her more clearly, for that single moment, than he could see the color of the soul that she had been born with, as all mortals were. The soul itself. The ultimate insult to the *Kialli.* To the kin. Were they to be ruled by cattle?

No.

No.

He lost the illusion a moment.

He did not answer.

She waited, and then the waiting was done.

She did not need to have his name to fight him; she did not need to take his name to destroy the presence the passage between worlds had given him, the flesh. She drew her sword back to strike, and it struck steel as she brought it round in a half-arc.

A sword went flying across the tavern's space.

* * *

Auralis swore.

Could be worse, he thought, drawing daggers as an afterthought. *I could have gone flying with it.*

The young man, the young *idiot,* was still rooted to the spot in terror. Almost, Auralis thought, as if his feet had been driven, like iron spikes, into the wood itself. "RUN!" he snarled.

The young man gaped at him. Just gaped.

Kiriel turned. Shadows fell, like drifting water, out of the corner of her eyes, darkening her face; her lips were gray, her skin white. White, he thought, as ice, as something that had never known life.

"What," she said, her voice low, as cold and colorless as her skin, "are you doing?"

"Look at him!" Auralis shouted, stepping back from the force of her words. "LOOK AT HIM!" He thought, as she raised the sword, that she would strike him. Knew that if she did, it was death, his death, no way to run from it this time.

He met her eyes; saw nothing at all in them but the darkness, the ice. Her lip curled in contempt as she looked at him, through him; where she was impervious to *his* sight, he knew, then, that she saw everything about him.

Why he did what he did next, he couldn't say, would never be able to say; it was the last act of a stupid man, and he would tell himself that again and again for months afterward, when he woke, with a half-scream choking his throat, from the nightmare of this tavern, this woman.

He dropped both daggers.

No *Kialli* would have disarmed himself in the face of such danger unless he meant to give up his name. And even then, to disarm oneself this obviously was to render oneself useless; it was more than a simple act of suicide. Much more.

It gave her pause. She stopped. Stopped for long enough to *see* him, to know who he was. The shadows had taken her vision to the fight; the fight had controlled it. What had Isladar said? Never let your attacker choose the method and the means of the fight. Never let him dictate the how, and if you can avoid it, the where.

"What," she managed to say, "are you doing?"

"Look at him," Auralis said. He was shaking. She could smell the fear as if it were old sweat, but it was an acrid fear, an unpleasant one. She shied away from naming it. "You're attacking

a boy, Kiriel. I don't care what you think he is—look at him. Look hard."

She turned, then.

Turned to see the creature waiting, a cool smile at play across his lips. Could feel his power, the taunting that lay beneath it. The dare.

"I know the kin," she said, her voice far darker than his. "I know what I do here."

"You *don't*."

The human was inconvenient. He was inconvenient and he was a threat to the plan that Lord Isladar had crafted. He was also not under protection, any protection.

But to kill him was to alert the girl to his presence, his true presence, and that, too, was a threat. He thought a moment as he heard their speech, the interaction of it, as he saw Kiriel tainted by human concern in a way that both pleased and surprised him.

And then he lifted his voice, and wrapped it in power, and said, *"There! Beside her. The man who controls the demon. The mage. Kill him and they will both be gone!"*

Auralis heard the death in the words; it was for him, after all. The whole tavern would know that Kiriel was a demon, and untouchable—but he, he was only human. The first dagger's blow glanced off his shoulder blade, driving chain and leather into his skin. Drawing blood. Would've been worse, but he knew how to move. How to run.

Auralis knew how to run.

There was one safe place in the tavern; he found it, hiding behind Kiriel di'Ashaf, a girl half his age. And behind Kiriel was the boy, the youth she had singled out for slaughter. It was not coincidence; he was now certain of it. One of these men, in this tavern, was no man—but if she couldn't see it, he was damned if he could. He didn't know how to look.

Don't do this, he thought. *Don't play into their hands. We'll have to hunt you down, or kill you ourselves. Don't give them that weapon.*

He was surprised when another blade glanced off his cheek. Her shadows hid the light he would have used to judge its trajectory. Strange, how one required light for so many things, and yet didn't notice them until it was gone. Sort of like breath, like breathing.

He raised a hand; felt another blow, something strike his ribs.

He saw her turn. He knew that she was going to protect him. It was the wrong thing. The wrong thing to do.

But he didn't want to die. That was the crime, knowing that she was being set up, and being unwilling to die to save her the trouble.

He fell forward, to knees, exposing his back and hiding his face. Wondering, briefly, when he had become so vain.

And she saw that they intended, all of these little humans, to kill Auralis. That they intended to kill *her,* which was laughable.

"How *dare* you?" she cried, and her voice reverberated in the tavern as if the tavern were far too small for its depth and its grandeur, her anger. She raised the sword she held, she brought the shadows with it; she called upon her birthright and it came.

Two men, the closest two, the two who had dared both her sword and Auralis' theoretical magic, stood frozen before her, disarmed, although it hardly made them more helpless than they had been.

They were his tools. Auralis was hers. She defended what she owned; those were the rules of the Hells.

Her blade rose, and her blade fell—

And light singed the air in front of her eyes; light blazed across the back of her hand, a burning white line of flame, a whip's crack up her arm. She screamed in a shock of terror— terror of what, she could not say—and the sword *went out*.

She was too well-trained to drop it. She held it, the way a man who's lost a hand will hold that hand, as if by holding it, he can somehow make himself whole. She did not forget the two men, the two unarmed men, but they had been rendered harmless—they were as frozen in shock as she by the light, by the pain, by the sense of terrible, terrible loss.

It was *gone.* The shadow; the power—it was gone.

And without it—without it, she was nothing. She was less than nothing. She turned, at once, the sword now steel that housed no spirit, no blood, no essence.

Auralis lifted his face and stared at hers. But she didn't see that. What she saw stood behind him, stood in the center of the circle she had carelessly forced the floorboards to surrender. A boy, not much older than Valedan kai di'Leonne, but infinitely less wise. His shaking hands clutched a dagger; his lips were so gray they were almost the color of death.

She reached out to touch him, because she couldn't—not quite—

believe he was real. He couldn't be real. He had no color. None of the light and the dark, the swirl and the movement, that *all* humans had, who had choice.

Shaken, she looked down; saw Auralis. Saw the empty shell of him, the familiar comfort of darkness, the closeness of twisted anger, loathing, fear—all gone. Fled.

And yet—she reached out—

And it was then that she saw it: The ring. The ring that had fallen from the hands of the seer-born witch, Evayne. Evayne a'Nolan. It almost hurt her, to look at that band, but once she did look, she wondered that she had not seen it before; it was burning with a white fire that at once scoured and tantalized vision. No gems in it; no engraving; nothing whatever to mar the perfection of its line.

No beginning, no end.

Just the ring itself.

The mantle was gone.

She grabbed the ring and almost cried out; she could not move it, and the attempt was more painful than any of the lessons that Isladar had tried, successfully or otherwise, to teach her in her youth.

"Boy," she said, biting back the pain, forcing herself to show none of it, "leave. Now."

He clambered sideways, between the distinctive edges of newly-cracked wood. Stopped. Unlaced the pouch at his belt and threw it at her feet as if he couldn't quite believe that she would let him go, and wanted to distract her for long enough that it didn't matter whether or not she'd changed her mind.

The tavern had drawn collective breath. Kiriel offered Auralis a hand—the hand that bore the ring—and he groped about as if in darkness before taking it. It did not burn him. He did not even notice its touch, he who was, of all the Ospreys, the darkest, the most lost. "I think," she said, "we'd better leave."

He was going to say something sarcastic. She saw it in the lines burned by sun and time into the set of his lips. But before he could speak, someone else did.

"What a clever, clever illusion."

And she looked up, across the room and the three tables that Auralis had told her the gamblers used. Looked across the empty chairs, the upended flasks and tankards, the low flat boxes that dice were thrown into.

He bowed, and she recognized him by the gesture. Auralis, she let fall; an afterthought, and a necessary one.

The sword that she carried was no danger to anyone now, expect perhaps an unarmed mortal. She lifted it anyway, lifted it in the hand that did not bear the ring, because it was the hand that was not on fire.

"You."

"But I believe," the *Kialli* said, "that the truth of your nature has made itself felt in this holding. We will put an end to your schemes and your murders."

"No," she said. Just that. "You will die." She leaped.

His laughter was slow and lazy; he moved far more quickly than she.

It shouldn't have been possible.

It wasn't possible.

Her hand was on fire.

CHAPTER THIRTEEN

Humans, once gathered together, often pooled their voices, made of cacophony a consensus, lumbering, larger than it had the right to be, a single thing. These humans, in their muted fear, were no exception. They spoke now, the cascade of indistinguishable words a whisper of anticipation. Sensing blood, death, defeat, they watched. Safe things to witness, when they were someone else's to experience. Humans were, in that respect, not unlike the *Kialli*.

Wood splintered in the distance outside of the immediate circle she had made by splintering wood herself; something heavy cracked as if struck by force. The door. Was he abandoning the spell that sealed it?

"What is this, little Kiriel?" the demon whispered, for her ears alone. "Am I so contemptible a target that you have chosen to divest yourself of *all* defense?"

Fear. Fear then.

She hated fear. But she lived with it, gathered it, beat it back; had always done just that, more than that. The arrogance in her enemy's voice was a warning and she had not always been a power in the Shining Court, although she had always been a fighter. What else was there to be? She could fight, or she could die.

His hand came down in an arc that ended with wood. Wood was weak; it splintered and flew—and this sound, this she paid heed to it; it changed the ground beneath her feet; it changed the lay—and therefore the law—of the fight.

She had no power.

It was not the same as having no weapon; she would have to show him that, should she survive. She *would* survive, to show him that. She swung, low, keeping the sword's play as tight and controlled as possible.

Do not fight in anger. You become anger's weapon; it is never *yours.*

His voice spurred her on; the wildness of this helpless state seemed a harmony to the memory of the teacher that, had he been here, would have saved her life only after she had proven that she was worthy of the salvation. Only then.

Never, never, never.

Vow it. Mean it. Never prove yourself worthy of him again.

But she'd proved herself worthy time and again, and this *Kialli* was no different from the rest, when it came to attacking the less powerful. Arrogant. Stupid. Dangerous.

She leaped.

She leaped, and the music carried her, the song that she had not known she was singing because her lips were pressed tight and thin, a white line over teeth too blunt to be useful, over words too thin now to carry the under-rumble of power, of power's authority.

Lightning leaped with her; leaped before her, branching at a point behind her back, but not above her head. It struck the *Kialli* shields, buckling them; driving the creature over broken floor and fallen furniture alike.

He was here.

He had seen no sign, in her, of weakness; no sign of the fear that she struggled with; no sign of the cost the power's loss, and the ring's burden, exacted.

She felt at once trapped and relieved; he *was* here. He had come. And she was, in all things, the student, his only student. He was, in all things, the only teacher. A test. It was another test. And she had passed it, somehow, or he would not be here. Was Evayne his servant?

She froze; she had often frozen thus when Lord Isladar of the *Kialli* had decided, at last, to intervene. His magic was finely tuned; she would feel its crackle and its build a moment before it would strike, and she would know, he'd trained her so well, when and where it would land.

This bolt singed her skin; she'd lurched to a stop—struggled for it, found it—but momentum carried her into the outer edge of a gold-tinged white light, whose heart was blue, blue fire.

The *Kialli's* eyes widened; his lips moved over perfect teeth, human teeth. He raised his arms above his face in a gesture of denial, instinctive, old as time and older than the *Kialli* themselves.

Spoke a word. Another word. The arc of mage's light hit him. Passed through him. He was gone.

A woman cursed, in time with Kiriel's curse, her voice familiar. "I believe," a man said softly, another stranger, another stranger's voice, "that you have all witnessed an illegal act of magery. Illusion, a complicated art." Noise returned slowly to the tavern, in whispers, in prayers. In music; the lute's gentle strum.

The man who spoke smiled softly as his fingers touched those strings. "The magisterial guards will be along presently; they have been alerted. We, my companion and I, would have arrived sooner, but we were . . . detained . . . by this rogue mage's companion. He is dead, by decree of an Order in Council of the Magi.

"Any information that you can provide us will aid us."

"But we *saw* her!"

The man with the lute tossed his ringed curls over his shoulder. "That's why they call it 'illusion,' " he said, the sarcasm in his voice sharp to wounding. "I am Kallandras of Senniel College. I serve the Kings."

She heard someone mutter the word "bard-born." She knew what it meant. Stranger or no, she had seen this man before, in another hall, in the Palace of the Kings themselves.

He met her eyes. Bowed, but not before she could see an expression flitter across his face, unfamiliar and unwelcome.

"My companion," he said, in a voice that carried the length of the room without ever becoming a shout, "is a member of the Order of Knowledge; she has the signs, and the writs, and any of you may question her if you wish to detain us further.

"But there is a man with murder on his mind—and it is of a particular type; he does not kill, not by his own hand—he plays you all for fools and has you do the killing for him. Let us take our companions from you, and we will pursue; keep us here another five minutes, and he is lost.

"You outnumber us, good citizens, and you have been through a darkness of your own, and a danger, and therefore the choice must be yours."

All the while he spoke, he played, and there was no doubt at all in Kiriel's mind that he spoke the truth, and all of it. And she *knew* that he lied.

But as the woman in midnight-blue robes approached her, she forgot that. "Kiriel," the woman said softly, "I believe we must go."

Evayne. A moment of confusion, there.

And then realization. Understanding.

Bitter disappointment, followed by bitter self-loathing.

Who had she thought it would be, after all? It could not, would not, be Isladar; she had betrayed his confidence, as he had betrayed hers; she had carried the war of the Court *to* him. And he?

He had taken from her the only woman in the Court she valued—the only one.

Could she forget that?

Could she forget the crime, the vow, the anger?

It shamed her, and it hurt her, so she looked at the truth very, very briefly and then turned away from it and refused to see it again. Hardened herself—she was good at that, if nothing else. He was not here. They were not allies. She was truly kin, now. She was alone among enemies.

Evayne a'Nolan had a soul that seared her eyes because it moved so quickly, becoming darkness and light in a cross of bands that brooked no observation, welcomed no intrusion.

Or she had had such a soul. Tonight she was as empty of light and color, of boon and bane, as one of the kin. Bad enough, but so was Kallandras. So was Auralis.

Her hand was no longer on fire, although enough pain lingered that she was certain it had not been seared to ash. She was afraid to look; it hurt to look.

"Kiriel." Gentle, gentle voice.

Her nod, when she offered it to the seer, was stiff and unnatural. "Auralis."

And Auralis, shaking, rose. He stared at Evayne.

"She's a—" She started to call her friend, or ally, to give her some title that humans would understand meant a momentary safety. But the ring burned her hand, and burned it still, and the words would not leave her lips. "Evayne. She's Evayne."

"We've met before," he said softly. Shakily.

The seer's violet eyes widened a moment. Narrowed. "In the Averdan Valleys," she said. "And . . . before. Auralis?"

"We don't have time," the bard said.

They left the tavern.

Meralonne APhaniel was waiting for them. He was bleeding, the rents in the clothing he wore exposed flesh too white to have known much freedom under the sun's light. Here, in particular, where the sun was harsh, the lack was obvious.

"You were in time." Not a question.

Kallandras and Evayne exchanged a glance that was both weary and wary. "A matter of definition," Evayne replied at length. "The demon escaped."

He said nothing.

Kiriel thought, at first, that it was because he was angry, but as he approached her, she saw the expression upon his face as if it was illuminated from beneath, and it was; he carried a lamp. The light did not gentle him. Indeed, it added a harsh edge to the cut of his features, darkening the shadows that made of it an angular, a dangerous, landscape.

"Kiriel," he said softly.

She did not trust the softness in that single word. He had never spoken her name with anything but respect. Could he see it? Could he see the truth of what she could barely comprehend herself: the nakedness, the loss of the power that had been hers since her father—no. No. What was she, without that?

She lifted a hand to ward him; she had never thought to do it before. How long had it been since the shadows had not nestled within her, coiled and tense with the desire to expand and consume all?

Memory was treacherous. It answered the question that she could barely ask aloud. But even before then, even before the power had been poured into the vessel that she had only then understood she had been fashioned to be, even then she had had the vision that she was born to. It was gone, now.

Sightless, she stared out at these, her companions, and she could see nothing at all but their faces, their bodies; they were leeched of the colors that twisted and danced within the shell of flesh, the body.

"Kiriel," Meralonne said, lifting a hand.

She stepped back, lifted her own.

He caught it. "Where did you get this?" he asked.

She would have cut him in two, for her free hand still held the sword that had been made for her by the only one of the *Kialli* who considered himself a smith. It had been a gift. A talisman of sorts, he had said, and although she knew that it had been offered only to curry favor with Lord Isladar, her master, she'd accepted it as that. Protection against such offense as this: an unwanted touch. As if any touch could be wanted.

But where his hand touched hers, the fires banked. She stared at him. Pain could not make her cry out; of all sensations, it was the one she was most inured to. He'd seen to that. But this: cessation of pain, unlooked-for—it startled a wordless sound from her lips.

"The ring," Meralonne said softly, intently, unaware of the concession surprise granted him. "How did you come by this?" And then he turned swiftly. "Evayne," he said.

The seer's offered answer was silence. They were not friends, these two, but they were allies; there was history between them; she could see it clearly, although she could see little else.

"Yes," Kiriel replied. "She dropped it."

"Dropped it?"

"It—it—" the fire that reddened her cheeks as she turned toward the now hooded face of the seer had nothing to do with magic, with magery. "You *tricked* me!"

Evayne said nothing.

Kiriel tore her hand free—cried out at once with the pain of it—and reached out for the woman who had, she dimly recalled, just saved her life. As Isladar would have.

And, as Isladar, for her own reasons. She played her games.

Kallandras said, "There was no trick, Kiriel."

Kiriel did not, could not, hear him. Roaring, although the sound was pathetic and weak, she reached out before the older woman could react, and grabbed her by the folds of her cloak.

"Kiriel, no!" Evayne cried.

But it was late, for that. The cloak opened wide, and into the night sky, with its high moon and its terrible heat, there spilled darkness and ice.

And she, with no protection, stood in its path, in awe.

She was not going to move. He saw it clearly. Whatever it was that Evayne held within the confines of the only clothing that he had ever seen her wear, it was revealed to Kiriel's eyes, and Kiriel's eyes alone. Bard-born, death-trained, Kallandras could make out nothing; what was there was reflected in the lines of Kiriel's face, and that, poorly.

He did not look at Evayne; he did not need to. Her voice told him all that he needed to know; that the girl was in danger, that she was not certain of her ability to protect the girl from the cloak itself. Had he never dared to touch her? He could not remember; it did not matter.

Certainly, he had felt Kiriel's anger before.

But he had never been asked to pay for it with his life.

He had been Kiriel's age when Evayne had destroyed the only life he wanted. That was probably the only thing that they would have in common, she and he—that and the rings. It was enough.

He was across the cobbled grounds, his feet touching stone once and twice; a third time, and he felt snow and ice and bitter, bitter cold—and he felt her, Kiriel di'Ashaf, demon-killer and darkness-born child, as he wrapped both arms round her and bore her to ground, rolling with the momentum of his jump.

Not gentle; he could not afford to be.

He released her before she could struggle, stepping back. Her eyes were still wide, and he knew why, he *knew* why. His feet had touched ground like that only once before, at Evayne's behest. In Scaral, on the darkest night of the Old Weston Year. The first rite, for either of them; they had both been younger then. Once had been enough.

And it had not been he that she had chosen to sacrifice; he had not paid the price of that night, except in this way—the memory could be called up by the touch of an old shadow.

Her cloak had stilled by the time Kiriel gained her feet.

"I am sorry," the seeress said, the word so low it carried inflection only to the bard. "But the cloak is . . . magical. It hides much, protects much."

"That—that was not you," Kiriel said, rising. "I have seen shadows like that—"

"It is the sacrifice and the knowledge," Evayne said, coldly now, though not so cold as that shadow, "of the Winter Road, may you never walk it."

"The Winter Road?"

"Enough, Evayne," Meralonne APhaniel said. "We do not speak of these things in so open a place. Not now, when so much is at risk."

The seer nodded almost genially; she did not speak. Kallandras knew that that was for his benefit. But he was not a young man, not in that way, anymore. "It is . . . all right."

"The ring?"

Reflexively, she looked at her hands; only one ring remained there now. "There were five," she said. "That one was the second to go. A year ago. Less."

"And the others?"

"I believe you already know where one of them lies," Kallandras said softly, speaking with the wind's voice, speaking of the past. "But for the rest, it is not for the guardian to say; she carries them, but she cannot use them, and she cannot see, clearly, to whom they go, and for what purpose."

"No," Evayne said, uneasily. "I cannot."

"The last one, then?"

"It is . . . it is the ruby. I am not Myrddion," she added. "He was a seer without parallel. The Oracle's path did not consume him; the price he paid her, she returned tenfold. He knew, and then chose. But in no way, in the years that I have labored in this war, have I been able to discern how he made his choice, or why."

"Yet you must know who the rings were passed to."

"Kallandras speaks partial truth, Meralonne. I *could* speak of it; I am not compelled in that regard as I am in every other in the life I was given to. But I will not speak of it. It is enough of a risk to wear the rings at all, and when the god—" and she stopped a moment to look to the North in the darkness, "when he walks these lands again, he will *know,* and he will begin his search. I will not willingly give to his followers a knowledge that they would otherwise not have."

"Do you know," Meralonne said, still speaking to Evayne, but turning his gaze toward Kiriel, who still seemed to stand in a state of shocked grace, "what those rings were? Do you know what went into their making, and how many lives were sacrificed to the process?"

"No," Evayne said, "and it would ease my heart *not* to know it. I know too much already that I must both accept and ignore, and it becomes harder to do what must be done with each bit of such knowledge gleaned.

"I will not ask you," she added softly, "how you have come to know it, oh, historian of the antiquities."

"This was his pride, his darkest hour," Meralonne said softly. "Of all the rings, unnamed, unadorned. The fifth."

Kiriel turned then, and it was clear from the shift in her expression that she had listened to them, let their words pass through her and yet remain. "I would give it back.

"Take it, if you can."

He shook his head. "No. It is yours, for better or worse, although you would satisfy a lifetime of bitter curiosity were you to tell me what the ring's power is."

She stared at it. Smiled, although the smile was bitter and much older than her face. "It burns me," she said, so softly that even Kallandras had to strain to catch the words.

"It burns me, and it steals my power."

He stared at her a long time, and then he said, "perhaps, Kiriel, the theft is a gift, and you have not yet had a chance to realize it." The words were kind, and the voice itself, kind as well, but alloyed with a terrible pity. Kallandras met the silver-gray eyes of one of the few men in the Order of Knowledge that he was privileged, felt privileged, to call friend.

"We are all tested," Meralonne said softly, turning his gaze, again, upon the girl, "and we are all tempered." Silver-gray was lost to the closing of eyelids, and when that color returned to his face again, his expression was neutral.

His voice, if he spoke, would be neutral as well. Meralonne, as many of the members of the Order, could rob his voice of the power that the bard-born were born to hear.

"What in the Hells happened to you?" The lights came on. Duarte, holding them in the cusp of his hand, fueled them with his magic. Quite a sight, especially in the dark of a night that had gone on far too long.

Unfortunately, Auralis had seen the sight enough to find it neither impressive nor intimidating. The palace itself, with its enforced quiet, its expanse of space, the height of its ceilings even in these, a wing given to guards and soldiers and not to paying guests, as the political members of the patriciate were called by the servants all over *Avantari,* was more intimidating than the lights clenched in Duarte's hands.

The change room was empty, and he was pretty damned certain the stewards would have his balls if he woke them up and demanded a bath—but his bed was still his bed, Duarte notwithstanding. All he had to do was get to it, and he'd worry about the rest later.

"Not now, Duarte." Auralis doffed his armor, scratching ineffectively at dried blood. He gave up after a while as he always did; he wasn't a patient man.

"No, not *not now.* Now."

That tone couldn't be ignored. Auralis tried for a full minute and a half before he gave up and met the eyes of his very tired leader. "I was in a fight."

A thousand sarcastic expressions flitted across the face of the Primus of the Ospreys. They were, judging from the silence that followed, inadequate. Which meant that he was in a bad mood. Poor Primus.

"Where were you in this fight?"

"The Cock and Bull."

"Ha ha."

Auralis shrugged; it hurt. "The Yellow Finch, then."

He was surprised when Duarte hit him. Too tired to be angry, although the anger came up and went down before he'd gained his feet. "Take a hint," he told his Primus. "I was on my own time. I don't owe you any answers." He rubbed his jaw reflexively.

"Don't even think it."

"I wasn't." It was truth. "I was thinking of bed. Sleep. Alone, even."

"Auralis—"

"I'm not going to tell you. You want to know, you can ask her."

"Ask who?"

Auralis turned to look over his shoulder.

"Ask who?"

"Kiriel," he replied thoughtfully. "When she gets back."

Duarte's eyes shuttered. Bad sign. Worse than being punched, cursed, or demoted. "Duarte—"

"You're on duty," Duarte said.

Auralis cursed. Loudly. He was wounded, although none of the wounds were deadly, and he was tired. But he knew that Duarte had fallen into Primus behavior, and wasn't about to fall out of it for the sake of his well-being.

Which was the price you paid in the army for saying pretty much what you felt like saying. A reminder that they were going South, which had all sorts of meanings to the Ospreys, one of which was this: you were about to put one foot across death's line and spit in its eye while wielding a dagger and wearing a thin undershirt.

It didn't stop him from using the full range of his vocabulary to curse the bastard—but he did it under his breath until he was certain that said bastard was well out of earshot.

And he made his shift on time.

Valedan kai di'Leonne was not sleeping. He had slept earlier in the evening, only to wake with the quiet changing of the guard. The moon was not quite full, but there were lights here, mage-lights and lamplights both, in plenty—a staving off of darkness and the meaning of darkness, both sleep and death.

Serra Alina sat beside the flat, low mattress that the Southern-ers used as a bed. He saw a faint, glimmering line as her hair caught lamplight. Her skin, powdered as a protection from sweat and oil, did not. Here, in the North, the beds were higher, and until he had chosen to declare himself—or had been chosen, the dis-tinction no longer mattered—he had attempted to live in the style of the people that had not been his people since his father had chosen to offer him to the Imperial Court. A long time ago. More than half a lifetime.

"You can't sleep," he said.

"I do not need to," she replied. "It is not I who faces the beginning of the Challenge on the morrow."

"You will not attend me?"

"I will watch, of course, with the women. But attend you? Not even Baredan will be able to do that, and he is beside himself with rage."

In the South, those words had different meaning than they did in the North; Baredan spoke gently, softly; his voice and his actions betrayed no rash temper, no immaturity of control. But, yes, he thought she was right: Baredan was angry.

"I will walk a bit, Serra Alina."

"Do you wish company?"

He thought about it a moment. Shook his head. Rose. She brought him night robes, something to fend off the chill of an evening in the Tor Leonne. Here, of course, with the humidity that forced the height of summer's glare to linger long after the sun had given way, they were not necessary, but he wore them without comment. She was teaching him to do this; to accept with apparent ease all of the niceties of a life that would be offered to him.

Should he win here.

Should he survive to win in the greater war, the true test. She fitted him with his sword, and this, too, he accepted. Perhaps sleep had not released him whole into the waking world; it happened, sometimes, that dream lingered, sapping him of the edge that a sword needed.

The walk helped. *Avantari* did not know sleep, and although it was almost silent, there were signs of the life of the palace; servants, its arteries and its veins. He would miss the palace. He did not think of it as home. It was unwise, having made his decision.

And yet, taking such care, he found himself again by the fountain beside which so much of his later youth had been spent. Silence and magelights reigned here, not Valedan, not Cormalyn or Reymalyn; night was peaceful.

On impulse, he cupped his hands and slowly lowered them into the ripple of fountain water, gently pressing the backs of those hands into the surface until, at last, a little trickle of water hovered on the edge created between the two, flesh and liquid. He held himself still for as long as the moment lasted; he had done this, time and again, as a small boy. Did not, in fact, remember the first time, or the last, it was so minor a freedom.

Water seeped into his palms; they sank beneath the surface until he chose to withdraw them. There, cupped, liquid trickled between the cracks of his fingers. He turned, hands still cupped. Knelt above the stones. Bowing his head, he whispered a benediction and a prayer; the one for the Lady Moon, the other for himself.

"Touching," a voice in the shadows said.

He did not freeze or pause; he continued to speak. To himself, for himself. Only when he had finished did he condescend to look up; to share his expression with a man who had meant to mock it, and who meant him more danger than that, although in the South, that was danger enough.

He thought he saw a glimmer in the eyes of Anton di'Guivera, faint but unmistakable, as he rose. "Ser Anton."

"Ser Valedan."

"You are prepared for the morrow?" Valedan touched the hilt of his sword, pulling his shoulders back slightly.

"You are a youth," the old man said. "You are a mere boy if you think that you can ever be prepared for battle. They did you no service, the Northerners who trained you."

Another insult. But it came from an enemy; he did not expect better; indeed, would have been thrown off his stride had better been offered. "I am," Valedan said, with a quiet dignity, "what I am, in the Lord's sight and in the Lady's. If you are more, or less, in either's sight, you must make peace with yourself, not with me."

The older man's eyes widened. "You are . . . bold," he said at last.

"I am honest," Valedan replied. "It is a failing of my upbringing." He bowed. "Unless you wish to detain me, or to prove yourself the better swordsman here, in the privacy of the Lady's night, I will leave you.

"But I would warn you against such a contest, Ser Anton. You serve not the Lady, but the Lord—and he the Lord of Night— and unless you believe the Lady to be a lie, as the Northerners do, you would do better to put your faith in the sun's hours. The Lord," Valedan continued, the first hint of bitterness in his voice, "favors brute strength and few causes."

He left, exposing his back.

* * *

Anton di'Guivera felt old. Just a moment, and the night's weight rested heavily, too heavily, upon his shoulders. He touched his sword, for strength. Pulled his hand away, as if that strength was not the strength he desired. He waited, until the boy was long gone, and the courtyard emptied of all but the relic of the fountain and the evidence of the Widan. And then he, too, stepped up to the fountain. The face of the statue in its center was blindfolded, and he found it a peculiar mercy.

There was something about the boy—the Leonne boy—that he could not face. Not easily.

The men that he had chosen for the test were sleeping, or if they were not, they were not so foolish as this young boy, to openly flout his wishes. Who were his trainers? Who was his master?

It was a weakness, to acknowledge such a lack of sleep's ease.

And both he and the boy had been lettered by the same ink, the same brush; they wore the same character. He knelt by the fountain's water, as if this were a circle of contemplation. It had served a would-be Tyr.

You came to kill the boy, he thought, dispassionately. There was truth in those words, and it, like his sword, was made of a tempered steel, hard enough to keep an edge.

But it troubled him. These few days—he'd been distracted, like a fool—as if he were the boy he accused the boy of being. His eye wandered, always, to where the kai Leonne trained. To the Northern men, the Northern *women,* who trained him; who bruised him, who advised him, in louder or softer tones.

He watched the Serra Alina, hovering like a protective wife, the boy's constant shadow. He wanted to have her killed, and did not dare, not yet. She was known for the danger that she had been to Mareo di'Lamberto, and no witless woman was a danger to that man. Only a wise and cunning one; a treacherous enemy.

He wished them all dead, but he faced the truth, because it was night, and because the boy had already seen it. He had lost the desire for the death itself; for the boy's blood on his hands.

Last of the Leonnes, he thought, plunging his aged hands into cool water, taking it up, spilling it almost wildly, *I made an oath and I* will *keep it.*

And then, perhaps. Then, peace.

The North was beguiling. The Northern gods, even more so. He listened to those of the Imperial Court who would speak, and he'd heard of his personal favorite: *Mandaros.* Lord of Judgment. Keeper of the Dead. They did not believe in the winds, in the North; it was another hand that guided them and killed them, beneath the sun's gaze. They did not believe in justice, not the true justice of death for death, life for life. But they believed in this: That the souls of the dead went to these—these *halls,* these things of carved stone that went forward and up on all sides, a great heaviness of age and weight, like the palace itself.

And there, the dead lingered who had loved ones who still lived. They watched, from their place by his throne, if they were deemed worthy enough to be granted such a place, and they waited.

Mari, he thought. And then, because he was old, he offered water to the Lady, and he prayed that it was the Gods of the North who had found his wife when she had been betrayed, so completely, by the man he served, and the Lord *he* served. For the gods of the South had failed her utterly, as he had.

Until now.

He walked away from the fountain less peacefully than the boy had, because a thought had been building in his mind, and he had turned away from it until this, the night before the contest, the last threshold to cross: That Mari, his Mari, would have liked the boy.

Winds scour him. Sun scorch him.

It rained.

The air had been heavy with rain all day, and Kiriel knew—because she'd seen it now, a dozen times, each one less shocking to her than the last—that the rain would give over to clear skies and heat in a matter of minutes; that these great, rounded blobs of water would fall into bubbles, puddles and nothing before she could make a dash for cover.

Not that she had ever dignified the summer rains with a dash for cover; let the Ospreys do it—and they did—and let them call her crazy for it afterward; she found it fascinating to stand beneath the downpour.

In the North, there had been wind, and the wind was cold; there had been sun, and the sun, too, was pale and chill in the Northern sky. Ice came, in the folds of wind; snow followed. But water was no gift of the sky; it was wrested from ice by fire, by magic, offered to those who were frail enough to need it.

She had been. She'd been made to feel it; to feel the frailty, the flaw in her that required food, air, water—and yes, sleep, although not nearly so much of it as Ashaf. But Ashaf had told her of a place—*the* place—where the rains fell, the land was green, and the people toiled under the open sky; that they were kin, and not kin; that they offered each other comfort as well as rivalry.

She stopped in the rain, drenched by it now, uncomfortable in the armor. Reached into her shirt; grabbed the only thing that Ashaf had left her: the pendant. Gripped it, its large heavy facets cutting her hand as she lifted it to her eyes.

It came to her, as Ashaf had once—only once, and only toward the end, when she was tired and afraid—showed her how it must; she called for *home* with a yearning that offered all of her emptiness, all of her isolation, all of the bitterness she felt toward the strangeness and the folly of the world she found herself trapped by.

She called; the pendant answered.

She saw trees there. She saw a woman, younger than Ashaf, smiling; heard her voice. *Valla.* She saw a boy rush up, rush past, laughing as if at great mischief, a blur of motion gone too quickly to be pinned by name. Saw a man, bent by furrows of newly turned dirt—dirt that she could smell, that smelled clean somehow— and as he looked up, and met her eyes, she knew that she could trust him, although somehow she shouldn't; that there was a difference of power between them, an old debt. *Daro.* Other faces. Other names. They returned to her, all Ashaf's.

Last, she saw the graves, and because they reminded her of death and loss, she let the pendant fall.

Burial was so important to Ashaf, and Kiriel had failed in even that. To bury the body. To perform the rites. But she hadn't known how important they were until the moment she'd caught and held this pendant.

The rain fell; tears fell with it; she could tell them apart because of the salt. She stood a moment, in the rain, and then the rain left her, wet and sodden, in the middle of the streets, in *Averalaan Aramarelas,* the high city.

She turned, turned again, caught between the palace's height and the shadows of the night—shadows that were darker to her eyes than they had ever been. Was this human night? Stumbling once, she began to run.

She heard the commotion outside of the healerie door. If she'd been lucky, it would've woken her; she wasn't; she couldn't sleep. Sliding her legs out of the left side of the bed—and into a wall, as that was where the bed rested—she righted herself and grabbed her robe, not much caring for lack of dignity.

Dignity had never been one of Jewel's main concerns. Wasn't one now, truth be told, but it was one she'd had to adapt to, as she'd gotten older and closer to The Terafin's Council. She could put it on, but she had to be more on edge to do it, and she had to have a better reason than a bunch of noise outside of the healerie doors.

Of course, it *was* the middle of the night, and Alowan *was* theoretically sleeping, and there was no doubt in her mind that Elonne was going to put in an appearance sooner or later, offering her that lovely mixture of threat and promise that Jewel had so learned to despise. But she didn't quite expect it here.

And anyway, if she had there wasn't a damned thing she could do about it—no dagger. No weapons allowed in the room by decree of one of the few people in Terafin that no one, but no one, wanted to piss off. She got out of bed on the right side, remembered that she *always* got out of bed to the right, not the left, and wondered if this were another thing left from Daine. From Daine's life.

She wanted to throw them all out and have done; to get rid of the bits and pieces of him that *were* her. Just the same as any woman would've done with a man's things who'd promised her everything and then left her.

Not fair, she told herself; it was true. She knew he was suffering as well, wherever the Hells he was. And that wasn't her problem now; the door was.

But when he opened it, she froze.

She would have spoken his name, but apparently her mouth, for once, was in phase with the rest of her body. He looked away first.

"I'm sorry, Jay—Jewel—Jay—"

Her toes curled at the awkwardness of his flush, his bent head. She knew exactly what he was feeling. Exactly.

"Jay," she said. "But it doesn't matter what you call me. You could call me rover or hunter for all I care, as long as you didn't pat me on the head and order me to heel. You *know* who I am."

"Jay," he said softly, pleased and discomfited at the same time. "There's someone here to—to see you. Alowan won't let her in, but she's—I think you need to see her."

"Who is it?"

"It's Kiriel," he replied. "But she's not the same as—as she was."

He knew that much about her. That much about her den. Just

from the healing. Did she know that much about him? Her gaze wandered to the left side of the bed, to the wall there. How would she know how much she actually knew, and how much she knew the way she'd discovered that? Left side, for Daine. The way his room at home had been set up. Would more come to her if she wanted it? She was tempted to try. Tempted more not to.

"What do you mean, not the same?"

"She's—she's—I think you need to see her." He took a deep breath. "Alowan's going to skin me alive."

"Alowan's no Levec," she replied, pushing past him and into the open door, hardly aware of the fact that she'd covered the distance between them at all—because, after all, yards or inches, what difference did it make? He was not *with* her, as he had been.

"No," Daine said. "That's why I'm worried."

They crossed the room, the ATerafin and her shadow; stepped into the arborium and stopped there. Alowan's shadow was short; he was not. She could see that his body blocked the entry from the manse to the healerie, and could further tell by the set of his shoulders—the tension of their line—that he had no intention of giving ground.

Made her nervous; she covered the ground that separated them awfully quickly. Trying, all the while, not to notice how close she was to the healer who had taken half of her with him into the partially unknown territory of the who that he was. It was easier than she'd thought it would be, and she had Kiriel to thank for that.

Kiriel was kin, her chosen kin. Den-mate.

"Alowan," she said, as she drew close to his back.

The healer turned only his face. She saw that his hands gripped the doorframe on either side of him. "Jewel," he said, a faint edge of disapproval in his voice.

Which meant, she thought, that Daine was right; he was furious. How had he known that, when she wouldn't have guessed it? She was the one who had known him for half her life. She might ask him later. She would ask him later.

If she remembered.

"Alowan, what's wrong?"

"It's the girl," he said quietly. "Kiriel."

"Yes?"

"She won't leave her sword outside."

Jewel frowned, stepped to one side of Alowan and wedged her face beneath his underarm and the frame of the door.

Kiriel stood in the hall, face flushed with anger, knuckles the proverbial white as they gripped the hilt of her undrawn—barely—sword. It was obviously with great effort that such control came to her; she was breathing as if she'd been fighting in the circle for half an hour—and that, against a far better opponent than a stationary old man.

"Kiriel?"

The youngest member of Jewel's den stared up at Alowan's face. Up, Jewel thought, as if only then noticing the differences between their heights.

"Kiriel, you've left your sword before. When you brought me. Or you wouldn't have been allowed in."

Kiriel swallowed. Nodded. Didn't take her eyes off the man whose healerie, whose territory, this undeniably was.

"Then what is the problem? Just leave the sword by the door; no one's going to be fool enough to steal it."

"I don't—I can't be sure of that."

"And you could before?"

Whatever had been holding her head up was pulled out from beneath her chin; her chin fell into the space between either side of the collarbone.

"Alowan," Jewel said softly, "I don't think you're needed here."

"And I," the old healer replied, affably, "don't think that it's your position, as patient, to dictate to the doctor." Steel beneath those words. There'd have to be.

She thought about arguing with him; thought again. Pride warred with time, and time won; time and respect for the healer. "I mean," she said quietly, "that I think I can guard the door a minute or two."

"You are not yet dismissed," he told her softly.

"I know. No, I mean it I *know*."

"Good." His expression seemed momentarily less glacial as their eyes met. It froze again, fast, when he turned away from her "Daine," he said. "I wish to speak to you in my quarters."

"But I—"

"That was not a request."

The younger healer followed the older one, and as they turned a corner, disappearing beneath the shadows and greenery of the arborium, she heard him say, "A Terafin can afford to be ignorant and irresponsible; *she's* not the healer. Do you know what you were risking by waking her yourself?"

"She wasn't sleeping—" He cut himself off.

Not, of course, fast enough. Jewel cringed. Pulled her attention away from the two as they walked, because they didn't need it. Kiriel did.

"Kiriel?" she said. She started to say something else, but the words died as this child den-mate lifted her face. "What's wrong with your eyes?"

She was mute; without anger to serve as brace, she seemed to have no way of holding herself up. No need to, now.

"You can leave the sword," Jewel said softly.

"I can't. If it's stolen—"

"It won't be stolen."

"But it—"

"It *won't be stolen,* Kiriel. I give you my word. This is the healerie."

Hesitant, Kiriel stood three feet across the threshold, like some creature of the night who needed permission to cross. No, not just permission. Jewel took a breath; braced herself a moment in the door, and then went to the girl. Caught her white hand, stiff-knuckled, grip-sure, and began to pry fingers from hilt. It wasn't hard work, but it was work; it was as if the girl behind the hand had vacated the body, and resided only in eyes that were as brown as Jewel's.

As brown as.

There was no trace of gold remaining in the edge of irises that seemed to have lost the light.

"What—what happened, Kiriel?"

She drew the girl in, and the girl came, wet with summer rain too old to reflect light.

"It's gone," she said before Jewel could speak again.

"Wait," Jewel replied. "Here. Come into the healerie proper. There's no one near my bed; Alowan's rule. Too many 'damned ATerafin' walking around mistaking their daggers for their politics."

"It's gone," Kiriel said again, as if she hadn't heard the words; as if Jewel herself was the only guarantee of privacy she required. "Not just the mantle, not the shadow, not just those—" She lifted her face again. "But *these.*" Cupped her hands over her eyes; pressed her fingers against closed lids as if she thought to discern something by touch alone. "I can't see. I can't see anymore."

Jewel knew that she wasn't blind. "What," she said softly, "can't you see?"

"You. I can't see you."

Jewel waited. The moment lengthened until the passage of time was more uncomfortable than any possible invasion of Kiriel's privacy. "Kiriel, I don't know what you see when you see me."

"More than just the darkness," Kiriel whispered, and then, before Jewel could speak another word, she began to weep.

Without hesitation, Jewel caught her in arms that remembered how to do just that; how to catch fear, how to calm it; how to take strength from the act of being strong. It was easy to be strong, just like this; it reminded her of the past; made Kiriel a part of that past as well. Made Kiriel, truly, a member of her den, someone that Jewel could take under wing and protect.

Later, much later, she would wonder about it; there was no pull away from Kiriel; no need to fight an instinct that screamed *don't turn your back* or *don't touch,* an instinct that was bred into blood the way only a seer's could be.

And later, not that much later, she would wonder how it was that unarguably one of the most dangerous people she had ever met could look so much like a child when she slept.

CHAPTER FOURTEEN

17th day of Lattan, 427 AA
Averalaan, Kings' Challenge: Gathering of the Witnesses

Here they fought.

And here, in roads remarkably similar to these, they fell, their bodies lining the packed dirt of red, red streets. Weapons were pried from their fingers, picked up by men and women who the shadows hid so poorly. The sense of last stand defined their actions; they did not flee anything but cowardice.

Were there children?

Yes. Evayne A'Nolan was the only person living who had seen them; who had seen that not all lays are lies born of large heart and little intellect. There had been smoke and fire that night, and death, of course; always death. Even after the enemy had been crushed, the burning continued; too many had fallen to bury decently, far too many.

She could almost taste it, the dark and greasy smoke of those fires—but then again, she had seen so many war-fires. Folly to think that one was more horrible than another, or more memorable. It was just that she stood in these streets, again, and recognized them for what they were beneath the layers of history laid down above them.

The fight was long past; four hundred years and more had a way of obliterating the most noble—or the most vile—of intentions. Story held some hint, song, more. But unless one had been there, or been somewhere very like it, that was all one had: some hint.

She stood in the dawn's light. The rapid rise of pink and deep blue brought with it the hint of day's heat. She would, if she were very lucky, be gone by the time heat came in earnest. Long gone.

All around her, as if she were a large rock, people passed; those that jostled her did so unaware of just how close the crowd they were part of had forced them into the circle of one who openly wore the mage's medallion. Order of Knowledge. Knowledge.

She watched with knowing eyes. Saw the past that they did not see, these people who waited on glory in the open streets, clutching their coin, their tents, their belongings great or small.

The battle for Veralaan had been here.

As had Veralaan herself; the mother of the Kings; the priestess of the Mother. She raised twin banners, sun and moon to the people of the city, day and night; they had come. To the Mother. To the Queen.

Here, the warriors gathered. Here, the enemy was met. One final stand. One final song. The women were as silent as the men. The children wept, but only the children, and they wept with cause, for the scouts of their enemy had come in a body and left their mark before passing. They were not careful to conceal their presence, and why should they be? The Blood Barons waited in force beyond walls that had already been breached. It was a matter of time, and a short time, before the city itself, the city of Veralaan's birth, was laid waste, laid to rest.

You were given your chance to recant and retreat, the Barons said, over the closing distance, their magery taking the words and giving it bardic strength without any of the bardic truths; *perhaps you will hear such a generous offer again when you return from Mandaros' hall.*

No one expected mercy.

No one expected clean deaths, although the prayers were littered thick and fast, said loosely, but with a passion that was astonishing in its mixture of anger and clarity.

She had come to save a life, just one. But because she was there to guard, because she was there to join in a fight, to be the shield behind which the children gathered and stood, to be the safety that parents otherwise occupied might send their children to— she was witness to the miracle of that age.

The horns. In the distance, over the clash of steel, above the thick, wet sound of bodies made and fallen, they came. Weston horns, they were called, high and clear; but she had seen them, and she knew that they were fashioned, and patterned, upon horns far older and far less noble in cause. But they were made for power, and power resided within them; they spoke, and the whole city heard the promise of their salvation.

Even Evayne. Even Evayne who had so often heard such sweet promise made a lie of, come too late.

This morn, as that one, there were people, but what weapons they carried they carried concealed, and there were far, far more of them than the city had held after its single chance to spare itself the fate of the pretenders.

And this morn, as that one, she watched over a child. Just one. He had been here two days—or rather, he had been here for the entirety of the two days that she was aware of. Hair a dusted white, eyes a deep blue, skin now red and white where it was peeling, he slept on the patch of ground that he had chosen as his own.

This day was the first day of the King's Challenge in the here-and-now. The challengers would come from their homes and their hotels, from their patrons and their tenting, to the West Gates. They would carry their tokens, and they would carry their helms; and in plain view, they would ride, armed and armored, throughout the hundred holdings.

And the pale-haired boy, his grim little face masking the building pressure of hope and excitement, would be there to watch and witness.

Because she chose to bear the symbol of the Order of Knowledge openly, no one tried to dislodge the boy forcibly from his chosen position, for she shadowed him, hovered at his side. Fewer than ten merchants had offered her money to move on. She was pleased.

It was peaceful here. It was so seldom peaceful, she took a moment to marvel at the quiet.

The boy stirred; he would wake soon. When he woke, the path would take her to a different here-and-now, one more urgent, more dangerous. Hard to remember, when life was that cutting, that close to death, that *this* life existed at all: People daydreaming, working, singing, and bickering; people eating and drinking and trying to find companionship in a city crowded to bursting. Kings' Challenge.

At sixteen, she had hated them for having the freedom that she felt had been taken from her, be it her choice or no. At twenty-five, she barely noticed them; they were unimportant, unassuming—meaningless. But at forty, at forty it was different. She could begin to see her own youth, the awkwardness in her own early life, in the lives that went on around her.

A woman pulling a wagon lumbered into view, cursing and swearing a path through the people who were even now trying to find a place to wait out the morning hours. Evayne lifted a hand

and called the woman, using just enough power—and foolishly, at that—to be heard over the woman's own voice.

She had coin of the realm, and she used it, purchasing apples, bread, cheese; they were fine and fresh for all that she was so sour. Evayne took these, halved them; woke the boy.

He started at the sight of her, heavily robed and girded with the medallion that mages wore.

"You've nothing to fear from me. Not here," she said, smiling softly. "And not today. It's the Kings' Challenge; almost everyone is here for the same reason. You've found yourself a good place, and I, a good place as well."

He didn't answer, but she didn't expect an answer; she'd seen enough to know that he was skittish and suspicious, and probably with good cause, from the yellowing bruise on his cheek. "If you will watch my spot until the sun is at its height, I will break fast with you at my own expense. If I am not returned by the time the sun is at its height, sell my place. Or give it up as you see fit." She held the food out of his reach. "Do we have a deal, Aidan?"

He rubbed the sleep out of his eyes and nodded, hunger making him less wary.

She knew he would remember to ask how she knew his name—but not until after he'd half-finished the loaf and the cheese. And by then, it wouldn't matter.

But she wanted to laugh because, hungry or no, he still waited to see her take the first bite. As if a mage might rely on common poison if death was what they had in mind. The imagination of young boys was bright and earnest and endless—but not, in the end, terribly accurate.

Here and there, the magi found men—it was almost always men and boys—who carried weapons that had been prohibited to observers of this year's Challenge. It was a general rule, although in past years ill-enforced, that spectators were not allowed arms of war; there tended to be too much drinking to regulate their subsequent behavior, and fights between men who had laid out hard-earned and soon to-be-mourned coin at betting tables across the city became steadily more violent as the Challenge progressed.

It was meant, Meralonne thought, as he pointed out yet another of these men to the four who served him in his duties, to be the test of a true warrior, this Challenge; how could anything but war surround it? Still, he was privately glad that the penalties surrounding the use of forbidden magics were harsher and less riddled with legality than those surrounding the possession of a sword—because it was magic that was his concern here, and he was one of the few members of the magi who was capable of dealing with an enemy quickly and completely. Unfortunately, those magics that were best used to defeat an enemy were not those best used to keep that enemy alive as an artifact for the courts to study.

The sun was cool, as of yet; the dawn had barely shaded the sky, but people were already waiting for the procession that would take these chosen contenders through the city—usually on horseback, although by no means always—to the high city, and from there to *Avantari,* where the Kings would grant their blessing for such endeavors as comprised the Challenge.

People had been waiting, Meralonne knew, since two evenings previous; the magisterial guards loathed the Challenge season as much as the rest of the citizens seemed to enjoy it. And for the citizens themselves, there was a single genuine reason to crowd these streets, waiting. The contenders were each allowed the choice of one "witness," and that spectator, granted the would-be champion's token, was allowed to join the procession, to be literally swept away by it into the high city.

Many of these people had probably been to the high city, for although they were not encouraged to loiter, nor were they to be barred if they could pay the toll. But the only day they dreamed of belonging to that city was on this one, when—if Kalliaris smiled— they would be handed a champion's token and allowed to walk, freely, across the bridge that separated the rulers from many of the ruled.

There was no way to stop them from gathering. No magisterial guards could have prevented it; not even, he was certain, the full force of the magi unleashed. Oh, they could *kill* easily enough, but they could not discourage dreams that were, for this morn, more bright and shiny than new gold.

He had seen them gather every year. At first, he was contemptuous of it; he remembered those days clearly, and wondered when they had gone. If they had. *Do you only dream of touching greatness?* he wondered, as he saw one boy's beet-red face. He had probably been sitting in the sun for at least two days, holding his place by some miracle that had nothing to do with money, or size, or power. *Do you never dream of attaining it?*

But of course there was no answer to such a question. The boy would dream because he could dream, and perhaps that's all he could do. One of thousands, of tens of thousands, he would be passed over by the parade of challengers as they chose—and they did choose—to best suit their own ideas, their own private dreams, the memories, fragmented and challenging, of their own lacking childhoods.

The child's fair hair gleamed in sunlight, pale as platinum; pale as Meralonne's hair. Over peeling red skin, it was striking, and he did not realize, until he cast a shadow across that pale wildness, that he had stepped in front of the boy. "What is your name, child?" he asked.

The boy was long in answering, and no parent or guardian stepped in to speak for him. But Meralonne was a mage; he wore his symbol openly, and the story-filled mind of a young boy could not help but understand what the quartered moon meant. He thought the child would not answer and prepared to turn, wondering why he lingered.

"Aidan," the boy said at last. No family name. Meralonne wondered if he knew it. "I'm Aidan."

"Have you been here long?"

Gap-toothed, the boy's smile was still bright. "Three days," he said. "I kept this spot three whole *days*. They'll be coming by here."

"You are so certain?"

"You're here, ain't you?"

"Yes. And yes, they will. Soon." He nodded. "I must attend my own duties; if I am held up here, they will not be permitted to pass."

The boy started to speak, and then stopped; he said nothing. Meralonne expected no less. It wasn't safe to talk to mages, and mages never did want to speak to young boys except for some evil purpose, some terrible fate. Stories said that; you were either a champion or a victim, a hero or a fool. And the boy was no hero; he probably had some idea of the dire consequences of a mage's notice. Death, something demonic.

Stories. He turned, taking the protective shade of his body away from the young boy's upturned face. He had not lied; not a word of it. The work was there to be done, and this year it had to be done exactly.

He did not expect to find the magic that he sought, although he was never less than thorough; Evayne had assured him that

the last of the kin summoned prior to this day had been found by
them. Found, destroyed; sent back to the Hells on the thin stream
of their name. A good night's work; a more satisfying venture than
this, this petty magical act of bureaucracy.

But this was the life he had chosen, and he was not certain, even
given the simplicity of the fight, that he would choose the fight
to live for; it was a warrior's life.

Sea salt was in the air; there was a time, a long time past, when
he had not lived by the banks of the ocean. Then, he had been a
warrior. In his youth.

"Member APhaniel?"

He shook himself. "Yes?"

"We're finished this street, sir, if you're ready."

He nodded, silent. "We're finished."

Valedan kai di'Leonne rose with the dawn on two scant hours
of sleep. Dreams had plagued him, and they stayed with him as
he struggled toward wakefulness; he had struggled with no less
difficulty toward sleep. Alina was there, to attend; to sponge his
back and shoulders, to oil them; to fit him with shirt and the
loose pants that were so uncommon in the North. Last, she brought
to him his sword.

It was not named, this sword; it had no history behind it, no
past greatness upon which he might rest some of his weight. But
it was, as swords go, a fine one; curved slightly, and single-edged,
but perfect.

"We had no time," she told him apologetically, "to have its
sheath or its grip or pommel redone with the appropriate insignia, but the blade itself, I am told by the Commanders, is beyond
reproach; even Baredan himself was pleased by it."

As very little had pleased General Baredan di'Navarre in the
last few days, he took it to be a good sign, and he bowed, very
correctly, as he accepted this last of her burdens. Of course, today there was no sword's test; the sword was, if all went well, a
statement, not a weapon. But it was a statement that he would be
judged by, and he would make it as well as he could.

Baredan struck the gong in the outer hall. He was certain that
it was Baredan because the General was wont to be louder than
necessary, and this was definitively *loud*. Serra Alina's brow
creased, momentarily, as she brought the smile up on her face. "I
will greet the General," she said. "Prepare yourself, Valedan. The
surcoat bears your marks, and the markings of the Leonne clan.

The sword, the sun in ascendance. They are finely done, and you may thank the Princess Royal for them; her gift to the man she calls the finest of her students."

"To the man," Valedan said softly, as she retreated, "she says *must* prove the finest of her students, because too much rests in the balance otherwise."

Alina did not hear the words. He found himself a mirror, re-arranged his sword, feeling self-consciously like a woman who preened and fretted. Princess Mirialyn did neither. Nor, for that matter, did Alina; it was as if the Serra had no need to ascertain what was, and what was not, perfect; she knew it, as if instinct beyond sight guided her in all things.

No, only Valedan stood like this, and only now.

"Valedan," Alina said softly, lifting the curtained door that separated him from the world. "It is time. The men are gathering for the procession in the holdings, and you are expected to join them."

"Guards?"

"There will be four, including the General." She frowned. "There appears to be some . . . difficulty with one of the Ospreys."

He rolled his eyes. "Not today," he said, through clenched teeth. Then he laughed, if slightly bitterly. The irritation blunted the edge of his nervousness. "Lead on, Serra Alina. I will go with the General, and I will look for you, with the women." He stopped, a foot over the threshold. "But you don't have to sit with them. You're of the North, now, in so many ways. Sit with the Princess; I know she's offered."

"I am of the North," Alina said, "And it would have been my chosen home. But you are of the South, and if I am to aid you at all, I must be seen to be of the South as well." Her smile was bitter. "And I *am* of the South. It has not left me, although I thought I had left it many years ago." She knelt, then, as if to prove her point. Knelt to him, pressing knees, palms, and forehead, into the cool stone, as gracefully, as naturally, as any Southern Serra might, and no Northern Lady. "Fight well," she said, as she lifted her face from this feminine contemplation of the floor, of his feet. "Please the Lord, and he will grant you what is yours by blood."

And what, he thought, for the first time but not the last, *will the Lord grant* you, *Serra Alina? What will you win, if I win?* He hoped that she had an answer for herself, because he could not ask it; not now, not so close to the beginning of the test, this first test.

He knew, as he turned, that it would not have pleased her to hear the question. And knew, as truth, that it would have pleased her to know that he thought it. Such contradictions were a way of life, in the South.

Baredan was angry. It was obvious to Valedan, and the kai Leonne was fairly certain that it would be obvious to anyone who saw him. Anyone of the Southern delegation. "Let me take this opportunity to remind you that the Ospreys are not suitable as dress guards. Not suitable as *guards,* not for a man who hopes to achieve—"

"Yes?" Valedan pitched his voice low, lending it a coolness that he did not feel. The word carried. The halls of *Avantari* hoarded noise as if they were so ancient, and so abandoned, that noise itself was a joy and a company. One word might echo in the heights above, at the peaks of arches and in the shadows carved creatures cast, for what seemed hours if the word itself was an unfortunate one.

As it was, however, the castle was so busy that echoes of old words could easily be lost to newcomers. The General, a man not used to correction, be it ever so subtle, took the hint, but he was ill-pleased.

Valedan himself was not certain that he was overjoyed. "The horses?"

"Readied. You will not find finer horses, Tyr'agar." Formal, now.

"Good. I will never need them, I fear, as much." He smiled, the expression as stiff on his face as the neutrality was on the General's. It had been a long night for both men, and it promised to be an even longer day.

He knew at once, although how, he was not certain, that the problem the Ospreys were experiencing had, for once, very little to do with their legendary lack of discipline. But more than that, he could not glean, because of their equally legendary protectiveness; they were hiding some fault or flaw in one of their own, and short of death—perhaps including death itself—he did not think he, who theoretically held their chain, could pry information about that flaw free.

Primus Duarte stood, armored, armed; beside him stood Decarus Alexis. At their side, or rather, a step back, the genial man that they all called Sentrus Cook, which must be a Northern term of affection. And beside him, the youngest of the Ospreys, the girl. Kiriel.

He hadn't realized, until the words left his mouth, how oddly comfortable he was with words, with these men. Because the moment he looked at the girl, he knew something was wrong. "What's happened, Kiriel?"

She flinched; Cook darkened; Alexis' glance flickered off the impassive side of Duarte's face. The only Osprey who could muster what it took to treat with nobility, Duarte's expression never wavered.

"And where is Auralis?"

Alexis flinched, and this time, Kiriel's gaze dropped groundward.

"Sentrus Auralis," the Primus replied, "was deemed unfit for dress duty."

"And Kiriel?"

"Kiriel is as fit as she can be for dress duty," he replied. His tone set *the* tone; they would tell him nothing. And he did not have the time, today, to pry. Wasn't even certain what it was he would pry into; clearly Kiriel was uninjured, and there was nothing about her that he could point to as obviously wrong. But it was there, and it wasn't until they had fallen in step, two in front and two behind, that he realized what it was; she walked behind him, and he was not forced to control the urge to look over his shoulder with every other step he took.

They emerged into full sunlight; the Lord's gaze, today, was to be unhindered by merciful cloud, his heat unalleviated, Valedan thought, by the fall of rain. It was not one of the official tests, to cross from Western gates to the high city in full armor, but men collapsed from less. He wondered, idly, if anyone would.

They were met, in the small courtyard by the stables, by Mirialyn ACormaris. She carried, of all things, a large basket; he half expected to see flowers tilting the round wooden lid up. The thought of the Princess with flowers, however, was too odd, and indeed as he approached her, he realized that the basket itself was *heavy*. She bowed, a Northern bow. "Tyr'agar."

"ACormaris," he said, returning the bow in kind.

"If you would do me the honor, I would be pleased to escort you to the West Gate."

"Today?

"Yes. I am to deliver this year's tokens." She frowned; no matter how still he was, no matter how certain his expression, she always knew when he was confused. "Tyr'agar, I'm certain," she said, in the voice of the drillmaster and not the diplomat, "you remember what I told you of the Northern custom."

"You may be certain," Valedan muttered, "but it is with certainty that I *don't* remember."

She did not roll her eyes; but she tilted her face skyward a moment, as if asking for patience. She, called wisdom-born, rarely needed it; it was a gesture, no more. "We ride from the West Gate. You will see the city and its hundred holdings in a way that you have never seen them. They will be lined with men, women and children—and should you desire it, you might choose to give one of the spectators your token. They will be allowed, by the guard, to join the procession; in the case of smaller children, they are often taken in immediately, because the token itself is easily stolen, and likely to be so.

"Those chosen will follow their champion to the high city, and will be invited to view all events, as witness. As proof," she said, smiling somewhat bitterly, "that there are things that unite us all, be we richer or poorer."

"And you tell me this now because you do not wish me to embarrass myself there."

"Yes. I assume that someone will have kindly told your compatriots of the custom." Her frown was delicate. "It presents a security risk, and it always has. But we have yet to dispense with it as a practice. There was some argument—"

Valedan lifted a hand. "Enough. If this is apology, it is more than unnecessary; if it is warning, it is warning enough. I have the guards of the Kings of the Empire at my disposal; I have the legendary Ospreys—and their name is probably the *only* name that is known to my enemies here more intimately than my own— I have my wits, my own strength, and the just cause. You cannot protect me from all risks. If they choose allies and assassins as their gesture of good faith, they so choose. It will do them no good."

She held his gaze for a long moment, and then she offered him something rare: a smile. A nod. "You will surprise them all," she told him softly, readjusting the basket she carried.

"Them? Not yourself?"

"I? I am ACormaris," she replied gravely. "I am rarely surprised."

The ride to the West Gate was not so quick as all that; although no traffic was allowed in the streets of the city, Valedan realized that what the ACormaris had said had been true: The streets had disappeared beneath the feet of more people than he had ever seen gathered in his life. It evoked silence, muteness; he did not have the words to lend dignity to his surprise.

Still, they let him pass; he flew his flag, and the flag of the Crowns, and besides that was well-protected. One or two of the young children—boy or girl, he could not tell—let out a whoop and a cheer; they knew that at least one of the party was destined for the Challenge, and the heat and expectancy of the dawn had brightened, not dampened, their spirit. That cheer was caught hesitantly, but it was caught; it passed before them and behind them, a gentle wave, presaging the day to come.

He was not a devoutly religious man. And had he been, he would not have prayed; it was not the Lord's way to accept with anything other than scorn an approach of supplication. He had his sword. His armor. His guards. He had his claim, and the battle which would define his life or end it—and that battle, *that* was Lord's gift, and Lord's weight. How many men's lives were defined by a battle that would, in its turn, take and shape the lives of those thousands that he might never meet personally, might never otherwise touch?

He knew that he was not a devoutly religious man because he *hated* the gift; because it was, to him, a burden. Their cries, this unlooked for jubilation, eased the burden of this first day, this seventeenth of Lattan, in the year—in the Imperial year—four hundred and twenty-seven.

Without thinking—and it could only be without thought, because the laws of the City were in no wise transparent or unknown to him—he drew his sword; the crescent caught light and sent it scattering, a flash against stone and cloth, against wall and dirt, window and stall. There was a drawn breath, a sudden cessation of sound, and then when it returned, it was louder—and carried on voices much deeper and fuller than the high fluting of children.

They don't even know who I am, he thought. *Who do they mistake me for?*

As if she could hear the question, and perhaps she could, Mirialyn said, "You are a hero come to test yourself against other heroes; in the eyes of these people, you are part story, part song. There are many men who come from across the Empire, often with little money, and few prospects. Each hopes to be found worthy of the Kings' Challenge; very few are."

"And the few," Valedan said, "are those who've had the time and the money to train well."

Again, the expression on her face was peculiar, almost bitter. "Remember that," she told him, as softly as she could over the street's noise. "In all of this, in anything that follows, *remember*."

Her words were too serious, but he was serious; it was a thing they had in common, this wisdom-born quarter-god and an expatriate Southern noble. He let them in, because he trusted her. There were few people he trusted, and they were almost all Northerners. Almost.

But trust was perhaps not a thing the Lord valued or encouraged. Certainly Baredan trusted no one; Ramiro trusted no one. Alina did not. He held the sword until his arm tired, thinking it foolish while at the same time thinking it wonderful that so simple a thing could cause this momentary happiness, this wave of excitement that seemed to pass from person to person as they traveled.

It should have passed. He should have seen the boy and moved on.

But Meralonne APhaniel felt his age. Felt it not as a matter of fact, an intellectual assumption that governed most of the Order's members, but as, at last, a thing beyond his control. For a brief moment he understood the folly of searching for immortality, although he had never been a man so trapped by that particular fear.

"What troubles you, Member APhaniel?"

Only one man in the Empire could lay claim to such a voice. Meralonne felt the fall of his shadow in the light of the climbing sun. Felt it pass though him, the touch of a ghostly hand, a hint of a brotherhood and a past long closed to him.

To either of them. He bowed to the master bard, Kallandras of Senniel College. "I did not think to see you here so soon."

"Or at all?"

Meralonne's smile was cold, but it was there.

"What has caught your attention?"

"What makes you assume that anything has?"

"I rarely see a man of your station—and relative wisdom—stand staring so long in a street as busy as this one. For one, it makes one too easy a target for thieves."

As they both knew no thief would dare, Meralonne felt no need to dignify this convivial prattle with a reply.

"In fact I think I've seldom seen that look on the face of anyone over the age of eighteen." There was play and light in the eyes of the man who said those words that robbed them of any edge.

Meralonne raised a frosty brow. "If the truth be told—"

"And what else, between two such men as we?" Sardonic words; smooth, smooth voice.

"—I was indeed stopped by something that would have given me pause in my youth." His hand rose as if at a sudden gust of wind, a touch of the element they both knew best. "That boy."

"The one with hair almost as pale as yours, but nothing else whatever in common?" The bard showed a rare flash of teeth; it changed the lines of his face. Oh, he knew how to smile; he could hardly be a master bard without that particularly necessary social skill. But this private half smile was unusual, seldom offered; it was too sardonic to be properly useful. At another time, Meralonne would have felt some echo of pleasure, dim and distant, at the bard's flattery.

Not today. The ring on the bard's finger seemed as natural there as flesh—or spirit—and he had never paused, not after the harrowing of Vexusa, to ask why that ring had become the bard's. He'd assumed that Myrddion, long dead, had somehow intended the ring to serve the purpose it *had* served. Had assumed that he, mage and loremaster, had intervened so that Kallandras might be spared the price that great magics demanded by their very nature.

But the fact remained, as the ring did: Kallandras of Senniel College was still its bearer, and over the decade and a half that had passed since the ring had almost killed him in Vexusa, he had learned to negotiate with the element the ring was fashioned from. Had learned to summon wildness in a quantity small enough to exhilarate but not to destroy.

An elemental mage would have learned as much, but would never have learned the control so easily.

We are all vain, all fools; none more so than I. I knew there were five rings, and each of those rings had a role. Yet I thought it was almost over. It has barely begun. Do you desire greatness, boy? You will see it. And someone will pay the price. He did not speak the words aloud because he wasn't certain to whom he was speaking; the youth in front of him, or the youth that he had long since left behind: his own.

The time is coming, he thought, and knew it. *In spite of all we have achieved, the Sleepers will waken.* It was true, and truth of a type that allows for no other; Meralonne could not be easily dislodged by the master bard's gently edged humor. And the bard, less stubborn by far than the mage-born man who was one of his very few equals, gave up.

"Why does he draw your eye? To me he would be one of many were it not for the color of his hair."

"To you, all humanity is 'one of many.' "

"Not all, old friend."

The silence that came between them was that of the gathered, expectant crowd: one they could watch, but could never join. But the cries, the expectation almost fulfilled, were not enough to still conversation to one born to the voice, as Kallandras had been.

What would you have been, Kallandras of Senniel, had you been given over to no other calling? You might have sung of life in a voice so loud that no man in the city could remain unmoved. He did not ask the question; he never would. Kallandras stood in death's shadow, and if life cast the shadow, it was not life he served. Not quite.

"The would-be Tyr is fifty yards away and we are called upon to join them." Silence. Then, "Meralonne?" Wind's softest voice.

"He reminds me of the hunger of youth, of being young. Of dreaming," the mage said, as if Kallandras had never spoken. "Of greatness. I fear that we will see all of these things, and I am old enough to have learned that almost no man is capable of bearing the burden of greatness without dying beneath its weight. And yet, bard, I will tell you this one secret: I have not grown so wise. I see that boy and I desire to see his dream fulfilled, at the same time that I learn to fear it." The mage shook his head. "A pity we are on display, I would like my pipe."

"A pity indeed. Miri is not known for her compassion."

They exchanged a quick smile, but the bard spoke again. "Perhaps you desire this because you have learned to take joy in the joy of others."

"Is that what you hear in my voice? I know how to hide the truth, but I do not know how to lie. Not to you; your gift is too great a gift. Tell me," Meralonne said softly, "what my truth is."

Kallandras did not reply. For a moment, he let the hush of the crowd carry them both. "You've never asked me before."

"No."

The bard turned to the crowd. "They say we can never go back."

"They are wise."

"If we cannot go back, are we damned if we also cannot escape?"

"There is always death," the mage replied.

Kallandras laughed. "And we two are still alive." He lifted a hand. "No more. See? They are upon us."

Meralonne nodded, but he did not move.

Kallandras shook his head, opened his lips. Spoke. And from a world away, crowded to either side by a sweaty press of people who spanned all ages, all shapes, all nationalities, came a red-faced boy with platinum hair and too-slender arms.

"Hello, Aidan," Meralonne said, inclining his head slightly.

"Am I going to lose my spot?"

"I believe you already have."

The lines of the young boy's face stilled suddenly, as if the ripple caused by dropping a large rock in placid water had been frozen in time for their inspection. "But . . . but I ain't done nothing wrong!" He came to life in a rush of motion. Turned to look over his shoulder, to see in fact that the mage was correct; he'd lost his spot. "I was there three whole days! That was—"

"Boy," Kallandras said softly, although any other man would have had to shout to be heard. "Hush. They come, and we are in their road."

Words left the boy's mouth and tumbled into the sudden shouts of the gathered crowd that lined either side of the road, the crowd that he'd been part of and now stood apart from, uncertain of two things: why he'd been called, and why he'd come. He looked to either side, searching open mouthed for the spot he'd abandoned, his stomach folding in on itself and falling as he realized that there was no room at all for him in that wall of people. *Three days.*

The riders were a shadow that wavered as he stood frozen, struggling with tears. Struggling to move before the soldiers who were walking ahead of the horses moved for him.

The man who had called him from the roadside— *why* had he come? Why, Kalliaris, why?—put a hand on his shoulder. "Wait."

The horses were flanked to either side by guards, armed men who wore a crest that was not quite noble. House crest. The boy didn't know which House. Didn't care. Because he did recognize the crest of the next visible rider: the Princess of the blood. He stopped trying to get out of the way.

Commander Sivari came next; Aidan recognized him and held his breath because the first and only time he'd ever met this man, there had been a moment of magic. This man had sparred with his champion.

He didn't recognize the horse. It was big, it was dark, it looked a little too wild to be ridden through streets as crowded as the hundred holdings were on this particular day. But that didn't matter. He recognized the rider.

The golden-haired man's hand was still heavy on his shoulder but that no longer mattered; he couldn't have moved now had he wanted to. He thought he might wait here while the horse and rider bore down on him and either crushed him or passed him by. If he'd been six again, he would have darted forward; shaking the parental grip on his shoulder he would have flagged Valedan kai di'Leonne down; he would have begged to be allowed to follow, to watch. Just that: to watch. He would have promised *anything*.

But he was old enough now to understand just how open to humiliation that left him. Old enough and experienced enough. He'd begged for food when things were really, really bad; had begged for work when they weren't. It tired him down, wore him out, made him desperate to be big enough, old enough, that he could *do* something: join the army, or the magisterial guards, or the merchant navy—anything but sit and beg, stand and whine.

He wanted this more than he had ever wanted food or money— and yet he knew that he wouldn't cheapen its importance by treating it as if it were just another handout. And as he couldn't think of anything else to do, he stood there, a stranger's hand on his shoulder, breathing almost forgotten.

Valedan kai di'Leonne had carried his sword from the isle, waving it as if it were a flag; he caught sunlight with the flat of the blade, sent it back to the ground where it was greeted as if it were gold by people who waited with outstretched hands. He couldn't remember feeling this excitement, this adulation, for anyone.

For anyone but his father and the man that all the young boys in the harem had worshiped: Anton di'Guivera. The man who had bested the Northern foes. The man who was honor and power defined. The man who had killed his father.

It soured his mood a moment; he stared at Mirialyn ACormaris wondering how it was that she, a rare child who bore Kings' blood, could bear to see the throne pass to brothers who did not. *They carry Gods' blood,* he could hear her say. *And half is as dilute as we want it, when there is so much to rule, so much to destroy when we make our mistakes.*

"You are here," the Princess said, as quietly as Alina might have, and as gently. "They are watching."

He lifted a mailed fist, wondering if any of these people understood who he was. Wondering if his own people would honor him so easily if no threat of death bound them. Wondering who his own people even were.

The streets opened up before him. People waited to either side, like the walls of a mountain pass. And in the tunnel they formed, he saw three: Kallandras the bard, Meralonne the mage, and between them a boy whose hair had been burned to light by the touch of the Lord.

The boy reminded him—for no reason he could think of, of the blindfolded boy. It was only when their eyes met that he realized that he'd seen him once before. At the first test, the winnowing of challengers.

The Callestan Tyran looked askance at him; he shook his head. No.

Both the bard and the mage bowed their heads and dropped to one knee, draping an arm across their chest. But the boy who stood frozen, his mouth half-open, his knees locked in a standing position, honored him by the absence of formality.

Can I live up to that?

Probably not. Certainly his father had not. Anton di'Guivera had not. The winds had scoured them, the sun had bleached them; both would scour and burn him in their time. So the ACormaris said, and she was seldom wrong.

"No," he said.

"No?" The Princess said.

He did not reply. Was barely aware that he had spoken the reflexive word aloud. There was nothing at all about this common boy that reminded him of himself; indeed, the opposite, with his pale skin, his lack of height, his obvious lack of wealth or rank. Nothing at all because the boy had been born free, and Valedan kai di'Leonne—the man who would be Tyr'agar—had been born to a slave, and freed at his father's political convenience because his mother was the least favored of his wives.

They had nothing at all in common, except the passing of hope. The belief in things greater and better than oneself at twelve.

"Valedan." Mirialyn's voice, heavy with wisdom and certainty.

You watched me fight. What did you see? Did you see what I saw when I watched them? Did I promise you some honor, some wisdom, some law that was greater than power, just by picking up a sword and swinging it well?

No. No more than Anton di'Guivera had done.

"No." .

"Valedan?"

"I am Valedan kai di'Leonne," he said, sliding down off the back of a horse that he knew should not be left without rider in streets as crowded as this. He handed the reins to one of the Tyran. "I ride to join my peers in the King's Challenge." He stopped speaking as he approached the boy who stood between two kneeling men—two of the most powerful men in the Kingdom. "I fly a foreign flag. It is *the* foreign flag; the crest that rules the Dominion."

"Valedan," Mirialyn said. He chose not to hear the warning in her voice.

"But it is the Empire that has sheltered me, and it is in the Empire that I have been tempered and honed. You were witness to the first step I took on this path, the first step I took on my own. I would be honored if you would continue to bear witness for me." He bowed then, bowed to this commoner, this sunburned, white-haired boy. "Because in watching, you will remind me of what I must strive for. And why."

He was not terribly surprised when the boy burst into tears.

Ser Anton di'Guivera arrived at the West Gate in good time; too good a time for his liking. Some handful of men had already gathered, armed and armored in the Northern style. He had studied them, where he'd had opportunity, and he understood their strengths and their weaknesses as well as any man not born among them could. They were the greatest threat to his students' desire to claim the crown—they always were—but they were no threat to him personally, and they were therefore beneath his notice.

The horse that he rode had come from the Mancorvan Plains shortly before the slaughter; he had seen to its purchase personally because he understood the measure of Mareo di'Lamberto well, and had rightly felt there would be no supply between the Tor Leonne and the Circle in Amar after the deed was made public.

Still, although he'd chosen the beast, he'd chosen in haste; he had meant for the new horse to better the horse that had once served him in his quest for bitter glory, and although the stallion had the appearance and the bearing, he did not have the spirit. *Things pass.*

His students rode beasts of only slightly inferior worth; they had been sent to make a statement, after all. But the man they had chosen to make that statement to was nowhere in evidence.

Carlo was having problems with his horse. A pity, since Carlo was a horseman without parallel. That he found the crowds intimidating was expected; that he fared so poorly at the reins because of it was not. Unfortunate. Andaro, where the horses would allow it, rode at his side, attempting to soothe. They would remain this friendly until they entered the combat itself. After all, only one head could wear the crown.

Where was the boy?

Others came, on horseback, or on what passed for horseback in the North; little beasts, bow-backed or too spindly, sweating with the effort of carrying a man in real armor. Still, their weapons were sure, and what the North lost in riding—and it did lose—it gained in weapon-crafting and use.

Forty-three. Forty-three men had passed the fine, old gates when he saw the Callestan banners take the wind. He snapped to attention at once.

"Carlo!"

The younger man turned, pulling at his reins, and pulling at the bit, invisible, that bound him just as surely as his horse was bound. Ser Anton nodded in the direction of the gate, and Carlo, eyesight still undimmed by the passing of youth, saw at once what he referred to.

They came together, snapping into the full height of their shoulders and backs. *This,* they understood well. Even Carlo seemed to relax.

The Callestan guards came without their Tyr; that was expected. A man of the Tyr'agnate's station did not condescend to join a common parade; it was too gaudy, too public, a display. But behind the Callestan banner flew another. He expected to see it; they all did. But it cut him, angered him.

The Ospreys. The Kalakar's House Guards.

Carlo's mouth opened; Ser Anton sliced the air as if it were the young man's impulse. Silence reigned.

And following the flags, Callestan and the well-known white bird on a field of black in the center of the Kalakar House crest, came the young Valedan kai di'Leonne.

"Where did he get that horse?" Carlo said.

Ser Anton frowned; it was a minimal expression. Had Carlo seen it—and he could not, from his vantage—he would have ceased to speak in that minute. Possibly ceased to breathe. He did not.

But Ser Anton had to concede that the horse was fine; dark, and of a color except at face and foot, where black markings spoke of its Southern breeding. It was not the horse that caught his attention, not really the rider, because the rider, he expected.

It was the boy who rode at his back, white-haired, red-faced from the combination of summer heat and lack of the hat that was so practical, and by children so despised. His expression was hesitance and wonder, joy and fear of joy's loss; it was the youth that Ser Anton did not remember possessing. The youth his own son—by the dictate of the kai Leonne—had been denied.

And would he have had such a youth as this, given his father? Not the first time he had asked such a question. Still, he was surprised at how pained he was to see young Aidan at the back of his chosen enemy. Because he knew that the simple boy would never understand, and never forgive, the success of his vendetta.

It passed. It always passed.

What did not was the determination.

"Who is the boy?" Carlo said, his voice muted.

"The same boy," Andaro replied. As observant as his teacher, which was a pity.

"Was he a spy?"

"Don't be an idiot. He is wind-brought, no more."

Idiot, indeed. Ser Anton turned to the wisest of his students. "Andaro, watch here. I go to receive the witness tokens."

Andaro nodded; it had been decided, long before this day, who would bear those tokens, and when those bearers would strike. Nothing, in the end, changed that.

Of Ser Anton's students, eight had been chosen to participate in the Challenge. Had he not witnessed the prowess of the Northern Imperials for himself, Ser Anton di'Guivera would have been personally insulted—and surprised. Matters political did not rule contests such as these; tests of excellence required no more than excellence.

As if to give the lie to even the thought, the large jolly merchant that Andaro had personally chosen as witness stepped forward to join him. His hair was streaked white and pressed flat to his forehead by what could only be, as he could smell it at this remove, scented oils. His face was half again as wide as it was long, and the line of the jaw was hidden beneath the weight of a thinning beard.

"We had heard that the Leonne bastard had joined the Challenge. Both fortunate and unfortunate. Many of my kin will be present in the coliseum."

By which, Anton knew, he referred to the merchants. It was true, but Anton felt a real, a rare, annoyance at the unwelcome intrusion. At the intrusion that should not have been an unwelcome one. They were here, after all, for the same purpose.

"Yes," he said coolly. "There are."

The merchant crossed his chest with the flat—and the fat—of large hands. They were ringed, like women's hands; the clansmen found this appearance, this mockery of Northern wealth, the least threatening. It was in Pedro di'Jardanno's best interest, and the best interest of his profession, to threaten as little as possible—unless that was his mission. "Have you taken his measure?"

"I?" Anton shrugged, turning his gaze to the boy. "In some things you must decide for yourself; do not turn to me for objectivity in this particular matter."

That Pedro was irritated by the tone of Anton's reply was obvious; that he expected as much, equally obvious. Anton maintained his reputation for a lack of any real finesse. Such lack had endangered his life before, but it had conversely saved it; and never more so than at times like this, when he truly despised the man so spoken to. Dangerous, that contempt; after all, he was a weapon, no more, and one did not waste one's brief time despising a sword.

Except here, at a test of honor, between men of skill. The sun was not yet gone; the shadows it cast should not have been so long. But there she sat, the woman whose love still defined his life, watching, as he watched.

What would she have said, had she known that he stood beside a man who was—in the end—a servant of the Lord of Night? The brotherhood. It was not named; it was rarely called. Rumor said that it never failed.

He was done with rumor.

"He is taller than I expected."

"And you had good reason, no doubt, to expect less."

Pedro di'Jardanno was silent again, which was a good thing. Ser Anton did not relish the consequences of killing him, but the act itself was beginning to have its strong appeal.

"You are an . . . unusual man, Ser Anton. I would believe, were it not for your legendary dedication to a cause of your own choosing, that you have become too enamored of the event itself."

"And if I were the type of man who cared what another thought, I might point out that legend indeed is the only home for such dedication as you claim for me." His voice grew chill, robbing sun of warmth but not blistering heat. "Because if I were such a dedicated man as you imply, I would certainly have remained dedicated to my original goal: hunting the bandits who killed my wife and son.

"A man of your intelligence would of course realize that the Tyr'agar who ordered their deaths was a weak man, not a stupid one. There is no way that he would have trusted such information to mere soldiers, especially not to men of power and ambition such as the former General, Alesso di'Marente. Marente, therefore, did not have access to that information. Were I he, I would have chosen to call upon the Lady's dark brotherhood—but had he, no word that they were assassinated would have escaped. They are not political creatures, that brotherhood.

"Which means he trusted only the perpetrators. And as that information did come to light, and so conveniently recently, it must mean that the man in the Tyr's service who was given the orders still survives."

Pedro said, "Your instructor—"

"Long dead." Ser Anton's smile was thin. "Which means, of course, that I have far to search, and that my answers will lie in the Court of the Tyr himself.

"Take for example you, Pedro di'Jardanno. I believe this is the first time that you have been under the command of the General."

"A wise man would remember the rank of the man he serves."

"We both know that until he takes the Sword he is called Tyr by the sycophantic, cowards, and serafs. He knows it as well."

"He would be greatly displeased to hear you speak thus."

"And will you run back to him like a harem child to carry the tale?" Ser Anton shrugged. "He will choose to ignore it; he is practical. He needs my skill and my public support. He needs your skill. Just as, perhaps, another before him did."

Pedro's deceptively soft face paled. "Ser Anton—"

"Dedication," Anton continued, unmoved. "Perhaps you are right. Perhaps I should examine more closely the men with whom our new Tyr surrounds himself. Perhaps I would find the hand responsible for the two deaths that have always driven me to succeed.

"You deal death at the whim of unscrupulous rulers. You always have. I am watching you—except, perhaps, on those rare occasions when something, such as this competition, catches my attention."

"I . . . see."

"Good."

Pedro di'Jardanno walked away, pulling his heavy silk robes around a girth that was more show than fact.

It was ill-considered, to have spoken so freely. Foolish, especially when he did not consider Pedro to be the enemy, that final death which might give him back what remained of his life. Perhaps he was old indeed, to know this and care so little for its truth. He turned to see the kai Leonne standing silently with his men, the flat of his blade exposed to the sun's light. The Lord's gaze. His posture was perfect.

What had Scr Kyro said?

He would have died with us, rather than choosing to save his own life, as the Northern Kings offered. We are his kin by that action. Anton, and you fail to understand that, if you have come to me for approval.

And he had. Not obviously, of course; a man of his stature could ill afford to plead like some wayward child for the approval of his elders. But Kyro was a man his youthful self, long since buried under the weight of wind-brought sand, understood. Even admired.

Mari had liked him.

Mari was dead.

CHAPTER FIFTEEN

Evening, 17th of Lattan
Averalaan, Guesthouse in Avantari

The witnesses were given quarters adjacent to *Avantari,* the Palace of Kings. They were also given guards, in a manner of speaking. These were placed at the doors, the street windows, the long halls; they were stationed in the kitchen; they were, in short, everywhere, and far more numerous than the witnesses they purported to be guarding.

Aidan couldn't understand it; not at first. He didn't expect to, though; the Kings had money, and no one who had a lot of money had to make sense if they didn't damned well want to.

And they had money all right. Aidan had meat for dinner that night, covered in weird sauce—he scraped his off—and after that, cream, sugar, fruit that was rare no matter what the season. Everything was pretty, and he regarded the food with a mixture of hunger, disdain, and curiosity before he was convinced that he wouldn't make an idiot of himself by eating it.

There were three boys his own age, and one girl; they sat together, ate the same way, and eventually went off to their rooms by some silent mutual agreement. The woman in charge of the guesthouse had put them all in the same stretch of hallway because, as she said, there was at least some chance that one of them was paying enough attention to remember it. Sam—funny name, for a girl—was.

So he found his huge, empty room, on the second floor of what was a huge, bustling building, and he sat in the center of a bed six times too large, wondering what it was going to cost him to be here. When she smiled, Kalliaris was the most wonderful god in the world.

But when she frowned, you kind of forgot what the smiles were like. *You beware,* his mother used to say, *of any luck you don't make.* He'd wondered, then, how the Hells you were supposed to *make* luck. But he almost understood what she meant: Things could go just that shade *too* well. Kalliaris liked the helpless and the downtrodden—and as long as you didn't forget just how helpless or downtrodden you'd been, she was fair.

But forget—just forget for a minute who you owed your life to, and she reminded you. If you survived it.

Things were going too damned well, that was the problem.

That and he'd eaten way too much.

Evening, 17th of Lattan
Avantari

The moon was high.

Devon ATerafin had nothing against the moonlight. But shadows had a way of gathering. He was always wary of the shadows, and tonight he'd spent almost an hour watching them. Instinct spoke with its own voice. If not for that voice, he would be sleeping in the relative comfort of his own bed. Instead he waited here, his eyes straying between window, balcony, and door; the doors to this particular set of quarters were notorious in a very small circle of men and women.

Devon disliked silent doors as a matter of principle, but the very particular Patris Larkasir insisted that they be well-oiled and otherwise perfectly maintained. Patris Larkasir's loyalties lay with the Kings, and in his job as the overseer of the Royal Charters and Trade, he was peerless. Devon had had the privilege of working with him for just over two decades, and he knew that the only security issue Patris Larkasir cared much about was that of his information. Whether or not someone could enter the office *quietly* was not a matter of concern; as far as Patris was concerned there was actually no such thing as too quiet.

Devon adapted. It was not one of the traits for which he was known in general, but it was one of the traits that he had found most useful in his long career.

The door, when it opened, opened, as expected, silently; had he not been watching for the movement he might have missed it, and he missed very little. But he swore under his breath when he saw who stepped through it.

And of course, being who it was, he heard; Kallandras of Senniel missed nothing that could conceivably be heard, distance notwithstanding.

"You were expecting me, I see. Did she summon you, as well?"

"She?"

In the darkness, the bard *was* dark, as much a part of the shadows as—as Devon himself. They were dressed for darkness, both of them, or rather, dressed to take advantage of it. Kallandras raised a fair brow. "If you did not see her, you must tell me one day what, exactly, you were waiting for."

"I'll trade," Devon said, with a smile that was slightly less sharp. "You tell me what on earth you thought you'd find here."

"You," Kallandras replied. He stepped back through the open door, leaving his voice behind. "I don't think we've much time."

"Time for what?" Devon followed him quietly; they moved, both men, as if movement itself were suspect.

The bard did not answer.

Aidan hadn't thought to tell his Da much; only that he was going to wait in the streets until the parade of champions had passed him by. He'd half-hoped his Da might join him; they'd done it less than two years past. But his Da was working, and as he said, the parade was the best time to catch up on the work that needed doing, what with everyone gawping like farm boys.

Three days. Da. You take care.

I will.

Three days, then.

He remembered this in the dark of night; the moon through open courtyard and half-closed glass—glass!—cast a weak shadow across the sheets as he sat bolt upright.

Da's going to kill me.

He lurched out of bed, hit the ground with a grunt. The beds were a lot taller here than they had been in the old house. In the rooms above the shop, bed was a flat mat that sat on the floor; didn't much matter if you rolled out of that. Cradling his arm, he got shakily to his feet. He'd bitten his lip to stop from shouting; everyone else was sleeping and besides, he didn't need them to think he couldn't even get out of bed without injuring himself.

He hadn't brought much in the way of clothing, and he'd spent the last of the evening trying to clean what he had brought. The shirt was still wet when he pulled it over his head. Nothing dried in weather like this.

But he hadn't taken off the medallion. Pulling it out from beneath the damp folds of shirt, he made sure it would be plainly visible; the guards would ask otherwise.

What are you going to tell them? That you have to go home and tell your dad where you are? That brought him up short. He stood there, hand on the door, sure he was going to look like a complete fool.

Better to look like a fool than to be *one.* His grandmother's words. His mother's. His Da never said anything like that; looking like a fool, or feeling like one, always made him angry. Made Aidan wonder if he was getting to be too much like his Da.

And that made him open the door.

It was unexpectedly dark in the hall. The torches must've burned down. It surprised him; the whole place just reeked of money, and money meant light. Torches, oil, mage-stones, windows the length of a wall and the height of the ceiling. But down the long hall some lights were burning, and he shrugged, closed the door, and started toward them.

Until he saw that they were bobbing. Moving. They dropped once to the ground, or rather, seemed to bend that way. Beneath the glow of lamp, he could see an exposed back, laid out, facing a ceiling entirely absorbed with night. It shimmered under the pale glow of lamplight. The light rose again; the body did not.

Aidan didn't know much, but he wasn't stupid.

He held his breath, backed down the hall. In the distance he could hear first knocking, muffled slightly, and then a creak. The whole hall wasn't in use. It wasn't. He told himself that. And maybe they weren't going to open every door. Maybe they were just—just looking to steal something. Something like that.

But he didn't breathe. He didn't put the full force of his weight on the flat of his feet, choosing instead to place heel down steadily and let the rest of the foot follow. Quietly, quietly. He didn't want to be seen, and he knew that if he was heard at all, he would be,

Had he wondered why there were so many damned guards?

He stopped. Wondered, instead, where in the Hells they'd all gone. And then he heard the first scream.

And then he began to run.

Kallandras froze for a moment, stopping in mid-stride as if men normally stopped that way, and at that, completely gracefully.

Devon was a second behind him and attuned to him; he stopped as well. The grounds were silent if the normal noise of the grounds could be disregarded—and during the Festival season, that was difficult.

"We're late," Kallandras said softly. He began to move again, quickly.

He recognized the boy; Valedan's witness. He hadn't spoken to him, of course; he'd observed him from a polite distance. All affairs that related to the politics of the realm were observed from a distance of one sort or another, but they were observed. The boy's white hair caught what scant light there was through the window of the guesthouse's upper storey. His hands were not so striking as his hair, not so pale; they came up, struck the glass, palm first.

Devon's eyes narrowed.

"Kallandras!" he cried.

The bard stopped, crouched low to earth, turned, all in a motion. "What?"

"Tell the boy to get away from the window."

Anyone else and Devon would have had to explain. What boy? What window? Why?

Kallandras raised his head slightly in the silence.

The boy disappeared.

Do not touch exterior glass.

The words came from nowhere and hung in the air like a sword. Like a sword wielded by no one, but sharp enough to kill, and suspended a little too close to the neck at that.

Aidan pulled his hand back from the window and turned his back to it instead. In the darkness, the torches were swaying. The hall was a long hall, beginning to end, but it was suddenly becoming a lot shorter.

They didn't shout for him to stop. That was the weird thing. They made almost no noise as they ran; if it weren't for the lights, he might not have heard them at all.

And he knew that was bad.

There was a bend in the hall, and stairs.

He took both.

The doors would not open.

In Devon's left hand was a completely useless ring of keys. Oh, the keys slid into the lock, all right; they even turned. But the click of authoritative opening did not follow that movement;

it was as if the lock and the key had been somehow sundered, as if they had lost the ability to speak the same language, although they retained the same outward appearance of compatibility.

Not bolted; not barred; not locked. Anything as simple as that would have been visible immediately in the light that Devon carried. Kallandras waited at his side in silence—and Devon knew it was the silence of the listener. He thought, as he rose from his slow crouch, that not all bards could listen well, even if they were born with the voice—but those men and women born to the voice who could listen, he was certain, could hear heartbeats and interpret them.

"Who are they after?" he asked, when the bard's gaze met his.

"I'm not . . . sure."

"What do you hear?"

"Nothing," he said. "Nothing except the feet of heavy men in the hall above."

"The guards?"

"Dead," Kallandras said, in a tone that held only fact, no emotion. "Or sleeping. I would definitely say sleeping," he added, again dispassionately. "Were it not for the scream."

"They can't all be dead."

"No, I concur." Kallandras surveyed the door.

"There's this door, three servants' entrances, and the main set of doors." The door that they stood before was the door by which the priest left and entered.

"Let us pretend that whoever our enemies are, they have the same dislike for the priests that they are once rumored to have had. I would try the servants' entrance closer to the Northern stairs."

Devon didn't ask Kallandras how he knew the lay of the building so well. They ran.

When Aidan tripped down the stairs, he wasn't even surprised: he *had* had it too good, and Kalliaris had noticed him and started to frown.

But when the blue light fanned out above his head, when it splashed the wall in a flare of light that was—he couldn't think of a different word for it—*sticky*, he figured she was just smiling with an ugly edge. Because the light dripped down like some sort of heavy liquid.

The fall hadn't hurt him. Hadn't really slowed him down; he'd actually gotten to the bottom faster. He rolled up, made damned sure that whatever was dripping didn't touch him, and threw open the stairwell's swinging doors.

Above him he heard cursing.

He couldn't understand a word of it, but he'd listened to enough of the language over the past week to know it for what it was: Annagarian. He offered a breathless curse—in Weston—which was all he had time for. He had to get out.

Whoever they were, they didn't bother to trip down the stairs; they came down it like full-shod horses; heavy and loud.

Where in the Hells are the guards?

As he flew clear of the doors, he tripped over his answer.

And this time, he *did* lose time.

If it hadn't been for the circumstances, Devon would have laughed. This door, simple and almost featureless—inasmuch as *any* door that stood on the grounds of the Kings' land could be said to be either—would not come down. Both he and Kallandras, in his own modest opinion, had had the training required to use their strength to advantage; the door was heavy enough, but it was hinged; there should not have been any way that it could stand—completely unperturbed—against two such men working, as it were, in concert.

But it wouldn't budge.

On the best of days, Devon could find two good words to say about mages if he struggled. This was not the best of days. Kallandras stiffened; his eyes, even in the darkness, took on that peculiar flatness that meant he was listening, he was giving something beyond Devon's hearing his full concentration.

"I think," he said softly. "I have an answer."

"To which question?"

"You wanted to know who they're after."

Devon took in some of the bard's stillness.

"They're after Valedan's witness. Aidan."

The guards were dead.

Or at least he thought they were dead; living men didn't usually lie in wait across the length of the floor. But these did. His foot caught on the unexpected underside of ribs, and he fell flat across two men.

Two men who, far from having fallen in a heap, seemed to be laid out, side by side, arms and legs straight. As if they were statues on the tops of those fancy cenotaphs that rich people bought by dying. Except they weren't statues. As his face grazed the floor, he could hear the whuffling snort of breath: sleeping. They were sleeping.

He desperately wanted to believe that they'd just fallen asleep on duty. Gods, he wished he were stupid.

But he wasn't, so he knew damned well that he didn't want to join them. His palm found cold links of cloth covered chain; he pushed himself up, stopping for just long enough to steal a long knife from the sheath of the nearest guard. It was big enough to be a sword to Aidan.

Awkward and heavy, but better than nothing.

He gained his feet. He started to run.

"Stand back," Kallandras said.

He wasn't Astari, but he was an equal, and in this, as much a comrade at arms as the Astari were. Devon asked no questions. He stood back.

Stood back while the bard stepped forward. Stood back while the bard lifted his hand, his right hand, and placed it palm first against the door. The line of his body stiffened, as if in pain. No, Devon thought; *in* pain.

"Be ready," the bard said, through visibly clenched teeth. "They know we're here now."

"They—"

From a clear and cloudless sky, lightning fell—and Kallandras was the conduit.

The door buckled, shivering under the flare of light, the heat of it, the weight of it. But it buckled the way a tent wall will; the way something flexible will; undulated in the darkness of night, in the light of Kallandras' hand.

For the first time in years, in more, Devon heard Kallandras of Senniel swear. He said nothing; offered no aid. Instead, he saw to his weapons.

In the darkness—and it *was* dark, even with the huge windows and the moonlight—the great hall looked different. Different enough that Aidan lost his bearings. He found it hard to run because the long dagger he held was ungainly, and the bodies that were lined up, neatly and evenly, in the hall couldn't quite be ignored. He had to know where they were.

But he knew there was a door here somewhere. Sam had pointed it out—she was a nosybody, noticed everything—and because he thought it was so stupid, he remembered it.

He wondered—because he couldn't stop himself from wondering—whether or not that scream had come from Sam's room. Because he didn't remember where her room was. Hells, he'd barely remembered his own. She had.

He didn't know her well enough to recognize her scream.

Door. He had to think. The *door*. Breath was painful, hard to take. He wasn't sure why; he'd run a helluvalot faster than this, and he'd certainly run for longer.

Someone shouted something. Foreign words.

But the meaning was clear enough.

They'd seen him. They knew where he was.

Kalliaris, Kalliaris, please—please let me get there before they do.

What did he owe her already?

The footsteps at his back stopped; the room fell into a silence that he didn't realize *was* silence over the sound of his own breath, the intensity of his internal prayer. No one moved. He should have been happy. He should have looked at it as a gift from the goddess.

But it was *too* quiet. It was just wrong.

He made the door with more than enough room to spare. Grabbed the handle, pulled for all he was worth. Which apparently wasn't enough. The door didn't budge.

"Well," someone said, and it took him a minute to realize that he understood the word, "you've led my associates a fine chase, but I believe, Aidan Cooper, that your dalliance is at an end."

He turned, the dagger clutched in both hands—both shaking hands. Standing in the middle of the hall, coming quickly toward him, was a very tall, very large man.

A man with hands as black as mourning, both outstretched, and both filled with something that seemed to be blue light, thickly pooled in palms and around fingers. "If you make this more difficult, you will suffer," the man said. "Suffering is not, however, required."

As the light he held grew brighter, Aidan could see that the man wore gloves, supple and dark beneath the moving flow of whatever it was he carried.

"What—what is that?"

"It is . . . a gift," the man replied smoothly. "It will do you no more harm than was done to the men who sleep here. You will feel no pain."

That's why you're wearing the gloves?

He turned to the side, either side, and saw that the foreigners—he recognized them now, and felt, of all things, betrayed—had come upon him. They did not seek to hold him—but they wouldn't let him pass.

He weighed the worth of the dagger against a man who was—who must be, although he didn't bear the marks—a mage, and men who were probably just thugs. Made his decision.

"Aidan, hit the floor. Now!"

And unmade it. His knees buckled almost before the words made themselves understood.

There was nothing so sweet in his life to date as the sound of splintering wood.

Devon stepped past Kallandras through the shattered door, the splintered frame. The boy lay aground at his feet, his back harbor to wooden splinters; blood had been drawn by the force of the door's opening. He saw that, although he spared the boy the second of recognition, no more.

"Do not interfere in what does not concern you."

Devon was not short, but the height of the man who spoke those words forced him to look up. The whole of the building was dark; he was haloed in a light that was unpleasant and cold; it drew the eye and repelled it at the same time.

Had he been almost anyone else, the whole of his attention would have been absorbed by this. He was Devon ATerafin. He counted four men to either side of the door; they had not drawn weapons.

Nine in total. How surprising.

Steel's rasp completed the thought. Not his, of course; when Devon wanted to draw a blade, he didn't give himself away so carelessly.

"You'll pardon me," he replied, "if I decide for myself what my concerns are." In the night beyond the words, the bodies of the Kings' Swords had been laid out against the floor. The heat of his momentary anger surprised him.

Why? Because war hadn't been declared yet?

"I would pardon you," the man replied, in flawless, uninflected Weston. "But I feel that my companion is less likely to be patient." Blue fire, shot through with shadow that was fine enough,

delicate enough, to be black lace, writhed in his hands, illuminated his face. "I will offer one further warning because I am
feeling generous and because I am at heart a peaceful man. Leave.
Now."

Magic had its own particular smell, its own taste. Devon ATerafin had spent much of his adult life studying it. There was a particular feel to a magery gleaned by years of developing talent;
the man who carried magic in his hands didn't—quite—have it.

There was no denying magic itself. Many men who were not
mages were versed in crafts similar in seeming. Few of those
worked with allies of the Shining Lord—and this man did not
look insane enough to be Allasakari. A puzzle.

Devon never appreciated mystery when lives were at stake.

The darkened great hall of the guesthouse could have been a
cathedral. The ceilings were tall enough to disappear into night's
shadow; the window, crossed by lead and filled by colored glass,
was built to catch the sun's rise and fall, from ground to beam.

The only fight he'd ever been in in a cathedral had nearly
killed him.

As if to remind him of that night, the large man—the only man
he was certain would not be among the roster of challengers'
witnesses—nodded. The movement was minimalist enough to be
significant. Devon crossed his arms, the movement a quick snap
of forearm and elbow.

Two men fell.

"I'm afraid," he said softly, "that I will have to disappoint your
less patient—and less visible—friend. Boy." he said, speaking to
the vicinity of his feet without once looking down, "I believe it's
time for you to leave now."

"A pity," the man replied. "Believe that my regret is genuine.
The matter, however, is now out of my hands." And as he finished the last word, Devon realized that he had, in a fashion, a
sense of humor.

He threw the blue fire.

Afterward he would be certain it only took a second to recover;
he could judge time by feel; they had trained him that well. But
the ring obeyed its own laws. He had learned over time that it
was not a tool, it was a wild ally. It did not negotiate. If you needed
its power, you took it; it took what it required in its turn.

Time. Which was bad.

He had not called the lightning in years. Not the lightning, which was difficult enough, and not the wind. The wind's voice was a terrible thing. It scoured him. It emptied him from the inside, and he understood, as he stood in the emptiness of the wind's voice, what the wind meant to the Southerners. Why damnation was an eternity in the wind's wake.

But he was already damned.

And because he was already damned, he could return to the world when he heard a familiar voice. Could recognize it, although he had, in fact, never heard Devon ATerafin scream before.

Devon ATerafin wore two rings; a gift of the magi. Wore as well a vest that weighed less than gauze, less, he thought, than the webs out of which it was woven, it was that fine, that supple, like captured light. However, none were remarkable to the eye; indeed, the rings were plain and of a quality rivaled only by the offerings of apprentices to questionable goldsmiths. No matter; they were not meant to adorn.

They were meant to protect, to ward, to guard.

To guard against fire, mage-fire, the magelight that brought not illumination, but death—or worse.

Devon *moved*. That came more naturally than breathing. As did seeing the boy, half-crouched, in the mage's path, his dull shirt almost white in the glow of traveling light. What did not: breaking the flow of the jump itself; halting the motion; changing its course.

Devon stood.

He was the wall behind which the boy might survive the blast.

Until the light struck, he thought it *was* light—some artifact of magery, dangerous yes, but not more so than a well aimed quarrel or swordmaster's weapon. He had seen mage-fire before, had, in fact, been burned by it. This had not looked that strong.

But when it struck, it clung not like fire, but rather, webbing—and it whispered in his ears as it climbed up his face in a moving, liquid sheet.

Devon ATerafin, it said. Just that. His name.

But he knew, hearing it, just how visceral a power the name of a demon held for the demon in whom it was rooted.

Because as the light entered him he felt that name begin to dissolve.

He could not stop himself: he screamed. Just once.

The light wrapped around him laughed.

* * *

Kallandras heard the laughter.

It was brief, but heavy, sensual; it lingered like a caress that is both unexpected and forbidden, but not—not quite—undesired or undesirable; there was about it a satisfaction and a cruelty that was so natural it was the most striking element of the voice itself. Wilderness there. Power.

It was also kin to voices he had heard before, in a past that was never far enough away.

Demon. *Kialli.* Kin.

Devon.

He armed himself. Lifted his hand and armored himself by that motion.

And stepped into the hall.

The man's scream had faded into a terrible silence.

Aidan was mute, as mute as the man, as terrified as he had ever been.

The man in black gloves came up to him then and grabbed both shoulders. He struggled; his captor released one shoulder for as long as it took him to swing an open hand.

Aidan understood the unspoken command better than most; he stilled at once.

The man spoke in the foreign tongue. No one answered.

He spoke again, his voice colder. Again there was no answer.

The next set of words was a question; Aidan thought his collarbone would snap at the momentary clenching of large hands.

No answer.

But that third time, that third time Aidan realized his captor was speaking *to* the light. The light itself seemed to be alive.

And it was wrapped around the man who'd come to help him. Wrapped around him, and then, somehow, sunk in as if it weren't light at all, but a shining, shimmering liquid, something thick and oily and heavy.

The man's body began to twitch and spasm; his hands reached up; he clawed at his face, drawing blood. Or it seemed like blood; it was dark a moment across a sheen of black-speckled blue light. The light seemed to pool there, where the wounds were, glimmering darkly.

Feeding.

This was going to be his fate.

He knew better than to struggle.

He knew better, but he did.

* * *

There were nine men in the room. Nine men, the boy, and the man that was—and he admitted this only to himself—of all his allies closest to him in nature, in ability. Devon ATerafin. Not a brother, never that; they had chosen different masters. But they had chosen masters, and they both knew the price and the value of service.

He walked quietly; silence was the first of the arts that he, a man born to speech and the vice of song, had had to master. His footfall did not disturb the man who seemed at the center of things, perhaps because his attention had been absorbed, momentarily, in the beating of a boy. A short task, that; not a challenge, not even a real distraction; he spoke above the sound of his own open palms.

It did not disturb his conversation.

But unfortunately, the creature to whom he spoke was not so absorbed, not so inattentive. "I believe," he said, in his nonlanguage, "that we have another . . . guest." He spoke in a voice that was in tone and texture so similar to Devon ATerafin's that were he not bard-born Kallandras might not have heard the difference.

The man whose most distinguishable feature was his stature looked up from the height of a boy's shoulders. His face was impassive. But he offered Kallandras none of the warning, none of the threatening conversation, that he had offered Devon.

Instead he turned to the eight men who stood adrift, and ill at ease, in the large hall.

"Kill him. Quickly."

They stared in surprise; most of their attention was focused upon the ATerafin. Had they responded immediately, it wouldn't have mattered. He had enough time to do what must be done.

Flicking the folds of his sleeve to the side, he pulled back his arm and threw an awkwardly shaped, ornate, dagger.

When it struck, Devon ATerafin screamed.

Screamed with its voice and his own.

The man in the black snarled in genuine surprise.

Then he lifted the boy—both hands still gripping his shoulders—and flung him half way across the hall; he was rubbish now, unwanted detritus.

A sword was drawn in the hall, a sword long and curved and slender of blade. It had a name; Kallandras thought he could almost hear the echo of it hang in the air between them. A bad sign, that.

In reply, he drew two blades of his own.

"I serve," he said softly, "the Lady."

"And I," the large man replied, "the Lord."

He did not like the odds; seven men to one. But he thought, as the giant closed, that at least four of those seven would wait for the sword's edge to decide who was victim and who was victor.

It would be a short wait. Kallandras had rarely seen someone so large move so quickly.

Fire.

Now the fire came.

It singed his skin, but not from the outside; *this* fire was liquid, and it bubbled in his veins. He fought against it.

He understood pain well. He was Astari, after all.

There, and there, and there; three scars whose pain still echoed when the air was sea-heavy. He remember the fight they'd been taken in.

He remembered.

His enemy.

His enemy's face. It came back to him in a dark so profound it seemed etched in light.

Pain, yes.

This was not the blade's pain, but neither had that been, and the scars that he counted deepest had come from wounds that drew very little blood, in the end.

Save us, he told himself. *Save us. Pull the blade. Throw it.*

His hands rose as if they were not his hands; they felt too heavy, too large, too stiff.

Save us, he said again.

Those hands trembled, spasmed. He could not force them to rise. He could not find the fire in time.

Throat raw with screaming, he could still taste both blood and dryness, dryness and blood. Something was missing from his memory of fire.

Kallandras admired the man's speed. Paired with his size, he thought it unmatched, possibly unmatchable. Sword flashed in the dimming light that coated the ATerafin who lay, knife in muscles of his thigh, across the floor.

The giant crossed over him as if he were a bridge, using the speed, the muscle, the weight—not of sword but of the arm and shoulder behind it. Kallandras had been trained to fight where fighting was necessary, but he was forced back by the speed of his opponent's sword, by the strength of blows that could not be merely deflected and forgotten.

He did not know where the pain came from. Fire? It had a source, he was certain it must—but a drowning man doesn't often ask where the mouth of the river is. The burning held him, held him, scoured him; he felt flesh singe and wither beneath its august touch, its ancient light.

Save us, the voice said again.

And this time he heard it, understood that it was distinct. *Who,* he thought, *are we?* Because he didn't know. He didn't know the answer to the question. Until the fires had come, he wouldn't have known how to ask it.

We will die, fool, the voice said, and he recognized it as distinct, unknown. Desperate.

The fire. The fire. The fire.

But he'd felt pain before this. There was a time before this.

No, the voice said. *There is only now, and we will perish in it if you will not act.*

But he heard a voice, saw a face: Dark, night-eyed, grim.

He almost died, then, although he did not know it. Because he knew where the pain was coming from, what the wound was; what he would see if he listened, if he watched—and he did not wish to live it again. Had it been taken from him? Had it? He would part with it willingly.

Everything you are, we will own, the voice said. *We are the Compact. We are the circle. We protect what* must *be protected. There is no duty that comes before our duty. Give your oath, and I will accept it. If I accept it, your life will no longer be your own.*

There was a knife in his thigh. It hurt, not so much because there was pain—although it was there—but because, if not for his training, it wouldn't have been the thigh that she hit. She. Black-haired, beautiful, wild.

He did not want to be here. He had suffered once, had lived through it once. He was bleeding. *Why? Why, Allia?*

She didn't answer, of course. Treachery of this nature was its own special explanation, its own torment. He tried to stand. His leg was on fire. *Poison,* he thought. He remembered thinking, *Poison.* He almost didn't care.

Make your decision. Your life—
Will no longer be.

Your own.

What more did he want, the heartless bastard? Had he not already *made* his choice? The proof of his cursed loyalty was there at his feet for all to see.

The circle widened, darkened. There was blood on his hands, the dead at his feet—the dead—Allia, dead, at his feet. Allia.

Pain. Fire.

He looked up, he remembered it now, looked up into those night eyes, those inhuman, unshuttered eyes, and he saw her killer. Saw—gods he had hated it then, he hated it now—that her killer *was* the words, that beneath the death with which he veiled every phrase and every silence, every move he made, he had fashioned himself loveless for the duty of protecting the Empire's heart and soul: King Reymalyn and King Cormalyn. The Lord of the Compact. The man who fashioned, who forged, and who tested the Astari.

Devon was bleeding.

She had wounded him, and the wound was burning, burning, burning. Poison?

"Decide," Duvari said. "After tonight you cannot avoid the decision."

The knife.

The knife was in his thigh. She had missed—had she missed on purpose? Had she missed because she had doubts, had learned to love him? He wanted to believe that, but honesty—with himself—was his fatal flaw.

Pain.

I thought I was in love with her.

His fatal flaw. *No, I* was *in love with her. Allia, what would you have been if you had chosen a different life, if you had chosen—*

Life.

They had both chosen lives of death.

"I choose to serve the Lord of the Compact."

"And what does that service entail?"

At his feet, the dead. He bowed his head. "Everything. Everything in the service of the Kings. No loyalty to any House will come before my loyalty to this service. No oath will come between me and the oath I make now." He took a breath, started to speak, to say more—but Duvari, cold and grim, lifted a hand, silencing him.

His single act of generosity, of kindness, in the face of loss. "Who swears this oath?"

"Devon. Devon ATerafin."

Devon ATerafin.

He was burning; his thigh was on fire; he understood what that fire meant now. His hands, twitching and shaking, rose; he could not see them; could barely feel them.

He knew that the dagger was in his thigh; that it was somehow working its way out of his flesh. Shaking, because fire was not the death he desired, he reached out and grabbed the knife's hilt.

And pushed.

The screaming was not his; the pain was.

In the silence of what was left of himself, of his memories, Devon ATerafin began to recite the names of the Trinity. And as he did, he began to remember other wounds, other scars; to hold these, to keep them, to remake what he understood himself to be.

He caught the blade once in the tines of his own weapon. Caught it a moment, held it there, straining, testing.

The man grunted in surprise.

Kallandras spoke. "You serve the Lord of the Night, but the night is my Lady's domain; if she is served in darkness, *we* are the brotherhood who serves her. But they do not know who you serve, nor who I serve."

The man grunted again, forcing his sword in, in, in, its sharp edge seeking Kallandras' exposed throat. "We both know there *is* no Lord of the Sun," he said. "It's a lie, it was always a lie."

Lower, his voice.

"The rules of the Lord apply to his people," Kallandras said, as if the giant had not chosen to speak. "And I will allow for those rules when I face men, and not the shadows of men. The light casts you, and the servant of the light casts you out."

The man shoved then, shouldering weight, risking the edge of his enemy's weapons. Kallandras broke free, dodged, ran nimbly over to the ATerafin's side. He felt all eyes upon him; he had been bard-trained, and knew how to draw the attention when it suited his needs.

Had been Kovaschaii-trained, brother-defined. He knew what his needs were, and he exploited everything to that end.

The tall man's eyes widened; he was not, Kallandras saw, a complete fool. "The Lord," the man said, "rewards power. It is only power that he values."

"Were you there, at Leonne's dawn?" the bard asked, the words almost a song in themselves. "Were you there, to see what he saw, to hear what he heard? Can you know the mandate of the Lord himself?"

"The Lord," the giant said, advancing slowly now, "rewards *men*."

"The Lord rewards honorable men, or so it is said. The South once understood honor; they have cast it aside. Why else would the Lord have abandoned Leonne?"

"Why," he continued, pitching his voice, "else would the Lord have brought us here, in the service of Leonne's rebirth?"

The man sneered. "You are fools," he said to the six who waited, armed, for some sign, some turn in the course of the fight itself.

"But," Kallandras continued, softly, "you have chosen to ally yourself with the Usurper, the Lord of Night; you are not a man; you are beneath the notice a man deserves."

He came, then.

And Kallandras smiled.

Because he had been trained to fight when it was *necessary,* and the fight here was not. There was no pride in him, no desire to do the right thing; there was a death, it was waiting for his hand to deliver it.

"Silence," he said, speaking with the voice. And then, as the roar left the man's lips in a rush, he added, **"Do not move."**

It would not hold him long. Kallandras knew it, accepted it as truth. The bardic voice worked best where its effects were felt but not noticed, where it encouraged behavior that was almost natural. Here, with death between them, there was no question of that; it was a test of wills, and in the end, the command the voice exerted would fail.

Had it been a matter of time, that might have concerned him. It was not. It did not.

Kallandras stepped in and gracefully separated the man's head from his shoulders.

The sword twitched and shook as the body, free from its compulsion, reacted. Kallandras stepped out of its way, wincing only when it fell across Devon ATerafin. He waited a moment in silence, his weapons, like his arms, at his side.

When he looked up, the six men were farther away. He spared them that glance, but no more.

Quietly, and with a reverence that they could not miss, he knelt before the corpse of the man. "Brother," he said softly. "You have been carried too long by a man who does not know your worth; too long by a man who serves your ancient enemies. Will you allow his killer to raise you? Or will the vengeance due your master's killer be meted out as you see fit?"

"I vote for vengeance," a voice said.

Kallandras smiled. "ATerafin. Kind of you to join me."

"Not really," Devon replied. He was shaking; Kallandras could hear the aftershock in his voice. But his body was almost still to the sight. "And I think I must be delirious. Tell me you aren't speaking to that sword."

"I think it unwise," the bard said gravely, "to lie to a member of the Astari. But I feel compelled to warn you not to touch the blade." He paused a moment, mock-gravity falling into its reality. "Are you—"

"I don't know."

All the answer he needed in those three words.

"We've lost the eight."

"No," a voice said, from the farthest reaches of the hall. "You haven't. No thanks to either of you."

Shining in the darkness was the orange glow of a pipe. And above it, face lit from beneath by a spark of natural fire, Meralonne APhaniel. "The eight have been taken by the Magisterium—"

"This is not magisterial—"

"And turned over immediately to the Imperial Guard," he continued. "ATerafin, you are far too predictable."

"And you aren't predictable enough." Devon rose, knees folding in toward chest and stretching just as slowly once he'd rocked his feet to touch ground. "What are you doing here?"

"Housekeeping. For all the thanks I receive in the doing. Although if the truth were known—and it will be, so I might as well deliver it myself—the young boy that Valedan chose as witness is largely responsible for my presence."

"He knew enough about the magi that he could run to the Order from the Imperial Palace, unchecked, and be turned immediately over to you?"

The pipe glowed; it showed the edge of the mage's smile. "Not exactly, no. I was . . . visiting an old friend."

"Or were being visited by her?" Kallandra's question.

"No, actually. In truth this escapade was met by you and he; she did not rouse me."

"But?"

"I'm afraid, ATerafin, that you serve too completely the interests of another master, and he is not known for his gentle consideration of the magi." He bowed, slightly. "I do not think that this is the time to ask, regardless."

"Why?"

"Because," he said quietly, "there are detections and blessings that I believe it in your best interest to voluntarily—and *immediately*—undergo."

Kallandras waited out the three-beat silence, thinking that it was always this way with men of a certain type: their quietest voice was reserved for a statement that allowed no opposition.

Devon bowed; the bow was stiff.

"ATerafin?"

"I think—if the boy is safe—that it would be in our best interests to procure the services of the magi or the Mysterium for the duration of the challenge." He took a step; Kallandras turned away so that he didn't have to watch his knees buckle. They did; but Devon was Devon; he continued to walk. He would accept no help, and in this, he and Kallandras were not alike: Devon was practical, but he had his pride, and that pride had not dimmed with either necessity or age.

"Member APhaniel," Kallandras said softly, as Devon and the mage drew closer entirely by the ATerafin's effort, "there is still the matter of the sword."

"Yes, there is," the mage said softly. His gaze was steely and distant. "But I am a mage, and if I remember my history correctly, that blade is not for me or mine."

"Your history plays you false," Kallandras said. "Or Southern history does."

Silence, there. One rarely corrected a member of the Order of Knowledge. "Perhaps," the mage said, "I was being too subtle for you. Let me try again: The sword is your problem." His eyes fell upon the back of the headless corpse that lay against Devon's feet. "That one, and his kin, is mine."

"You recognize him?"

"Yes and no. He is of an order of mages that dwells South of the Empire; the Sword of Knowledge cannot contain them, and the Order has never tried. They are assassins," he added, his eyes flickering a moment over Kallandras, "of a common type—but they use what they learn to advantage. It seems that there is truth to the rumors."

"Those?"

"They mastered the forbidden arts." He turned to Devon. "ATerafin?"

Devon said quietly, "I'm ready."

"Member APhaniel?"

"What, Kallandras?"

"If it's not too much trouble, do you think you might wake the rest of the guard?"

A white brow rose in a pale face. "I think," he replied, still somewhat frostily, "that the Kings' own mages can attend to the trivialities." His face softened momentarily. "Kallandras, we cannot wait. I do not know what occurred, but from the young boy's rather panicked description, I can guess.

"We have time, but not much of it; what is at risk is not Devon ATerafin's life, but his experience."

Kallandras fell silent at once. *Devon,* he thought. Their eyes met. *You are better than I knew at concealing yourself; I did not hear this in you.*

They left him alone, with a corpse, a sword, and the sleeping bodies of Imperial guards.

He knelt before the sword again.

Meralonne took the light with him, but as night settled, the clarity of moon and stars made everything less harshly visible. Still, in the darkness, in *any* darkness, he would have seen this sword.

It was not for him. The life that he led, the path that he had chosen, the path that he had chosen to walk away from, all of these things had ill-prepared him for the life a wielder of such a weapon should have.

The only thing that worked in his favor was the war itself. He remembered old stories; older stories. Remembered that the swords of the desert cities were swords that took a man's name and bound it, almost as his had been taken and bound. And he remembered that the swords themselves could avenge the deaths of the masters they had chosen. Magic, old magic.

Southern magic, blood magic.

It was said that men were killed by the thousands to build such a weapon as this. That they were taken and measured and stripped of all essence, that they were somehow used to give the sword a measure of life. It was said, and said, and said, and each telling held something of the teller's fears or desires in it.

No such magics existed in the here and now.

And no such weapons.

But looking at the crescent of slender blade, he wondered that any of it could be true; the blade itself seemed the essence of steel, something perfect, too pure to be quenched in blood.

Why? It is only a weapon. It does not care how it was forged, or tempered. No more than Kallandras himself.

And yet . . . he bowed again.

Reached out, his hand hovering in the darkness a moment. He lifted the blade.

And to both his relief and his profound disappointment, the sword remained silent.

CHAPTER SIXTEEN

Early morning, 18th of Lattan, 427 AA
Avantari

Ser Anton di'Guivera waited for the sunlight in a grim, a bleak, silence. Those who knew him well—and they were few—would have seen the blackness of the rage in the stillness of his face, in the silence, the forced economy of his movement.

At his feet, thrown there like so much refuse, were eight medallions. Eight, stripped from the throats of their bearers, who now resided in the magisterial courts as common—and dangerous—criminals.

The man who delivered them had been most insulting.

But that, of course, was not what angered Ser Anton; he expected poor manners and poorer grace of the Northerners. No; that man had departed in a proper Northern snit, in the dead of the Lady's night.

They had not left it at that.

They had sent him envoys that could not, not quite, be ignored.

"Ser Anton?"

He lifted his face, smoothing the lines of his mouth to a taut straightness. "Princess Mirialyn," he replied.

"We realize, of course, that you are not to be held responsible for the behavior of the witnesses that your students have chosen."

He was so weary of politics. The night sky was still in ascendence, and the temptation to be impolitic under the Lady's moon was strong, strong, strong. He wanted the dawn, the steadying influence of the Sun; the touch of the Lord.

"Of course," he said at last. "That is why you are here. To assure me that no blame attaches to me or my students."

"Of course," the pale-haired man said, speaking far more smoothly, and far less expressively, than the Princess. Ser Anton was certain that this man was born with the twisted tongue of the

Northern bards. "But we wished to warn you, Ser Anton," he said. "because there will be rumors attached to the evening's events, and because it appears *all* of your students' chosen witnesses, were involved in the unfortunate event, you will be under suspicion by people who are less open-minded."

"Of course." He folded his arms across his chest like a shield, unconsciously choosing to take advantage of his height and his size. "And you now speak for the Crowns?"

It was the Princess who replied. "I was not, unfortunately, witness to the events, Ser Anton. Had I been, I would have, of course, confined the interview to persons of appropriate affiliation." She shrugged elegantly, casually. "Kallandras of Senniel happened to witness half of what occurred.

"And although I do not believe you have met him, we have a young boy who was witness to all."

She turned, spoke a word to the two guards at her back. One of them disappeared for a moment, but it didn't matter. Ser Anton knew who he would bring back.

He did not pray to the Lord for anything but strength, and he did not pray from a position of weakness.

Bruised, definitely black-eyed and swollen, the face was a little less familiar, a little more of a shock, than he expected. But he recognized Aidan. He knew failure when he saw it.

Ser Anton di'Guivera was not a man accustomed to failure, but against common wisdom, he acknowledged that he *was* merely a man, and had failed in his time. Still, he was not a man to be glad of it, grateful for it, when the failure was his own.

He did not know, therefore, how to feel at the sight of the boy.

He listened to the bard recount the evening's events; he even listened intently, wondering how much of it was true, and how much false. He would have to speak to the men himself, if they survived their incarceration.

Then he turned to the boy.

"So," he said, inclining his head, "you have seen your first battle, have been party to it. Do you still want a warrior's life, young Aidan?"

Aidan, grim-faced and hesitant at the same time, showed his age. He squared his shoulders, lifted his bruised chin—possible cracked jaw, from the look of the bruise's color, and said, "Yes."

"Then you are very brave, very foolish, or both."

Aidan shook his head. Glanced up at Kallandras of Senniel,

whose gaze was trapped by Ser Anton's expression, or lack of it. "If we don't fight 'em, they win.

"I don't know how to fight yet, but I will." He was silent for a moment, then.

Too silent. Too still.

It was not yet dawn; the sun was half an hour away. He said, "Did you know what they were going to do?"

Such a desire in those words, such a ferocity, such a quiet waiting. Lady, Lady, help him. He crouched—a posture distinct from kneeling, separate from it.

"Aidan," he said softly, "there are no rules in war. I ask you to remember this."

He knew that he would have caused the boy less pain if he had struck him, full out; if he had deepened or added to those bruises.

What he had not realized, or what he had prevented himself from realizing beneath the Lady's Moon, was that he would have caused himself less . . . discomfort as well.

Was it a sign?

And if it was, did it matter? He was Anton di'Guivera. No odd occurrence, and no discouragement, had ever served to sway him from his course. How was this different?

The light was shrouded in smoke; fire burning the last of the night, and its oil, away. Behind, in the rooms down the long, stone hall, he could hear the echo of early rising. Almost certainly Andaro and Carlo.

Today was the test of the river, the first test. They, all of his students, felt it auspicious to begin their exercises when the dawn lapped the edges of the night. It still surprised him. He wondered whose idea it was, because he could not conceive the pragmatic and political Andaro choosing such a superstitious course—but Carlo was a man of the open sky, the high sun; it defined him.

Still, whoever chose the hour made a statement: for the hours between the Lord's ascendence and the Lady's descent were the hours in which a man was free to be himself, a follower of neither, a child of both.

He stood, listening to the sounds of the day herald the day in. How, truly, was this different?

Killing bandits, of course, was easy. Killing Tyrs hardly less so, in the end. She would have accepted their heads, in her name, and if not in her name, than in the name of the son—her son, the one territory in which she was ferocious in her protectiveness.

But his Mari, his Mari would not, in the end, gladly accept the head of a boy.

Did it matter?

Surprising how the answer could change with the direction of the wind.

Aidan was silent.

Valedan was silent.

The woman—the Princess, the ACormaris—was silent.

Aidan had never realized just how loud, how uncomfortably loud, so much silence could be. He was miserable. He wished, although he wasn't stupid enough to say it, that he had been ordered back to the guesthouse. He hadn't, and everyone was so damned busy he was afraid to interrupt them and ask them the only question that really ate at him.

That scream. Had it come from Sam's room?

He wasn't stupid enough to think he could've made any difference. Hells, he'd seen what had happened to the ATerafin. But he hated that he'd run to safety when he'd heard the scream, because he thought—he was pretty sure—that it had come from her.

He looked up, met the unnerving, and unblinking, gaze of the Member of the Order of Knowledge, and looked down at his feet again. They were all tense with waiting, all of them. But the Member of the Order of Knowledge had been the only person here to insist that Aidan be sent away.

Valedan had refused the request.

Problem was, it didn't sound like much of a request to Aidan, and he knew better than to trust a mage. Especially after last night.

Valedan turned to look out the window. The sky across the whole of the visible ocean was purple-pink.

"You don't have much time," the ACormaris said quietly.

"No."

"Your presence here is not, strictly speaking, necessary."

"It is not," the Member of the Order of Knowledge broke in, "necessary at all."

Her eyes were narrowed slightly as they met his. She said nothing, and he shut up. It surprised Aidan, that the mage would shut up like that; the ACormaris didn't look particularly dangerous. Maybe rank counted for something.

"I feel that the responsibility is partly mine. Unless you specifically request otherwise, I will wait."

"And the Challenge?"

Valedan said nothing. Aidan's glance bounced between them until he realized that that *was* his answer.

The sky grew paler, and paler still.

Commander Sivari found them. "You're popular," he said, but only after delivering a very correct, very formal bow. "I didn't think they were going to let *me* in, and it's career-limiting to refuse a Commander of the Kings' Swords entry into any portion of *Avantari*. ACormaris," he added, bowing.

She smiled. "Commander."

"We're . . . almost ready."

They both looked at Valedan. Valedan stared at the door.

Beyond the door was Devon ATcrafin, with another gods-cursed mage. The master bard was with him as well.

"Ser Valedan," Commander Sivari said, "this is admirable. And you must decide, now, whether or not being admirable to a handful of Northerners is what you hoped to achieve at this Challenge."

Silence.

"I will be required to give notice to the adjudicatory body if you choose to forgo the test of the river." He waited. Frowned. "But if you forgo the test of the river, then your enemy, in failing, has still found some measure of success." His frown deepened, and after a moment, he bowed. Left, his steps mincing and loud in the huge room.

Aidan looked past him to the ACormaris, and she met his eyes. She smiled, but it wasn't a happy smile.

He sidled up to her, taking care to stay as far away from the mage as possible. "How long is it going to take?"

"I don't know," she said softly. "What you saw—what he underwent—we have no history of it here. The effect of the dagger makes clear the nature of the attacker, but the nature of the attack itself is of concern."

He dropped his voice as much as it could possibly be dropped and still be heard. "Why won't Valedan leave?"

"You must ask him that."

"I already did."

"And?"

"He didn't answer."

"Then I should not." She smiled gently, "but I will. It is not his answer, and it is not perhaps the answer he would give; remember that." She drew closer to him, and he thought—he thought her incredibly beautiful. As beautiful as he had once thought his mother was, when she had been his whole world. "Valedan is going to be King in the South. The word for King is 'Tyr'agar,' but either word—King or Tyr'agar—is just that, a word. He is not old."

He seemed old enough to Aidan, but Aidan didn't choose to correct her; and besides, the way she said it, it sounded true.

"He chose you as witness."

Aidan nodded; she seemed to expect that.

"And were it not for his choice, your life would have been in no danger. He wishes to keep you at his side because there, he feels you will be safe. And if not, he will be there to fight a battle he believes to be his own." She looked over the top of Aidan's head. "He also wishes to know that . . . no permanent harm was done to the ATerafin. Or if there was, the method by which it was done; it will be used against him again, and the knowledge is as much a weapon as his sword."

She stopped speaking, looked up and past him, and then looked back down. "He must learn, for himself, the difference between personal responsibility and power. If he is to take a country, he will have to sacrifice parts of it; there is no way that this war will not be won—or lost—without the deaths of thousands."

"But he *knows* that. There's going to be a *war.*"

"Ah, yes. Of course." She smiled again, sadly. "But you know—we all know—that our parents will die. It's fact, but we weep when the truth of it cannot be escaped."

She might have said something else, but the doors opened again.

Commander Sivari stood between them.

And at his side, the dark-haired, veiled woman. She stepped over the threshold, and fell at once to her knees, lowering her head into the stone. It made Aidan nervous, because there was something about her that just didn't look like it should be on the floor.

He heard the ACormaris mutter something under her breath. He'd've paid money to hear what it was, but she'd gone too quiet.

"Serra Alina," Valedan said. "Please, rise."

She did so at once. As if he was the one in command. "Ser Valedan."

"Why have you come?"

"I would speak, if you would permit it, in private."

"I will not."

He couldn't see all her face, but he could see her eyes. They narrowed a minute like sharp blades. "Very well."

"Speak freely," Valedan said, clearly annoyed. It had the feel of an old discussion—a sour one.

"You have ten minutes to join the Challenge. I have come to remind you of this fact."

"I will join the Challenge when I know the extent of the damage—"

"You will damage yourself, and doom both the General and the Tyr'agnate over a matter of pretty principle." She was still, and her voice was as cold as the Northern wind. "I do not understand what you hope to gain by waiting here, by *insisting* on waiting here, but I will tell you what you accomplish in the eyes of the men you *must* impress. They will assume that you are weak, or frightened, by a single attempt on the life of a seraf."

"He is not—"

"It does not matter what he *is;* it matters only what they think he is."

"Alina—I'm in large part responsible for what happened—"

"And you fulfill this sense of responsibility by waiting?"

"I—" he fell silent, and Aidan recognized the silence for what it was. A wall. A decision.

So did she. And she wasn't going to accept it the way the others had. The way Aidan himself had. "Then give up, Valedan. Give up the title, forsake clan Leonne, give up the claim to the Tor Leonne and the lake within it. Because I tell you now that to hold that throne, even were it given to you in a joyous time of peace—" her words made it clear exactly how likely she thought that was, "—will cost lives. And if you are not willing to spend them, you cannot take the reins of power; leave it to men who understand what the costs are."

"There has to be—"

"A better way?" Ice. Near silence. "I think," she said softly, "that it is best that I . . . excuse myself. Kai Leonne." She knelt again, the stiffness of her body wholly at odds with the posture it adopted.

Everyone was looking at a different corner of wall. Everyone but Aidan himself.

"That's it, then?" Valedan asked, bitterly.

She was silent for a long while, but in the end, she relented. "Yes. Do you think the Northern Kings wait here, in a room, for news of their trusted servants? They rule. They prepare for a day in the open sun. A day in which they will be under the scrutiny of men and women over whom they hold the power of life and death. They will dress well. They will speak perfectly, regally. They will accept that the most important thing that subjects such as the ATerafin *can* do is protect them, and they will be above public worry over the fate of a single such guard."

"But they have to be worthy of that protection."

"Do you think them otherwise?"

He was uncomfortably silent. When he spoke at last, his voice was muted. "No."

"Then," she said, and her voice had quieted, softened, "learn from them. Wisdom, Valedan. Justice." She lifted her gaze. "Boy," she said.

"Aidan," Valedan corrected her.

"Aidan, then. Come, and come quickly. You have your duties, and he has his, and we have very, very little time in which to complete them gracefully."

For the first time in Aidan's life, being a king suddenly didn't look like it would be a lot of fun.

The Ospreys were angry. Not that they'd cared much about the stray boy that Valedan had chosen as his witness, but an attack carried out for the purpose of somehow harming him—and through him, Valedan—reminded them of old actions.

Duarte, of course, was wise enough not to tell them any of the salient details, and anyway, he wasn't all that certain that he knew them himself. But he'd forgotten about the boy, and they weren't above using children to get at what they needed; they were Ospreys, after all. The boy told them everything they wanted to know in the five minutes before Duarte gave strict orders forbidding such communication. He expected trouble, and hoped, briefly, that it wasn't the type of trouble that would force his hand; they weren't even on the field yet. It was too early to start killing his own.

But to no one's surprise—or rather, none of the Ospreys—the eight men who had been taken captive by the Imperial guards failed to survive to be questioned. The questions they had answered in the brief first interview were the only questions that would be answered.

It was rumored that the Astari were beside themselves with rage at the clumsiness, the carelessness, of the Imperial guards. The guards themselves did not let any chagrin at the loss show; they stood up as bullishly as possible to the Lord of the Compact. The jurisdictional squabble was tense enough to make itself felt. Bad, that.

Worse, Valedan had arrived late—and the late arrival sealed his fate. He was, of the contenders, to jump first.

But he was political enough, Duarte noted, to accept the placing with enough grace that it was clear he felt he deserved the unspoken rebuke. And that always played well with judges who were far enough away from their own youth to frown at a more natural reaction.

It was hot.

Kiriel stared at the sweat that dampened her sleeves as she lowered her forearm from its sweep across her brow. She was *sweating*. In the background, as new to her as the fact of this physical infirmity, the Kings' men were setting up.

Not that there seemed to be all that much *to* set up; the champions had come, with all due respect and ritual, to a wide field, grassy in all places except for the long pits of white sand. While the bards sang, and they *did* sing, their words blending into each other in a harmonic chaos of history and emotion, the judges came forward to speak with the would-be champions—or their trainers.

She knew this because such a judge came to speak with Valedan kai di'Leonne. The heat was ferocious, and she felt it so strongly she almost separated the man's head from his shoulders because he happened to be the only outsider who'd dared to present himself to their over-large group. Unfortunately, Duarte stepped on her foot, and Cook stepped in front of her, and the judge, ill-tempered no doubt because of the same heat that Kiriel faced, was taken to speak with Commander Sivari.

They'd lost the Princess, which was a pity. She was one of the very few women that Kiriel had ever met that she felt almost comfortable around. There was no odd rivalry, no fear, no foolish fixation on beauty as a means of power—although, to Kiriel's growing chagrin, she realized that that fixation was not entirely as foolish as she had once believed—between them; Mirialyn ACormaris simply was.

And Kiriel?

Was simply hot.

"Sentrus," Duarte said, after the judge had passed, "What exactly *is* the problem?"

She'd looked up at him, at the etched lines of his sour expression, and she'd said—before she could stop herself, "I'm sweating."

He stared at her blankly, as if the answer and the question were completely unrelated. Waited, while his shadow grew shorter in the rise of the the midday sun. "You're . . . what?"

"I—I'm *sweating.*" The dampness between her skin and her underpadding was so terrible she wanted to strip herself of its protection entirely.

Alexis and Duarte exchanged a single, long glance. Duarte lifted a hand to his forehead. He did that, Kiriel knew, when confusion kept him from being furious. Almost. "And this is new to you?"

"Yes."

The tenor of their second glance was different.

"Cook," Duarte said.

"Primus." He lifted his hand and belted his chest soundly. Duarte winced; Kiriel wasn't sure why.

"Please keep an eye on the Sentrus. I believe she is feeling . . . ill."

"Sir."

"I told you," Alexis whispered. If there'd been any sibilants whatever in the short sentence, she would have been hissing loudly enough for venom to have appeared on the flat edge of her teeth. "I told you that sonofabitch wasn't telling us everything."

He sincerely hoped that Auralis, usually quite healthy, had the money stashed away to see a healer after the previous evening's escapade, and more, the wisdom to do so—because no one took Alexis on when she was at full-strength and they were almost dead. "Decarus," he began.

"Don't start, Duarte. We can't afford to be ignorant, not here. He can play his games when there isn't so much at stake."

Which is true. But he knew, watching the white lines around her thinned lips, that wasn't all that was bothering her. "Alexis."

She didn't look at him. Wouldn't, not when he used that tone of voice. He did not know how to be gentle with Alexis. He wondered if any man did. If anyone did. Not a comfortable thought. "She's one of us," he said at last. "And Auralis looks after his own."

"And what are *we*?"

"We're officers, love," he replied, half-coldly, which was as coldly as he could. "They're not."

"He was."

"He was never an officer. Killing got him the rank, the first time. Killing lost it. Nothing owns Auralis. Especially not something as intangible as rank. Alexis—"

But she was already gone. She'd mastered that skill, to be absent while standing an inch or less away and he—he was suddenly aware, was Duarte AKalakar, that he'd lost it. Love, he thought, made fools and weaklings of them all, and always when they could least afford it.

CHAPTER SEVENTEEN

18th of Lattan
Averalaan Aramarelas, the Test of the River

She couldn't *see* anything. Oh, she could see bodies, living ones; she could see the rise and fall of chest that spoke of breath and breathing. She could hear voices, could see the exchange of words that passed from man to man. But all she could see was the color of hair and eyes and skin, the height at which the body stood, the attitude it adopted on the outside. She could see clothing.

"Kiriel?"

Cook's voice. She remembered that she hated it. "What?"

"Valedan's ready for his practice."

"They've barely started!"

"They've started. He drew early. He gets three attempts."

"At what?"

Cook's skin lost color. It meant—it meant that he was afraid, although he didn't look afraid. Her nails bit her palms as she balled her hands into fists. She couldn't *see* anything but the face. Not the colors that twisted beneath its surface. Beneath any of their surfaces.

"*Kalliaris,* Kiriel! You told Duarte that you'd read what he'd given you."

"Auralis told him that," she said curtly. It was true; Auralis *had* said it. He was lying, but he'd said it.

"This is the river's test. River vaulting?" His eyelids compressed into a fine line before he managed to pry them open again. "Kiriel, I can't believe that of all the Ospreys to imitate, you chose Auralis. The man's got a death wish written all over his face, and in enough languages that no one misses it. Okay, pay attention. You see those long, thin frames that are set up over the sand pits?"

She squinted, feeling the brightness of the light. Hating it, because it caused her eyes to tear. *Her* eyes. Sweat ran. "Yes?"

"See that long pole on the grass, there?"

"No."

"There, right underneath—you see the guy with the flag? He's straddling it at the moment. What an idiot."

She couldn't see it. She, who'd been able to see almost anything, could not see this. Her fingers were white, and around one of them, like any harmless piece of precious metal, a thing that could not be removed. Not even by removing the finger.

She'd tried it, cutting the finger off; had had to steel herself to the act. She could still feel the ice of blade's edge, the call for blood, but it was more distinctly separate from herself than it had ever been. The sword was it had been made. The sword's master was not. And the sword knew it.

She was afraid of very little—she would be damned if she'd be afraid of wielding her own sword. But although the sword had been willing, the flesh was not; the ring protected the area of her body around which it had found purchase.

She notched the blade.

So, she was here, a defender of an earthly lord. She had one sword that would aid her, and very little else. No vision. No shadow. Her power had been the only thing about herself that she'd understood.

Not true, Kiriel, a voice from the past said. *You have more about you than power. You have curiosity. You have honesty, of a kind. You do not seek pain for pain's sake.*

But I do, Ashaf. I force myself not to seek it for your sake. And how is that honest?

We all desire things that we feel in our hearts we should not desire. It isn't the desire that defines us, Kiriel. Never that. It's only the action.

Today, she stood very still beneath the sun whose heat she could suddenly feel. Because her whole life had been defined by those words, that exchange: to struggle against desire, to win through, to beat it, so that   and this was the truth—Ashaf would not be hurt. It was cowardice of a type; she had been afraid to hurt Ashaf.

The struggle itself hadn't ended with Ashaf's death, and perhaps it should have. Perhaps she should have accepted the truth and learned to live, in the city that was her only heritage, the life that she had been born to, or would have been without Ashaf's interference. She hadn't. She'd fought herself, pushed against herself, every day of her life. It had become so very much harder when she'd knelt at her father's feet to accept his gift; when she'd risen, literally a changed person.

But she knew the struggle.

What she did not know was this: What she should do, what she *must* do, when the thing she'd fought against simply gave up, rolled over, and died. There was no desire, now. For anything.

"Kiriel?"

And the sweat was running down her forehead. She'd never really understood the bands that the Osprey wore beneath their hair, and above their eyes; that it had been practical hadn't really occurred to her. How much of human life was like that? Practical in ways that hadn't occurred to her?

Sivari watched his charge. Watched the boy—no, that wasn't the right word, but he couldn't quite bring himself to think of Valedan kai di'Leonne as a man—as he lifted the long, slender pole that would be his first challenge. It was heavier than it looked; hard and stiff with just enough flexibility to carry his weight in an arc several feet above ground—if they were lucky. He'd drawn poorly, but the draw was what it was. He had three chances to clear that stupid stick. If he did, he progressed. If they all did, they all progressed—but Sivari knew they'd lose at least half—if not more—in the first round. He just prayed that one of them wasn't Valedan.

"Are you nervous?"

General Baredan di'Navarre. Sivari gave him a half-nod; it was all the attention he was willing to spare. The more correct Southern General did not choose to feel slighted. The Tyr'agnate, Sivari thought, was that hair's breadth less practical. But the South was bred into them both.

"From here, he'll go on to the river's banks."

"And that's safe?"

Sivari snorted. "General, we are not in disagreement here."

Baredan clearly did not believe this, which was just as well; it wasn't—quite—true. *Admit it, Sivari,* the Commander thought, with just a twinge of shame. *You know the boy's almost good enough. Hells, he might be good enough. He's no Anton di'Guivera—but he's maybe one or two years away from being* that *good.*

And you want to be a part of it. You miss this.

River vaulting was a Northern trial; Commander Sivari said it had come into being as a time-honored way of crossing a river when the people involved in such an enterprise were too barbaric to have developed an understanding of the simple concept of bridges.

Valedan, having spent some time at court in *Avantari*, understood that this was exaggeration, a thing said because the Northerners were the men who set the trial's standard; the men to beat. Alina, however, found it graceless, tactless, and untrue.

Why is it, she said softly, *that the Northerners feel a need to belittle their opponents? A worthy opponent, and the ability to master him, is the rank of one chosen by the Lord; to beat weaklings and fools is the sport of weaklings and fools.*

Spoken, Sivari had countered, *like a person who's never had their life saved from the wrong edge of a sword because the person who was wielding it was stupid. You thank Kalliaris for whatever saves your life.*

This is not a contest about life, *Commander. It is a contest of display and challenge.*

And then she had stilled, remembering even in the privacy of their odd war council that she was Southern. Or so Valedan thought, until she spoke: *No, you are right. This contest is about life. Your pardon.*

But he felt, as his hands gripped the pole, that the argument was already beyond him; that he was, in their eyes, a child, to be advised, to be coddled, to be protected where possible—and, as all children of power, to be feared in some small way.

He prodded sand with pole, putting his weight against it.

Looked into the stands for sight of Alina and Mirialyn. The former, he could not see, but the latter sat with the Kings in attendance, waiting, her eyes clear and steady across the vast gulf of grassy field.

I cannot take the test for you, she had said.

I don't want you to. But he knew that she would fly where he might fall; that she would remain steady, where he might falter. He took a breath; filled his lungs with sea air that seemed more natural to him than the dry stretch of harsh land that had surrounded his home.

He cast a shadow as he walked to the starting position.

Cast a shadow as he ran, steady, bending slightly into his knees as he approached the lip of the long furrow of white sand. He leaped before pole touched ground, almost anchored by it; the sun was in his eyes, and the crossbeam—the height was before them. He twisted, flat in the air; passed over the beam.

He remembered—as he had not done the first dozen times he had tried this—to let go of the pole. The sand was hot when he hit it, and he hit it with poor grace, grazing face and forehead as he rolled in it.

At this rate, there won't be a pit—just a bunch of would-be champions carrying sand in the folds of their clothing. He rose, shook himself, and made his way back to Sivari who stood, arms folded across his chest, lips pressed across into a thin line.

"Well?" Valedan said.

Sivari shrugged. "It's the first round."

The younger man nodded, wanting encouragement, and hating the desire for it. Someone came with silks and water, and he scrubbed his face clean of sweat; his moment had passed and already another man stood in the sun's glare, casting a thin shadow.

The river jump itself was different, but there was only one path to the river.

First test. Ser Anton was not impressed with the jump itself; it was stiff, and very close to the bar. Still, he had to admit that he thought it likely the boy would edge his way into the middle of the pack, and this was only the first jump. He did not need to cast a backward glance to his own students to see them clearly in his mind's eye—and that was about as much, in this particular event, as he needed to see. This test—it was Northern in invention and Northern in execution. Short of removing the men from their families for years—as had been done with him—he could not expect them to fare as well.

He wondered, idly, how long the kai Leonne had trained for. Wondered it when his own students were called out of the stands to take their place in the jump.

It was hard not to be caught up in this, not to feel, as he watched, that history's roots were *here,* in this contest, at this place; that the course of whole nations would be decided by the outcome of the Challenge.

He took a breath; the air was heavy with salt, almost wet enough to be water itself. He had been young, here.

It was hot by the river's bank, and the sea breeze that often alleviated the summer heat was absorbed by the wall of bodies that had formed behind the line of the Crown guards. In front of those guards gathered the guards of the contestants, and among these guards, the hostility of warring nations. One or two of the contes-

tants, true to their roots, had no such entourage; the only attendants they had brought were their witnesses, and the witnesses
stood as far apart from the armed men as they could without crossing boundaries into the event itself. It was easy, actually; they were
given a spot at the forefront of any such crowd.

But when their contestant was given leave to enter the ground,
the witnesses were escorted from the enclosure to stand, like a
living shadow, by the judges. They could watch, then, although it
was frowned on to actually say anything.

Aidan was fairly good at lying low. He was good at avoiding
people who were too much larger than he, and he was good at
showing deference when he least felt it.

They thought he was a polite boy—for the inner holdings, although they never added that in so many words—but they still
thought he was a boy. That irked him. Still, no one thought to pat
his head or tell him how much he'd grown, which was better than
he sometimes got.

"I see that you are still watching foreigners," a voice said, softly, at his back. He jumped; he knew the voice's odd accent, the
way it said the right words with all the wrong breaks and pauses,
sort of like a river running uphill in its riverbed.

"Yeah," he said, reddening. "You don't—"

Ser Anton di'Guivera frowned; the frown was a cool thing in
the day's heat. "Here," he said softly, "We do not speak of the
wars we may be fighting. This is the Kings' Challenge."

Aidan nodded. "But—"

"But?"

"Your men, and his men—they're separated by the Kings'
Swords."

"Yes," Ser Anton said, "they are. Do not be foolish enough to
think that the Kings are disinterested parties in this affair. If Ser
Valedan kai di'Leonne chooses to attempt a return to the Dominion, it will be with the blessings of the Northern Kings—and
quite possibly with their martial aid."

"Martial?"

"Armies."

Aidan said nothing for a moment. And then he turned to look
up into the face of the most famous man in the Dominion. "Why
do you hate him?"

"Do I?"

"Don't you?"

Ser Anton shrugged. "Watch the games, boy. They start, even as we speak."

Gold caught the sunlight and hung it a moment round Aidan's neck like a pendant; it was heavy.

"Look, Andaro. It's the Northern pawn."

The words were theatric, overly loud, certain to be heard by anyone who spoke Torra. Thankfully, on this side of the river, they were few; three men, to the best of Valedan's knowledge, and Valedan himself was one of them.

He knew, from his days in the Imperial Court, that to ignore the taunts of older children was, in the end, to best them; they learned that short of physical violence, they received no pleasure from him. But wisdom was only knowledge, and if knowledge could save a man from himself, the world would have been a different place. His knuckles were white against the pole that lifted, momentarily, from its slanted perch across his shoulders.

"He's pretty enough," the voice continued, "If you like white skin and big eyes. A bit thin, I think. Probably has the same water for blood as the rest of the Imperials."

I am the kai Leonne. He heard other words. *I do not have to respond to this.*

"Pretty," the same voice said; his unseen audience remained conspicuously silent, but Valedan was certain that silent or no, he had no friend in that unknown quarter. "Pretty and white. What else is pretty and white? Harem women, of course. Women.

"What do you think, Andaro? Doesn't he look like a woman?"

Valedan didn't hear the next words because there weren't any. He tilted the pole on his shoulder and then pivoted tightly, lowering it by the center, hafting it to a weapon height.

He knocked his enemy off his feet; hit him hard enough that the wind forced itself out of his open mouth in a small, satisfying huff. Winded, the face was slightly flat, broader and coarser than the faces of the Imperial hostages, and definitely ruddier. Or perhaps it was flushed; hard to say.

"Get up." Valedan threw the long pole to the ground and picked up the half-pole that was used by the boatmen to push off from the bank. Picked up a second, and threw it at the dark-haired man who had propped himself on one elbow.

"Get up."

The man rose. "I am Carlo di'—"

"You are *nothing*."

Silence, edged on one side by white lips and on the other by a face bleached of color, emptied of sneer that had passed for smile. The man that Valedan had denied a clan name gripped the half-pole and rose, his cheeks regaining some color, and it an ugly red.

"Carlo—" the shorter man at his side said, speaking for the first time. "Carlo, this is not wise."

The man so spoken to slowly put up his pole, straining a moment as if at a great weight.

Valedan said, coolly, "I see that you are not content to fight your own battles; you hide behind the skirts of your . . . companion."

He was prepared for the charge when it came.

The sound of wood striking wood was distinctive. Aidan recognized it. although to him it was oddly distorted, and not just by distance. But it was clear that the man at his side recognized what that difference meant at once. And why wouldn't he? He was Ser Anton di'Guivera; the only things he didn't know about fighting were probably things that weren't *worth* knowing. Even the Northerners respected him. Even them.

"Boy," he said sharply, "my eyes are not perhaps as keen as they once were. Please tell me that there is no fighting across the river." As he spoke, he reached out for Aidan, slid his hands under his arms, and *lifted* him, acknowledging by that gesture Aidan's slight build, his unenviable smallness.

But because it was Ser Anton, Aidan schooled himself not to mind. Wasn't hard, really—because the minute he got a clear view over the heads and shoulders—mostly shoulders, of the people who had edged their way just in front of him, he forgot there was anything *to* mind.

"Aidan?"

Commander Sivari appeared beneath him. His eyes were obviously better than the old man's—he started to swear.

"Boy?"

"They're fighting, sir."

" 'They'?"

"I think —I think it's Carlo, sir."

"And?"

"Ummm, Valedan, sir."

It was strange. Until he head Ser Anton begin to curse alongside Commander Sivari, he'd never realized how similar their tongues sounded.

* * *

They were neither of them masters of the art. The poles that they were wielding might as well have been clubs. But even so, they knew how to move; they had been trained, one in the South and one in the North, exactly this way: one on one, beneath the open sky. Carlo was older and had the advantage of weight; Valedan, lighter, had the advantage of speed. Experience lay between them, but how wide the gulf was only the combat itself would determine.

Their sticks clashed and rebounded with the authority of their weight; they struck, pivoting stick and self in an attempt to land the definitive blow. They exchanged no words.

Words, after all, were just a way of reaching this point; they'd done it; they had no further need of them.

Bets were being made. As the boat reached the flat platform set up for this single week, Sivari could hear the numbers being shouted. A side glance at Ser Anton made it clear that the older man's Weston was not up to translation over a great distance. Or perhaps he understood the numbers, but could not put them into the proper context. Whichever was true, it was just as well.

At the moment, there was no competition, no combat, between Sivari and Anton di'Guivera; they were, he was certain, bent on a single purpose. Or perhaps two.

First: Stop the fight before one of the two young men had injuries to something other than vanity and pride. Second: Find a damned good reason not to kill them for the humiliation of this completely disgraceful behavior.

Sivari thought that of the two, he would find it easier. Valedan was not, in fact, a student who had come to him, and upon whom his reputation rested. The Flight wanted the war itself to take place, and Commander Sivari, theoretically of the same rank, was far less valuable to the Crowns—and the Kings, having acknowledged the boy as a peer and a monarch in his own right, were unlikely to turn a blind eye at his untimely and ungraceful death-by-throttling.

He was not as certain that Ser Anton di'Guivera would find so compelling and so accessible an excuse—at least not in time.

The adjudicatory stood in a thin line—they were few—around the area traced by the movement of staves; they were grim-faced and silent. Listen, and Sivari thought he might be able to hear the words that had already been said. He stepped forward to speak them himself, and froze.

Very few of the adjudicators—none, this day—had ever been the Champion of this Challenge; Sivari had. And he saw something akin to memory, but somehow more personal for its reality, in the moving faces of the two men who fought here. He recognized Valedan's opponent at once; the surly, ill-bred student who was one of the best of those Anton had traveled with.

And he recognized, better than that, that they had both—Carlo and Valedan—found the invisible center around which the contest pivoted; they held to it. He was not certain that he could separate them. Not certain that he wished to try. There was no friendship here; no false pretense; there was no overt bloodlust, but there was much to be proved.

None of it was pretty; all of it was real.

You could watch these two fight and remember that the Challenge itself had been bred for warriors and bred by war, although it eschewed both. He had been angry that the men who had been set to judge the quality of the cross-river jumping should instead, sit, idle, while the two fought. None of that anger remained. There was just this—and to a man who had been there, there was an almost visceral need to see its natural end.

And then he heard the voice of Anton di'Guivera, a man who had twice been Champion, and who had never once offered insult or dishonor to what that title meant. He stood forward, stood tall.

When he spoke, he spoke in Torra.

"You will cease this *at once.*" He waited; the grunt of his student, almost caught off his stride, was his entire answer. Another man would have given up at that point.

"You dishonor your vows. You forget yourself. You forget the purpose of the Challenge that you have agreed to embark upon. There will be *no war* to mar the games."

Valedan's turn; a near slip. The slope of the banks themselves were six inches beyond his right foot, and Carlo had almost managed to use superior weight to bear him back; to force him into the river. Clever; the river was the signal of the failure of a jump.

But Valedan slid to the side; Carlo stumbled forward an inch or two; there was give and take in the combat.

There was no response. He had not expected a response; Sivari couldn't believe he would be that stupid. Not Ser Anton di'Guivera. But expect it or no, he was obviously ill-pleased not to receive one.

He turned to the oldest man present—a man who was perhaps six years his junior. He bowed, a Northern bow, and said, "With the permission of the adjudicatory."

"Ser Anton," the man said. What else did one say to legend?

Anton di'Guivera stepped away to the boat that had carried him, Commander Sivari, and the quiet young witness that Valedan had chosen, from the far banks of the river to the heart of the action itself. He bent a moment at the boat's side, and when he rose, Commander Sivari saw that he carried a boatman's pole loosely in his left hand.

He bowed again to the judges, and they nodded to him; the glimmer of curiosity, the sudden cessation of breath, was not lost on Sivari; indeed, he was part of it. This man, this man was Anton di'Guivera.

He walked toward the two men who struggled with the weight of their weapons, and their opponent's, and the pole came up in his hand. It was a pole, no more—until he swung it.

And then it leaped up; it shed weight; it seemed somehow thinner and more supple. Was it of hardwood? Sivari thought bamboo would look more cumbersome than the pole in Anton's hands. As he lifted it, as he swung it in a tight, deliberate circle, it almost flew.

The pole that had been Carlo di'Jevre's did.

And the student himself followed, heavier, his body landing audibly in the soft grass and dirt. His teeth were clenched to force silence, but Sivari noticed that his arms were wrapped round his side. The young man with whom he had often sparred in the fifteenth holding, the man their spies had correctly identified as Andaro par di'Corsarro, came at once to his side; he began to kneel there.

Without a backward glance, Ser Anton di'Guivera barked. It was barely a word, but it was a denial.

The young man hovered a moment over his fallen companion; their eyes met, and Carlo nodded quietly. Anton did not see this interchange—or chose not to be aware of it. Andaro withdrew.

And that left Valedan, his pole gripped and lowered, his cheeks flushed, his expression almost unreadable.

"Put up your weapon," Ser Anton said, in Weston.

Valedan drew himself up to his full height. He had height, but it was always a surprise to Sivari to have his attention called to it. "If you wish the weapon," he replied—in Torra, "it is yours by the Lord's Law. If you can take it. There are no clouds in the sky," he added softly. "There is only the open sun, and the Lord watches."

Sivari had never before understood the force of the words, *there are no clouds in the sky* so clearly. It was a Southern phrase; it meant, as far as he could tell, that all masks had been set aside. Or it had meant that. But here—here it was that and more.

"Put up your weapon," Ser Anton said, again in Weston. "I have been granted permission to intervene by the adjudicatory, and as a contestant here, it is not in your interest to deny their command."

"Let them make it, " Valedan said. "Between you and me, there is only one judge."

And he swung.

It was sudden, the movement; unexpected, even by Sivari. He had seen tension gathering in his half-student; he had seen the line of his jaw stiffen to shaking, the knuckles on his hand whiten. But he had not seen the small clues that spoke to him of movement, of attack.

He forgot that; a pole flew.

It was not Valedan's.

Silence struck them all, an unexpected blow, an unlooked-for attack. Ser Anton di'Guivera, in the history of the Challenge, had never once been unarmed.

Bitter truth, there. Sivari was first to recover. First to acknowledge that age made a difference; it took what experience built, ate away at it like the Northern rivers against the mountain beds. He hated age. For a moment, he *hated* it. Not in and of itself, no—but for what it had done to Ser Anton di'Guivera; what it had taken from him.

Valedan himself stepped back.

And Ser Anton di'Guivera stepped forward. Unarmed, he was not without weapon. Not without grace or speed or strength. He did not attempt to grab the pole that Valedan held; he did not throw himself to this side or that; he simply turned, pivoting on a foot at precisely the right moment. Valedan was raw energy, skill just being honed; Ser Anton was . . . the Southern Champion.

The sun was watching; there were, indeed, no clouds.

No words, not from the judges, not from the student who had managed to raise himself up from the damp grassbed, and had limped to safety.

If he could have spoken to Valedan, he would have. He might

have given him the pointers which would have extended the combat; might have given him the confidence to see that Anton chose to wear him down, and how. But could he, he might not have.

Ser Anton di'Guivera ended the combat with the open palm of his hand. He raised it, snapped it shut at just the right moment. In it, for all to see, was the end of the pole's blunted hook.

They stood, swordmaster and pretender to the Southern throne, separated by the length of a boatman's pole—and joined by it.

"Valedan," Ser Anton said—speaking in Torra. "I sit under the cover of no cloud today. What I have said is the truth, no more, no less; I do not speak it for my own purposes, and perhaps I should not speak it at all if it serves yours. But I will speak it. My student, my Carlo—he is a foreigner; these lands have taken life from his family in war, but they have given him *nothing* in return. The respect he owes these people is the respect of manners, and his are, understandably, poor.

"You are different. The North has sheltered you; it has protected you; it has granted you the only legitimacy you are likely to see. The rules of the combat here are not the Lord's, and you have, by your existence here, agreed to respect them, foreign as they are.

"You owe them honor." He opened his hand.

The unsupported end of the pole fell heavily to the ground.

Valedan said nothing at all.

"Ser Valedan kai di'Leonne," the older man said. He bowed.

"Ser Anton di'Guivera," Valedan replied. The pole fell then.

CHAPTER EIGHTEEN

18th day of Lattan, early evening
Avantari

Andaro was mutinous.

And that, in a person of his control and skill, merely meant silence; the silence of a slightly turned head, a turned back, a stiff jaw.

Ser Anton was not amused. "Andaro," he said.

"Ser Anton." His tone of voice robbed the three syllables of any warmth of familiarity or respect due a name; they could have been foreign babble, children's nonsense.

"You will practice."

"I will practice," his best student replied, "when Carlo is ready to join me."

They stared at each other; the distance between them was measured by anger. Sadly, in Ser Anton's case, part of that anger was turned inward as well as out. He hated disobedience; he hated lack of respect. Yet in this case he felt it was—almost—deserved. He had bruised Carlo's ribs, and quite possibly cracked two of them. The blow he had struck he had struck in anger, and anger had controlled the connection, not skill, not intent, not prudence. The physician had been quite clear: it was in Carlo's best interests to withdraw from the Championship and rejoin it again the following year. Carlo himself refused, as Ser Anton would have expected.

"Andaro," Ser Anton began again. "We both know that Carlo is not in appropriate condition to continue with this practice."

"Or with this Challenge?"

Challenge was there in his words. Ser Anton's hand came to rest, lightly, upon the hilt of his sword. Andaro did not blink.

You are, Ser Anton thought, *too much like your master in his youth.* And in his youth, he would perhaps have been equally imprudent defending those he cared for. He tried to remember this.

He tried to remember the young man he had been, before his life
had been buried by the sands the wind brought, blistered by the
fire, scared by the sword.

Tried and failed. "Carlo chose his course."

"He chose," Andaro replied coolly, "to accompany the man he
most respected—"

"He respects his desire, Andaro, and my skill. Little else."

Andaro's silence was long and thin, a thing that seemed easily
broken until a man tried.

"Is that what you think, Ser Anton?"

"Pick up the sword," Ser Anton said softly.

Andaro measured his resolve against the resolve of the swordmaster. He was no fool; in the end, he was no fool. He picked up
the sword.

But he did not stop speaking. "Do you believe that he came just
for his own glory, that he came because he desired the crown?"

"Yes."

"Do you think that your name means—*meant*—nothing to either of us?"

Ser Anton bent to ground; he came up bearing the practice blade.

They stood, two armed men; that was enough, in the eyes of
the Lord.

"My name had nothing to do with his behavior. I've met harem
children who were less disgraceful in *private*."

"Your name," Andaro said, "had nothing to do with his behavior. But your behavior, Ser Anton, affects us all. Carlo is not—is
not from the ruling clans. Neither were you. He follows you as
he can, he worships you, as he must. You are honor to him. You
are the goal he seeks to attain. Do you understand what you've
done to him? I do not expect you to be other than what you are.
But you have always been more than that to Carlo."

He did not refute the truth of the words; there was nothing to
be gained. "Carlo is a fool," he said at last. "A skilled, a skillful,
a competent, fool."

It was meant to anger; it angered. But it did not fluster. It did
not distract. Because they both held swords; because they both
stood on even ground in the sight of the Lord. Because Andaro
was everything that Carlo was not.

"We did not come here to serve the Lord of Night, Ser Anton.
We came to serve you."

"And you feel that somehow my service and His are conjoined?"

"Tell me, on your word, swear to me by the dead that you value, that this is not true. We are not fools, Ser Anton. We could not help but note the absence of the eight. And we have heard the stories that the Northerners are even now passing among themselves. You are not the only man with the presence of mind to learn their tongue."

Not the only man, no. But one of the few.

"Yes, he is hotheaded. Yes, he is impulsive. Yes, he lacks control, and self-control. But none of these things changes the truth: he lives for you, he lives to cast your shadow.

"To see it bent and twisted, to see it—"

Enough.

Ser Anton *moved*.

And Andaro proved himself to be the best of his students; he was not there to greet the blow; not there to parry it. Proved himself to be perhaps better than the swordmaster knew, because in the end, he set the terms of the contest; there was anger between them both, held in check, kept in its place, but evoked and invoked. A binding.

18th of Lattan, 427 AA
Aramarelas, Magisterial Court

"What were you *thinking?*" Commander Sivari kept a lid on the words that he might otherwise have spoken had he not been in the company of ladies. It was, in Valedan's opinion, a poor conceit; neither Mirialyn ACormaris or Serra Alina di'Lamberto had any delicacy that he could easily offend. Or quite possibly offend at all. "Valedan?"

They waited in the courtyard of the magisterial docket that had been commandeered for the games. Here, crimes such as cheating—or brawling, which was far more common—were dealt with, complaints against the contestants were heard, fines were meted out, where fines were appropriate and not too politically difficult.

That I was tired of listening to Carlo-the-imbecile. He did not, however—and wisely—choose to speak the words.

The complaint against Valedan had been formally issued in front of the three men whose task it was to pass judgment. It had not been issued by Ser Anton's student; it had been issued by the judges themselves. And they bore witness.

"Getting into a fight is bad enough—but *starting* it?"

There was very little he could say. So he said nothing. He knew that that wouldn't make Sivari any happier, but was fairly certain at this point nothing would.

The sun's shadows were getting shorter; the midday break was approaching. Valedan had been forbidden the rest of the test of the river; that hadn't been in question. Whether or not he would be disqualified from the rest of the tournament was what they waited to hear. And Commander Sivari did not wait patiently.

"Valedan—"

"Commander," Serra Alina said, more sharply than was her wont. "Someone approaches."

He looked up. A man in magisterial robes nodded in their direction; they rose from the shaded stone benches upon which they'd been sitting and followed him.

"This is not an unusual offense," a very bored looking judge said. "In fact, it's so common it's a small wonder there's any Championship at all. Usually, however, the contestants have the good grace to do two things. First, they *leave the grounds*. Second, they get drunk so as to have some semblance of at least a pathetic excuse for their behavior."

"Yes sir." Valedan said, bowing his head.

"However, they are usually far more truculent about their misdemeanors, and as an old man I know that the Championship is its own punishment. Therefore I have fined your party the standard fee—" Valedan had no idea what the fee was, but Sivari obviously did by the under-the-breath deprecation, "and because I am feeling exceedingly mellow, it being the start of the season and not the end of it, I will allow you to finish last, beneath the man with whom you were brawling, in the portion of the river-jump that you did not complete."

Commander Sivari's exhalation could probably be heard in the courtyard.

"If you, however, choose to continue this particular and unfortunate behavior, you will be disbarred not only from participating, but from even witnessing the events. Ever. Do I make myself clear?"

"Yes, sir."

"Good. Dismissed. There are two men who were knife-fighting in the spectator stands who are next on the list, and I consider their practical crime to be graver, if less insulting, than your own." He looked down the edge of his nose. "NEXT."

*   *   *

"Sivari," the Princess said, "he still has some chance of winning."

"If he places well in the rest of events, yes."

"The judge could have chosen to place him last in the event, period. There has been some agitation for exactly that punishment. Were it not for the request and the recommendation—" she stopped. "Never mind. As it is, Valedan," she said, turning to the kai Leonne, "you've been ranked twenty-fifth of the twenty-five who were selected to compete in the river-vault. Do well in the rest of the day's events." She glanced to the center courtyard, where the sundial cast its shadows. "We have little time; come."

As they made their way out of the public courtyard, Commander Sivari turned to Valedan. "If you ever do anything like that again, you won't have to worry about being disbarred. I'll strangle you with my bare hands." He passed the Princess, and the Serra who had been standing quietly by Valedan's side.

"Valedan," she said softly. "A word of advice."

"Serra Alina?"

"You cannot have men in your service who show such a disrespect for your rank that they would dare to speak like that in the presence of any witnesses."

Valedan shrugged, the movement elegant and quick. "It's Commander Sivari," he said. "He didn't mean it."

"It is not whether or not he meant it that concerns me." Her words were ice. "No man but one who courts death speaks that way to a Tyr. Not even be he par to kai. Only the powerful speak of death to the powerless in the South."

"Alina—"

"I understand the Commander," she said, the words cold. "I understand the North. Rule in the North, Valedan, and you may do as you please. But you will go South."

"Alina, he has been a much valued friend here."

"Yes," she said, and her expression softened. "Valedan, in the North, the greater the affection a man feels, the less respect he offers."

"Then he—"

"Lose his affection. You cannot afford it. Without respect from the Southerners, you have nothing, and if even one of the men whose support we require hears such a speech as that, you will indeed have nothing."

And her words, so softly spoken, so elegantly, so quietly, were sharper and far more inflexible than the Commander's had been.

Valedan kai di'Leonne would have bowed to the woman who

was his Southern teacher—but men did not bow that way in the South, and she would only correct him.

"Aidan."

He was quiet. Very quiet. Aidan hated it when grownups were quiet in that particular way. He'd seen it before. His father, first, and then Widow Harris. You were quiet like that when you had words you didn't really want to say. Words that were going to be said anyway.

He was grateful: The Princess of the blood had actually taken the time to send word to his father the morning after. He wasn't certain what she'd said, but he had a feeling it was something quiet. Like, Aidan is fine, and is staying as a guest at the palace because he's been chosen as witness. Nothing about demons. Nothing about death.

He was fairly certain about it; his father could be rough—and was—but if he'd heard about the killings, he'd've been down at the gates of the outbuildings raising Hells' own city.

He would. Aidan was certain of it. Almost certain of it. And that was as much as he wanted to think about his Da.

He shifted, uncomfortably hot in a room that was far too big, far too grand, for someone like him. The guesthouse had been a dream, but this was a dream that had gotten too large. It was like being at a banquet and being *forced* to eat when there wasn't any room left for food.

And he thought it was going to get worse before it got better.

So he tried to ignore the voice.

"Aidan," Valedan kai di'Leonne said again.

But he couldn't ignore it. Couldn't; didn't know how. And he knew that he was going to hear what he didn't want to hear. He looked up. "What?"

"We're sorry about—about your friend. We're not completely certain what happened but . . ."

"She's dead."

Valedan bowed his head. "I'm sorry," he said quietly.

Aidan shrugged. "It's war," he said, because he'd heard it said so often today that it seemed the only thing he could say.

"Yes," Valedan said. "War."

But she *wasn't* a soldier. She wasn't a warrior. She wasn't even a woman, yet. She was just—just Sam, the girl who remembered where the rooms were. And they both knew it, he and this foreign prince.

"What happened?"

"We think—but we're not certain—that she was killed by the same . . . thing . . . that nearly killed the ATerafin. She—" He bowed his head again, turned away. "She killed four Imperial guards; snapped two necks. Almost escaped. And there was very, very little that was human about her when she finally died."

"But—" He stopped. "Is that what they meant for me, too?"

"I think—and I'm told that you are *not* to discuss this with any but myself—that they meant exactly the same thing for you." He turned to the low table and lifted the jug of water that seemed—'cause the dozens of servants that came in and out never touched it—to just keep filling itself. Given the money the Kings had, it wasn't impossible. "We think that they intended to use you—what was left of you—as an assassin."

"But if the magic—"

"Yes. We don't understand it. And it is . . . worrisome. It can be detected, if we know exactly what to look for. The Kings' people have begun to interview the candidates. We should know by the end of the test of the javelin, whether or not any others were affected." He poured water into a large goblet. Handed it to Aidan.

"This is war," he said quietly.

And it sounded, to Aidan, as if he was trying to convince himself of that.

"Do they want you to lose *that* badly?"

Valedan's head rose again. "I think so, yes. Winning is important in the Dominion."

Aidan snorted. "It's important everywhere." He drank the water; it wasn't exactly cool, but it wasn't as warm as the air. "Do me a favor?"

"If it's within my power."

"Win this. Beat the bastards."

Valedan laughed. Then, as he saw the expression on Aidan's face, he grew somber. "I will," he said. "For your Sam, and for my own, because I'm certain by the end I will have many, many of them." He rose. "I will require your services in the morn; break fast with me."

19th day of Lattan, 427AA
Averalaan Aramarelas, the Test of the Javelin

The Ospreys were both pleased and furious.

Pleased because Valedan had given the "other" Southerners

something to think about, and furious, of course, because he was judged to have started the fight in the first place.

"Ever notice how political these unpolitical events are?" Fiara said to Alexis' back. "Everyone knows they're here to try and kill him. All *he* does is try to hit one of them with a bloody stick. Wasn't even Valedan who laid the bastard out."

"Everything's political. Welcome to the Imperial Court. It might not have escaped your notice that he's very much part of it, hostage or no. Frankly, I'm impressed they didn't sink him."

"They did! He went from tenth—"

"Fifteenth at best."

"Fifteenth, then. But they dropped him to last place, behind that—" She managed to stop herself from using the word "Annie," but it was a close thing. "Behind the other one."

"They dropped him to twenty-fifth, Fiara."

"That's last."

"They could have dropped him into the hundredth position."

"They wouldn't dare."

The silence was short and a little bit too warm.

"Fiara, try to look at it slightly differently. Duarte has volunteered your services as dress guard to The Kalakar. You accept because it's a direct order, and he's already in a foul mood."

"And?"

"The Kalakar is going to meet The Berriliya. They go off into a room together for a discussion. They take half of their guards as plumage, and they leave the rest behind. You're one of the lucky ones. You get left behind."

"Alexis—"

"One of the Hawk's guards is a man you recognize; he's been pissing you off for almost a decade. He starts to make smart, and you deck him."

"Duarte would kill me."

"Right. Or at the very least bust you down to sentrus."

"I'm already at sentrus," Fiara said, although they both knew it.

"Pity, that. This is *war,* Fiara. It's not a little bit of infighting or a bit of ugly rivalry. And you know what Duarte's like in a war." She shook her head; stray strands of hair clung to her face like black filigree.

"Yeah, I remember," Fiara said distantly. The distance, the sudden quiet that took the words, made it clear that she *did*. "But you know something, 'Lexis?"

"What?"

"You were worse."

Alexis' turn to be silent, to let silence acknowledge the truth in the words that might have been an accusation had they come from an outsider. "We weren't really talking about either Duarte or myself. We were talking about Valedan. He's not at liberty to start a fistfight because he feels like it. Not now. Not ever.

"They're letting him know it, probably as gently as they're allowed to get away with letting him know it. Certainly a helluvalot more gently than Duarte would've. Oh good."

"What."

"They're back. Heads up. Look sharp. You've got your orders."

Kiriel di'Ashaf, off-duty for the moment in the shadows of the tented awnings that had been put up by what might have been a small army of men and women had they been carrying something other than tent poles and fabric, stared at Fiara, then Alexis, her head bobbing back and forth between them as they exchanged sentences.

She did not understand the Kalakar guards.

"Was he given an order, then?" she asked Cook.

"Who, Valedan?"

"Yes."

"About what?"

"About how to behave."

"No."

"Then the example Alexis gave makes no *sense*."

"Kiriel—" Cook brought his hands up to massage his forehead. Or at least to cover his face; Kiriel couldn't quite tell which. "Valedan wants to be a King."

"He wants to rule, yes."

"Kings don't start fistfights."

"But—if they want, and they rule, who would dare to stop them?"

"No one."

"Well then?"

"Valedan doesn't rule *yet*. He has to impress a lot of people before he gets to be ruler." Cook's expression shifted slightly; he smiled as Kiriel stared at him. The smile cracked when she spoke, though.

"And he's going to impress people by allowing himself to be belittled in front of witnesses?" It did not occur to her to keep the scorn out of her words. "Are these judges trying to weaken him? Are they in the thrall of his enemy?"

Cook covered his face with his hands again.

"You two!" Alexis shouted.

They both looked up.

"Look sharp!"

Cook straightened out. Kiriel stared at him. "But we're off duty," she said at last.

She understood, by his reaction, that he was not pleased with the outcome of their conversation. That he had not, in fact, been pleased with the outcome of most of the conversations they had beneath the open sky, on this terrible, hot, wet, endless day.

Neither was she.

They made no sense. They made no sense at all. The men were here to prove they had power and skill—but they were forbidden to fight. Absolutely forbidden to kill.

That there were levels of 'forbidden' was new to her. New as this city. New as these strange, confusing and irritating people that called themselves Black Ospreys. In the Shining Palace, forbidden had only one meaning.

She would have remained silent, but she had to ask one more question. "Cook?"

"Yes, Kiriel?" His voice was almost inflectionless.

"What's the purpose of ruling if everyone you surround yourself with has more say in your existence—more power—than you do?"

Morning.

The second day of a trial that had been more of a trial than Valedan could have imagined. He had thought—and he knew, now, how stupid he'd been—that he might display the skills he had built, over time, with the aid of Mirialyn ACormaris; that he might distinguish himself in the eyes of his people.

And then what?

Be admired? Be held in high esteem?

A completely innocent girl was dead—and he had no reason to believe that that death had not been a hideous one. In her wake, eight men, eight unquestioned and unquestionable men, followed. The work, he was told, of the Dominion. He believed it.

"You're thinking again," Commander Sivari said.

Valedan shrugged.

"He's brooding," the ACormaris said gently.

He started at the sound of her voice.

"I cannot stay," she said; it was true. Here, only the personal trainers and the witnesses were allowed to gather. He had offered to cite her, and Serra Alina had emphatically refused to allow it; to be trained, it seemed, by a woman was worse than no training at all.

He started to speak, and she smiled, shaking her head. "I've brought you a gift; I wish you to both use and keep it." And turning to the men who accompanied her, she lifted a spear by its thick wooden shaft. "It is not magic," she said, "but it has been crafted by a master, and it is a simple enough thing." Her smile faded. "I gave you your first sword," she said softly, "but it is not up to any of the tasks you have chosen to face. I am glad of it, and I would replace it equally gladly—but I fear that you will have no significant sword until you raise the Southern one." She bowed. "Do well today, Valedan. You can."

He was surprised by the gift, although he shouldn't have been. He bowed in return. "Are you—"

"Allowed this? Yes, of course. There are similar gifts being given throughout the coliseum. No weapon, no artifact, is brought to the field that doesn't pass beneath at least three sets of mage-born eyes. And for this Challenge, given the events of the past nights, I would judge that estimate conservative."

He took the spear. Held it tightly in both hands.

At his side, the young witness gaped at the retreating figure of the Princess Royal.

"I don't like it."

"You've said that one hundred and twenty-seven times since I got out of bed this morning."

"I wouldn't have said it at all," Avandar Gallais replied smoothly, "if that bed hadn't been located in the healerie. You've been—"

"I've been fully healed," she replied. Of course, as she'd said a variant of those words one hundred and twenty-seven times as well, she knew they were a waste of breath. And on a day like this, hot air was unpleasant and unwelcome.

Torvan ATerafin's face was stiff from the effort of not laughing—and if she could've been certain who he was almost laughing at, she'd have made sure he paid for it somehow. After the Challenge; until the Challenge was over, she was going to need him. Of all of the Terafin's Chosen, Torvan was the guard she felt closest to; she had saved his life at least once, and he—he had saved something more precious to her than her own life. Arann's. One of her den.

Jewel was renowned for her long memory.

She thought, looking at Torvan, that age had not yet found a way to settle on him; his shoulders were broader, and his face a little more lined, but his hair was still dark, and he had about him that hardness that death, and not age, diminished.

Now if she could only do something about the sense of humor, she'd be set.

"I did say it was all right," Daine said, speaking softly, measuring his words as if words were precious.

"And Alowan overruled you."

Daine winced at the memory, and then shrugged. "I'm here. She's here. You can hardly call that being overruled."

"Say that," Jewel muttered under her breath, "when this is all over and you've been locked in a healerie with an angry healer."

He laughed.

And his laughter sounded so familiar to her, she joined in. Kept laughing, even when she realized why: it was a deeper echo of her laugh, full of bass and volume.

"Besides," she added, "Carver managed to get Angel the head list."

"The what?"

"Head list. List of the contenders," she added.

Daine looked confused. Avandar looked disgusted. Torvan looked away.

"Why," the healer asked, "is that important?"

"Those are the up-to-date lists we use for betting. There's money riding on this year's Challenge—and mine is some of it."

Avandar looked even less amused. He hadn't reached the bottom of his limited tolerance yet; the decade and a bit had given Jewel a very exact sense of how far she could offend his sensibilities. "Jewel," he said, "I must say again that I think this unwise."

"Must you?" She looked up, and between the opening and closing windows milling people made in the crowd, she saw a familiar face. "ATerafin!" She shouted, and then, as she looked around her, she added, "Devon!"

She knew at once, and didn't bother to question that knowledge, that something was wrong.

It wasn't that he was tense—although he was if you knew him well enough to look for all the right signs—it was something other, something else. Maybe, just maybe, it was the fact that he looked as if he hadn't slept a wink in the last day. Or week, she amended, as she finally drew close enough to examine him.

She had thought to be cool. She remembered that before she opened her mouth to speak. This man had been a friend, and he had refused her the aid that she'd all but begged for. Begging didn't come easily to Jewel, ATerafin or no; it had never come easy to her; she would never do it for anything less than the life of one of her own. Her own life, and she'd probably spit in the face of all danger. But she still had to pull herself up short to stop the greeting that had been natural for her.

I must be getting soft. "ATerafin." She bowed.

He bowed in return, and the bow was stiff. As if he were wounded, and hiding it. Or as if—

She turned her head slightly, ever so slightly. There, in the shade provided by trees that had not yet grown too tall, lounging like one of the visible idle rich, was a man that she had seen only a handful of times in her life—and had intensely disliked each and every one of them.

Duvari.

The Lord of the Compact.

"Tell me," she said, all personal business forgotten.

"Not here," he replied. "And not in front of so many."

"I'll have to take Avandar."

"Your domicis has been cleared, as is usual. The Lord of the Compact will be in attendance. As will, with your permission, a member of the magi."

"Meralonne?"

Devon nodded. Stiffly.

"Done."

They met in a room that Jewel had never seen the inside of—and instantly regretted entering. There were, of all things, no windows here, and although the room gave the impression of size, she thought it due to the fact that the walls were painted a flat, pale white. White that color was hard to come by, and a good thing, too.

Unfortunately, it seemed that while the rare, pale white was found here in abundance, common things that usually made up the interior of any room were not: chairs, for one. Tables. There was a fireplace, and she supposed that in a desperate pinch she could crawl up it and escape.

Avandar, as usual, was unflappable. And as he normally chose to stand, the loss of chairs were entirely cosmetic to him.

They weren't to Jewel; every man in the room was a good eight to ten inches taller than she was, and she hated to be at a height disadvantage; she was aware that it made her feel a bit defensive. That never worked to her advantage.

"Tell me," she said, turning to Devon, forcing herself not to dwell on her growing irritation by taking control of the meeting.

"We were hoping," Duvari said—not much surprise, really, as that son of a bitch never ceded control of anything to anyone, "that you might tell us." She hadn't expected to like Duvari much better now than at any other time in her life, and in that at least, her expectations weren't disappointed.

"Why don't I tell you I'm recovering from a grave—illness. This means that I tire easily."

Devon's momentary expression was halfway between frown and grimace.

Duvari's was all ice.

"What Duvari means to say," the ATerafin said smoothly, "is that we have news. It is of a sensitive nature; it has not been cleared, and is not to be made public." He paused. "Insomuch as that is possible given the witnesses to the event itself."

"What event?"

"We will require, of course, your word."

What she wanted to say made it suddenly clear that her previous words were true. She was tired. Biting the words back and swallowing them was harder than swallowing the vile concoctions of lunatic herbmasters, but she managed. "You of course have not only my word, but the pledge of my House. The Terafin herself brought me the request; she's promised you full cooperation and wishes to assure you that any member of her House will likewise cooperate."

She felt Avandar's eyes on the side of her face. Tough. "But I can't cooperate with innuendo, and I've *also* been requested to oversee something by the magi."

"We know what the magi require," Duvari said. "It was our suggestion."

She wanted to ask him if the We was royal. Didn't.

"Is there anything unusual about the man you know as Devon ATerafin?"

She started to answer. Stopped. The wording was incredibly

awkward, and for all that he was a bastard, he was a well-spoken one. She turned her gaze to Devon.

To Devon ATerafin.

He met her eyes, almost flinching from them. As if he expected her to see something. As if he expected her to be able to read the secrets of his past, the embarrassing ones, or the painful ones. As if he expected to be somehow exposed. But he knew better. He knew how her gift worked.

And that, of all things, made her nervous. He *knew*.

She didn't look at people this closely. Not often. Both she and they tended to find it uncomfortable and unnatural. But Devon stood, as he always stood when business was at hand; unflinching and quiet. It made it easier for her to forget that she was staring at him; he'd all but vanished from behind his eyes.

His eyes were light; the light of sun on a blade or on water; nothing gentle there. Nothing vulnerable. The lines of his face, worn into the corners of eyes and mouth and the stretch of brow, told his age, but not to Jewel; as she watched them, they twisted, jumped, vanished.

Vanished into shadow and darkness.

Although she knew she wasn't touching him, she could feel his hand in hers, hear the steadying murmur of wordless whisper. The tunnels beneath the city had devoured half her life in the space of a few short weeks: Lefty, Fisher, Duster, and Old Rath. They had given her her life: ATerafin, part of the governing Council.

But while she'd been in them, that one time, with Devon, she had had little thought of what she had lost, and little enough thought of what she might gain. Balanced there, between life and death, the only alternatives *were* life. Death.

She could hear her heart, feel it as if it were alive, a thing so foreign to her daily existence that it was beyond her control. She might as well have been sixteen years old again, in the darkness, looking for the demons who were closing the ways —and by closing them, opening the gate.

Except that this time, in the darkness, she heard his heart as well. ATerafin, Astari. Kin.

He lifted a hand and opened it, she heard the movement more than she saw it, but the glow in his palm was mage-stone, light that could be contained without pain, hidden with ease, called upon when needed.

"Jewel," he said, using the silent motion of lips. "The light."

She lifted her free hand. Opened it. Reached for the stone—

And cried out as it touched her skin, devouring it. Mage-stone lost all illusion; she looked at the shard of someone's soul, someone's brilliant, sharp-edged soul.

In shock, she looked up, and she saw that his eyes were golden, that his hair was dark—that he was, in fact, not Devon, not a man at all.

"You cannot see clearly," the woman said, and she knew this woman, with her dark blue robes and her pale skin, violet eyes. "Take the test, Jewel. Walk the path."

The fire ceased to burn her; all that remained was the light, pale and oddly menacing. That light caught her eye as if it were a trap set for just that purpose and she gazed into it. It shuddered, as if gaze were touch, and that touch unwanted, undesirable even in nightmare.

But she looked anyway, because at its core was Devon himself. He carried a long knife, not a sword, and a buckler; he wore no armor, and he'd obviously seen fighting; he was bloodied. Unbowed, though, and grim—as she might expect.

She wondered what he was fighting.

"The light," he said, his eyes tracing the confinement of its shining walls, her cupping hands. "The light. Can't you see it?"

She did. She thought she might speak to him for longer, thought she would gain answers in this twilight that she had never gained; access to a part of Devon that was as hidden to her as his role in the Astari was hidden to most people.

And she wanted to know. That was the worst of it. She wanted to know because here, in this place, she didn't have to expose anything of herself to get those answers. It was one of the very few times in her life that the power of the seer-born had truly seemed like a weapon to her.

She knew what that meant.

She looked away. But not before she understood what exactly it was that he wanted from her; how exactly she could come to his aid.

She looked up, and her eyes were watering; she knew it. Evayne nodded, as grimly as Devon had probably fought. "You *are* ready, Jewel. I am sorry for it, but I can no longer bear this burden alone. What you do here today, you will have to do, and the fate of much more than a single man's soul will depend on it."

"I'm too old to be tested like this."

Of all things, the seer-born woman laughed; it was bitter and at the same time warm. "I am—by my path—almost two decades your senior, and I am always tested, always on the edge that you have just walked a moment, looking at the ATerafin's . . . struggle.

"I will come for you, and when I call, you will make the only choice you *can* make."

"You've seen this?" Jewel asked bitterly.

But the darkness was gone, as was the midnight of blue and black and painful, handheld light. The impression of stone tingled in her palms a moment: magic's gift and leaving. The room returned. Duvari. Devon.

She was tired. "I don't know what you're looking for," she said at last, "but you're still the same ATerafin to *this* set of eyes. Whatever it was—it's gone, if it was there at all."

"If he weren't—if he were somehow . . . hosting something unpleasant, would you see it?"

"I probably wouldn't see ringworms unless they were killing him," she replied, forcing her jaws not to clench as she spoke. "But I take it you're not speaking about ringworms."

"No," Meralonne APhaniel said softly.

Jewel spun on a foot at the sound of his voice. She hadn't seen him enter the room; hadn't heard the door swing in to announce his presence. That presence, today, was different. He was not dressed formally, although the make of the simple clothing he wore was fine, and what he did wear was covered with the darkness that spoke of sweat or labor, the blackness of ash or fire. As if aware of her surprise—for it had been a long time indeed since this member of the magi had turned his own hand to hard work in Jewel's memory—the mage bowed; the bow itself told her much. He was tired.

"Member APhaniel." Duvari could make an unpleasant command out of anyone's name. Even Meralonne's. In spite of herself, Jewel was impressed.

"I am hardly likely to tell her something she can't figure out for herself," was the mage's cool response. "And we gain no allies by treating the people we need as if they were imbecilic."

"Or," Duvari said, "politically astute. There are some things that it is not necessary to mention, and the wise person—" and he stopped to stare at Jewel a moment, "—does not wish to know more than she needs."

"The wise person," the mage replied, "understands the value

and the temperament of those he uses, and treats them accordingly. This particular ATerafin is not at her most useful when she's hooded."

"And she doesn't like being talked about in the third person unless it's by herself," Jewel said. "It's the kin, right?"

Silence.

Meralonne nodded.

"We've seen prior evidence of the use of living bodies as hosts," she said.

"Yes," Meralonne replied, but hesitantly. "Yes, we have."

"But?"

"But in this case . . . it's different. Worrisome." He removed a pipe from his robes. "Do you mind?" he asked, waving its stem in her general direction.

"Not at all," she replied. It wasn't true, but she knew Duvari hated it, and she was willing to suffer if he did. Petty. "What could be worse than what happened with—than the ability to take a body and some of its memories?"

"To take a body and all of its memories," Meralonne said, softly. "The creature that destroyed the—" He shook his head. "The creature that we are both speaking of *was* a distinct form, with a distinct set of abilities." He began to stuff dry leaves into the deep bowl of the pipe, nestling them there with a meticulous care that he showed in very little else that was not directly involved in his speciality of study.

She shrugged.

"The creature that has caused us difficulty at the Challenge is bound by no such form. It is almost as if—" He lit the pipe with a careless snap of fingers. Or rather, he tried. "Ah, yes,' he said dryly. "Duvari's famous room. I do believe that I had forgotten some of its less natural properties."

"I don't believe you," Duvari said coldly. "It is exactly the sort of detail that a mage of your renown does *not* forget."

He shrugged. "As you will." He pulled flint from his pocket, sticks of dry wood. She had seen this done before, but not often. Fire from a natural source was harder for a man of Meralonne's talent to obtain, but he worked at it in the heavy silence.

Pipe smoke and information hung in the air between them as the mage turned his attention back to Jewel ATerafin. "It is almost as if the Lord of the Hells himself could somehow reach back across the wide bridge to the Abyss and draw his followers here, whole; that he could deny them the form and the shape of the world, the heaviness of it, the flesh."

"Why bother?"

"I am not completely certain," Meralonne said softly. "But I believe—and my knowledge of the kin is not, fortunately, complete—that creatures of the type that were used some fifteen years ago are actually rare. To infiltrate where necessary, it would require far more of them than are likely to exist. But stripped of flesh, denied a body, most of the *Kialli* would seek whatever they could find, regardless of their learned or developed abilities.

"It is," he added, "a hunger, and a protection."

"Stripped of flesh?"

"Jewel," Meralonne said quietly, "you forget your theology. The kin have no natural forms; they force a form of flesh from their imperfect memory and the magic of *this* world combined, and they wear it. It reflects them, and they reflect it. When a demon is summoned, the moment he bridges that gate created by his name, he takes his form. There were old experiments done to stop the *Kialli* from such an arrival; it is why we have some meager understanding of this at all."

She didn't ask him about those experiments; she didn't want to know. "Did 'they' succeed?"

"No," he said softly. "They did not have the power required to keep the creature from its form."

"And you're telling me that something here does."

Silence.

She was suddenly glad that this room had no windows, that it allowed for the casting of no magic, that it had one door, and that door an easy one to keep an eye on.

"Yes," he said at last.

"If I ask you what has the power to do that when a group of rogue mages doesn't—"

"They weren't rogue," he said. "They were seekers of knowledge under the reign of Vexusa."

Silence. Terrible, long, silence.

"Why does it always come back to this?" she whispered. "The cathedral. The Shining City."

He put the pipe to his lips and inhaled. Some answer. At last he said, "You know why."

And the terrible thing about it was that she did. She knew. *Allasakar.* Lord of Darkness. Lord of the Hells. Ruler of the kin.

"If he can do this," she said faintly, "he'll have hundreds of . . . of kin that can take human shape. Thousands."

"I believe that is the fear."

"Are they detectable?"

"Yes . . ."

"But it's worse than the last one."

"Yes. Because the creature does not create its own flesh."

"Rath was—"

"Beneath the skin, the flesh was not his," Meralonne replied quietly. "I'm sorry."

She looked up at Devon then, sharply, gaze like the edge of a knife. He met her gaze anyway, fencing with his own, unwilling to give ground.

She was silent a long time. "That's why you need me," she said softly.

"Yes. What a seer sees is nothing as simple as magic, or the creation of magic; it is far more complex, far more reliable."

The pipe moved. Jewel did not.

"He's really here," she said at last. "And if he can pull any of his subjects across the divide . . ."

"Yes."

CHAPTER NINETEEN

"Then what can we do?" she asked, straightening out, lifting her chin slightly. She felt Avandar at her back; had forgotten, until he moved restively, that he was there at all. Was surprised by how natural it felt, how unnatural it was. "I think I've listened to every bardic lay there is about the Shining Lord. How do we stand against a god?"

Meralonne shrugged elegantly. "The same way," he said softly, "that we stand against any enemy. I pity you; I pity any man or woman who is not a member of the Order of Knowledge, for it seems to me that it is easiest for them to continue their labors in ignorance. I would have thought—I *do* think—better of you."

"If he were all-powerful, we would be ash," Devon said quietly.

But she could hear a child screaming across more than a decade, and the screams were more real than the nightmares that threw her out of sleep. Because she'd lived them.

With him. With Devon.

"Maybe he just needs the sacrifices," she said softly.

"Maybe." He smiled, and as the smile fell into place, the last of his unease seemed to give way before it. He bowed, ever so slightly. "But I think that you forget the end of all bardic tales."

"Oh?"

"Moorelas," he said quietly. "Moorelas rode."

"Moorelas fell," she replied.

"Does it matter? So did his enemy, in the end."

"Who gets to love a hero who does nothing with his life but prepare to lose it?"

He raised a dark brow; it changed the shape of his eyes. Blue eyes. And then he laughed. "Touché," he said softly. "But I believe that the Lord of the Compact now requires your service, and in earnest. There are . . . two ways, or so we believe, of detecting such infiltration.

"First, and easiest, is you. Second, and more difficult, is the healer-born."

"No," she said. There wasn't any question at all who he was talking about, and she felt a chill, and an anger. Daine had been at the healerie for only a few days, and he had met, outside of her own den, almost no one. Almost.

"Jewel—The Terafin has given her permission, in case of emergency, for all members of her House to cooperate to the fullest extent with the Crowns or their chosen representatives."

"Fine. I'm cooperating. But he hasn't given his yet. And he's *not* ATerafin."

"Oh?"

"He's one of mine," she said, and her voice was low, quiet. "Not that that means much to you, as we've both seen." She wanted a reaction; wasn't sure which one. Didn't matter. He didn't give her one. After a minute, she continued. "He's been through enough lately. I won't risk him."

"If the rumors are true," Devon said softly, "he'll only be able to tender one answer if we make the request. You and he are said to have . . . much in common, at the moment."

She was surprised at just how angry she was.

She was especially surprised at the white mark her hand left in the side of his face; it had been years since she'd hit someone. She was not, however, sorry. It had been done; she'd live with it.

"You can ask him," she said. "But without my say-so, he won't do a damned thing for you. Try to force him," she added softly. "Try to push. I'll make sure every healer this side of the Western Kingdoms knows about it. And knows that you have the support of the *Astari*."

The drawn breath she heard at her back was Duvari's, not Devon's.

Devon was absolutely still.

And then he raised his hand to the side of his face, touched his cheek, met her eyes. Smiled, although because the smile was one she'd never seen on his face before, she couldn't place it and didn't know what it meant. Danger, maybe. Something.

"A temper like that," he said softly, "won't hold you in good stead in the arena you want to play in." He bowed, stiffly, correctly. "You understand our need better than almost anyone here. You're right, of course; the decision cannot be forced. Should not be." He turned to Duvari. "With your permission, I believe it is time to adjourn. The contestants have yet to be . . . screened, and we've left ourselves little time."

Duvari was slow to nod, but the nod—when it came—was definitive. "Member APhaniel," he said curtly.

"Of course, Lord of the Compact." His eyes skirted the tense lines of the two ATerafin faces. Came to rest on Jewel's. "Your pardon, ATerafin," he said quietly. He ceased to draw on the stream of smoke, and the embers began to fade. "I was summoned in haste from the duties I have undertaken to both the Order and the Crowns, in order that I might answer questions deemed pertinent to your investigation. The matter we are discussing is not generally known to the magi. Currently, there are three, and you will be delivered into the hands of Member Mellifas should the need for such consultation arise."

"What are you doing?"

"I," he said, sardonically, "am put to uses which mere apprentices would be deemed too intellectual for." He set the pipe aside a moment and stretched, the movement as languorous a display as any Jewel had seen from a man who flipped from dignity to cantankerousness and back without warning. "It has been an interesting discussion; I am grateful for the opportunity it afforded me to relax."

And she knew, as he spoke the words, that he was lying. "You're worried," she said bluntly.

"Perceptive, as always." He bowed. "I am pressed," he told her softly. "My services are required to put your services to use, and my time here means that we will not be well-coordinated without cost."

"Go, then," the Lord of the Compact said.

The chill in the air was evident in the magi's wake, but he went. Jewel wondered what it would be like, to have Duvari's power.

Daine was waiting for her beneath the arched stone ceilings of the untraveled wing. The isolation robbed him of height and age; he seemed younger than Jewel thought possible as he walked back and forth, staring at his reflection in the shine of the polished wood beneath his foot. His hands, she saw, were locked behind his back. *That* one, that wasn't hers.

He looked up as they approached; the door hadn't been enough to catch his attention.

"Well?" he asked, as Jewel approached him.

"It'll wait," she said. That was all.

But he fell in line at once, no further questions asked.

The Terafin had never seemed this comfortable with Alowan, or he with her. She wondered why.

Avandar was seething. Quietly, of course; he wouldn't dare reprimand her in public. But she knew that she'd stepped over a very thick line when she'd reached out and slapped the only other ATerafin in the room, and she was already beginning—albeit a little—to regret it. Avandar's stare was sharper and harder than a dagger's edge, and far more persistent. Because, of course, part of his job was to protect her from making gaffes like that one. Gaffes which, she was certain, no patriciate-born woman—or man, for that matter—would ever make.

You can take the girl out of the street . . .

"What'd you do?" Daine whispered as Devon and Duvari pulled slightly ahead and their heads met a moment in an exchange of information that seemed far too stiff to be called conversation.

She almost laughed. "What makes you so certain I did anything?"

"The invisible daggers you-know-who is launching into your back."

"Oh. Those." She shrugged. "Nothing much." The chill in the air grew increasingly thick. She sighed; stopped short. "I want to ask you something."

He stilled at once; tone of voice, probably. "What?"

"Were you in Averalaan seventeen years ago?"

"I think so," he said quietly. "But I don't remember much. Why?"

She started to say something sarcastic, and then looked at his face. Hard to remember how many years separated them. "It made me," she said softly. "It made me everything I am." She closed her eyes and the shadows took her vision, opening them again almost immediately. The smell of ancient soil, rotting timber, worn and cracked stone, lingered in the air like a vision.

"Your parents might have told you about the Henden of the year 410."

He paled then but said nothing.

"Well, it's back."

"Jewel, this is not the place," Avandar said coolly.

"It's the only place," she shot back. "And it's your job to see that we're not heard."

"There is the matter of legality," he replied. "You may recall what the penalty is for using unauthorized magic in *Avantari*."

"I'll keep it short. They need me to tell them if everything they see is what it seems to be. Because, of course, I see differently."

"I thought your talent was a secret?"

"It's an open secret. Not a good thing, but something I don't have much control over. I live with it."

"It's been worth three attempts on her life in the past seven years as the information has filtered out," Avandar offered. "But please, continue.

She ignored his interruption; Daine couldn't. "Three attempts on your life?"

"Did they succeed?"

"Well—uh, obviously not."

"Good. Forget about them. Politics demand no less."

He stared at her for a minute. Stared past her shoulder to where Avandar stood like a bouncer, waiting for someone—anyone— to make a wrong move. "This is worse than that."

"Of course, it's worse than that." Jewel ran a hand through hair that, no matter what was done with it short of shearing, fell into her eyes. "I—I'm not going to make the decision for you because I can't calculate the risk. How much damage can a healer take without dying?"

Daine's face shuttered at once, and then she remembered that hers wasn't the only life he'd been exposed to—merely the most recent. "A lot," he said at last. "I can't lose my head, but short of that—*if* I'm given the time, the place and the food—almost anything. Time's important, though."

"You've tested this."

"No."

"Fair enough. Are you willing to?"

"What she means to say—"

"I know what she's trying to say," Daine said, before Avandar could finish. "Why me? I can't see—."

"You can touch 'em. I don't know how the healer's talent works. Hells, I barely understand how the seer's talent works, and I've *got* that one. But I think you can tell if a person's—uh, not quite what they should be—just the same way you can tell they've got a disease."

"As long as you don't expect me to cure it," he replied.

She'd remember those words later—she knew it the minute she

heard them. "Never mind," she said sharply, some fear forcing the words to form.

"What do you mean never mind?"

"We don't need you."

"Look, Jay—if you're talking about demons—"

"That is *quite enough*," Avandar said.

"—and if you're talking about that Henden, that's what you're talking about—"

"Daine, Jewel, I must insist—"

"—then you've asked me about it for a very good reason. You can't just change your mind in the middle of the question!"

"I can change my mind any damned time I please," she replied, shorter than she'd intended to be.

"No, you can't, not about this—"

"Avandar Gallais," another voice said, one that tickled Jewel's ear, but fell short of the rest of Daine's sentence, "you've been granted royal dispensation to use your magics appropriately; shut them up."

It was Duvari's voice. If one of her den hadn't been questioning her authority, she was certain she'd have died of shock. As it was . . .

"I will assume by that," the domicis said softly, "that you mean 'protect them from eavesdroppers.' "

"Very well," Duvari replied, his voice as friendly as falling stone, "you may assume that. But *do it*."

He did not recognize the woman who came by the side of the ATerafin; he did not recognize either of the older men—both dark-haired, both far too deliberate in their movements and the way they casually scanned the crowd to be anything other than dangerous—either. He did not recognize the man who was probably about his own age, but he *did* recognize the symbol that man wore: Two palms, face up, in a platinum field. Gold hands, and somewhat stylized, but it didn't matter—the healer-born were known, loved, and perhaps feared a little for their power of refusal, in any kingdom, any country. Even in the South, where they rarely announced their presence by such obvious emblem.

He bowed; he bowed to all of them, mindful of the need now for manners and decorum. It was hard to remember that need when his only company was Commander Sivari and the Ospreys.

"My apologies, Tyr'agar," the ATerafin said, bowing quite low, "but we have need, at the moment, of your indulgence."

"Of course," Valedan replied. "Is there a problem? I've heard that the contest will not begin until after the sun's height."

"Rumor, in the rare instance, is correct. Please summon your men."

He nodded, turned, and made a brief statement to Commander Sivari.

The man to Devon ATerafin's right leaned over and spoke a few words.

"Ah, apologies, Tyr'agar. We do not wish to speak to the men you have on duty; we wish to speak to *all* of your men."

"All of them? But they are not all available—"

"All of them. I believe that you are currently protected by the Ospreys. Ask Primus Duarte—is that his name?—to gather them. Tell him that any man who is not here for this inspection will no longer have access to the grounds upon which the Championship is contested."

"But the—"

"We will wait," the unknown man said softly. "We have need of the magi before we start."

"Carlo," Ser Anton said softly. "Be still."

"What game are they playing?" Carlo said in return. It was not a reply, but it was as much of a reply as the young man was capable of. Indeed these words, or a variant thereof, had been the only words he'd been capable of for the past two hours, and they wore thin indeed, even though Ser Anton's thoughts had not been dissimilar.

"I imagine they will let us know shortly," the swordmaster replied.

"That's what you said an hour ago."

Ser Anton could almost hear Andaro cringe, although he knew he wouldn't actually see it should he turn around. "Carlo," he said softly. Too softly.

Happily, Carlo was impatient, but he was not suicidal. He managed, for five minutes, to be silent. In this, as in most things, timing was everything.

The day proceeded poorly; Ser Anton was mildly concerned. Had he not known that the Imperials had in fact sent out guards—in force—to every party in the arena, he would have been actively worried. He felt some fear that they might discover what they were seeking.

No—fear was too strong a word, and he was Southern enough

to correct himself although there was no one to hear the half-formed thought. He was *concerned*.

Still, there were reasons why one did not choose to threaten a master of his skill; he acknowledged this truth with both pride and a twinge of weariness.

"Ser Anton," a familiar voice said. He shifted both gaze and stance and offered a correct, if somewhat stiff, bow to the Princess of the Blood.

"ACormaris," he said. Wisewoman. Still, for all her claim of wisdom, she had about her none of the Voyani trappings, none of the sense of their deep mystery, their hidden certainties. This was wisdom as the Lord might have it, not the Lady—but there were few indeed, even among the Radann, who granted the aspect of great wisdom to the Lord.

"Forgive us for this intrusion and forgive us for the delay in the test. We have had a complaint laid by an authority that it is not within our power to ignore. It seems that the lives and the safety of the athletes and their witnesses are at risk, and we have undertaken the responsibility of guaranteeing their safety." She paused, offering him the edge of a smile. "We will request that your students, yourself, and those who form your following, present themselves, momentarily, for inspection by three of our experts."

"And if they refuse?"

"Then they will be refused entry into the test."

"Impossible."

"Unavoidable." She shifted slightly, bending at the knee, taking on a stance that—were it not for the lack of a weapon—he might have recognized immediately. "We will tender apology and possibly compensation should your students feel it necessary to refuse."

"And how will we be certain that your . . . inspections . . . do no harm?"

She met his gaze, but she did not parry the blow. Instead, to his chagrin, she sidestepped it and struck home. "That is beneath you, Ser Anton."

He raised a brow, surprised at the sternness of her chosen tone. Surprised by it, amused by it, but set off-balance for a moment. There were no Southern swordsmen who could throw him off his game. And perhaps, had she been a man, she might not have succeeded. His weakness, not hers, and like any good opponent, she exploited it.

Even if unaware of its existence. He bowed, and this bow was fluid, all grace; no sign of age marred it. "It was," he replied softly, "as you say. You will forgive me, but we did not realize that you wished to see our entire retinue."

It was her turn to frown. "I apologize. Word was sent—"

"It was not sent directly to me; it was intercepted by one of my students." Carlo, of course; it had to be Carlo. "And the messenger's Torra was poor. Sadly, Carlo's Weston is poorer."

"We act in haste," she said, "But not with the greatest organization. This is the first time in the history of Challenge—" He lifted a hand to correct the sentence that she had not, quite, finished; she smiled ruefully. "The first time since the inner city difficulties one hundred and sixty-three years ago, then. I spoke for brevity's sake."

"And I interrupted for form's sake. The point is yours, ACormaris. If I cannot assemble the retinue, what penalty will we be required to pay?"

"No penalty—but those members of your retinue that are not assembled and witnessed will not be granted passage into the arenas or the palace for the duration of the Challenge."

"I see."

"We still have the spectators to witness and to pass," she said softly. "We can return."

"We will be assembled," he said. "I assume that free passage is being granted?"

"To enter, yes, at the moment. To leave . . ."

He raised a brow.

The smile left her face. "The charges and the complaint are serious. We will not ignore them, and no amnesty, should the guilty party be found, will be granted."

He heard the fall of the sword in her words, and he smiled.

He smiled.

Goldwork, in the heat of a day such as this, was not the choice of any sane man. That was work for either apprentices or the rainy season, although it was perfectly acceptable to acquire one's wares when the merchants traveled. Gold worked at the hands of a maker was exceptionally rare, and the makers worked as they pleased; no man or woman had the right—or the lack of sense—to tell a maker otherwise.

And yet.

In the courtyard sheltered to the west by the outer wall of the Hall of Wise Counsel, beneath awnings and tents set up for just that purpose, the makers worked.

And what they produced was not, in fact, art; it was craft, pure and simple; craft of a kind that the most humble goldsmith's apprentice would not boast of. Indeed, it might have been less insulting, and less politically unwise, to assemble such an army of apprentices.

But for one thing: the makers made their home on the isle of *Averalaan Aramarelas,* and the makers did not make an error. Not one. Even in this, the most simple and unseemly of tasks, they were lost to the world; the gold mattered, the simple molds mattered; the cooling mattered—and each thing in turn, end over end, was repeated beneath the open sky.

The magi worked in concert with the makers, and this was an uneasy, even a terrible, alliance. Neither magi nor maker were used to being dealt with harshly, and neither were used to being forced to false courtesy.

Meralonne APhaniel, who oversaw both the making and the finishing of the rings, was exhausted before the work was half done. It was simple work; it was work that, at one point in his long life would have been entirely beneath him, or worse, an insult to his particular capabilities.

He was glad of that; as a youth, he had never dreamed of enchanting such a number of things, and only the fact that they were insignificant at all—that it was a magic meant to linger ten days, no more—allowed him to survive it. He would face the fevers for it; he was certain of it. He was fairly certain he would survive them—but he knew that he could say this only because some of that burden had been passed on; five men worked at his command. And each of them wore, as adornment and office, the symbol of the Order of Knowledge: The moon in three phases, and the elemental symbols in the quartered full face.

"Member APhaniel," a voice called gently.

He looked up and met the blue eyes of the most renowned bard that Senniel College had produced.

"The ACormaris sent me to you. She says that the task is almost done."

"And you had to come in person to deliver this message? I'm exhausted, Kallandras, not stupid."

The bard smiled. "No. Not stupid. I chose to deliver the message in person."

"Why?"

"This is the first making, but it will not be the last," he said softly. "And perhaps I wish to see it to capture it fully. There will be a song at the end of this battle, and a song at the end of this war. Whose voices will carry it, I don't know. But this is the first opportunity that anyone has had—to my knowledge—to see this many makers at work in concert."

"Or mages?"

"No," Kallandras replied. "I have seen the work of mages before. I mean no disrespect, old friend, when I say that the province of the makers holds more interest for me; they make magic out of things ordinary."

"There is a magic in the ordinary," Meralonne said. "I will concede that to you. To watch them at work on something worthy of their grand obsession is probably as close to a glimpse of the gods at work as we are likely to see in this age." His gaze narrowed. "And I am old enough and feeble enough—at the moment—to pretend to believe you. Tell the ACormaris that we will be ready shortly."

Kallandras turned and spoke a moment, and then turned back. "I think," he said softly, "that Jevrin can manage from here."

"Jevrin," Meralonne replied succinctly, "is a clod."

"A talented clod. Meralonne. Enough. We have not passed through the fires together to surrender to obsession and overwork."

"I believe," the mage said, "that I know my own limits."

"Knowledge and acceptance are two different things. Come."

The mage held the bard's gaze. Found it unwavering and cool, and found that fact comforting. "Very well," he said quietly. "I think that perhaps—just perhaps—there is some merit in what you say."

And before he could make his way from around the wide, flat bench, before the first rays of the overbearing light could mark his pale skin, his treacherous knees gave way completely.

He cursed, and cursed again.

Kallandras was beside him, his arm a support. Humiliating that it was necessary.

"How did you know?" he said, from between clenched teeth.

The bard was absolutely silent. Then: "The infirmary has been put at your disposal. The Lord of the Compact desires your continuing presence in *Avantari*." He called out, and the man that Meralonne had pronounced a clod nodded. Grimly.

"I told him," he said. "But he's one of the magi." As if that were explanation enough. It probably was.

"You came to stop me," Meralonne said.

"Does it matter? I'm here, and I'll be of use while I am." Silence descended as they walked, sharing his weight between them. At last, Kallandras said softly, "You are not the only mage I know. Even before I came to this city, I understood the price of their power. It is not very different from the cost of my own."

He spoke in a voice that no one, no one but Meralonne would hear.

And they were, in Meralonne's opinion, acceptable last words to hear; the chills came suddenly, far faster than he had expected; his collapse was complete, and completely beyond his control, long before the healerie's doors opened to contain him.

He carried the rings. At the last minute, an ornate box was found to contain them; the obvious method—a large sack—was deemed, in the end, unsuitable for public display. The fact that the men who so deemed were also men who had not lifted the box itself was not lost on Kallandras by the time he approached the arena.

Mirialyn met him, her expression the only thing about her that was serene as always.

"The Master apologizes," he said quietly, "but says that the remainder of the rings will be ready within the hour. It has been—it has been a difficult two days, ACormaris."

She shrugged, then took one of the boxed rings and pressed it firmly into the palm of her hand. "Hard to believe," she mused, "that something this plain and this thin could be worth the political penalty we may well pay for its creation." Turning, she led him down the hall, the command to follow inherent in the motion.

"Valedan," she said, just ahead of his vision but not his hearing. "We've done. We'll finish with athletes and trainers first, work our way to the spectators by the end of the evening. There will be room for error," she added, although it was obvious, "but we're watching."

He rounded the corner then, and saw Valedan. The boy was pacing like a caged beast.

"You'll forgive me," she added, "if I do not choose to don the ring yet; we will all be forced to wear them, but a demonstration of their function might save us some difficulty where the Northerners and the Southerners are involved."

He nodded. Held out a hand, palm up.

She smiled, and Kallandras saw a flash of warmth in an expression that he would have thought, this day, had none. "You're the first," she said. "Be honored. The makers have been slaving in our service for almost a day and a half, without pause."

His eyes widened slightly. "But the rings are—"

"I know. Put it on."

"I don't think it's going to fit—"

"Valedan, we're now four hours late to start; we'll be five hours late before this is over, and *only* if we work quickly." She took a breath. "My apologies, Tyr'agar."

"Accepted," he said. "Alina's not here." He slid the ring over his finger, and Kallandras, watching, saw it widen to fit him, moving not as a metal, but as a shining clay. Light limned it momentarily, a brightness and a warmth that seemed the essence of gold itself. And then it sat upon the ring finger of the young Tyr's sword hand.

"Thank you," Mirialyn said quietly. "You can't remove it. It is attuned to you, and if for some reason you cease to be *you*, it will . . . let us know."

"How?"

"Best not to discuss it," she warned. "When you see it, it will be obvious enough."

He nodded to her.

"All right, the rest of your guards will have to wear them as well." She raised a hand to her brow.

Valedan moved at once, and Kallandras thought, watching him, that he had not noticed—that none of them had noticed—that the ACormaris had said not *if* but *when*.

To say that the Ospreys were mutinous was inaccurate; had they been, Duarte would have been forced to act. But to say that they were happy or complacent would have been to miss their point entirely, and they made it. He was willing, for the sake of peace, to actually don the first ring.

It helped that his magic was capable of telling him that the power of the ring was defensive and informative, and that the transformative magic that resided within the gold—not an easy spell, in his estimation, because it was so very subtle—was meant *for* the gold itself, no more. But even knowing this, there was something very wrong about watching gold—one of his favorite metals—curl around his finger like a snake and then harden there. It was . . . disconcerting.

Alexis followed his lead. Auralis obeyed as well, although he couldn't refrain from cheap theatrics when the ring fit itself to his hand. Had the Princess of the Blood not been in attendance, Duarte would have rewarded his fake cry of agony with a good reason for a real one. But that did the trick as far as the magic-suspicious Ospreys were concerned—because any cowardice on their part would now be seen as worthy of Auralis' mockery, and no one subjected themselves to that willingly.

Unfortunately, when Kiriel took the ring and slid it around her slender finger, it exploded.

She felt nothing when the ring touched her palm, and she had been trained so well, magic should have set up a shiver that started there and passed through her as if she were a bell and it a clapper. Oh, she knew it was magic; gold didn't move like that without cause—but she couldn't feel any of it.

"What are the rings for?" she whispered to Cook.

He'd shrugged. "Don't know how they work—but I'd guess they're supposed to help us separate people from demons, somehow."

Made sense. She didn't know how she'd accomplish the task had it been made hers—but then again, there was a reason the Empire was respected, even feared, among the denizens of the Shining Court; the speed with which they approached their crises did not surprise her as much as it should have. As it might have, once.

Her fingers curled up round the edges of the gold as she made a fist, driving its cool lip into her skin. A moment of clarity gave her pause: this ring was meant to detect the kin, or their master's work. And what was she, if not the latter?

She started to speak. Lifted her hand to catch the Primus' attention. It caught light instead; light along the rounded curve of polished platinum.

All right, she thought, lowering her hand. *You've deprived me of what I am. How far does it go?*

"Cook, do the rings *do* anything?"

"Don't know. You heard Duarte—or weren't you listening?"

She said nothing. He rolled his eyes.

"Person's not the same as the first person it fit itself to, it'll let the Kings' men know. If the body's the same, but it's been tampered with somehow, it'll let the Kings' men know that, too." His eyes narrowed. "Why are you asking all of this?" he asked suddenly, as if only just remembering that Kiriel never asked an idle question.

She met his eyes. Smiled softly. He stepped back from that

smile, and that made her smile deepen and lose its edge. "Let's find out," she answered. She slid the ring onto the ringless hand. Because, of course, it was her less-favored weapon hand. Old habits, deeply ingrained.

The light came.

Burned.

Expanded in a ring of white fire.

She had the time to cry out, and the strength not to, as shards of hot gold scored her clothing and her flesh.

The pain itself was like a cloud of smoke; it cleared with air and time. And as it did, she looked up to see that Primus Duarte was covering his face with both hands. Her hearing was not what it had been—a gift, no doubt, of the cursed ring the seer had 'dropped'—but she knew that he was swearing under his breath.

"Well," Auralis said, filling the silence before anyone else could, "that answers that."

"What answers what?"

"We know what the ring does when it's not on the right hand." He laughed, speaking to Duarte, whose hands had come down and now rested at his side. "Anyone stupid enough to try to take her out, or worse, take her over, deserves whatever the Hells they get."

That caused laughter, even hers. It surprised her enough that she stopped. Stared at her hand, which was bleeding and messy.

"The ACormaris is going to be pissed," Alexis said, from the corner of the room. "What do we tell her?"

"To get us a ring that goes on the normal way. Auralis is absolutely right," the Primus said.

"Which means," Cook whispered, for Kiriel's ears alone, "it'll be his fault if something goes wrong." He stopped then, stared at her hand, and swore. "Med!"

"It's nothing," she said curtly.

"There's a reason they don't let soldiers self-diagnose." He reached for her arm, stopped himself an inch short, and frowned. "You're an Osprey, you follow his orders. Duarte!"

"What?"

"That light was a bit more than just pyrotechnics."

"What?"

"Kiriel's hand has been fried."

"Tell her to get to the medical division, post haste." He paused. "Make sure she *doesn't* see a healer, just in case there's one on site."

"Right, sir." To Kiriel, he added, "You heard him."

She frowned, but it was half-hearted. The ring had exploded upon sealing itself round her finger. No one else had had that effect on it. Somewhere, buried so far within her that she couldn't reach it no matter how desperately she tried—and she had—she was still *herself*.

Funny, how much that mattered.

Ser Anton watched as Mirialyn ACormaris slid a ring that he had chosen from the clutch of slender, simple adornments onto her finger. She made the movement masculine, graceless, and public, lifting her arm so that the men here, most of whom were taller than she, but not all, could see what followed.

It wasn't particularly pleasant; the gold itself seemed to shudder at impact with flesh.

"Now," she announced, "the ring itself is proof of my identity. It will change in appearance if it is removed, and it will . . . warn us if the rings change hands. It will also alert us to the presence of foreign, but hidden, magics.

"You may, of course, desire to test the truth of my words. A word of advice: Don't. After this event, no athlete will be allowed into the Challenge grounds should the ring be altered."

Ser Anton did not bother to soften the words she spoke; he translated truly, keeping up with their sense rather than their exact tone.

"At this point, you may feel free, any of you, to leave the grounds should you choose not to wear the rings that we have made. We understand your suspicion, and ask your patience and understanding for ours. We have no choice. A young girl has already died, and it is only our vigilance that will prevent a similar death. If you choose not to bear such a ring as this, you will be escorted to the bridge, but you will not be stopped or questioned." She turned, bowing to Ser Anton di'Guivera.

He watched her rise. "I am impressed," he said. "If I were in the South, ACormaris, I would almost suspect, by the speed at which you responded to the threat, that the threat was somehow manufactured by you as well."

She did not speak; did not choose to frame a reply to an accusation that was, in the end, no accusation.

He held out his hand.

"No, Ser Anton," she replied, her lips devoid of smile, "I will not choose the ring you wear; choose it yourself, as you chose mine."

He nodded, thinking that she was, in the end, a very perceptive woman. That she understood that women had no visible power, no authority, in the South, that they were considered fairer and weaker in many, many things. That by understanding that truth, she had used it against them all. For she *was* a woman, and she had donned the ring he had chosen without flinching. Any man here who now did less unmanned himself in front of his compatriots.

Cleverly played, he thought, as he picked up a slender circlet of gold. And then, unbidden, another's face came to him, another's name. *Serra Alina di'Lamberto.* He placed the ring on his finger and turned to his students.

"Put them on," he said, in a voice that brooked no refusal — and no questions. "The test of the javelin will proceed when all contestants and their chosen trainers and guards bear such trifles."

Tyr'agnate Ramiro di'Callesta did not wear the golden circlet upon his finger; Baredan di'Navarre did. It said much about these two men, and that saying was lost on neither when they met to observe the contenders in the coliseum below.

What was interesting to both men was that the Serra Alina di'Lamberto was so adorned, although she had chosen, for such public display as Serras were subject to, to ring her hands with such gold and gems as had been given her by her family. It made the ring hard to spot unless one knew what to look for. Both men did.

"Is there truth," Ramiro said softly, "to the rumors?"

"There is truth," was Baredan's less stern reply, "to *all* rumors. But if you refer to the attack upon the guesthouses, yes. Your information is good, even here."

His sources of information within the Empire were unrivaled across the length and breadth of the Dominion, and both men knew it. It was Southern, to stand thus, knowing so much and saying so little. Peaceful, in its way, because it was normal. So very little was normal in the world these days.

He found himself missing his wife. Serra Amara the Gentle. And his wives, his concubines. He did not yet miss his sons; they had reached the age where the wildness of their youth was second only to their determination to prove that they were, in fact, unimpaired by that youth, and it was tiresome to argue with boys who could only barely refrain from speaking the words that might force him to kill them.

Yet he had been such a youth, and had become a man, having survived his father's increasingly justified wrath; he had hopes that his sons would do the same.

"My son," Baredan said, "would have appreciated this far more than I; he would come to it with new eyes."

"And not eyes weary of spectacle? General, I am surprised."

Baredan smiled, the curve resting easily on his lips. "The Northern air," he said. "It affects us all. All," he added, with a sideways glance, "except yourself and the Serra Alina. A sword is softer than that woman, and less sharp."

"I would not have suspected that the North could provide such ease of spirits; had I, I might have convened a meeting of Generals here, claiming neutral territory."

"And I would have refused such a request, thinking it either insult or trap," the General replied. "But I find it odd, to stand beside the man who, of all Tyrs, I least trusted—"

"Garrardi, surely."

"Garrardi is dangerous in his fashion, but easily predictable; his cunning is turned to his pleasure and his pride, not his power. But you interrupt me, Tyr of Callesta."

"To defend my honor, surely. But continue."

"I stand beside the man I least trusted, surrounded by the Northerners who follow the demon Kings I've fought against for half my life, watching a hundred youngsters heft spears across a manicured waste of greenery. It is . . . not what I expected." He laughed. "I have to be given *leave* to wear my sword, not to meetings between men who have much to fear from each other, but on simple errands, on a stroll from one end of this ancient palace to another. In everything, this life confounds my experience."

"And yet you sound suspiciously content."

"I am content. I feel the war in the air," he added. "I feel a battle. And it is not a battle of convenience—I say this now, who have never said this, either to the other Generals or to the Tyr we then served—but a battle that *must* be fought, against an enemy, finally, worth killing; worth dying *to* kill." He laughed again; it surprised Ramiro. Had they been in the Dominion, it would have worried him. Such laughter, unconcealed, was either ruse or an inexplicable loss of control—for they had never been friends, and given the roles they occupied, were unlikely to become any closer than they were now.

Not if they were wise.

"I feel young again, Tyr'agnate. I feel young, and on the edge

of a battle that will define not only my life, but life itself. And he,"
he added, "bearing the blood of the Leonnes in his veins, has
brought us to it. The demons have been called, and if the golden-
eyed serve the demons in any form, then I am the Lady's son, not
the Lord's. They cannot best us if we stand together, and so, for
this war, we *will* stand."

Ramiro's gaze glanced off the General's shaded profile, and
then down to where the contenders gathered.

Valedan kai di'Leonne had come up to the line drawn across
the grass with fine, white powder. He bowed, courteously and
with obvious grace, to the adjudicator who bid him wait. All this
they could see clearly.

And this is the boy who is worth such a war?

"The brawl with Anton's boy was costly," Baredan said, as if it
needed saying. "But they watch each other now."

"They watched each other," Ramiro replied, "because that
'boy' has at least one broken rib; he will wait out the wrestling,
but will ride and fight. If he cannot take the crown for himself, he
will make certain that the kai Leonne cannot claim it either."

Silence.

Valedan stood as the adjudicator rang the heavy, perfect bell.
He drew his arm back, his shoulder stretching in the sunlight, his
skin exposed a moment from beneath the white tunic. No armor
here, nor any need of it. Not in the North.

There were three throws allowed with the spear. Two were for
targets, and one for distance. The sun was in the wrong place for
the former; for the latter, it mattered less. The kai Leonne lifted
his hand to shield his eyes from sunlight. He stood a moment—a
long, tense moment, and then he let the spear fly.

They granted him silence.

The rest of the crowd did not. At least in this, there was no difference between the North and the South.

"My eyes are not equal to yours," Ramiro said, lying baldly.
"How did the spear fly?"

"Who cares? It's the landing that counts," the General said.
"And he's hit the target faster, and more accurately, than any before him."

"Good." The Tyr smiled. "But I confess I do not understand
why the measure of strength is the last test, not the first."

"In the North," a third voice said, "we value control over raw
power."

Both men turned to face the Princess, Mirialyn ACormaris. She smiled, the smile reminiscent in many ways of Alina's.

The Tyr'agnate shrugged. "At least you acknowledge that raw power has its value."

"Yes," she said. "In this world, at this time, there is no choice but to acknowledge that fact." Then she bowed, respectfully, to the Tyr'agnate. "I must deprive you a moment of your companion."

"Oh?"

Her gaze lingered a moment over his unadorned ring finger. "I beg your indulgence and your understanding," she said, "but it is a matter Southern, and it is to be resolved in the arena and beyond; you have chosen not to venture there. General Baredan?"

He nodded.

Followed.

Ramiro di'Callesta cursed, but inwardly. He could not trust himself to Northern magics.

The Serra Alina was waiting for them, and at her feet was the body of a man dressed in the Southern style; armored, although the weather was poor for it. Unarmed, however. He wore no flashings, no colors to mark him, no crest that might attach to a clan—yet the value of the armor he wore was such that the clans were certainly involved.

She looked up when Mirialyn entered the enclosed room.

"Valedan did well," the Princess said. "For the medium-range target, no one else has come close. I believe that Eneric will match—but not best—his throw."

"Eneric?" Baredan said.

"The Northern favorite," she said. "The man considered most likely to take the crown."

"Ah. The man who won the River jump."

"Yes."

Alina, however, having received that much news, looked back to the body. "General," she said, "I beg your indulgence in this."

"This is a Northern affair," the General replied, knowing well that she needed no indulgence of his, save for form's sake—and knowing further that one did not withhold such indulgence from a woman of her reputation. "And you must, of course, feel free to interact in a method the Northerners find acceptable. I am not your brother, and not your husband; you are not my responsibility, Serra Alina, save in the way that all women in need of aid are."

And he knew that she would die before she required his aid, or the aid of any man. He bowed.

And she surprised him by bowing as well. "I am . . . less familiar with these things than I should be," she said softly. "My training with the Lamberto clan is not the equal of the training other women of powerful families receive.

"But this man is one of the men who made their attack upon the Tyr'agar's chosen witness. Or rather, he was."

"What is he doing here?"

She was silent for a moment. When she spoke, she spoke as if there had been no hesitation. An honor, he realized, but only later. "I asked to see him."

"Pardon?"

"I asked the ACormaris for permission to examine the body."

"And you felt that you might have some insight into the manner of death that the Northern mages and their experts did not?" He did not bother to hide the incredulity in his words.

"Obviously." Nor she her sarcasm. He was surprised. Refreshed by it. "However I am not completely familiar with all of the signs."

The signs. He froze, unable to mistake her meaning however much he might have desired otherwise. Then he pushed past the ACormaris, and knelt at the side of the Serra Alina.

She folded her hands in her lap as if they were a fan; lowered her chin, straightened her back and waited. Waited as he brushed the hair above the left ear lobe aside, turning the rigor-released flesh so that he might better examine it.

There, on the inside of the lobe, scored there as if by brand, was a single mark. A five-pointed star. He spit to the side and stood as if the touch of the mark against his flesh was beyond his ability to contain disgust for. It was.

"This mark," the ACormaris said. "Is it as the Serra fears?"

"It is *Kovaschaii*," the General replied. "And marked in such a way as to claim that credit."

"The *Kovaschaii* do not mark their victims," the ACormaris said, frowning. "Did they, we would have known what the marks meant on our own."

"They do not mark men who are not meant for marking, no. In the Empire, I imagine that such a mark would be anathema to those who would seek the brotherhood's aid to begin with. But from what I have heard, the brotherhood of the Lady's dark face will grant a death that you specify, at a cost that *she* specifies.

Easiest by far, and for that reason less costly, is to ask for the death and to allow them to openly claim it for what it is: a gift for the Lady." He let the hair fall, and sat back from the body, the warmth of the sun having deserted him completely beneath this sky of stone and wood. "We were meant to know this."

"Why?"

"Because," the General replied, "demonkind has failed far more often in its attempts than the brotherhood has."

The spears that had been passed before the eyes of the mages were passed beneath them again upon exit; they would, should the contenders choose the same weapons, be inspected again when they lifted weapon by shaft and walked up to the line drawn in grass. Easy enough to control that, here.

Easy enough to control everything, Valedan thought, save the flight of the spear itself. Wind helped him, or rather, its absence—but breeze or no, each contender was granted a space of minutes in which to ready his spear, minutes in which to throw it. The adjudicatory body, made restless and a little too sharp by the day's delays, were strict in their enforcement of these laws, and at least five men had been disqualified from the medium-range throw because they waited for the wind to lessen.

None, so far, had been removed from the long target; one man's public failure was another's—several in this case—lesson.

Still, Valedan waited, not so much counting the seconds as feeling them, sinking into them. The long target was more difficult than the medium target, and far more difficult than the test of distance. The Serra Alina likened it to the life he had chosen, and she was probably right.

He was aware that to his left, fifty feet away, Eneric was also lining up his shot—also waiting, playing the time out until it came close to the edge, to see how Valedan threw.

He recognized it, of course, because he did the same; they might have been one man in an imperfect mirror, caught waiting.

Waiting to see who would flex arm first, who would put shoulder behind motion, who would loose the shaft.

And how far it would fly, how true.

It was not uncommon in the test of the long target for all men to fail, but there were degrees of failure.

No wind, none, and the sun scorching its way into the unwelcome distance. He hated to squint; he squinted.

It's hard to strike the right balance, Sivari had said. *Tough. Pay as much attention as you need to to your enemy; never pay more. And how in the hells am I supposed to know what 'enough' is? If you win, that's enough.*

It was a game, to wait; a test of something.

He counted. As carefully as he could count while waiting, while watching out of the corner of his eye, while glancing at the unblemished center of the target that Eneric of Darbanne needed to strike.

Thirty.

Ramiro di'Callesta watched from his seat at the curve of the coliseum's height. He heard Miko say, although he was not close enough to see who the benefactor of his words was, "What by Lord's Fire is he doing?"

There was no answer, but the Callestan Tyr smiled.

Young, that boy; young and hot-tempered as the young arc—they had seen evidence of that during the River Jump. The first thing he had done, striking the arrogant, ill-mannered student of Ser Anton di'Guivera, that had been likable. Oh, he was admirable, and Ramiro granted him admiration with ease, but he admired many men. Even, although he did not say it loudly, the General Alesso di'Marente. Especially the General, who played his game so well he might indeed gain for himself what none of the Tyrs could ever have taken: The Tor Leonne. The Dominion's prize.

Yet if he admired Alesso, if he thought him a man worthy of regard, he did not *like* him. This boy, by being—for that instant, no more—*a* boy, like any young man, had made his mark on the Tyr'agnate.

"Why isn't he throwing the spear?"

Because, Miko, Ramiro thought with some irritation, *he waits to see who throws first: The Northerner who thus far is his only competition, or himself. They have a limit of time imposed upon them; step over it by a second and the throw is lost entirely. But throw too early and all advantage is lost. Let the other expose his power and his skill first for your inspection.*

"Maybe he's too nervous to throw," another of his guards said — and Ramiro was grateful for the existence of Torra, regardless of the language barrier that was so difficult to surmount, because it meant they could only humiliate themselves by displaying their ignorance among the few Annagarians present.

                              *   *   *

The adjudicator lifted his hand; there was a grimness about his expression that could be easily seen in the half second Valedan spared him. Time.

Fifteen.

No movement to his side. No shadowed flight across grass, no spear's arc.

Ten.

The spear had to leave the hand before the last of the time was counted. In the space between breaths he had time to wonder if his count was correct. Only that much time. The sun was hot, the wind scant.

Five.

He pulled his arm back slightly; his breath, he deepened. Close now.

Three.

Close enough.

Valedan kai di'Leonne threw the spear—and as it flew, he saw that it did not fly alone.

Ramiro smiled.

His men were a great deal more effusive—far too effusive, given the behavior expected of Tyran—and that broadened, rather than lessened, his smile; there were, after all, no women present to note the breach of manner and sensibility—and no Southerners of rank close enough to judge him by their enthusiasm.

Neither spear flew completely true; neither hit the center of the target, which was, after all no bigger than the heart of a large man—but they hit the targets well.

Valedan kai di'Leonne frowned. He heard the roar of the crowd; heard Weston, some Torra, some of the Northern tongue, syllables blending and disappearing in the tumult.

But he was not satisfied.

Not even when the adjudicator returned to him and bowed. "Your throw," he said.

Eneric of Darbanne appeared at his side, expression as cool as the sea in the rainy season. But he bowed, and then extended a hand in the Northern style. "I have not heard of you before," he said, "but I will not forget the name now that I have heard it. A pity that you did not compete in the River Jump."

Was it meant as an insult?

Valedan shrugged. Did it matter? Form was form; he had forgotten that at the River's test, and he had paid for it. He took the offered hand. He had expected the Northern man to do what many Northerners do—to make of this shaking of hands some primitive contest of strength.

Eneric did not. He brushed pale, pale hair from eyes that were almost too blue to be real and smiled. First smile. "You are not satisfied."

Valedan shrugged again.

"You bested me here, and equaled me in the medium throw." He started to speak, stopped, his smile broadening. "In the North, your displeasure would be an insult; to me, it is not."

"An insult?"

"Yes. It is clear that you consider the throw inferior—and we were both off our mark today. But to consider it inferior when it bested my best—it implies that I am beneath notice."

"You speak well for a Northerner."

"And you speak well for a Southerner." He released Valedan's hand. Bowed. "I believe that you have been underestimated, Valedan di'Leonne. But I believe that this next test is mine."

Valedan looked at the size of the Northerner, torn for just that moment between the competition and grace. To his surprise, grace won. Eneric was larger than Valedan, with the longer reach—none of which mattered; he was well-muscled, bulkier; he carried a momentum through size and strength alone that, for distance, Valedan could not match. "Yes," he said. "If someone challenges you there, it will not be me."

He bowed then, Southern style—and then when he rose, he struck his chest with a curled fist.

Eneric returned the latter gesture, and they parted.

Ramiro watched.

"Well?"

He glanced up, surprised at the interruption. Beneath the shade of a wide brim, his par waited in silence.

"The . . . hat . . . it does not suit you."

Fillipo met his brother's eyes a moment and then removed it. "You were lost to wind," he said.

"Or sun's glare," Ramiro replied.

"He threw well," Fillipo said politely.

But they were kin, these two; he knew that the throw itself

could not demand this attention from the Tyr'agnate of Callesta. He waited patiently.

At length, as the contenders began to assemble for the last of the three tests, he was released, and turned to his brother, rewarding patience. "I do not know who that boy is," he said. "I thought—we all thought—that he was seventeen, and weakened both by thinned blood and Northern life.

"And then, I confess, I thought him a Lambertan pawn—the student of Alina di'Lamberto, no more."

"And what has changed that?"

"That man," Ramiro said softly. "That pale-skinned, pale-haired man. Do you recognize him?"

"Eneric of Darbanne, I believe. He is said to be the Champion in waiting," Fillipo shrugged. "You did not hear what passed between them, surely?"

Ramiro frowned. "Of course not. But in watching it, enough is clear. The kai Leonne has made a friend, if I am not mistaken."

"Men make friends," Fillipo replied. "It is hardly worthy of remark."

"It is worthy when that man is your enemy."

"Ramiro—this is the Kings' Challenge, not the Lord's. The competitors are often friendly."

"Granted," the Tyr'agnate said, unmoved. "But Valedan is a stranger to tests. I would have said, the first time I saw him, that he was a stranger to the sword as well. But now I understand that he is a stranger not to its use, but its allegiance. He has the Lord's grace."

The third throw of the day belonged, decisively, to Eneric of Darbanne. The Northerners who occupied the northern side of the coliseum as if it were a recently taken castle, filled the whole of the isle with their jubilation when he took to the white line. It seemed impossible that their cries could grow louder, but they did, and almost immediately. He played no waiting game here; he threw with an ease that was dismissive, that acknowledged no competition.

Indeed, there was none. The spear fell just short of the line of benches occupied at times by the judicatory body, some ten feet, possibly twelve, from the next closest spear.

The test of strength gave him the lesser crown and closed the event for the day; Valedan kai di'Leonne, who had given him pause in the first and second throw gave him no pause in the third—although Captain Sivari was quick to point out that nothing short of a quarrel at close range would have done so—but in spite of his poorer placement in the third, he came second.

Andaro di'Corsarro finished best for the Southerners at tenth, and people were privately surprised at his finish; the Southerners did not favor spears or their use, and they were also poor archers.

No, the tests at which they excelled, always, were yet to come: The rider's test.

And the sword's.

CHAPTER TWENTY

The streets, during the Festival season, had a life of their own, a rhythm that sleep and work and the demands of a day's labor could not suppress. The magisterians were out in force—and for the most part they were honest enough; they took little ease from the wine merchants or the sellers of ale and late-night food.

This wasn't always the case, but the events of the evenings past had made of their patrol a necessity far more urgent than stopping drunken brawls. They were on edge, and that edge demanded, and received, their best. Whether you liked them or hated them, in the end they were almost all honest men. Tired, hot, overworked—but honest for all that.

The bards were out as well. Many of them, Kallandras recognized by sight, but a handful—a very, very few—had come new to the city from their colleges, Morniel and Attariel, and although they wore those emblems and carried new—and less valuable—instruments, it was easy enough to mistake them for revelers, wide-eyed and brilliant with youth.

Easy for one who was not Kallandras. He listened to the sounds of their voices, hearing that youth in them. Wondering why it was that the gods saw fit to gift so few with such voices, and even then grant them their full range and glory for so short a time.

His own voice had not sustained the easy tenor of his youth, but his gift made up for the lack—to most ears. His own, dispassionate, could hear the difference enough to remark on it. Enough to regret it, and he would not have thought, in a youth far, far different from the youth of the Morniel and Attariel students, that he could regret any loss. Any loss save for the one that had shaped his life: his brothers.

He held Salla in his arms with the easy familiarity of a master, but her strings were still.

"What, no song, Master Bard?" the wine merchant called, affecting a merriness which implied that his wines were better than

Kallandras knew they were. Good or no, they would sell; it was the Festival season. They might sell late, rather than early, from the looks of the merchant.

"A moment, Varren," the bard replied. "I see an old friend, and we might be persuaded to sing a duet."

"Well, sing here, sing here if it pleases you," the wine merchant said. Kallandras would have laughed under other circumstances; the man was literally rubbing his palms together with ill-contained glee. But the bard that he saw was, of all bards, the retired Sioban Glassen—and the only familiarity she granted him upon sight was that of relief.

He moved through the crowd toward her, murmuring quietly as he did; carving a delicate, almost unseen, path with his words, the subtleties of his voice.

"Sioban," he said, as he reached her. "Why did you not call for me?"

She shrugged, and he smiled slightly. Of all bardmasters, Sioban Glassen had become famed, in her time, for her use of the bardic voice—or rather, for her lack of its use. *I'm not bardmaster because I can order any idiot around,* she had been fond of saying. *I'm bardmaster because I'm the only one here—next to Solran—with enough of a sense of responsibility.*

Solran Marten had succeeded her, and Solran was voiceless—but not powerless. Never that.

"What is it, then?" he said, bowing. Knowing that she did not speak because her voice would give something away, although she was skilled enough to hide it from almost anyone else's hearing.

"I've been sent," she began, and he did hear it—the tremor of an old fear, "by Sigurne Mellifas. To find you."

"Sigurne Mellifas? Why?" He wanted to ask a hundred other questions, for he had not seen her in literally years, and she had been among the most important of his masters in Senniel.

"I don't know."

Lie. He let it pass.

"If you would accompany me, Kallandras, she requests your presence upon the isle."

He nodded at once, and she smiled. The years fell away from the corners of her lips, although the lines the smile rippled were many. Had she been beautiful in her youth? He could not recall; she was beautiful to him now in a different way. "How could I refuse? You found me, Sioban. It was . . . needed."

They both knew that he spoke of his youth.

"You gave me all the life that I have now."

The shadows flitted beneath her eyes; she turned, and then turned again. "But it wasn't the only life you'd known." No question, there.

He said nothing, old habit. They walked some ways together through the crowd, Kallandras sweeping it gently—always gently—aside.

"I have heard," she said quietly, "from Solran."

He waited, patient now, although it had never been his way to interrupt her.

"And I have heard from an . . . old friend. I desired to see him," she said quietly. "I did not realize how close to the eve of war we've come. I'm glad, master bard of Senniel, that I am no longer the bardmaster. Once was enough."

And he knew that she spoke of a Henden in a dark, grim year. Some memories had a life of their own; they could be cozened and reasoned with, but they could not be laid to rest.

They crossed the bridge; he almost offered his arm, and he would never have presumed that when she had ruled the college. Because she had never needed it then. She probably didn't need it now. "I think you should know," she said, "although Sigurne did not tell me this in so many words." Now the hesitation was strong; as strong as the curiosity that had always been part of her voice where he was concerned.

"Yes?"

"Meralonne APhaniel wishes to speak with you."

He frowned. "He is—"

"In the royal healerie, yes. And if Dantallon sees you, you'd better be prepared to use your voice and pray; he's in a foul temper."

"A healer has no effect on the fevers. He knows that."

"And he always deals so well with loss of control where life is concerned." There, more of her edge, that snap of her words whiplike and familiar.

But beneath that edge, truth.

"How bad?"

She did not answer.

"Sioban. How bad is he?"

She did not answer, and by that, he knew she wouldn't. But she had met him here, instead of calling him, instead of asking another bard who knew him well to call. There were at least two who could reach him across the length of a city alive with the noises of just such a celebration, and possibly farther than that. The fact that she had summoned neither, that she had come *in person,* suddenly said too much. He began to walk quickly.

In the darkness, Meralonne APhaniel toiled. Sweat speckled the length of his brow, reflecting light and fire; the heat passed, and the cold was upon him, as terrible in its way as any demon could ever be, but closer, far closer.

Watching him, Kallandras knew all these things as intimately as only those who had suffered the fevers could. But he knew, also, that no one suffered as the mage-born did, not even the healers. And he knew, further, that the only men and women to whom the fevers were often fatal *were* the mages. Still, in his life he had heard of it only thrice.

Three times was enough.

Sigurne looked up from the bedside as he entered, her face pale with lamplight, although he thought it would be pale regardless. She looked frail; she always looked frail. But beneath that, part of it, a steel surer than almost any other. The moment her eyes met his, her shoulders slumped.

"Kallandras," she whispered, "thank you for coming."

Sioban was at his side, and that was enough to make him cautious. But he bowed. "I would not refuse a request of yours, Sigurne, were you a seamstress and not one of the magi."

"It was not my request, but his," she said, looking away. "Both the ACormaris and Devon ATerafin have been to see him, and I believe—although I cannot be certain of it—that the ACormaris thought it germane to speak with him, even given his state."

Anger, there. Brief, but certain.

"The circumstances are complex," he said.

"Yes. But so is an old woman's anger." She granted him his gift, and the truth of it. "He has not rested since she came; he desires no company but yours."

"Why?"

She turned away again, as if she could not meet any gaze, not even under cover of darkness. "He is not doing well, Kallandras," she said at last. "And what strength he had, he . . . expended."

"Pardon?"

"Dantallon came to see him."

He started to speak. Stopped. Paled. "Was the healer injured?"

"His pride, and if he chose to press it, the magi would answer for Member APhaniel's use of unauthorized magics in the healerie. But Meralonne is deemed to be—or was—in a state of dementia, and therefore I have been asked to ward and guard him. He will not have Dantallon in the room."

"No," Kallandras said.

"But he used strength he did not have to make that point. And he uses it now, to speak, to ask for you." She rose. "Come, then, and speak with him, and perhaps he will be at ease." Her voice cracked on the last word.

Is it to be here, Meralonne, that you meet your end? Here, in the courtyard of Kings, and not there, upon a field that needs your skill and your knowledge of ancient magics? He moved round her gently, as aware of her presence as he was of the presence of Sioban.

He sat. "Member APhaniel," he said. "Meralonne."

There was no response other than the shuddering of a man who could not be kept warm. Kallandras lifted a hand, raised it, reached out—and hesitated, there, an inch from the pale, wet curve of Meralonne's brow.

They did not touch, these two. They did not offer comfort except as it must be offered: On the edge of death, or just beyond it. And he did not want to acknowledge that this was indeed that edge. "Meralonne."

Gray eyes widened, sudden, like the flaring of magical fire. "You must . . . investigate . . . what I cannot," he said.

Kallandras frowned.

"You will . . . have heard this . . . no doubt. The men who died." He lost the thread of words; Kallandras waited, listening. No one listened as well as he. "The ACormaris came. The Lord . . . of the Compact . . . has forbidden interference in this affair. She thought . . . to warn me . . . not to interfere."

The frown fell a moment; it was like Miri to spite Duvari in some things, and he could hear her now: "I am not allowed to speak about the circumstances surrounding the death of the Annagarians because Duvari finds it strange that they died in captivity, apparently within a few minutes of each other . . ." She had told him as much.

But he did not understand why she had come to Meralonne. Not now.

Not until he spoke again, laboring over each word. "You have heard . . . their names."

He reached out then, caught Meralonne's hands in his own.

Felt them shaking with fever's strength. "APhaniel," he said, voice low, denying nothing because in the end there was nothing to be gained by denial. "There were not nine names."

"No . . . I did not think so. But there were at least eight." He slumped, then.

Ice, here, as if the cold could be transmitted by touch, and perhaps it could. "Brother," he said quietly, his word for Meralonne alone.

The mage smiled, lips moving up in a rictus of emotion so alloyed with pain it was impossible to separate them. "Go."

He released the magi's hand, and then turned back. Speaking with the bardic voice, speaking with a fury of something that he had thought himself beyond, he said a single word.

"Live."

Eight names. Eight names.

Had he been stupid? They were eight, and he had thought that number high, and it had been weeks ago—but he had not thought that those eight would be part of this nine. And why?

Because the names had been taken in Annagar; of that he was certain. They had been taken, and they had been given back, to the Lady. To *his* Lady.

Over the years, he had come to peace, of a kind, with his life, and the death that would follow it. He had betrayed Her. He had betrayed his brothers. There was truth in it, but it was not so bitter now as it had been. He had come to peace, of a sort, because he had seen the demons, and he understood the whole of what they presaged.

Still, he knew when another brother became one with the *Kovaschaii*, for he was still one with them, in his fashion. And he knew when one died; that, too, was given to him. They dwindled, those that he had loved best, those that he had known.

Years had passed since he had been given a task such as this. Years, and the passage of time had dulled his senses, had given him a false security. One of his brothers was here, in the city. And somehow, although he did not understand the how of it, the Lady had given him permission to take those lives. She had refused it for the Kings, and for the Exalted; he knew it for fact. She had refused it for Valedan kai di'Leonne not once, but twice.

The stars were light and low above the seawall.

"Kallandras," she said, and he did not turn; he knew her voice, knew her age by it, knew everything he needed to know.

"Evayne."

"He is not finished yet," she said quietly. "He is not finished; they have come, and he will be given four names. Four names, and you will recognize all of them.

"I am not your master here. I have not come to order you; neither you nor I are what we were when we first set out upon this road."

He turned then, bitter, angry as he had not been angry for decades. "How generous of you, Evayne. Am I now so well-trained, to be trusted to kill my brothers without even the threat of the end of everything?"

She flinched; it surprised him into silence. They stood a long moment, the sea's waves gentle against the seawall.

"It is almost over," she said softly, with a bitterness to rival his own. "I thought we were beyond our beginnings." She raised a hand to the collar of the robes by which he—and any others of her victims—knew her best. "Three names, Kallandras; the fourth will take care of herself."

"Does it matter?" he asked, containing the emotion in the cold of the words. "Does it matter, if *he* walks the world? Have we not already failed?"

"We are alive. We are free. While these two things are true, there is no failure." And then she lifted her hands to her face, and he saw, in the moonlight, that her left was slick with blood.

"Where have you walked, Evayne?"

"Does it matter?" she said. "Your suffering is so much greater than mine, after all. You must meet again the men that you betrayed once, a lifetime ago—and I must meet anew people I have yet to betray. You loved your brothers, and your Lady—and I?

"I leave behind those that I barely know at all. Barely."

Rawness there, anger, and hurt, all rushing inward to fill a terrible, terrible emptiness. He had taken two steps before he could stop himself. *I am not what I was,* he thought, and knew it for truth. In his youth, he had had no pity.

"Where were you?" he said, and she said only one word, and because he was a bard, it was enough.

Askeyia.

He had heard the name before, once or twice, although he did not immediately remember from where. It didn't matter. The word itself was like a curse, a prayer, a darkness, and a secret; it was a wound that had scarred, that would scar, when it healed. If it healed.

She did not weep because she was far too old for weeping. But he heard the youth in her voice this eve, as he felt the youth in himself, tangled up with the mesh of experience and the certainty of necessity—and the terrible burden of guilt, the desire for peace.

What world, he thought, although he did not say it, *is worth this? What world can we leave behind that can justify what we have done, and what we have yet to do?*

Beyond the question itself, the answer came back over the hush of the sea's night lull: voices raised in merriment and in argument, in joy and in anger, in hope, in glee, and in momentary despair. Softer, but not completely hidden to a man who knew how to listen, the blend of those sounds as acts of love.

"Are you finished with me?" She tried to keep her voice as neutral as possible; it was hard. It was hard to speak at all. The day had been longer than she had thought possible and the end of it kept receding as she watched. She could barely believe that Duvari had no more use for her.

If she'd had the energy, she'd have been angry. Didn't.

Devon ATerafin looked up from the balcony; his hands tightened a moment on the simple stone rails. The only acknowledgment at all that he'd heard the question.

Daine and Avandar waited in the room at her back in the uncomfortable silence the domicis often produce with people who feel some need—no matter how slight—to converse politely. Avandar was worse than most. She wondered what he would be like as a man stripped of responsibility; she couldn't imagine that he would be any friendlier than Duvari.

Or Devon, this eve.

"ATerafin," she said.

"I am not the seer, Jewel. You are. You are the best judge of your duty here."

She waited; music was being played, and song sung end to end, out of sight of the balcony, but below it all the same. No night was a quiet one, not during the Challenge season. She had thought that somehow *Avantari* would be different; it was the Palace of Kings, and the Kings were dignity defined.

On the other hand, King Cormalyn at least was probably smart enough to cut his losses.

"Yeah," she said, speaking into the night. "I'm finished."

She turned, almost angry; moved too quickly. Must have.

She heard him say something, brushed his words away with

the heavy wave of a hand, took a step toward the doors and teetered there, on the edge of night.

And fell in.

The darkness when she woke was alleviated by light, but the
light was gentle and soft-edged; the sleeping room of a rich or a
powerful woman might be lit in just such a fashion.

And she noticed it, too. Because when she woke out of nightmare, when she woke out of the grip of a dream that propelled
her through all levels of sleep and its nuance in her need to flee
it, the first thing she wanted was the light.

Avandar, who was no comfort in anything else, was a cold comfort in this; he came with light, either lamp or, on rare occasion,
open fire. He had, in the beginning, carried magelight—but she
took no warmth and no calm from its sight; things magical were
often no small part of the fears that drove her.

"Jewel," he said, and she realized the moment she heard the
voice that it *wasn't* Avandar who held the lamp aloft.

It wasn't Avandar because she wasn't in her room, her wing, or
her house. She was in a small room, in a small bed, with an open
window to her left; the window was her height, from the floor up,
and three times her width. Real glass, although two of the leaves
had been opened to the cool night air.

"Jewel," Devon said again, quietly.

She turned to look at him; he hovered in the doorway, and she
saw that his foot was almost, but not quite, across the threshold.
She pushed the bedclothes away and stood, shakily; important to
get her footing and keep it.

"Where am I?"

"You collapsed," he told her. "I had you carried down to the
healerie."

I carried you. She blinked. "This is part of the healerie?"

"It's a room reserved for convalescents. As you well know, the
healer himself does not attend everyone who enters." He lifted
the lamp; it illuminated the side of his face. "You called me," he
said softly.

"I was having a nightmare," she replied, equally quietly.

The silence was almost painful.

"No," he said again. "You called *me*."

She shrugged and looked away, to the open window. "Maybe,"
she said at last. "Where's Avandar?"

"He's outside the room. As is the young healer. The healer,

though, is wise enough to sleep. He would have come to you himself had you not called me."

"Devon," she said, "I can't trust you. You've told me as much in more words than I care to remember. And in less."

He said nothing in reply; she turned back to him, spread her hands out in front of her, palms up. "But I'm stupid. I *do* trust you. I don't know why."

"Why did you call me?"

Her eyes flickered, much as the lamplight did, off the side of his face. "We were down in the tunnels," she said, averting her gaze. But that wasn't the dream's point. "You need to get Meralonne."

"Meralonne is indisposed."

"I'm not kidding, Devon."

"Neither am I. At Dantallon's best guess, there's a greater chance that he perishes from the mage fevers than that he survives."

She reached up and cupped her face in her hands; sat back on the bed as if her legs wouldn't support her. "Mage fevers?" He started to explain, and she wanted the explanation, but she knew it wasn't the time or the place; he couldn't come. It didn't matter why.

"Why Meralonne?"

"I don't know. But there's—there's a demon somewhere, waiting for Valedan. I saw him."

"You . . . saw him?"

She nodded.

"What did he look like?"

"I don't know. We were too far beneath the surface; it was too damned dark. And I knew—I knew that if we could reach Meralonne, we'd be safe."

There was a long pause; a longer pause.

"Kiriel?" he said softly, almost—but not quite—hesitating. As if he knew that she was one of the den, and he was trying—damn him anyway—to leave her what little bit he could. He probably did know. Living as close to power as she did, she'd come to learn that nothing was secret. And nothing, not a single thing, was safe.

"Not Kiriel," Jewel replied. "I don't know why—but that was a death, and not the demon's. Not her."

He stood there, in the doorway, as if he were part of it. As if, Jewel thought suddenly, he had closed the world out for a moment, while he held light with which to banish nightmare. How could he offer her this and refuse her aid when she needed it so desperately? At last, he bowed, stiffly. Formally.

"Where, Jewel?"

"I don't know." And then, taking a deep breath, she added, *"the Challenge."* It came out of her as if it were a force of its own—and that force, all the strength she possessed. Good damned thing she'd already bent her knees enough to touch bed again, because she knew, by the distinctly wobbly feel to them, that they'd no longer support her weight.

"Sleep."

"But Meralonne—"

"Sleep, Jewel."

The damnable thing was that she was *so* tired. "But—"

"We'll take care of it."

She wanted, very badly, to ask him who *we* was. And for all she knew, she might have.

He did not tell her, not then and not later, that the moment she'd begun to speak in her hesitant, angry way—precious anger that, for all it stung—he'd *known* about the attempt on Valedan's life; did not tell her that he was certain he'd recognize both the site and the assassin if he saw either. Because, of course, the memory, murky and insubstantial as it was, wasn't his.

It wasn't cowardice on his part, although he examined his fear dispassionately before he at last set it aside. Caution dictated silence; he was silent. The Astari, after all, prized discretion highly.

He knelt, on stone and marble pattern, before the altar of the Mother's finest temple. The stone there was cool, shadowed as it was by ceilings so high it seemed easier for them to deny the sun. Or the moon, giver of thin, silver light, echo of brilliance.

How much of the life he'd lived was left him? He was certain there were memories that had slipped between his fingers, unanchored and examined by *Kialli,* so much flotsam and jetsam. Did it matter?

He knew who he was, and if he did not remember clearly all of the hows and whys, he was old enough to know that the memories that he did have, that he was as certain of as any man can be certain of anything, were not a simple truth; they had been shaded by years and the perspective of years, changing and growing as he did, aging as gracefully.

Ah, there. Footsteps; a heavy tread for a lighter foot. They came from the left of the altar, growing steadily louder as the arches above caught and echoed them in the silence of prayer.

"ATerafin," a young man said; he looked up as if only now aware of his presence. "The Exalted will see you now."

"I am honored," Devon replied.

The man bowed in return and waited patiently while Devon rose. Together they went into the hallowed chamber of the Mother's stronghold.

She was Exalted, and he was merely mortal; he knew it so completely the fact was like air: necessary, unavoidable. He knelt at once, and the posture made his earlier supplication at the altar look stiff and wooden, although he was certain it had been neither. This woman, with her eyes of gold and shoulders that appeared too slender to carry any but the flimsiest of weights carried burdens that even he, sworn to protect the Kings and die in their defense if need be, had never considered.

She wore no finery; she was not expected to speak publicly on this day, or the next, or the one after. But to say that she took her leisure was untrue; she was like the Kings. The finery that her public office demanded did not define her authority, as it did for so many of her priests or the patriciate; it merely underlined the obvious.

And yet, even so, she was tired.

"I have heard," she said softly, "that Meralonne APhaniel has fallen victim to the fevers."

He grimaced. "Truth."

"And I have heard that a young child has fallen victim to worse."

He bowed again. There was very, very little that the Kings knew that the Exalted did not.

"I have therefore taken the liberty of speaking with my brothers, the Exalted of Reymaris and the Exalted of Cormaris; we have begun our labor, but we fear—"

"I know," he said softly. "But the girl's body was completely destroyed." He would have looked away, but her eyes gave him no such permission. "It was the only way," he added softly, "and in truth there was very little—if anything—left. It will not rise again to be used against us."

"Then you have done well, ATerafin." She turned; the balcony doors were open and breeze trapped in the billow of pulled curtains. "The Exalted have acceded to the request of the Lord of the Compact to the best of our abilities."

"And will you then accompany the Kings' party to the Challenge?"

Her frown was slight, but it pained him nonetheless.

"It is not our way," she said softly, "to attend the Kings' Challenge; there are no healers on the field, and none allowed. Such an event is a throwback to the warriors' days."

"Men war," he countered softly. "It is our nature."

"Many things that are our nature are avoided. Dying," she added, with a sharp smile.

"In the end we can't avoid that."

"No. In the end." She folded her arms across her chest, and for that moment looked like a mother, not the Mother. "I have little patience for the games, but given the risk and the danger—and given the indisposition of Meralonne APhaniel and the unfortunate age of Sigurne Mellifas, I do not see that duty allows us any avenue of escape.

"You may tell Duvari that we will, indeed, attend."

He bowed. It was the only way to look away from her face.

"ATerafin."

He rose.

"Your other request has also been granted, but I will now confess that the daggers that we give—and the five bolts—are all that we can give. Member APhaniel is adept at arts considered ancient, even by the Churches, and the metal will not take the summer enchantment unless it is properly treated. The bolts," she added, "are of a tree that is only found twice a year, and only then by people who know how to look for ways that man does not walk.

"We pray," she said quietly, "for Member APhaniel's quick recovery."

"He is not the only mage, surely?"

She did not lie; such a stern woman had no need for subterfuge. "He is not the only mage," she agreed. "But the arts that he has made his speciality were considered of little use four hundred years ago; he has begun to teach, but only since the Henden fifteen years ago have any been willing to actually study what he offers.

"He says he has two apprentices who may—in ten years—be as competent as he."

They both knew what that meant.

He wondered, briefly, why Duvari had not chosen to impart that information to him.

But only briefly. It was impossible to distrust the daughter of the Mother; it was almost as difficult to trust a man like Duvari. Especially if you were one of the magi; Duvari was notorious in his suspicion for and distrust of mages.

As had Devon been, once.

Kallandras of Senniel was waiting for him when he at last returned to the office, carrying his precious burden. He lifted a pale brow as the ATerafin dropped his ungainly sack across the desk's surface.

"I see," he said wryly, "that ornamental chests are in short supply this Challenge season. And," he added, eyeing the rumpled but sturdy sack, "that the Mother is more practical than the officials who serve the Kings."

"More merciful," Devon replied, with a quick flash of teeth. "Neither she nor the officials have to carry either burden—but she's aware of the weight regardless." Magelight, as even and smooth as a patch of cloudless sun, washed the room in a color close enough to green that it was clear Patris Larkasir economized where he could; moonlight had been denied by the pull of heavy curtains.

Kallandras slid off the perch the desk's surface provided, sliding his palms forward slightly. He didn't bother to ask what Devon ATerafin carried; it wasn't necessary. Beneath the momentary amusement, he heard urgency. They had little time.

"You sent a message to Solran. She sent me."

"Yes."

"In what capacity, ATerafin, do you wish my services?"

"Is there any question?" He unknotted the sack. Reached in. Pulled out an ornamental dagger, a heavy, awkward, jeweled display piece. His eyes rested on the scabbard as if caught by the finery there. As if.

"Devon," Kallandras said quietly.

The man he knew as Astari closed his eyes a moment. "Meralonne is indisposed," he said at last.

"I know it. He sent for me."

Gaze flickered off gemstone, like tongue of flame. "Is he as bad as they say?"

"Yes. Possibly worse."

"Do you know what the full implications of his death would be?"

"No," Kallandras said, certain by the question that he didn't. "Does it matter?"

Devon said nothing for a long moment. When he spoke again, Kallandras heard something familiar in his voice; an edge that reminded him that the Astari *were* weapons. "Valedan kai di'Leonne faces death at the test of the sea."

The master bard looked down to the knife that had become, in Devon's hands, that rarest of things: perfectly still. So had the ATerafin. "The Astari?"

"They watch," he said softly, "but it is not the duty of the Astari to protect a foreign monarch—or pretender. They watch the Kings."

"And you?"

"I watch the boy; he is, after all, of interest to the Kings and their future security." Light, that. Light and easy, said without inflection. Without passion.

Devon ATerafin was a silent man; a still one. He had better control of his speaking voice than most bards, and he gave little away, save when he chose to do so. Kallandras had rarely seen him unguarded. But if he was neutral by choice, unknowable by discipline, he was a man whose convictions could be felt.

It comes, he thought, *to the boy. To Valedan kai di'Leonne.* "Very well, ATerafin," he said quietly. "Arm me. Arm us both. The dawn is scant hours away, and I am not a youth, to forgo sleep with ease."

"Before the Challenge?"

"By the basin, yes." He rose. Made his way to the balcony the curtains obscured. As his hands touched the material, drawing it noiselessly to one side, he heard his name. He turned his head, acknowledging it.

But the ATerafin seemed to have lost his thought, or to have decided the better of offering it for inspection; silence fell, uninterrupted, as he left.

CHAPTER TWENTY-ONE

20th day of Lattan, 427 AA
Averalaan Aramarelas

Sun.

Light on the waves as bright and pale as platinum, the wind in lull. It was unseasonably cool an hour past dawn, which meant it was bearable to the men who stood waiting. At the break of dawn, the officiants—among them the Kings themselves—had in solemnity and gravity declared the start of the day's events. An hour had drifted away, and it was a rare hour indeed, in the company of speech makers and men whose identity was defined by their clothing, that passed with so little boredom on his part.

Golden-eyed, the Kings were called demon-born in the South— but Valedan thought their eyes very like gold, the sun's metal; he could not countenance them as demons of any nature.

But Valedan kai di'Leonne was only one among many.

The Kings had made their speeches, offered their salutes, granted their permission, and the procession had moved from *Avantari* to the edge of the docks themselves—or rather, the boardwalk which led to the docks. These docks were short and squat; low to water, unlike those used by the famed vessels of the Empire. Wide and solid, they were kept for the purpose of the Kings' leisure: Swimming, fishing in small vessels, watching the sunrise with nothing at all between water's reflection and vision. Valedan had seldom seen wood so rich in color and so seemingly new that had obviously weathered decades; the work of the mage-born, no doubt.

He hadn't long to marvel or to wonder; the contestants formed up across the length of the boardwalk, waiting, waiting. His guards and his watchers outnumbered them.

"We cannot protect you here," Baredan had said. "Forgo this test."

His eyes flitting across the mages who patrolled the water in little vessels that moved as if oared by madmen—none of whom were visible—he spoke to his first General. "And will I forgo the marathon as well? Without either, I have no hope of winning."

"This isn't the war, Valedan; it's a battle. At this early stage, we can afford to lose everything but you."

"We've had this conversation before," Valedan replied.

As Baredan had not expected to have an effect, he bowed stiffly in the morning's light. He turned his head to either side, counting and taking the measure of the men who had been chosen to guard the kai Leonne—although he knew both number and measure well enough by now.

Ser Anton's students were in evidence, but the threat they presented had nothing to do with their scant abilities in this challenge. A mage had been stationed by their retinue, and they were "protected" by several of the Kings' Swords.

Ser Anton did not appear to notice; Carlo was actively annoyed. He was so much like an Osprey in temperament that Valedan wondered if he'd truly been culled from the South at all.

"Third heat."

Valedan nodded at Commander Sivari's words. They weren't necessary, but he found the sound and tone a comfort. Here, the challenge was simple: Swim from the isle to the mainland and back. Quickly. The javelin had served him well; the water, he hoped, would serve him well again. In this test, neither far North or South were well-served by their natural environs. Not so the heartlanders, as the citizens of the strip of land that surrounded Averalaan liked to call themselves; oceans and rivers in the center of the Empire, especially here at its heart, were warm and calm. Swimming was a pastime of leisure; if a swimmer were pressed, it was also an activity that welcomed practice, and it rewarded skill over bulk or muscle—although muscle and skill combined would almost of necessity win.

Valedan cast a glance at Eneric, and the Northern barbarian waved, his hands splayed wide in an open palm gesture that was not unlike flailing.

He, too, was in the third heat.

Fifteen men stepped forward onto the lowest portion of the boardwalk. No seawall here; the seawall fortified the eastern edge of the isle, petering out to either edge. Behind each stood their chosen witness and a single trainer; the witness watched, and the trainer waited to receive the clothing they wore. They stripped to skin beneath the sun's glare. Only one of them appeared to find it amusing, and Valedan was immediately embarrassed for those women he knew with certainty were witness to the event. The man's companions in this swim maintained their dignity and their seriousness, ignoring him and each other. Or trying to.

The judges counted.

Numbers had been one of the first things that Valedan had learned in this land of the two Kings, the demon-kings, the golden-eyed scions of foreign gods. Numbers, spoken with painstaking care, a finger and a toe at a time, under the watchful eye of both his mother and the Serra Alina.

Counting.

He watched the fifteen. Wondered if the water were cold, although he knew it would not be.

The judges counted, and he counted, in Weston, in silence.

Time.

The first man to break water in this event was also the man whose sense of play had seemed so out of place. Obviously dignity wasn't everything.

He crossed his arms. Set his lips. Watched.

They searched.

They searched in silence, and they searched in a quiet of simple movement as they slid through the crowds that the city, high and low, had assembled for the benefit of the challenge of the sea. Neither man was particularly modest; modesty was a profession of incompetence.

Devon ATerafin chose the lower city boardwalks as his hunting ground. He did not choose to explain his choice, and Kallandras did not choose to question it, although it was clear that the lower city was by far the more difficult terrain. For one, the boardwalks were wider and rougher, and the Kings' men had less visible control over the crowd that had gathered, in high spirits and with not a little money riding on the outcome, to watch the sea's test. No man gave up his place easily, and few moved with anything like the normal social graces that accompanied movement in a crowded city street—and there were few enough of those when the heat was high. Worse still, there was *no room* for fighting, and if a fight occurred, not only the enemy would die. Life would be lost drawing sword in the cramped spaces people made for themselves.

But Devon seemed comfortable with his choice, and Kallandras, measuring the Astari carefully, nodded. He preferred the open space to the closed one, although death was death: In either open space, with a full-run hunt, or in close quarters with barely room to lift a wrist, Kallandras of Senniel, who had once been somewhat different in the Lady's service, had no difficulty killing.

But he thought that Devon would have no difficulty in a similar situation; the Astari trained their own, and well—and in arts other than death's. Or so it was said. He knew better than to ask.

He carried Salla with him; it was a risk that he was loath to take, but he could see little way around. As a favored bard of Queen Marieyan—and as the foremost master bard of Senniel College—he was given leave to wander as if he had been born to the patriciate's heights, but to wander without a lute was to be uncrowned in front of a people that expected a King. Important, in games like this, not to disappoint expectation.

And therefore, he was polite, friendly, peaceful, and soothing by turns; he offered attention to one and all with a fealty to song and festivity that rose above the boundary of nation or competition. He was aware of the two Morniel master bards, and the single master bard from Attariel, and he coaxed a duet from both.

But he kept it as short as possible; the sweetness of voices so intertwined, so inseparable, was a special type of pain all its own—and he could not afford that distraction now.

He made his way slowly, from the full width of the well-kept stone streets to the flawless boardwalk, his hair beneath the brim of a wide, round hat that hid nothing but his cheeks from the slowly rising sun. He cataloged faces, adding names to them where names were appropriate: Northerners, their champions, their trainers, their witnesses; Southerners—all; and the men and women from the heartlands, some of whom called this city at the center of the world their home.

And all was as it should be.

The sun cast long shadows at dawn and dusk; any good bard knew that such shadows as these were both protection from the sun's lack of mercy and a negation of its light. Double-edged, like a Northern weapon; he wondered briefly what the Southerners used as a metaphor for just such a thing. If they did, at all.

And he had the time to wonder.

The Kings, he gave nod to; the Queens he actually stopped a moment to bow before. Queen Marieyan laughed when he sang a quiet chorus beneath her ancient chair. Of all the women of power

he'd met in his life, she was the woman whose laughter he most
enjoyed evoking; he wasn't certain why.

But the Queen Siodonay the Fair chased him off, and rightly;
his cheek would be noted, and no doubt less fortunate and far
more callow youths would attempt such familiarity without the
background and history needed to serve as root and platform.

It weeds them out, he would often tell the Queens. He did not
say it now, not surrounded as he was by so many callow youths,
half of them near naked, all of them eager for the chance to prove
themselves. Or to prove themselves worthy, as if this—a swim
across the bay—could in fact do that.

And should he criticize?

After all, to prove himself worthy, had he not, instead, quietly
taken a life?

He felt no shame in it now, but no unearthly joy; it was a fact
of his life, the edges of it, and the sharpness, lost to youth. He
shifted, restless, and caught sight of Valedan kai di'Leonne again,
but there was nothing out of place, nothing amiss, in either the
boy or his entourage.

The boardwalks could do, Devon thought, with a thorough cleaning. To start: the people could be swept aside and into the bay itself. Then the merchants' stalls—most illegal, and he would know,
given the office at which he worked—and the wandering acrobats
who played so artfully with fire.

He had half expected that they would turn up as demons or
kin—for legends were explicit in the duplicity of fire, and the
way the kin were drawn to it. But each and every such entertainer
had proved to be merely that: entertainment. Passing entertainment, when one could back out of the crowd and escape it.

He heard the splash of the first heat hitting the water almost to
a man, and he felt the whole of his body stiffen, although the
noise was lost quickly to the cheering, whistling, and jeering of
the crowd itself, speaking with so many tongues, so many voices,
so many purposes that language and meaning were almost lost.

He swept the boardwalk in a great semicircle, flattened himself to the side as a merchant's wagon, with its suspiciously
Southern draft horses, muscled its way through the crowd by implied threat of trampling. Not that the horses themselves were
likely to be such a menace, but they were restive and ill-pleased
at their surroundings, and they had the advantage of height and
size to add to their perceived threat.

He wandered there, to the wagon, where the merchant was setting up. Two large, dark-haired men barred his way with gleaming crescent swords. They would have looked down upon him, but he was of a height with the taller of the two, and not in the mood to underplay height for the sake of peace.

Besides which, these men were clearly from the Dominion and not likely to look kindly upon any peaceful overtures.

"Eh, Patris," the merchant said, standing and wiping his hands on the red-and-white silks that covered his body from head to toe. "Have you come to sample the wares of a simple merchant?"

"Simple? You are too modest," Devon replied dryly. He meant it: No merchant found their way here, *late,* on a day like today and made a space for themselves—without death or the threat of death, and he had seen neither—by being simple. And the merchant, for his affected joviality and his large, unassuming proportions, did not look like the sort of man who arranged favor by the simple expedience of popularity.

There was something about this man that was familiar.

He cursed himself, because he did not know *why.* Devon ATerafin had no false modesty: he was one of the best members the Astari had ever produced or trained. And he had no false pride: He *had been* one of the best.

Now, his memory splintered and fragmented by the death-throes of a demon, he didn't know why the man was familiar: was he spy? Assassin? Friend? Had he been used by Devon in some fashion in the past, or had he been warned against him?

Or had he been somehow essential to the plans of the *Kialli* who had died at the thrust of a dagger? For it was the shadow memories of the creature that drove him now. He shook himself.

The merchant laughed. "Heat," he said.

"Spice, rather," Devon replied neutrally, as what little breeze there was stirred the scents of a few—a very few—open jars. "Your wares are potent."

"And expensive," the man agreed with a deep, dry smile. "But you are attired like a man who is destined to be a customer."

Meaning, of course, that he knew enough about cloth and cut on sight to know money when he saw it. "We are not without such niceties on the isle."

"Oh-ho, and you a man of the isle! Come, then; no doubt, you recognize the finest of wares, and I have them in abundance. No simple bay leaves, no basil and cloves, no sweet greenery here."

"Pedro," one of the two guards said.

The merchant froze, half-word already formed on his lips. "What?"

Speaking in fluent, bass heavy Torra, the guard said, "The second heat is stepping out onto the boardwalk."

"What of it," the merchant replied, in Torra that was arid as the deserts. "I am on the trail of money, you fool, and I'm not to be interrupted. Tell me only if something interesting happens." He frowned. Added quickly, "Or if that Northerner—Eneric, I think—is losing. You're paid to watch my money after all."

With a smile that was all teeth and little eye, he turned back to Devon. "Pedro di'Jardanno at your service, Patris."

"Devon ATerafin," Devon replied. "I am the second to Patris Larkasir, a man whose name—if you are so well renowned—you must have heard."

The merchant's smile dimmed; Devon doubted that it would ever gutter entirely, it was so patently nailed to his face. "That would be—"

"Yes. The lord who oversees the traders' commission, among other offices."

"Well, sir, you can see—"

"Your fine wares, yes. Please."

Something here, he thought. *Something.* He tensed as the merchant's hands disappeared from view, relaxed as two stoppered flasks were brought forward in the shade of the wagon's awning. But in that moment, between tension and its uneasy death, revelation. Not here, the death. Not here.

He turned as the cries and shouts of the crowd grew louder. The second group of men was approaching the seawall.

It was much past dawn when she woke, but it might as well have been midnight; the shadows were strong. Strong as this, and what woke her was the sensation that she couldn't *breathe.* She woke gasping and flailing. She woke to Avandar's face. It was the only thing about the room that was familiar; his face, and the lamp he carried. Where he'd gotten the lamp from, she wasn't certain; magelights were far more common in the castle itself than lamps and what lamps there were weren't idly picked up and carried off. But he was Avandar. He was good at some things.

She was already sitting, but that didn't last long; she lost all feeling in her legs and sort of slid down, down, down, until her face was in her knees and the world was white, thin silk.

He waited impassively, having learned over time that touching her in any way was not acceptable; there were dreams she had to struggle out of on her own.

"Jewel?"

She shook her head, trying to find enough air to speak with. "It's bad," she said at last, doubled over, into the bed itself.

You could always count on Avandar to have good hearing. It was rarely useful, but you could always count on it.

"It's daylight," he said. "The Challenge has already started."

"Can we stop it?" Gods, this was humiliating. But at least the satin was smooth against her cracked lips. She turned her head to the side, so that she could see Avandar's midriff, robed and covered as it was.

"No."

"We need Meralonne," she said then.

"Out of the question, Jewel. Devon made it clear—and Dantallon made it *quite* clear—that the mage is not to be disturbed."

"We need him," she said again.

"If rumors are true, he's going to be far less useful than you are now."

"Help me up."

He was silent. And still.

"Avandar, we're going to fail if we don't get to Meralonne. Help me up!"

Without another word—although she had to admit that his strongest disapproval was reserved for his silences—he put both hands under her armpits and hauled her into a more-or-less sitting position. She was still wearing the clothing she'd come in, thank Kalliaris, although her feet were bare. She lifted her arms to slide them round his neck for support, but they tingled and ached enough that they wouldn't quite connect at the hands. She was one step up from dead weight.

"Where are we going?"

"How the Hells should I know? You're the man who notices everything—take me to where Meralonne APhaniel is. Now."

Valedan heard the cries of time cross the ocean from mainland to isle as if they were a sentence. He had first learned to count in Weston.

She had taught him that, the Serra.

The Princess had taught him to speak. It seemed natural to him then, to be surrounded by women—even if the women were strange and harsh and not at all the graceful, hidden creatures of his father's harem, not the beauties for which the harem was famous.

But he could remember, if he tried, a time before Weston; a time when the language of foreigners was the buzzing of malignant, demonic spell. Even after he'd lost that fear, he could hear it as taunt, as control that he could not wrest away from the speaker.

He felt that now, as he stood.

Felt it as Sivari touched his shoulder, wordlessly, and pointed to the boardwalk and the grim-faced, sun-darkening officials. He did not wear armor, not this day, and he knew that he was being asked to strip down to what he might swim in—but he did not wish to surrender any of his clothing to the sun.

Because, of course, he did not wish to be exposed.

"Valedan kai di'Leonne," he heard a man say, the pronunciation hard and workmanlike.

The Third Heat began to form up, a line of fifteen men.

"Valedan?" A small voice—a foreign voice—said.

He looked down and met the eyes of his too-red, too-young witness. Forced himself to smile. "Yes?"

"I think they've called you twice now."

He didn't bother to add that there were only three calls.

"I can—I can hold your stuff for you. I won't let anyone else touch it."

That wasn't the duty of a witness, but the offer calmed him. "I'd be honored," he said gratefully. Because he knew, in so saying, he would also confer honor. The boy seemed unnaturally proud of his position, whatever it meant. Witness.

And he could take the time—quickly, quickly—to add to this boy's joy. Because he had indirectly added to his sorrow. Balance. He ungirded himself of sword, and handed the weapon to Aidan, who managed, just barely, to look as if its weight were insignificant.

Stepping up to the line, he pulled himself free of his tunic, his underclothing, his boots. And then he turned, because he couldn't help it, to see Eneric. The Northerner smiled broadly, as if the gravity of the situation were entirely foisted upon him and none of it his own making. He stepped out of line, while the officiants were not looking, and for one moment, Valedan thought he was going to piss in the ocean.

He was shocked.

The other Northerner in the heat laughed, and that drew attention; Eneric stepped back into the fold as if he had never left it.

"Get ready," the officiant rumbled. He lifted the Kings' flag.

Kallandras saw them line up, and he almost called Valedan back. But the boy wouldn't come; that much was clear. He had found nothing, seen nothing, that indicated the presence of an assassin, and the one he most feared to meet, he knew for fact was not present on these grounds.

But he knew that Devon ATerafin had not found the death he feared either. And they had very, very little time.

The second heat straggled in from isle to mainland, and then, spinning and using the seawall as a launch, propelled themselves back, back to the beginning of their quest for recognition in this challenge: the boardwalk itself.

At the far end, the third heat was preparing itself for the waters; a breeze was toying with them, but it was a weak one.

"A fair day," the merchant said, "for such a task as this."

He nodded, force of habit strong enough to carry him when inclination failed. They were too late. He knew they would be too late.

They had set a dragon at the door of Meralonne's secluded room, but Avandar Gallais didn't recognize her. Old, silvered, her skin wreathed in lines, she seemed frailty defined—and perhaps she was, in some other dream or delirium, some life that wasn't this one.

Age and a certain irascibility could destroy elegance and grace, and certainly it destroyed the patina of power by which so many men made their name. But it did not daunt the mage Sigurne Mellifas, born a commoner, bred a commoner, and raised half a childhood to be victim. She had risen above too much to fall back to it, and age was not the indignity that a gentler life might have made it.

Still, she looked mildly surprised as the would-be visitor appeared, carried in the arms of her domicis like so much dead weight. It forestalled some of her grimness, and removed the edge from the set of her lips.

"I should tell you," she said softly, "that Member APhaniel is in no fit condition to see anyone."

"Except that I'm not either?"

She smiled rarely; she smiled now. "He is fitful; he wakes seldom, and when he wakes, we *must* use that time to feed him."

"Understood," Jewel said, forcing what strength she could find into her voice. It wasn't much. "But I'm Jewel ATerafin," she continued.

"The Terafin adviser. We've met."

"Then you understand that when I say I must speak to Meralonne or a man will die, I mean it, and know it for fact."

"And if you speak to him," Sigurne replied, "do you know for fact that a man *won't* die?"

"We can never know that for fact, but—"

"Jewel," Avandar said, interrupting her. "She speaks of Member APhaniel."

"Oh."

Sigurne frowned, but the frown was mild. "I will see if he wakes," she said reluctantly. "Follow me."

They did, or rather, Avandar did; Jewel came by default since he apparently had no intention of putting her down.

The magi was not awake. He was not asleep either; he was in that fitful, restless state a sick man hovers in, neither here nor there. Sigurne had folded her arms across her slender chest, which was comment enough in itself, but fell just short of order: She knew who Jewel ATerafin was. She knew what she did. She knew Meralonne well enough to know that this particular visitor could not be protected against.

"Meralonne," Jewel said, struggling with her voice. Struggling to sit up. Again, only marginally louder, "Meralonne." She looked up at the underside of Avandar's chin. "Put me down," she said.

"Let me wake him."

"You know the rules, Avandar. Put me down."

He did, upon the edge of the sick man's bed, crossing his chest with his arms in a brooding parody—an accidental one, Jewel was certain—of Sigurne Mellifas' pose.

She touched his face.

His eyes snapped open at once.

"NO!" she said, and it *was* loud. "It's *me*, Meralonne. It's Jewel!"

Nothing changed but the sense of imminent death. His eyes were wide. "What . . . brings you . . . here? This is not a . . . safe place for a . . . young woman to be."

His hand was on her wrist.

She swallowed. Jewel ATerafin hated to be touched, and especially not like this: the fevered grip of an insanely strong man was very difficult to break. She endured. Had to. "It's Valedan," she said softly. "They're hunting him."

He started to rise. Fell back.

"Meralonne," Sigurne said, speaking for a moment like a Guard Captain and not a member of the magi.

"Ah, the lovely Sigurne. Who hunts him?"

She hesitated before speaking. "Kin," she said at last. "Devon is out looking for them. But—"

"Where is Valedan?"

It was Avandar who answered.

The last of the men were hauled out of the water; there were two who gave out in mid-passage and had had to be rescued by boat.

The flag, faltering in a breeze that was not quite strong enough to lift its weighted end, came up in a strong hand. Valedan let his arms drop to his side; let his muscles, shoulders, and back relax. He bent at the knees, feeling the bend itself, sinking into the posture. Breathing.

"The challenge of the sea?"

"Yes. The magi are out in force, patrolling the waters *and* the crowds. But they aren't going to find whatever it is, and it'll kill him." Wasn't a doubt in the words because she had no doubt; she had seen it, had been woken from dream by it, had humiliated herself by asking for Avandar's aid—as if he were her father—to get here to say it.

"Get Sioban," he said urgently to Sigurne Mellifas. "Now. Get her now."

"But—"

"Sigurne."

She left.

"What?" Jewel said, as she lay in his shadow, the length of his hair across her arm as smooth and soft as if fever had no purchase there.

He looked exhausted, far paler than she had ever seen him, and he was not a man whose skin took to sun at all. But his eyes, gray as steel, were clear, and his words, heavy with weariness, surprisingly cogent.

"You need my knowledge of the kin," he gasped, struggling for shallow breath. "It must be knowledge that I have, and that others do not possess; the summonings are against our law and against our edicts of study." He closed his eyes then. "If it is studied, we are doomed, and if we do not study, we are doomed.

"Choose your doom, Jewel," he said softly.

"Tell us."

The flag fell.

The men dove.

Water was broken by the fall of their bodies, the clean position of arms and hands, the thrust of their feet.

Sioban Glassen had come at a run; Sigurne, she had left behind at the moment she'd been given the summons. She knelt by the bed, her face red from exertion, her expression at odds with it. "Member APhaniel," she said.

He was silent a long moment, and then he said, "Call Kallandras."

She started to speak; he raised a hand. "No—do not summon him here; we will lose. Tell him only this, tell him quickly:

"A handful of the *Kialli*, to the best of our knowledge, do not need to breathe."

Her brow creased. "This is an emergency?"

"Please, Bardmaster. Master Bard." He sunk back then, and his grip on the arm of the youngest woman in the room finally failed. But she knew, as it did, that some part of what he had said had been, in fact, a lie.

"Kallandras, it's Sioban."

"I'm here."

"Meralonne APhaniel bids me tell you this: Some of the *Kialli* do not need to breathe. If it's useful, you have to tell me how over a good, stiff drink."

He was already in motion. The first words she'd spoken sank roots and then spines, drawing his blood from heart to surface like metal shavings to magnet. He was not of an age with the competitors, but he knew—who better?—how to move silently, quietly, *quickly*. As he raced across the boardwalk, he spoke, and the words carried to only one man.

The water was in his ears, and it buzzed and tickled.

"Do not stop swimming, kai Leonne."

He recognized the voice; it was the bard's voice. Kallandras of

Senniel. A man he trusted, and had reason to trust, for all his magical ability.

It might have cost him time, to hear the words, to process them, to recognize their speaker; but it carried command, to continue, and he did.

"No matter what you see, below or to the side, your duty and your challenge is to pass the test of the sea."

He cut the water like a knife.

Felt it, bracing in its sudden chill, as salt reminded him of the day-to-day scrapes and scratches that were normally beneath his notice. He carried—like a pearl diver—a single blade, but there was no blunt edge to take hold of between his teeth; he held the handle.

The bay was not shallow. Fishing villages along the coast had sand bars and whole stretches in which a man might wet no more than his knees for braving water—but the waters around the isle and the bay itself were not so gentle. They were clear as far as the eye could see.

The eye, in this case, couldn't see far enough.

The sand beds weren't flat; there were rocks here, large and smooth, which overlapped and stood atop each other. He cast his glance in two directions, first up, to where the swimmers passed above him, their bodies floating in a layer of water that seemed, from his vantage, clear and white, like liquid light. Beneath him, as he turned his gaze down, the rocks, and their shadows, a darkness cast by lack of light in the ponderous movement of water.

He started to swim up for air, and felt a stab of pain. His hand. His left hand.

In the element of water, the elemental ring was sun seen through diamond, made painful by the lulling shadows of the ocean. He grimaced. Grimaced and understood the call of air. He did not hesitate; he drew breath, and water did not pass his lips.

The air had claimed him, after all.

Clutching the knife in hand, he began to swim in the water beneath the swimmers, pacing them as he could. Guarding them.

Had he been in the element to which he'd been trained, he would have been in no danger at all, but movement in water was different. What he could see—and he *could* see, for night was as much a part of his training as day had been, and the light here was much like it—he could react to. But his reaction time was *wrong*.

And because of it, he could not turn and face the enemy that passed by him like a shadow—not quite.

Sharp pain, stinging salt, and a billow of murky cloud.

The cry went up from the isle.

Blood. Cormaris' Crown—there's blood in the water!

Devon heard it, heard the voices that carried it; they stood out in a shrill, a sharp relief against the blurred murmur of the crowd. What the watchers saw, the crowd would see soon enough.

He tensed slightly, but even in this proved true to his own training; the glance that he cast toward the merchant, Pedro, was furtive. And it was unseen.

The merchant's face had gone smooth as fine steel; he was as tense as Devon, and as casually nonchalant about it as a man with much practice could be.

"Your pardon, Merchant," the ATerafin said quietly, bowing. "But it seems there's to be some unauthorized form of excitement this Challenge, and I for one am curious."

"You've money riding on it?" the merchant asked.

"And more," Devon replied.

He made his way to the seawall, and no one—although the crowd was thick with bodies large and small—attempted to stop him.

He adjusted.

This was at the foundation of every lesson he had ever learned: flexibility. He took no time to argue with the facts, or to panic because they did not correspond to what he knew; they were facts. He had been cut to bone, and had he been slower—had he, in fact, been one of the swimmers above—he would be dead from the casual strike of a claw that seemed almost invisible in the water's swirl.

Or not.

The ring seared his flesh as the claw had cut it. Like a slap across the face, it braced him, cleared a vision obscured by too much water.

He could see, in the movement of the current above him, and in the blood that eddied within it, the slender figure of a creature that seemed made of glass. Glass—sharpened, streamlined.

There were no rocks beneath his feet. But the ring was on his hand, and he felt it burning there; he leaped up into water as if, for a moment, it were air.

* * *

The blood caught his attention because he had to swim *through* it. There was a moment, a single moment at which the men to his right and left gave ground at the shock, and to his shame, Valedan kai di'Leonne did not. He passed by it, thinking of the seawall, of the rise and fall of his arms, the straight line of his leg, toe to knee, the way his limbs sliced water with as little resistance as possible.

He didn't have to think of breathing; breathing came naturally. He didn't pray. He didn't wonder whose blood it was. He swam.

Just as Kallandras had . . . asked.

Devon saw the kai Leonne break ahead of the heat; it surprised him. Eneric was not favored to win this challenge, but he was a strong swimmer for a Northerner, and he had stuttered a moment. Four of the fifteen had—the four who were swimming in blood.

Whose blood?

He jumped up to the seawall's height and stared down at the waves not ten feet below. The desire to order Valedan out of the water—to order them all out of the water—was strong; so, too, was the knowledge that to use that authority, for he had it, was to expose himself to the merchant who also watched and waited.

Valedan, he thought.

And then, *whose blood?*

The creature was a water creature, or so it seemed to Kallandras; it moved with the easy grace of something familiar with water's lift and weight. It had a face; the lines of eyes, of high cheeks, of slender face and long jaw, could be made out as if the movement of light had been caught in just those places and frozen there. It also had two arms, two legs, and a swirling cloak that seemed made of the water itself.

At any other time, it might have looked like a man, displaced by an element, and handsome for it.

But it was death, merely death, and he was not yet ready to face his Lady; not this way.

The creature raised a glass brow. "You *are* impressive," it said mockingly, the words more of a sensation than a sound. He cast a glance upward, to the receding bodies of the swimmers above, and then to the shore.

When he smiled, he froze water. Or he should have. "They will take their time returning," he said lazily. "Come, then. Come and play."

Kallandras was prepared, this time, for the sudden, swift motion of the creature. After fifteen years together, he and the ring had an uneasy understanding of each other's limits—but it was imperfect. He moved before the creature did, and the water sizzled at his hand. But the pain was gone; he thought the price the ring would exact would not be too high this day.

If he survived.

Survival was everything. He took a breath; the air was so sharp, so sudden in its rush he might have been flying—or falling.

He gave himself over to the dance, to the fight.

Valedan touched rock and rolled, head over foot and side to side, aiming himself at the isle. He was arrow straight by the time the movement was finished, his hands above his head in a point, the tops of his feet flush with the line of his leg. Someplace between touching the rock and using it to give himself momentum, he cleared the water enough to take in the air.

He did not hear the roar of the crowd, or the hush of it. He did not see the ATerafin who stood upon the wall itself.

But he saw, clearly, in the depths of the water below, a man whose voice he had heard before he touched water this day: Kallandras of Senniel.

Not all of the men who had been granted permission to enter the Kings' Challenge entered all events. It meant, of course, that if they won the single event, they claimed the crown for that event—but they could not win the title of Champion, regardless of how they progressed in the events they chose as their own.

Ser Anton di'Guivera had, after some minor consultation with his students, chosen two men to face the test of the sea. These two: Andaro and Carlo. Carlo had, after all, come from the Averdan lands closest to the waters, and knew them well enough to have taken some boyhood ease there.

They stood on the edge of the pier, watching; they witnessed the sudden spill of pale crimson rise up, as if carried by the dying gasp of some huge, unseen creature, from the ocean's depths.

If it gave them pause, they showed nothing; it was not in their nature, and their training—in this, Carlo was acceptable—was to deny any display of weakness, such as surprise.

But when the man rose, bleeding, from the water's surface, shedding salt and sea and blood as if all liquid were one thing, one of the two men froze in place.

The adjudicator bid them hold at once; the mages—and the mages were ever-present, turned in their crafts of heavy wood, their hands raised as shields and weapons, the words breaking their silence, leaving their lips, in much the same way as the man broke water.

Wood splintered and shattered in that moment.

Screams now. Screams that did not quite carry to the men who, trapped in the third heat, toiled under cloudless sun and shadow.

The man who rose fell, his flight cut short by some ill wind.

The Southerners understood better than any the caprice and the malice of the wind. But Carlo cried out to his brother, lifting a bronze arm.

Ser Anton followed the direction of that pointed hand, and he saw—as Carlo did, curse the quickness of his vision—the water creature that stood, momentarily, like a pillar in the air. Easy enough, to miss such a creature; easy enough to assume that the water had risen in the wake of the bleeding man.

Easy enough, Ser Anton thought grimly, for a student that he had not trained.

The man broke water again, and behind them all—behind the standing tableau of fifteen naked or near-naked men, the Kings' men were coming, their voices both raised and controlled, army voices. Fighting voices.

He shaded his eyes against the sun's light; looked beyond the dispersing blood and the gush of breaking bubbles to see that the front-runner, the man by far in the lead in this contest, was indeed the kai Leonne.

Helpless target. Unarmed.

With just this ease, he thought, cold in the summer's heat, the fight was over. He had all but vowed that it would be *his* hand that ended the line; had, in fact, were he honest, vowed it.

He felt no anger as he contemplated the death; no heat. Just the chill, perhaps of water, perhaps of true night.

He was slow; that was it. Slow, his gaze turned to the interior landscape and not the exterior; the battle within and not the slaughter without. Whatever held his attention, it kept him from seeing the obvious until it occurred.

Carlo di'Jevre broke the line that comprised the fourth heat. He spun, neatly, took five steps, kicked aside the robes and the tunic that passed for Northern modesty as if he couldn't stand the sight of them. He bent, turned, faced the water again, and leaped.

Ser Anton cried out. Andaro cried out. Both voices blended in words of denial that only the water heard.

Carlo di'Jevre had taken his sword into the watery domain.

He had never enjoyed the kill.

That was the truth, and it was the assassin's truth: Men who enjoyed the kill too much were wed to the death, not the Lady, and the Lady was jealous by nature. Such men as those, she did not take in, and if she did, she did not keep; they joined a different brotherhood, and served a darker purpose. In the darkness of sun striated by the movement of heavy water, he remembered that truth.

And although he couldn't afford it, he remembered more: The tenth time he had woken in the night at the brotherhood's home in the deep South. One of the soft-spoken boys he had—hesitantly—allowed himself to become close to, lay awash in so much blood the silks and the mats couldn't swallow it quickly enough.

All that was left of the moment following it were impressions. Hand on a dagger, in the darkness. Dripping, bloody dagger. Lamp, poor light, on a face. Another boy's. Grimness there, and deep satisfaction. That boy, like Kallandras, had been taken off the streets of a Southern city, a place where a seraf was not quite a seraf, and a clansman not quite free. Then.

Now.

The *Kialli* moved, sensing the things that the bard could keep off his face, out of his movements, out of his voice entirely—but never, never out of his thoughts. It was a mercy, to strike at him, if not an ease; it had been years since he called upon the power of Myrrdion's ring. Years since it had called upon him, and he was comfortable with its absence.

The creature moved lazily out of his way.

So, too, had that young man moved. Lazily. Easily.

He waited, with that dagger, with that death. The masters had come, bearing light to alleviate night's cover. They witnessed the work of the boy they had thought to take in, and to teach.

In silence, they had listened to his claim: *I have proved myself worthy of you.*

Kallandras felt the grieving anger that he had felt then, even now. That he had risen, from ground and mat-side, to speak, to give voice to before the turn of robes and feet carried these men from him—they, so elevated, he so desperate.

"You have killed your brother!" he cried. "And the brother-hood is the only thing that separates us from common killers. We have each other!"

Something in his voice, even then. Something in his voice caught them all, masters and would-be *Kovaschaii* alike. Maybe that's when they had first realized what his voice could mean to them.

"What is this brotherhood that you speak of?" the oldest Master said softly. "We have the Lady." But he bowed to Kallandras, not yet novitiate, not yet initiate, just a child a step above serafdom.

Then. Now.

The creature struck him, and he—he missed; his blade made a wave, a swell of water, that fanned out across his cheek. He knew that he had caught the creature's attention; that his anger, unearthed and somehow still alive although it had been more than three decades laid to rest, was a hook. That and his pain.

Assassins don't enjoy killing. The truth.

But they use whatever weapon they have at hand when a killing must be done.

The old man had bowed to Kallandras, and when he rose from that bow, his lips were curved in an odd smile. "See," he said softly, "to your brother."

He had been left with the dead then. Left there, with no idea of the honor, oblique and painful as it had been, that the old man had conferred upon him.

He had understood the value of the brotherhood, the desire for its society and no other, before they had taken him into their number and made him one with it. He understood it now, and it burned him; the pain made him careless—or as careless as one can be who has been trained by the *Kovaschaii* masters.

Did they curse him now? He knew that one, only one, of those masters remained alive; the others, age had taken.

He knew the loss, of course, but today he let it in.

Beneath the moving waters, beneath the theater of their sun-harsh light, he let it in.

Above them both, the assassin and the kin, Valedan kai di'Leonne was in motion.

He reached Andaro in time.

Caught his wrist in the grip of a man who was both older and undaunted by that difference in age. The sun had darkened him, the wind had hardened his skin; he took from time; time did not take from him.

But if Andaro's hand had been stopped short of gripping his sword, he could fence with his eyes, the gravity of his expression, the accusation it contained. He did not, however, demean them both by begging.

"The adjudicators gave their order," Ser Anton said softly, seeing the wreckage of splintered wood upon the water, the corpse of a single mage—the others had somehow survived both the weight of their robes and their underwater enemies, and had made it ashore. "The magi will act when the waters are clear; they cannot risk magery in the water; it may well kill the challengers."

Andaro made no reply. Nor would he.

He stared out into the still spot in the water where he thought Carlo must have dived.

Watched as, less than a minute later, that familiar—completely drenched—head bobbed up, seeking air.

It was not enough.

Kallandras lived through the pain, offering it to the demon like a drug; he used himself, as he had been taught to use himself, mercilessly.

Kallandras saw the expression, so appropriately glassy, that held his enemy's face; saw him slow and shudder a moment. But the assassin was accustomed to pain, and in the end, so, too was the *Kialli;* he looked up, and saw as Kallandras did: the passing of his intended victim. He smiled, he only paused to smile, and then the water took him beyond Kallandras' reach.

Air wrapped him round; enveloping him, like a stream too thin to be seen, it answered his call. He followed, but not quickly. Not quickly enough.

But there was one other in the water, with a single crescent sword, a sword that moved too slowly given the water's pull; a sword that dragged him down with its weight. He struggled, but he kept himself near the air that was his life.

Saw the first of the swimmers.

Waited, in the water, and then, with one last breath of air, gave in. Slid beneath it.

He saw, as clearly as he could, the man who had come out of the water, followed by the unholy water itself—only this time, the positions were reversed.

No question; none whatever. The creature was here to kill the kai Leonne.

Lord of Day, Carlo di'Jevre thought. Gripping his sword, he waited. Beneath him, beneath the approaching kai Leonne, the man whose golden hair now filled the water with strands not unlike the legendary mermaid's suddenly pursued; he carried something too small to be a real weapon in his right hand, and in his left, nothing.

The creature turned, lifted a hand that was slender and long, and hurled something, something unseen—but not unfelt.

The water rocked with its sudden unfurling. But the target, the man, had somehow stepped aside. As if water were something that offered him purchase.

"HOLD!" that man cried, and Carlo froze. So did the creature; or rather, it slowed, as if waking to water for the first time and realizing that it had weight.

The creature's snarl was carried by wave; he raced up now, up toward the kai Leonne.

Carlo waited. Held his sword. Readied it—as much as he could in water like this.

He would regret it later—if ever—but the creature's back was toward him, its attention divided between the kai Leonne and the man who pursued him. Carlo was certain that such a thing must realize that he was there—but perhaps not, or perhaps he was only another swimmer, another fragile, easily killed man, with no magery to protect him.

But it didn't matter; he did not call the creature; did not demand the right to face him in honorable combat. This was no creature of the Lord's, no creature meant to stand and fight beneath the open sky. Night here, night in the depths; all *men* fought a night such as this. He heard its terrible gurgling; saw the kai Leonne pass above them both, and struck, as true as he might, the creature's transparent spine. Then, because his body wished air more than he wished the sword, he rose up, leaving its weight behind. Leaving his *sword.*

And because he did, its claws cut his calf to bone, drawing blood, but not life's blood.

He had the privilege of knowing that his strike was not wasted; the man struck, with the dagger that seemed so beneath notice, and even surrounded by water as it was, the creature began to burn.

Lord of Day, Carlo thought, as he reached for air, gasping. *Lord of Light.* He made his way to the open boardwalk, reached up, and was hauled onto his feet by two angry men.

He laughed before his leg collapsed. Laughed in the face of their silence, their anger, their concern.

"What does it matter," he told Andaro's grim, white face, "about the Challenge? What will they do? The Challenge is a game, Andaro—but I—today I have faced the first *true* enemy."

"And was it worth your life?"

"I'm alive."

"You might not have been."

Carlo grimaced as Andaro lifted him. "What do you think?" And he laughed.

"I think," Ser Anton said, looking into the water's deeps as if all that lay beneath its moving surface had been laid bare to him, "you've lost your sword."

The third heat made it to the boardwalk. The fourth heat was delayed.

And perhaps because of the delay they swam poorly when they did at last receive permission to swim. So, too, did the fifth heat.

Valedan kai di'Leonne was, against all odds, the winner of the event. And no victory, not even the fight with the young boys of the Essalieyanese court, had ever been so galling, so contemptible, so empty to him.

CHAPTER TWENTY-TWO

Serra Alina came to him in the humid, cramped waiting areas adjacent to the open glory of the coliseum. The Princess brought her; the two women cast long shadows as the sun left the sky. It had been years since he had believed in the Lord and the Lady, but he yearned for the night now as if, indeed, it were that mythical Lady's bower, a place for peace.

Not yet.

Serra Alina publicly prostrated herself before him, as befit his rank and her own; it made the Ospreys uncomfortable—or worse, made her the objective of their insinuations, their colorful innuendo. She was a Serra, of course, and rose above it.

But he was Valedan. "Primus," he said, in as formal a voice as he ever used, "if you cannot teach your men to speak respectfully of a woman who is the ACormaris' equal in every way, I will kill them."

Silence, there. Decarus Alexis whistled softly under her breath, but her smile was sharp with approval—or with what came as close to approval as she ever offered Valedan.

"Tyr'agar," the Primus said at last.

"Dismissed." Valedan turned to Alina and said, more shortly than he had intended, "Rise."

She rose. Lifted the veils that separated her skin from the Lord's view. "Valedan," she said quietly. "You won."

He made no reply; she glanced at Mirialyn.

At last she said, "You joined this contest to win; to take the title. This is your first victory."

"If *this* is victory," he replied, his voice a low snarl, "I wish I had never entered the Challenge to begin with."

Mirialyn and Alina exchanged glances again; the glance told Valedan that Mirialyn had summoned the Serra.

"How so?"

"To *win*," he said, "I kept swimming. A man was fighting for his life against a creature that wanted *mine* . . . and I kept swimming. I offered no aid, no resistance, no battle."

"To *win*." He spit.

She frowned, a ripple of lines around mouth, eyes, forehead.

"And worse—worst of all—one of the men I believe was sent here to kill me *did* intervene. On my behalf. He struck the creature, and probably saved not only my life but Kallandras' life as well."

"Had Kallandras not been present," the princess said, speaking for the first time, "that man would have perished. As it was, he was injured badly enough we believe he will now no longer be a contestant in any of the remaining tests." She was silent a moment. "He was favored," she said at last, the words oddly hesitant, "to win the test of the horse."

He knew what she was telling him, and hated it.

"Valedan," Alina said quietly, "you must come to the podium; they will call for you shortly. And when you go, you must honor the spirit of this competition."

"Is that why you came?" He turned away from her then.

"Yes," she said, unflinchingly. "You made your choice. You must now live with it, with grace. That is the mark of a man."

"You have come here to tell me that?"

"I had hoped," she said coolly, "to offer merely my congratulations." Reproof.

He was angry with her; angry with them both. But he valued her enough—barely, this one afternoon—to hear the truth when it was spoken, no matter how little he liked it.

The crowds that opened up before him shook with applause as the challengers entered the arena. The voice of the ocean itself seemed to run through the benches in waves, rippling and breaking against unseen shoals. Fitting, here.

Witnesses.

They had seen the blood, they had seen the shattered wreckage of both a mage's craft and a mage's life—and they had seen that the challengers themselves continued on boldly and without apparent fear of the dangers beneath them. *This* was the stuff of champions and legends, the place where the one met the other and stayed wed.

And the man at the lead of the third heat—the heat which marked the turning point in the challenge, that made of it a blood sport—was Valedan kai di'Leonne. He was called last, and his name was lost to the crowd, taken by it, and carried on its tremendous voice. That such a thing could be formed out of disparate splinters—old voices and young, soft and harsh, male and female—seemed to the young kai Leonne a thing of wonder. He stood a moment, as if the voice of a god had been turned upon him.

And then he remembered why he had earned it, and the wonder left him completely; if a god's attention was upon him, the judgment rendered could not be favorable.

He walked the narrow path made of honor guards and witnesses. At the head of that path, Aidan, a young boy. Had he dreamed of heroes at Aidan's age?

Of course he had. He turned away from the boy's regard. Took his place upon the podium. Lifted his hands in twin fists.

The "merchant," Pedro, was beside himself with rage. It was a quaint phrase, that—a Northern phrase. It was also accurate; he seemed to have somehow stepped outside of himself and left only the anger behind. In the Dominion, the cost of such a display was not easily measured—or rather, it was measured by the power of the men in front of whom you chose to expose such a lack of control. And power was something that ebbed and flowed, a thing whose future could not be predicted.

Or so it had been in Ser Anton's experience.

Who, after all, could have foreseen the death of the Tyr'agar, and the fall of the clan Leonne?

"Why didn't you stop him?"

Foolish, to ask that question here. The crowd's roar was broken a moment as the kai Leonne took the podium; as the officiants in their brightly colored yet somehow somber robes began their crossing from podium to Kings.

The man Pedro referred to with such ire stood stiffly, his left arm slung over something the Northerners called a crutch. He had been offered something far less dignified—a chair, with wheels, as if he were merchant offal and it a tiny wagon—and had in the end chosen the rounded curves of hardwood. He could support himself, and he did; not even Andaro was allowed to publicly offer him aid.

The sword was awkwardly worn, and the leg bandaged in gauze that had just been dressed and changed. He would scar, of course—but with luck, he would not limp or lose the use of the leg; the bone had been chipped—or so the physicians said—but not broken.

The Kings had offered them the use of a healer, and Carlo had refused it. Because he knew too much of what they had planned for the kai Leonne, and he could not allow that information to pass into enemy hands.

Thus did he prove himself.

"Had it not been for his interference, we would not have *failed!* Do you even understand the cost of his action?"

Ser Anton stared at the profile of one of his two most promising students, aware—*well* aware—that in the South, healers were not trained to the same use as they were in this, this huge ancient city; that they, in fact, would not have the skill to repair this injury if too much time passed.

Was he aware of the cost of the action?

Oh, yes.

This man would never be his best, or his best student, again.

And they both knew it.

"Ser Anton—"

"Pedro," he said. "I know the cost." He would have said more, but the silence that fell made him realize how exposed the words they exchanged were; there was an unnatural silence, in a coliseum of this size.

And it had been called for by the kai Leonne.

No fists of victory, no Northern gesture. He called for silence, and he received it.

But what he did with it robbed Ser Anton of words. Of more.

"The test of the sea is the test of Averalaan," Valedan said, pitching his voice so that it might carry to the heights as well as the depths. "And men have proved themselves through it since this great city was founded.

"The first men to lend themselves to the sea's mercy were warriors; men who had fought and survived the Baronial Wars. They fought on land and they fought in mountain passes; they fought in great vessels upon the ocean's face.

"Today, I took the test of the ocean, and before you all, before my chosen witness," and he smiled at Aidan, "I was judged first among challengers. And for that, for that I am grateful."

He let them in, then, and they came, filling the space between words with his name.

"But if the spirit of the warrior is a part of the test of the sea, then I will tell you now that if I won the race, I cannot—will not—stand alone."

He took a breath, thinking now, balancing his desire to behave honorably with his desire not to insult the men and the women who had judged, and would judge, the challenge; to offer gratitude, to expose to light the excellence of, yes, an enemy—without exposing to ridicule the heart of the championship itself.

"For while I swam above the blood, the blood itself was spilled.

"Honor Tallosan, the mage whose life was shattered alongside his small vessel." He bowed his head. "Honor Kallandras, the master bard of Senniel College, whose skill with song and word is unchallenged, unchallengeable; whose dance in the depths rid the depths of danger.

"And honor, last and most, a man who had nothing to gain and everything to lose; who came to the Challenge from the South, the far South, and will return that way without facing the rest of the Challenge in which he hoped to prove himself.

"This is a warrior's test, and the man who proved himself worthy of it is the man who dared the waters with a sword and no hope of reward, although the responsibility to protect the challengers was in no way his."

He turned, then, seeking the face in the crowd and finding it, slack-jawed, almost stunned.

"Honor Carlo di'Jevre!" He stepped down from the podium then, and held out his hand, not in command, but not in supplication either.

And then Carlo di'Jevre straightened out, gaining inches and something else: pride. He did not look back at Ser Anton, although he cast one glance at one of his comrades. He stepped into the coliseum from the side, and the people answered his step, and Valedan's request.

He heard the name of his enemy, and he smiled; he began to chant it himself. To offer honor where honor had been offered; to offer it where it was due.

The Southerner drew even with Valedan, although it was a slow process, the movement hobbled by injury and stiff pride.

He did not speak to Valedan, and perhaps that stung, but when Valedan mounted the podium again, Carlo di'Jevre allowed him to do what he allowed no other: offer him a hand.

Clasped, their hands were a knot of dark and light, sun-stain and pale nobility. They were of a height, and their hair and eyes of a color; they might have been brothers, separated at birth, and returned to the fold shaped by two different hands—whose intent, in the end, could not eliminate the similarities that were there.

The crowd came to life as if it had been a slumbering, single creature, and the roar it raised went on and on, deafening, frightening, and comforting by turns.

The officiants returned from the Kings' box, and as they returned, they carried not one cushion but two, and on it, two crowns. Two wreaths.

Baredan di'Navarre offered no name, and no adulation, as the words of the crowd washed around him. Neither did the Tyr'agnate, who stood beside him in the box. But the Tyr's men, even the much admired and much respected Fillipo di'Callesta, had been carried away by the tide and the moment—and in that moment, Baredan could see that Fillipo was the younger of the two men. It had not been obvious to him until now.

They waited, the General and the Tyr, until the applause and the approbation came to an end; they waited a long time. But as the Kings finally rose to speak, for they spoke after each event— both to congratulate the winners and, in Baredan's practiced eye, to remind the spectators of whom their rulers were—the crowd gave up its voice, and there was room in which two men might speak.

The Tyr'agnate said, "He is not the boy we were led to believe he was."

Baredan replied, "He is not the boy *he* was led to believe he was. But he is not yet what he must be to lead armies."

"No?" The Tyr shrugged. "Not armies, perhaps. But twice now, twice, General, he has proved that he can lead men. And few indeed are the boys who lead men." His frown, subtle, was still evident. "They will see it," he said softly.

It was not the turn in conversation that Baredan had been expecting, but he followed it. "His enemies?"

"And his friends, but yes, his enemies. They have failed a second time. There is only one other event at which they might have success."

"The marathon."

"The marathon, yes. And it must be clear to them—as clear as it is to either of us, now—that they *must* succeed. He is more capable than any of us thought, perhaps even the kai Leonne himself.

"He has fire," the Tyr'agnate added, "but not wisdom."

"The Lord values fire."

"True enough," the Tyr replied quietly. "But death is the domain of the Lady, and she values wisdom."

The evening was upon them.

21st of Lattan, 427 AA
Averalaan Aramarelas

Jewel Markess ATerafin sat in the open halls of the Queens' healerie; the sunlight, from the height of cut glass, was broken by lead crossbars as it came to rest upon the floor by her feet; short as they were, those feet cast shadows. It was early, and she had slept most of the previous day, but fitfully, as befits the ill.

Avandar was by her side, and Daine; both men wore the night poorly, for she had been offered a bed, and they had made their way through the night cramped by the backs of chairs or a hard length of floor. Torvan waited just outside of the healerie, no doubt to escort her back to Terafin.

Unfortunately, without the permission of Dantallon, that escort would have to wait.

A meal had been brought, but it had been brought for Jewel; Avandar and Daine were, of course, free to come and go as they pleased, and their keep was not the responsibility of the harried palace staff. At any other time of the year, they would have been better treated and tended—but at any other time of the year, Jewel would not be in the Queens' healerie.

She tried not to feel too guilty, and succeeded—in Avandar's case. He could take care of himself. She did offer Daine part of the food she'd been brought, but it didn't particularly surprise her when he refused with just a hint of offended pride; he was not starving, just hungry.

The door swung open. She sat up quickly enough to knock cutlery and dishes off the uneasy perch her lap made. Luckily, they were empty.

Unluckily, the visitor wasn't Dantallon.

It was Devon.

He bowed. "ATerafin," he said, softly and formally.

She nodded in return; etiquette didn't demand a bow, and even had it, she didn't particularly feel like giving one. But she stopped short of open hostility; she was curious. There were questions that she wanted answered, and she *knew* he had the information.

"You've heard," he asked, "about the outcome of the sea's test?"

"Valedan won."

He nodded to himself.

"And chose to share the podium with one of the men sent from the Dominion. I don't think anyone—even a man who hid in the most deserted place in Averalaan with his fingers in his ears—could avoid knowing that much."

That provoked a smile from the ATerafin, albeit a thin one. "I do not know what was said or done, but Kallandras of Senniel College, with the information that Meralonne APhaniel somehow provided," and at this, he raised a dark brow, asking and not asking the question, "with the aid of the Southerner that Valedan chose to honor, found your *Kialli* threat and ended it."

"Is Kallandras—"

"Both he and the Southern man were injured, and in the same fashion."

"I'd heard—"

"Yes. The Southerner will withdraw. He was offered—and has refused—the aid of the healers here. As did Kallandras, but he is legendary for that."

"He's . . . a private man," Jewel said softly, her glance drawn to Daine's stiff profile. *Would I do that again?* She thought. *Would I risk that with anyone else?*

She already knew the answer. *Yes,* and *never.* Some part of the healer was a part of her, and only because she was older and somewhat more experienced could she easily pull strand from strand and know whose was whose.

"Yes. The fear of a healer is a great fear—even though it is well known that a healing less than the call from death is not nearly so invasive. Men are superstitious by nature."

"And with cause," she said softly.

As did Daine.

There was an awkward pause. He blushed; she didn't.

Devon granted them their silence as if it were a natural part of the conversation. He looked away, and when he looked back, it was gone. "I must ask you a favor," he said reluctantly, as if it pained him. It probably did.

"What?"

"I want you to stay here until the end of the Challenge."

"In the healerie?" she asked, half a smile tugging at her lips.

His smile met hers halfway. "No. *Dantallon* wants that."

"You?"

"If there's going to be a fight, I want to stand beside a woman who understands what the cost of both fighting—or refusing to fight—will be."

She waited then. "You realize you've got no right, no damned right at all, to ask that of me?"

He said nothing.

She looked away from him, the wall suddenly fascinating in its flat lack of anything interesting. The silence stretched out for minutes on end.

It was her domicis who broke it. "I will inform the Terafin," he said.

She cursed him, but in silence. Nodded.

He watched her profile, waiting. Knowing that he had to wait, and liking it about as much as anyone would. He knew why he had to wait. Teller's near-death stood between them, between the woman who—and he admitted this bitter fact without bitterness because it *was* just that, fact, no more—had, at heart, begun to learn the price of rulership. It was a lesson that too few rulers ever truly appreciated, and a lesson that The Terafin had always understood. He would not have chosen to take her name otherwise, and he knew that the House Name *was* hers.

But he also knew, when the answer came, what it would be. Because they had stood in a darkness that was timeless, beneath the streets of a city ignorant of the danger it faced. And she had seen what that danger was, when he could not—it irked him, even now, although this, too was simple fact.

Betrayed by him or no, she could not *unsee* it.

Duvari had already informed The Terafin, of course. Devon had counseled against; it was the surest way of pushing Jewel ATerafin away from the duty that she would otherwise embrace. Duvari's compromise: Give Devon leave to tell the young ATerafin of her duty in any fashion he chose. That it was a compromise for Duvari spoke volumes about the Lord of the Compact, but the Compact had its own rules, and the Astari were there to follow them.

The Astari were Duvari's as much as Terafin was The Terafin's. He served both, as he could.

And if she rules the House? He thought, watching Jewel's stiff anger as he waited. *What then, Devon?*

It was the domicis who spoke. Avandar Gallais, a man that Devon had never particularly liked. That, if he were honest, no one particularly liked, not even Jewel herself.

"I will inform The Terafin," he said. His eyes crossed Devon's, and it was clear to Devon that the domicis, at least, understood the situation. But if he conveyed the message to the House itself, he could also inform Jewel's den. Her den.

Her own little coterie of Chosen. He wondered if she ever thought of them that way; knew that she didn't. Wondered what she would be like when one of them finally died.

Because no one of power took the service of men and women without expecting to lose them. Not during a struggle for succession.

Not during a war with kin.

He waited; she gave him nothing except, through the rough nod of assent, her commitment to fight their common focs. It was enough that he gave her this: his continuing presence, a means of allowing her to vent an anger that he both regretted and refused to change.

"Angel is *pissed*."

"Not . . . not upset?"

"How'm'I supposed to tell the difference?" He shrugged.

"Good point." She remembered the look in Alowan's eyes, and wondered how much of it was reflected in her den-kin. She'd never know; that much, about Angel, was fact. If he suffered he kept it to himself, and there wasn't any way, short of knife point, to pry it out of him.

Carver shoved the hair out of his eyes. All these years, and he hadn't gone sensible on her; neither had Angel. Teller, Arann, Jester—even Finch—they'd adopted the practical look of the ATerafin, but Carver and Angel, long hair cropped in odd places as if it were sculpture, were determined to hang on to their roots.

Or their youth.

She appreciated it. Her own hair was still a mass of loose curls that tightened whenever the humidity was high. She kept it short when she had the time to sit still and be sheared, but otherwise, she kept it twisted up in a roll, with a wooden pin as anchor. She didn't keep bangs, but strands of hair always managed to be just long enough to get in her eyes.

She mirrored his gesture. Grinned. "I bet."

"He'll be allowed up in four days. You haven't heard that much swearing in a healerie in your life!" He was laughing. Good damned thing Angel couldn't hear him.

"Teller?"

"Mending. Better, although I think it'll be a week before he's up and about."

"The House?"

"It's only been two days, Jay."

"The House?"

He laughed. "Still standing. No one else has made any political moves. I don't think we'll see action again until after the Challenge, for what it's worth."

"Good."

"You?"

"One true dream," she said softly. "No, two. I'm exhausted, and I've been in a foul mood."

"She has," Daine said, quietly and helpfully.

"So what else is new?" But he stood. "When are you up and about?"

"As soon as Devon can find the damned healer," she replied gracelessly. "The Lord of the Compact wishes my services. The Lord of the healerie wants the Lord of the Compact to drop dead. Obviously, he can't quite say as much in as many words, so he's absented himself. If *I* weren't the one being inconvenienced or used to make a point, I'd think it was really funny."

"Well, keep yourself well, then. I'm going to get food."

"Good. While you're scrounging, take Daine."

"But—" the healer began.

She'd already lifted a hand. "Don't argue with me. Eat."

"But—"

"You heard the lady," Carver said, laughing. "She's just done two things. First, she's generously told us both she's in a foul mood. Second, she's given you an order. When the first is true, the second had better be followed." He caught Daine by the upper arm. "No one's going to hurt her here," he said. "Avandar'll be back any time now."

Daine allowed himself to be led away because he knew her well enough to know Carver was right. She was in a foul mood. The only answer to an order when she was in a foul mood was "yes."

Her third visitor was Kiriel.

The day had worn on; the sun was past its height. Dantallon had still managed not to be found. Jewel contented herself with imagining the expression on Duvari's already rather dour face, but it was a meager contentment. She was not ill enough that she found bed rest restful, not well enough that she didn't find the irritation wearing.

But both of these things fell away when the youngest member of her den stepped fully into the room and closed the door behind her. She rested against that door a moment with her back, her hands obviously clasped behind it.

"Kiriel," Jewel said. She spoke tentatively. She always did, around wary wild creatures.

"I'm off duty," she said, as if she needed an excuse to be here. She probably did. "Anything interesting happen when you were on duty?"

The younger woman looked vaguely surprised, and then shook her head. "No."

"Good."

Her forehead creased a moment, as if the weight of thought took effort. "Why?"

"Why is that good?"

"Yes."

"Because it means that no further attacks, or attempts, occurred."

"Oh." She stood there, door at her back, as if she needed to be close to the only escape there was.

"Kiriel?" Jewel said softly.

The girl raised her head slowly. "I didn't even know he was there," she said.

Which made no sense, but Jewel knew better than to interrupt her. Conversations with Kiriel were rare enough they seemed fragile, and if they were going to be broken, it wasn't by the den leader. She waited.

Kiriel let her wait, and it became clear to Jewel that the unidentified "he" was so obvious it never occurred to her that the confession wouldn't immediately make sense. *Who, Kiriel?* Jewel thought. Time stretched; Kiriel's shoulders slumped as if the silence itself were judgment. *Come on, Jay. Who?* And then she knew. "Maybe," she said gently, "he wasn't actually a demon."

Kiriel's smile was bitter. "Maybe," she repeated, "I'm not actually god-born." Then she stopped. Lifted a shaking hand. Stared at the ring round her finger. "I recognized him," she added lamely.

"Oh, you're god-born, all right," Jewel said, wondering how many of the demons they'd meet were creatures Kiriel *personally* recognized, but unwilling to ask. "I don't think the magic's been created that can rob a person of their talent, if they were cursed or lucky enough to be born with one; with you it'd be even harder. But I didn't know there was any water in the Hells."

"I don't know if there is."

"You weren't—"

"No. I spent my life surrounded by demons, but they were all *here*. I've never been to the Hells. I don't know if—I don't know if a mortal *can* travel there and survive it. I don't know what they'd be if they came back." She shrugged. "I think he must have used a lot of his power to cloak his presence—because he must've known I'd be here."

Another pause. Longer, this time. "Why didn't you tell *me?*"

Awkward, the silence between them. "It was a vision," Jewel said at last, stepping around each word as if they were broken glass. "And visions make their own choices."

Kiriel's stare was long, unblinking.

"Jay," she said at last, "If you don't even trust me to fight the kin anymore, than what *am* I good for?" She spread her hands out, palm up, in unconscious mimicry of either Jewel herself, or someone very like her in gesture. Rawness there; Jewel half expected Kiriel to bolt.

So she got out of bed, pushing the coverlet—which, given the season, was meant more for modesty's sake than practicality's—back and swiveling her legs to the side of the bed Kiriel was nearest.

"What," she said, as she stood and walked toward a Kiriel who, surprisingly, waited for her, "are any of us good for?"

"You've got your sight," the younger woman said, in a tone that made her seem, suddenly, every year of her fifteen or sixteen years—and not one day more.

"True. And it made me, I won't deny it. Even before I understood what it meant, it made me. But Carver? Angel? Teller? Any of the rest of us?"

Kiriel said nothing.

Jewel said nothing.

This time, Jewel won the waiting game.

"It's different."

"Yes," Jewel said again. "It's different. But we got by on nothing. That sword—you still know how to use it?"

Kiriel nodded.

"Means you can earn your way in the world. When I was your age, we did our best to get by by cutting the purses off of stupid, monied men and women who were careless enough to wear them in open view. We fed ourselves by stealing from farmers' stalls, clothed ourselves as much as we could by getting wool or cloth the same way." Something struck her. "Is the sword special?"

At that, Kiriel smiled, and the smile hardened the lines of her face. She was the only woman Jewel knew on whom a smile could look so much less pleasant than empty neutrality. "Yes," she said. "A gift."

"And it?"

"No other could wield this sword."

"You can?"

The smile vanished. "I don't know," she said, and the admission obviously cost her. "I haven't been in a fight since—since the ring." She paused. "I can—I can still pick it up."

"Isn't that the same?"

"Don't know." The hardness returned a moment, lending the cast of her features the patina of age and power. "I tried to cut my finger off. Didn't work."

Jewel looked at the ring that seemed plain and harmless enough; ignored the comment. "Could you use a regular sword?"

She hesitated. "Yes."

"Is The Kalakar looking to kick you out of the House Guards?"

"I—I don't know."

"Kiriel," Jewel said, drawing close enough to touch—but not touching. "Not a single one of them can see a demon half a city away. I can't either. And I've seen you with that sword."

"When?"

"When you rescued Valedan from the demon in the Great Hall. Every noble of any value at all saw you."

That seemed to please her.

"Why do you think you have no value in and of yourself?"

Kiriel stared at her for a long, long time, and when she answered, there was a wariness, and a weariness, in her voice that aged her, when most of her questions seemed to rob her of adulthood. "I don't understand the rules of power the Empire is run by. In the Shining Court, they're simple. If you have power, you survive. If you have a lot of power, you rule.

"I *had* power, Jay. Now, by the standards of the Court, I have nothing."

"By the standards of the so-called Court, most of the men and women of this City have nothing," she replied almost sharply. "But you'll notice it's the demons who lost."

"Last time," she said slowly, and Jewel knew she was speaking of the events that preceded her birth.

"Last time," Jewel added, "there was a big fight, there was also a god present."

"Not one," Kiriel said, parrying. "There were two gods present. Without Bredan to fight for you, diminished as he was, this city would *be* the Shining City, and Allasakar its ruler—diminished as *he* was. He's not what he was in the Hells. But he's more than he was when he was trapped in a gate at Vexusa—and you?

"Your god is in the heavens. He has nothing to offer you. No followers. No children, and therefore no power."

"First of all, he's not *my* god. Second of all—"

"Don't let me interrupt you," another voice said. Carver stood lounging in the doorway, his arms across his chest, his eyes narrowed.

"What?" Jewel said irritably, half-glad to be pulled out of an argument that she didn't want to have because she was, dammit, getting really angry, and she knew that that was the one thing she couldn't be where Kiriel was concerned.

"Our boy actually managed to scrape a tenth-place finish."

"Our—you mean Valedan?"

"Unless you were rooting for someone else and I missed it."

"How?"

"Gods know." Carver's shrug was economical and elegant, but he still paused to brush his hair back over his eye. "If we were betting event by event, I'd've lost my House crest."

"Not even as a joke, Carver."

"Yes, sir." He paused. "Aren't you supposed to be in bed?" And was gone through the open doorway before he could hear what she had to say. Good thing, too. It wasn't pretty.

"Kiriel," she said, not looking at the younger woman, "My life is in this fight. I get to keep it if I'm lucky, I lose it if Kalliaris frowns—but the fight is worth the loss. It's worth my loss, and it's worth the loss of my den, possibly even my House.

"It's that big. It's that important. I wouldn't have chosen a fight like this for the world—but having been handed it, I couldn't walk away no matter what it cost. Do you understand that? This is a fight *worth* dying for. Even more important, it's a fight worth killing for. If we've got nothing else, we've got that."

"Is that important to you?" Real curiosity now; all anger, all proud display was gone.

She started to answer. Stopped. Thought about it for a long time, feeling the shadows; Evayne's. Terafin's. Her den's. "Yes," she said at last. "It's important to me. And in the end, I'd rather fight a fight worth dying for than not, a fight that puts blood on my hands I can actually live with. But more than that, I'd rather the fight weren't necessary at all." Jewel shook her head, her grin half-rueful, and totally unlike any of Kiriel's expressions. "But it *was* really important to me, when I was younger. You make me feel like a youth again."

"Is that good?"

"No, it's very bad. Because a youth can't run a House in the middle of a war."

Kiriel left Jay in the healerie. The news about Valedan didn't matter to her; winning was everything, and he had, so far, won one event. She didn't understand betting, and had allowed Auralis to take some of the coin of the realm—the coin by which she was paid for her services, although so far she'd done nothing but stand around and wait a lot—and place a "bet" for her.

Betting was something that Jewel apparently did as well. It seemed like anything else the Ospreys did for amusement—harmless *and* pointless.

This is a fight worth dying for.

Even more important, it's a fight worth killing for.

Kiriel understood the first concept well enough; there were fights it was worth risking death for. Obviously that risk had never born fruit, but she had undertaken it no small number of times coming of age in the Shining City.

It was the second concept that was odd. *All* fights were worth killing for. To enter into combat, one declared, by action, a desire for the death of one's enemy. What had Jay meant, "worth killing for?"

"Kiriel!"

Interruptions were rarely welcome. Whoever called her name was met with the frown that all the Ospreys had become accustomed to.

"What?" she said shortly.

Auralis, sword sheathed and unarmored, fell into step beside her. "You look," he said, "like I feel."

She'd heard that one before. It meant . . . it meant . . .

"You look pissed off," he added.

That one, she knew. "You're angry?"

"You aren't?"

"Not really. Confused."

"Because we humans are so stupid?"

She shook her head. "Not all of you, no."

"Well, thank the gods for small miracles." He had an edge to his voice that was also familiar; it meant that he wasn't really thankful for anything. Sarcasm. Yes. She wasn't a fool; she understood sarcasm when it was used to wound. She didn't understand it when it was used for nothing. No reason, like betting, like standing around with a sword waiting for a fight to come to you, and getting gold for it.

"Somebody told me that we're involved in a fight," she said at last. Auralis, used to her by now, failed—just barely—to roll his eyes. "She said it was a fight that was worth the risk of losing everything she cares about—and she cares about a lot of things the way Ospreys seem to care about each other—but more."

"More?"

"More." A word of warning in her voice. It surprised her. She tested it as the streets brushed past them in the growing darkness. Power or no, it was still to the darkness she turned for comfort and anonymity. "She's important to me, Auralis. She trusts me."

"We trust you."

"She trusted me before. Before the—before." Lifted her hand; let the ring catch his sight. She could not speak of the loss openly.

"I trust her," Kiriel added, uncertain why she spoke to Auralis at all. And then, because she was honest, she added, "I trust you in a fight, but I don't trust you, Auralis. There's too much about you that wants power and death."

"And she doesn't have that?"

"No. She *has* power, if I understand the Empire—"

His clear snort was comment enough, but he didn't interrupt her further. "But the power—she's afraid of it. Afraid to take it. Afraid to fail it, I think. I understand the fear of losing power. It's the fear that any normal creature has. That anyone I knew growing up had—except for one woman, and even she—even she was afraid of losing the influence she had with me.

"But she's not afraid of losing power. She's afraid of what she'll lose if she has to take power."

"And she told you this?"

Stung, irritated, Kiriel rounded on him. "I understand *power*, Auralis. I understand its use, and its lack. I am not an idiot because I don't understand your childish phrases and the way you use words to mean the opposite of what you've said. *I am not a child.*"

The sound of metal against metal woke her; he was still. But she—she had drawn her sword. It was a crime, in the city streets, to draw sword as she had done. But Auralis didn't reply in kind; he waited. Waited, shoulders tense, his body ready to answer the thrust or slash of a wild blade.

The bower of night trees were high, high above them, and all around them a stream had opened in the press of bodies that the city had become since the challenge. She had thought it crowded and oppressive when Evayne had first brought her—and now, now the temptation to cut herself some space was something she constantly fought against. Harder, when a sword was at hand and ready. When *this* sword was at hand. She struggled a moment to sheathe it.

Realized that she had drawn it. That she *could* use it. But not here. Not in Jay's city.

"No," Auralis said, when the last click of tang against sheath ended that struggle. "You aren't a child. Believe it or not, Kiriel, it's not my first thought." He shrugged, as if the sword had never left the sheath.

Someone tried to sell her something. He opened his mouth, got halfway through the sentence, and then stammered his way into invisibility.

"But you were talking about someone?"

"Yes. She says we're involved in a fight. She means, of course, a war. But she said it was a war worth losing everything she values for—everything. I think she meant that she wouldn't regret the loss, if the war itself was won. She's wrong about that," she added. "But she said that this fight was a fight worth dying for."

He did roll his eyes.

"That's not confusing, not to me."

"And?"

"She said it was a fight worth killing for, and that's what she needed, in the end. A fight worth killing for."

"So?"

"You don't understand it either?"

"Not hardly. Most wars are worth killing for. That's why we're soldiers, after all."

Her shoulders hunched as she tensed. And then they relaxed completely.

Kallandras had no time to recover.

No time, although until he found his seat beside a crowd-weary Sioban Glassen, he did not realize it. His leg throbbed; at the commands of the physicians, he kept it elevated by the simple expedient of sitting on the earth in front of a few free inches of bench and dropping his foot, heavily, next to the bench's other occupant.

She didn't mind, and she didn't ask questions. Years of friendship had taught her that they were both useless and uncomfortable.

Years.

A young woman from Morniel College was singing a delicate lay; he heard it drift up from the rhythmic movement of the nighttime sea, a dream of love and death, a hint of history.

"She's not bad," Sioban said. "Not as good as any of my old students, but not bad."

He smiled. She'd said nothing else for most of the Challenge about any voice she didn't recognize, and it was understood by everyone, except perhaps for the unfortunate journeymen so discussed, to be high praise indeed.

"Your memory is kinder than you were," Kallandras said, and she laughed. Her laughter, earthy and rough, was almost a sensation; he was surprised, often, at how much he enjoyed the sound of it.

Layered between amusement was her experience, the depths of sorrow, the years of fear and responsibility, the wisdom that both had forced upon her. Experience, sorrow, fear—they underlay her joy in a moment's words, somehow strengthening, rather than weakening, the mix.

"You've grown wicked with time."

"I've a fair distance to go to catch my first master."

"What, me? I stand still, Master Bard, since my retirement."

He raised a single brow until it was completely obscured by the edge of his hair.

She laughed again.

And over the ripple of laughter, he heard a distinct sound. Or rather, just as her laughter had been a sensation, he *felt* it: the peel of a bell, the tolling of a death.

Jewel ATerafin.

A second time.

Bruce Allen.

A third.

Ellora AKalakar.

And a fourth.

Devran ABerriliya.

He smiled as pleasantly as he could; it was easy; he enjoyed the company of the woman who sat at his side. "I fear," he said softly, "that I must retire. I'm not a young man, and the minor wound I took is causing some pain."

"Nothing good wine won't cure."

"No, but good wine, I'm afraid, is hard to come by at this time of year."

She smiled, but her eyes were sharp and hard as a sword's edge; she could hear something in his voice.

Duty.

She rose. "Well, if you'll plead pain and exhaustion, I'll plead age and infirmity. I think I'll turn in as well."

Distracted as he was, he had to smile and shake his head.

"If you need to find me, you know how."

He had to return to his lodgings, find the ointments and the herbs that the evening required. He must now be wakeful, watchful.

The four names had been taken; the deaths sounded.

And he had been given the task of preventing them. One man. One man against his brother.

There was a fourth visitor.

Jewel had expected one. Expected, in fact, two: Dantallon and Duvari, either singly or side by hostile side. She'd eaten and drunk—or rather, she thought sourly, been fed and watered—and she'd managed to get rid of Avandar at least three times on various thinly disguised pretexts.

The fact that there were six armed men at her door at all times, two of whom were Carver and Torvan, didn't hurt either.

Sleep came and went. The shadows lengthened as the sun came to rest on the horizon's blurred edge. This far away from the Challenge activities, she could still hear cries and cheers, most wordless, all faceless. Best was when the music, carried by bardic voice, drifted up through the glass. Bards could make themselves heard if they so chose—and to *be* heard in the tumult of a Challenge night, they did choose.

Even when she had lived in the lower city, she had enjoyed the Challenge season; people made merry with alcohol were far less sensitive to the clumsy fingers of nervous thieves.

That was a lifetime away; funny it should come to her so clearly here, in *Avantari,* as far away from her life in the twenty-fifth holding as she could possibly get.

The door didn't open. There was no knock. The sounds of

merriment—all of which excluded her—without did not diminish or change. But she knew when she was no longer alone; it happened in a half-breath, between wandering thoughts, fragments of memory.

"Jewel."

"Evayne," she replied quietly. Her hands stilled; they'd been rearranging the thin coverlet into something small rivers might travel—peaks and valleys, twists of cloth that caught shadows and light from the lamps on the wall.

"You are in danger."

"So what else is new?" She looked up then, feeling the difference in their ages. As if she were still sixteen, still ignorant, and still powerless. There should have been humor in the words; she'd meant to wedge it between them somehow, to make the statement flippant, a proper armor. But the words came out unadorned, and she was exposed by them.

"You must go South," the woman in the midnight-blue robes said, raising a hand to the hood that framed—that hid her face.

"You aren't telling me anything I don't already know."

"No." She bent, this older woman, this living mystery, and reached into the folds of her robe as if they were a closet.

Jewel knew what she'd see. The orb. The sphere. The crystal which was said—in children's stories so old they were almost never told anymore—to be a splinter of a seer's soul.

It hung between Evayne's hands, a silver glow in the coming night.

"Go South, Jewel Markess ATerafin.

"And when you have discovered what you must discover, answer the call."

"What?"

"You have started so many lives, and finished none of them. When the time comes, you must walk a path I walked when I was barely sixteen. Face the same doors, Jewel, and pass the same tests."

"Why?"

She held aloft the shard; it flared white, a terrible light that made of the rest of the world a darkness. Transfixed, unable to look away, Jewel ATerafin heard the seer say, "Because if you're to have the ability to control what you see, you must expose everything you are to her, and let her slice and cut what she will."

Bitterness there, and pain that seemed so much a part of her that Jewel suddenly couldn't imagine she'd ever lived without it. "Who is this she?" She asked softly.

"The Oracle," Evayne said softly. "And now, Jewel, if you will?"

"Will?"

"It is time for you to leave."

She started to speak. Not even to argue, because to argue with someone required some shared knowledge, and it was clear that Evayne held all the cards. But before words left lips, she felt it, sudden and sharp; saw the ghostly spill of blood just left of the center of her chest.

"Quickly," Evayne said.

Jewel reached out with a hand; the seer gripped it.

She spoke two words as the window shattered. The lead that had held the beveled glass crumpled as a figure emerged from the wreckage; a dagger flashed orange in lamplight and flew the length of the healerie's room.

But its intended victim was gone.

She appeared in a well-lit hall. It was an old-city hall; the ceiling was flat, rather than arched, but it was tall, with a catwalk around its perimeter and windows around the catwalk. The lights were far too bright, and the ground a little too uneven; she stumbled, her knees apparently having been left behind in the healerie.

"Jay!"

Before she hit the ground, an arm caught her around the shoulders; the arm was slender, but it shored her up more easily than Arann's would have.

"Kiriel?" she asked softly.

It was Kiriel. But the girl's gaze went past her—hard to do considering how closely they stood—to the woman at her side. Impossible not to see the hostility in the glare. "Evayne."

"Kiriel," the seer said, her voice heavy, even tired.

"What are you doing with Jay?"

"Saving my life," Jewel said, more shortly than she'd intended.

"So she can do what with it?"

Hard, that question. Angry.

"Kiriel," Jewel said, in her best den leader voice.

"You don't know this woman," Kiriel replied, in a voice as close to the darkness as she'd used since she'd lost all her precious magic.

"I know her better than you'd think," Jewel replied. "We've met before, and under darker circumstances than this."

"She doesn't save anyone's life for free."

"How do you know?"

"I—I know."

So did Jewel, suddenly. "The fight's worth fighting," she said tiredly. Not sure who she was trying to remind—herself or her den-kin.

"Kiriel," the seer said. "I give you back your den-kin. She is your responsibility now. The kin are not hunting her this eve, but the brotherhood of the Lady is."

Kiriel's grip on Jewel tightened.

Great, Jewel thought, as Evayne took a step into nothing and simply ceased to exist—in front of about a hundred people. Luckily, in the noise and the clouds of gathered smoke, only about twenty of them now stared at her with that wide-jawed curiosity that can get ugly really quickly.

"Who are the brotherhood of the Lady?"

"Hells if I know," Jewel answered. "But I think we can discuss that somewhere else."

Kiriel nodded. "Wait a minute," she said quietly—which meant that Jewel could see her lips form the words but couldn't actually hear them without an active imagination. "Auralis!"

One of the quiet strangers separated himself from the long tables that were used for overcrowding during the Challenge season. He eyed Jewel with the same trust one offers a dog with a foaming mouth who hasn't done anything remotely aggressive— yet. She returned his regard; he was a tall man, bronze with sun, copper-haired, blue-eyed. *Attractive,* she thought, *and he knows it too damned well.*

She hated that in a man.

"Kiriel?" he said, speaking to her but pinning Jewel with his not-quite-glare.

"We've got to go. I . . . owe you money, I think."

"You do," he said, folding his arms across his chest. "Where exactly do you think you have to go?"

"Somewhere," Jewel replied, "where a hundred people aren't getting ready to report illegal use of magic?"

He laughed then, although the edge of suspicion still hardened both stance and feature. "In this part of town?"

"Even here," Jewel replied. "I know this 'town' like the back of my hand.

"Hands like that?"

She looked at her hands involuntarily in the light. They were paler than they had been when she'd made a life for herself—barely—in the twenty-fifth. And on the left ring finger, she wore, thick and heavy and shining with craftsman's perfection, the signet ring of her House—the jeweled and platinumed gold ring that marked her as part of its Council.

"Yeah," she said. "Hands like this."

"Jay, do you know who the brotherhood of the Lady is?"

"Of course. I always pay attention to orders of assassins." She bit her lip, and before Kiriel could speak said, "Sorry, Kiriel. No. I have no idea who they are. I don't really care either—I just want to know which bastard was responsible for hiring them."

But Auralis had gone deathly still. "What did you say?" he said softly, his gaze demanding Kiriel's reply.

"The brotherhood," she said quietly, "of the Lady."

He turned to face Jewel ATerafin then. "You're wrong," he told her quietly, all hostility muted. "You *do* care who the are. We call 'em the *Kovaschaii* here. Ring any bells?"

"No."

"They're an elite bunch of assassins. They cost the worth of a small barony—an old-style barony—or so it's rumored."

"Fine."

"They don't fail."

She rolled her eyes. "Assassin," she said. "Meet seer."

His eyes widened. "You're *that* ATerafin!"

She flushed. Ego had gotten control of her mouth. She felt young again—and she remembered, her cheeks hot, that she hadn't particularly liked being young. "And you must be one of Kiriel's Ospreys."

"Good guess." His face had lost a little of its glacial quality; none of its danger. "Duarte told us about you. You're the former thief." Measured words.

Some men could say them with honesty; certainly they were true. But this man was using them as a weapon—or rather, he was handling them the way he would handle something unfamiliar but quite probably dangerous. Testing. Trying to cause discomfort or embarrassment.

"Yes," she replied distantly, as if acknowledging a truth that bored her, or worse, a truth that only children toyed with in such a fashion.

Very little got through to Jewel when malice was behind it.

Honesty could hurt her, but even then, only from those she already valued and respected—something she was pretty damned certain she'd never feel for this particular man. She turned to Kiriel, her expression softening slightly. "You can stay here if you want, or you can follow. But I'm leaving. I have to get home. If that bastard thinks he—" She stopped speaking, albeit with some effort.

"I'm leaving with her," Kiriel told Auralis quietly. "She's—she was confined to the royal healerie. If she's here, it's not because the healer gave her permission to leave."

He shrugged. "Well," he said, "it's hot and boring here, so I might as well tag along."

"Wonderful," Jewel said.

CHAPTER TWENTY-THREE

Ser Anton di'Guivera waited. The courtyard was full of the men and women whose power and authority granted them easy access to *Avantari,* fragrant with the scent of new sweat and rich wine; the lamps and the magelights that the Empire was so fond of imparted a color to gown and tunic, to shirt and surcoat, that hinted at the revelries of day.

Night was a time of peace.

But not here. Not in this palace, and not in this city. He found it vaguely distasteful that the city itself chose not to sleep. And chose, in its wakefulness, to treat *every* night with the abandon reserved, in his homelands, for the Festival of the Moon. The Lady's time.

Perhaps it was understood that he felt this discomfort, perhaps not. But it was the Princess of the Blood—the only true child of the men who ruled this Empire—who came to him in this sea of friendly distances. She spoke Torra; that he expected, but she spoke it flawlessly. Had she offered him more than the respect of a fluid, formal, and very Imperial bow, he would not have been surprised.

But then he remembered: Alina.

"ACormaris," he said quietly.

"You are unescorted this eve."

"I have—I had a wish for—privacy. In this city, it appears that the courtyards of the Crown halls are as private an open space as one can find."

"There are quieter spaces," she said secretively. "And the moon's face is almost full. Come, if you will."

He watched her, unblinking, for a full minute. And then the bards began anew, and although their voices were hypnotic and compelling, they sang about war in a tongue that war was not meant for: Weston.

I am old, he thought, and he felt it: the fear that experience exposes. Younger men—men like Carlo or Andaro—see costs measured in their lives alone. Nobility in that. Freedom.

And what of Ser Anton? Was not the cost of this measured in his life? Ah.

"Forgive me, ACormaris," he said softly, "but I see a person I wish to speak with."

Her eyes followed his, seeing as he saw, and with just as much comment. But before she acceded with her customary grace, she touched his arm. It surprised him; he looked at her; met eyes that were a little too brown to be golden, and a little too bright to be entirely comfortable. "Ser Anton," she said at last, "we have all, in our time, been asked to put aside the injuries done to us by our enemies."

The words of a foreigner and a woman. Protocol did not demand that he answer her; politeness did. It was an easy battle. He remained silent.

"In my life," she continued, "I have learned that those injuries that we cannot put aside devour us; they unmake and remake us in such a way that we cannot clearly see ourselves." He started to pull away. "An indulgence," she said softly.

"I am not a Northerner," he replied, but he waited, the sea breeze sudden and strong for just that moment, a reminder that the wind listened.

"It is a common story. An old one; we call it a Lattan tale."

His smile was stiff. "You will tell me," he said softly, "of a young man who faced a creature that could not be killed."

"Indeed."

He could not keep the edge out of his voice, nor the mild contempt. He was not, after all, a child. "Such a young man was a seraf, a common villager. He had wife and child, mother and father, a good lord—all these things, the blessing of the Lady."

"That is not as we tell it, but yes."

"He went to face the monster—a creature twice his height, several times his weight, with sword-length claws and an appetite for human blood."

"You've heard this story before."

"I used to tell it to my son. But perhaps it is not the same. Let me finish, and then you may judge." He could not keep the condescension out of his voice, although he knew she was ACormaris and, because of it, worthy of more. It was night. The Lady's face was full.

"The Voyani matriarchs had come and gone, and they had judged this one man to be the only hope of the Terrean. In the South armies amassed and were slaughtered to a man; the villages were defenseless. But the Havallah Voyani—it matters not which Voyani clan it was, and you can start a war by using the wrong clan name if you're in the presence of Voyani—had looked into the future.

"You are the only one," he said, lowering his voice, "who can do what must be done. Take this sling, and take this rock." He stopped then, bitter, a momentary fire in his regard of the quiet princess. Because, of course, he knew the story. He knew the point she was trying to make; had known it before she'd begun. But he'd thought his irony and his condescension, along with that foreknowledge, would protect him from acknowledging it.

We know ourselves so well and so little.

"I forget the rest," he said.

"Ah. And I remember it. Might I continue?"

"No. No, I am an old man, with no desire to hear harem tales. Your pardon, ACormaris, but I am weary. My most promising student has been removed from the Challenge rolls, and his partner is aggrieved. I had hoped for a moment of peace in which to reflect."

She bowed again, deferentially and without comment. "I believe," she added softly, "that he is still waiting for you."

And, like a woman, she missed *nothing*. His Mari had missed nothing. She had probably seen the bandits long before the rest of the village. He often wondered why she hadn't fled, although he knew the answer. She had led such a protected life, first with her doting, foolish father, and then with him, with her doting, more foolish husband. She understood that death waited on every breeze or in every gale, and that it was impartial—but understanding it and *knowing* it in your core were different things. No hand had struck her with intent to harm; no man had touched her with intent to kill. As a child, her eyes had been shielded from every death a child can be protected from seeing.

It had made her brave, the way fools are brave.

His fault.

She had thought—he was certain she had thought it—that she might somehow help her son and the other children. They said—they said that she had died *fighting*.

The boy looked on; he had not looked away since their eyes

had first met across the thin crowd, and he did not, in fact, look away until Ser Anton came to stand in front of him.

"Aidan," Ser Anton said. "It is good to see you well. I do not see your champion."

"He's not here." Silence. Watching the boy's face, Ser Anton could see him weighing the words and the anger behind them; trying to decide how to throw them.

He could not believe—no, truth now, under the Lady's face—he *had not* believed that a boy could injure him in any way. That a foreigner, blond and red with sun, the dark colors that were a man's legacy in the South watered down by exposure to Northern sea and Northern indulgence, could matter to him in any fashion.

"You heard about Carlo?" he asked, changing the subject.

"Yes." That softened the boy's face slightly. "He's withdrawn."

"Yes."

"And he won't see a healer."

"No."

Silence. Then, "Valedan says it's because he knows too much about the plans to kill him, and he's afraid the healer will tell."

He had not yet offered this boy a lie. He tried now. "No, it is because, in the South, it is unmanning to be touched by a healer. They take from you, boy, just as the wind does. They expose you, they read what they like out of your life."

Credulous, the boy replied, "You mean the death call."

"Is that what you call it here?"

"Isn't that what it's called everywhere?"

"No."

"A healer—the Princess says a healer can't betray the healed. Not if they both agree to it."

"And you believe her," was the unguarded reply, "because you are a Northerner. In the South, we understand war."

He had not meant to say it. But the anger was back in the boy's face. "You don't understand *war*," he said, and his hands, smaller than Ser Anton's because of years and possibly the scarcity of nourishment in his background, curled into fists and shook with the effort of containment. "You understand *murder*. It's not the same thing."

"Is it not?" Ser Anton said softly. "Men are paid to follow orders, and they are ordered to kill. They kill until there are either no more men to be killed or their leaders come to terms. Do you think you understand war from watching *this*?" He raised an arm, to take in the Challenge, its revelers, this palace of politeness and invisible weapons.

Aidan took a step back, his white hair suddenly brighter beneath the halo of magelights. And then he said, coldly, "You were all about Southern honor. You came here out of love for your wife and your son, and you won two crowns because of it.

"But you don't love anyone now, and if you're what Southern honor is, then Southern honor is a lie." He stopped. "Except for Carlo's. Because he knew—he knew that he couldn't just let you murder Valedan. That killing him, and having him killed by a— by a *demon*—isn't the same thing.

"Do you know that you killed a *girl?* Do you know that you killed her horribly, because your men helped to feed her to a demon? Do you even care that she was someone's daughter, just like I'm someone's son? You were the *defender* of the helpless. You—and your fight—and the bandits—" He dragged a sleeve across his eyes. "It was a lie, I guess. A lie, like anything else."

A boy of his age was not as young in the Dominion.

"I admired you, Ser Anton," the boy said, and tears mingled with anger, shaking the voice yet making it stronger at the same time. "I thought you were so—"

Ser Anton surprised both the boy and himself. He heard the slap as if he were the clapper and the boy the bell—or perhaps the other way around; it resounded in him, the act of striking a weaponless young boy.

They froze; he watched the white mark on the boy's face gradually redden. His hand. He expected guards to rush in to the boy's defense, but Aidan straightened himself to his full height. "Why are you doing this?" he asked. He said it quietly; the tears were gone. It was as if that blow bound them.

And it was an act of intimacy, that slap. Only intimate anger could force the hand of a man like Ser Anton to something other than lethal violence. No; not true. But this, this strike of hand across face—this was reserved for errant children. His own.

He bowed. Bowed to the boy whose company he wanted, and whose company he now knew would be far, far too costly.

You are the only one who can do what must be done. Take this sling. Take this rock.

And what good, the young defenseless man had asked, would a rock do, where horses, swords and arrows had failed?

Oh, yes, he knew it. He knew the story well.

*The creature has three eyes. It sees all that happens around it.
Only aim, hit true, and you will turn one—just one—of those
eyes inward.*

So he'll be blinded. They tried *that.*

*No. He will not be blinded. He will be forced to see what the
chaos of fighting and death has allowed him to escape—why else
do you think he kills and kills and kills? In the fight for survival,
only the sword counts; the warrior's trance is everything. Why
do you think he chooses a life in which he can do little else?*

Take the rock, boy. Aim true.

*Because this creature was a man once, and made foul by the
sorceries of his choice and his desire.*

And the boy took the rock, and faced the monster.

And the monster's eye turned inward.

And he died of what he saw there.

They were quiet, these two men. Wine had come their way,
and it was of a very, very fine vintage; so, too, had fruits, chilled
somehow against the summer heat—and cream, something thick
and rich and sweet that had no equal in the Terreans they made
their home. No equal in Raverra.

Even women—and in the North, women were by their very nature both repellent and exotic in their forwardness—had made it
clear that they were available.

The food, they accepted, but the women they merely flattered
by gentle rejection.

"I have failed him," Carlo di'Jevre said quietly.

Andaro di'Corsarro said nothing. There was nothing to say.

"Do you think he'll forgive?"

"I don't know. I would have thought—I would have said, had
you asked me this a month ago, that he would have killed you for
interference. Now . . . I just don't know." He was older; the two
years had seemed so vast a gulf when they had first met under
the old man's tutelage. Now it was nothing. Twenty-one. Twenty-
three. Nothing.

"It is the kai Leonne," Carlo said, breaking silence—for they
had found a silent place.

"You think of him because of where we are," Andaro replied,
and it was in some ways true: they sat in the small courtyard in
the Arannan Halls, their backs pressed up against the rounded
curve of the fountain's short wall, the alabaster figure of a boy, a

sightless boy, behind them. Water fell from his hands, a continual thin downpour, an offering or an obeisance. They knew the value of water. And even if the kai Leonne had been raised here, in the weak wastelands of the North, he knew it as well. His blood knew it.

"No," Carlo said softly. "I don't." He lifted a hand to the wreath that he could not quite bear to be without. He had sacrificed the full use of his leg in exchange for it, and he bore it like a scar: proudly. "We helped him," he continued quietly. "We helped him kill the Tyr'agar."

"And that?"

"It was not the same."

"His wives and his daughters were with him."

Carlo shrugged. "Neither you nor I were wasted on the women; we fought his Tyran, and we bested them. That was clean."

"And he fought the Tyr'agar." The words that left him next were quiet, soft words. "Beneath the Lady's Moon. She judged, Carlo."

"We're beneath the Lady's Moon now," Carlo replied. "Or I would not tell you what I think."

Andaro smiled in the shadows because Carlo, of the two, felt the need to express everything. Not always with words; indeed often words were an impediment and a waste of his time—but by action, reaction. He was wild, impetuous, his court skills at very best half-formed—in all things, unlike Andaro di'Corsarro.

"Then tell me what you think," Andaro said. "I will not speak of it to Ser Anton, and I will not be offended."

"I think that the kai Leonne would never stoop to the use of demons. I think the kai Leonne serves the Lord of Day, whether or not he has the Radann creeping up his backside with their commandments."

Andaro laughed, but quietly. "You've had too much of that very fine wine."

"Or not enough, is that it?"

"Or not enough. But you can drink more than any man present; enough would beggar them." His smile fell away like clothing at day's end. "Carlo, we've come here to serve Ser Anton. Not the new Tyr, or his new Tyrs."

"Yes." Carlo picked up the glass—for glass was everywhere in *Avantari,* or so it seemed to the two men—and drained it. "But had you asked me—had you asked me, even that night of slaughter, I would have said that Ser Anton served the Lord of Day.

"But he knew about the demon, and the demon is no part of the Lord of Day, and no part of the Lady; the night that is falling is His, and I—" He stared at his hands. "And if the death of the Leonne clan is the final stone that brings the wall down . . . maybe I'm happy to be a cripple."

"You're hardly a cripple," Andaro replied, but he was troubled. "We made our choice."

"Based on what we knew."

"And now?"

"Now, the only thing that would keep me here is you."

They stared at each other a long time in the darkness.

And then Andaro turned, the movement sudden, a snap of neck and shoulder. His sword made more noise than he did as it left his scabbard.

Carlo rose at once; they were a single person in time of danger, and the injury was forgotten. No; that much pain could not be forgotten. Ignored.

"What is it?"

"We were heard," Andaro replied quietly.

"By who?"

"I'm not sure. I saw him leave. He was too large to move that quietly." He sat on the fountain's edge.

"Ours," Carlo said, "or theirs?"

Tonight, under the moon's open face, Andaro said, "I don't know. But I think—I think we would be safer if, this one time, it was one of theirs."

It was not.

Pedro, the merchant who was not a merchant, could move silently when he chose, and he had so chosen. That one of the two was aware of him at all said much of Ser Anton's training.

I told them, he thought, fingering the slender dagger that was as much a part of him as the multiple rings that adorned his fingers, the ostentatious display. In honesty, he had been wrong. Ser Anton di'Guivera had proved himself worthy of their trust, dedicated to their goal.

Cortano di'Alexes had foreseen that much: that his hatred would prove far greater than his title. Pedro himself had not seen that. Ser Anton's reputation was obviously greater than the man himself, and that amused Pedro. Very little amused him these days.

The conversation between the two men angered him.

He was a vain man in his fashion, but not without cause; he knew that it was not wise to anger him, and wished at times that his role was a more public one; if it were, people would understand the risk they took when they interfered with his plans.

But no matter.

He served the true Lord, the *known* Lord, in his fashion, and when the time came, his role would be known. In the streets beneath these streets, when the City was brought, once again, to light.

Watching the two men, Carlo and Andaro, the seeds of the final contingency plan had been planted, and as he walked, as he returned in leisure to the lights and the lovely noise, they began to sink roots, to grow deep. To carry the analogy, and he had a great love of such things, he knew that that plan would bear fruit if all others failed, and indeed, it pleased him, for there was a rough justice in it.

The Imperials had robbed him of his first victory, and the Imperials had robbed him of the *Kialli* who would have lined the marathon's route, thus robbing him of the easiest access. But the third attempt— that was betrayal, pure and simple. Had it not been for the interference of Carlo di'Jevre, Valedan kai di'Leonne would be dead.

Pedro forgot little. And forgave nothing.

The names of the Lady's chosen were the foundations of his early life. From the moment that the *Kovaschaii* masters had opened their doors to him, had anointed him with the grail and the star in a labyrinth under a city that was old as time, he had heard what they heard: The Lady's voice, chiming the deaths she desired.

What he had not heard, what no man but the brother granted the responsibility for the death could hear, was the name of the man who hired the brother. The name was not spoken; it was taken, taken by consensual touch. Many were the men who refused that touch—and the service—for what it represented: Intimacy. Invasion.

Kallandras did not, therefore, know who summoned the *Kovaschaii*. But he knew the names. No one who spent time in this court could not. *Jewel ATerafin.*

He dressed for the revelry and he dressed for the night; the flash of color that was his overcoat could be easily discarded, as could the large boots. Salla, the lute by which he had earned his title, was not so easy a thing to set aside; for that reason he did not carry her, although he had chosen to take that risk at the height of the sea's challenge. He had not always been honest with himself in his youth; he could be honest now. He had preserved that lute through every battle, every bardic challenge, every contest. She had been Sioban's gift, and although he had felt disdain for it then, the music had already trapped him.

Such were people; they either died or grew to love their cages.

He was halfway across the palace when he found Mirialyn, and she carried the news: Jewel ATerafin had disappeared from the healerie. There was no evidence of a struggle, but a dagger had been thrown into the headboard of the bed she'd been in. They were searching for her, assuming that she had somehow managed to flee.

It would not be easy to kill the seer-born.

But if one knew that's what she was, it wouldn't be impossible either. He bowed to Mirialyn; she said nothing. Her way of wishing him well.

Bruce Allen. The Eagle. Of course.

"Miri," he said softly, before she could move away.

"Yes?"

"Where does Commander Allen currently reside?"

"I think—if you must know—he's staying with Sioban."

There were so very few things in the world that surprised him. This did; he would not have thought to find Allen there. But the fact that his brother knew to look for Jewel ATerafin in the healerie implied much about the man who wished her dead. He knew his victims well.

"My thanks," the master bard acknowledged.

With Sioban.

"Sioban," he said, into the wind, into the silence that the bardic voice could penetrate without breaking.

Silence returned; the unnatural silence that gathered around words of power.

"Kallandras? This had better be important."

"Are you with Commander Allen?"

The pause was awkward, but there. He relaxed. Until she spoke again. **"No. He's off with the Flight."**

The Flight. The three together. **"Where?"**

"Why?"

Cursing did nothing but alleviate irritation; Kallandras rarely used it. **"Sioban."**

"Avantari," she said at last. **"Hall of Wise Counsel, in the East Chamber of Resolution."**

Which meant, of course, that The Kalakar and The Berriliya were fighting. **"Thank you,"** he said.

"Your Ospreys tried to have the boy killed!" The Hawk's voice was taken to the heights of the profoundly simple room, there to echo and swoop. "Did you think the rest of us wouldn't hear the truth?"

"The boy made no complaint, formal or otherwise—which means it's none of your gods-cursed business. Or have you so few of your own men that you've nothing better to do than spy on mine?" The flats of her palms slapped the top of the fine grain, emphasizing the fall of her own reflection across the room's single table. It was polished, this table, and heavier than ten good men; it didn't even rock at the force of the blow.

Commander Bruce Allen was certain it had seen worse.

"No, Kalakar. I find little joy in the escapades of your men, and no desire to learn more of them. But this was brought to my attention by an external source, and I was forced to answer it. You've made no attempts to discipline the Ospreys."

Silence. Ellora's lips were white. "It always comes down to the Ospreys, doesn't it?" she said tersely.

"Not particularly. Your men were always a discipline problem. The lack of enforced discipline caused friction for myself and my Verruses. I do not wish to see that difficulty reimposed when we take our armies to war. There have been few border actions, and it has been twelve years since we've seen battle. Many of the men we've recruited during the Challenge are unformed— and I will not see them turned into the chaos that *you* call an army!"

"Devran," Bruce Allen said, raising a hand. "The Ospreys were used by *the* army."

"They were also formed out of the men who would otherwise have faced the Kings' Justice—and died doing so. But I understand their use; they are devoid of any moral sense or purpose and they make a fine weapon against an enemy more like them than the Kings' men."

"Yes," Ellora said starkly. "They do. They protect your boys. They keep their hands clean, so they can pretend they've fought the 'better' war."

"Ellora," the Commander said. "They keep the hands of *all* of our armies clean, most of yours included."

Silence.

"And the discipline they face has always been legendary and severe."

She shrugged. "I won't—before we've even entered the field—be told how to form my units. They operate under the rules of the Kings' Justice—"

"Barely!"

"And they fight to the death where they have to."

"They fight," The Berriliya said, and Bruce Allen knew they were coming to the core of an argument that would haunt them all, again and again, over the course of the war, "for *you*. Not for the Kings, and not for their Justice; not for the Empire. They fight for Commander *Ellora*. They don't even give a damn that a House name follows the rank."

"And should they?"

Both the Kestrel and the Hawk were bent over the table now, straining across its length as if to reach each other. Commander Allen stood between them, consciously aware of two things. That he admired the woman and the man immensely; that the woman did, indeed, drive an army with the force of her personality, both giving—iconically, of course—and demanding devotion and loyalty. Legend: That if she was on the field, she did not leave any of her own, fallen or dead, for the enemy. Truth: She didn't.

The man was a military man; stiffer, and without the personal charm, the rough openness, that The Kalakar offered. He left the dead when the cost of bringing them in would be *more* dead, and he expected his men to see the value of that exchange. Most did. The Berriliya's men were loyal to The Berriliya—partly because of their competition with The Kalakar's. He held them, he demanded their respect but not their love or filial devotion. And of the two, it was Devran whose mind was quicker; he could make the coolest of decisions without the pain or the anger that came with surrendering the lives of his soldiers. Thus, in the end, he fought the less costly war. And yet . . .

Together, when they weren't actively trying to have the other removed or disciplined, they formed an army that had both head and heart, that reacted intelligently and instinctively; they were a team.

And they were a team that responded to *his* command because, in the end, he could see where they could not.

There were two great windows in the room; two, open to darkness and the muted sounds of the night.

Instinct made him fall to the ground an instant before the window shattered.

CHAPTER TWENTY-FOUR

Crossbow. A simple weapon, elegant and easily carried when the target was on flat ground. No such weapon had been used against the ATerafin, but she had escaped unscathed.

Kallandras saw the light from a tall window give his brother's face the grace of gentle glow. It made him beautiful, and the master bard hesitated for just that second; the bow was trained. The *Kovaschaii*—and he struggled, now, to think of him as that, as that and not more—lifted a hand, pressed it flat against the pane.

Held the bow.

Glass shattered.

Quarrel flew.

And wind nudged it, wind nudged it a hair's breadth off its perfect course.

There were three people in that room; gender ceased to matter. They were the heart of the Kings' army; a good choice of deaths. Kallandras froze a moment, staring at the mild consternation, the lift of brow, the compression of lip across a brother's face. This was not one of the younger brothers.

No point in conversation; there wouldn't be any.

He armed himself.

On a bad day, he could arm himself completely silently; he could draw metal against metal as if it were feather against skin. Power was not the reason he killed; he had no desire to make another suffer by forcing them to witness the death he was about to grant them.

But there were other desires.

On rare days, he lied to himself, and that angered him in the here and the now, his brother yards away.

Perhaps that anger betrayed him, for the first lesson taught was that there were two things that must never precede a killing: pleasure or anger.

His brother turned.

His brother.

"Tallos," he said, because he could not help himself.

And Tallos said, "Kallatin," as his arm left his side.

He had been from his brother long enough, and there was no like longing in Tallos; there was hatred, anger, a bitterness that, living as he had always lived, had had no chance to fade. Not as Kallandras' bitterness had done, exposed to time, to sun, to a life outside of the *Kovaschaii*. A life he had never wanted; a life he did not want.

And did.

He was in motion, and if the flying metal blade struck him, it drew scant blood. First blood.

He offered no other words. Tallos was the Lady's. Kallandras was less and more. *After what they did to us,* he wanted to cry out, *how can you serve the Lord of Night? How can you serve His purpose? She all but made her vow!*

But there would be no answer to that question.

Out of this, out of this night there would be a death. A death, that was all.

He called upon his reserves; Tallos called his. They had both used their training this day, and their energy, and they both knew that behind stone walls perforated by lead and glass, three men would soon be watching.

The master bard called upon his voice.

The *Kovaschaii,* expecting it, called upon his will; the voice was stronger. It slowed him.

Kallandras struck; Tallos parried. Second blood, first for Kallandras.

He had not put the whole of his voice into the fight. Could not, more fool he. For no other necessary death would he fall into the trap of honor.

He fell here. Blood fell, too; his.

And if he died, this brother would leave him, fallen refuse, he would be trapped within his corpse, no brother to guide the Lady to him, no dance along the hidden star to light her way. No Lady to return to him his name, and to see him to her halls or the halls of Mandaros.

Tallos was three years his elder, and a master of the second tier; so, too, was Kallandras. They seemed born and bred in different lands; where Kallandras was fair in color, Tallos was as Southern as the Serra Alina. As hawklike, as merciless. But they had both been taken from Southern streets.

Blade-dancers played their games, in the South, danced on death's edge. Were any watching, had any witnessed, they would have thought that Kallandras and his brother *were* such blade-dancers, for Tallos deigned to draw weapon and close. Hard, to speak with the bardic voice when every breath you drew was necessary; harder, when the voice could never—never quite—be made as instinctive a weapon as a sword. There was a power in it that did not lend itself to death. Even by Kallandras.

Tallos was no fool; the deaths at the broken window were deaths he had promised—but unlike Estravim so very long ago, he made no attempt to throw his life away completing the task that had been promised to the Lady. A single death, and he might have.

But he might not have.

The *Kovaschaii* were human in their fashion.

This death was not a death that had been promised to the Lady; it was a death that had been promised to the brotherhood, by the brotherhood, decades past. Tallos would not forget. As Kallandras could not.

These two, they had trained together. Worked together. Taken flight on their first—and only—task together, as brothers were allowed to do when they had not yet been deemed capable enough.

Kallandras remembered.

He started to offer the ritual greeting, the respect due a brother. At least the last *Kovaschaii* he had met had given that much. He snapped his arm up, and in the night's scant light, gold and silver glinted; the ten-point star that neither man needed to see to understand the presence of. He lifted his sword to draw the sigil and the challenge; to declare his tier, and his ability.

Not so Tallos; not so, a man for whom the betrayal was both collective *and* personal. He came at once, the swing of his arm, the slight doubling of his step, unmistakable. All nicety, all hope for even the convention of the brotherhood here, was gone.

Kallandras replied in kind.

Bound in memories, bound in the anger that comes *only* from memory, their swords struck and slid off one another, strike and slide, strike and slide; timed, as all things were timed—by the heart, the heart's beat, the movement of air into lung: the rhythm that marked their lives.

Ellora was first off the floor.

It wasn't that her hearing was keener—or so she would later say—it was that she loathed the smell of stone. And this close to stone, side of mouth and cheek pressed into its flat, cool surface, air dragged into mouth along its length, she'd argue that it damned well did have a smell.

But she also heard the blades dance.

"Ellora," Bruce said; he and Devran had retreated to a safe place beneath the table. Silly thing—none of the Commanders had thought to carry either crossbow or longbow to a private, if heated, meeting.

They had swords, though. The scabbard of hers made an unpleasant noise as she dragged it up across ground with her. The blade made a different sound as she separated it from scabbard; she held it, knees bent, the sound of a dozen blades filtering in through the broken glass.

"Ellora."

She heard the scrape of chair against stone; it grated. She knew that Bruce was going to be annoyed. Oddly enough, he'd be more annoyed than Devran; Devran ABerriliya—The Berriliya now—expected no less from her, and probably privately hoped she'd get pincushioned for her lack of caution. Her ostensible irresponsibility.

Slowly, she made her way to the windows, cursing the fact that the Kings had enough money to make the damned things so grand—and so very long.

Blood and blood; blood and blood; they exchanged these cuts as lovers exchanged caresses; angry lovers who are not quite distant enough to let go of what they had when what they have is so bitter. They called upon the reserves of their training, not for strength, but for *speed,* burning that reserve in a flare of motion, of movement.

No fight between brothers ever lasted long.

Or rather, no sparring did; how many brothers fought, and how many killed each other?

He was weakened by the morning's flight and the loss of blood; Tallos should have been able to kill him. Should have. But the wind was strong in this small courtyard; leaves were torn from trees out of season, falling in swirls like a green rain, at his whim. He would pay. He would pay for it all. *This* power had come a little too easily.

He could not speak; he desired it, but the price for speech was death. Here, Tallos knew his weaknesses and his strengths, and he had, it seemed, never forgotten them.

Blood and blood; touch and touch.

He thought there might be no distinctive strike, no final blow; they would whittle each other's lives away in this courtyard, in a battle that showed the bruises of Kallatin's choice, decades past, across both of them.

But he was wrong.

In mid-strike, Tallos lost his rhythm; his sword flew *back* inexplicably, and Kallandras heard, as if from a great distance, metal striking metal, and the curse, cut short, of a woman's voice.

Heard it at a distance that did not allow him to stop; his sword was in motion; Tallos was in motion; the two connected perfectly.

No last words, even. He found the assassin's heart, and stilled it with the runneled steel of blade. It took a long moment for the body to fall, and in that moment, Kallandras had dropped his sword. His arms were under the arms of his brother, to ease him in his fall.

"I don't think," he heard someone say, and hated her for it, "I've ever seen you fight, Master Bard. You're good."

The Kalakar stood in the moonlight.

Holding his brother under both arms, he acknowledged the compliment with a toss of the head. Acknowledged what lay beneath it as well; suspicion, curiosity.

"Who was he?"

He shrugged. And then he did what he was sworn, by Senniel's oath, not to do. **"If you would, Kalakar, the Kings' Swords should be summoned."**

She didn't notice, or didn't appear to, the use of the bardic gift, the laying of compulsion beneath words that were reasonable in their own right. Kallandras *was* a master. In the poor light, she bent, searching the flagstones, and then the tamed wild blooms, for the sword that Tallos, in breaking his rhythm to deflect, had lost his life to.

He could be patient; patience was an art that the *Kovaschaii* worked hard to force their younger brothers to develop—for death required patience, of a sort, and an attention to detail that only the patient ever achieved.

But he could not be patient now, not with this woman, not in this place, the body a demand and a responsibility.

He lifted his brother as she lifted her sword; held him as she sheathed it. "I will send for the Kings," she said, and she left him. Left him for just long enough.

He carried the body into the shadows, cursing her, cursing the

Challenge, cursing the crowds that robbed him of the thing he most required. Privacy. Peace.

Framed by the waved curve of broken glass, Commander Bruce Allen watched the master bard leave. "I think it's safe, Devran," he said. "Ellora will join us shortly."

The Berriliya, dour, was silent; Commander Allen laughed. Ellora was a woman who could fall face first into a pigsty and come up with a rose between her teeth—or at least a wholesome meal; she habitually challenged wisdom and common sense as if they were her enemies. It did not always work, but she had never quite been humbled enough to fall prey to the mixture of fear and experience that most men called caution.

No; that was unfair. She was cautious much of the time.

And had there been AKalakar here, they would have served her purpose. But in a room with only two men, neither of whom were under her direct command, she did what she felt she had to do.

Remarkable.

As remarkable as the fact that she had taken the request of the bardic master as if it were an order. He made a note, and kept his own counsel.

He danced.

In a tiny room in Senniel College, a place that defined him, and that he—against his early will—had come to define, there was refuge and privacy. Journeymen crowded the walls, of course, and the hopefuls who might be chosen as apprentices should they impress a master, but as he *was* such a master, they neither questioned him nor followed when he bid them go.

He had passed beneath the arch of the great hall that separated the masters from the rest, and rested a moment there; death had achieved what his brother had never achieved in life: Tallos was graceless and heavy.

But at last he found his room, and pushed the door wide; he carried Tallos across the threshold and closed that door behind him, as if it were more than aged wood, iron hinges.

Then he'd laid the body out in the five point star.

He danced, his body not so graceful as it once was, nor so artful. But if youth is passion—as all songs suggest—there was a wild quality to the dance that showed any who witnessed it that there were parts of his heart that were protected from age and time, from change.

And *she* witnessed it, of course. She heard the song that words didn't carry; saw the way he leaped and landed, each strike of foot against floor a part of the star that was hidden, the secret self.

The room was given to mist, to the half-world, to the land where the gods might roam freely and the mortals might join them. And standing in shadows that were colder than the Northern seas, and far older, stood the Lady.

"Tallos," she said, and her voice was a revelation, "born Simeon, I return to you your name." A gift. But not for one such as he.

Tallos rose, shedding his body as if it were clothing in which he had traveled months of dusty road. Kallandras could see his back, and not the expression upon his face; he did not know if there was rapture at being, finally, united with the Lady, with his name—this true self—and with the brothers that lay beyond death, above death.

But he knew, when Tallos turned, that not all of his life had been left behind. He did not speak.

"You have summoned me," the Lady said. "You have freed your brother." Her voice was cool. "I have not forgotten," she added softly, "that you braved the ruins of Vexusa to free two we could not find." She placed a hand upon Tallos' stiff shoulder, drawing him closer. "I have forgotten nothing."

He knelt, the force of desire sapping the strength from his knees, as if a desire that strong left no strength for anything else.

And this, too, she understood. It was not for her; it was for Tallos. For his brothers. "Lady," he said, belying the truth in the only way he knew how.

"One of my own would have found him, bard," she replied softly, a warning there.

"I did not dance his death because no one else could dance it. I danced it because—" He looked up.

Met the eyes of Tallos, the Tallos of his youth, the man-boy whom the sun had darkened. Tallos said nothing.

"You danced," she said. "It is enough."

"No one will dance for you," Tallos said, speaking at last.

"Do you think I don't know it?" He could hide bitterness when he chose; he could make a mask of his voice just as most men made masks of their faces when the situation demanded it. He spoke softly, the words measured, the truth, or the fact that he had accepted it long ago, evident.

"No, Kallatin," Tallos said softly, "I think you *do* know it. Of all my brothers, you were the one I—" He glanced at the Lady; Kallandras heard the shift in his voice, but did not curse it; he was bard-born, and heard what had almost been said. "The one I least understood." He bowed, then.

"Lady," Kallandras said, still upon his knees, abased in every way a man could be abased and still be what Kallandras had become. "A question."

"Ask," she said.

"After— After Vexusa, I would not have thought—I would not have thought that you would take the deaths requested by those who serve the—the Lord of Night."

Wind howled a moment from the folds of her robe; the bird upon her shoulder rose with a screech in its wake, settling only when silence had returned. He bowed his head.

"I choose to answer this question because I am aware that my brother did not return to the Hells; aware that he has not yet paid for the crime that he committed against my chosen. But *you* will not question me in that fashion again."

"Lady," he said.

"What you . . . dare . . . to accuse me of is a falsehood. I have taken no deaths from the men who collude with your enemy, unless it be their own."

"The eight."

"Eight, yes."

"But these—"

"No. These deaths were offered to me, and I accepted them, from a man of the place you call Averalaan." Wind was the voice of her ire. "We may meet again," she said softly. "But it will not be at your death."

He was not a young man anymore.

It did not break him to watch Tallos walk into the mist, with no further acknowledgment, no farewells, no hint of understanding. It did not hurt him because the loss was so much a fact of life it had become all that he expected.

Until Tallos turned back to him, and he could see, in the otherworld, the light that danced along the thin trail of his tears.

"Has Sigurne died?"

"No."

"Then I'm amazed you managed to gain entrance into my chamber," Meralonne said, his dry voice thin as old leaf. "She's let no one in except Dantallon and the boy who brings what passes for food in these parts."

"You are . . . well." the bard asked.

"And you are a liar," the mage replied. "Bring me my pipe."

"I'd as soon bring Dantallon a noose and a yardarm," Kallandras said, laughing. He could see that mage was shivering. "You recover well, Meralonne. I have seen men felled by—"

"Carelessness. Go on."

"By fevers such as yours who were racked for two weeks before they either recovered or succumbed."

"I have enough pride not to die making children's baubles. Not an end for me, I'm afraid." But he pulled the blankets up in hands that shook. "I will confess," he added, "that I am weary."

Kallandras bowed his head.

"And that I will not sleep until you tell me whatever it is you came here to confess."

"Confess?"

Meralonne coughed. The weakness would hold him yet; Kallandras did not think he would see sunlight without the filter of glass until well past the end of the Challenge. "I will speak," he said softly. "You are tired."

The mage snorted. It was an oddly comforting sound.

"Tonight, an assassination attempt was made upon Jewel ATerafin and upon the three Commanders: The Kalakar, The Berriliya, and Commander Allen."

The mage was still a moment, then the trembling set in and he stifled it. "Success?"

"None."

"Good. Why is this significant?"

"To you?"

"Clever bard. Yes, to me."

"Four deaths, Member APhaniel, and they were called for—and accepted—by a man in this City."

Meralonne's eyes were silver steel. *"Kovaschaii?"*

"I believe so, yes." Neutral words. Safe words.

Safety could be such a lie.

"That would take money."

"Rather a lot."

"And the knowledge of how to reach the brotherhood at all."

Kallandras nodded quietly.

Meralonne swore. "Can you find Dantallon?"

"No," a stern voice said. The dragon, silver-haired and fragile, had returned to the den.

"Valedan, you've done well," Serra Alina said, her hands as soft as her voice. She lay oil against palm, and then palm against skin, and where her hands passed, a warmth seemed to seep into the muscles of his back, his shoulders, his thigh. The bruises, she passed over. He wished she'd passed over the words as well, and said nothing.

Aidan was in the witness house; Aidan, whose wide eyes had seen both his victories and his falls with a kind of fascination that evoked, in Valedan, a sense of what he must have been like at twelve.

And *that* made him think of Ser Anton, which was uncomfortable enough—but from Ser Anton, his thoughts went to Ser Carlo di'Jevre, and that destroyed the lull of the Serra's hands. She knew it, too; her hands paused a moment; she lifted them from his body, gathered her strength, gathered her oils, and then continued.

As if she were in truth his wife, a wife.

Which she would never be, in fact.

Eneric of Darbanne had won. No surprise there. Had he the habit of placing bets—and had Commander Sivari less fierce an eye—he would have put his money on the Northerner. He had offered his congratulations, and that offer had been received with self-confidence. With pride.

But Valedan's attention had been drawn, time and again, to a man who had entered a challenger and become a witness: Carlo di'Jevre.

"Valedan," the Serra said.

He could not discuss this with her; he had tried. She was as severe a taskmaster as Sivari, but the bruises she left in their training exercises were more subtle. "Serra Alina," he said, groaning slightly as he rolled off the mats and found his feet, "my thanks for your efforts."

She did not mar the stillness of her face with a frown, but he felt the night grow darker in the stillness of his rooms. "And you will sleep now?" she asked coolly.

"Yes," he replied, "but let me take in the sea air a moment."

"Do you wish company?"

"Thank you, Serra, but no; tomorrow is the test of the horse, and I desire to gather my thoughts."

All lies, all of it. It was funny how two people could speak so

pleasantly, mean so little by it, and still understand each other
so well.

He went, as he habitually went, to the fountain of the blindfolded
boy. Justice.

And there, in the darkness of moonlight and night sky, he found
that there was no privacy.

"Where are we going?" Auralis asked.

"For a walk," Jewel replied.

"Damned long walk."

She rolled her eyes. "Where does it look like we're going?"

"To the High City." His voice made plain what he thought
of that.

"I used to live in the twenty-fifth," she replied, "but I don't
live there now. You're a soldier. I'm a soldier. Different wars."

"And?"

"I'm going back to the command post before I head out again."

"Avantari?"

"No. Terafin."

He missed a step, and then smiled. "That should be interesting."

Something in his words pulled her up as short as he'd been
pulled up; she froze, for just a moment, as if a dagger's edge was
at her throat, a man's voice in her ear. And her throat was dry, dry,
dry. Nightmare crowded her vision; waking version, just as real.

"Jay?" Kiriel said, but Jewel shook her head and began to run.

"Mother's blood," Jewel said, the words short and labored.

"What? What's wrong?"

"I should've known—damn Evayne—I should have thought—"

"What?"

"She never does anything without a reason. If she'd just wanted to save *my* life, she could've dumped me outside the healerie
doors in *Avantari*. She took me to *you* and to *him*. And you're
here. What do you think that means?"

Kiriel fell silent.

Auralis said, "A fight?"

But she didn't answer, couldn't answer. *Healerie.*

Andaro heard him first. He was listening, after all, to the rise
and fall of Carlo's chest, the quality of his breathing, the quality
of his silence. Carlo was seldom quiet in this fashion, this thoughtful contemplative retreat to a place words wouldn't quite reach.

The idea that the Lady and Andaro were not his only audience had obviously not occurred to him; they were both disquieted.

And both unwilling to face the crowds, although the rider's test would demand everything Andaro had to give it come the dawn. And how much, he thought. How much was that?

Footsteps grew louder, although they were not by nature loud footsteps, not the heavy, cloddish Northern tread. He felt comforted by it, although he did not recognize the sound of the gait. They'd been trained to that; to recognize a man by the approach of his step.

And so it was that they stayed, silent and waiting, while Valedan kai di'Leonne approached the fountain in the otherwise empty courtyard. He came to its edge and stopped there.

They rose to greet him. Should not have, perhaps, but they rose anyway.

He surprised them both; he bowed, and the bow was low, completely Southern. "Ser Carlo," he said.

"We didn't realize," Andaro began, but the kai Leonne lifted a hand.

"This is all the lake I have," he said, gesturing to the fount and its thin stream of ever falling water. "And compared to the waters of the Tor, it is not so very great." He turned to face the statue in the fountain's center. "But it was fashioned by the hands of an Annagarian maker, and the name he gave it was Justice.

"It seems fitting," he added. "And the water is sweet water, if not so wholesome as the lake's."

"This is yours?" Carlo said.

"It belongs to the Kings," was Valedan's reply. "All things in *Avantari* do. This fountain, these halls, the footpaths. They don't own people," he remarked, "but everything else that can be owned is theirs."

"And have you survived, with no serafs? How can you be served by people who neither fear you nor grant you the respect of devotion?" The words left Andaro before he could stop them, and once uttered, they could not be called back. He stared at this man, this Valedan kai di'Leonne, and surprised himself by seeing past the youth. He was, to the best of their knowledge, some seventeen or eighteen years of age; he might be older. Certainly not younger.

But the years that separated them—six at most, four at least—usually made themselves felt, made themselves known. Not tonight. Tonight, this boy was the kai Leonne.

Is this what Ser Anton sees in you? Andaro thought. *Small wonder he is disquieted.*

"How have I survived?" Valedan shrugged. "Well enough. Perhaps there is less to fear in the Northern Court than there was in the Southern Court. These people," he added, lifting an arm as if to take in the entire Empire, "do not make their reputations by the behavior of the serafs they own."

Carlo shrugged, impatient; he was a clansman, but only just, and he owned no serafs. "Not all of the men of the South do, either."

"No," Valedan said. "I know." They were silent. At last he said, "You were sent here to kill me, as my father was killed." Not a question.

Andaro was impassive, silent. He would not be forced to a lie by this man.

But Carlo was . . . Carlo.

"Yes," he said, before Andaro could catch his glance. Intimacy, in honesty. Something to avoid.

"And now?"

Half-bitter, half-proud, Carlo looked down at his leg. "Now what?" he said. "I am as you see me; I've done what I've done. You judge."

"Because you can't?"

That raised hackles; Carlo's eyes narrowed and he drew himself up to his full height—a height that had not been seen since he'd stepped down from the only podium he would stand on in this Challenge.

Andaro felt comforted.

Until Carlo di'Jevre spoke. "How am I to judge?" he asked, his voice the low burning of fire's ember. "Your father was weak. His weakness weakened *us*. He led us not to victory in the war against *these*," his arm swung wide, as Valedan's had done, but the movement was faster, harsher, "but to defeat. The only man who had a measure of success in that war now rules us."

"By what means?" Valedan asked fiercely, eyes narrowed, expression half-hidden in the shadows cast by magelight and moonlight.

Carlo lost the height he'd gained. "I don't know," he admitted, turning his face to the Lady Moon. "I knew—I thought I knew—until I came to this sun-scorched land. And now—I just don't know."

"I owe you my life," Valedan said again.

"You owe the Lady your life," Carlo countered. "I wouldn't have raised sword to save *you*."

"Yet you did."

"For *her* honor," the swordsman shot back, his voice sharp as blade's edge, eyes as narrow. "For her honor, and for the Lord's."

Valedan bowed. "And whose honor did Leonne serve in the time of Darkness? Whose were Leonne's enemies? The Lord's. And the Lady's." He rose. "Carlo di'Jevre, I would be honored—"

"Be damned first," Carlo said.

But Andaro heard it: the waver in the voice, the division, the guilt and the desire. Carlo hid nothing when a weapon was not in his hands, an armed man before him. Even when he tried, as he tried now.

Valedan said smoothly, "I may well be. But not for lack of trying. I'm honored to have you here, in this courtyard, by this fountain." He bowed. "The Lady's Moon," he said, "is shining brightly this eve."

And darkly, Andaro thought, although he did not speak. And darkly as well.

Damn you, kai Leonne.

Night.

Moon in courtyard, impaled by wrought-iron fence. Often seen, from Terafin, but just as often accompanied by silence. Silence—in the streets of the High City, so close to the Challenge itself—was the one thing that money apparently could not buy, nor power ensure; even here, at the heart of the Empire's power, men and women flowed through the streets, the night itself their destination.

Jewel was used to running through crowds; she'd done it a hundred times before; a thousand. But it had been half a lifetime away, and if old habits didn't die—and they didn't die completely—they didn't cling as strongly as they could. Perhaps it was the night, the lack of easy vision, that made the run so difficult. Or perhaps it was the destination: Terafin. Running *to* Terafin always seemed fraught with this terrible lack of speed, this certainty of the terrible consequence of failure.

Kiriel and her friend followed. She was grateful, grateful enough that she paused, in the holdings and directly before the bridge, to wave them on. Best not to lose them, not here. Kiriel knew the way in broad daylight, but night?

She would smack herself later; magic or no, night was Kiriel's element.

The guards at the gate were ATerafin, of course. She flew between them, lifting a hand; torchlight glinted off worked gold, worked platinum.

"Hey, Jay!" a voice called, and she skidded—literally—to a halt across damp grass.

She turned to face Arann.

"Where's Torvan?"

"Hells if I know—*Avantari*."

"But—you—"

"The *healerie,* Arann—we need to reach it. *Now.*"

He left his post. She'd remember it later; he left his post. And followed.

They were four people: Jewel, Kiriel, her friend Auralis, and Arann of the House Guard. They could not move quietly, but they could, having cleared the checkpoint, move *quickly*. No tangle of weed here, no dip in road, no web of crowd to either side or, thanks to alcohol, underfoot. Here, the halls were wide and well-lit, and they went on in relative peace and quiet.

Relative peace.

Relative quiet.

The healerie.

Kiriel heard it first, or at least, Kiriel said it first: *Swords*. Jewel couldn't hear it at first, and she cursed her talent-born blood, cursed the fact that she couldn't summon vision. It was master and she was not—like a horse, she waited to be ridden.

Was this Evayne's lesson?

Hard to hear anyway; Auralis and Kiriel in half-armor, and Arann in the full armor of the House Guards, thundering at her side with each heavy footfall. She had no time to summon other guards. Took no time. Kiriel heard swords.

And swords were forbidden in the healerie.

They took a corner, took another one; the halls in Terafin were wide, and they could run four abreast. Jewel should have been the fastest; she should have gotten there first. But Kiriel, wearing armor, carrying a sword—when had she unsheathed it?—was somehow lighter on her feet. Devoid of shadows, robbed of the menace of the supernatural, she retained *something*. And something, tonight, was a blessing.

Jewel was next; she drew no weapon. First, she still didn't know how to wield a sword. She'd taken a lesson or two—could hear, now, Angel saying, *you fight like a girl!* just before she decked him—but both she and the swordmaster concurred; she wasn't large enough or young enough to become a master.

And at sixteen, newly ATerafin, it was master or nothing.

At thirty-three, at thirty-three she hated the hubris of her younger self. Breath began to scorch the sides of her throat. Too much soft living. Too little real labor.

She heard Arann's intake of breath. They were close enough now that he could hear it: Steel against steel; the short cry of a man's voice. Neither he nor she recognized whose. They put on a last burst of speed.

There: the healerie's solid, simple door. Closed.

But no question, no question at all. Beyond it, the sounds of fighting, distinct. Swords in the healerie. And one didn't take swords into the healerie without Alowan's permission. The consequences were simple: Cross the threshold with the weapon, and never cross it again as a patient.

Jewel knew what it meant: Whoever had opened the door didn't give a rat's ass for the consequences. That meant one thing. *Alowan.*

Or two.

She hadn't said it. Hadn't spoken it aloud, because in the Empire, and in the mind of a superstitious girl in the twenty-fifth holding with a Voyani mother and grandmother, words had power—what was said could resonate through the years, scarring the speaker. Could catch the attention of the winds—or in the Empire, of a capricious, an irritable godling.

She said it now, a prayer, a promise, her shaking hand on the healerie door.

"Teller. Angel."

The door was locked. Arann kicked it in.

The first thing she saw made no sense—but fear did that to her; heightened immediate images into a sharp clarity of here-and-now that sometimes robbed them of context. Men were at a door. Men in armor, with heavy swords. Chips of wood were flying—they were using their swords as axes.

Context tumbled in.

Alowan's door.

She thought—would remember thinking—*why don't they just kick it down?* before Kiriel jogged her elbow.

"Jay?"

The metal against metal wasn't coming from the men at the

door, obviously; it came from inside the healerie itself. "Them," she said thickly. Kiriel bobbed, head rising and falling; she cut a path through the greenery as if she *were* a demon and the word a dismissal.

But Arann and Auralis were armored, Arann for duty and Auralis for gambling houses full of drunkards who had lost too much money, and the opening of the healerie door had finally caught the attention of the men who labored, notching and dulling their swords. They looked up. They were four.

Four men, and she recognized the armor at once. Recognized the surcoat. House Guards. *Terafin* guards.

One of them swore.

"Kill them," he said. "Kill all of them except her."

Auralis and Arann exchanged a brief glance, and then their faces set in expressions characteristic to them, a hardening not unlike the taking up of a shield. Auralis smiled; that was all, the smile a broad splash of warmth across a face a bit too self-satisfied to otherwise be handsome to someone like Jewel.

Arann's face became a mask; a slight narrowing of eye, a stilling of lip, a setting of jaw.

Both men lifted their swords. She fell through the crack between them, although neither man spoke a word, and when she did, that gap seemed to close on its own as four men rushed in.

No taking of time, here; they had numbers—two to one were never good odds—and probably little time. The healerie door was open, after all. Someone would hear them. Someone would have to hear them.

She pulled her dagger and spun on heel, teetering a moment between this fight and the one that she could hear. And then she ran. It almost killed her, to run—because she didn't run toward the beds either.

She ran for the door, the exposed stretch of empty hallway. She ran for Captain Alayra of the Chosen. Alayra was always in.

There were four men in the healerie proper. They carried swords, wore full armor, and circled two men, both armed, neither dressed for combat, who stood back to back. One was small, too small for a fight like this; a slash crossed his chest from shoulder to waist, staining shirt and skin. His face was bruised and yellowed— old bruises, to her practiced eye. He was barely standing. Would not, she thought, stand long.

Teller.

The other, wilder beneath his tight control, was unwounded, had caused pain. He was taller—as tall as Auralis although not as broadly built—and although he bled, it wasn't completely clear why. His sword was stained.

Angel.

The other beds were empty. No—not completely; three beds were bumpy; the sheets had been slashed end to end, much as Teller's chest had been. She'd have to ask. Later.

Two to one. Poor odds.

Four to one were poorer.

She stood in the room like a small storm, and then, of all things, Kiriel di'Ashaf laughed.

Arann was the largest of the den. Heaviest. Strongest. He'd been in fights before that had almost killed him—and they were fights like this, not contests of honor, but simple attempts to end his life. The fact that these men wore armor and carried swords didn't change those rules. What changed them slightly was this: Arann himself had been trained, by Alayra, by Torvan, by the sword-master of Terafin. He wasn't the best—but he wasn't far off.

Two of the men were younger than he was; two older. He'd recognized all of them. Knew how they fought, as he'd drilled with the two younger men in the ring. Never for keeps.

This was for keeps.

They hadn't the time to build momentum, nor the time to build speed; but they were used to taking advantage of superior numbers. Alayra's gift. He was used to defending against superior numbers. Torvan's gift.

He took the first blow with the flat of his sword, side-stepping the man who delivered it; twisting him; using the slight lack of control momentum built against him. Almost worked.

The second blow—unparried—was glancing; it slid down armor and caught a moment in surcoat. That was all. He responded in kind.

Alayra was sleeping.

Figures. Middle of the Challenge, all of the men on tenter-hooks, the streets full, The Terafin engaged in whatever it was The Terafin did during a season that saw the influx of every merchant and politico you'd want to see—and a whole lot more you didn't—and Alayra was sleeping.

Or at least that's what it looked like to Jewel.

But the minute she touched the bed—not Alayra herself, just the bed—she knew that the Captain of the Chosen was gone.

It hit her like an assassin's blade, shoved suddenly and deftly between her ribs in a single strike. She stepped back.

No time left. No time to honor the dead; no time to even speak of it clearly. She ran back from the room, retreating as if at the discovery of fire.

Ran to the door where two members of the Chosen—not too young, but you didn't get Chosen by being young—were standing. She didn't recognize the woman. But the man, the man was an old friend. Arrendas. Captain.

"What are you—"

"Julia summoned me," he said.

"But you're in armor—"

"Jewel, it's not that late. But you, *you,* not any other ATerafin, don't go running hellbent through the halls for no reason."

"You were—"

"I was. I'm back. What's wrong?"

"Alayra's dead," she said. Lifting her ring, showing it although it wasn't absolutely unnecessary, she added, "and Alowan's going to be if you don't go to the healerie *now.*"

The ring gave her words authority and command.

Or something. She wasn't certain; her throat closed after they'd left her mouth and she couldn't have spoken them again had she wanted to. She turned, and she heard them at her back.

"Jewel?"

"Arann and a man you won't recognize are fighting four of the House Guards. And—and at least two of my den. Girl, armed, our side. Probably Angel."

They left, then.

House Guards were trained by the same people. Same way. They were good, these two. Younger, older. Good. He was wounded. Twice, a gash across the cheek, a strike, heavy enough to send him back, across shoulder. Two swords sought entry between the joints of armor, or through the armor itself; could be done. He'd seen it.

But it hadn't, *Kalliaris'* smile, been done yet.

At his side, the stranger fought. Arann didn't have thought to spare beyond this, but he prayed, briefly, that the stranger could hold his own. Because he thought it was just a matter of time, and if the stranger fell, he didn't even have that.

* * *

Four men against two.

Four men against three. Kiriel smiled.

And for the first time in her life, the result of her smile was this: one of the four men turned to another and said simply, "Kill her."

There was no sudden cessation of motion, no hesitation, no subconscious deference to *felt* power; there was unadorned order, as if she were of less consequence—obviously less consequence—than either Angel or Teller. One man—*one* man—broke away from their attack, his sword firmly, confidently held, his expression just a shade off bored.

"Don't you know who I am?" she cried, swinging her sword in a slow arc that was level with her chest.

"Doesn't matter," the man said. She heard the weariness in his voice, and that made no sense to her either. Weariness.

The ring on her hand was flat, lifeless; it had betrayed her once and had gone to sleep. But she knew—she knew that beneath its sullen, flat platinum, she *had* power, she was what she had always been. Hadn't Meralonne's ring proved that?

When you fight, Kiriel, you always have something to prove.

Not his voice. Not here. She parried the man's first blow as if it were a fly.

But if you fight as if you have something to prove, you will fail. The reasons for beginning a fight must be left outside of the fight itself, or they will devour what you need: concentration. Control.

And she had always followed his advice. Because she trusted him. Had trusted him.

Trust no Kialli, Kiriel. Not even me.

She roared and the sound was a whimper, a failure of power, a weakness of breath. Human. But her enemy had been expecting no such thing and he paused a moment, stepping back from the engagement as if she were mad, as if the madness demanded an attention that her sanity was unworthy of.

He died, that expression still upon his face.

If Kiriel was not all she had been, the sword hadn't changed.

When he took the third wound, his left leg almost buckled beneath him. Almost. He held it straight, but the effort cost him: fourth wound. Glancing slash. He could feel the sweat running down his brow; hoped it wouldn't reach his eyes. He was tired.

The minutes were as intensive now as hours; he wasn't certain that he could actually—

Ah. Fifth blow.

He fell back, staggering, parrying.

Lifted his sword as a sword caught the light; caught it, although his swing was wild enough he had luck to thank, not skill. He was going to die.

He didn't want to die.

He had prayed to *Kalliaris,* the only god any of them really did pray to when they stared death in the face. But this was beyond that; death was too close to him to even *see* clearly. And that close to death, that close, he forgot prayer entirely.

Prayer, after all, had never done him as much good as *she* had.

"Jay!" he cried, half-plea, half-pledge.

Metal slid off metal in a long, slow blur that ended with the hilt of his sword. It was a good sword. But so, too, were theirs; they were Terafin swords.

Jay answered.

To either side of him, the shadows silvered and moved; he blinked, blinked again, wiped a gauntlet across his forehead—which did exactly nothing—and then lifted his sword, almost renewed by what he saw: The Chosen of Terafin.

For the first time since they'd arrived in the healerie he had a chance to actually look at the stranger who had come with Jewel—and he saw, to his surprise, that a dead man lay on the floor at his feet. He fought one on one with a Terafin House Guard—and Arann thought he was winning.

Would have put money on it.

He didn't feel her hand on his shoulder—not through the armor—but he heard her voice and turned toward it. It was surprisingly gentle.

"Do I look that bad?" he said, or tried to.

"Don't speak," she replied, which was as much an answer as he needed. She led him, and because he had always followed her when things were darkest, he followed her now, giving over the responsibility of action and decision.

And shortly thereafter giving over the light, the greenery in the arborium, the sound of water's gentle fall, close enough now to be heard above the din of sword.

He heard a scream, something shrill, from the rooms where the beds were. Bolted up; she pushed him down. "I *said* lie back."

More like the Jay he was used to. She pulled the helmet free from his head and he felt water, blessed and cool, across his forehead.

And that was all.

The silence from the healerie was awful. She wondered, as she cleared the arborium and headed toward the beds, whether she'd ever be able to come here again and find the quiet peaceful.

Probably. People had memories like sieves.

Kalliaris, she thought. *Smile. Smile, Lady.*

The three beds closest to the open arch had been slashed by two blows; sheets had been torn back and exposed. A body lay here, on the floor, a sword still gripped in its hand. She didn't recognize it. So far so good.

She stepped through the arch, passed beneath it, and steeled herself.

Kiriel stood a few feet away, cleaning her sword with a bed sheet. Alowan would have been furious.

"Kiriel?" she said briefly.

"They're alive," was Kiriel's terse reply.

She took two steps, two quick steps, and then stopped six inches away from the youngest member of her den. She was always shy of touching this one. "Kiriel?"

The girl looked up, warily. Blood flecked her cheeks, her forehead—none of it, on first inspection, her own.

"Thank you."

But Kiriel looked away, turned away. Not much she could do to change that.

She left her. Deeper into the room, to the left, she found Angel attempting to bind Teller's wounds. Both men were as white as the sheets they were using, if you didn't count the green tinge to their skin. Or the blood.

"What— what happened?"

Angel didn't look up from his work—and Teller didn't look up either. They seemed to be absorbed by this simple attempt at doctoring.

"Teller," she said.

He shook his head. Closed his eyes.

It was Angel who answered, and he answered with a jittery, a single, motion. Pointed.

Beyond them both, beyond them were the dead. But they weren't simply bodies; they had lost arms, legs, half a head; they lay strewn across the breadth of the room as if they were dolls an angry child had destroyed in a fit of berserk rage. Armor was rent as if it were cloth, and there were two blades that were sheared in half.

She closed her eyes.

Squared her shoulders. Opened her eyes again. "What happened?" she asked, taking a breath. "Not—not that. I can see that with my own eyes. But I heard swords—"

Angel nodded.

"That woman," he said. "The one that came during our fight with—with the Allasakari. In these halls. She came tonight. She had two swords and a warning. Dropped the swords on the bed and disappeared.

"We had enough time to hide; to make mock bodies under the sheets. I think they thought—Hells, of course they did—that they could just walk in quickly and kill us all."

"They sent a lot of men for a quick kill."

He shrugged. "Guess you can't be too certain."

"Jay—" Teller said softly, eyes still closed.

"I know," she said just as softly. He reached out for her hand and she gave it to him—but her attention was with the youngest member of her den. Kiriel.

CHAPTER TWENTY-FIVE

"All right," Jewel said, knocking at what remained of the door—and there wasn't much of it. Swords weren't effective axes, but they'd almost got through.

"I don't know who built these doors," Auralis said, his syllables blending into a long, slow drawl, "but if I ever build a fortress, I want him." He bent, touched splintered wood, and whistled. "They should have been able to knock the damned thing down."

She hit the door, and then kicked it; both sounds were curiously flat. "Alowan!"

"Jay—"

Finch. Finch had come from somewhere to lay a hand on her shoulder. It should have been comforting; it was a touch she couldn't have mistaken for anyone else's. But she shrugged it off.

Because Alayra was dead.

Had it been so long since she'd seen death? So long since she'd felt its presence, and worse, the lingering shadow it left in its wake?

Yes. Too long. They weren't even *her* dead; they were just dead. She drew breath, sharply. *Answer the door, Alowan,* she thought, curling her hands into knuckled fists. *I won't have had it all be for nothing.* As if the eight dead men were sacrifices; not hers, and therefore lives she could offer up.

Squeamishly. *Get a grip,* she told herself. No one else would have dared.

And then she heard it, something grunting and creaking, the sound of something heavy being dragged or pushed across the floor. She almost laughed. But it would have been too close to the edge of hysterical, and she didn't want to go there. She bit her lip and smiled instead.

"Jay?"

The noise continued, and before it was finished, The Terafin joined them in the healerie. She came with six of her Chosen, and her domicis; the former were armored and weaponed. The

Terafin herself was dressed very, very simply—in a pale gown, something that the light bleached of color. Which seemed fitting. Morretz was in the loose but perfect robes of a servant, albeit a highly valued and valuable one. If he was armed, it wasn't obvious.

Nothing about the man was.

"You'd be best," Jewel said to the Chosen, "to leave your weapons outside."

One of the Chosen was Arrendas; she hadn't remembered him leaving.

"I believe," The Terafin said, "that the healer will forgive us this trespass." She stepped forward then. Knelt a moment beside one of the fallen. Arrendas knelt and flipped the corpse over.

"Do you recognize him?" The Terafin asked.

"Yes," her Chosen replied, his voice carefully neutral. His glance strayed to Auralis, Kiriel's friend. Osprey. AKalakar.

The Terafin's followed. She nodded and rose.

Auralis showed himself to be only half a fool. The Terafin and The Kalakar were not a study in opposites—not the way The Kalakar and The Berriliya were—but they were very different women. What the Osprey rarely offered the ruler of his own House—if reputation was anything to go by—he offered The Terafin. He brought his hand to his chest, sharply. Smartly. Bowed.

"I owe you a debt," she said quietly.

He smiled broadly, but the smile faltered. "I was . . . pleased to be of service," he said at last. "But I like a debt as long as it's not mine."

"And I," she answered. She turned, then, to Jewel herself. "ATerafin," she said.

Jewel nodded.

"The healer?"

"Whole, I think."

"Whole," the healer said, as what was left of the door swung open. There was, in fact, a thinning of wood that allowed the light to shine through. Jewel wondered, idly, what the swords looked like. Forgot about it the minute the old man stepped beneath the arch of his doorway and into the brighter light of mage-stones that rivaled sun for the clarity of their glow. He had aged—and she had always thought him ancient.

He bowed to her. Bowed low. "Forgive me, Jewel," he said.

"Forgive *you*—but why?"

"I—had enough warning to move the armoire into the arch to

block the door." He did not look up. "But not enough time—not enough to leave my rooms in search of your kin."

"Then be at peace," Jewel said quietly. "Those kin are my den and my responsibility. If you'll forgive them for having swords in the healerie, I'll tell you that they're alive and whole."

"Swords?"

"They had enough warning to pick up the arms that were left them." She paused. "Teller's bleeding, but I think he'll survive."

"Who left them arms?"

Jewel hesitated.

"Jewel," The Terafin said, "I would be interested in the answer to that question as well."

When she'd first come to the House, she'd been afraid of The Terafin; when she'd been given her name and had settled in—had become as much a friend as the woman who ruled the House allowed herself—she'd found this quiet way of giving orders a contrast to the surliness of merchants or magisterians in the streets.

But she'd learned that there was a steel behind those words that surliness or temper couldn't hope to contain.

"Evayne," she said quietly.

"So," The Terafin said resignedly. "It's started. At least in our day we had the decency to wait until the corpse had cooled."

"Or at least until there was a corpse to add to," Alowan said gravely. "No one of you stood still, Amarais." He bowed. "Let me go to see to my two patients; we will have time to talk later. Whoever the attackers are—or were—they've failed, and they will not try again this eve."

He left the room, and The Terafin let him go because he was Alowan, and because his name was his own. He did not serve the House; he served *her*, and that choice was his own, had always been his own, to make. Or to walk away from.

But Jewel put a hand on his shoulder. "Alowan," she said softly.

"Yes?" He froze; he did not look back, either to Jewel or her Lord.

"There were four men in front of your door. There were four in the healerie. They are—dead. But not pleasantly."

"Oh?"

"I—no. Please wait—I'll have Teller and Angel brought to you."

He shrugged himself free of her hand. She knew better than to stop him.

Because she wasn't The Terafin, she tried anyway. "Alowan, please—"

"Do you think I haven't seen death?" he asked, and this time, he peeled her hand away. "I'm old enough, Jewel, to need no protection. A healer is a man whose touch heals the injured; the act itself is merely talent, like song or dance or even love—it says nothing whatever of what else these hands have done."

But the healerie was his heart; it was here that he worked his craft in peace. He adored the arborium, adored the light that shone through the windows at its heights—the costly, costly windows—the fountain whose voice could only be appreciated in the near-silence of a place of healing.

"It's not you I'm trying to protect," she said.

"Who, then?"

Jewel lifted her head. Let it fall to her side. "I don't know," she said quietly. Because there was only one name she could fill his silence with, and she didn't want to use it. *Kiriel.*

He walked away from her, from them, and into the healerie itself.

She listened for his words, but there was only silence.

For the first time in her life she wondered exactly what he *had* seen in the House war that had propelled Amarais Handernesse ATerafin to the high seat.

The Chosen brought Alayra to rest in his healerie, laying her upon a bed over sheets downturned by Alowan out of habit. He touched her face, which was slack-jawed now and quite cool, given the weather. The veins of his eyelids were green-blue and purple under the white of his skin; he seemed for a moment a thing of foreign marble, shot through with cracks of color, bright and dark.

When he spoke, they were almost surprised to hear it, but he did speak. Alowan was one of a handful of healers that could get the body to reveal the truth of a death hours after all life had passed.

"Poison."

"Thank you, Alowan," The Terafin said. "Arrendas." The Chosen bowed. "Accompany me. Jewel, I require your presence as well. I thank you for your intervention, Auralis AKalakar; your needs will be tended here by those who are in a better position to fulfill them." As she turned back to Jewel, she frowned. "Where is Torvan?"

"*Avantari.*"

"You left without him?"

"Alowan wasn't the only one *she* visited tonight."

Silence. Then, "Arrendas, send for Torvan at the Palace at once. Tell him his presence is requested."

"Terafin."

"They're—they *were*—Haerrad's men, every one of them."

"You are certain of this?" The Terafin asked.

Arrendas nodded grimly. The moon was almost full, and the light it cast still considerable in the personal library of The Terafin. At her back and to the left, Morretz stood, arms behind his back. He looked up as the sound of heavy steps broke the silence.

The Terafin nodded, her eyes dipping to tabletop and back. Morretz detached himself from her back and walked toward the door. After the events of this evening it was almost disquieting to see them separated; it was as if shadow cast by light had peeled itself off the ground and gone its separate way.

Which was stupid. Fanciful. Jewel was too old to shake her head, but not too old to call herself an idiot. She did so freely but quietly as she watched The Terafin's face.

Tonight, she looked old. There were lamps, both on the table and the wall; there were mage-lights, but they'd been spoken into a softer glow, being of the expensive variety where words actually had an effect. Combined, they cast the worst kind of shadows— the ones that brought out the hollows rather than hiding the flaws.

Arrendas rose; the sound of his chair brushing floor caught her attention.

Torvan ATerafin entered the room. He walked to where The Terafin sat and fell to one knee before her, bowing his head. Breath didn't come easily to him, but that wasn't surprising; Jewel hadn't expected to see him for another hour at best.

"Terafin."

The woman who ruled them all reached out then, placed a hand on his head. He lifted his face, and their eyes met. Jewel couldn't see his face; his back and the table obscured it. But she could see The Terafin's, and it scared her.

"You have not failed me," The Terafin said, "and you will not. Rise."

He rose; in all things, he did as she commanded; he was one of her Chosen, and would do no less. "Captain Arrendas," she said softly, and he nodded; he had already risen, as if expecting something.

"Captain Alayra was poisoned tonight, probably by the same hand that sought the death of Alowan. My apologies, Jewel, but I believe it clear that Angel and Teller ATerafin were an afterthought, a way of ensuring no witnesses to the deed." She raised a delicate hand to forehead, fell silent a moment, then took a breath, bracing herself by the arms of her chair.

"We have had two captains for almost ten years now."

But Alayra had been retired. She was accorded the honor of her rank, and more; she was given the responsibility of training the House Guards from which, in time, the Chosen would be selected. She was an excellent weaponsmaster; she had been an excellent Captain. They had been together, Alayra and Amarais, a long time.

That was what was wrong. They had been, in as much as they could be from such disparate backgrounds, friends. The Terafin had just lost one of her oldest friends. That was not a surprise to Jewel. What was—and she was ashamed to realize it—was that The Terafin was grieving.

She had never seen grief, not like this, not from this woman. She'd resented the Hells out of its absence time and again, but she had accepted it; The Terafin was, in the end, the woman against whom all strength was measured. And against all odds, she'd been strong.

She's allowed, Jewel thought. *She's allowed to be human, gods curse it.* But she felt it as a blow, as a loss, to see this woman laid bare, even in as subtle a way as this.

The lamplight caught the tears that hovered in her eyes; they were unshed, yes, but they were there.

"Torvan ATerafin," she said, "you have served me well; you have survived the most difficult events that the House has yet seen, and survived your unwilling part in them."

Old history: Torvan had once been a demon's momentary vessel, and the weapon by which that creature had struck at Terafin. At *The* Terafin. Arrendas bowed his head. Torvan did not bow his.

"It was not easy. But I think it will be easy compared to this."

He said nothing, waiting. She looked at his face, and then beyond it. Beyond them all. "Do you remember what the House at war was like? Were you there, Torvan?"

"Barely," was his soft reply.

"I remember," she told him. She took a deep breath and then seemed to shake off the gloom as she straightened her shoulders.

"I choose, therefore, to continue the tradition of two Captains for the Chosen."

Jewel glanced at Arrendas; he had grown still.

Torvan was silent for a moment. And then—typical of Torvan to be so slow, in Jewel's opinion—he realized what she was offering him. "But—"

The first smile of the evening graced The Terafin's face. "You think I honor you. You think I offend Arrendas, and you may well be correct—if you believe him to be so small-minded as that."

He offered no reply, and her smile broadened. "You have not yet said you will accept this honor."

"I am—I am Chosen," Torvan replied. Then, with more confidence, "I am Chosen; I will do whatever you believe is necessary."

Her smile dimmed somewhat. "I know it," she said softly. "All of my Chosen would. Do you remember what happened to his Chosen?"

It was such a strange question they all stared at each other in confusion before they realized that The Terafin spoke of her predecessor.

"No," Torvan said softly.

But Arrendas bowed his head.

"Captain Arrendas?"

"Yes," he said. "Alayra made it clear to me when I took my rank."

"When I die," she said quietly, "what do you imagine will happen to my Chosen?"

"If you die at the hands of one of them," he said, tossing his head in the direction of the library door, and through it, the ATerafin who were gathering for war, "we'd die." He shrugged. "One way or the other, we'd die."

"Yes," she said starkly. "You are all ATerafin, and when I die, those who seek the high seat will not be able to trust you enough to keep you as part of the House—but they will not be able to expel you either; to take your names from you in such a fashion devalues the name, and my memory—it is too public. Easier by far to kill you all."

"And you made that choice?" someone said unexpectedly. It was, of course, Jewel.

"I? No," The Terafin said softly. "But The Terafin before me did not fall to unnatural causes. The Chosen—*his* Chosen— retired; they left the House, or at least the city, because they had no desire to choose another master to serve—because the choice would have split them, and they had served most of their years with the Chosen as an indivisible unit."

"Would you do that?" Jewel asked abruptly, turning in her chair to face this newest of Captains. "Would you retire if she died?"

"No," The Terafin said softly, "they will not. The Chosen of my predecessor retired because he died peacefully—and they ascertained that by whatever means necessary; they were not, as my Chosen are not, stupid. Had he been murdered, they would have had one more duty."

Jewel stared across the table at her Lord, finally hearing what had been said, although she'd been trying to ignore it. Maybe they all had. She bowed her head, and when she raised it, there were tears on her cheeks. Because she knew, she *knew,* that The Terafin was right.

"They won't choose well, you know," she said softly.

The Terafin met her gaze. Waiting.

"They—none of them—are capable of choosing men and women who are *worth* the title of Chosen. What kind of a man or woman chooses to work for a murderer?"

"Jewel—" Torvan said, lifting a hand.

"They've proved tonight that they aren't even worthy of the name Terafin."

"One of them has," The Terafin replied reasonably. "And now," she added, rising, "I would have two men summoned. Gabriel, because I wish his strength and wisdom, and Haerrad." The two Captains exchanged glances. "No, gentlemen, it is not as simple as that. I like Haerrad no more than you, and in fact, a good deal less. A good deal. But I have never understood him to be a stupid man. To use his own, his easily identifiable men, in a slaughter of this type—that would be, in my opinion, inexcusable stupidity.

"Therefore we are looking at someone who had already managed to offend Alowan, and who fears that Haerrad is the most likely contender for the high seat in my absence."

"That would be all of them," Jewel said, without thinking. Jewel, who wouldn't admit for the world that she had assumed that Haerrad was the guilty party.

Captain Torvan—Captain in the space of minutes—said, "But, Terafin, it's clear that they didn't expect resistance. Had the eight arrived with no warning, they would have easily killed Angel and Teller, and almost as easily removed Alowan's head from his shoulders. Done quickly, they could have left."

"They were eight men. They were seen by someone on the way

to the healerie." She lifted a hand to her forehead. "I am concerned, at times, but I have faith in my retainers. Jewel, you will
attend as well."

Jewel ATerafin bowed her head. "I don't suppose," she said,
turning to Torvan, "that you brought—"

The door swung open. Avandar stood in its frame, two Chosen
at his back. He was, from her brief inspection of his expression,
in a *foul* mood.

"Never mind."

He understood what it meant. When Jewel ATerafin left the room
at the side of a domicis who was as close to murder as he'd ever
seen one come, Torvan turned to The Terafin. Watched her watching the doors as they closed, in a strained, an uneven, silence.

"We didn't all retire," he said softly.

"No."

"You didn't tell her all of the truth."

"No."

She met his gaze squarely, evenly. Arrendas came to stand beside her. It was the Captain—the acting Captain who spoke
first.

"You know Jewel ATerafin better than any of the Chosen," he
said quietly. Clear to Torvan, then, that The Terafin and this particular Captain had already spoken. "You know the other . . .
candidates."

Torvan was as stiff as Morretz; he offered nothing.

"She trusts you," Arrendas continued. "Of all of us, were she
to choose a Captain, you know who she'd offer the position to
first."

Torvan ATerafin was silent a long time; he was habitually honest in the presence of both his best friend and his Lord, and they
waited.

At last, he said, "Yes."

"Yes?" Arrendas; The Terafin had already closed her eyes.

"Yes, she would offer me the rank of Captain. Yes, I would
accept it. Yes, she would take the Chosen of Terafin as they stand
now, and keep them intact. And yes," he added, for he thought he
understood The Terafin now, although she had not, and would
not, speak further. "If your death were not natural, she would use
us against your killers, and she would *take* the House. She would
have the only force that has trained together, in adversity and
otherwise, for decades: The Chosen. The others have House

Guards, their own factions—but they are not our equal. *If* we stand together." He met Arrendas' gaze squarely. "What would your guess be?"

"If Jewel Markess ATerafin takes the House," the Captain replied evenly, "I believe that we will lose less than ten percent of our number—to retirement. We will lose more than that to the succession war." He smiled grimly. "But it is rumored that she is the chosen heir of *Terafin*, as well as of The Terafin. At heart, I believe that she will lose no one, and that the continuity of the House and what it stands for will pass unbroken—" He stopped. Stared back at his Lord as if realizing only then that he was openly speaking of her death.

The Terafin smiled grimly. "And if I offer her the House? The Council waits my decision, and it is mere weeks in the making."

"If you offer her the House," Torvan ATerafin sad quietly, "she will accept it. But, Terafin," he added, "you have done the best you can do: You've let her come to that decision herself. Give her a little more time."

"She's made that decision?" A quickening of expression across his Lord's face caught the light, sent it out.

He exhaled. Turned his back upon them both to stare at the closed doors. "Yes. Yes, I think she has. But she doesn't know it yet, and Jewel Markess ATerafin is not a woman who can be forced to admit in public what she's barely begun to admit to herself."

"That she wants the House?" Arrendas again, the clank of his armor drawing closer to Torvan's turned back.

"No," he said starkly. "That war costs lives, and that she's beginning to be willing to fight a war." He turned back to the woman who sat, Morretz a motionless statue at her back, and he bowed. "I will be your Captain, Terafin, and after you, I will be hers."

He saw her nod, then. Thought that—*hoped* that—the relief in her expression wasn't just a trick of both light and his imagination.

News traveled. Servants carried it. ATerafin carried it. The men and women who frequented the healerie with their pathetic aches and scrapes carried it.

The Terafin spoke at length with each member of her Council; with each man or woman of power who had already begun the negotiation of the dispute that would end in several deaths and a new House ruler. He had not expected that. Should have seen it; Amarais was a cunning woman, and not to be tricked by foolish display. Of course he'd intended to have the men killed once they finished their duty. They would be silent bodies—bodies that he, in fact, had some part in apprehending for their heinous crime. He could produce proof of their loyalty to Haerrad—but it was useless now.

Useless.

He was not a man given to grand gestures or to grand rages, but if anything could drive a man to either, this was it, this failure.

"My Lord."

He turned quietly, irritated that he had been unaware of the messenger's interruption. That irritation had already fallen fast beneath the surface of a benign expression. He turned. "Rise," he said.

"I bring word from the merchant Pedro di'Jardanno," the messenger said. He did not hold out a roll of paper, did not offer a scroll, which was common in the Empire. There was no privacy between the man who sent the message and the man who received it, and he liked it not a bit.

But to kill another man's property was not, given the abject failure of his internal plans this evening, a wise decision; he refrained.

"Give your message," he told the waiting seraf, "and then leave quickly. I am already under some suspicion."

The man bowed in the Southern fashion, and had to be ordered to rise again before he would speak. A lifetime of slavery to another's will probably had that effect. Or a certainty that failure in any little grace was death.

He was fascinated by the Imperial culture. Repelled by it. He wished to rule *men,* not these shadows of men, not these intelligent cattle.

"Speak," he commanded.

"Jewel ATerafin, Commander Allen, Commander Ellora, and Commander Devran are still alive."

He'd seen at least the first for himself, but he'd assumed that the assassin had had to hunt them separately; indeed he'd sat through the interview with The Terafin, her right-kin, and Jewel ATerafin thinking about the fact that she would not have the younger ATerafin as a weapon for much longer. Amused by the thought.

"Yes?"

"And the brother who was hunting them has died."

"What?"

"It was reported to the Kings' Swords. He is said to have been killed in the attempted commission of a crime."

This profound a failure.

"Thank you," he said softly. Wondering, idly, if he now had either the contempt or the enmity of Pedro di'Jardanno to worry about. Neither was desirable. He alone of all Terafin had seen what that man might do. Could do. Had done.

"Do you have word to send to my master?"

"I will send word as I am able. Tell him . . . he has my profound apologies. It appears that there are forces at work here that neither of us are fully aware of."

He rose, this seraf, this half-man, and was gone.

22nd day of Lattan, 427AA
Averalaan Aramarelas, Coliseum

It seemed incongruous to Serra Alina, watching the foot race, that men of ungainly size and stature should in fact be faster than those whose build seemed, on the surface, to suggest fleetness of foot, grace of movement, light quick steps.

The Northern barbarian, for instance, was large and broad; he was tall, for he cast a tall shadow, but seemed shorter than his height to the eye because he had that barrel chest that seemed so admired in Imperial standards of male beauty. She thought he looked heavy, and heaviness implied lack of speed. Clearly, her sheltered life, both here and in the harem of her oldest brother, and her father before him, had not prepared her for the truth of the race: Such size and such muscle counted, yes, but for more, and not less.

Valedan's muscle was youth's muscle; he was taller, or seemed taller, to the Serra, and—although she never said it aloud—he was graceful in the sinuous, unaffected way few men are.

She also knew that he was fast.

The oddsmakers had placed Eneric of Darbanne in the lead, and indeed, these men were men who knew how to make their money, although they had lost much in the test of the sea.

Here, they placed Valedan either first or second, but with a greater likelihood of second place. Carlo d'Jevre had actually been ceded third place, but he had withdrawn, and that left Ser Anton with only Ser Andaro. He was ranked lower, between fourth and seventh, with some probability of either third or second, and some very small chance at first.

Miri had once explained these numbers to her, the why and the wherefore of them—but she had barely listened then; she had a head to remember numbers, and to listen for results. That was enough. She rarely forgot a thing once told.

The Serra Marlena en'Leonne was wringing her hands. Alina wondered idly, and not for the first time, whether or not this woman had been striking in the bloom of youth; she was not at all attractive now. She made of weakness a virtue, but not one to Alina's liking. For the sake of the event itself, however, they endured each other's company.

Short of leaving the box that had been set aside to provide a maximum of privacy to guard the modesty of the Annagarian women, they had little choice. Alina would have made her way to sand and ground and open sea wind—were it not for Ser Anton's presence.

Two reasons to dislike him, although she knew that the latter was unworthy of her.

"Look, look, Alina! He starts!"

"He is lining up, Serra Marlena," she replied. "The mages will be brought out first, and then the judges; there is some time yet before he runs." The older woman's grip on her arm was astounding in both its ferocity and its familiarity.

"Look at him—is he not the image of his father?"

She made no reply. It was both prudent and wise to make none. As always, this silence was taken for agreement. Privately, Alina thought Valedan favored neither mother nor father, although she had seen the Tyr himself only a handful of times in her adult life, and could not in fairness draw a good comparison.

He was taller than either, and wise enough to know when to accept a limitation; wise enough to know when to challenge that acceptance. She thought he would make, of all things, a *good* Tyr, and shook her head at her own folly. *I show my blood,* she thought ruefully. *Lambertan, for all the clans to mock.*

Good, after all, counted for little. *Powerful* was definitive. She believed it; it was, after all, truth. Serra Marlena was rare among the Serras; she clung to half-truths as if clinging was a type of salvation. As if, indeed, salvation could be gained by such pathos.

And yet . . . and yet . . . she could not name the emotion that she had felt the night the crowns were offered to those men who had braved the test of the sea; to the man who had won it. She had been angry at Valedan's lack of grace, and she had delivered the rebuke that only she could deliver—but she had not expected him to rise to the occasion in the fashion that he had: With grace, and without, in the end, absolving himself publicly of his private shame.

Mareo, she knew, would be proud.

Mareo, the brother for whom she felt such ambivalence.

Winning, she had told him *defines us. As does losing*.

How we win, he replied, seeking the sunlight with his eyes, *defines us. And how we lose*.

They had argued, of course. And in the end, he had chosen to relieve himself of the strife in his home by sending her, expendable and in fury, to the North as a hostage.

A kindness, although no doubt he had intended no such mercy.

She remembered that day clearly.

As wars go, the last war between the Empire and the Dominion was a short war, but a costly one; it had divided the Callestans and the Lambertans, guaranteeing a border in chaos for the Northern Lords. The harvest—the harvest had been taken by those serafs who had miraculously survived either side of the closing armies; who had survived the fires and the burning embers carried by wind.

She had been attended by her serafs; she claimed three, but was allowed none of them in her exile, by the will of her brother, the kai Lamberto.

"The Northerners do not believe in slavery," he had said; she could hear it now, as if the words had been trapped by malicious breeze to be carried over and over again when the sun was at this height, "and they will free the serafs to their Northern cities. I will not lose them in such a fashion."

She was insulted, of course; those serafs she had chosen and trained on her own, and she knew, she *knew* that they would never leave her. It was their duty, after all, their reason for existence: to serve.

Wryness, that. She was not too proud to admit—in the silence of thoughts, beneath Northern bowers where no spy of her brother's might witness it—that he had probably been right. She had seen it happen, here. And she could not even condemn it.

Had the North not changed her?

The winds were sharp today, they carried a chill in the shade that belied the summer heat, the summer humidity. As if she knew what that unlooked for coolness presaged, she looked up, her face half-veiled, her posture perfect.

Mirialyn ACormaris stepped into the box and bowed, Northern style, to her. "He will run," she said, "and I thought, if you wouldn't mind, I might join you."

"You are not needed below?"

"Would I be here, otherwise?"

Not an answer. Never an answer with her, although she was counted wise and spoke truth when she chose to speak directly. Serra Alina frowned as the Serra Marlena began to speak. She raised a sharp, slender hand as if it were blade, and the older Serra subsided, although her irritation was plain to see.

Plain, and an embarrassment. Ser Fillipo's wives did not deign to notice her lack of grace; neither did Ser Kyro's wife. Graceful manners required no less than such feigned ignorance. Therefore Alina's response was almost as rude—although it was welcome, she had no doubt of it—coming as it did in front of a foreigner. An outsider. A stranger.

She rose. "I would be pleased to join you a moment while we watch the Tyr'agar," she said. Miri offered her a hand, and she accepted it; the dress that the Serra wore did not reward quick movements with grace. They walked to the front of the box and sat at its farthest edge, briefly exposed to sun as they gazed down upon the ground of the running field.

There, men lined up in a single row cast long shadows. They had run several races each today; this would be the last.

"ACormaris," Serra Alina said quietly.

"Serra."

"Four days."

"Yes. Four days, and there will be an end to this, one way or the other."

"You are prepared for the hundred run, as they call it in the city streets?"

"The marathon? Yes; as prepared as we can be."

Silence was awkward. Profound. "Ah," the ACormaris said softly. "The mage is finished."

"The ten men?"

"Will run. Look. The adjudicator has taken up his position."

The noise that had blanketed the coliseum lifted like a curtain; there was silence, tense and anticipatory. The men knelt. Lowered their heads. Touched the earth with both hands—she did not understand the significance of either the hands or the kneeling. In the Dominion, men who hoped for victory did not abase themselves in the eyes of the Lord.

But this was the North; how could she think otherwise, who

stood beside Mirialyn ACormaris in the salt-laden air of the High City?

The adjudicator lifted a hand; a woman came up to the podium to stand beside him. Her hair was gold and gray, the color of wealth and wisdom. She opened her lips. Spoke. The entire coliseum could hear her as clearly as the contestants.

Bard-born.

"Prepare."

The men shifted almost in unison.

"Hold."

They were tense; she could see that now. To start before her given word was an offense in the eyes of the adjudicatory body, and that body held all power here to athletes whose lives depended upon their success. She played out the moment, as if inspecting them at a safe distance. Waited. The silence dragged on.

They were holding their breaths, and they two grown women, and no young girls to be impressed by a foot race. Mirialyn ACormaris had doubtless never been that young girl, but Serra Alina had been, and if she struggled, she could remember it clearly. It was humiliating in its fashion, as all weakness was; she rarely struggled that hard.

"Start!"

Sound returned in a rush as fleet as the men who now covered the ground with shadow and foot.

Don't look back.

He leaned forward, bent into the run, let his knees take his weight; he used his arms almost without thought, keeping time with the movement of his hips, his legs, the length of his stride. The sound of all breath was lost to the roar of the crowd, and he heard his name, time and again, made fuzzy by the number of voices that carried it.

Valedan.

The shadows fell the wrong way, though; it was later in the afternoon. He could see them across the ground, although they were distorted enough that he couldn't—quite—attach them to the runners themselves.

Didn't matter.

Nothing mattered but this: Run. Fast. Faster. *Faster.*

It was closely run.

Close, but not so close that it couldn't be called.

Serra Alina would have liked to think that the Northern men were bred and trained only to this purpose, there was nothing else that might excuse Eneric of Darbanne. But she knew, having seen him between events, that he was not a decoration—and this contest, in the end, this pitting of skill against skill, was a decorative contest.

No wars were decided here. No power given or granted; no armies destroyed or created. Pride was served, be it national or personal, but that was all.

And Eneric of Darbanne was no one's decoration.

Valedan kai di'leonne had to settle for second, and second was not without value. Interesting, to her, that Ser Anton's student took third. Two Southerners on the podium, a miniature war in the making, and each standing behind the Northern Champion.

I must not, she chided herself, *make analogies out of everything.* But she had been raised in the South, and in the South, all such detail had significance.

She noted—how could she not—that Valedan kai di'Leonne was greatly pleased with the second-place finish; more pleased to her eye than he had been with either the tenth place or the first.

Mareo, she thought, with apprehension, for she knew what his objections to Valedan kai di'Leonne would *and* must *be, you would like him. You would honor him, if you met him, if you took the time to watch him.*

You would come to understand that he is no Northern pawn. Or you would come to understand that your concept of Southern honor is Northern to the core.

And that, he would not do.

But to watch the boy, to watch him run and take second and be proud of it because his first place win had been so tainted gave her her first hope.

They did not need her brother's support, no.

But she knew well that if they did not have it, they would be forced to destroy the reigning clan of the Terrean of Mancorvo.

23rd day of Lattan, 427 AA
Terafin Manse

They faced each other, The Terafin and her domicis. Years had passed; years had marked them in ways that they barely knew themselves until they stopped to look and to question. The sun was a pale luminescence across the sky's edge; dawn soon.

Morretz carried a lamp, one glassed-in and therefore protected from the caprice of breeze or wind. Not that either existed in plenty at the height of this sullen, still season, but he took precautions with fire regardless; these were old habits, and old habits, for Morretz, had acquired a strength that was akin to a force of nature.

They sat in silence, bowed by the weight of things unsaid.

At last, she spoke. She would speak first, or no one would, and Morretz had perfected the art of waiting. Especially at times like this, when she chose to don the worn cloak of her dead grandfather, the blood relation of whom she had been so fond. It was too hot for such a cloak.

As if she knew what he was thinking, she said, "It still smells like him."

In the darkness, her voice might have been a young woman's voice.

He said nothing, knowing that this was not the time. And knowing well that she had paid a great deal of money to a mage of the Order to preserve the cloak in just such a fashion, to keep it as a living memory when her own memory failed as all memories do.

After a moment, she said, softly, "Alowan."

"Yes."

"How will I die, Morretz?" So cool her voice, so calm, the meaning of the words were almost lost to the tone.

You could not comfort this woman. You could try, but you could not do it, and he had long since given up the awkwardness of trying. He brought her the cloak when she desired it, or more often put it away when she had finished with it. She exposed so little, it was impossible to believe that she was afraid.

"Morretz," she said quietly, her hands settling into stillness in her lap.

How to answer such a question? He had not asked it of himself, because he had chosen to serve her, and her death was, literally, the end of the life he lived. Perhaps the end of his life; he could not see it.

"You are my most trusted servant," she said, "and one of my wisest. And before you speak to me of Gabriel—and I know you are thinking of him—I will only say that I regret the weakness that allowed him to persuade me to grant Rymark ATerafin his entry here. Rymark is Gabriel's blood son, and proof—if any had ever been needed—that blood does not run true.

"Yet he is the boy's father, with all that that implies, and he was close to the mother, who is dead. He sees . . . less clearly at the moment than I would like."

"And that leaves me?"

"That leaves you, Morretz."

"You are wrong," he told her firmly. "You should ask this of Jewel."

Her silence was long, and broken by a rueful laugh. "I should, yes. But I won't. To ask you is to ask a man of some cunning and some intellect to guess at what I guess at, to reach a logical conclusion in some fashion that I understand.

"But to speak to Jewel is to have an inexplicable, unreachable answer writ in stone—if she answers at all. I want an answer that *I* can reach, Morretz. An answer that intellect, confidence, or knowledge will take me to. I am not looking forward to death," The Terafin added quietly, "But I have seen my own death in at least three places in the last month—and in nothing so clearly as the attempt upon Alowan's life."

He would have argued with her. He wanted to. But he saw as she saw. He bowed his head in the dawn's colored light, exposing streaks of gray.

"Will you not change your mind," he said at last. "Will you not prevent Jewel from going South?"

She waited until he raised his face to meet hers. "I would," she said, "but I believe in the end that to call her back is to destroy the House; to let her go is to destroy only a single ruler."

"But the House—"

"The Terafin spirit," she said softly, softly, "gave her permission to travel South; indeed, he gave her the responsibility of it."

He knew her. He knew her, and he hated this in her: That she was the House Ruler, and that everything—*everything,* gods curse her—was done for the good of the House. He saw as she saw.

CHAPTER TWENTY-SIX

This was the only test at which Eneric of Darbanne was certain to fail. And not to fail in a minor way, not to take second or third or fourth, but to fail, period. He would not make tenth unless some catastrophe occurred; he would be lucky, in the estimation of Commander Sivari, to break twentieth.

But he came, and he prepared, the same as any of the other contestants. Valedan admired that. He rode a horse that was, on sight, inferior to at least fifty of the horses that Valedan had himself glimpsed or inspected; it was too old a horse for such a race as this, and it was, simply, too short in stride, although it seemed rock stable, a dependable mount in a crisis. It was a gray, bleached by time of color.

Eneric of Darbanne smiled as Valedan's pace slowed.

"She's a good horse," he said.

Mare. "You don't—you don't take a mare—"

Eneric laughed. This man, this man who was favored to win the Challenge, knew he was going to lose this race. And he didn't seem to care.

"Valedan," Sivari said, bowing brusquely in acknowledgment of the Northerner. "Your horse—"

But Valedan stopped in front of Eneric. "Why?" he said.

The Northerner could have ignored the question, or he could have misunderstood it; it was, after all, a single word. But he shrugged instead. "I bought a new sword for the competition," he began, and then laughed when he saw the Southern shock spread across the younger man's face. "And a new shield. I had new armor made. New clothing. Even this," he added, hands momentarily tugging at a leather pouch that hung from a broad belt, "I had made new."

"But—"

"But none of them are alive, kai Leonne. None of them have seen me through battle and skirmish against bandit and encroaching noble the way she has." He scratched her broad head with a proud affection. "She's not what she used to be when she was a filly. But I've had her eight years, and she's never faltered and never failed me.

"I won't win with her," he said, acknowledging the truth that Valedan had not—and would not—speak. "But winning without her just wouldn't be the same. But truth—this is the truth—be told, I'd take another horse to race with if I thought I'd come close to the front, but there are too many damned Southerners here for that, and I won't slight her for less than victory." He paused. "Your own horse is a fine beast. True Southern blood there; I'd be surprised if she wasn't Mancorvan."

"I'd be surprised if she was," Sivari replied, before Valedan could. "You know how the Mancorvans feel about the North."

"True enough. But he's a fine horse, and he'll give the others their only real challenge." He leaned forward, held out a hand. "Good luck, kai Leonne. You're *our* Southerner. Win."

Valedan nodded almost absently, staring at the dark eyes in the white head. And then he followed Sivari.

When he said, "I don't understand," for the fifth time, the Commander laughed. Here, under the open sky, over a bed of flat grass that had been sheered into something so fine it felt like cloth, he said, "Eneric is a Northerner. First, they value the loyalty of living things. Second, and if you're a cynic, more important, horses are rarer, and more expensive in the Northern clime. To buy a beast like yours would beggar all but the high nobility, and Eneric, for all his worth, doesn't approach theirs in wealth. He might, in time, should he win here." He shrugged. "They have a rough honor and a rougher sense of justice—but you've managed to impress him, or he'd have spit just as soon as answer your question.

"They like an underdog in the North," he added.

"But—"

"Winning is almost everything, Valedan—but you yourself now know it *isn't* everything. If it were, you would never have chosen to share that podium. You've declared yourself, like it or not. It isn't a declaration that Eneric of Darbanne—that any of these contestants—could have made, but having seen it, they're impressed. Now come. We're testing the patience of the adjudicators as it is."

Valedan nodded.

And stopped again, in front of a waiting Southerner. Andaro di'Corsarro. They bowed to each other stiffly, and if Valedan rose first, the bow was not shallow. Andaro was, with the withdrawal of Carlo, the best horseman in the palace. No exceptions made.

This man, he thought idly, *is here to kill me.* But it didn't matter—not at this moment. The track mattered, and the men who tended it were nearly done. The horses mattered. The race itself.

He said softly, "I would wish you luck, but you require none."

Andaro shrugged, and they both turned to their tasks. But as he walked away, he heard a soft voice say, "Carlo is watching us both."

The sun was not to the liking of the horses; not in the early morning, and not in the afternoon. But they were run, and run the way the men had been the day before: without pause, if they won or came close to winning. Of the races, there were ten in total, and the track at the end of the day was smooth by the artifice of those whose responsibility it was to tend those things.

Eneric did not progress to the finals; did not, in fact, place at all in his heat. He seemed content, his horse, upset. They looked an odd pair, this Northern barbarian whom everyone secretly bet on to win the Challenge, and his frost-haired, slightly-too-short-in-the-leg mount, but they did, in Valedan's opinion, suit each other in a way that made no sense to him.

His horse, standing over seventeen hands tall and covered head to foot in a gray-blue coat that was broken only at boot and forehead, was named Lightning—probably one of a hundred horses so named in the Empire—fared better, far better than that; indeed it was hard not to let the horse lead the race, let the horse make the decision. The animal did not desire to be left behind; he knew what he was doing. Racing, and at that, to win.

Valedan had thought him built for war, not for running; he seemed heavy when examined beneath a bridle. But in motion his weight was the muscle that propelled him, and he knew it, too.

He wasn't as certain that he would want this animal beneath him in a pitched battle, but in a race, Mirialyn ACormaris' choice proved, as if there were ever any doubt, wise.

Valedan knew that Aidan was in his glory. It was almost as if, building up to the final event, everything had weight and meaning. This horse was no normal horse in the young witness' eyes; it was a *noble* horse, a beast of great power and strength, a suitable mount for a *hero*. He could almost hear the words that Aidan never embarrassed either of them by actually saying.

Still, awe had its uses; Aidan was afraid of the horse, and stood well enough back from it, which was probably wise; Lightning had no use for the timid, and made it plain by snapping at air with a speed that matched his name, or worse, by bringing his head round like a giant fist. It was between the races—leading up to and afterward—that Valedan's real work was cut out, for the adjudicators allowed no fighting between the stallions, and if the rider could not control the horse, the horse was banned. As simple as that.

He counted the riders who were banned on two hands.

The kai Leonne watched his Southern enemies, the width of the field dividing their camp, and he saw that Andaro di'Corsarro and another man, a younger one, had horses as fine as his own — neither of whom seemed to need the force of control that Lightning did. He envied them their easy handling, their complete ease.

It made him feel truly foreign. Truly Northern.

"Valedan," Commander Sivari said softly. "The line-up begins. This is where you will make your mark against Eneric; his only true weakness is this test. He will run in the marathon, and he will probably win it; you will have a chance to best him at archery, although that contest is by no means foregone.

"Ride well."

"Ser Anton."

"Ser Pedro."

"You've been inordinately silent lately."

"I speak when I have something to say."

"And you have nothing to say? A change, I fear, and not for the better. I see that your students have fared well at *this* particular test."

The urge to kill the man and have done had not been as strong as this for a number of days, a sure sign that he had been in the so-called merchant's presence for far too long. "They fare well at this test, yes. They will fare well at the test of the sword, and they did well, given the field, at the foot race. They will fare less well at the marathon, and will probably fail to place with the bow.

"Is there any other information that you require?"

Ser Pedro shrugged easily. "You have not yet chosen to call

the test of the sword—the only test that really matters, as we both know."

"No," Ser Anton said curtly. "I have not."

"The Northerner, then?"

"You may call—and bet—as you'd like." He shrugged, the movement too stiff to be called graceful. Anger did that, when it was ill-contained, and it irked Ser Anton to *be* so obvious. "I hear rumors," he said, changing tack.

"Rumors?"

"Apparently there was an attempted—and failed—assassination."

Ser Pedro's easy silence became sharp at once, edged and frosty.

Have care, Ser Anton thought, but whether as warning to the merchant or himself, he was not certain.

"That," the swordmaster added, "is commonly known; that is not the interesting rumor. What is interesting is this: the assassin, apparently, was killed in the commission of the crime."

He turned then, giving the field his attention.

Ser Pedro offered his back a complete silence. One turned one's back on a man of his kind very, very seldom—and usually only like this: as a blow, to make a point. What Pedro might have replied—and the merchant was so rarely at a loss for words there was, doubtless, a reply coming, was lost: the horns were sounded across the field. There were no gates here, although in the North, gates were sometimes used to contain horses. Nothing separated the horses from the running field but an indelible, wide white line that every eye, be they on the ground or in the farthest remove of the coliseum, could see clearly.

There was a penalty for crossing that line early, and several riders had paid it during the runs leading up to this one. It was notable, and expected, that none of the better riders would fault in such a fashion.

None did.

The horses *moved*.

Just as they had when he sat among them, so many years ago.

"This has been a long time coming," she said, and Kallandras stiffened at the familiar sound of her voice.

She was old, this time. Old, wise now, and gentler for it—but no less resolute. She was certain of her power. And when he saw her, at this age, when he saw her at all, she was like the gathering storm; a whisper could make the hairs on the back of his neck stand on end.

"What do you think of the boy, Kallan?" She gazed out into the field where the horses were being prevented—some poorly, and Valedan's among that number, but prevented nonetheless—from jockeying for position in a way that would disqualify their riders.

"I think," he said, his voice subdued and for her ears alone, "that he has been a surprise to all of us." His eyes narrowed; the words that he had spoken were, he realized not true. But speaking them to *her* brought out the flaws, the cracks between their whole facade. "Every one of us but you."

She smiled. There was no blood on her hands, this moment; no blood on her face, no repairing rents in the fabric of a cloak that her father had given her when she had come of age in a world that he did not know.

"I would not have suspected," he said quietly. "I thought it perhaps the intervention of *Kalliaris*." And perhaps it was.

"I had no hand in him," she said softly. "Not even to influence the ACormaris when she chose to begin his idle training so many years ago. She pitied him, I think, and she has often been fond of those who carry their quiet with them."

"You speak as a woman who knows her."

"I know her better now than I did in my youth, yes."

"Whose hand, Evayne?" he asked softly. Almost without conscious thought—to an observer who did not know him—his gaze flickered to the Ospreys, and to the demon-child who stood on duty among them. "Whose hand had part in the boy, then? We've enough shadow and shade for this battle, I think."

"Yes," she said as softly. "He is not god-born; you would see it. Had he been, he would have been drowned at birth, in the waters of the Tor Leonne, a fitting tribute to the Lord of the Sun."

"Say, rather, to the ignorance of the Southerners." But he turned to face her; to catch the violet of her eyes with the blue of his own, pale now; they both had steel in them that the light exposed, no matter how they might try to hide it. Kallandras was better at hiding, of course, when he so chose. "Whose hand, Evayne?"

"Let me ask you, instead, a different question, Kallandras of Senniel."

"I am almost done with your questions," he said, the mildness of his tone belying the edge the words themselves contained. He felt it; the weariness. He did not hate her, however, for the death of one of his oldest brothers. Did not, in fact, blame her, as he would have in the anger and heat of youth. But he wanted the luxury of mourning, and during the Festival, he would have no privacy for it, beyond what he had already taken.

"Ask a question yourself, then. Whose hand shaped me?" And for an instant, she spoke with weight, with depth, with a feeling that she displayed so rarely in her years of power, as if feeling itself was the thing that she had finally managed to extricate herself from.

"How?"

"For myself, I am not yet permitted to answer you—and I feel that I will never be permitted an answer to that question, not while you live to hear it." She spoke without bitterness, but her lips were thinner. "And for Valedan, I do not know."

"Then how do you—"

She only shook her head, and he subsided. "I have a request, Kallandras; a request." She opened her hand, and in it, gleaming beneath baked, white clay mud, a single ring. It was not a fine ring, and not a Northern one; it was made of jade and gold, an intertwined coupling of bands.

Poorer men gave such a gift to their wives in the Dominion; poor, but free, men.

"What is this?" he asked.

"It is what I have been sent to give, and I have been sent to give, obviously, to you—although you would not have been my first guess." She paused. "Let me tell you a story." She was seldom so expansive; he was wary at once. "And let me answer a question in the doing.

"There was a young woman who was adored by the husband who had chosen her. She had been raised free, although poor, and she was of some will; she had neither the perfect grace nor the perfect manners of women of high birth, although she had been born no seraf. She disdained the wearing of shoes, and her nails were often split or dirty."

He raised a brow, but he did not interrupt her.

"She had a father who adored her, foolishly and openly, and she found a man not unlike him, but much younger, whose open adoration made her father's seem placid and distant by comparison. In and of herself, she might have become many things, but the love of these two men protected her in a land where so few are protected." She turned to the South a moment, and then resumed her telling, her face to the shadows cast by the combination of sun and hood.

"She was a vain girl, as girls are at the dawn of adulthood, and she desired him to prove that he loved her, much to the disgust of everyone except her father. The young man was a poor man, and he killed bandits for her, and defended her father's clan against the Voyani who raided in that season, but she was interested in nothing that had been looted or taken as just payment for crimes; she wanted something that came from *him*.

"He had no money. He was not the head of his clan, and he was an honest man; the things that were looted were turned over to the kai of his clan.

"But he desired her happiness, and he was young enough to want to prove to her that he did love her."

The horses were in a line; the judges were waiting beyond the edge of Evayne's tale. His eyes saw that, but his ears heard only the soft cadence of her voice, the *truth* in it.

"So he went to a jeweler, and finally found one who would consent to make him a ring. He had wanted a necklace, of course, one fine enough that she might publicly wear as a token of his great affection—but short of killing the jeweler and absconding with his pieces, which would have touched off a long and bitter feud, that was not an option.

"So he had a ring made, of jade and gold, twined just so. And when it was ready, he took it to her, and offered it. At first, she was disdainful of it, as she had been of much else, but he said, "I am what I am, Mari, and this—this is a symbol of our lives, for *I* am the jade and you, you are the gold that gives my life value—see, here, the bands cannot be separated.

"And she was touched by that, and the sentiment won what the ring itself would not and did not. Approval. Trust. Faith. She had set him a young woman's cruel test, and he had passed it."

Horns blew across the field, and the coliseum crashed and thundered with names, as they were called in louder and louder voices. But he was bard-born, and he could hear her as she continued to speak.

"And so she was happy.

"But one day, while she was working with the clays—for this is what she did to help her family—the ring itself was lost, and only after she had finished tossing the last of three fine jugs and had set them to bake did she realize that it had left her finger; that it was probably buried in wall or base of one such creation, and baked there.

"She could not afford to lose the time and the labor, but she felt as if she had given her heart away, and when he returned, she was inconsolable. But he had returned with fine news, fine news indeed: he, and his wife, had attracted the notice of the sword-master of the realm, and they were to travel—at the expense of the clan Leonne, and in a style fitting the clan's expense—to the Tor.

"She was shocked, and then overjoyed; she told him what had become of her ring, for there was now no reason why she might not destroy her work to retrieve it. But he caught her hands—ringless now—and he told her that, if she was willing, he might take these three jugs with them, for one—one alone—held their hearts, and in a secret place that no malicious wind, nor sun, nor moon might disturb; that they were the product of her hands and her labor, the last work of its type that she might do unless she otherwise desired; the last tie with the old life that had brought them together. And these vessels were treasured in his house above all else, and filled with the waters of the Tor, when the Tyr'agar chose to show his generosity.

"And of course, she was given finer jewels, as befit her rank."

He looked across the field; the horses had lengthened from a line that ran the width of the track to one that ran its length. And at their lead, the Southerner, and at his hooves, and closing, Vale-dan. Clods of dirt and stone flew at their feet; they were bent into their horses, into the winds that swept past them.

He spoke, softly. "This is that ring."

"Yes."

"And you have yourself discovered it and removed it from one of those vessels."

"Yes."

"No wonder," he said softly, "you were required now, at the height of your power."

"Yes."

"But this story—if it were commonly known—"

"It was known only to the man and his wife; it is now known by four, and not two, for I was told, and I have told you."

"And who told you, Evayne a'Nolan? The man? I doubt it. And the wife is dead."

"Yes. The wife is dead. But the gods guard and shepherd the dead," she said softly, "and the gods speak. They speak in a language that occasionally we are given leave to understand. From Mandaros, at the behest of this woman, this story came to the hand that has fashioned so much that is so bitter about my life. And from Him, to you.

"Take this ring, and tell him. Tell him that she loves him, that she waits for him, and that she does—as he suspects—like the boy. Tell him that she says she's still not very patient, and she won't wait for more than a lifetime, so she respectfully requests that he not do so much that he has to live through another one in atonement."

He turned then, to see her face, and before she pulled the hood low, he could see the faintest glimmering in her eyes. He felt it in his own. They, neither of whom were moved at death or causing it, were moved at this—this act of sentiment.

Of love.

He missed the race's finish, although he heard it announced in a roar that shook earth, it was so loud. Anger there, and jubilance.

He turned back to the track, and he could see that Andaro di'Corsarro held his head particularly high as he sought—and found—someone in the stands closest the ground itself, and raised his hand in proud salute. First, then. But Valedan, somehow, was second.

His hand curled protectively around the ring that Evayne had given him, but his thoughts were for that young man. *Whose hand,* he thought, *and how?* And, unbidden, *What price will he be forced to pay for anything he's granted here?*

Ser Anton's students were louder, by themselves, than the whole of the Northern contingent. They had entered the coliseum for the first of the two events by which real men were known, and they had showed their strength: Andaro di'Corsarro, born to and of the Dominion of Annagar, carried the crown on proud brow. He had placed third in the foot race, but he had placed behind the northern pawn that they had come this far to defeat. Had, in fact, placed behind him in every event but this one.

There was not enough wine in the city for the men who followed Ser Anton di'Guivera. Luckily, they were not given much chance to prove it. Ser Anton was still their master here, and he looked not to the past day's glory, but to the next day's event.

The hundred run was so named because the path the runners took led them through every holding in the city, high and low, rich and poor. They would run through a pass made of people to either side, people held back by the flimsiest of barriers and their ancient belief in the authority of the city's many guards.

Hours. Hours away.

He rose from his silence like a man shedding water after a long dive. Shook himself and made his way out to the edge of night. There, Andaro di'Corsarro, the much celebrated hero of the hour, sat beside Carlo di'Jevre. They were quiet, and between them there was only one glass, and that in Carlo's hand. Andaro would not risk the run to Northern wine and the excess of celebration.

He had been much like Andaro in his youth, but Andaro in his wisdom attached himself to no helpless woman, no helpless babe.

They looked up as his shadow passed them.

"Ser Anton," Andaro said quietly.

"You did well," the swordmaster said.

He was too old to be pleased by praise, or rather, too old to show it. He nodded, kept his head bowed that extra half-second that spoke of respect.

They were silent beneath the face of a moon unfettered by cloud.

"Tomorrow?" Carlo said at last.

"The hundred run, yes."

It was not the question he'd asked; not the question that hovered beneath the single word. The silence stretched awkwardly between the swordmaster and his students. It was the master who was forced to retreat from them, the brightest of his students, the two of whom he had been most proud.

The moon was high and bright, almost impossible to ignore.

And so he found himself by the fountain, staring into the stone cloth that covered the eyes of the blindfolded boy. The water here was heavy; it was abundant. The sea did not taint it with salt; the winds did not cover it with sand or dirt.

He would not have said he was waiting, had any chosen to ask, but he *did* wait.

And in time, the waiting was rewarded.

The boy, Valedan kai Leonne, came out of the shadows like a shadow, into the glow of mage-stones and moon. He started as their eyes met, but the surprise rippled over his features and was gone.

They had spoken in the clipped fashion of Southern men in anger; some of that remained in the boy's bow. The bow surprised him, and he returned it with a nod, much as he might have returned the regard of a—student.

"You ride well," he said grudgingly. "But you chose your mount poorly."

"Or undermastered him," Valedan replied. "As a horse, he is fine, but high-strung."

"He is Mancorvan?"

The boy shook his head. "Callestan."

"That, I cannot believe. He was probably Mancorvan originally."

"He bears no brand."

"The Mancorvans do not brand their horses. They count on the quality of the beast itself to tell the tale of its breeder."

The boy stood quietly, awkwardly, in the moonlight. Watching made Ser Anton weary. Where had it gone, the fire of his youth, his younger self? Where did the determination that had carried him through not one, but two, of these Challenges now reside?

To kill a Tyr had been remarkably easy.

To kill this, the least of a Tyr's seraf-born sons? In the moonlight he lowered his eyes.

The boy cut him. He said: "You must have loved your wife a great deal."

It was not what he expected to hear. Not what he desired. He did not speak; the shock began to give way to something akin to anger. But when he raised his face, he saw no hint of cruelty, no hint of mockery, in the boy's face; there was nothing there at all.

"You were raised in the North," he said at last, but softly.

"Yes," he said. "And born in the South, in the harem of a great man, to a woman he grew quickly to disdain. If there was love between my father and his wives, he never showed it in a way that we could clearly understand."

"You were a boy," Ser Anton said gruffly.

"And a boy knows nothing of love, of course."

Silence.

"Did any of his wives survive?"

"No. But you must know this."

Valedan bowed his head a moment. "Yes," was all the reply he offered.

The silence was thick. Heavy.

The boy threw it off first. "Tell me about your wife."

"Yours is the line that killed her," was the swordmaster's reply.

"And your son?"

"The same."

His own students might have been put off; they might have read the warning in the cutting edge of the words. Not so this one, who owed him nothing, certainly not respect or obedience. "Did she follow the Lady?"

"No." He rose. "She followed me. And I led her, in pride, to the Tor Leonne, for my first audience with the Tyr'agar." He could not call her back; could not unmake the choice that he had made. He could only do this: strike out. Kill. Avenge.

But before he had cleared a courtyard whose meaning he attributed to the malice of the Lady, the boy spoke again. "Ser Anton."

"Yes?" He did not turn. Something in the boy's tone told him he would like the question no more than any of the other questions he had asked this eve.

"The hundred run tomorrow."

"Yes?"

"Will there be more assassins?"

Wind take the boy. None of his own students had dared to ask the question so boldly. "I don't know," he said, offering the boy ignorance. It was truth, after all; he could not be certain.

"Thank you."

Lord scorch him. He turned, thinking to catch the boy's back. Caught his eyes instead, and held them. "Take care," he said quietly. He himself was not certain whether or not he meant the words in warning or threat.

CHAPTER TWENTY-SEVEN

"I'm sorry, Devon," Jewel said for about the twentieth time. "But you can't just point me in the right direction and expect me to start seeing for you. Doesn't work that way." *As you should damned well know.* And he did know, that was the Hells of it; he knew, but he obviously felt he didn't have much choice.

There were a hundred holdings in this city, some older than others to listen to the residents bicker, and she'd come nowhere close to traversing all of them. But Devon ATerafin had somehow managed to get her a horse—she wasn't comfortable on horseback, probably never would be, and the damned creature *knew* it—and permission to trace as much of the route as the runners would be following in advance of their actual run. Where permission was sort of like an order, but less easy to refuse.

Not that she would have tried. Because she knew what Devon didn't: that Kiriel couldn't sense demons anymore, the way she had with the first few.

Kiriel was as certain as she could be—which wasn't very—that they'd destroyed all of the ones she'd pointed out to Jewel what seemed years, but was in fact weeks, ago, but they both knew that the creature that had come close to killing both Jewel and Angel hadn't been detected at all—whether or not because he hadn't been *there* Jewel couldn't say, and Kiriel wouldn't.

Beyond the slim barricades, people gathered. They stood beneath awnings and wide-brimmed hats, huddling, when neither were available, beneath the shade of trees, as if sunfall were much like rain. At this time of year, it was worse.

She shook her head. Smiled jaggedly. "It's the twenty-fifth," she said. She'd traced the route on horseback, seeing the same crowds as the hours dwindled and the sun rose; there were more people visible than cobbled stones. Challenge season.

Devon nodded quietly.

She shrugged, almost embarrassed. "It's different for you,"

she said at last, lamely. "You get to go home if you want to." Not, if she were honest, that there was much to go home to: lack of food, shelter, and safety; a lot of hiding from magisterians and trying desperately to become good enough at theft that you could survive another week or two; the one friend she'd had outside of her den was long dead, and her den whittled down to bloody size before they'd managed to make their escape. But desperation had its own rules, its own stark simplicity. Nothing at all like life in Terafin.

Her hands stopped on the reins; the horse stood a moment beneath the sun, as if she had finished her journey through the city, rather than just interrupting it. She sat up straight, seeing the past in the thin arms and thin faces of the watchful spectators; seeing herself at their backs, her shaking hands attempting to pull money from their pockets, food from their baskets, anything at all that might help her den survive another day.

Dreaming, she remembered, of a day when they'd have enough, and she'd never have to be less than her father would have approved of again.

"Jewel?"

"Nothing here," she said softly. "Nothing."

"Member APhaniel," Sigurne Mellifas said, in the tone of voice she usually reserved for pronouncing sentence on rogue mages, "I caution you against use of magic—in fact, use of *anything* at this early time."

"It's been six days, Sigurne," the member so lectured replied.

"And must you do that?"

"We are in the open air." But in deference to the mildest member of the Order of Knowledge, Meralonne APhaniel ceased to stuff the bowl with fresh leaf and tucked his pipe—with obvious regret—back into his satchel. "Sigurne," he said gently, "it's been *six* days. Most mages are taken with fevers for a good deal less time before either recovering or succumbing. Age and infirmity don't really change that." He paused for effect. "Dantallon himself pronounced me fit for . . . exercise."

"At the knifepoint of the Astari," she replied pertly, "and against his better judgment. You know he thought you'd be abed until at least the end of the Challenge."

He grimaced. "I feel much better," he began.

"And I suppose—"

His gaze flickered a moment over the crowd; his expression lost that long-suffering frown that spoke of rare friendship.

And hers, that vaguely maternal air.

He crossed the empty street to the barricade itself; Sigurne stood back, a lone old woman beneath a wide-brimmed hat—a practical hat that somehow seemed perfect for her, as most practical things did—arms crossed, eyes open. He had never been in a fight that involved Sigurne before, but he did not feel uncomfortable with that member of the magi at his back; her frailty was physical, if it existed at all; it was hard to tell with Sigurne.

He was met at the barricade by guards. They were, almost to a man, Southerners. Their gathered presence invoked the magisterial guards that had been assigned this section of road, and *their* presence called the attention to the youthful core of inexperienced mages sent by the Mysterium. They, he'd been instructed, were to *be* his power; his recovery, such as it was, was suspect, and fragile.

Luckily, such a gathering of men wielding authority—or at least swords and magic—had the end effect of pushing anyone of relative sanity as far to either side of the roadside as they could go. Unluckily, in a gathering for an event of this nature, there wasn't all that far they *could* go without actually losing their long-defended places streetside, and only the actual use of said swords or magic would cause them to abandon their positions entirely.

"Is there a problem?" a voice from behind the Southern guard rang out.

"Preferably not," the magi replied softly.

The voice switched over to Torra, and one of the guards turned to face it. The exchange was quick and short, and obviously held on one side by a man who expected to be understood. He was, of course.

"*Magi? You idiot! Get out of the way!*"

Huffing as if from great exertion, a rather portly merchant appeared between the ranks of his guards, who moved to either side of his girth, but did not choose to forsake their ground—or their point.

They had become inconsequential the minute the merchant appeared. He bowed theatrically. "Ser Pedro di'Jardanno." The bow was Northern in style; the affectation existed beyond national boundaries.

Meralonne offered a clipped bow in return; a thing of relatively little substance. As if lack of show could balance overt show-manship.

But power recognized power; that was a rule older than any-thing but time. Their eyes locked a moment before the member of the Order graciously requested permission to view the mer-chant's supplies.

"You must understand," Ser Pedro said, with an apology that fair gleamed, although it was made up of the usual parts: insin-cere expression and over-pronounced word and gesture, "that I did not come here to *sell*. I came to witness the hundred run, one of the few events that a common merchant has easy—and inexpensive—access to." He did not wring his hands, for which Meralonne was grateful.

The magi nodded quietly. "Of course," he said, with about as much force of meaning as the merchant's words contained. He followed the merchant, and the Southerners closed at his back.

The merchant's stall was impressive, given the lack of space the marathon usually afforded anyone, guards or no. It was not quite a wagon—too small for that—but not for want of trying, and it had enough fabric strewn this way and that a careless man might have mistaken Ser Pedro for a cloth merchant. Velvets, silks, heavy cottons, and fine spun wools, were artfully arranged within the stall's protected interior; there were cushions here. Food. Two decanters, one filled with water in the Southern fashion, and one with wine. He wondered if the merchant would claim that the waters came from the Tor Leonne itself. He did not ask; there was a tension in the air that forbade it.

But although he examined the stall itself with care to detail, and with the magic that was his birthright, he found nothing out of place, nothing remiss.

"Your pardon," he said softly to the merchant.

"Of course," the merchant acknowledged, bowing in return.

He left the stall, wondering what had called him to it, through the crowds and the rows upon rows of men. Wondering what he had responded to, what inside of him, beneath open sky, had felt that momentary twinge of danger.

One step. Two steps.

The third step did not fall; he turned, his hand flying back, palm open, his lips, wordless, calling the only defense he had—or needed—as the answer came.

The stall exploded; fragments of wood, burning cloth, ruined food followed. People screamed, but it was not the explosion that invoked those cries; it was what followed. And they fled, where they had not fled for guards or swords or magic.

Writhing a moment in sunlight, smoke from the fire grew dense and dark, a black maelstrom. He called—he almost called—his shield; felt the emptiness of its loss, a reminder of a recent battle. And then the darkness solidified, took shape and form—a shape and form that he had never seen before, but knew intimately regardless.

"*Illaraphaniel!*" the creature roared.

"Allaros," he replied. His sword shivered and crackled like blue ice on fire. His eyes scanned the crowd, but the merchant had dissolved with it, carried by its fear, sheltered from vision. *Decanters,* he thought. *We should have known.*

In the distance, he heard, of all things, horns. For a moment he stiffened in exultation, and then he remembered: the run. The hundred run.

The *Kialli* was caught by the same fancy, and the same realization, as if they were part of the same storm. "We will play the game of mortals and the game of gods," the creature said, folding great wings behind his obsidian shoulder blades, "but at *our* leisure. Come. This has been too long denied us."

And from the center of his palm, red fire flared and took form, even as he himself had done. Sword. It was followed by shield. Full shield, fully formed. The mage did not waste time or breath cursing, although the desire to do so proved that his time in this city had taken its toll.

"You made the wrong choice, Allaros," Meralonne said, measuring the strength of his enemy—and the time it would take for the last of the people closest them to flee. Yes, he had been in this city a long time, if he could spare thought to them, but it did not concern him; once they joined combat in earnest, he would be lost to it.

"Speak to me of choice," the creature replied, its visage twisting into runnels of expression that seemed almost—but not quite—natural. "When this is done."

Meralonne opened his mouth to speak, and fire came in the wake of the *Kialli* words. The time for hesitation was destroyed in the blast.

Meralonne APhaniel *moved.*

* * *

Valedan leaped forward, into his knees; he could not—not quite—force himself to give up the burst of speed that the competitors chose to put on at the run's beginning. He knew better than to be left at the back of the pack, but he also knew better than to attempt to pull out in the lead—not from the beginning. No one here knew his full strength, and their ignorance was his advantage.

Sadly, the same could be said of any competitor in this run.

Speed didn't matter here. Commander Sivari had said this time and again—but it was impossible to believe it when the starting line moved so abruptly, surging into the streets as if the finish line were already well within sight. His competition knew what he knew: you surged ahead, found your place near the front—but not necessarily at it—and paced yourself until the end.

The end was hours off, half a day.

The sky was clear. Bad, that; the sun would make itself felt as the day progressed, and not a few of the hundred would collapse along the route in the holdings. He only prayed—to Kalliaris, and this caught him almost by surprise—that he wasn't one of that handful. Too much at stake. Too much to lose.

The streets opened up; he caught sight of the man ahead of him and pulled forward along the stretch of cobbled stone, his lips turning up in a smile of recognition. The runner spared a backward glance—obviously not one of Sivari's trainees—and returned the smile. He even moved over a bit to give Valedan some room.

Eneric of Darbanne was shorter of leg than Valedan, but not by much; he was also, of the two, sun-darkened, his skin was near brown and his hair almost white. They didn't waste breath with speech, although Valedan spoke Eneric's name in greeting, and Eneric lifted a hand, the motion rippling his stride slightly.

Valedan kai di'Leonne had grown up in the North. The Empire had sheltered him. He had been taught that it spanned the length of the coast from the edge of Averda to the frozen Northern wastes, that it stretched in breadth from the isle of *Averalaan Aramarelas* to the amorphous and little-understood buffer that the free towns formed. That, with political will and strength, it could grow to encompass the little cluster of Western Kingdoms.

Everything about the Empire was big.

But knowing it—and he had learned from the tutors appointed

by Mirialyn ACormaris—was a distant experience to this: the hundred run, as the citizens of the Averalaan called it.

Riding through the streets from the West Gate to the isle had not given him the intimate sense of the city's spread, although in many ways that ride and this run would mirror the same route. There, he was mounted, he was part of a pageantry of sight and sound, of banner, of heraldry and display. Here, he was on foot, and the height of buildings, the nearness of the men against whom he had competed shorn of anything but simple, light cloth, made the task enormous.

The city of Averalaan became, for the moment, the Empire: larger than life, larger than a single glimpse, or a hundred glimpses, could contain. There, along the barriers, the rich and the poor alike pressed against wall and road, seeking a glimpse of the contestants. Skin, dark and light, smooth and wrinkled, hidden and exposed, melted into a distinct pageantry of color and life that *was* the Empire.

He took energy from it, somehow. He, the Southerner, running at the side of the Northern giant, running behind a man he vaguely recognized as a young free towner. He forgot that there was anything but this: the run itself. He found his stride. He kept it.

The two swords thundered like summer storm where they met, and a single fork of lightning, edged in red, shot up from the ground. They were driven back, mage and demon—Meralonne into the open street, and the *Kialli* into the building which had shadowed the merchant's stall.

The merchant himself was gone, his guards scattered as if they were commoners with no means of protection, no training to prevent them from fleeing in blind panic. The magisterial guards scattered as well, but deliberately, drawing and hefting their flat, lifeless swords as they took up distant positions at the magi's back. As if the circle had been drawn, and they did not—not yet—dare to interfere in the battle.

All of this, he saw in a glance; he had that time; the *Kialli* lord had, after all, disappeared *through* the wall at his back.

He did not choose, however, to reemerge from that hole.

Magic, when it came, came down in a rain from above.

Two of the magisterial guards caught fire, their voices raised in twin screams of pain.

That would be Allaros, Meralonne thought. He bit back the urge to curse and lifted a hand in response—but not more than that; the fires guttered before the spell—and the power, desperately needed for the fight, for he had no shield—came into focus.

It was not his way to thank gods; he did not thank them now.

But he rose upon the currents of the heavy air, forcing it into a breeze, shaping it to his will. The *Kialli,* it was said, favored fire, and in most cases, that was true.

Fire and air were often cunning allies, poor enemies.

But he had air, and it howled as he rose, wrapping himself in its splendor.

Jewel ATerafin swore.

She swore loudly and rudely in a box exactly four feet from the Kings' box, into a silence that had fallen as the last of the runners disappeared from her view.

The Kings did not deign to notice. Of course not. But two men did: the Lord of the Compact and her companion, Devon ATerafin. He caught her arm—the arm that faced away from the Crowns—in a grip that was a bit too tight to be friendly. "Jewel?" he said, accenting the first syllable, the question multilayered.

She pointed skyward, into the distance that had swallowed the runners, a distance littered with treetops and buildings. "You'll see it soon enough for yourself," she said, pulled her arm free. "Come on, we've got work to do."

"Jewel—"

Lightning, in a clear sky, tinged red and blue as it streaked into emptiness *from* the ground.

Devon ATerafin, curse him, *didn't* swear. Oh, well. That was what breeding did for you—put you at a loss for words.

He didn't argue either.

They appeared from out of the crowds as she hit the ground and signaled, Angel—out from under the watchful eye of Alowan, and probably unwisely—and Carver. These were her denmates of choice in a fight like this: they knew the value of running, they weren't stupid when they chose to be brave, and they followed *her* orders. Not Devon's, not The Terafin's for all that Carver had chosen to take the House name, but hers. She didn't need the stress of worrying about the politics of giving a command at a time like this.

Devon raised a brow as they fell in behind Jewel like shadows cast by twin lamps. Her lips compressed in a thin line but she said nothing.

"We can't outrun the runners," Carver said.

"We're not following their route," Jewel replied. "They aren't exactly going in a straight line." Thank Kalliaris for small mercies.

Angel whacked Carver in the shoulder. "He knew that," he said. "He was just *trying* to look stupid."

"Tell him to try something that'll actually take effort."

They were in high spirits. They shouldn't have been. She should've stepped on them. But there was a freedom here, on these packed and crowded streets, that they didn't have in Terafin. And in the end, the danger didn't seem any less; they risked their lives. But it was to a known enemy, not the act of a treacherous hand in their own midst; it was to darkness—and they'd fought that before, they'd fight it again—not people who all converged on the nexus of power that *was* Terafin. Clean fights were always the best fights, but you got them so rarely.

"Over there!"

Devon's voice. She looked—they all did—in the direction he pointed.

Fire tufts decorated the air in an aurora of angry color; the winds at the tops of buildings were obviously a lot stronger than the tepid breeze they could garner at ground level.

That meant something to Devon. He relaxed—although exactly what difference that made she would have been hard-pressed to say.

"What?"

"Meralonne," he said. "Meralonne APhaniel."

The moment he said the name, she knew he was right. "One of these days, you'll have to tell me how you knew that."

"One of these days." He picked up speed, and then slowed again. "ATerafin," he said at last, "I believe you've got a better idea of where we're going than I do."

She nodded. Took the lead. Was happy to take it. The sun was hot, the air was still, and the fire that burned in the distance had nothing to do with the weather. But she knew where it burned—or close enough—and she began to circle the city that had once been her home like a bird of prey might circle the air above its intended kill.

Only one thing broke that mood, but as often happened, when it was broken it was shattered.

As she crossed the brewer's road, as she stepped through the cart-empty streets—and cart-empty streets at this time of year

were a blessing that only occurred during the hundred run itself—
she heard it: screaming.

She cursed herself, because she remembered then that no fight
is clean.

They knew it, too. Angel and Carver came to rest on either
side of her, daggers drawn, faces and sudden silence completely
somber.

"Split up," she said.

"Signal?"

She nodded; whistled something short and sharp.

Angel whistled back; three tones, quick succession. She shook
her head; changed the middle tone to something that *her* lips
could get around. They melted into shadows, right and left; went
their own way.

"Next corner," she said to Devon.

He stared at her a long time; she pulled her hair up under his
scrutiny, twisted it into a knot, and pinned it back almost in a single motion. Then she drew her weapon as well.

"Fancy dagger," he said.

"Probably not much different than what you're carrying."

"Me? I've decided to try something slightly different." He
shrugged his shoulder, and the straps that crossed his chest grew
slack. From over his back he pulled something heavy and almost
clumsy. Crossbow.

"Is that why you're wearing that stupid cape in this weather?"

"No." His smile was brief, lean, a thing that glimmered around
the corner of his mouth and was gone. "See you there."

Beneath his feet the people were like the cobbled stones; so
much a part of the landscape they could be forgotten. The air was
more important, and to step on it, to be granted firmament in its
eddies, was a giddiness and a joy of its own. If the element re-
proached him at all, it would wait until after the battle.

They were alike, in that: death first.

But so, too, was his enemy.

The fire fell, and where it fell, it burned; the screams of its victims bore witness to that. He had not the time—and barely the
inclination, to stop it; there was *Allaros,* there was himself, either caught in their chosen battlefield.

But he was aware that the fires were guttered; aware of the use
of magic below him. The power was noteworthy enough to draw
his attention from blade and wind.

Sigurne.

Unfortunately, she was noteworthy enough to draw his enemy's attention from blade and fire as well.

"You choose human allies, Illaraphaniel? How pathetic." He lifted a smooth, obsidian hand. Fire fell from it casually, like an afterthought or a statement of careless fashion.

And just as carelessly, wind buffeted it, pared it to nothing. "You have been away a long time," Meralonne said, lifting his sword. "Your command of the element is . . . almost theoretical. And we're taught that fire *is* the element of the Hells."

Allaros darkened; anger twisted his features. "You say that," he said, "who stand before me shieldless?"

Meralonne shrugged. "I do not face a *Kialli* Lord. I need no shield."

Sword struck sword in an instant; attack and defense, although who struck first and who parried, it would have been hard to say.

She hadn't known they'd be fighting in air, and she took the lack of foreknowledge personally; she was probably the only person in the Empire who could. Of her den, only Finch and Teller had less experience with a sword than she did, but they were all equal in the ranged weapons department: None, if you didn't count daggers. At this distance, she didn't.

The problem with mages and demons—well, one of the problems—was that they didn't need a weapon to be able to attack in safety at a distance. The air was a perfect place to be for a short and bloody fight.

A longer fight on a day like this, and, well, the mages that informed the adjudicatory body would be all over the site like locusts to harvest in a bad season. But it would take them more time than it would take either Jewel or her den; they took longer to prepare for a fight.

Fire flared in an aurora of white-orange light. She *felt* the heat; sucked her breath in and stopped moving a moment as if, by freezing, she could avoid it. Idiot.

The people around her screamed.

The streets weren't deserted—they'd been far, far too crowded for that—and Jewel used the ring that gilded her hand to grant herself authority. That authority played itself out in short, sharp barks as she directed people who were—almost—capable of fleeing without crushing the slower or the smaller beneath their thousands of heels.

The magisterians were all over the streets, and she used her authority—although it was purely theoretical at this point, as no one had authority over a magisterial guard by leave of title or Family save the Crowns themselves—to put them to useful work dealing with the press of people who slowed and calmed the farther they got from the fight itself.

She pushed on.

Devon ATerafin found shelter in the shadows of the ruined building. He found bodies there as well; the creature's ascent through the building had been fast and brutal. It had also, he thought, caused death as a side effect, not an end in and of itself. The people whose bodies had fallen with the rubble and blackened joists were indistinguishable from the ruins to the demon.

Devon thought—although he could not be certain—that there were survivors.

And he would find them, in a minute or two.

Less.

He raised his bow; raised it, grateful the sun was at his back and not his brow. In the clarity of sky there was only fire and lightning to complicate the shot—and they weren't enough to obscure friend from enemy. Meralonne APhaniel was silver and white, steel-gray and pale-blue; his foe was obsidian and shadow, white and red. Where their swords clashed, they spoke with the voice of the storm.

The storm was not his concern.

Two.

One.

Fire.

He *moved*. Reflexes that had not been as sorely tested as this in years propelled him the length of a hall exposed to sun and sky; he rolled head over heels, coming up with his hands on the body of the empty bow.

Where he had stood, the rock and the dirt had been fused into a glowing patch of red liquid.

He had no time to speak. The fire followed; he leaped out of its reach.

She stood in the empty street, casting a shadow that inched west as the sun progressed. Of all the gathered men and women—and there were few, very few, who had stayed to witness this combat—she was the woman most versed in the study of magic. Most versed in its practice, and in the consequence of its practice.

She stood as stiff as a corpse, and indeed, when Jewel ATerafin first saw her, she thought, somehow, some spell had either killed her and left her standing or had immobilized her completely—for she recognized Sigurne Mellifas, the soft-spoken leader of the Order of the Magi, if such a disparate and chaotic group could be said to have a leader.

But as she approached, the sweat across the older woman's brow, the creases in forehead, the quick blink of lid across eye, told a different truth; her gaze, her silver-blue eyes, were turned up, to watch the glory of Meralonne APhaniel embattled.

Almost against her will, Jewel joined her.

She lost fifteen years; more. The white-haired mage was death and glory; he had walked through fire and lightning, earth and air, to reach the combat of his choice, and having reached it, he had given himself over to it with a wildness not unlike the forces of nature that had been called upon to stop his progress.

He was magi, mage and scholar, but he fought in the air with a sword, like a common soldier. No, of course not that, not common—but not like a man of magic. And he looked, to her unjaded, practical eye, unaged. Unaging.

He also looked as if he were giving ground.

The creature that he fought was as unlike Sor na Shannen—the creature that she had first seen him fight so openly—as night from day, but he had about him the same beauty, the same darkness, the same command of shadow; if power could be defined by appearance, it was defined by his, by Meralonne's. She stood transfixed by them, by the crescents their swords carved in air, by the visible trail their weapons left in their wake.

It seemed inconceivable that either should falter, but she knew the color of blood when she saw it. First blood.

It fell in silence.

It fell across Meralonne's brow.

First blood. She could not remember, in that earlier fight, if she had seen the color of his blood or not. In fact she felt the shock of seeing it fall, this time, as if it were a first, or as if it were something that he could not shed.

And why not? Power did not deprive the man of mortality. If he lived, he bled. If he could bleed, he could die. Could die there, at the height of the buildings, below the bowers of the trees that lined the Commons in the distance.

She started to cry out, to promise him aid if his feet touched the ground—but the words fell far short of her lips. She had seen the fire fall, and although she didn't understand why, it had not fallen on Sigurne. She would not willingly call attention to what had not yet been considered worthy of it.

She turned to Sigurne, for mages knew how to speak in silence, just as bards did when one could be found. But she fell silent again as the old woman—and she looked it now, looked *old*—raised both of her shaking, lined hands.

Raised them as if in supplication. Except that when they reached their height, the open fingers furled in toward palm, leaving shaking fists. Around those fists, light, the light a muddied brightness that Jewel ATerafin had come to understand, over time, her particular vision—and not natural sight—made clear to her.

There was orange light, and around it, a patina of golden brilliance—but although it had been more than fifteen years since she had seen that particular gold, neither concerned her; she knew orange well enough to know that Sigurne had woven a protection of some sort. There was green light, deep and dark as fine emerald, and it was lovely, a color that Jewel rarely saw when magics were summoned; it felt cool, a coolness that the fires above wouldn't damp or destroy.

Yet even this did not stop her. What did was the color she saw beneath the green, for it shed no light, but rather seemed to devour it.

Sigurne Mellifas was calling the shadows.

Or being used by them.

Her hand was on the dagger that the Mother's Daughter had given her; darkness did that to her, when it was *this* darkness, this magic. But contained as it was by the fragile form of Sigurne, she stayed her hand, incapable of believing Sigurne Mellifas some practitioner of forbidden arts.

As if her sight—hers of all—could deceive her.

"Stay your hand," a voice said, and she turned, willing to look at anything that was not Sigurne, her dagger hand trembling. She was alone, but she recognized the voice.

"Evayne."

"Yes, and I am not close to you; not close to where you are. I . . . cannot travel. This is costly enough. Sigurne Mellifas has

seen darkness that you have only dreamed of, Jewel. Of all here, save Kiriel—and perhaps notwithstanding—she understands the nature of the Hells, and the force that drives men to it, willingly, life after life.

"*Ask her, ask her if she survives what she intends—for she is no young woman—who her first master was.*"

"She won't answer; she's never answered that question."

"*But do not doubt her motivation any more than you doubt your own, Jewel ATerafin, and guard what you see here wisely, for only you will see it.*"

The dagger fell; the sun rose.

And Sigurne Mellifas *spoke*.

She spoke syllables, but they were syllables that Jewel clapped her hands to her ears to avoid hearing; there was something about them, like an animal roar, but somehow darker and older and deeper, that contained a horror worse than one's own death. Worse, in fact, than death.

No human voice could speak like that; no human voice—but Sigurne Mellifas was undeniably human.

She spoke.

Kiriel di'Ashaf froze.

Flanked by Auralis and Alexis, on patrol in the ninety-seventh and ninety-eighth of the hundred holdings, she raised her head as if waking from a dream or a reverie.

"Kiriel?"

She turned, put her hand to her hip, gripped the haft of her sword. The sun had lost all warmth, all light; there was shadow upon the horizon, a spill in the sky like a cloud gone awry. And she knew its *name*.

A hand gripped her arm, pulled her round; she almost drew the sword before she recognized Alexis' face.

"Kiriel, I asked you a question."

The syllables of the name faded, but the echo still traveled the length of her spine. For a moment—just a moment—she felt shadow; she felt at *home*.

The moment passed. The sun returned, and with it the weakness that plagued her. Glowing in the reflected light, the band upon her hand—the ring that protected itself from this immortal-forged sword, caught light. "I—I think someone's found our demon," she said quietly.

Alexis and Auralis exchanged a look over the top of her head.

"Where?"

She said, "You didn't hear it?"

"Didn't hear what?"

"His name."

The second look that traveled between the two senior Ospreys was more pointed, but it answered her question. Which was good, as Alexis wasn't going to bother. She knew the Decarus well enough to know that.

"Where, Kiriel?"

"I don't know. I don't know the city well enough. It's that way," she added, pointing.

"Can we get there in time?"

There was a stillness in the air; even the fire seemed to freeze at the chill of the magi's shadow-bound syllables. The magi herself was stiff as steel; was standing, in fact, except for raised arms, in exactly the posture she'd assumed when Jewel had first set eyes on her.

"Allaros," Sigurne said, through gritted teeth, her voice raised as much as a voice could be raised that had spoken a name not meant for mortal throat.

The demon turned his gaze to earth. "Do you *dare?*" he demanded, his voice the thunder.

"Yes," was her tired, tired response. "That, and more, if it is necessary."

Fire flared, erupting from his hands as if he were ornamental font, and it, liquid. But it fanned around her—and Jewel, for which the younger woman thanked Sigurne—in a circle; it melted ground, but did no damage.

"I have," Sigurne said softly, "some purchase upon your form. While you wear it, I have your name."

Meralonne APhaniel came then, riding the crest of air that seemed to still echo the syllables Sigurne had spoken with such difficulty.

The demon parried, but it was slowed, slowed by the weight of something that Jewel could not see.

"This . . . is . . . not . . . possible . . ." the creature snarled, parrying, striking, parrying. "The hells have no purchase over *me!* I did not traverse the ways through the circles or the mages. I am here, I exist in the *now*."

She was growing paler by the second. She spoke anyway. "You gave up your life. Such a decision cannot be revoked by mere presence, or the existence of an open passage between that world and this.

"Did he tell you otherwise? You will not be the first to believe the words of a Lord who decries such credulity. *Look at yourself,*" she said. "Look at the form you have been *granted*. No summoner's trick, this, no burden of circle and passage, no mage's rapture. *Look!*"

And the word was a command.

Jewel knew it.

She wondered if Meralonne would strike then, while his enemy was held in the grip of another's compulsion. Of the many things that she admired about Meralonne, pragmatism was one: He was not a man to waste his life on a point of honor.

And yet he stayed his hand.

As if seeing himself only truly at the force of her word, the creature's gaze dropped. She waited a moment, and then saw that something else dropped as well: his shield. It flickered, as if struggling for life, before its fire went out completely.

"It will not be the same," he said softly; the wind carried the words away from her ears, but she heard them all the same. She'd wonder how later.

"Allaros—"

"Did you know it, Illaraphaniel? Did you humor me?"

The white-haired mage said nothing.

"Or did you think that I knew it?" An obsidian profile that was suddenly achingly beautiful in its momentary vulnerability gazed out, out beyond the city to the sea itself. "Do you know what I most miss?"

"No."

"The worthy foe."

Silence. "And . . . I," the mage said.

"And second?"

"No."

"Life. In all its aspects. I miss ending it. There is no death in the Hells, no satisfying closure; although the pain of the damned is intoxifying, it is also endless." He bowed his head a moment. "And I miss beginning it."

"Allaros—"

"Meralonne!" Jewel cried out, sudden in her panic. "Now! Kill him now—Sigurne is almost past holding him!"

And the creature's lips turned up in an unpleasant smile. Ugly, but respectful. "But victory is better than failure, and you *will* fail, and if we have no life in the Hells, and no life here when we leave it, we will at least end *yours*."

He struck, then, and Meralonne struck as well; their blades passed through each other as fire was finally consumed by lightning.

Jewel barely saw it; she had turned her back to the fight with just enough time to spare that she managed to catch Sigurne Mellifas before she hit the ground.

Kiriel came round the corner far in the lead of Auralis or Alexis. Her sword was unsheathed; she held it a moment as she looked at the bleeding magi, at Carver and Angel, at Jewel—here!—and the woman whose weight she struggled with.

Of the demon, there was no sign.

She sheathed the sword. Stood in the open road a moment, waiting.

Jewel ATerafin raised her head, as if that silence were a question. In a fashion, it was. "Kiriel."

The younger woman nodded.

"Help me."

She walked across the open ground, and as she approached, saw who Jewel was struggling with. The old woman. Sigurne Mellifas. Without thinking, she put out both arms, caught the whole of the old woman's weight, and hefted her as if she were an infant and Kiriel, her mother.

"So," Jewel said softly.

"What?"

"You've still got your strength."

She almost dropped Sigurne as weight returned to her arms. Almost—but not quite. "I—I didn't," she said softly.

"Doesn't matter. We've got to move. The runners will be here, and the magisterians have to have enough time to clean up."

"Where are we going?"

"The isle," Jewel replied. "The isle or *Avantari*."

Meralonne joined her, bowing stiffly to Kiriel, his brow still slick with blood. She'd missed this fight, and now wished she hadn't. "You must have—fought well," Kiriel said, awkwardly.

"Did you know the *Kialli?*" he asked.

"Not personally, no. But I—I knew his name when I heard it."

Steel-gray eyes met hers; held them a long time before he deigned to let them go. "Take her to the Palace," Meralonne ordered. "If she survives that far."

CHAPTER TWENTY-EIGHT

Valedan came in third. Eneric came in second. Andaro di'Corsarro came in first, driven as if by the demon that Meralonne had faced. He was a surprise to them all, judging by the look on his trainer's face; a surprise, that is, to all save one man. Carlo di'Jevre looked on with a pride that had no bounds as Andaro found the speed necessary—somehow—to cross that margin, that narrow, man-made boundary, first.

He collapsed immediately, his legs spasming, his body twisting into stone and dirt as it struggled for air. The crowds along the street took up his name with a roar that only the ocean in fury could match; they understood what they saw—both victory and collapse—and they appreciated the effort.

Neither Valedan nor Eneric were so indisposed, and both men must have wondered what it would have taken to push them across that line first.

Commander Sivari wondered it, but he wondered dispassionately. He had watched the race, riveted only in the last fifteen minutes; his thoughts were still anchored to numbers, to the probability— the possibility—that Valedan might walk away with the crown that Sivari himself had once claimed.

To that end, Valedan's position crossing the line was all that mattered; he could not go back in time and reclaim the race. He could only go forward. Tomorrow: archery, and of that, he felt more confident.

The day after, the test of the sword.

He had seen Valedan fight. Had wondered, the first time, how he'd ever missed the boy's singular skill; had even been surprised that Mirialyn ACormaris had not. But having seen Valedan in action, he also knew that battles that counted were different in subtle ways from the battles that didn't; Valedan had never really been in a battle that *counted*. There were too many men who came to this competition with the sword as their chief strength;

who struggled to take only that crown, of the ten, and not the crown for the event itself.

The Southerners, for instance.

He could not help himself; he glanced across the enclosure to Ser Anton di'Guivera, feeling it: The pang of loss. *Idiot*, he told himself. But there had been about Ser Anton that patina of nobility—a nobility of spirit that birth and circumstance could never duplicate—when the Southerner had taken the Crown. Not once, but twice, and in the name of love.

Much is done in the name of love, he thought, and looked away.

"Valedan."

The water played through his open fingers as he held his palms up in supplication beneath its fall. He knew the voice; knew by the near soundless fall of perfect steps that the Serra Alina was drawing closer to where he knelt. He wanted to order her away; he almost did.

But the fact that he *could* order her, and she—Southern-born and -bred—would be forced by some nicety of law and custom to obey, where in the North she might laugh or stand her ground with ease, silenced him.

"Valedan."

He did not look up. He knew what he would see; could hear it in her voice. She was silent a long time, and at last he spoke. "An old woman is almost dead," he said, each word flat and uninflected. "And a dozen more *are* dead, because they were standing in their windows, watching the streets below. Hoping for a sight of the runners."

"Valedan, you take too much upon yourself. It is a type of arrogance."

Palms became fists. "Arrogance? There would be no demons on the streets, Serra, had I not chosen to join this contest."

He waited for her denial; there was none. What could she say? She was no fool, and no liar; she knew the truth when she heard it.

"And did I choose to join it so that *others* might fight while I run or play at fighting?"

"That is your arrogance," Serra Alina said, but not as unkindly. "That you think that raising sword in a battle you are not yet equipped to win is somehow more noble than letting men fight and die who *are* capable of doing so.

"Do you think you will lead an army and defend each man,

each common soldier, with your own person? Do you think that because your cause *is* the noble cause—and it is that, Valedan, and I do not mistake it—no one need die in its service? Do you think that whole villages won't be slaughtered, in either your name or your enemy's?"

"No!" He turned, then. Rose in a single motion to face her, to face the words that she alone could speak aloud to him. "But I *think*," he said, through teeth that were clenched so tight it was hard to speak at all, "that they should not be dying while I am *playing*. That they should not be facing death and darkness, while I run for gold-plated *leaves* beneath the Lord's gaze!"

She did not take a step back. Did not, in fact, appear to notice his anger, the obvious lack of control that he showed by expressing it so openly.

His mother would have fled in tears.

"Valedan, I am not your mother, and I am not a part of your mother's harem; nor am I—nor can I be, to my regret—a part of *yours*. I say this, then, as an outsider, and you must take it for what it is worth.

"You made your choice. You made it with what wisdom and knowledge you had at that time. You *knew* what the risks were."

"I knew they'd try to kill *me*," he said.

"And you thought that that wouldn't cause deaths outside of your own? You have been too young, Valedan. You are gaining wisdom now, as any of us must do: by experience. You no longer have the comfort of such naivete. Your choices will always cost lives; you are pawn to power, but if you succeed, you will be Northern King, Southern Tyr. Men will kill for you, and die for you, on days when you do nothing more than drink the waters of the Tor Leonne."

Stillness, an utter economy of motion, fell like a mantle on his shoulders as he met her unblinking gaze. "And am I, who rule, to have no say in this?"

"What do you think, Valedan?" She asked, softly, surrendering some of her harshness because—and he knew it—she had spent too long in the North.

"I think," he said softly, "that I can't stop making choices, so it doesn't matter. Is that what you wanted me to say?"

"I? No. I want you to come to your rooms. I want you to sleep. Commander Sivari says that you must do well tomorrow."

"In the *games*," Valedan said, bitterly.

"Even so. Perhaps this is the most important lesson you will learn from this, kai Leonne. You have made the commitment, Valedan; you must continue it now, with grace, and if you are not pleased with the commitment itself, learn from it for the future."

Jewel ATerafin sat beside Meralonne APhaniel and Sigurne Mellifas, or rather, sat between them; they had both been laid out in the healerie by a rather short-tempered Dantallon.

"You again!" he said, when Meralonne walked, washed in blood, through the healerie's modest arch.

But he'd fallen silent when Kiriel had come bearing Sigurne Mellifas. And his silence had become more dour when he realized that the cause of her ailment was beyond his ability to cure.

He'd seen to Meralonne's wounds—inasmuch as Meralonne, who loathed healers for reasons that Jewel couldn't fathom, but would never have argued with, would allow him to. He'd brought cloths and blankets for Sigurne, and had sat by her side, carefully wiping her damp brow, until Jewel had offered to take over for him.

"It's just make-work," he told her quietly.

"I know," she said. Their hands met, and he smiled wryly.

"She has that effect on people. I—she's not young, but I want her to survive."

"I know."

"And will she, Jewel ATerafin? Will she survive?"

"Yes."

He froze a moment as the word died into stillness, and then his eyes closed and he let his head fall into his hands. "Will you need a bed again, ATerafin?" he said, a moment later.

"I hope not. Not that I have anything against the beds here," she added, "but I've spent way too much time in healeries in the last month, and if I never see one as a patient again, it'll be too soon.

"I'll stay a few hours."

"Your domicis?"

Avandar stood close to the largest window, a grim shadow against the glass.

"He'll stay until I'm gone. He's . . . not happy with me at the moment."

"I'm not sure I'd want him unhappy with me," Dantallon replied. But Jewel had seen him face down a room full of upper nobility when he felt his cause—usually the health of a stubborn patient—required it; she couldn't imagine that Dantallon would particularly care if anyone were unhappy with him, given the right circumstances. She watched him leave.

And when he was gone, a hand touched her hand.

She turned to meet the open eyes of Meralonne APhaniel, unsurprised by his convenient wakefulness.

"Jewel ATerafin," he said, his voice soft rather than weak. Dantallon was convinced that the fevers had him again, or that they would—but possibly not as badly. She couldn't understand why; the rings seemed trivial compared to the fight with the demon. But she wasn't magi, and she knew better than to ask.

She held his gaze. And then, acknowledging what he had not yet spoken openly of, she turned from him to look at the troubled face of Sigurne Mellifas.

"Yes," he said softly.

"Did you see what she did?" Jewel asked, her eyes tracing the lines in the old woman's brow with a mixture of fear and affection.

"I did not need to see it," Meralonne replied, his voice failing to draw her attention away from the woman of whom they spoke so obliquely. "I heard the name."

"I thought it was myth—the name thing."

His answer was a trifle frosty. "You have spent too much time with Kiriel to be that stupid, but I forgive you your transparent attempt at protection."

Silence again. At last, Jewel said softly, "What will you do?"

And she heard, of all things, a chuckle. She turned then, his hand still on her hand.

"What will *I* do? What will you do, Jewel ATerafin? Of the two of us, *my* history, I believe, is somewhat less sterling than yours."

"*I* was the thief," she countered.

"True enough, but there was a certain purity even in that; you were a thief when you had no power. And therefore the thieving did not define you; what defined you then still binds you now."

She wanted to know what he thought that was, and even started to ask, but there was something in his expression that made her pull back. Made her ask instead, "And what shadows your history, Member APhaniel?"

"Perhaps I have dabbled in the same arts," he replied softly.

She stared at him until his lips turned up in a smile.

"Your particular talent gives you the advantage in this conversation."

She shrugged. "It wouldn't have mattered at all had I been the one trying to wield your sword." She was quiet a moment, and then she said, "Sigurne knew you wouldn't make it on your own. She knew it."

His gaze grew remote; passed beyond her to the woman on the bed. "Yes," he said softly. "And no, I don't know how."

"I do. She knew who that creature was."

"I think it . . . unlikely."

"Why? You seemed to know who that creature was."

"That is why I think it unlikely." He rose, stiffly, releasing Jewel's hand.

"Meralonne—Dantallon's going to kill me if you collapse."

"Probably." He passed her bed; came to stand at the foot of Sigurne's. She saw the shudder take his slender frame; twist his features. He forced it aside. Dantallon would have been *furious*. "The magi suspected," he said, "but we did not know for certain.

"Sigurne has seen much in her life, and—like you—she may have done things she now regrets at a time when she had no power. What she has done since she gained true power defines who she *is*.

"I will not betray her, if it is possible not to betray her; I believe that the arts she learned, she must have been fated to learn for just this reason: battle is coming, Jewel. Beyond it, the war that will forgive all, or destroy all." He bowed his head. "And truthfully, I have become fond of Sigurne, and I am fond of very few people in my dotage."

The funny thing was that *was* the truth; so few people spoke truth when they announced their intention to do so.

"Well," Jewel said, "you're a member of the magi, one of the wise. If you don't think she's any danger, who am I to argue? Besides, if I take this complaint to the council of the magi, and you deny it, they'll have to side with you."

He was utterly, completely silent.

And then she understood, and she understood completely. She felt a chill in the room that emanated entirely from his eyes. It wasn't much lessened when he bowed, although his subsequent collapse into the bed that Dantallon had designated his did take a bit of the edge off his unspoken threat.

Why, she thought, as she returned his bow, acknowledging the threat that he had chosen not to make, and that she had chosen—by so bowing—not to take offense at, were powerful people always so cold-blooded when they made their decisions?

25th day of Lattan, 427 AA
Avantari

In the morning, things were clearer.

He rose with the dawn, having seen too long a night, and when he left his chambers, it was the Princess and not the former Kings' Champion who was waiting for him.

The halls were empty; the air was quiet.

On just such a morning as this, for several years now, Princess Mirialyn ACormaris would meet him. Just as today, she would carry a bow; he would carry nothing. They would walk—as she walked—down the quiet hall, and at the end of the hall, not the middle, and not near the door where the discussion might drift backward into the occupied halls, she would turn to him, and she would ask, "Are you ready?"

And he would shrug.

And she did. And he did. It made him laugh.

The sound startled him. She answered it with a smile, a rare warmth that travelled the breadth of her face, changing very little.

"I spoke with Alina," she said, as they continued to walk.

He stiffened a moment. Sighed. "And?"

"Valedan, she understands what it is to be a Southerner. She does not—she *cannot*—understand what it is to be Valedan kai di'Leonne. None of us can. You were born in the South; you were raised in it until your eighth year. Some elements of that remain. But you've come of age in the North, among the patriciate, the Northern nobility. You have learned our ways.

"They will become inseparable, North and South, within you, if you succeed."

"And if I fail?"

She turned to face him. "Death." Before he could reply—and there was no guarantee that he could have—she removed the bow from its resting place across her shoulder. It was unstrung, almost unbent, but he could tell just by looking at it that it was, if unornamented, a very fine weapon. "I would be honored," she said, "if you would use this."

He caught it in both hands; was surprised by its weight. It was heavy, much heavier than it looked.

"I will not be able to go with you," she continued softly.

He knew that she spoke of the Dominion and the war.

"Alina will go, and that will cause comment. I believe that Sivari will take his leave and travel with you as well. The Commanders will go. Listen to them, Valedan; they do not give poor advice."

He started to speak; she lifted a slender finger.

"Listen to them, but remember that in the South, *you,* and you alone, must be seen to rule. If you disagree with anything they say, choose to speak privately, and quietly, no matter how strong the disagreement is. To disagree, and then to be persuaded to their way of thinking will not be acceptable to the Southerners who watch, who weigh the Northern influence in your life.

"But," she added softly, "if you make a decision, and the Commanders are arrayed against you—if you are certain in your convictions, declare yourself publicly; they will bow, because they have no right to be there without your request."

"I will have Baredan," he said quietly. "And Ramiro."

"Yes. And Fillipo as well; he is cunning, but I think has more of a heart than his brother."

"He can," Valedan replied without thinking. "He doesn't have to rule."

She stared at him a long time, and then she nodded. "Truth in that, kai Leonne. How much of your heart will you give away to become power's vessel?"

"I don't know."

"You know that there's a choice, now. Don't forget it."

"Will I be allowed?"

She smiled. "Probably not. But I would say, no, I *will* say, that you will take Jewel ATerafin with you as well, and when you are troubled, you might turn to her, if only to listen to what she has to say."

"Because she has the so-called sight?"

"Because," Mirialyn said gravely, "she is caught in the same struggle that will bind you: the choice between power and compassion, between wisdom and justice, between duty to a cause and loyalty to yourself. She has the advantage; she is older than you are, and she surrounds herself with people she can trust.

"But you, Valedan, can trust so few that it might be better if you did not trust at all."

They were waiting for him.

The Ospreys, the Commander, the Callestans. Even the General, Baredan di'Navarre, seemed to exhale and gain his ease only when Valedan came into full sight.

"Am I late?" he asked, although he knew full well he was not.

The General understood the rebuke, softly spoken though it was. His smile was brief, almost rueful. "You are not, kai Leonne." He fell into step beside Valedan; Commander Sivari joined them.

"Are you ready?" Sivari said.

Valedan nodded.

The strange thing was, it was true. He heard the muttering of the impatient crowd that waited beyond the gates; heard the adjudicators, their voices sharp and sudden as the lash of a whip; heard the song of a dozen bards, rising and falling as if it were part of the tide that waited beyond the seawall. All of this, for the day, the penultimate event: the test of the bow.

And yet this one day, he felt a calm settle across his shoulders like a mantle. It was as if he had somehow taken the peace of the courtyard in which the blindfolded boy held sway, had swallowed it with the cool running water, had carried it here.

"That bow," Sivari said, his voice coming from both a long distance and less than three feet away.

Valedan took the bow from his shoulders. "Yes?"

"It—it looks familiar."

"Mirialyn gave it to me," Valedan replied.

"Can you string it?"

It was not the question he had expected, although as a trainer, Sivari often asked odd questions. Valedan started to answer carelessly and stopped the words from coming; there were Southerners here: Baredan and, at a greater distance, the Callestan Tyr. *Of course*, he thought. And then: *Why is he asking? He knows I can string a bow.*

As he often did, he found refuge in truth. "I haven't tried."

"I would try," Sivari said, his voice as neutral as Valedan ever heard it, "before the competition starts."

Sivari, what do you know about this bow that I don't?

"It's not magical, is it?"

"If it were," Sivari replied, "it would be taken from you by the adjudicatory body—as would your place in this competition." But his eyes were narrowed, unblinking; his hands were conspicuous in their sudden stillness at his side.

Valedan set the bow on end, wrapped the string half around his ankle, and bent the aged wood.

Something as heavy as this he expected a fight from; he put his shoulders and his upper body into the motion, holding the bowstring's free end. The dark, polished wood caught sunlight, returning both that and the shadow of his bent reflection to his narrowed eyes.

"Valedan?"

Beyond it, he saw a darkness that was broken by starlight, by the clarity of constellation; he felt, at his back, the cold, cold wind, and he realized with a start that he had never seen a night so crisp as this, a sky so utterly clear.

This had been her gift to him: Archery.

As he struggled to join string to bow, he remembered the first bruises such a simple task had given him, and with bows much, much lighter than this. Oh, she had offered him sword, had watched his progress with Alina's daggers, had taught him the rudiments of combat with shield and with scant armor—but *this* had been her gift: The watchful kill.

"Wait, Valedan," she would tell him. "The wind is not right." Or, "Wait, Valedan. The grass is not moving, not the right way." Or even, "Wait, and we will eat well."

Later, she had taught him speed, but the grace of the weapon was in this: Watching, seeing, waiting—and then, only then, letting fly.

"Kai Leonne?"

He shook his head; his dark hair sent a shadow over the bow's reflection, bringing back the heat of summer sky, the approach of the Lord's Hour.

"Well done," Sivari said, his voice a hint of that cool breeze, that night sky. "Do you know what it is that you hold?"

"A bow," he replied, no more. But he *did* know. She had given him, somehow, the heart of the North, a North unblemished by the heat of the summer sky, the humidity of the open sea, the bitterness of the political squabble and the coming war.

And for the first time in months he was not afraid of taking what she offered; of holding it. She was the North, Alina the South, and he had never, in the course of his hybrid education, been separated from either.

Commander Sivari bowed. "Kai Leonne," he said, as a familiar might, "I think that you will never cease to surprise me. Come. They are waiting for you."

He had never been calmer than he was that day.

He thought he might never be as calm again, for the time in which he might draw the bow, fitted with arrow, and wait out the manipulative malice of wind and sea breeze, was fast coming to a close.

There were targets, painted in gaudy colors so that their import might more easily be gauged by those who watched. They could not move, of course; could make no attempt to evade.

Contestants came and went; they were allowed three shots; they were allowed their choice of which of the three they attempted to hit. Valedan took his time.

It *was* his time.

The crowd's chant became the chatter of gulls, of something so natural it faded into the background. His rivals were not rivals; they were there for their own reasons, and they met their own tests. But not one of them saw as he saw, felt as he felt: This was his time, and when he loosed the last arrow, it would be over.

His first shot flew true, piercing the dark, deep blue that stained the heavy targets. He drew another arrow after the first had settled. Pivoted slightly, staring down the shaft a moment to the target twenty yards to the west. He heard the judges, heard the crowd, heard the deep resonance of bardic voice.

But more than that, he heard the wind, the rustle of leaves at the edge of the stadium and beyond it; saw the dip and flight of gulls above. He watched them as they swooped to ground and eddied up in the current, and when he felt the time was right, he let loose the second arrow.

It, too, flew to the target's heart.

The crowd was louder now; the only human noise he could hear. He waited them out, waited as patiently as he knew how. He fitted the third arrow, the third shot, and pivoted again.

The last target.

It wasn't necessary. He knew it. But it was the last one. He felt a cold, cold wind cut his cheeks with razor fingers, freezing blood instead of drawing it. He saw his breath hang like a shroud of mist in the air before that wind blew it out of his sight. He shivered a moment, knowing that cold, like heat, was a killer. Understanding the lesson.

And then he watched. He waited. He felt the moment approaching.

The arrow flew.

The target accepted it, swallowing wood and ending its flight perfectly: the heart pierced.

Three shots.

Three targets.

He knew this was a Northern skill, a Northern sport. He would gain nothing for it from the South, save the acknowledgment of victory. Knew that there were few in the Dominion who could do a third so well on a lucky day, and knew as well that it counted for almost nothing in their eyes. Alina would have frowned, but Valedan didn't care.

This was still his, this skill, this test, this time.

He turned away from the targets toward the spectators' boxes. The Kings were there, and the Queens; the man known as the Lord of the Compact and hated for it; the Kings' Swords. But beside them, the only person he wished to see: the Princess of the Blood. Mirialyn ACormaris.

He walked the grass for her, crossing white lines and gold lines with equal regard: none.

And when he reached as far as the grounds—and the guards—would allow, he paused before her. Raised the bow that had been her gift in both hands.

She met his eyes, and her smile was dim, a mixture of pride and loss, an acknowledgment of both his time and its passing.

He bowed, first to the Princess and then, only then to the Crowns.

Turning, he let the noise of the crowd in.

Lamplight, filtered by fine glass in too many shapes to count, touched the table, distorting its rough surface.

Pedro, who was so much more than a simple merchant—and now, with far too many mages searching for him through the breadth of the streets above, much less—gestured, guttering the lamp. The small, windowless room was plunged into darkness.

Yet even this was not so very dark, although he couldn't, without appropriate spell or ornament, see the hand in front of his face. He gestured almost absently and the light returned, flickering as if it were some serpent's lazy tongue.

Why?

This was to have been his triumph, and through it—through it the return, after centuries, of the brotherhood of the Lord. Let the cities laid to waste in the vast desert stand; let the ancient enmity between the followers of Lord and Lady at last end their bitter feuding. Already, the Voyani were being turned from their guardianship and their folly, and this boy—this boy was one of the few things that stood in the way. There was nothing personal in it; death was rarely personal, not to a man who wished to *be* a power.

The plan itself had been simple, and had the cursed creature *followed* it, the mages hunting him through Averalaan would find nothing: He, Pedro, would be long gone, his goal attained. The boy would be dead.

Instead, he sat here, his instrument—the highly prized gift from the Shining Court's Lord Ishavriel—having failed him utterly. And the failure would sting less if he understood it. That mage, that member of the Order of so-called Knowledge, had seen *nothing.*

True enough, the voice said. *He saw nothing. But Allaros saw* him.

Pedro resisted the sudden urge, the visceral urge, to make the light brighter. Steeling himself slightly, he reached across the table to one of the many stoppered flasks that stood there, reflecting and absorbing the light. He lifted it gingerly, aware now— how could he be less?—that whatever resided within the bottle could free itself.

That, Ishavriel had quaintly neglected to tell him.

The Lord would be angered by it, no question; the flask itself lay in shards against the cobbled stone. And it had a value, both to Ishavriel and to the Lord, for its magic was a thing so contained in the workmanship of its glass that it gave away nothing. It was not magic as Pedro understood it; nor magic, in the end, as the *Kialli* did. It was a work, a thing so utterly itself it could not be corrupted, although it could contain anything at all that its owner might choose to pour into it. Even the essence of the kin themselves, undiluted by contact with the world.

Voyani magic.

They were our enemies, the voice said smoothly.

"Everything was your enemy," Pedro snapped back. He regretted it before the words had time to echo, but did nothing to attempt to withdraw them. Weakness enough, to show irritation. Unforgivable weakness, in the presence of the *Kialli*, to show contrition as well. And the Lord knew he felt no contrition.

The time is coming, human.

"And you're so certain that you won't decide on whim to destroy the last of your Lord's plan?"

Ishavriel is not my Lord.

"I spoke of *The* Lord.

Silence.

The test of the so-called Sword.

"I know."

Tomorrow. All he had to do was evade the magi for one long night, and reach Ser Anton di'Guivera in time to join his party before the start of the event.

CHAPTER TWENTY-NINE

The Serra looked upon the sword from a distance of both experience and distaste. She had come—as she so rarely did—to speak a few, a very few, words to Valedan kai di'Leonne, the man that she had unofficially tutored for over half his life. Ospreys were sent scattering at her unspoken desire for privacy—but they watched. They'd accepted the job, after all, and if they'd accepted it with their usual poor grace, they'd do it well.

Alexis saw the slight flicker of sun-lines across an otherwise smooth brow; it took her a moment to match that ripple with the blade that Valedan now girded round himself.

As if aware of her lapse, the Serra looked up, her gaze as direct as an unexpected dagger's thrust.

But of course; Alexis was a woman, even if she was an Osprey. Serra Alina di'Lamberto observed the nicety of Southern custom without—quite—invoking its spirit.

I heard you were traveling with us, Alexis thought. She wondered, briefly, if it were true. Thought it must be, although hands as smooth as that had never done the heavy work of blade's lift and fall.

"I do not find fault with the blade," she said softly, and Alexis felt honored in spite of herself. "But rather, with the blade's history."

"It doesn't have much of any."

"Exactly so."

Valedan shrugged. "It doesn't matter. You know why I can't use a blade with any history other than—" Silence. He did not name it. "It's good enough, Serra Alina."

There was a tang of salt in the air, a taste of it in the mouth; hard to differentiate, for a moment, between blood and water, here at the edge of the Challenge's last test. He drew it, his single blade; the motion was almost silent.

Alexis found herself smiling.

"And you told us," she said, the edge of accusation nonetheless evident, "that you were better with a dagger than a sword."

He met her gaze, and the familiarity of her tone, coolly. "I am," he replied.

They locked stares; Alexis broke first, more out of consideration for his rank than any discomfort on her part. But she shook her head as she turned, the smile creeping back over her lips. *The little bastard,* she thought. *And knowing Valedan, it's probably true.*

The fountain ran at their backs. This courtyard had become a second home to Alexis. She had despised it on first sight, both as a home for monied Annies and a bastion of authority. But it was a fundamental truth of Alexis' character that she despised everything on first sight. Only those things strong enough to weather her withering disregard stayed around for long enough to earn her approbation. In this case, the fountain itself—like any natural formation—was above her like or dislike. Easy, in that case, to learn to like it, because there was no risk involved.

But still . . . she saw Valedan kai di'Leonne pull away from the Serra Alina beneath the rising glow of gold and pink and orange at the edge of sky turning blue. Pull away and come to stand by the fountain's edge, the lip of carved stone that was so perfect only the hands of a Maker-born could have fashioned it. He knelt, casting long shadow, the water beneath his spread hands. As if he was saying good-bye. As if that stone boy, blindfolded, blind, a figure of supplication, was more alive than they were.

He looked his age.

Not once had she truly seen him look his age, and it shocked her more than nudity would have. She wanted to turn away, but did not.

Because when this boy walked through the open arch, when he left this courtyard, he was leading them—Ospreys and Empire—to war. His were the shoulders that would bear the cause behind which tens of thousands. Southern and Northern, would flock, and for which they'd die, the meager coin they earned unspent.

The cause for which the Ospreys themselves would once again lose numbers.

The valley came back to her then, as it often did. The visible scars had faded with time; the hidden ones, never. It worried Duarte, and she let it. Let weaker men let go of their anger and their pain. She needed both, and she faced this truth fully, here on the morning of the last Challenge day. Anger and pain were the rod and the crown in her life, the things by which she governed, the links that made her, at heart, an Osprey.

She did not kneel beside him, although she came to stand at his side. Kneeling, supplication of any type, was not her way.

But she spoke with muted respect when she did choose to break his silence. "Kai Leonne," she whispered.

He looked up. Met her gaze, his already losing the vulnerability that at once made him both appealing and disgusting.

"Commander Sivari is waiting for us."

He rose. Turned to the kneeling—when had she fallen to hands and knees in so debased a manner?— Serra, and bowed, correctly. Exactly.

The last day had started.

Ser Anton di'Guivera had named his sword after the first man— and he differentiated between men and the bandits that he had spent so much of his life hunting—he had killed. It was not the way of the Southerners to name their swords in such a fashion, and at that time, he had been much censured for it. Had he not been a favored student of the weaponsmaster who ruled the Tor Leonne's best warriors, he might have had many, many names to choose from that day.

But he had chosen, and the sword had served him well.

The day that he had had his discussion with Alesso di'Marente and Cortano di'Alexes—Sword's Edge, and a man that Ser Anton had always privately disliked—he had forsaken that chosen name; he desired another. Had come, in fact, bearing a nameless blade seeking no less than the right to name that blade anew.

Leonne.

The test of the sword was upon him, upon them all. At his back, steel rang in the early morning air; Andaro's sword, tracing an arc of air and sunlight so swift the sword itself seemed insubstantial. Until it struck, of course.

Much to be proved today.

But the sun's fires had burned so high—untended, it seemed, and carelessly so—that the taste of ash was in his mouth. Here, on the day of his triumph, he could not hear her voice at all, and it was her voice, the texture of it, the softness that concealed a precious edge, that, reached for at need, had sustained him.

The ache was profound.

What had he thought would alleviate it?

Ah, as always, death. Death.

He turned lightly on foot then, his blade's arc promising just such a death. The edge of blended, tempered steel came to rest against exposed skin, cutting it ever-so-slightly.

The man so struck did not move a muscle. Their eyes met in the silence of perfect control, one man the supplicant, and one the danger.

Ser Anton lowered his sword. He did not sheathe it.

"Ser Pedro."

"Ser Anton."

"You come late."

"By the Lord's will, I am here," was the smooth, rather chill reply. Gone was the fat, the dark hair, the rounded face; all that remained of the merchant Ser Anton had traveled North with were the eyes; sharp as a blade, and possessed of the same light when the sun struck just so.

Ser Anton shrugged. "I had expected you earlier."

"I am flattered," Ser Pedro said, in a tone that conveyed precisely the opposite, "that you expected me at all, given the nature and force of my opposition."

The older man shrugged. "Given the nature and force of your allies, I chose to have . . . faith. But, Pedro," he added, the coolness settling around the words and hardening there, "if you deny me my kill by drawing the attention and the fires of the Northerners before my time, you had best hope that the master you serve is all the mad priests promise him to be."

"A threat, Ser Anton? How distasteful."

"It is merely information," the swordmaster replied. "And you gather information in your skein. Make of it what you will." He turned then, and left the man under the sun's open glare. He was surprised at how much the slender man's presence irritated him. But it did, and he accepted this truth: This was not a day that he wished to share with an assassin. With a man who felt so much akin to enemy.

And why not? His sword-grip was white-knuckled. *Do we not now serve the same Lord?* The open sky waited. The Lord watched. The Lord had no patience for weakness.

No love for the women and the children who had not yet grown into their first sword. No love for the men who had served long and faithfully on the battlefields of the nation. No love at all, as far as Ser Anton had been able to determine in his adult life, but at least one great hatred: The Lord of Night. For only at the advent of the Night had the Day come into its strength and chosen to reveal itself in glory to Leonne.

To give Leonne the founder the Sun Sword; to give Leonne's Radann the Five.

What was Mari, what was Antoni, compared to that?

Perhaps the Lady loved her. Ser Anton had never truly been the Lady's man, and he did not know how to ask—for in the South, one thing was truth: One did not ask a question if one could not bear the answer.

It was almost done.

Almost time.

He did not leave his students, but he felt a sudden sharp yearning for sweet water, for the silence of its trickle in an empty courtyard where privacy was a physical thing and not merely a state of mind.

When had he noticed the boy?

Now, the last of the tests upon him, and unarguably in Valedan's case the most important one, Sivari had no choice but to stop and wonder. Miri had seen something in the boy from a much earlier age—that much, the Swords were privy to. She had trained him passingly well, but he had always carried the impression that she had offered him the skill that he displayed the previous day: the Northerner's heart. The bow.

Mirialyn ACormaris was no mean slouch with a sword; she had the caliber of a champion, but not the experience, and none of the drive that brought a man—and a very few women—to stand at this place on this day. He might have thought she disdained it, although no disdain was ever evident upon her unusual features.

And yet she gave him Valedan.

Train him, she had said.

I do not have the time to train a boy to the level—

Test him, then. I ask it, Commander, as a favor; even if you find nothing of promise in the boy—nothing exceptional, I will consider the favor granted. And in her tone, unspoken but obvious, the other truth: that she had the rank and the power to order it should he attempt to refuse.

The curiosity was stronger than the pique. He had tested the boy. The Southerner, the foreigner caught between cultures and people, shorn of family by treachery and deceit. *Meek boy,* he'd thought. *Too quiet.*

Meek or no, he found his support among the Tyrs and the General Baredan di'Navarre. He had the respect of Serra Alina and of Princess Mirialyn ACormaris. He had surprised each and every one of them, quietly, as befit his nature.

Boy, he thought, because to him Valedan was a boy, *surprise us again today.*

He put the force of prayer behind it.

Exhaled when Valedan kai di'Leonne, flanked by his Ospreys and a rather testy looking General, came through the cloistered arch and into the main ground that would house his final practice.

"Kai Leonne," he said, his voice sharp with respect and impatience—the perfect blend of drillmaster and man of inferior status.

"Commander Sivari. One last time?"

"I doubt very much it will be the last time," Sivari said, drawing his blade with the edge of a smile, "but yes. One more fight that doesn't count before the judges call you for the ones that do."

Heat.

Sun, pale and luminescent. Shadows short and sharp and dark, the wake of sun's light. Clash of steel; horns and bells—sounds of judgment in the slow, long day.

Sweat, heat, the taste of salt in air too close to the sea, too far from its cool surfaces.

Lord's light.

Lord's judgment.

Water came.

It came in gourd and jug, in decanter and wineskin, in stoppered flask and bottle, in bucket and in roughly shaped ladle. It came in heavy cloth, and in tubs meant more for fine bathing than public sport—and everywhere that water was carried to the men who labored or who waited, honing their skill and later, their state of mind, there was cheer.

Not all of it loud, of course.

The Northerners were rousing in their appreciation; they were foolish and excessive in their glee. They lost focus as they made rivulets of sweet water from head to toe, setting their blades aside to revel in relief.

The Southerners were not so foolish, not so disrespectful of the Lord's glare; they took what was offered both thankfully and watchfully, and if it was offered with rougher grace than many of the men were used to—no serafs here, after all, and Kings Swords made servitors of infinitely inferior grace—it was still gratefully accepted.

This heat, though—this was not the heat of the summer heartlands; it was not the heat of the South. What the Northerners found so exceptional, the Annagarians found only barely worthy of note. Were it not for the presence of the damnable sea and the sea's heavy air, it would be unworthy of note at all.

"Andaro."

Ser Anton di'Guivera's premiere student looked up at the only voice he had yet acknowledged that did not, in fact, belong to the swordmaster.

"Water?"

He couldn't help but smile. The flask that Carlo held was still stoppered. "You've not had any yourself."

"I'm not in the running; I'm as useful as any other Northerner here. Let the water go to the warriors."

He caught Carlo's wrist in his shield hand; his sword, leather throng damp with sweat, did not leave his fingers. "You've proved yourself in the eyes of the Lord. You've fought his enemy, and bested it. What will I fight? Men. Northern men—and the North, while not the Lord's, has *never* fallen to the wiles of the Lord of Night. Never entirely. Be proud of your accomplishment, or be quiet."

Carlo smiled, a flash of slightly crooked teeth in an otherwise perfect face. "Will you win?"

"For you, yes." He cast a cooling glance in the direction of the swordmaster. Then he released Carlo's arm. "Drink if you're thirsty," he said. "I will take water later."

"This is it," Duarte said.

Auralis said nothing; Alexis nodded. Kiriel split her attention between the rest of the Ospreys and their leader. The Primus was finely dressed and sharp as a good blade; the men who followed his command—and they did, if with poor grace—were discomfited in the sun's glare.

As was she.

But as Duarte did not condescend to notice it, she hid her own discomfort as best she could. Duarte knew when to show weakness in the face of humans who were, by their very nature, weak, and he chose not to show it now. She was learning.

"Sentrus," he said, and she knew by the slight edge in his voice that he was referring to her.

She snapped a sharp salute—sharper, in fact, than was the wont of a regular Osprey. She felt Auralis rolling his eyes at her back.

"You know what we're looking for, Kiriel. I give you dispensation to deal with an emergency as you see fit. The *rest* of you," he continued, his voice both louder, firmer and somehow less stinging for it, "will follow standard procedures. There will be no heroics—"

That was interrupted by catcalls and jeers; he allowed it—for three seconds.

"Admittedly a poor choice of words, given the audience. There will be no *grandstanding*—"

She did know what he was looking for. The problem at the moment seemed to be giving it to him. Her practiced eye swept the hands of all Ospreys present, looking for the thin band of gold that separated her from them. But all she had to go on at the moment *was* her vision, and her vision was not what it had been.

The guardian of her weakness—and she had come to think of it, perversely, as just that—sat upon her finger, as bright and unmarked as a newly made promise. Beneath it, inseparable from her life itself, was the thing that marked her as tainted—or as strong; her father's blood and gift. It was a distinction that she and Ashaf had often argued about in her fourteenth year.

And here, again, *again,* Ashaf came.

She could see the old woman's lined face, sun-bitten and windburned; ancient compared to the faces of the other human women who gathered in the Court. She was not afraid of age, but she was afraid; Kiriel had sensed it early. Had sensed also that it was not a fear that was—quite—satisfactory to feed on, to encourage, to incubate. It was a thing of wonder, that fear, and of curiosity, and she had spent many a night wrapped in Ashaf's frail arms, drawing warmth from the questions she asked her old friend.

Ashaf, what are you afraid of?
Would you be sad if I died?
Would you be sad if I killed a demon?
Would you be sad if I killed a human?
Would you be sad if I didn't love you?

Her face was so clear in the heat of the Challenge day that Kiriel had to close her eyes and turn away from it. Which only made it worse. Always did.

How much do you love me, Ashaf?

Will you love me forever?

And Ashaf would answer while Kiriel was rocked there, cradled in the weakest arms in the Shining Palace as if they were the only safe haven, the only true strength.

"Kiriel?"

Auralis' voice. He knew better than to touch her to catch her attention—they all did—but he could make a slap of his words by the tone he chose. This was more of a forceful nudge.

She looked up at him.

"Your hand," he said softly—and he almost never spoke softly.

She lifted her sword.

"Not that one."

Her other hand, then. Balled into a tight fist.

Ah. That was the problem. It was bleeding. He didn't ask her any questions—she thought he might; Cook would have. But the silence stretched out until she realized that he intended to stand a moment, as if he were already in combat, and guard her back.

Exposure. That was Auralis' fear.

And he shared it with her now. It struck her, numbing her hand, her arm, the lines of her face, that that was exactly what he was doing: He was sharing his fear. But not the way that scared humans usually do—no weeping, no wailing, no gnashing of teeth. No; his was a different gift. He blanketed her with the protection that he himself might have desired in the face of vulnerability. She had never, ever expected to see this from Auralis, the darkest, the most crippled, of the Black Ospreys. Had never, in fact, expected to see it from anyone but Ashaf and Jay.

But because he offered, she answered the question that he would never ask.

"I was thinking of the only woman who ever cared about me while I was growing up. A *Kialli* lord killed her."

She saw all the darkness in his unblinking gaze before he turned away, and she wondered how much of the kinship she felt was to that darkness, and how much to the flash of recognized pain.

Jewel Markess ATerafin was *tired*.

But when the silver shadows crept beneath the surface of her closed lids, she shook it—and fast. She sat up in bed, in her wing, surrounded by walls, doors and windows she was familiar with.

And standing before her, in the haziness of after-sleep, was a woman who belonged to none of these things, but was recognized immediately.

Evayne.

"Jewel," she said.

"Evayne." She was torn a moment between staring in stillness and silence to catch every word, every gesture, every nuance, and rushing to cover herself with the clothing most convenient to reach. But Evayne never came for a friendly chat; there was always something at stake. She dressed.

"I am . . . hampered, Jewel ATerafin."

Jewel frowned.

"There are forces at work, now, that I should have more clearly foreseen and did not. I had thought—" She frowned. "You are not yet what I have envisioned you to be. You have the power that I, too, was born to—perhaps, because it is so natural to you, you have the stronger gift.

"But it has lain fallow."

This Evayne, then, was younger than the woman who had come to preserve her life in the healerie; there was no demand and no command in her voice. She did not mention the oracle, and Jewel didn't ask.

Evayne shook her head and her hood fell away from her face, as if that minor gesture was a command.

"I did not see the events that would rob Kiriel of her essential birthright at this juncture. I see," and here she pulled her heart— for so Jewel thought of the crystal orb—from her sleeve, "*Kialli*, and death. I see the most dangerous of Valedan's enemies in Averalaan finally making his stand."

"But—"

"I cannot cross that threshold today; the coliseum is forbidden me."

"What?"

"There are rules, Jewel ATerafin, and vows; I have followed the former in every way *I* can, and I have made the latter. The vows of the god-born are . . . particular. There is a power at work— about which I cannot speak—that interferes with my ability to walk the path of the otherwhen. I can give no aid when aid is needed.

"And Kiriel is blind."

There was a knock at the door.

"Not now!"

"But there's someone here for you—and I think you probably shouldn't piss him off by making him wait!"

"I have asked Kallandras to come," Evayne continued, as if the interruption offered by Carver and the door were beneath her notice—or beyond it. "But I fear we may already be too late."

And she did fear it. That much was obvious to the eyes of a seer-born. "I'll go," Jewel said.

Evayne smiled, the expression thin and half-bitter. "I know."

He prayed for a worthy enemy.

It was a true warrior's only prayer: to be given an enemy of worth against which to pit the skills of a lifetime. A true warrior did not pray to *win;* he prayed to be allowed to prove his skill, beneath the eyes of the Lord.

But he wavered on the definition of *worthy*.

Certainly Valedan kai di'Leonne had proved himself to be a completely different man than the one that Andaro had been led from the South expecting: He was quiet, yes, but he did not have that placidity, that weakness, that implied he was another's puppet. He stood beside General Baredan di'Navarre, called traitor by some, and the Callestan Tyr, called traitor by everyone, and it was clear from the Tyr's watchfulness that he did not consider Valedan to be his. He did not flatter; he rarely spoke.

And at least once, to Andaro's knowledge, the boy had done something that had shaken both of his chosen supporters. Real anger, there. He had faced the servants of the Lord of Night. No question. He was *Leonne,* after all; the scion of the *only* bloodline considered worthy enough by the Lord that the Lord had come down from the heavens to anoint it in blood.

Valedan kai di'Leonne's father had been a weak man. They had said—all of Anton's students had said it—that the bloodline had been lost in that father, and in the son; that the line was at an end.

And here, in the heart of the much despised North, they had come to make truth of that certainty, that youthful contempt. This was the day, this the hour: The Test of the Sword. The Lord's Test. The man's test.

Andaro di'Corsarro was a warrior. He prayed for a worthy enemy.

* * *

The healers were on the field.

Their twin palms, gold and platinum in what was almost certainly maker-made reliefs, hung round the neck, exposed for all to see. This was the test in which men were lost, and lives taken by overzealousness, by accident, by stroke gone awry or out of control.

No man was required to die for the test, but the use of a healer disqualified the contestant; he could—should he somehow find himself empowered to do so—merely stand, brush off the proffered aid, and continue in his quest for glory. But the healers were that quest's end.

No one was certain where such a custom had come from, although it was widely believed to be a dictate of the first Kings, who felt that the expense of a healer would separate the monied and titled patriciate from their less fortunate competitors. Dantallon, Queens' healer and lord of the healerie in *Avantari,* thought differently. For the sake of a game, for the sake of men's ego and men's vainglory, this contest had been created. And it had served its purpose—but no healer-born would fix a wound and return a man to battle over and over for such a poor cause.

For any cause.

There were two healers present; himself and one other that he was certain of. He had suspicion that the Astari had planted another, a man they might make use of in as advantageous a way as possible without answering for later. As the aim of the healer was to preserve life, he frowned at the politics, but was not openly critical.

His aides from the healerie were with him; his supplies were in the bundles they, and their chosen servants, carried. Things were complicated by the fact that those entering the grounds were required to bear the rings that the magi had given as a mark of security. He was understaffed because of that requirement, and none too pleased by it, although he did claim to understand it.

His own talent he had been privately "requested" to use only in the case of mortal danger.

The sole exception to that: the young man upon whom the entire Southern war rested. Valedan kai di'Leonne, raised as a hostage in the Arannan Halls of *Avantari.*

What will we see, boy? What will try to kill you, and who will die because of it?

He did not ask the question aloud because he knew, without knowing how, that he would already get more of an answer than he liked. Although the sun was high and bright, there was a storm in the air, a crackling of energy that had yet to be released.

Of the hundred, there were at best a handful of swordsmen who Ser Anton could—and did—dismiss as mediocre. Not hopelessly so, of course; it was clear that they had some experience or they would not have been allowed entrance into the Challenge. But their strengths had been split among the ten tasks, and only a very, very few of them had the time and the fortitude to hone those strengths, sharpen them, make of them a weapon.

Eneric of Darbanne was one such contestant. His style was purely Northern; it was a thing of speed but little grace, of accuracy that seemed—almost—to be luck and afterthought more than the result of deliberate action. And yet.

And yet.

He was unbeaten in this hazy day, unblemished by anything but water.

So, too, was Andaro di'Corsarro. But the two men were cut from different cloth—were cut, Ser Anton thought with a momentary wryness—from rock and silk, from sackcloth and ironwood, from things so different the only thing that forced a comparison at all was the fact that they *did* cut, that they wielded the blade well.

He felt a pride at his student's achievement that he had not thought to feel. It vanished slowly as Andaro left the field. Another Southerner—Nicco—took his place; another Northerner faced him. There would be, if he were judge of it, blood shed in this fight.

It was significant that so far neither Eneric nor Andaro had drawn or shed blood. He himself had taken this last test without leaving a mark on an enemy, and without being marked by one. Skill.

Blessing.

He turned away, closing his eyes as contestant's steel began to clamor for attention.

He was not a contestant now. He was not on a mission to prove himself, either to the South or the North—but the one link remained between that man, that long-dead man, and himself: He had much to prove to the dead; he wished to offer them a victory and have peace.

He raised his head. Straightened his shoulders. *We pay a higher price than we envision for peace,* he thought. But that was a truth he had discovered years past, and he had never flinched from the search. He opened his eyes.

Met the eyes of a young boy, white-haired, skin patchy with flakes of skin that suggested sun's burning.

Had the clouds obscured the sun's face, the Lord's vision? He felt a hint of the night breeze, the night's hand, as the boy lifted a hand in greeting and then froze there, caught by the sudden indecision of a child who has only just remembered he is supposed to be addressing an enemy, and not the Uncle he had played with quite happily for most of his life.

This was how it started, Anton thought, feeling no such indecision in the touch of the Lady's proffered circumstance. He crossed the distance that separated them. It was not great.

"Aidan," he said, offering the boy the iron smile that he had offered him the second day they met.

"Ser Anton." The boy hesitated a moment longer and then thrust his hand forward. Ser Anton wore light armor—which, in this heat felt anything but—without gloves; the gloves were at his belt. He clasped the smaller, smoother hand and shook firmly.

"I should have thought to find you here. This is where the swords are singing."

Aidan's smile was instant, unaffected; it had a depth to it that only a boy's smile could. Unalloyed. Bright. A thing of wonder that he had not quite learned to conceal. Wonder and vulnerability were so closely twined they might almost have been the same thing.

And yet it was safe, in the presence of the dour swordmaster, to share such a thing. He stared at the boy dispassionately, thinking only that, at twelve years of age, he was probably too old to truly master the sword—but that, had he been born in the South, Ser Anton might have tried to teach him anyway; the instincts were there and an instinct and passion like Aidan's couldn't be taught, no matter who the teacher might be; one was born with it, or one did not have it at all. He had met very few born with it.

"Your Challenger?"

"Five fights," Aidan said. And he answered so enthusiastically, so proudly, that Ser Anton realized it had not occurred to him that Ser Anton himself was paying at least as much attention as Aidan had. "Five fights, and not a scratch on him. But it's almost impossible to get near him in between the fights; the Ospreys are thick as bees 'round honey."

"His sixth fight?"

"Soon. After these two. No, after the two *after* these two."

"Do you know who his opponent will be?"

At this question, perhaps a little too obviously disingenuous, Aidan fell silent a moment. His face hardened into the expression that children the world over wore when they lived too close to the streets and death. "You already know," he said curtly.

Ser Anton, unfazed, nodded. "Andaro. My own. I should have liked to see him face Eneric first, I think. That man is better than I would like to admit."

Silence. Then, "See who faces Eneric first? My Champion or yours?"

Anton laughed; the sound was short and sharp, rare enough to draw attention to them both. He waited until that unwelcome interference had passed before replying. "Your Champion, of course. My own, whose strengths and weaknesses you have seen today, I would save for that ultimate test.

"He is here, after all, to prove to the men who watch—the men from the South, the merchants and the cerdan who guard them, the Tyr, the Tyr's Tyran, the General—that those born and bred to the South are superior in every way to those whose blood is dilute at best and who have lived a pampered and soft life in the Courts of the feminine North."

"I thought," Aidan said, with perfect dignity, "that he was here to kill him."

Anton's turn to offer silence in the place of words. At last, rather gruffly, he said, "Ser Andaro is my best student; he was rivaled by Carlo, and he has always claimed that their skill is equal; it is not true. He is my best in every way.

"He has taken the field, Aidan, and he understands well what is at stake—but in the end, I do not believe that he will turn this from the test it is into the killing that it might otherwise be. I have had him for too many years, and in those early years, I was a different man."

No question of it; in those years, he would never have explained himself to a mere boy, and at that, a boy one step away from serafdom—if that. He knew he should leave. "A question, Aidan."

Aidan shrugged.

"Who do you think will win when Andaro and Valedan finally face each other?"

Another boy would have answered with boastful pride. Aidan

grew thoughtful, and this distance in his expression gave way to the compulsion that had, in the end, drawn him to Ser Anton's camp.

"I think," he said carefully, "Andaro has the best chance of beating him. Andaro's skill is always the same, no matter who he's fighting. Valedan—Valedan seems to get weaker with weak opponents and stronger with strong ones."

"As if the fight itself were a conversation, some sort of give and take, rather than an absolute skill set?"

Aidan frowned.

Anton suppressed a smile. "Never mind, Aidan. I understand what you said. It is a habit of the old; they make everything as difficult as possible when they choose to discuss it—and if something is stated simply, they cannot help but adorn it with more words.

"Do you think Andaro will win?"

Silence. Then, "No."

Ser Anton nodded quietly. "We shall see," he said. "But I would concur with your evaluation. Valedan kai di'Leonne has an instinctive response and a fluidity of style that I have only rarely had the privilege of seeing in action. He is not what I expected, Aidan.

"And you are not what I expected. I had forgotten how surprising the North could be. Come; I believe it is two Northerners who are to compete next, and I would be very interested to hear you speak of the difference in style between my own students and Master Owen's."

He shouldn't have been speaking to the old man. He knew that the old man was an enemy.

But did it really matter now? There were so many guards and mages all over the damn place a *fly* couldn't get through to Valedan—and there wasn't ever much harm done by watching.

He remembered being angry with Ser Anton. If he worked hard at it, he could be angry now—because Ser Anton had, dammit, been a *hero,* not just another Southerner. But if he watched the swordplay, he didn't have room for anger, and the moment the anger left him, he was standing beside the only man in the audience who probably felt the same way that he did.

So he said nothing.

When Ser Anton moved closer to the field itself, he followed, standing closer to the old man than the man's shadow, which at this sun height was pretty damn close. The guards were perfunctory; they examined Aidan's medallion and looked carefully at both Ser Anton's and Aidan's rings. But they knew both Aidan and Anton by now—who wouldn't know Ser Anton once the fight had started?—and they were willing to allow him to be as close to the fight itself as the judges.

After all, the contestant was his student.

The only uncomfortable moment for Aidan was in the chance meeting with Commander Sivari. Also King's Champion, although once to Anton's twice, he had come as Valedan's trainer. He raised a brow when Aidan's glance skittered guiltily across his face before he bowed very respectfully. Bows were good for that—they hid your face if you did 'em properly.

"Ser Anton."

"Commander Sivari."

They bowed as formally as the contestants themselves would have; Aidan could almost imagine that these two, and not their students, were the combatants. They took each other's measure while he watched in awkward silence.

"I was going to send for young Aidan here, but I see that you've saved me the trouble. Will you join me, or will you join your own camp? They've lined up as close to the circle as the judges will let them; two, in fact, have been disciplined."

"Crossing the line?"

"In the opinion of the guards; the adjudicatory body was not called."

"My thanks, then." Ser Anton nodded. "I will, of course, take my place with the rest of my students." He turned to Aidan. "You are welcome to join me; I would welcome your observations. But I would welcome those observations at Challenge's end just as happily if you chose to remain here."

He wanted to go.

He wanted to watch the two men meet at the side of the only other man who he was certain heard the same song that he did when the swords finally met. The desire made him miserable.

But Commander Sivari laughed. "You have a student in this one, Ser Anton."

"He is old for a student," Ser Anton replied, but there was a glimmer in his eyes, a softening of the line of his lips, "but if circumstances were different, I believe I would take him and make a swordsman out of him that even your student today would have trouble besting."

"Then if you want my blessing, you have it, Aidan. Valedan himself would be pleased for you—and proud of you, if he heard Ser Anton's words. Go if you want."

He almost reached for the old man's hand, just as if that old man were the father of his younger years, or the grandfather he'd lost to death. Did—and then froze, and then forced his hand to his side. He hoped that Ser Anton hadn't noticed it, but he knew that Ser Anton noticed *everything*.

But the old man shook his head, said nothing.

The distance to the coliseum wasn't far.

She'd taken Angel and Carver with her. Kallandras waited patiently throughout. If he heard The Terafin's private words—and it was said that some bards could hear the spoken word more than a mile away—his face betrayed nothing. Face like that never would. It was beautiful, in its way, but it was impenetrable; better armor than the Terafin Chosen were given when they were selected for their duty.

She found Kallandras of Senniel intimidating, although he had rarely been anything other than charming and polite. Of all the master bards she had met—and she was willing to allow that, even as a member of the Terafin House Council, she'd not met all that many—he was the most dangerous.

To a seer, danger had its own feel, and the men and women who wore it, wore it like a translucent mask. A warning. A statement. A fact.

She felt particularly uncomfortable with him today, and put it down to the harried way she'd stepped from bedroom to meeting room with a pause—at Avandar's absolute insistence—to add the finishing touches to clothing that might, just might, be seen by royalty who would judge the House by it. But she noticed that this day of all days, Kallandras the bard was shorn of his famous lute. He carried daggers and a slender sword so naturally she had failed to understand their significance at first sight.

As if understanding the thought and the direction, he nodded, offering no smile, no easy camaraderie.

Kalliaris, but she hated battle.

They were given a carriage; both Avandar and Kallandras could live on a horse if need be—Hells, Avandar looked like he'd been born to it—but although Jewel's den had learned to mount and ride, they'd never taken well to it, and the horses—damn then all—knew when they carried nervous riders. Jewel was the best of the lot—she could manage just fine as long as there weren't many people underfoot. She thought of the typical streets at Challenge time. Snorted.

Just how in the Hells you were expected not to be nervous when you had a couple of thick hunks of rope and leather as your only method of controlling something that probably weighed ten times as much as you and could crush you flat with iron-shod hooves, Jewel had no idea. But Avandar managed with annoying calm.

Unfortunately, Jewel found the carriage ride to be the far more comfortable of the two methods of travel—which wasn't saying much given the speed of the driver and the roads beneath the wheels. The streets themselves were, of necessity on this last Challenge Day, packed; it was hard to negotiate them without having to come to a halt.

Too many halts.

"Jay?"

Angel's voice, tense with sudden knowledge.

Her sudden knowledge.

"ATerafin?" Kallandras' voice, asking the same question that her den-mate had, but with an edge to the word that brooked no silence, no time to gather thoughts.

"We're late," she said, her eyes caught by the edge of a ghostly vision that was torn from her by sunlight and movement and color.

They all froze, but in different ways. Carver and Angel drew breath, but Avandar and Kallandras seemed to settle into the edges that made them dangerous men. If they were afraid of any possible outcome, they hoarded their fear jealously.

"Someone's already dead," she added, "and he doesn't know it yet."

"ATerafin—"

"I don't know. I don't know who. They'll kill the boy—"

Kallandras reached for her; Avandar's hand was in his way in an instant. Their hands met, bard and domicis. Jewel knew that she could not have moved as quickly as either man had in response to her or each other.

They did not argue. "Which boy, ATerafin?"

But while the certainty was not fleeting, the details were. She looked at him, and then looked out into the streets that now seemed more impassable than the twenty-fifth holding had when it had been littered with magisterians looking for her den. "I don't know," she said, in helpless frustration.

And then, Kalliaris smiled.

"Aidan."

CHAPTER THIRTY

The voice came to him on the wind.

"Aidan, I do not know where you are, but you are in mortal danger. If you are not with friends, flee if you can hear me at all."

No identification followed the words, but he didn't need it—he'd heard the voice on one other night, and the events of that night still lived in the depths of the type of sleep a dreamer *can't* escape. Kallandras the bard, the master bard of Senniel College.

Voices at a distance—especially raised ones—were a matter of fact in his daily life, a life which seemed so far away from him now he could almost forget he had one. But voices like this—voices that spoke in a whisper so close to his ear he leaped up and back at the shock—were like childhood stories—the ones that give you the dreams you can't escape from.

"Aidan?"

"Aidan, we are coming as quickly as we can."

He looked up to see the concern in Ser Anton's face. *Am I with friends?* No. No, he wasn't. He was just with a man that he wanted, desperately, to have as a friend. An old, a very tarnished, hero. Gods, but he was being stupid. Hadn't Ser Anton already as much as said he knew about the attack on the Witness House? Hadn't he already admitted that he knew about the demon? "It's—it's nothing."

"But not for long," Ser Anton said. "Look. That is definitely the Leonne standard, rendered in the Northern style."

"And in the Southern. Over there. I think it's being carried by General Baredan."

"Bold boy," Ser Anton said softly. It took Aidan a minute to realize that he spoke not of Aidan, but of Valedan kai di'Leonne himself. He didn't see what was so bold about carrying a standard; gods knew that Andaro, when he did show, would be carrying—would, rather, have carried—a standard of his own.

But then he looked up at the old man's expression, saw that the focus lay at a distance. He remembered to breathe as he followed the old man's gaze.

Sure, he could run. He could listen to Kallandras. But he'd miss it. He'd miss the start of the fight. He'd miss the fight. And the only person who was anywhere close to him now was Ser Anton di'Guivera. He could not believe—would not believe—that Ser Anton would personally harm him.

Not when they had this thing to share: A testing of the two men whose skill they both valued.

The adjudicators and the magi moved in, in greater number than Aidan had yet seen. He exhaled. It would be a few minutes yet.

But the swords were being unsheathed; he could hear the metal. Light helms were being raised, donned, visors lowered. Heat— and there was heat—was being denied. They girded for war, these two, and they accepted the terrain that had been chosen for them almost as if it were beneath notice. Almost.

He felt a sharp pain in his hand. Brought it up to his face in surprise and saw the knuckles were so white, he'd somehow managed to drive at least one of his flat little nails through the surface of his palm.

"Aidan?"

"It's—it's nothing."

Ser Anton nodded, and then his gaze fell upon the circle that the magi circumscribed. Aidan was certain that he wouldn't look away again.

She had seen the bardic voice before, but she had never *seen* it like this. Kallandras of Senniel College bowed to her, a drop and lift of head. "With your permission, ATerafin," he said, in a voice that brooked no refusal—and no questions.

Her gaze glanced, skittishly, off the side of Avandar's face, but the domicis seemed to understand what Kallandras was about; he said and did nothing.

The bard swung the carriage door wide, and in the same motion, rolled out of the cab and *up*, where he disappeared from view.

"What is he—" Carver began, but the bard himself answered their question in a voice that might have rolled in during an ocean storm so strong it could have broken the seawall, it hit the crowded street in such an undeniable wave.

"Get out of the way of the carriage."

She had time to steady herself given her gift, but only just; Carver and Angel came out of their seats and landed rather gracelessly as the carriage lurched into sudden flight.

It began.

Not with a blow, not with a strike, not with a sudden rush of movement—although both Andaro di'Corsarro and Valedan kai di'Leonne had used both tactics in their previous bouts. No, it began in silence and stillness; not even the breeze cared to move through the sluggish humidity of the sea air. The circle that contained these two men contained the world in microcosm; the South and the North, the echo of old wars, the premonition of new ones.

They took each other's measure in the subtle things, waiting, waiting, waiting.

Sivari watched as Scr Anton's student broke the tableau. It surprised him; Andaro was perhaps six years older, and therefore more experienced, than Valedan, and it had seemed to him, as observer, that the first contest within a contest would be decided by who struck first, or rather, who moved last.

"Remember to breathe," someone said at his side. For a lesser man, he would not have turned.

But the man who addressed him—in a fashion that bordered on the familiar—was the Tyr'agnate Ramiro di'Callesta. Dangerous ally. Deadly enemy. Not friend and not foe, because no Southern man of power could be trusted enough to be called the former, and no man in his tenuous position in the Dominion would make himself the latter. Not yet.

"I'll breathe," he said, irony weighting the words. "And you?"

"The Lord watches," the Callestan Tyr said. "And I. I will tell you now that even my par is much impressed with the kai Leonne's showing today. Ser Kyro is beside himself."

"Ser Kyro watches?"

"It took some effort to gain both permission and space, but yes—the entire hostage contingent has been present from the start of the day. A gift," he added. "A Callestan gift." He raised a hand, his expression wry, even—although it was hard to be certain with a man such as Ramiro di'Callesta—self-deprecating. Upon his finger, glittering in a thin band of maker-worked gold, the magic of the North that he had refused to don. Until now. The test of the sword made its own demands, and they spared no one.

Sivari had spared the time he could. He turned back to the sound of glancing steel. Strike and parry, but the parry was a sliding movement that ended in a strike of its own. Low movement, and fast.

In earnest, the two men closed.

Serra Alina di'Lamberto sat on the edge of the witness box, surrounded not by silent women—although all the women were present—but rather by Callestan cerdan and even Tyran. They had rightfully taken up the position best suited to guarding the married women from the eyes of the idly curious. They had also, and this did not escape her attention, chosen the best vantage points from which to watch the combat that unfurled below.

Not the last combat, no.

Not the one that would decide the Kings' Challenge.

That was to come, and that featured the very prominent Eneric of Darbanne, an oddly pale giant of a Northerner with frightful manners and a bearing that any mother might secretly be proud of. The Lord would love such a warrior as he, if the Lord knew love at all.

Her face she obscured by spread fan, but she had lifted the veils that were so often worn in public; her brother would have been irritated at least, beside himself with rage at worst, for the public display she made of herself, the momentary disregard she showed.

Today, it did not matter.

Southern eyes—and they were, after all, the only judgemental eyes that she need fear in this crowd of gathered spectators—were all turned groundward, to the two men who fought within the confines of the prescribed circle, beneath the eyes of judges both earthly and more.

Because this combat decided much more than the Challenge; it was the banner that would be carried into the war by one side or the other.

And the hostages had, by the evil of circumstance, been forced to choose a side in that war, or perhaps been chosen by one. Their lives unfolded here, with the slashing and striking of light scattering steel.

Valedan.

First blow, and probably first blood. The kai Leonne staggered back, gaining his feet—and his sword arm—before Andaro di'Corsarro could take advantage of his luck. General Baredan di'Navarre watched, unblinking, as the boy side-stepped the brunt of the attack, also pirouetting out of the danger; almost using the momentum of the blow itself to carry him.

His hands—the General's—were fists.

He had seen dancers who were less well-matched than this.

But the dancers were fighting for the same goal; they drifted on sword's edge—and death's—seeking a precarious balance.

These two were each trying to push the other over.

Mirialyn ACormaris sat in a chair at the foot of the Kings and Queens, beneath her half brothers but separated from the rest of the Royal entourage. She had sat in chairs such as this for most of her adult life, although the chairs for the Princes were a later addition. Oldest child, she, and not wisest for it.

But wise enough to begrudge her brothers nothing.

It was her own life that bit her here, that caused her a momentary pang; her life in the form of a young man. She had no children. She had never missed them. But Valedan kai di'Leonne had been, in his way, the outsider child. Much as she had been in a youth as awkward as any child's.

Her brother, she felt, would have responded differently; she was both proud of the difference and chagrined by it. That had been her life. Was still her life now. Wise, she was called. Child of wisdom.

The memories of her childhood had lost their teeth, but those teeth had still had some bite in them when she had first set eyes on the eight-year-old boy and his hysterical mother. When she had brought him to bow and spear and the Northern hunt.

It was the sword he had wanted, at first, and therefore it was the sword she had denied him, perverse as she was. She knew—or thought she knew—that he would spend his life in the Northern court. There would be no home for him in the South; that much was clear. It had seemed the wisest course to offer him the breadth of her own experience; to let him choose.

He had come back, time and again, to the sword.

She had taught him.

And as she watched him now, the truth bit her, as those memories of early girlhood could not.

This was not the boy *she* had trained. What she had given him, in those early, crude circles, and what he had achieved, even given the aid of Commander Sivari—they did not seem, to a mind bound by wisdom and the dictates of experience, to be congruent.

Yet what hands could be at work but his own? The magi were

out in force, and the Southerners watched like hawks; no sword could give him what he had today, no matter who had crafted it, save perhaps the sword the first-born had forged at Myrddion's side at the dawn of their age. A sword such as that fair cried "magic! magic!" or so wisdom had it. It could not be used without being seen.

Valedan, she thought, gripping the arms of her chair too tightly.

The carriage careened into the courtyard of *Avantari;* it teetered a moment on its left wheels and then rocked to a stop, shoving the horses forward.

Jewel's door flew open as if it had lost both hinges—it hadn't—and Kallandras stood in the light. He held out a hand, and she took it almost without hesitation.

Almost.

"Jay?"

"Follow!" she cried, half the word spoken from within the carriage's confines, and half without. There was more than the pressure of his pull upon her; there was an urgency, a sudden pang much like the stab of an invisible dagger.

She flew. Or as near to flew as she could on two legs.

It was Kiriel who sensed it first, and even she did not immediately place it—the ring's curse. Had she been in the Shining City, had she never fled through the path along the bottom of the unnatural crevice that served as both gate and barricade, she would already wield every weapon at her disposal.

But she had fled; she did wear the ring. Her senses were quieted, her attention held by the frustrating and tantalizingly comprehensible men and women with whom she struggled to serve. The Ospreys were as silent as men and women could be—which was almost a shock in itself—as they watched the fight stretch out, a clear victor undecided. They held their breaths, collectively sighing in relief, collectively inhaling in dread, almost afraid to break the silence with their cheers. They hadn't been so hampered in any of Valedan's other fights.

But two men could not fight forever, and while Valedan had landed a blow, Andaro had landed two. They were nervous. *She* was nervous.

That's when she should have known.

But she didn't, not immediately.

Not even when she found her gaze pulled momentarily from

the spectacle that held the entire coliseum in thrall to see a Southerner approach the judges on the periphery of the circle.

She noted his standard, but more, noted him; he was Andaro's comrade, and if she was a judge of humans—and she knew she was not—a friend or perhaps a brother.

But she should have known then, because he *was* so unremarkable and because he caught her attention, regardless.

Aidan knew.

Aidan *knew*.

He was the witness, after all; he was the boy that Valedan kai di'Leonne had chosen—from horse height and a distance—to gift with the medallion that now hung in the open around his neck. Hadn't he watched? Quietly, of course. The Ospreys scared him, the Callestans intimidated him, and the crowd of mages that visited randomly made him melt into the shadows—but he watched, mostly unseen, mostly forgotten.

It was his *right*.

The unnamed fear gripped him tightly.

He glanced up at Ser Anton, and then across the field, uncertain now as to what he knew. That Carlo di'Jevre had never been friendly? That Carlo di'Jevre spent as much of his time as close to Andaro di'Corsarro as possible? That Andaro had *won* the marathon for Carlo, because of the injuries that Carlo had sustained fighting the demon under the water?

They all knew that.

But the bard's voice had come to him, only him, carried by wind, heavy with warning and fear. He knew both of those—that warning, the fear behind it—even if the bardic voice was soft and smooth, where his mother's or grandmother's voice grew harsh or shrill with the burden. He was in danger *because* he knew.

You are in mortal danger. Flee

He almost did. He knew how to run. He knew how to hide. He knew how to survive.

But another truth occurred to him, because he'd listened to his mother's stories, his grandfather's stories: the bard somehow knew there was danger, but he didn't see what that danger was.

Carlo di'Jevre had, as usual, no interest whatever in Aidan. But Aidan, like moth to flame, could no longer look away from Ser Anton's other student.

He left the swordmaster's side, his hand sliding over the dagger that he always carried—the single dagger that had been a gift from a grandfather he'd watched settled into earth too many years ago. They'd let him keep it, that first day across the gates into the coliseum. He'd thought no one would be allowed to carry weapons, but the adjudicator had only laughed when he'd asked about it, and Aidan didn't much like being laughed at, so he hadn't asked why.

Didn't much matter, now. Maybe it was just Kalliaris, and it was up to Aidan to decide whether the dagger was an act of her smile or her frown. Gods, it was suddenly so *cold*.

He followed Carlo, moving across the grass as quickly as possible. It wasn't easy; there were men all round, men of magic, men of knowledge, men who were set to guard and protect the traditions—that was the word that Ser Anton used—of the Challenge, and they were all a head taller than Aidan, even the shortest and widest of them. He lost sight of Carlo di'Jevre once, and he put on a burst of speed, dreading the feel of a hand on his shoulder, of anyone trying to stop him.

But they didn't, because it was his right, as Valedan's witness, to approach. As Valedan's chosen.

To approach as closely as the judges did.

Because he was there, because he was afraid, he was not surprised when Carlo di'Jevre threw his arms wide and sent the nearest judges—three men of equal size and stature—almost flying to either side.

But he knew what it was that had caught his attention as he saw the raised arms of the Southerner: the hand, the right hand, was adorned only by a black-and-red circle of scorched and blistered flesh.

When he spoke, he spoke with the voice of the storm; the clouds gathered as the first syllable left his lips.

Aidan didn't have time to think.

He understood more than he could put into words; the storm that was gathering was blacker than nightmare, more certain a death than any death he'd ever seen in his life. But he'd heard of others, and those tales lay buried in childhood, hidden so far from thought the memories responded as if they belonged to another boy, in another place.

Valedan kai di'Leonne was in front of both him and the creature who was starting to speak, caught in the purity of a fight that Aidan had been chosen to witness. Luck, he'd thought it.

He never thought that there was another reason for the choice, another hand behind it. Had no time to feel honored, no time; he could feel the weight of the momentous fear begin to shift beneath his feet and rob his limbs of strength.

Valedan kai di'Leonne was fighting Andaro di'Corsarro in the Kings' Challenge; his back was turned; he saw nothing of what happened behind him. Just as Carlo di'Jevre saw nothing of Aidan. Neither blindness would last for long.

Biting his lip, he drove the dagger neatly into Carlo di'Jevre's back before the last of the syllables left his lip.

Thunder, then.

Lightning.

Aidan had the privilege of meeting the eyes of the beast; Carlo di'Jevre roared and turned. The dagger itself was lost in the flesh of his back, locked there by the sudden tightening of unnatural muscle. Not that Aidan thought about the dagger for long. The whites of Carlo's eyes had been devoured. As had the rings of brown. What was left: darkness.

A more certain death than the clouds of shadow gathering above them all like some Hells-spawned storm. A more certain death than he had ever seen, and he had seen death. His mother's death.

He thought to wonder, as his knees chose that moment to fail him, if he would see his mother again, soon. If she would be proud of him.

A certain death.

He felt a terrible pain as his chest dissolved and the creature turned away.

Meralonne APhaniel cried out.

Sigurne was instantly awake—a bad sign, in her condition. But bad or no, she was attuned to the battle that had begun over fifteen years ago beneath the streets of Averalaan's oldest holdings; her eyes went to the soaring heights of the healerie's only truly grand windows.

She lifted a hand, but he had gained enough control to catch it; to touch her lips.

"Yes," he said, and he knew his face had lost all color.

"How?"

"Obviously," a humor so dry the words might catch fire if rubbed together returned to his voice. "I don't know. I was here."

She struggled to rise; he helped her. It was either that or struggle to hold her down, which she could ill afford. Which he could ill afford. The fevers had come, as Dantallon had surmised they would; he had kept hidden what could be hidden. For a man who professed a great disdain for the practice of the magical arts, *very* little could be hidden from Dantallon.

They sat in the silence, and then Meralonne APhaniel said, "We're in the healerie, Sigurne. It is a room that protects itself from the casting of magicks, or so Dantallon has often hinted." Meralonne waited for some words of wisdom to come from her; they were two magi, after all, two of the few members of the Order considered among the Wise. She offered him muted silence instead. Determined silence.

He lifted his slender hands, cast them skyward.

Cast.

His own power was so very, very weak; it had been a full-day and perhaps a few hours and the chills had barely abated. But power was there, and he could catch it, thread by thread. Bind it to his will. Will, after all, was the foundation upon which all of his magic had been built.

He faced an old woman, worn by time into a shadow of her former height, granted by power a crowning glory that she could never have attained in her youth. He was . . . fond . . . of Sigurne Mellifas. He respected her. There was no other reason to sit before her, half a body space between them on her wide, dignitary's bed.

The spell, he lay before her, before them both.

"Meralonne," she whispered, "No. It is too soon—"

The air began to twist, as air did in the haze of too much heat, too much sunlight.

"Who calls?"

"Meralonne, idiot."

"Master APhaniel! Thanks the gods—we—"

"I don't have time for idle chatter, Cahille—let me *see.*" He did not have the power to travel to the coliseum itself; the casting of the spell—and he did have it—would kill him in his weakened state. But he would not sit in ignorance.

"Let you—oh, of course. Sorry, sir."

The magi looked apologetically up at Sigurne. "Cahille is a model student—for a member of the Order. He is also by character and inclination the perfect librarian. It's a small wonder he's still alive."

"I've taught Cahille," Sigurne replied, her voice as weak as his magic. "Look," she added. "He's let you in."

The clouds that stood between them took on form, color, a sense of place in miniature. Costly. Everything was costly.

But there was no mistaking the tableau on the bed, captured by Cahille's vision.

They both heard it. The best of Ser Anton's students. The best of Commander Sivari's. Southern born, bred to the lives they had been chosen for, caught in a fight that was, inexplicably, a step or two away from the complicated intimacy of a blade dance, they heard the roar.

Almost nothing else would have caught their attention simultaneously; almost nothing else could have broken, so exactly, the cadence of their fight in such a way that no death or injury resulted.

Valedan turned; Andaro froze.

The rag-doll body of a small boy covered in blood flew across the heads of the gathered, silent, crowd.

The roar turned into words, guttural harsh utterings that neither Torra nor Weston could boast.

The darkness closed round them both, then.

Death, there.

Death.

Meralonne did not understand what happened next. There should have been death; a quick, painful death, a thing of blood and excess. A statement. There was enough power contained in the seeming of a Southerner to rouse his awareness a mile away. Easily enough power to crush the lives of two human men.

But although he saw the darkness erect a shield that both he and Sigurne had seen one time before, that shield did not buckle and fold, crushing the two trapped within it; it expanded. It grew to contain them all: Valedan kai di'Leonne, Andaro di'Corsarro, and the creature that had been Carlo di'Jevre.

He did not curse his own stupidity as he watched, but he wondered, aloud, whether or not this had been a part of the plan of the Southern contingent.

"They play at politics here, the fools; they play at *justice* and *wisdom*. What wisdom now? Kill them all, as I suggested, and there would be no harboring of such a creature in the heart of the Empire."

Sigurne reached over the vision; touched his arm. Brought him back to the present. "Men play at many things, Meralonne. I would rather they play at justice and wisdom than brutality and dominion. And I have seen what I now believe you have seen. Enough to know what the cost of the failure of the game is."

"Why did he not destroy them?"

"I do not know."

Andaro's cry followed the cry of Carlo di'Jevre.

Of the thing that had been Carlo di'Jevre. Valedan recognized his face, and the proud line of his Southern body, but the eyes were guttered by a darkness so profound they would never hold light again; he was certain of it.

But where the first roar had been an animal cry of fury and frustration, Andaro's cry was one of disbelief, of despair. It cut Valedan; cut him deeply. There was no intimacy between them, Southerner and Southern hostage, and only an intimate should ever have to bear witness to a cry that contained so much.

But he hadn't much choice. His grip on the sword was tight, tight, tight. For the first time since he had walked to the Great Hall, surrounded by guards that had become, overnight, watchful enemies, he longed for the Sun Sword.

Sun Sword or no, he was Leonne, and the enemies of the Lord of Day were the enemies of his bloodline; he knew that now. He would not die without a fight. The creature opened its mouth, raised its arm. But his hand fell open palm up, a menacing supplication.

He spoke.

"I . . . am . . . not . . . dead . . ."

Carlo di'Jevre's voice.

"This . . . is . . . our . . . battle. Finish . . . it. For . . . me."

Labored, that voice, those words. The words, Valedan knew, of a dying man.

"Finish . . . it . . . and . . . he . . . will . . . set . . . you . . . free. I . . . would . . . never . . . let . . . him . . . kill . . . you."

"And what of you?" Andaro cried, and again, Valedan would have given much to be anywhere else, not to avoid the fight, but to avoid a pain that he had not earned the right to see.

The creature—the creature that was somehow still Carlo di'Jevre—did not answer. Its lips moved, and then stopped, moved and then stopped, a grotesquerie of attempted speech.

"What of you?"

Valedan spoke then, spoke carefully. "He is already dead, and he knows it. But whatever is left of him won't let the creature lie to you, even to save your life."

"Na'Carre? Na'Carre, the *truth*."

"There . . . is . . . not . . . much . . . time."

He should have attacked. He knew it. But he held his sword

up, as if awaiting, at the circle's edge, the signal to begin. Andaro di'Corsarro stepped forward, stepped toward Carlo di'Jevre. His sword he still held, but his arm was slack with its weight, with the weight of things intangible that were still obvious.

To Valedan's great surprise, the creature took a step back, into a darkness that he had thought, until that moment, went on without end. It appeared to be a wall. A wall, a barrier. He had heard something of such a thing in the Northern Court.

Allasakar.

When the creature stopped, Andaro stopped; they stood inches apart, but even so, Valedan could see the darkness that had been Carlo's eyes. What Andaro saw in them, he did not know—but he must have seen something, if not in the eyes, then in the line of face, the twisting of muscles into familiar spasms of expression, that spoke of something other than the demonic, for he raised his hand, his empty shield hand, slowly.

Touched the face of Carlo di'Jevre very, very gently.

"Na'Carre," he said, his voice a whisper. "How did this happen?"

"Pedro . . . gave . . . us . . . water."

Andaro nodded gently. Carlo's hand, shaking, rose to touch Andaro's; they stood a moment in the darkness, and made of the darkness something other than the death and the terror that it was.

"I will fight our enemy," Andaro said quietly. "For you. No matter what the cost."

Complicated by shadows, Carlo's expression shifted. Valedan couldn't read it.

"Thank . . . you."

Andaro di'Corsarro's hand fell away from Carlo di'Jevre's face. He stepped back, and turned toward Valedan kai di'Leonne, his expression shifting into lines as hard as his sword's.

Valedan waited, thinking that the circle had become much smaller—and that the boundaries had been writ in shadow; there would be no crossing the lines without a death, no quaint surrender. *This* was real. *This* at last was the fight that he had been seeking.

And it was not.

He waited. *Is this war?* he thought, but there was no one to ask the question of, not here. He hefted his own sword, waiting for Andaro. Waiting for Andaro's first move, just as he had done when the sun had beat down upon them.

Andaro di'Corsarro made that move.

Lightly, pivoting on his left foot. He swung round, his sword in motion, his face white as the Northern snows that Mirialyn ACormaris had given Valedan sight of as a gift in his youth. *You see,* she had said, *how the snow reflects the light even in the darkness.*

Yes, he said, silently, as he lost sight of Andaro's face. *Yes, I do.*

The Southern swordsman thrust his blade into the waiting body of Carlo di'Jevre, piercing the heart.

They heard the roar through the veil of magic that gave them any vision at all.

It eclipsed the sound and fury of magery in all its glory, the chanting and the cries of the priesthood's sons and daughters, as both magi and priest tried to break through the barrier that had denied them all so many years ago. Memory, in that frenzy. Had he been there, had Sigurne been there, they would have counselled reserve and caution.

"Was that ours?" Sigurne asked.

"How should I know? We see the same thing, you and I."

"You are an expert on ancient lore; *I* am only an expert on demonology."

He snorted. "If I had to guess, I would say that there is a fight of some sort beneath the barrier, and the creature has been dealt a blow."

"Not fatal."

"No." If it had been, the barriers would fall. Power such as this, localized and brought into immediate existence, was commonly believed to require a physical focus, a living vessel.

Ser Anton di'Guivera crossed the field. He carried his sword; he wore his armor. He paused only once, when a man with long hair and Royal insignia knelt in bloodied grass beside the body of a young boy. Flashing at his neck, catching the sun in sharp, sharp relief, the Northern symbol of the healers.

He did not ask about the boy.

Did not, in fact, want to know.

The end was in sight, and he was not certain what that end was. But he knew that his place was there, by the darkness—or in it. His unnamed sword caught light just as harshly as the healer's medallion had. Sun's light. Lord's light. He was a proud man. He knew what had happened, knew even what the role he had played had been.

Had never thought, not once, that it would come to *this*. The Allasakari and their pawns had been his means to an end.

Well, he had one. An end.

He did not pray. There was no point. He did not offer the Lord his obeisance, did not give any sign of his fealty. The Lord judged as he judged, after all.

The Kings' Swords denied him access until Commander Sivari waved him through.

Even in Sivari's face, accusation. Suspicion.

I owe you nothing, the swordmaster thought. But he found himself saying, "My apologies, my profound apologies. I did not know."

It was truth. And because it was offered to a man who spoke so little of anything else, it was accepted.

"Tell us," Sivari said, waving another man over. "Tell us what you *do* know."

Valedan kai di'Leonne was already in motion.

The move had been made; his response had to be as fast, as decisive. No matter that it was not the move that he'd expected. Andaro had time to pull his weapon free and step back before the creature's roar died into darkness.

"Don't let it touch you!" Valedan shouted.

Andaro nodded.

The darkness shifted. Constricted. The creature snarled, and its hands became living fire. Red sword, red shield, sparkling with a brilliance that never truly alleviated the shadows.

It kept the wall at its back, and began to shift along its periphery.

Devon ATerafin nodded as the Southern swordmaster finished speaking. "Then he is . . . infested. We have some experience with that."

He turned. Sivari caught his arm, turning him back. "ATerafin," the Commander said.

"I don't know," Devon replied. "But if I had to guess, I would say that the creature that inhabits the body has not yet had the time it requires to fully absorb identity and therefore control."

"And *this?*"

Devon stared into a darkness that seemed to devour all light cast upon it. Remembering. "He's here," Devon replied softly.

Silence, then.

*   *   *

"I would have spared *you!*" No hesitation in the voice; none.

"You killed Carlo," Andaro replied, the anger buried beneath the cold edge of the words.

The creature snarled with Carlo di'Jevre's face. But the face itself was changing slowly. Elongating. The jaw subtly widening. The blood splashed along his chest was red and dark, but the wound that had caused its flow was no longer visible.

Valedan stepped forward, coming in at right angles to Andaro di'Corsarro. He did not speak. His sword did.

The creature parried.

Andaro struck. Blade hit shield and, as the creature shifted weight to his shield arm, Valedan struck again.

Blood.

What had once been Carlo roared in anger, and then it *threw* the shield.

Valedan ducked, deflecting the flashing fire with the flat of his blade. Overbalanced, he fell.

His arm burned. And burned. Leather gave way to skin, and skin to bone.

But it was not his sword arm. Not that arm.

He rose, bloodied, barely able to control the spasms of the injured limb. Barely, but he managed. He had been waiting for this fight.

Andaro struck.

Valedan struck.

Although they had no time to speak, no space in which to exchange words or plans, they began to time their attacks, never moving in alone.

Ser Anton waited by the circle's side. The grass, not surprisingly, had died, and a wave of slowly creeping brown radiated out from the centre of the darkness. Above, there was screaming and silence, a mixture of panic and fascination; the field itself was scattered with the men and women who defined power in the Empire, and the tourney had become something older than a game, something real. Something deadly.

Bards walked among the crowds, calming them; bards spoke and were spoken to in a silence that brooked no eavesdropping.

He wondered what might have happened had this event, and this attack, occurred in the Dominion. Wondered, but distantly; his thoughts were turned inward and outward, and both inside and out there was darkness.

The darkness without shifted.

A great cry, some mixture of triumph and fear, rose from the priests, and they called for aid. For the first time, Ser Anton di'Guivera was privileged to witness the interference of Kings.

They came, golden-eyed, the demonic rulers of the Northern Empire. Avoid their eyes, and they appeared to be nothing more— although certainly not less—then men; not giants, but tall and of warrior bearing. But avoiding their eyes was not a simple task; where they looked, they saw, and he felt, as the eyes of the Wisdom-born King swept across him, that they saw much.

Much, in fact, that he himself was unwilling to see.

It had not taken Ser Anton di'Guivera long to understand that the golden-eyed were not the spawn of demons, but the spawn of Northern gods, weak gods, gods who would see their people ruled by women and half-men and the aged and feeble as their unnatural law demanded.

Before he had come to the North, he had memorized the stories—and they were legion— of Northern weakness, of Northern decadence; he had full expected to see sniveling excess acted out upon the corner of every street. But he had come for the Kings' Challenge. And as a Challenger, he had met the Kings.

At that instant, kneeling in the formal Northern posture, his back straight, his sword at his bent knee, he realized that he could not—not then, and not ever—raise his sword against these men. Golden-eyed, enemies. The sun was high that day, the sky clear, and he knew then that the sun did not shine in the same way over lands that had never known desert.

The Kings had nodded; the moment had passed. He had thought that nothing could revive the sense of wonder and dread that the Kings conveyed that day, for even at closing ceremonies, his composure, his elation, his weariness, had robbed them of their grandeur.

But today the moment came again. He was young.

They shed their robes, their crowns, their regalia; they set aside the weapons that were part of their finery. But the one king retained the rod, and the other, the sword, and as they approached the struggling priests and the exhausted mages, they turned, one to another, and crossed the items they carried. Rod. Sword. Light flared at the intersection of metal and metal.

Wisdom. Justice.

The balance of an Empire.

He sensed it. He thought Andaro might. The creature shifted
on both feet, swaying as the wall at his back seemed to buckle.
Hard to tell with darkness, but it was there—a moment of weakness. A lessening of the power of a god.

Valedan kai di'Leonne uttered a single word and threw his
strength into a frenzied assault.

Leonne.

They heard it. The word seemed to resonate in the air, witnessed
by the open sky. The dark shield seemed to shy away from the
combined effort of the Kings, casting groundward for death and
lack of light. The light was golden; the blood shed to capture it,
red. The Kings had joined the combat.

At just that moment, Ser Anton understood why the Shining
Court, whose Lord claimed godhood, and whose generals were
Kialli, feared the Northern Empire. He understood why they had
chosen to ally themselves with the South, why they had promised
aid, in war, against the Kings and their people.

And he understood what his own role in that must be.

A fire burned him, just as the Kings' light burned at the darkness. But the darkness resisted.

She could not approach its shell. Could not approach the shadows, although the shadows had been her strength and her power—
her survival—when she had been a Queen in waiting in the
Shining City.

The Ospreys, Duarte, Alexis, Cook—the men and women she
knew—kept a distance enforced by Kings' Swords and magi. Only
Auralis sought to break that edict, and he had been detained. There
would be words and, if she was any judge of Kalakar, Auralis
would lose a rank. Rank in the Empire was a concept she was
only beginning to understand; it was like having power, except
without any.

The darkness itself was heaving under the assault of Kings and
magi, of god-born priests. She knew it; she could almost taste the
way it snapped and struggled. Her mouth was dry. The Lord's
power was here; somehow, whoever had taken Carlo di'Jevre had
formed a link with Allasakar across the distance between the isle
and the Shining City itself.

If the vessel had been stronger, she thought no one would be able to stand against His shadow. No one but she, and she could not approach the darkness.

"Kiriel!"

She turned; all the Ospreys did.

Jewel Markess ATerafin, chest heaving, ran across the green, her domicis and Kallandras the bard at her side, her two den-kin, Carver and Angel, not far behind.

"Jay."

But attacking together or attacking alone, they were losing ground. The blows they landed did less damage, caused less pain; the creature was gaining in power.

It became easier for Valedan as the demon's face lost the last vestiges of Carlo di'Jevre's; he wondered if it were easier for Andaro. But he wondered briefly; the creature's strikes were still aimed at him, and he had now been wounded three times. Armor meant for the Challenge was not meant for a darkness and a demon such as this.

"Can you bring it down?"

Kiriel was silent.

"Kiriel?"

No one else had thought to ask her. No one else had thought of who she was, of what she could do. She had become, for the fight, an Osprey—half-twisted Houseguard with a past she didn't want to own.

Jay caught her by both arms. She allowed it, meeting brown eyes with brown eyes.

"Kiriel, please. Valedan's alive—but he won't stay that way."

"The Kings are having an effect."

"I know."

No doubt in the two words; she did.

"And I also know that they'll succeed in the end; whatever the power is, it's not completely connected to All—to its host. But that won't matter if Valedan's dead." She met Kiriel's gaze, her own unblinking, intent. "Tell me what you need me to do," she said, her voice low and steady, "And I'll do it."

Kiriel knew, then, that Jewel *knew* she could take the shield down. Kiriel herself hadn't known it for certain until that moment; the ring on her hand was throbbing as if it were a wound. She felt something ease within her; felt the dryness in her mouth catch her tongue, it grew so strong. But she managed to speak regardless.

"Tell them—tell them to stop."

Duarte, present and silent, frowned. "Tell who?"

But Jewel understood her. Jewel almost always understood her. She swore. "All right. Can you—can you come with me?"

Kiriel gazed at the darkness and then shook her head. "I don't— I don't think so. If I can—if I can do what you've said, I don't think I can be that close to their power without—"

"Never mind. I'll get them to stop. But Kiriel?"

"Yes?"

"Be ready, and be *fast*." She turned to the men who now waited at her back like a small army of a shieldwall. Taking them, Kiriel saw, for granted. Because she could.

"Okay, little bit of difficulty," Jewel told them. "We need to call the Kings and the priests off."

CHAPTER THIRTY-ONE

She caught his eye immediately, although later he wouldn't have been able to say why—and Devon ATerafin was almost never at a loss for an explanation.

Maybe it was the cadence of her step; in the middle of this madness, surrounded by magical fire, smoke and golden light, facing a barrier whose strength and whose appearance they had encountered together before in the darkest Henden the Empire had ever seen, Jewel ATerafin walked as if she were avoiding the market chaos on a busy Selday.

And she walked toward him.

Business as usual.

It was strange that after all their arguments and unease, that mattered. "ATerafin," he said, as she came within earshot, having lifted her hand twice to show the House Council crest to waiting Swords.

She nodded. No formality from Jewel; she was all business. "The barrier can be brought down," she said, curt and to the point.

"But?"

A small smile tugged at the corner of her mouth. "*But* you need to get the Kings and the priests away from it." She paused for effect. "*Now.*"

He turned, then; she followed him. Duvari stood not ten yards from the backs of the men he had made it his life to protect. "You realize," Devon said, "that he's not going to like this."

"That's why you're going to ask. I don't much like the idea of getting into a fight with him, and it's all I can ever do to speak politely at him when he's around." She shrugged. "That, and he trusts *you.*"

"He trusts you, in as much as he ever trusts a member of the powerful patriciate. But stay here." He left her then, and she obeyed, trusting him.

* * *

Three minutes later, the Kings put up their arms. The god-born priests, golden-eyed and weary, retreated.

Andaro cried out in pain; his leg buckled, flesh sheared to bone in an instant. Valedan cried out as well, but it was a war cry. His voice was hoarse with it. Not long now, and he would have no strength for words. But he was Southern-born, after all; a warrior's heir.

Kiriel di'Ashaf saw the light fade. The hair on her neck stood on end, then. Jewel came back for her, and she caught her den leader's hand in her own, squeezing it too tightly. Jewel said nothing. They crossed the green together, making their way past Kings' Swords, past exhausted magi, past priests who had laid down the symbols of their Order and the foci of their power.

She saw all this, and more; saw the Kings as they stood back from the barrier, arms crossed in front of their chests, shoulders straight. The war was not over in their eyes, but she had joined it, and she guessed that they did not quite trust her. Which was well enough; she wouldn't have.

Ah.

There it lay, exposed, the heart of her power. She slid her free hand to her sword's hilt, and left it there.

"You aren't afraid of the darkness," she said softly to Jewel.

"No."

"Why not?"

"Because this time," Jewel replied, with an intensity that Kiriel had rarely heard in her voice, "we're not helpless."

This, Kiriel understood. It was one of the few times she felt that she understood anything about Jewel ATerafin. "You'll have to stand back."

"How far?"

"Far enough," Kiriel said softly, "that I can't touch you immediately after." Her grip on Jewel's hand tightened, if that were possible. "Do you understand? It's important."

Jewel nodded. "Far enough back, then. Kiriel?"

"Yes?"

"Now."

Kiriel frowned and shook her head; she let go of Jewel's hand. Then, taking a deep breath, she drew her sword. Raised it, in the sun's light. She stood a moment, perfectly poised, the barrier a blade's length before her, the sun above, a woman who was almost a friend not fifteen feet from her back.

She almost couldn't believe where she was. To be here, yes—but not like this; that had never been the plan. Hers was a position at the head of the armies that would march to destroy this city, the heart of this Empire.

She had never told Ashaf that. Ashaf would have hated it, and she could not—not quite—bring herself to cause the older woman pain.

In the end, it hadn't mattered. Pain was caused, and death, and both because of her.

The sword dipped in her hand; her hands lost their steadiness. They always did when she thought of Ashaf. Ashaf had no place in war, no place in combat, no place in the lives of the powerful.

With a cry that was too incoherent to be a word, Kiriel di'Ashaf brought her sword down.

The creature cried out as if struck, although in truth neither Andaro nor Valedan's weakening blows had landed. Something in the air shifted; something changed.

It meant nothing to the Southern warrior, but Valedan kai di'Leonne's eyes opened in wonder as he felt, for the first time since the darkness had closed in, the sea breeze. He found strength then.

The sword shivered, rebounded. The barrier denied her an easy victory. No one could see the smile that turned her lips up, and just as well. Kiriel di'Ashaf did not sheathe her sword, although the sword itself became useless as she made her decision.

She reached out with her free hand.

Touched the shadow.

Jewel started forward; Avandar pulled her back, catching her by both shoulders in a grip so sudden she almost lost her footing.

The shadow touched *her*. She felt it seeking purchase in skin, in the flesh beneath skin, and she laughed, although the sound came out as snarl to her ears, to her human ears. Here, in the sunlight, she was ascendent; the power to conquer was hers.

The ring did not defy her; could not contain her. Had it ever? She forgot. This smallness, this shadow—what matter where it came from? Her father's, her teacher's, her enemy's—it was power.

And Kiriel di'Ashaf had spent her life training so that she might take it. She began to absorb the darkness; instead of fighting it, she let it in.

Jewel didn't struggle against Avandar. She waited. But he knew her well enough—no surprise after this many years. His hands remained where they were; on either shoulder, tightly. She knew there was no point telling him to either let go or loosen up; she didn't try. To speak would have been to somehow break away from Kiriel, from the Kiriel she *knew,* viscerally and completely, could never be called in truth di'Ashaf. Oh, she'd known it the moment she met her, but she hadn't seen *this*. This was a test of a den leader's faith and strength.

She wondered how many of the magi could see what she saw. Wondered what they would do if they could. Wondered, in fact, what Kiriel would do when the shadows consumed her. Or when she consumed them. She was grateful that she couldn't see the younger woman's face. Cowardice, that, and she knew it. But there are some things that friendship doesn't survive unscarred.

Or at all.

"Meralonne."

The magi looked up.

"I asked you a question."

"Ah. Apologies, Sigurne. I was—"

"Transfixed. Yes. I noticed. Clearly what you're seeing through Cahille is filtered in some way." Disapproval in the words, but not as strong a disapproval as he might have expected.

"What was the question?"

"Do you understand what the young girl is doing?"

"I believe so."

"Do you think that she can survive it?"

"I have no question of that whatever."

"Good." Sigurne paused, and then lifted a frail hand; she brushed silver strands of hair from her eyes, and then looked back at the spell cloud that gathered on her bed. At the man who held it there, hair as silver as hers, skin as translucent in quality, but somehow unbowed by the age that she had reached uneasy truce with.

She knew that his power would fail him soon; that in truth he was being irresponsible—dangerously so—by continuing to fuel the spell. But she was what she was: Magi, and a seeker of knowledge. Where curiosity and concern clashed, curiosity won.

"Will we?"

He gave no answer.

The barrier, to Jewel's eye, was getting thinner and thinner. She couldn't see past its darkness, but she knew that in a minute or two it wouldn't matter; the darkness was almost entirely Kiriel's now—or she, its. Kiriel had still not turned to face them, but her sword hand was slowly rising, the weapon clutched in such a way that it might have been made of bamboo for all the difficulty its weight caused her.

The shadow spilled from shoulder to ground, rolling off her back like the finest of cloth, a thing that spoke of power, of stature, of rulership.

Ah. There. Her free hand rose, and when it rose, it pulled the last of the darkness with it, uprooting it from soil, from grass, from anything that was not her.

Valedan saw the light first.

Andaro saw the demon.

Between them, they made a single warrior; they were too injured, too damaged, to stand as two whole men. But when the light came, Valedan rallied for the last time.

Before the Kings, before the Ospreys, before the Southerners and the people who had come to watch a pretty contest of skill, he cried out the name for which he would become known, and swung his sword in a wild arc—

—that ended with the creature's neck.

The head itself rolled across the grass, its expression shifting slowly from stricken squinting to rage. Not dead, not yet, but aware that the final blow had been struck.

There was a thunderous silence; the priests, who had until that moment been frozen, practically flew into action; the magi joined them almost as quickly. He saw all this, and then turned his back on it; Andaro had time to bury his sword in—through —the standing, moving body before mage-fires and something older than that began to cleanse it. He rescued his sword in time, and they stood, Andaro di'Corsarro and Valedan kai di'Leonne, in the Challenger's circle—a circle now marked perfectly by dead, brown grass.

But they didn't face each other. Valedan started to turn, and something caught his attention. Caught it, held it, pinned it struggling to the ground.

He saw the darkness that had had solidity now moving, now seeing, breathing, *living*. And it was less than five feet away.

She jabbed Avandar's insole with her heel and drove her elbows in a one-two thrust into his rib cage. That was enough to make him let go, and that was all she needed. Jewel ATerafin ran. There wasn't much space to cover between her and her target; less to cover between her target and Valedan kai di'Leonne, the man lives had already been sacrificed to protect. The boy, really; he was only a handful of years older than Kiriel—if that—and he was bleeding from a half-dozen dangerous wounds and a host of little scratches. In no condition at all to face darkness.

Of course, if she'd been thinking rationally, she'd have admitted that neither was she. That was her worst problem at times like this: She didn't remember to *think*. She just acted. Always just acted.

How could you rule a House when you didn't have the brains to rule yourself?

What had Kiriel said? *Far enough that I can't touch you immediately after.*

He raised his sword; hers was there, limned in shadow the way steel is often haloed with reflected light. It wasn't the sword that was terrifying; it was her face. Because he almost thought he recognized it, that face, but he could not bring himself to put a name to it. He wasn't sure why. Wasn't sure why the recognition frightened him.

But as he stood there, unable to either attack or retreat, some gift was given him; she staggered; took a step—an involuntary step—toward him, and then turned.

Gaze broken.

Valedan turned as well. He offered Andaro a hand; the Southerner, exposed to public regard, stiffly refused it. They retreated to the far edge of the circle, but neither of them crossed it.

He knew they were fools. But to cross the circle was to end the contest; to admit defeat. Instead, they sat—and they did sit; Andaro could barely stand—and watched.

This was what she hadn't wanted; to face the darkness head on. But she faced it because it was Kiriel, and because Kiriel was hers—her responsibility, for better or worse. Hers to save, and if

salvation somehow proved impossible, hers to kill. She knew that
now. That was why Evayne had woken *her,* sent *her.*

She also knew that Evayne didn't know it, and that brought
her comfort. Cold comfort was better than none.

Kiriel's face was wreathed by shadow, blessed by it, awful, terrible in its beauty, its seductive death. Jewel almost took a step
back. But she didn't. Instead she took a step forward, grabbed
her den-mate by either arm.

Stupid, stupid, stupid.

She could feel the shock of cold ride up her arms, numbing
them. Locking them in place.

"I know you're afraid, Jewel Markess ATerafin," Kiriel said
softly, softly. She touched Jewel's face with the palm of her hand.
*"I can see you so clearly, I can see all your fear. None of it is
hidden from me."*

"Then tell me," Jewel said, although her teeth were chattering
from cold—and worse. "What's the worst fear, Kiriel. What's
the worst fear I have?"

Silence. The familiar and completely foreign brow furled. Then,
"Me."

"R–right the first time. What about you?"

"Death."

Jewel snorted—an act of bravado which was becoming more
difficult as the seconds passed. "Good guess. Look deeper."

The palm against her cheek became fingers, became claws. She
was pushing. Knew it. But desperation makes a woman stupid,
and Jewel was desperate. She could feel the magi gathering at her
back; could feel the Kings, the god-born, the whole of the Empire's power staring down at them, waiting.

Waiting as she waited, but with so much less to lose.

The darkness readied itself. She saw it in the lines of Kiriel's
shifting expression. But it didn't pounce; it didn't strike. Kiriel,
darkness-born, found what Jewel had sent her looking for.

With a wordless, a strangled, cry, Kiriel di'Ashaf pushed Jewel
ATerafin away. Unfortunately, that push sent her staggering
ten feet back. It was not meant to injure; it was meant to preserve.
Avandar caught her again, and this time she knew he'd bind her
before he'd let her get away.

But she didn't try. She watched as Kiriel crumpled slowly into
the ground, the lifeless ground, at her feet. Watched as the sword
fell from one hand, watched as both hands became fists.

Watched, in sadness and with a pride that she knew she had no real right to feel, as Kiriel began to fight.

Our worst battles, Jewel thought, *are always with ourselves. No one else can fight 'em.*

And as she thought it, she knew she was both right and wrong. Something changed; something about Kiriel; something inside of her. The ring on her hand, unnoticed until now, glittered in the sunlight. No; it was flashing as if it, too, were struggling to come to light.

It succeeded.

At first the ring's glow was gentle; soft and somehow comforting. Jewel wouldn't have noticed it at all if she hadn't had the eyes of a seer. But she did.

Platinum ring. Oathring.

Kiriel's hands stopped shaking although they didn't unfurl. She touched the ring with her shield hand. Touched it. Held it.

A light that gentle, that pale, still shone brightly in the darkness. In a darkness such as this, it was a lighthouse, a beacon, a warning. And as the ring continued to shine, it seemed to grow brighter, and the darkness to grow less. Day broke, for Kiriel.

"Avandar."

"We'll speak later," the domicis said, through clenched teeth. But he, too, knew that the danger had passed. He let her go, this time.

She didn't make it to Kiriel's side before the Ospreys did.

The shadow was gone, the ring remained.

Kiriel flexed her hand, looking for charred flesh, for burning, for signs of the pain the ring had caused her. This time, there weren't any. There was the ring, a blurred line of metal that seemed to separate her finger from her hand. She looked up, hoping to see Jewel.

Afraid to see her.

The Ospreys were there instead. They surrounded her gravely, with a watchful silence that spoke of their suspicion and their concern. Had she been watching them with the vision she'd been born to, she would have latched onto the suspicion, made of it fear, manipulated it and used it if she needed to. But she saw them as they saw each other, and she knew that there was more there than fear, and more than just one kind of fear.

Who would have thought that fear could have so many faces, and that one of them could be—

Ashaf's face.

The ring wasn't blurring; she was, or rather, her eyes were. And her arms were shaking, as if she'd used too much power, too quickly. Isladar had always warned her of that particular risk. She rose quickly, turning away from the Ospreys and toward the two men who sat at the far edge of what had once been a combat circle. She turned away from them just as quickly.

Auralis came to her rescue.

Not that she needed rescue, not now—but he came anyway, shielding her from both his own sight and the sight of prying strangers or helpful friends. He didn't ask her any questions. Didn't want to know the answers, she thought. But it didn't matter.

He knew that she was close to tears. Knew that that weakness was not a thing meant to be shared with anyone. He was very careful when he touched her, but he *did* touch her; she'd remember it later, that he'd dared to put his arm around her shoulder and lead her away.

The strange thing is that the only person who tried to stop him was Jewel—and she only tried for as long as it took to make eye contact.

They rose.

He watched them: his student, gashed to bone at knee, thigh and calf, and his enemy, gashed likewise at forearm and rib. A cut across the forehead would heal cleanly if tended quickly; it would scar otherwise, but it was a scar that many Southerners would be proud to bear.

And many prouder still to see.

Valedan kai di'Leonne had bested the creature in full view of the spellbound coliseum.

They turned to each other, these two competitors, bleeding and weak with the lack of blood. Neither made a move toward the circle's edge, as if—having fought for their lives—they might somehow return to the contest that had brought them so close to death.

Or, more likely, as if neither one of them could bear to be accused of surrender.

Outside of the circle, the body and the head remained. Ser Anton's knowledge of demon lore was a child's knowledge, hoarded over the years—and that child within said that demon's bodies returned at once to the evil that had created them. At once.

"Andaro," Ser Anton said.

His student, warily, turned to face him, and Anton knew, as their eyes met, that he was student no longer. His no longer. It stung, which surprised him. The more so because it was absolutely deserved. Whatever he had promised this man, he had in the end only given betrayal, albeit unintended.

"Ser Andaro," he said, bowing his head. "Shall I tend to the body?"

That brought him to life, as Anton had known it would. The circle was his pride and his strength, the test of the warrior beneath the gaze of the open sky. But the body was all that was left him of something that he had valued at least as much. He hesitated on the boundary, and then said, "Don't *touch him.*"

Ser Anton clasped his hands behind his back.

Waited.

But here, he found Valedan kai di'Leonne unexpectedly graceful. It cut him, just as Andaro's anger did.

"Andaro," the young kai said.

The man who was not much older turned.

"You struck twice; I struck once. If the match is to be judged at all, that will be remembered." And before Andaro could move, he bowed. And stepped out of the circle.

There was a sudden whisper from the Southerners who watched, a growing rush of sound, muted and indistinct. Andaro, sword in hand, stared at the kai Leonne's moving back. And then he shouted a single word.

"Tyr'agar!"

The kai Leonne stopped. Turned back. Their eyes met, and Andaro understood that what he could not have taken in combat, he had been given in compassion. Not a thing to burden a Southern warrior with.

But his word, unlike the moving hush of whispers, was loud. Distinct. It traveled the breadth of the coliseum and any who understood its significance held breath.

Andaro di'Corsarro took his sword. Lifted it, beneath the open sun. Plunged it, point first, into the dead grass, the circle's edge.

He knelt—staggering as his wounded knee took his weight and held it—and bowed his head. "If you will have my service, it is yours. Your enemies are my enemies, and my death is yours to command." Loud, that voice. Ringing. Almost *too* clear to be unaugmented.

The Northerners were clever. Ser Anton had never accused them of anything less.

"I . . . apologize. It is not the formal oath, and it is—it is not done well. I am offering—"

"We have been blooded in the same kill, against an enemy no man should stand beside. I will take your sword over your pretty words—when you find them—any day." And then he lowered his voice, the words falling into a wry smile that seemed just a bit too old for his face. "And besides, it means we don't have to face each other on the field. I've now seen what you can do with that sword."

Andaro smiled in return; the moment stood until the sea breeze blew it away.

"Tend your dead," Valedan said quietly. "I—" and he turned to look across the field, "I have my dead to attend as well." The young Tyr'agar walked back to the circle's edge. Grasped the hilt that was damp with sweat and a trace of blood, and *pulled*. For an injured man, Andaro had planted the sword with a little too much strength.

Andaro nodded. Rose, with difficulty, and retrieved the sword he'd planted so visibly, so forcefully, in the ground from the hands of the man he had pledged it to. He would have eyes for only a headless body for the next several minutes.

All that Anton needed, really.

He saw his moment, and he, too, accepted it.

"Kai Leonne," he said, in a voice that was deeper and fuller than Andaro di'Corsarro's.

Valedan turned at once. There was no friendship in the look that Ser Anton met; there was nothing but steel and distance.

The swordmaster drew his weapon—and stepped into the circle.

The boy had not sheathed his. But he lifted a hand, waving away the Callestan Tyran—and the Ospreys—who might otherwise attend him. Waving away the magi, the priests, the powers that could sweep across them both with ease.

"Ser Anton."

And he, too, stepped into the circle.

Brave, that. Anton thought he might—if he were wiser—refuse the fight; it was risky, but had he chosen to invoke the presence of demons and their historical association with the South—a South that had sent Anton and his students—his reputation might not have suffered.

But he played no games, this boy; not here.

* * *

"As acting judge, it is my duty—"

"I have been offered combat," Valedan said quietly. "I will accept it."

"You are not in the South, with all respect, Tyr'agar," the nameless judge said. "You do not have the right—"

"I have claimed the rulership of the South, and this man is one of my subjects, not yours. The rules of suspension dictate that there are customs and rituals observed within the South which, when they do not interfere with the liberties of Northern citizens, may be observed in *Avantari*. Or am I mistaken?"

"No," a voice he did recognize said. "You are not mistaken, as you well know."

He almost didn't recognize the man who came with the voice, for it was Kallandras the bard, but dressed in darkness and bereft of the lute for which he was famed. He bowed, and the bow, as always, was perfect. "Tyr'agar," he said softly.

"Kallandras."

"The rules of suspension allow it, but your injuries—"

"Are my own."

He heard it, of course; it took no bardic talent to recognize the rage and the anger that overruled common sense and pain.

Turning, he met the eyes of the swordmaster of the South, the only Southerner to ever win the Northern crown—and at that, to win it twice, once each for the woman and the child that he had loved. And lost. To politics. To ambition, very little of it his own.

Or perhaps not; perhaps the ambition had lain there, lain fallow, and he was aware that although it had cost his wife and child their lives he *could not* give it up. Such a guilt had driven men greater than Ser Anton in their time.

Or so legends said.

"Ser Anton di'Guivera," he said softly, "will you do this thing?"

"I have offered challenge," the old man replied in a rock solid voice.

Kallandras' hand curled tight around a simple, inexpensive piece of jewelry. Closed there, unwilling to expose it to light. He heard the cracks and the fissures, so less evident in the old man's voice than in the young one's, exposed to him by talent, by blood, and not by any slip of the swordmaster's.

Evayne, he thought, *I know why you gave me this ring and this message.*

But he heard the voices beneath the words—young and old, raw and concealed—and he understood then what Evayne did not, or could not, given the burden she had so unwillingly undertaken. Ser Anton di'Guivera was about to be tested; was about to discover his own measure, his own depths.

So, too, was Valedan kai di'Leonne.

As a bard, Kallandras made his decision. He bowed. "The circle, gentlemen."

The Ospreys were, as usual, beside themselves with rage. "What in the Hells is that supposed to mean? We're supposed to *let* them fight?"

Duarte's lips were a thin line. "Good. I see, Fiara, that your comprehension is improved by a night's heavy drinking."

"Valedan's injured!"

"Yes."

"But the old man—"

"I don't need to hear it, Fiara. Alexis."

Alexis had said very little.

"Put the daggers down."

She folded her arms across her chest. "Duarte—"

"No."

"But if he dies, it's for *nothing*. All of it."

"Thank you for pointing that out."

Silence.

"All right," she said, and her arms slowly dropped. "But we kill the old man if he wins."

"You can kill the old man the minute he steps into the city streets. You touch a hair on his head while he's in *Avantari* and you won't have one. A head, that is."

"Got it without the explanation."

They were left to witness, to watch. The Ospreys were not good at games of patience.

Baredan di'Navarre brought the healer.

He dragged him through the crowded aisles and past the Kings' Swords, taking him by the hand minutes before Ser Anton di'Guivera's voice had been raised in challenge. Or Valedan's raised in acceptance.

He was not the man that Alesso di'Marente was—in any way. That General, first among the three who had served Markaso kai di'Leonne, was gifted with an intuition that no amount of experience or skill could equal; he was blessed by the sun, able to bask in its glory without being burned by the ferocity of its light.

Not so Baredan—but Baredan's skill was of a different type. He was canny, not so much in the field, although in the field he was able to hold his own, but on a more personal level. He understood not men en masse, but men, and watching Ser Anton's slight stiffening of the shoulders, even over the long stretch of grass that separated them, he knew what the swordmaster intended.

He had been afraid for a moment that the swordmaster would disgrace himself entirely—but only for a moment. Anton di'Guivera might consort with assassins—they all did, who played games along the political edge of the Lord's sword—but he could never reduce himself to being one. And that left only the challenge itself.

Had Valedan been an older man, had he been Ramiro or Fillipo, or even Mauro, who was not so much older in years as wiser in his acceptance of experience, Baredan would have stayed his ground, and left the healer alone; left him unexposed, unrevealed.

But he was Valedan, the too-young kai Leonne, and his first, his only, General was beginning to understand his measure well.

The sun was high, the sky was clear, two swords had been raised from the earth.

"I am sorry," he told his friend, as they approached the kai Leonne and began to slow their frenetic pace.

"He is not dying," his friend replied. "I will not call the dying."

"And this?"

"For you, Baredan, because the debt between us is no small matter." The man paused, his Southern throat unadorned by the Imperial symbol, the two famous palms that spoke of the healer's presence across the breadth of the Empire. "And because I am not . . . unimpressed . . . with the boy you came North to save." His teeth flashed in a white, white smile. "My foolish wife," he said, in a voice so heavy with indulgent affection it pulled an answering smile from Baredan, even given the grimness of the situation. "Watches from the stands, and she would never forgive me if I denied you what you have not yet asked. She thinks I am fearless, although she should know better; she thinks of me—" he laughed, "as a hero.

"And you know the cost of disillusioning such a wifely fantasy."

That wife had cost him his family in the end; his country. If there were regrets, they were not evident.

Baredan nodded. He straightened his shoulders and approached the kai Leonne. "Tyr'agar," he said, choosing the formal address because it would be witnessed.

Valedan turned. "If you have come to dissuade me—"

"I have not. But I have come, as your first General, to ask you to consider the use of a healer before you enter the circle. It is not undone, in a circumstance of this gravity."

Silence. The refusal gathered around the young man's lips, and stayed there, held in abeyance by something that might, in time, become wisdom. "Do you know what you're asking?"

"Yes."

"The use of a healer is strictly forbidden in the Kings' Challenge. I will have come all this way, and cost—" he fell silent again, struggling not with words, but with the enormity of what they meant. But he did not blanch, and after a moment, he continued. "I will have come this far for nothing."

"Yes."

Silence again.

I don't know you, Baredan thought, for he had steeled himself for argument. *I wonder if any of us really does.*

The Tyr'agar, Valedan kai di'Leonne, looked across the field; what he saw there, what he sought, was not Baredan's concern.

"I owe my life," he said very quietly, "to a boy. To a boy who has probably never raised a sword in his life, but loves them anyway. But this was a game, a way of catching the attention of the clansmen who were allowed to come this distance.

"And this," he said, quietly, in just such a way that Baredan knew he referred to Anton di'Guivera, "*is* the war. The start of it. Yes, General. I will accept the services of any healer that you trust enough to offer me." His smile was bitter. "I hope Aidan is still watching from some window in the halls of Mandaros. And if he is, I hope he forgives me."

Baredan frowned. "Mandaros?"

"Northern god, Baredan."

"Ah, yes. Death god."

"Lord of Judgment."

Baredan bowed. Nodded a man forward. "Valedan kai di'Leonne," he said softly, "I would like you to meet Ser Laonis di'Caveras." He watched closely, but the name seemed to mean nothing to the boy. Just as well.

"Can you be of aid," Valedan asked, stepping forward, "to another as well?"

It was not the question that either expected. They were silent.

"Ser Andaro di'Corsarro was much injured, and I believe that he, too, will forsake the crown."

"You show a great deal of concern for the fate of an enemy," Ser Laonis said quietly.

"A former enemy. But it doesn't matter. In the end," Valedan replied evenly, "they will *all* be my subjects, enemy now or no."

"A good answer," the healer said quietly. "But I believe that you have been in the North a long time, kai Leonne." Before Valedan could speak, the healer added, "It pleases me to fulfill your request; I will see to Ser Andaro if he will, indeed, permit it. I, too, have been in the North a long time—longer, I think, than even you."

The match was not a part of the event; Ser Anton was not a contestant, and by accepting the aid of a healer, Valedan was no longer one either. But although the challenge—offered and accepted—was no part of the Kings' Challenge, the adjudicatory body fell silent when King Cormalyn gave his Royal assent to the application of the young Tyr'agar.

Fell silent and repaired to the stands as any spectator might, even the Royal ones. There was to be no judgment here, save the Lord's judgment. No rules of fairness, save the honor that the two men, older and younger, brought with them. The circle itself, a thing of dead grass and dry dirt, served no true containment; it was symbolic, and no one watching felt that it would be anything but that: symbolic. Symbols, however, in time of war were often of value.

There was no surrender here, except a surrender unconditional.

Valedan kai di'Leonne took his sword back when the healer finished. He was pale; however the Lord had touched his skin during this competition, it was nothing compared to the healer's touch. He did not speak; not to offer thanks, nor to offer the court pleasantries in which so little can be said with so much.

Baredan had never subjected himself to a healer's touch before, and seeing the kai Leonne withdraw from Ser Laonis so quietly, seeing Ser Laonis lurch forward, almost as if to prevent the separation before realizing where he was and what he was doing, he reconfirmed his silent commitment. There were some things a man risked; death was one.

But there were some things that were too great a risk.

Valedan took a breath, steadied himself, and lifted the sword. The sword seemed to give him strength. He met the healer's eyes only once, and when he did, he offered a wordless nod.

Ser Laonis, not the most silent of men, returned that nod. Returned it with the fullest bow, the most proper Southern respect, that a clansmen of power can offer. Baredan was almost shocked. Not that the bow had been offered—although it was a shock to see it, so correct, from a man who had forsaken the Dominion— but that it had been offered with such sincerity.

A moment later, it didn't matter.

Nothing but training did. Training, experience, and the will of the Lord whose merciless gaze covered every sky, Northern or Southern, in its judgment.

Two men stood alone in the coliseum. Their attendants stood far enough to either side that they vanished from the view of intent spectators. Not everyone understood what had transpired; not everyone understood who the old man was, although they knew that the young man had recently fought—and beheaded— some type of mage or magebound man.

But the Southerners understood two things: that the rules of this fight were not the rules of the combats that had preceded it in the circles across the coliseum, all of which had been emptied during the fight with the Lord of Night's servants, and that this fight, unlike the others, was no pretty test of superficial skill; it was bloodsport.

It was honor, and there would be a death to seal it.

Two men stood, waiting, taking each other's measure in the silence of stillness and tension. The older man was obviously a man of experience and worth; those who recognized him as Ser Anton di'Guivera—and they were many—knew just how much that experience and worth counted for.

But the younger man was the man who would be first among Tyrs. The man behind whose banners armies would fall in, or in front of whose banners armies must fall. He was the scion of a weak clan, but he had proved himself, in the fight with the servant of the Lord of Night, and in the Challenge itself, to be worthy of regard.

But not necessarily worthy of the title.

This fight, *this* fight would decide that for many, many of the observers.

For Fillipo par di'Callesta. For the Tyran who served his kai, Ramiro, the Tyr'agnate of Averda. For Ser Kyro di'Lorenza, for Ser Mauro di'Garrardi. For the men who followed these men.

But more: for the students of Ser Anton di'Guivera. For the merchants who traveled under the banner of the clans of the South, all the way from Oerta and Raverra.

Significant, then, that it was the younger man who made the first move.

Two swords were raised in the circle below.

One fell; the other rose; the clash of steel was the defender's reply.

The next move was slow; testing. It, too, ended in that metallic conversation; attack, parry. Subtlety was introduced into the interplay of blades—feints, high and low, and evidence that both Valedan and Anton were capable of fighting with the hand that they did not favor.

Ser Anton landed the first blow, but it was glancing; the tip of the blade escaped the near impossible parry to land, to touch. Experience.

Valedan changed styles unexpectedly, he moved from the intensely ritual deliberation of the Dominion to the frenetic—the deliberately frenetic—attack of the Imperial North. Eneric's strength. Mirialyn's gift. Sivari's edge.

Ser Anton reacted as if he expected no less. But here, his age and experience were blunted by Valedan's youth, and a loud intake of breath escaped the crowd as Valedan replied.

Two swords were raised in the circle.

Two shadows cast, by sun, against the dead grass. Those shadows, just as the swords, met and parted, met and parted, stood and staggered with the force of attack and defense, a play within a play.

No one spoke; not even the Ospreys.

They watched the swordmaster. They watched the pretender. And more than one wondered what they would have been like, these two, as master and student, as liege and lord.

There could be only one lord in the Dominion, save the Lord of the Sun. That was the unwritten law; the truth that men understood.

In the light of the Lord's law, Valedan kai di'Leonne began to extend the fight, choosing stamina over experience, choosing, as he would become known for, the ability to wait out the enemy.

To make of waiting an art, an action rather than an inability to act. Sweat graced his brow, and blood from the third of Ser Anton's glancing blows.

But the third blow had been a lucky blow—and if luck counted, it counted only if absolute, and Valedan still stood, still lived. There would be no fourth blow, no fifth; but the blood drawn by the third would mark the Northern-raised, Southern-born Leonne, as no crown, no title, given by Northern Kings, could.

Ser Anton di'Guivera began, under the heat of the open sky, to tire. Valedan kai di'Leonne pressed him, pressed him hard. It seemed that he, too, was flagging.

But it was, as so many of his opponent's attacks had been, pretense, a feint. He found energy; he found strength. He pressed his attack, this last round of blows, with a stinging fury, a sudden passion, a driving, precise anger.

The unthinkable happened.

Ser Anton di'Guivera lost his sword and fell in a single motion.

One sword was raised in the circle. One hand.

Kallandras nodded quietly.

The first test had been met, had been passed. But the second, and perhaps the greater, had only just begun, and it would be passed or failed in a sword-stroke.

Ser Anton had fallen outside of the circle; his body lay half on green grass and half on brown, marking the division by its crossing.

He saw the swordmaster lift his hand, not in supplication—for that was neither his way, nor the way of the combat he had chosen—but as a shield, the only one he had chosen to carry.

And Valedan kai di'Leonne carried the sword, the single weapon remaining them. Carried it in a combat in which a death had been promised. He paused a moment, the sword raised in sunlight, the man unarmed beneath it no longer an opponent, just a defeated enemy. Just the man who had become the sword that killed Tyr'agar Markaso kai di'Leonne; the man who had shown no mercy at all, and therefore deserved none.

Kallandras did not speak. No one did.

But he was surprised to find that he was holding his breath.

There was one sword raised.

* * *

Ser Anton di'Guivera would not speak for himself.

He did not ask for mercy; he did not offer surrender. But he did not scramble away, did not choose to end his life without the dignity with which he had lived it. Life and death were the sword's edge. It was strange, that a man could offer death to so many, and could meet it only once.

There was no triumph in the face of the first man in history to best him. But there was anger there, and not a little of it.

Ser Anton wondered, as he watched, if the sword was suspended in time, if time indeed had stretched out the last second of his life beyond imagining, or if the kai Leonne was still fighting some struggle of his own.

He said, because he felt compelled to say it, "Kai Leonne, this is not an execution. It is combat; it is the Lord's work. No fault accrues to you—and no guilt—by my death."

The younger man's face darkened; his knuckles whitened. Ser Anton drew breath.

He faced the man who had killed his father, and he found, as the sword began its descent, that he could not strike for his father; not his father. Not that man. But there were other reasons to kill.

For Carlo di'Jevre, who had served Ser Anton faithfully and had, by his choices, been betrayed.

For Andaro di'Corsarro, who had lost Carlo to the *Kialli*, and who would be scarred by the loss forever.

For Aidan, whose family name he could not recall ever knowing, whose life had been lost because he was stupidly full of romantic notion and a belief in the nobility of *this*—this trial by combat, this test of steel. What had it proved? Nothing. There was no nobility in it.

But death. There was death. And he had chosen to face it, thinking—stupidly, as stupidly as Aidan had—that he could face the war and be the only one to pay the price for it. Idiot. Child.

He was no child now.

He was the victor.

He was the *Tyr'agar*, the *kai Leonne*, the last of a line. And he knew, because he could be honest with himself if no one else, that the real reason he wanted to kill this man was because this one man had been a hero to him, and it was his action, here, that had destroyed his ability to believe in the heroic.

In the noble.

This challenge almost always ended in a death.
The sword fell.

"Valedan, *don't!*"
The sword stopped. It stopped with such a force of will and sudden lack of motion it sent a snap up his arm and shoulder—both of which had been severely tested in this trial. The sun cast the blade's slender shadow across the length of Ser Anton di'Guivera's motionless face.

The kai Leonne lowered his sword slowly, as if waking. He met the eyes of the man on the ground, and then stepped back.

"Ser Anton," he said. Sheathed his sword. Turned.

There, by the circle's edge, supported entirely by the Queens' healer, Dantallon, stood Aidan. He was absolutely white, and his cheeks and eyes were surrounded by gray-black hollows that looked suspiciously like bruising.

The healer didn't look much better. "We had to watch," he said softly. "It was . . . necessary."

"He was—"

"Dying, yes. I thought he was dead."

Valedan bowed to the healer. Stood. His own brush with a healer's touch gave him some understanding—and he wanted no more than that small enlightenment.

"Did no one explain the nature of the challenge to him?"

"No."

"It was to the death," he said quietly, turning to Aidan, the witness that he had chosen in the streets of the hundred holdings in what seemed another lifetime.

"I know," Aidan said softly, swaying like a young tree in a heavy storm. "I know it. But . . ."

"Yes?"

"But he'd stepped outside of the circle."

Just that. Valedan turned and saw that Ser Anton di'Guivera had indeed crossed the boundary. Strange, that he'd missed that. "The circle is not a Southern custom, Aidan," he said gently.

"You aren't fighting in the South," Aidan replied. "Neither of you stepped outside that circle for the whole fight. And anyway, he—he didn't have a weapon. You couldn't just kill him. It'd be murder."

"It would be justice."

Aidan said nothing.

But Dantallon said, "It would be murder of a different sort, Valedan. We believe in the heroes of our choice, even when they have to struggle to live up to our beliefs. It was not just Ser Anton's life that you spared today." He stiffened. Lifted a hand. "I will take Aidan from you now; I have need of the healerie and the privacy it provides. If you wish to see him, he will be there, although we will be forced to keep him for at least a week, at best guess."

"My thanks, Healer."

"And mine." The healer did not bow. He couldn't, without dropping Aidan.

"Valedan—"

"Yes?"

"Could you tell my Da, do you think? I—I haven't sent any word for a couple of days now. He might be worried."

"Yes. I can do that." He turned away from the boy, unable to speak. Unable to describe in words the peculiar knot that had settled around the base of his throat. He walked over to his enemy, to this man that he had admired so much in his youth, and he realized that he wanted what Aidan had wanted. Still.

He walked past Ser Anton, and retrieved the swordmaster's fallen sword. It was heavier than he had thought, looking at it in action, and it was infinitely simpler than many a fine blade; the hilt was unornamented, unfilagreed, unremarkable.

"I had heard," he said, turning carefully, the blade extended, "that you had forsaken your sword's name."

Ser Anton rose, then, as if the comment were permission. "It is true."

"That you had come to seek a new name for it."

"I had."

The young man offered the older man the blade; the older man bowed and accepted it. The anger between them was gone; it had been guttered in the fire of the Lord's Test, and what remained was, if not peaceful, then at least quiet.

There was no accusation Valedan could make that did not sound childish at best. He said, instead, "A sword can be a sensitive thing. If I were you, I might choose to give it back its name."

"I have chosen a name for it." He bowed. "You have not named yours."

"There is only one sword that I will wield that will be significant," Valedan replied.

"Yes." Ser Anton di'Guivera gazed at his sword's edge. "The Sun Sword." He knelt, his sword still in his hand. "Tyr'agar," he said softy. Their eyes met.

Without looking away, Ser Anton di'Guivera planted the sword he carried deliberately into the earth at Valedan's feet. There was silence in the crowd that, almost forgotten, watched.

"Did you not promise allegiance and loyalty to my father and his father before him?" Valedan said softly, a reply that the wind did not carry.

"I did."

"And what of those oaths? Why should I now accept what has already been betrayed?"

"The father of your father," Ser Anton replied, without flinching, "murdered my only wife and my only child. Had I known of that risk before I made that vow, I would never have made it. Had I known the truth of their deaths before I made that vow to your father, I would never have made it.

"But I know the truth, Valedan kai di'Leonne, and I have taken both the measure of my allies and the measure of the man who would rule the Dominion, and what I give you now I did not think I could—ever—give. You will accept it or reject it; either way, this will be known: That you bested Ser Anton di'Guivera, and that he offered, in his turn, to serve you."

Valedan was silent for a long time; his gaze drifted down to the sword that stood in the dirt, and then up again to the man who had planted it there.

"What name," he asked quietly, "have you chosen for this sword?"

Ser Anton paused a long while before answering, but he did choose to answer. "*Mercy.*"

They stayed, one standing, one kneeling, while the sun inched toward the horizon. Ser Anton knew how to wait, but Valedan knew how to wait as well; they measured each other in the stillness.

But, as in the circle, it was the younger man who spoke first. "Be what you were," he said. "Be all that you were, and I will take your service, and your legend, and I will honor them both."

"I am not my legend," Ser Anton said. "You have seen the truth of it here."

"I have seen it tested," Valedan said. "Part of your legend was the love that you bore your wife and your son—and what you were willing to do in order to avenge their deaths."

Ser Anton bowed his head, and when he raised it, he offered Valedan a glimpse of vulnerability—the first. "She would have liked you, my Mari. She would have approved of you."

The sun began its descent as the last sword was sheathed.

EPILOGUE
AIDAN

For the first time in his life, Aidan felt self-conscious going home. It wasn't that he wanted to stay at the Palace—although part of him did—it was more the company that he brought into the holdings with him. They were used to a very fine life, one that Aidan had seen at their side for long enough that it wasn't quite a dream anymore, and nothing in the holding he called home could in any way match that life. Nothing.

Up above them, the matchless trees of the Commons gave way to the lesser trees of the twenty-fifth, and then the twenty-fourth. The streets weren't empty, but they'd lost the crushing press of people evident everywhere during the Kings' Challenge. The city had returned to normal.

He brought a hand to his chest. Touched it, surprised to feel anything beneath his palm at all. Almost unconsciously, he cast a nervous glance across the road to where the healers walked. Neither of them were Dantallon, of course. Dantallon attended the Queens, and he left the healerie in Avantari only when the Queens left the Palace. Like on the last day of the Kings' Challenge, the Challenge that had been won—and like all Challenges, would be confined to his perfect memory just as every winner in the history of the Challenge—by Eneric of Darbanne. Not by Valedan kai di'Leonne, but that didn't matter. Valedan had won the important battle.

That was the only thing that Aidan truly regretted: that he hadn't *seen* the battle with the demon. No, he'd been curled in the arms of Dantallon the healer, in a place that death couldn't quite reach, and life couldn't touch at all without a healer's help.

Hurt, to think about. So he thought about something else instead. Homecoming. And that didn't help much, either.

Please, Lady, he prayed. *Please let him not be drinking.* His worst nightmare: Walking into the two rooms where he and his father lived to a raging, drunken father. It didn't happen often, but it *did* happen. Only let it happen any other day, and he'd live with the bruises.

"Aidan," Valedan said.

Aidan jumped. Straightened his shoulders out of their almost forgotten cringe. "Yeah."

"It doesn't matter where you live; it's what you do with the life you have that counts."

Great. He needed platitudes like he needed—well, maybe more than he needed a drunk father. But not by much.

Valedan caught him by the shoulders and turned him round; Aidan didn't even try to resist. "Do you think this is so very terrible?" he asked, nodding in an arc that was meant to take in the tall, cramped buildings of the holding.

Aidan shrugged. Then, because it was Valedan, and because he spoke quietly, he answered. "No. It's just that—I've seen the way you live. I don't live like that."

"You've seen the way I live in the North," the would-be ruler of the entire Southern Dominion replied. "And to be honest, I remember finery as a way of life in the South as well. But I remember this: That I was born to a seraf—a wife, but still a slave. I was a very well-kept slave, freed only to be a hostage in the North."

Aidan was silent.

"You don't even understand what freedom is."

Aidan shrugged, stung slightly. "Hunger," he said. They stared at each other a long time. It was Valedan who broke the gaze. But he said, staring at the space just to the right of Aidan's shoulder, "I do not judge you, Aidan. I can't. I owe you my life. It doesn't matter to me where you come from." He paused for a long moment. "I am going away to war."

"I know."

"Ser Anton is coming with me."

"So's half the city."

Valedan winced, but continued as if Aidan hadn't interrupted him. He often did that. "He asked me to tell you that after we've won the war, he is thinking of coming North for a time, and if he does—and if you're willing—he'd like the opportunity to see to your training."

The words only made sense gradually; taken all at once they

were so enormous they were almost impossible to understand.
Ser Anton di'Guivera, the swordmaster of the South. Training—
Aidan? The lesser trees, the ancient buildings and the newer ones
in poor repair, the rutted roads, the poorly dressed people edging
out of the way of Valedan's well dressed—and more noticeably
well-armed—party, vanished. He saw a sword, and a circle, and a
man who had twice won the crown the Kings offered once a year.

"But—but the cost—"

"He says to remind you that he has no son. And that he owes
you a debt greater than mine." Here, the kai Leonne smiled almost ruefully. "Even in that, we are competitive. I, of course, think
my life is at least as important as his honor."

Aidan turned away and started to walk because he had a sudden urge to cry and he couldn't, couldn't, couldn't embarrass himself that way in front of Valedan. Or anyone.

"Are we almost there," the older healer said brusquely, "or are
we going to stand and talk in the street while frightening the
pedestrians?"

"Uh, almost there, sir."

Everything about the older healer was short-tempered and a
hair's breadth from rude, even his look; he was covered in dark
hair from brow to chin, and his jaw was squarer than the courtyard
of the biggest merchant bank. If he'd come off a ship in the port,
and was surrounded on all sides by angry magisterians, he'd've
looked more at home.

But there was no arguing with the twin palms that hung round
his neck like a beacon. Wasn't much approaching 'em either, but
that was probably best—this man, this Levec, was going to have
to heal Aidan's father. Somehow he couldn't quite see Dantallon
knocking his father over and sitting on his chest.

But Levec had promised that he'd do just that if that's what it
took. Promised it, not to Aidan, but to Dantallon.

Dantallon, of course, had been horrified. A healer couldn't force
a man to accept a healing he didn't want. Aidan believed it. Of
every healer but Levec.

The healer met Aidan's half-defiant, half-hopeful gaze. Rolled
his eyes. "Well, we don't have all day. Or at least I don't. I've
students to tend to, and people your age are *always* in need of
discipline."

"Healer Levec," the younger man said.

"You can't let these people waste your time. How many times

have I told you this, Daine? You'll be turned into a cushion for fat patricians before you're thirty if you don't develop some—"

"—ill humor. I know." The younger healer grimaced, sharing some of that expression with Aidan.

"I'm not blind," Healer Levec said gruffly. He turned on heel and stalked off, in the direction that Aidan had pointed.

"He's not as . . . bad as he seems," Daine said, wincing slightly. "And he's had a rough quarter."

"Why'd you come with him?"

"Because I wanted to see him actually heal," the young man declared. "He'd kill me if I told you this, but he's got a soft heart buried under that ugly exterior. I—he taught me. He saved my life at least once. He gave me a chance to make something more—much more—out of it. But he's always seemed uncomfortable as a healer, and when I heard he was going to do this—this healing, I asked permission to come."

"I'm surprised he said yes."

Daine's smile was pained. "He said no. But in harsher words, and more loudly." He looked up then, at the broad, retreating back. "I'd like to go to him." And he did.

Made Aidan glad he wasn't healer-born. It was probably the first time in his life, since his mother's death and his father's accident, that he'd any cause to be glad of it. He juggled his embarrassment at his home and his possibly drunk father and his fear of the Healer Levec; embarrassment dropped like a heavy stone.

He moved.

First surprise: The stairs were clean and cleared.

The hall was also clean; no empty baskets, no empty jugs, no garbage to be carted down to the streets. Aidan hesitated a moment as he reached the closed door.

This time, Valedan said nothing. Levec said nothing. They waited while he put his hand on the door's tarnished handle, drew a breath as deep as his still-tender lungs would hold, and pulled.

The room was *clean*. The chairs—both of them—were tucked neatly beneath a table that held two bowls, two spoons, two forks, and two mugs on either side of a basket full of fruit that was, to Aidan's jaundiced eye, no more than two days old. The windows were clean; the curtains—curtains?—pulled back.

He detected Widow Harris' firm hand in every corner of his home; he hardly recognized it. But it lacked one thing: his Da.

Valedan and Levec came in, and the younger healer—the self-professed unwanted company—followed; two of the Tyran and two of the Ospreys likewise forced themselves into the vanishing space near the door. The rest of the honor guard were forced to wait on the stairs; there simply wasn't room for them to move, let alone be effective should the need arise.

"Ummm, wait here," he said. Wasn't like there was all that far to go, after all; there was only one other room, and the door was closed. Aidan walked up to it and hesitated for a long time. Then he knocked.

"Da?" he called through the closed door. "Da, are you in there? I've brought a couple of friends I'd—I'd like you to meet 'em."

He wanted to say more, but he couldn't; his mouth had become completely dry between the first word and the last. What if—what if his father weren't here?

But Kalliaris was listening, and, frown or smile—he'd find out which soon—the door to the sleeping room swung open, creaking a bit on its hinges.

His father was dressed to visit the Mother's own temple. Not as finely as Valedan, but almost as finely as the Healer Levec—which probably said more about the healer than it did about his father—and his breath was mercifully free of the heavy, sour scent of too much ale.

Aidan stood there, his mouth half open, staring up at his father's face.

"I—I had word you'd be coming," his father said, both gruffly and lamely. "I'd've come to the Palace but I—but I had work."

He was lying. They both knew it. But they both knew he hadn't come because he didn't want to be embarrassment; a half-whole father to a hero son.

"She sent a letter, you know. Widow Harris—she recognized the seal."

"She?"

"The Princess. I kept it. She says you saved a King's life."

Aidan shrugged, uncomfortable with the truth now that it was actually in his home. "If it hadn't been me, it'd be someone." Before his father could continue, he added, "Da, I'd like you to meet someone." And he turned to see Healer Levec, arms folded across his chest, sitting on table top. He wished—he really wished—that it had been the *other* healer who'd agreed to his request. But that other healer was quiet as a mouse beside a large, angry cat.

His father's eyes narrowed and then, seeing the symbol around the man's neck, widened. Aidan had done the same—for different reasons, though. It was hard to think of Levec as a healer.

"This is Healer Levec."

His father limped forward, struggling with crutch that he rarely, if ever, used in the confines of his own home. "Stev Brookson. Pleased to meet you," he added, sounding anything but. Still, he held out a hand, and Levec gripped it easily.

"You probably won't be after we're finished," Levec replied.

His father's head whipped around.

Aidan didn't say anything; Valedan, waiting in silence, did. "I owe your son a great debt. I offered him money, of course, because money is the way most debts are paid, in either Empire or Dominion."

"You—you're that Southern King!"

Valedan's easy smile was years older than this face. "Aidan didn't want money. He figured you could make that on your own. But he did ask for the services of a healer."

Aidan's father frowned, and then his entire face froze. Aidan knew exactly what that meant, but this time he didn't cringe. The healer's grip on his father's hand whitened as he attempted to pull away. "Aidan—"

"Da, he says—he says it'll hurt 'cause it's old. The break, I mean. But he says that, swear to Mandaros himself, he can fix your leg."

"You asked for *that?* Without asking me?"

"Da, I—"

"You just went out on your own, just asked for charity for *me?*"

"It's *not* charity. I *earned* it!"

His father was that shade of red-purple that was ugly for so many different reasons. Aidan stopped a minute, caught between a cringe and the silence that he so often hid behind when his father was angry. Stopped a minute longer, angry himself, angry in front of the healer and the Ospreys and the Tyran and Valedan.

It had been easier to stop the demon. Easier to make that damned decision than this one. Easier to act. And *that* was just stupid.

"That's what *I* want, and I'm the bloody hero," Aidan replied fiercely, aware that all eyes were on him. "I want my father *back*."

"And what if that's not what I want?"

"Then," Levec said, speaking for the first time, "I will knock you over and sit on your chest and heal you without your permission." He was among the largest men in the room, even unar-

mored. Had his father been whole, it would have been a good
fight. But he wasn't, so it wouldn't be.

"Levec—" the younger healer said.

"Aidan—" his father said, at the same time.

Aidan said nothing at all. He stood, mute, the triumph of his
homecoming exactly what he'd been afraid it would be. In time,
maybe in time, his father would forgive him.

But this time, his father's face slowly lost its red, ugly color,
lost its frozen, growing anger, lost almost everything.

He said, "You come then, boy. You come here, and you give
me your hand. You're my son, you're my only son. You stand by
your Da while he does this."

EPILOGUE:

SER ANTON DI'GUIVERA

6th of Seril, 427 AA
Averalaan Armarelas, Avantari

Kallandras came upon him in the full light of the Seril moon.
Moon at full, a time of mystery and promise, a hint of wildness
and hunger.

Yet although he knelt beneath the moon— the Lady's Moon—Ser
Anton di'Guivera showed no wildness, no hunger. No movement.

The Arannan Halls were quiet; the Hall of Wise Counsel in
Avantari proper was not. Valedan kai di'Leonne, Ramiro di'Callesta, Baredan di'Navarre, and the Kings and Queens were se-
questered with the Flight—Eagle, Hawk, and Kestrel. Voices had
been raised, voices had fallen; there was a rhthym to the heated
anger that was carried by breeze and night air when the words
themselves had been carefully obliterated by the magi who served
the Kings directly. Only a bard would catch it.

There would be no drawn swords; no direct challenges. Not
yet, not here. But Kallandras knew that the blood between the
Callestans and the Kestrel was bad; sooner or later that rift would
open, and that blood spill. Sometimes it was considered wise to
bleed a patient. He would see.

But it was not of Valedan's council that he had come to speak,
and not of war, although war was the order of the hour, the day,
the month.

He waited, the shadows his cover and his counsel.

But Ser Anton di'Guivera did not move. The moon cast a soft shadow, hard to see at this distance, of the blindfolded boy who graced this courtyard in the Arannan Halls. That shadow touched the swordmaster like a benediction, it fell so gently.

The water from his cupped hands did not.

We were both trained, Kallandras thought, *to bring death. Not pain, not torment, not freedom—but death, the simple fact of it.*

He stepped into the moonlight. Before he had moved five feet, the Southern swordmaster had risen, turned, drawn his blade in near-perfect silence, and frozen, becoming as much a thing of stone as the boy carved by maker-born hands at his back.

And around the stone, beneath it, within it, the waters of life. They were alike, the fountain and the swordsman; it was no wonder that he was drawn here to find peace.

Peace.

Kallandras held it in his hand, roughly made and still flecked with baked clay. He bowed.

"Ser Anton."

"Master Kallandras of Senniel," the swordmaster replied, returning the fiction of the bow politely but maintaining his grip on the sword.

Silence, then. A meeting of equals.

"You are . . . astute, Ser Anton."

"You are a bard of the North. In the South, I do not believe we would suffer you to live."

"Ah?"

"A man cannot tell men what to do by voice alone. Or so it is said."

"It is said. It is not true even in the South where no bard is suffered to live, of course, but it is said."

"Not true?"

"The **Tyr**'agnate of Callesta orders a death, and his Tyran obey, regardless of what they deem correct."

Anton's smile was dim with night colors. "You are right, and you are wrong. Of the Tyrs, Callesta is the most dangerous. He sees too sharply, and he understands his people too well. The binding he places upon them works both ways. He would kill to a man any man who did not follow the orders that he gave—but he would die before he gave orders that would destroy that binding, and he knows their measure well." But the swordmaster seemed to relax. He did not, however, sheathe the sword. "If you have come to find the kai Leonne, he is not present at the moment."

They both knew that Kallandras had not come to speak with Valedan. But the bard understood manners, especially Southern ones. "I did not come to speak with the kai Leonne, Ser Anton."

"Ah."

Silence. At last Kallandras said, "I am not a young man, not anymore."

"I would be surprised, Bard, if you had ever been a young man."

"The young, if protected, have the luxury of vulnerability." He shrugged, a deflection of the truth in his opponent's words. A parry. "The old have the luxury of wisdom."

"Hard won luxury, that."

"As is any crown."

Silence, broken by the falling patter of water, the ripple of wave against stone. Kallandras raised a curled fist to the scant light and opened it slowly. Something small glinted in the flat of his palm. "My apologies, Ser Anton. I was . . . asked . . . to give you this during the test of the Sword." He curled his hand into a fist again. "But I hesitated at the appointed moment."

The older man's curiosity was nowhere in evidence, and he did not speak for a long moment. When he did, the desire to know more was a hint at the farthest edge of his voice. Ser Anton obviously knew how to be careful when he spoke, but he was so rarely that careful. "And that moment?"

"The moment before you challenged the kai Leonne to a combat that any Southerner in the coliseum knew must end in a death."

"And would it have stopped me, Bard?" The swordmaster asked, a fine vein of genuine amusement evident in the rigidity of his voice.

Kallandras inclined his head noncommitally. "It is not, in the end, for me to say; I am messenger only."

"But you chose not to deliver the message." Greater curiosity here, and sudden suspicion, the latter of which he took no trouble to hide.

"No."

"Kallandras of Senniel, you are unlike any bard I have met in the North, and I have met many. You walk like a killer, move like a killer, speak like a man who knows death at least as well as song—perhaps better."

Honesty. Complete honesty. "The Lady is strong," Kallandras replied softly.

"Tonight, yes. She is strong. And you, you stand like one of the brotherhood who serve her darkest face."

Kallandras took a step back, and then smiled almost ruefully. A genuine expression, although he did not believe Anton would recognize it as such. He knew that Anton did not accuse him. And yet. "We are both revealed by our talents; you to me by your voice, and I to you by your gift."

"Then by the Lady's grace, I will be blunt. I am tired, Bard, of politics and games; I am tired of the cost of the choices I have made, and I bear their burden—and will—until I am at last carried by wind to the winds.

"You have come to speak, and I will listen, but I will not listen for long. Deliver your message, or explain yourself if you desire it; leave if you do not." He turned his back, although the sword was still in his hand, and faced the fountain.

Easier, then, to speak to Ser Anton. The vulnerability of facial expression was difficult between two strong men, and something that was often not forgiven.

"I did not choose to deliver the message because you were about to test your own resolve, Ser Anton. To be tested, to find your own limits. To set them."

"Tested?" the swordmaster said. "And tell me, Bard, did I pass?"

"Oh, yes," Kallandras said, his voice so soft that the only man who would ever hear it was Ser Anton himself. "I watched you fight the boy. I watched you cut him. But before that, I watched you take his measure during the long day of the test of the Sword. He is almost miraculously good with a sword, but you, Ser Anton, were better.

"*Are* better."

The older man stiffened. Stiffened and then raised the sword slowly, almost casually. To a lesser observer it might appear that he was preparing to sheathe it.

"Do not," Kallandras said, and the warning edge was in his voice. It was not his intent to perish here. "You will protect no secret by my death. I do not speak in a way that others may hear, and I will not."

"Then why have you come with this . . . interesting supposition?"

"Because you are Ser Anton di'Guivera, and the legend that

attends you attends you for a reason." He bowed. "I offer you that respect, Ser Anton."

Silence, and against a bard, silence could be a weapon.

But Ser Anton di'Guivera was used to taking the measure of his enemy; used to making life-or-death decisions based on his estimation of that measure. He sheathed the sword in one easy motion. But he did not turn.

"I could not be certain," he said softly, "that the kai Leonne would accept my offer of allegiance. I could not be certain. There was only one way that I could give him my support that *was* certain. The challenge, witnessed by all, and lost. By me."

He shook his head, still facing the statue named *Southern justice*.

"He almost killed you."

"Yes."

"You were prepared to die."

Ser Anton shrugged. "Any man who lifts a sword is prepared to die. Or should be. But you spoke of a message, and you've obviously come to deliver it now."

"Yes." Kallandras walked to the fountain's edge. He did not look at the swordmaster, not directly. But he bent by the stone, placed his curled fist upon it, and then relaxed each finger slowly. Carefully.

"We say, in the North, that love binds the living. We say, when we sing, that love can bind the dead, hold them in the halls of Mandaros, where they wait and wait and wait until their loved ones join them."

"In the South," Ser Anton whispered, "we talk of the winds that sweep the howling dead across the deserts. The dead rage against the living, against their loss. Only the Lady can intervene. And I have prayed, Master Bard. Could you," he continued softly, without looking to the side upon which the bard stood, "lift your voice to the heavens itself, so that the Lady might hear it? I would count any debt paid, and all debts owed you, if it were possible."

"It is not."

Silence.

"But I am from the North," he said lightly, "and in the North, the tradition is different. There is Mandaros, who sits in judgment, and there are the dead, who seek what he has to offer. A woman told me a story, and I hope you will forgive us our presumption, for I may not reveal her nature, or her name, and you will want both."

"Continue."

"She traveled to the Tor Leonne, and spent some time in your home. She came to take an item of value from it."

The swordmaster stiffened with real anger. "I . . . see."

Kallandras stepped away.

"She knew, or thought she knew, what to look for, it had been so carefully described."

In the moonlight and the magelights, something flickered. Something caught Ser Anton's eyes. As Kallandras cleared the fountain, the older man turned. He froze, and he did not speak, and Kallandras was glad of it.

"But she found, in a room preserved as if it were a shrine, the three things she sought, and she broke them. Because she was told that something of value had been left in a casement of clay, wept over, and kept as a reminder of things valued. Things loved."

Ser Anton di'Guivera touched the ring that lay exposed to night and moonlight. It was too small for any of his fingers; that much was clear. In the darkness it was still possible to see the tremor take his hands. The shaking. Harder to tell whether it was due to rage or something else.

"She was told—my compatriot was told—that no one else knew of this, and that no one else knew that of all possessions, save perhaps your sword, this was the one you most highly valued."

The swordmaster turned then.

Turned, his hand a fist around the delicate, inexpensive ring, an inseparable joining of jade and a twist of gold: two bands. Two lives made one.

"I am sorry," Kallandras said softly, "to expose what was so well hidden—but proof was needed."

"Proof?" A single spoken word. An accusation. A cry of—grief? Anger? Loss?

"Mandaros is a Northern god, but perhaps your wife was a Northern woman, born into a land of harsh sun and harsher people. I cannot say. You have heard—no doubt you have heard—that there are places where those born to gods, and those who in truth worship them, might meet the gods themselves, and speak, and be heard.

"The message is from Mandaros, and delivered because there is a woman in his halls who natters at him endlessly, and who has finally worn away his patience—but not his affection.

"This woman begs leave, through the living, to deliver a message to the swordmaster of the Dominion."

Ser Anton looked away. "Continue."

"She wishes him to know that she loves him, and she waits for him in the halls of Mandaros. That as she can, she watches him, and that she does, as he suspects, like the boy. She guesses that he will know by the actions taken here—by myself, by my compatriot, by the Lord of Judgment—that she is still not a very patient woman, and that she will not wait for more than a lifetime—so she respectfully requests that he not do so much in this life that he has to live through another one in atonement. He'll have only himself to blame, after all."

The swordsman did not speak.

Kallandras bowed in the darkness. "Ser Anton," he said. "Marianna en'Guivera says that you are not jade and not stone, and that she was not gold. But I believe she desires happiness for you, or peace."

He walked away into the night.

And because he was a bard, a master bard, because he was Kallandras, he heard the whisper of a voice at his back.

"Bard."

He stopped. Spoke across the distance without breaching it. "Ser Anton."

"Is this true?"

"Yes."

He left then, because there are some things that brook no witnesses.

The moon's face was high and full in the Seril night, and it rose over a lone man in an empty courtyard beside a quiet fountain.

Michelle West

The Sun Sword:

☐ **THE BROKEN CROWN** UE2740—$6.99
The Dominion, once divided by savage clan wars, has kept an uneasy peace within its borders since that long-ago time when the clan Leonne was gifted with the magic of the Sun Sword and was raised up to reign over the five noble clans. But now treachery strikes at the very heart of the Dominion as two never meant to rule—one a highly skilled General, the other a master of the magical arts—seek to seize the Crown by slaughtering all of clan Leonne blood. . . .

The Sacred Hunt:

☐ **HUNTER'S OATH** UE2681—$5.50
☐ **HUNTER'S DEATH** UE2706—$5.99